I0590343

the Masters of Mystics

For those who need the adventures and experiences of fictional characters to better understand themselves—this story is for you.

Isle Oum

Prologue

A double eclipse was a sign from the Forgotten—that a generation of immensely powerful magic wielders were forthcoming. Burdened or blessed, depending on who was asked, with extraordinary abilities. They were highly sought after—coveted for the strength they brought a Kingdom or the destruction they wrought. They blurred the lines for what a magic wielder should be capable of, pushing the boundaries of the natural world.

Destined for greatness—or perhaps great wickedness.

It was impossible to know which until it was too late.

* * * *

The days of this reign draw nigh in score minus half,

The Long Night shall fall, smiting all in its grasp,

Death is wrought by thine own hand,

Thy Kingdom will fall as Destruction clears the land.

When Hope seems lost and doom is spelled,

The Power of Love will prevail.

* * * *

Last prophecy issued by Malakai Nader, former Court Seer

Part One:
The Desert

Chapter One

A s the blood ruby dropped into the merchant's hand, Kasper knew that he would be dead before the day's end.

The inescapability of that truth turned Kasper's stomach. He hated himself for it, but did nothing to warn the merchant as he took the tonic for Kai. The shopkeeper's hungry gaze gobbled up the vibrant gleam of the cursed gem now clutched between his fingers. Kasper pursed his lips at the man's elation, contemplating telling the merchant what would inevitably befall him, but Kasper remained stalwart. The shopkeeper's doomed fate was sealed. He didn't want to linger in the merchant's presence a moment longer, but the parchment nailed to a board behind the merchant caught Kasper's eye—more specifically, the reward snagged his attention.

Five hundred gold coins to anyone with

information about persons practicing

necromancy, shadow-work, and or blood magic.

That kind of money would change Kasper and Kai's lives—it would change a lot of people in Desmorda's lives. Kasper continued scanning the other announcements and decrees, but the rest were more of the same. Employment opportunities for magic wielders, royal decrees, more rewards offered for the capture of pirates, and—

"Get on out of here, boy, I want to close up." the merchant sneered and waved his hand at Kasper. A retort danced on his lips—remembering that he had condemned the man. Kasper swallowed past the lump in his throat and hurried out of the shop.

He ignored the cramping of his empty belly and slipped his hand into his pocket. Calloused fingers slid over and grabbed the amethyst residing there. A pulse of tranquility washed over him as he stalked further from the shade of the stalls and into the blazing desert sun. He grimaced at the sweat dripping from his nape, soaking into his shirt while the heat of the city smothered him. He wanted nothing more than to take the few goods he had purchased with what little money and gems were left and return to the caravan, but leaving was not an option.

The early morning crowd had already been sent scurrying for the mezzanine cooled by the Elementals—magic wielders that bent the breeze to their will. But there were still a few stragglers that held some promise. Kasper slipped the amethyst crystal back into his pocket. It knocked into the remaining two cursed gems—an emerald and a sapphire he had called up out of the earth days ago. A last resort. That's what they were supposed to be anyway, but necessity forced him to utilize the gems more and more these days. He wished he remembered how he had learned to draw up the gems and if there was a way to thwart the curse. The curse that condemned whoever received the gems as payment to a horrible fate. Death, illness or injury, that was the true price of Kasper's magic. But those childhood memories were closed to him. And not using the gems...

No. It was that or starve. There would be time later to better understand his magic and maybe find a way out of the crushing guilt. For now, though, he had no choice—unless he could secure some clients for Kai. Kasper fixed his face into one of disinterest. He relaxed his eyes, taking on an indolent and idle gaze. The aloof posture slid into place as he meandered closer to the sparse stalls that managed to entice a handful of customers. Tan fingers danced over the trinkets and wares, none of it intriguing to Kasper save for the handcrafted leather pouches. The rich, supple leather beneath his hands bordered on sensual and he had to hold back a groan.

He glanced at his own satchel that hung by his side. The straps were frayed and there were worn patches so thin that Kasper could almost see the outline of the contents within. He sighed through his nose. Affording any of these goods was out of the question so he placed the unmarred satchel back with the others. Kasper moved around the stall, feigning interest in the other items. A young couple wandered toward the stall—the perfect target for his brother. A leather water flask was within reach.

Kasper took it and said while inspecting it, "I wish I knew how this would hold up." He peeked at the couple and smiled as their eyes met. "I'm going on a journey toward the coast at the end of the week. It would be nice to know how the weather will be so I can plan better."

The man nodded, "Yes, that would certainly make things easier."

Kasper continued examining the flask, replaced it, and picked up another. He looked once again, marking the distended belly hidden behind muted brown fabric. He licked his lips, his tongue catching on the chapped flesh, and said, "Are you expecting?"

The woman's smile widened; she pressed a hand to her abdomen and shared a look with her husband. "We are. In a month or so."

"That's wonderful," Kasper replied. He moved around the stall and picked up another flask. "Wouldn't it be *more* wonderful if you knew the exact day? Or the sex of the child? Maybe even what was in store for them?"

The woman's smile faltered. She glanced at her husband again. Kasper cursed himself. He had come on too strong. The heat and grumbling in his stomach were fogging his mind. His desperation was bleeding through. The man slipped his arm around his wife's shoulders, nodded toward the vendor, and began steering them away.

Kasper dropped the flask and started after them, "Wait!"

The woman threw a glance over her shoulder and waved him off. "We don't want any trouble, please."

Kasper raised his hands in surrender. "I'm not trying to cause trouble, I promise." He turned and gestured back to the city limits and the desert beyond. "My brother is a Seer, a legitimate one. He could tell you whatever you want to know about—"

"We're not interested," the man said forcefully, pulling his wife tighter. "Leave us alone, or I'll call for soldiers."

Kasper froze in his tracks and pursed his lips. The last thing he or Kai needed was for soldiers to get involved. Even if it wasn't for their previous association with the Abadi family, the decree forbidding any unsanctioned form of soothsaying would certainly be an issue for them. The man and his wife continued further away, walking back to the perceived safety of the city proper, and Kasper remained still, doing his best to come to terms with his latest failure.

"You better get out of here, boy," the merchant said, narrowing his eyes at Kasper. "Mirador is no place for riff-raff like you."

Kasper tensed. He knew it wasn't his objectively impoverished appearance–the jutting collarbone and threadbare breeches screaming his destitution–that the merchant found off putting, but rather his association with the caravan. More specifically, his association with Malakai Nader—a renowned Court Seer.

Well, formerly renowned, anyway.

The merchant was still glaring at Kasper as he grimaced and waved the man off. He was uninterested in incurring his wrath and possibly alerting imperial guards to his presence. He turned, walking away from the clay shops and homes. The cotton tunic he wore clung to his sticky skin. With a heavy sigh Kasper willed his feet to carry him into the desert and to his brother's tent. A stone settled in his gut at the thought of the disappointed look that would shadow Kai's usually bright eyes.

Mirador hadn't been as profitable as they had hoped. With the unrest brewing in cities to the north, people were less willing to part with their coin—making Kasper's job of enticing people to the traveling caravan all the more difficult. People were growing less and less amused with the parlor tricks of their troupe, and even with the years and distance–physical and metaphorical–from the royal family of Desmorda, people were wary and fearful of Kai and his visions.

Kasper squinted and sighed. An invisible weight pressed down on him, his shoulders sagging, and his feet protested as he began the quarter-mile walk from the market to the city's outer edges. His eyes skipped over the individual faces of the people—their features blurring and blending in a haze brought on by the blazing sun. The buildings finally gave way to ramshackle lean-to's and then clumsily erected tents. The people he passed also became more forlorn and weary, but Kasper kept his pace even as he passed through the caravan's encampment.

A measure of the tension clinging to his shoulders released as Kai's tent appeared. They had been forced to camp on the outer edges of the caravan. A muscle ticked in Kasper's jaw. Even amongst the rabble, they were outcasts. He inhaled sharply, reached for the tent's flap to pull back the thick canvas, and braced himself for the cloying incense Kai preferred. Instantly, his eyes watered and stung. His lungs burned and screamed against the assault of fragrance. A sputtering cough escaped his lips. He waved a hand in front of his face, a poor attempt to dispel the smoke. It took several moments for his eyes to adjust to the dim candlelight of the tent after spending hours in the blinding sunlight of the desert.

"Have you considered wearing a turban or shade to protect your eyes?" asked an amused voice from within. Kasper blinked several times before a figure swathed in white and gold fabrics appeared before him. A dazzling pearl smile matched the extravagance that poured from Kai. Kasper suppressed an eye roll as he beheld the golden rings that gleamed from Kai's fingers, the feathered earrings cascading down to his shoulders and brushing against the ends of golden-brown curls that tumbled from the strip of hair that ran down the middle of his scalp from his forehead to his nape.

He looked ridiculous. But Kai wouldn't dare dress like a peasant.

Kasper shook his head and moved further into the tent, careful to avoid the burning incense dispensers and crystal orbs that dominated the space. He spotted a stool unoccupied by cloth or trinkets and set his leather satchel on it.

"A turban would mark me as a traveler," Kasper intoned as he removed a leather-bound book, Kai's tonic, and a package of wrapped shisha, "and that would give me away when luring people to you."

Kasper glanced at his brother, who had the audacity to look offended—a hand raised to his chest, his many bracelets clinking in response. His mouth was agape before he said, "I am a legitimate Seer. People should be clamoring to have their futures read by me."

Kasper did nothing to stop the snort that erupted from him. "Perhaps they wouldn't need so much convincing if you didn't lean into the theatrics of your profession."

A smirk reached Kai's lips, and he gestured to his hair and outfit. "A little flair for the dramatics never hurt anyone."

Kasper crossed his arms. "Yeah, no one but us."

Kai gave a long-suffering sigh and sat at his table, tarot cards splayed before him. Another bit of pageantry. Kai divined nothing from the slips of painted paper. No, his power originated from something else—something that still terrified Kasper.

"I can't help that the simpletons take me for a charlatan or that the King issued that heinously unfair decree. Besides, anyone who has received a vision or prophecy from me can speak to its truth. If I am to be burdened with such an ability, I might as well enjoy some aspect of it."

"Yes, and I love having my livelihood be dependent on it." Kasper mumbled under his breath.

Kai smoothed his hands over the cards before him, the Empress smiling up at him. "Were there any potential customers on your little walk?"

Kasper absentmindedly rubbed at the tiger's eye gem strung around his neck. The gem warmed and hummed in response, his thoughts becoming sharper in his mind, but Kasper released the gem—he had no interest in recalling his failure of an afternoon.

"No, I don't suppose there was," Kai said softly. Kasper's silence was all the confirmation he needed. His fingers skimmed the deck before shuffling and stacking them, the slapping of the cards the only sound in the tent.

Kasper cleared his throat, attempting to dispel the tension, and said, "The market is dead for the day. Why don't we head further into the city and explore?"

Kai pursed his lips, but nodded. "Yes, that sounds nice. Besides, a sandstorm will hit the city at the end of the week, so the caravan must be heading out before then anyway."

Kasper paused. No matter how often Kai revealed the future, it caught Kasper off guard momentarily. Kai had explained to Kasper once the difference between visions and prophecies. In Kai's words, visions were certain to pass because the events that preceded them had already occurred.

Prophecies, on the other hand, were…trickier.

"Prophecies are more profound events, warnings of things to come based on a person's current path and assumed choices. People can always change—can choose differently," Kai explained.

"Free will," Kai had said, *"that's ultimately the deciding factor in whether a prophecy will come to pass—and humans changing their ways are a horrible gambling prospect."*

Kasper returned to the items he had procured, grabbing the shisha from the stool. He turned and set it down on the table in front of his brother. Some of the shadows clouding Kai's eyes dissipated as he beheld the delicately wrapped package and said, "I simply do not want to know what you had to do to get this."

Kasper flashed a brief smile. No, Kai wouldn't want to know, and Kasper didn't want to share. Shame burned in his cheeks at the memory of handing over a cursed sapphire to the hookah dealer. Every exchange weighed on him. Kasper remembered every face. He marked the glimmer of delight in the eyes of his victims as they eagerly took the gems, believing they had pulled one over on Kasper. But he knew the horrible fate that would ultimately befall them—an injury, illness, or even death. He prayed to the Forgotten–gods whose names had been lost to time, but who many still believed wielded influence–that his sins would be absolved.

He knew deep down he didn't deserve it.

Kasper rubbed the back of his neck and asked, "Where's Cal?"

Kai tore his gaze from the shisha. He had already taken his hookah from the shelf and placed it on the table beside his beloved chaise. The only piece of furniture that Kai had ever bothered to take care of. Kai waved dismissively toward the back of the tent.

"Through there. But I'll warn you, he's in a foul mood."

Kasper chuckled and picked up the leather book; the stale aroma of parchment and ink floated through the air.

"When is he not?"

Kai bobbed his head. "Very true," he hummed. Then he dumped the shisha into the opening in the hookah. Kasper hurried his steps, anxious to be away from his brother before he began smoking. The whisper of canvas was a welcome sound as Kasper entered the back section of the tent.

If Kai was light and opulence, then Cal was darkness and depravity. Their birth coincided with the double eclipse nearly twenty-seven years ago, and it seemed that the heavenly bodies themselves were imbued in Kasper's brothers—Cal the cold and distant moon to his twin's ever-flaming sun. The typical, sweltering desert heat that permeated the air was notably absent in Cal's section of the tent. The sweat soaking Kasper's robes cooled, sending a shiver down his spine and pimpling his skin. Or perhaps the shudder was brought on by his brother's hunched form. He was bent over an archaic text splayed on the table before him, and shadows clung to his too-still body—the sight chilled Kasper to his bones. Immediately, Kasper's eyes went to the clay jars littering Cal's space, unable to stop himself from imagining their unholy inhabitants. He quickly averted his gaze, noting the neatly made cot and the bedside table that displayed a framed portrait of a beautiful blonde girl. He narrowed his eyes, trying to place her.

Pain throbbed through Kasper's skull. He sucked air through his teeth and winced. He shook his head and looked away from the portrait. Kasper blinked away the pain and shifted his focus to the numerous scrolls and tomes that Cal had scattered in front of him. Kasper's blood chilled at the titles he saw: *Necromancy, The Arts of Dark Magicks, Pirates Tales of the Isle Oum, The Swashbuckling Adventures of—*

"What?" Cal grunted, snapping Kasper's attention back to the dark figure before him.

Kasper swallowed. He peered at his brother, but only saw the monster lurking beneath the surface—the one that was crafted of darkness and terror. Cal's shadows swirled and gathered, and Kasper's mouth went dry. Necromancy, shadow-work, and blood magic were illegal for as long as Kasper could remember. Meaning nearly everything in Cal's tent was contraband and warranted execution—including Kai and Kasper. He knew that, of course, but knowing something and seeing it outright were entirely different things.

"Kas." Cal said more forcefully.

Kasper shook himself, took a tentative step forward, and gently placed the copy of *Heavenly Bodies: Celestial Events and their Magical Properties* on the table's edge—the book the one of the lesser illicit items among them. Cal straightened, not sparing his brother a glance as he lifted and inspected the book. A tan finger slid over the spine, and he flipped it open, thumbing through the yellowing pages. He turned, set the book atop his towering pile, and returned to the text before him. Kasper hadn't expected any thanks or acknowledgment from his brother, but he lingered anyway. Since Cal began traveling with them some months ago he had been withdrawn, often spending time sequestered in his tent section, not bothering to take meals with his brothers or speak to them outside of required interactions. Even still, Kasper swore that late at night, he heard him conversing with someone—or *something.*

There wasn't much of their lives before their banishment that Kasper remembered, but it was clear Cal had taken the exile particularly hard. Cal never said as much, never said much of anything, for that matter, but his rage was permanently evident—it was in his stalking gait and the rigid set of his jaw. In the darkness and shadows that clung to him, seemingly seeping from his skin. Cal's whereabouts prior to joining their caravan were still a mystery to Kasper. Cal was very secretive; if Kai knew, he kept it to himself. But whatever he had done or wherever he had gone did little to assuage the tension that limned the planes of his body.

"Was there something else you needed?" Cal asked, shattering Kasper's thoughts. Cal's voice was rough and scratchy, like wind whistling through a ship's sails or echoing throughout a cave. He wondered if it was from years of disuse, or if communing with the dead had taken its toll. Necromancy was not known for being particularly kind to the wielder.

Kasper clamped his mouth shut. Once, he might have tried to foster a relationship with Cal, but they were beyond that. Whether it was Kasper's fragmented and pocked memory or Cal's disdain for all living creatures, Kasper didn't know. But it didn't matter. He shook his head and turned—leaving Cal to his death-magic. The canvas whispered as he moved back through the tent to find Kai slumped over in his chair, shisha scattered across the chaise and hookah on its side on the sandy carpets. Kasper jolted and jerked toward Kai, closing the distance to his brother in seconds. The shisha must have been laced with something. Someone must have recognized him. Or they had followed him—an agent of the King, or some other opportunistic assassin. Kasper's trembling fingers clutched at Kai's robes. Curses fell from his lips. He should have vetted the supplier. He gave his brother a hard shake, to no avail.

He should have been more careful.

He should have been more thorough.

He should have—

Kai bolted upright and sucked in a violent breath.

"Thank the gods." Kasper exhaled, moving to get a better view of his brother. White light was fading from Kai's eyes and the bulging veins in his neck and arms were returning to normal. Kasper was again thankful that his magic didn't demand so much of him. Physically, anyway.

Kai's chest moved up and down rapidly as he recovered from the vision that had overtaken him. He spared Kasper a pitying glance as he said in a tight voice, "We have company."

Chapter Two

Rhea moved wordlessly through the caravan's encampment. Her mouth watered and her stomach grumbled as the nutty scent of fried foods floated through the air, tempting her to abandon her quest of finding Malakai Nader, former Court Seer.

For weeks. And weeks. And weeks, she had waited and waited for the caravan he traveled with to come close enough to Mirador that she would be able to leave the palace and locate him. She had no other thoughts save for finding him—but now the trinkets and oddities of the caravan drew her eye. The people–both their clothes and their features–were unlike anything Rhea had seen before. People of varying skin colors and professions dotted the narrow paths, all eyeing her with interest. The strapping bare chests of the strongmen. The fearlessness of the fire-breathers. The scrolling and incomprehensible tattoos that covered a number of the performers called to her—beckoned her to look closer and remain for a spell.

"Stay close to me, Lady." Brander–her guard–muttered under his breath from her side.

Rhea blinked, not realizing that she had strayed toward one of the stalls boasting hand-spun silk scarves for sale. Rhea pressed closer to Brander. But she absentmindedly fingered the fraying edges of the burgundy scarf currently swathed around her head and chest.

"Sorry." she said softly. Her gaze returned to the hastily construct-ed paths snaking between the temporary stalls and tents. Twitching fingers reached toward her neck, taking her gold pendant–her family crest—between her fingers. The pads of her fingertips slid over the ridges. They reminded her that she was here risking her safety—and her father's wrath—for the sanctity of her people.

Rhea took her bottom lip between her teeth, but immediately released it. The thick, metallic taste of blood flooded her mouth. She gently prodded the inside of her split lip with her tongue, testing the soreness of her still healing flesh—an injury courtesy of her father. His ragesome black eyes flashed in her mind. They had bore into her just moments before the back of his hand had connected with her face. Rhea shook her head. Fixating on the past would not help her save her country. She ceased her ministrations and lifted her eyes up to the sun that was slowly dropping from the sky. They needed to find Malakai soon, or they would have to return to the city. Which meant another day wasted. And another day that her people suffered and starved.

Sneaking from the palace and staying in taverns was one thing, but being caught outside of the city limits with the unrest that was stirring amongst the villages? That was another thing entirely. But she couldn't deny that the heat and exertion were taking their toll. Her throat was ravaged and her limbs burned with fatigue.

"We can stop, Your High—I mean, Lady. Allow you to get some water and rest." Brander spoke softly from her side.

Rhea spared him a glance. Again, she was thankful that he had agreed to wear plain clothes rather than his uniform. He was already a hulking presence with his broad shoulders and muscled limbs. The permanent scowl didn't do him any favors, either. And it didn't matter that he was nearing the end of his fourth decade; he still exuded the strength and deadliness of an imperial soldier. Rhea had the good sense to wince at what it took to hone that type of obedience and discipline.

Rhea looked down at her own attire. She too opted to wear less opulent clothing in order to blend in with the commoners. Despite that, she still kept her few pieces of jewelry that she wore daily. Though she tucked them under the scarves and shawls that the city women donned. A half-hearted smile graced her lips and she waved dismissively.

"I am fine. Besides, the sooner we find him, the sooner we can depart on our journey."

Brander said nothing, but his watchful eyes seared into her. He had been resistant to let her go on this venture, but she had made it clear she would depart with or without him.

They walked for another half hour, the tents becoming smaller and more drab as they wandered. The sun continued making its descent toward the horizon, but it did nothing to cool the scorching air. Rhea took a sip from her canteen, relishing the cool splash of water as it coated her sand-clad throat. Her stomach, though it had cramped earlier from hunger, now fluttered as their time to find the Seer continued to dwindle. Even the soles of her feet burned with the blazing sand beneath.

"There, my Lady. Just past that tent on the left," Brander said.

Rhea lifted her eyes, following where Brander pointed. There, the last tent before the expanse of the desert melted into the sky, was the location she sought. A wooden sign, smoothed by the sand-filled winds, swung from a precariously thin rope secured to the front of the tent. Once, long ago, it may have been ornate and beautiful, but it had been ravaged by wind and time. The faint markings revealed a carving of an all-seeing eye. Beneath it was an inscription that read:

Master of Fate, Seer Extraordinaire.

Rhea's heart kicked up in her chest. She fought the urge to sprint,

closing the remaining distance between her and her nation's salvation. She willed her legs to maintain their pace as they approached the tent. Up close, she saw the dire state of the canvas. Small holes peppered the outer flaps, and the color—clearly once a vibrant red—had faded immensely to a shade of muddy pink.

She turned and led Brander a few feet from the entrance. Her eyes darted toward the flaps and she licked her lips in anticipation before she said, "Remember, we don't want them to know who I am. Do not use my title or my name. If he recognizes me, we'll have to adjust from there."

She had debated the merits of being honest about who she was, but there was too much at stake if she placed her trust in this man before knowing he deserved it. Malakai could sell her out or use her for leverage against her father. The King would, of course, pay nothing for her ransom. He would just as soon see her dead than give over a coin for her. No, it was safer, for now, to conceal her identity.

Brander nodded solemnly and recited with a grimace, "Yes, Your Highness. You are Lady Hera, a noble friend of the royal family. Not our Princess Rhea."

"Exactly," she replied, taking a moment to collect herself. "I am a Lady-in-Waiting. You are my personal guard, and we are here on behalf of the Princess." She murmured the words softly. A prayer or plea to the Forgotten that her plans wouldn't be undone before they were truly underway.

A muscle feathered in Brander's jaw.

Rhea pursed her lips. "I know you disagree with my methods." Rhea glanced around, ensuring no one was nearby enough to overhear them. The wind whipped through the tents, sending the canvas flapping and fluttering, but there was no one to be seen. "But," she continued, "we have to find Izor's Lamp. Those wishes are my last chance to try and save my people."

Brander held her gaze for a moment, his eyes revealing the war within himself that his stiff posture attempted to mask. "As you wish, my Lady," he finally sighed, "but if anyone so much as looks at a blade, I will get you out of here. Nothing is worth your safety."

Rhea smiled tentatively and uttered a quick, "Thank you." She inhaled deeply, noting the faint scent of cedar and a hint of clove wafting from the dilapidated tent. The scent struck her as familiar—to that of her father's court, she realized. She prayed the smell wasn't indicative of her imminent meeting with the man inside. With a final steeling breath, the future Queen of Desmorda gave her guard a hopeful look.

"Let us see if Malakai Nader can help us find a lost treasure."

Chapter Three

The humming visions quieted in Malakai's mind. Kasper's concerned stare was still fixed on his face, but he didn't dare tear his eyes from the shadows that danced a few feet outside the entrance of his temple. Malakai stood and brushed the perpetual layer of sand from his alabaster tunic and breeches. His attire wasn't conducive to their environment, but he couldn't bear to wear the drab robes of muted brown that everyone but the wealthiest patrons donned.

Kasper sighed. It was a frustrated sound, tinged with grief, but Malakai paid it no mind. He was used to people doubting him, even if he always knew what was coming. He spread out the tarot cards, his fingers sliding against their worn surfaces, and plastered a brilliant smile on his face.

Kasper's sandals scraped over the sand. "Kai, I was just out there. There wasn't a soul in sight. They've all gone back to the city."

Malakai's bracelets slid toward his elbows as he raised his arms. He flared out the white knee-length cape hanging from his shoulders.

"Kai, what are y—"

"Shh."

The canvas folded, and blazing yellow light poured into the dim space. Kasper raised his hands to shield himself from the sudden brightness. Malakai lifted his hands higher, allowing the sun to glint off his worn and weathered gold-plated jewelry.

Malakai sent Kasper a wink, hoping it conveyed the importance of this meeting, but Kasper's wide eyes revealed nothing in return. Malakai's blood buzzed through his limbs. His smile grew wider because he knew precisely who was in his presence before the tent flap fell back into place, returning the space to its still darkness.

"Welcome, friends!" Malakai announced in a lithe voice. "How may the Master of Fate serve you?"

To Kasper's credit, he didn't snort at the airs Malakai put on—at least not this time—and neither did the Princess of Desmorda and her company. Which meant they were there on serious business. Malakai remembered very clearly a time when his counsel was sought with only the most serious intentions. He was consulted for serious political decisions and military campaigns. Now, he read whether a ship would arrive on the next tide.

Oh, how the mighty have fallen.

The Princess, dressed in a simple, wine-colored dress and scarf, scrunched her nose and raised her hand to her mouth to cover her cough. The man's expression remained guarded and alert—watchful for any sign of danger. She waved her hand in front of her face and cleared her throat, her composure wrestling to take control of her features. Her eyes, finally adjusting to the dim lighting, landed on Malakai, who still stood with his arms upraised.

"We would like to have our fortune read."

Malakai scanned them, his eyes wide and unblinking. Consuming each little detail. It was all too obvious to Malakai—the paltry attempt at passing as commoners. The woman's speech was too proper, too rehearsed. And the man carried an imperial sword—a dead giveaway. But who was Malakai to spoil the fun of the future Queen?

Malakai cleared his throat and swept out his arms toward the pair. "Ah, lovers perhaps? Do you wish to know how many children you'll have? Years left together? I fear it won't be a tremendous amount given the age difference, but love is fickle! Perhaps you would like to know what kind of lover—"

"No." the Princess said, her cheeks a bright crimson. "We aren't romantically involved. He's my…protection."

"Ahh," Malakai replied, enjoying the way she squirmed under his gaze, "what interesting people have found themselves in my presence. Still, love may blossom yet. I could tell you for only—"

"We're not interested." the Princess ground out.

A feline smile spread on Malakai's face. "I am most intrigued at precisely who would be important enough to warrant a guard, and," he gave the man a once-over, "from the looks of it, a former imperial soldier."

The man stiffened at Malakai's assessment and he knew his words rang true.

The Princess huffed. "We're not interested in your appraisal of our perceived professions. I would simply like for you to read his fortune."

"Then, please, have a seat, so that I may be of some service to you." Malakai said as he swept his hand out to the chairs opposite of him. The Princess flicked her gaze from Malakai to Kasper, who stiffened at her attention. She quickly looked away and gestured for the man to have a seat. The guard's mouth twisted as though he'd rather stick his hand in a starved lion's mouth, but he obeyed nonetheless. Dust motes plumed in the air when the man sat.

Malakai grimaced. "You'll have to forgive the state of things. It's tedious work trying to operate a business out of a mobile caravan that is only allowed to exist on the periphery of society."

Kasper coughed, a sign for Malakai to get on with things before he scared off their only customers in three days. Malakai smirked. If only his baby brother could use those crystals of his to sense the desperation reeking from the pair.

Malakai could keep them there for hours if he wanted.

The Princess stood behind her guard, her rich brown eyes peering down with an intensity–and familiarity–that made a shiver run up Malakai's spine. Her ebony hair was tucked under the wine-colored scarf, but wisps of curls peaked out at the edges. The scarf matched the flowing dress that stopped above her ankles and cinched in the middle of her forearm. Malakai had to appreciate her taste in clothes, which were nearly as good as his own. Elegant pieces of golden jewelry adorned her fingers, and a gold pendant hung from her neck. To someone raised outside of the palace, it was simply a necklace. They would think nothing of it, but Malakai knew better. The delicate swirls depicted the floral design of the clematis. Despite her efforts to conceal her identity, the image was clearly that of her family crest.

His attention also caught on her swollen lip. He bet his cherished chaise that her father, the King, gave her that injury. And from the angry red color and still healing skin, he suspected she hadn't received it all that long ago. Malakai looked away, refocusing himself on the task at hand. Literally. He reached out his hand, his palm upraised.

"If I could have your hand, Sir…?"

The woman cleared her throat and spoke, "Brander—and I'm Hera. Lady Hera."

Malakai pressed his lips together as he fought the urge to scoff. "Ah, Lady *Hera.*" he rolled the name around his mouth, trying it out. "Lady Hera and her faithful guard, Brander." He didn't miss the subtle panic in the Princess's face as he forced himself to play along with her ruse. Malakai let a hint of his smile shine as he said, "Let us divine what Fate has in store for you, Brander."

Malakai allowed his magic to wash over him. It filled his veins as he succumbed to the visions that always tugged at the edge of his consciousness. An audible gasp emanated from the Princess.

"Don't be alarmed, this is all expected." Kasper assured from somewhere behind him.

Malakai blew out a breath, bracing for what the Forgotten, or whatever forces governed his magic, wanted him to see.

Saliva flooded his mouth. The delectable scent of honeyed cakes filled his nose, warmth from the hearth seeped into his bones, reaching into the parts of him that he hadn't realized were hollow—

Memories of Brander's life engulfed Malakai, but he gritted his teeth and pushed beyond them, looking for the future that awaited the guard. Pain seared across his ribs and tore at his skin, but he focused on the vision and not the discomfort it evoked.

The sea, crashing and violent, flashed in his mind—

Metal clashed, thunder cracked, wood groaned, and the wind howled—

Malakai released Brander suddenly, pulling his hands under the table and wiping them down his breeches. He shook his head and tried for a smile as he said, "I see a journey in your future. The path will not be easy and danger lies ahead."

The room was silent, save for the wind still wailing beyond the tent's entrance.

"That's all?" Princess Rhea said, her eyebrows arched in indignation.

Malakai tilted his head and let some of his magic flare in his eyes. "Would you like for me to read your fortune, Lady Hera? Perhaps your future–or maybe your past–holds something far more interesting."

Princess Rhea's throat bobbed, her eyes widening slightly.

Malakai sent her a wink.

"That's enough." Brander growled and shot up from the chair, the lines around his mouth and eyes deepening.

"I couldn't agree more," Malakai intoned and reclined in his chair, "so, why don't you tell me why you are really here? You can't possibly expect me to believe you came all this way, seeking me out specifically, just to have some common palace guard's future read."

"Palace?" Kasper breathed.

Rhea lifted her chin, looking down her nose at Malakai. He wondered if she would now give up the ruse of pretending to be someone else.

"We are here on behalf of Her Royal Highness Princess Rhea."

Malakai arched an eyebrow.

Apparently not.

Fine, he would keep playing the game.

He sat forward, bracing his arms on the table. "And how could I possibly help the daughter of the man who exiled me from court? And then added insult to injury by outlawing mine and my brother's magic?"

Princess Rhea stiffened for a heartbeat. Her gold-flecked eyes held his own. She shook her head gently and reached up to touch her pendant. "She seeks a treasure." the Princess said.

Malakai dared a glance at Kasper, whose attention was honed in on the Princess, his brow furrowed. "What treasure could she possibly want? Her father owns half the continent, surely no jewel or amount of gold is closed to her."

"It is not ordinary wealth she seeks."

"What then, my dear Lady?"

The Princess hesitated, her eyes sliding to her guard. "I'm not at liberty to say."

The chair and Malakai sighed as he leaned back once more. "Then I'm afraid I can't help you."

"What?"

Brander was suddenly in front of Malakai. His hand fisted Malakai's tunic and yanked him from his chair as if he were a feather pillow. Kasper's bloodstone dagger glittered in the candlelight. Unsheathed and at the ready.

Brander's soil brown eyes bore into Malakai. "I think you better reconsider, Charlatan." the guard sneered.

"Brander, release him." the Princess commanded.

Brander held Malakai for another heartbeat before he shoved him away. Malakai went tumbling backward, but Kasper was there, catching him by the elbow.

Princess Rhea glared in Brander's direction before she stepped closer to Malakai and clasped her hands in front of her. "We seek the Cave of Splendors in search of a treasure rumored to grant its possessor immense power. The Princess wishes to have it to stop the doom that you foretold nearly a decade ago. She believes that since you gave the prophecy, you can also help to stop it. She needs you to help us find it and retrieve it." Princess Rhea held out her hands to her guard, who produced a tome from a satchel at his side. The Princess brushed her fingers over the worn cover and said, "She lent me this book, which holds tales of the Cave and its treasure."

A vision flashed through Malakai's mind.

It was brief, almost too quick, but he saw enough to understand what had suddenly become possible.

Malakai wetted his lips and straightened. Kasper's hand fell away. He nodded and said, "And what of payment? Since this is of such importance to Her Royal Highness, I have to assume that she is prepared to pay well. The journey ahead is quite arduous. I must ensure I am appropriately incentivized."

A muscle ticked in the Princess's jaw. "You will be compensated accordingly."

Malakai smiled. "Well then, I will discuss your proposition with my associates."

Princess Rhea unclasped her hands, her eyes wide and searching. "What is there to discuss? I have made my ask clear and concise. And you are being offered *payment.*"

Malakai didn't miss the emphasis that the Princess placed on the word. Nor did he miss the way her eyes danced over the mismatched and shabby furniture. Malakai stood a little taller and said, "I need to discuss their price and availability."

"But I only need you." the Princess retorted.

Malakai sighed and placed his hand on his chest. "While I appreciate the confidence, my skills do only extend to predicting the future. And I doubt your guard dog will protect anyone other than you. I do have myself to look out for, *Lady Hera.*"

The edge returned to the Princess's gaze. She crossed her arms defiantly over her chest. "Fine, but I need my answer within the hour."

Malakai's smile widened, and he bowed dramatically. "Of course, my Lady."

Princess Rhea moved toward the tent flap, her guard shifting with her on instinct. "We will be waiting outside; let us know when you've decided."

Malakai nodded, and the Princess swept from the room. Her guard gave Malakai and Kasper a threatening glare before vanishing into the evening sun. The smile dropped from Malakai's lips and he rubbed at his temples. He knew the arguments, confusion, and distrust that would ensue, but he had *seen* it. A future that promised a better life and redemption.

He wouldn't let his or his brothers' fear prevent it.

"What in the Forgotten gods was that?" Kasper whispered harshly. Malakai moved away from the table, opting for his beloved chaise that sat flush to the far wall of the tent. Footsteps followed. Kasper was proving relentless in his interrogation.

"What did you see, Kai? What treasure does she want? What's the Cave of Splendors?"

The wooden frame of the chaise dug into Malakai's spine as he leaned back. What little cushion there had been when they found the chaise was long gone.

"All will be revealed in time."

Kasper scoffed. "Don't recite that drabble to me, brother. If you plan to involve me in your schemes, I need to know what I'm risking my life for."

Malakai ignored him. He waved a hand, gesturing toward the back of the tent. "Please retrieve Caliban from the back. We will need his particular expertise for this little adventure."

Kasper went deathly still.

Malakai agreed with this sentiment. Nothing good ever came from involving Caliban, but Malakai knew in this instance it was necessary. Kasper lingered for a moment longer before disappearing through the opening toward Caliban's hideaway.

A breath.

A heartbeat.

That was all the time that Malakai allowed himself to revel in the glimmer of hope the Princess had given before his trepidation wholly replaced it.

Chapter Four

Kasper's faint cursing could be heard before Cal saw him. Cal sighed, and blinked his eyes, trying to force moisture back into them after hours of staring at the endless scribble of runes and ciphers. The canvas rustled and Kasper's sandals slid against the sand, sending dust dancing in front of his feet.

Cal flipped a page. "I'm busy, Kas."

"I wouldn't be bothering you if I didn't have to."

The quill clutched between his fingers dropped to the desk, and Cal directed his full attention on Kasper. Kasper went wholly still, his eyes pinned on Cal's face. Cal guessed at what Kasper saw. Dark, purple smudges shadowing under his eyes, and the hollowness of his cheeks from days of forgetting to eat or drink. He supposed it looked a bit like the monster that the King's lies and propaganda painted him as. A demon. A devil. A blood witch bent on destruction. Wrath Incarnate swathed in death and shadows, but Cal knew the truth. He was *far* worse than the King gave him credit for. Several heartbeats passed, and Cal finally arched a brow and signaled with his hand for Kasper to proceed.

Kasper shook himself from his stupor and mumbled, "Kai wants to speak with you."

Cal snorted. The sound was oddly mortal to his ears. "And my dear twin had to send an ambassador to retrieve me? It must be dire indeed," he drawled with all the false concern he could muster.

"Just come talk to him." Kasper whined with a narrowing of his eyes. Then he turned on his heel, aiming to leave. But he paused just before the threshold and muttered, "Maybe you can make him realize how asinine the proposition is."

"Well, if you think it's outlandish, then it must be worth it." Cal added with a dark chuckle.

Kasper didn't bother turning to give his brother a glare.

Cal sighed through his nose and glanced down. The words of the tome blurred and bled together. He closed his eyes and leaned back in his chair, tipping it on its back two legs, contemplating the merits of heeding Kai's request. There wasn't a thing he owed his twin, and he was not obligated to appear. However, Kasper's anxiety was intriguing. He was accustomed to Kai's usual schemes, but for Kasper to suggest that only Cal could talk him out of it was…interesting.

Cal opened his eyes and rocked forward, the chair slamming into the dirt. He glanced at the text once more, but he was beyond comprehending anything at this point. He pushed away from the table and stood. His joints barked in protest. They were stiff from being in one position for too long. He stretched and his eyes flicked toward his nightstand. Soline's portrait smiled at him. A pang echoed through his chest like a death knell, but he shoved it down, next to his shame and guilt. He turned away from the room, aiming for the breezeway that connected his smaller tent to Kai's.

"Ah, there's the shadow to my light!" Kai said in a way of greeting, not bothering to pull his focus from where he lounged, painting his nails. Cal paid him no mind and leaned against the far support beam, crossing his arms. Kasper's features were fixed into a pout. His shoulders sagged, looking to all the world like a dog about to be whipped for chewing the furniture as he leaned against the support beam opposite of Cal.

Kai took another swipe at his nails, gave a satisfactory nod, and sat up. He beamed at them both and said, "We have been presented with an opportunity to regain what we have lost."

A pregnant pause filled the air. Malakai was clearly waiting for Cal to prod him. Cal only stared at his twin—doing everything possible not to let his anger get the best of him.

Kai glanced at Kasper, who was staring intently at his sandals. Giving up the game, Kai cleared his throat and continued, "I have been asked to help locate a lost treasure. If we can retrieve the item, we can use whatever reward we receive to set our lives back on the correct path. I've seen the possibility."

Kasper remained quiet, his gaze drifting from Kai to Cal and then back again. The soft, worn leather of his boots gave little protest as Cal crossed one ankle over the other, his intense stare never faltering as he beheld his brother.

"Who's the client?" Cal said, his voice still gravely.

Kai's eyes fluttered, and he nonchalantly waved his hand. "An associate of the Abadi family."

The temperature in the room plummeted around Cal. The light in the lanterns gutted and sputtered out. "Absolutely not," Cal said with deathly calm, his shadows gathering at his back.

Kai huffed. "You're overreacting, Caliban. It's not—"

"It doesn't matter, Kai. That family took everything from me—*enslaved* me. There's nothing I want from them." Aiming to return to his room of darkness, Cal turned on his heel. Kai's hand shot out, wrapping around his arm.

"You aren't considering the possibility—"

A sneer curled on Cal's lips. "You are just dying to return to that life, aren't you, Malakai? You want nothing more than to be their faithful servant once more. To beg for scraps at their feet." Kai withdrew his hand, but Cal didn't move. His chest rose and fell as he waited for his pathetic excuse of a twin to defend himself. "Well, not me. Unless it's his head you're offering, I want nothing to do with it." Cal hissed.

Cal started off again toward his room, but Kai—miraculously regaining the use of his tongue—spoke once more.

"The treasure that they seek is in the Cave of Splendors."

Cal paused. Murder still blazed in his blood, but some of his rage banked at the mention of the fabled destination. Kai smiled tentatively and spoke softly, as if his words alone could shatter whatever fragile understanding had fallen between them.

"I know what you have sought all these years, and I know it lies in the Cave. The woman has a book about the Cave."

A jolt ricocheted through Cal. His eyes darted to Kasper, who had barely breathed, let alone uttered a word in the past several minutes.

"You know this for a fact?"

Kai nodded. "I saw it. We can all get something that we want from this. You just have to trust me."

Cal and his younger brother flinched at the same time. Kai may act flippant, but he knew well enough what those words would mean to Cal—what memories they would evoke. If he was willing to risk Cal's wrath…then perhaps he really did know that the Alakhira resided in the Cave of Splendors. And if Cal could get his hands on that book…

Kai looked to Kasper and then back to Cal expectantly. "Well, will you both help me? Help me right the wrongs of my past?"

Silence filled the space as Cal flicked his gaze to Kasper, who swallowed hard before nodding. Cal wanted to laugh. It had never been a question for Kasper. He would do whatever his brother asked. It had been that way since their exile. Another tense breath passed between them before Cal gave a terse nod. Some of the shadows nipping at his clothes dissipated. A wide smile spread on Kai's face. A thunderous clap resounded through the tent, then the light and warmth suddenly returned to the space.

"Wonderful! We shall let the Lady know our price. Please invite her and her companion back inside, Kasper."

Again, Kasper's eyes darted between Cal and his twin, forever caught between their endless schemes. Kai returned to his relaxed position, further examining his nails. Heat burned in Cal's face, and his jaw ached from clenching it. The muscles of his neck were taut as he kept his eyes trained on the wall, not bothering to acknowledge Kasper.

Kasper sighed, stood, and scooted in his chair. He headed for the entrance to the tent, carrying out Kai's bidding. Cal wondered if Kasper would always be Kai's lackey. The go-between and messenger.

Perhaps that was all he was good for.

Once that hadn't been the case, but those days were long behind them all. But maybe whatever price they could negotiate with the Lady would allow Kasper to finally find his path. Staring after his younger brother, Cal mused if Kasper would ever know the truth and, if he did, would he have the courage to change his course? Cal didn't know, and he didn't have time to ponder it as Kasper disappeared into the desert sun. The tent fell back into place as he left to retrieve their newest employer back to the Master of Fate.

Chapter Five

There was no movement in the surrounding tents. No humans or creatures alike. No life at all. The rough trunk of the palm tree dug into Rhea's spine. She stared at the sun as it descended further toward the horizon. She drummed her fingers along her thigh. She ran her eyes along the outline of the hazy mountains in the distance, but the passage of time did nothing to ease the need to do *something*. She tried to focus on her people and how their lives might be.

Rhea was no fool.

She understood that suffering was widespread and rampant. There were food shortages, little money, and limited opportunities for people to earn a living—and then there were those forced to eke out a living on the fringes of society. These were the people her father had doomed to a half-life, condemning them a lifetime of hardships and struggles.

People like Malakai and Kasper.

Rhea moved to stand, unable to endure sitting still a moment longer.

"Princess?" Brander asked, concern laced in his tone.

"Hm?" Rhea turned to him; her arms crossed stiffly over her chest.

"You really should rest."

Rhea dropped her shoulders and returned to her spot next to him on the ground, defeated. "I know, I just want to know what the delay is. He obviously has no customers, and he has to know that I'll pay handsomely." Rhea shook her head and bit her bottom lip. A moment too late, she remembered her split lip and cursed as she released it. Blood once again danced over her tongue.

"You should have put the salve on that before we left."

"No," she said between poking her lip with her tongue. It ached to the point that tears began welling in her eyes, but even then, she didn't stop. "If he sees no issue with striking me, then I will bear it for the world."

"Princ—"

A shadow fell over them, and Kasper was there. Rhea sucked in a breath at the sight of her childhood best friend. It had been almost ten years since she had last seen him. They were just children then, but she still thought that he would have remembered her—

"Kai, uh," he stuttered over his words, like he saw the way they interrupted her thoughts. "I mean, Malakai the Master of Fate, Seer Extraordinaire, is ready to see you now."

"Perfect," Rhea replied curtly and moved to stand. She brushed the excess dirt from her skirt and lifted her eyes to find Kasper watching her intently. She froze, unsure if he recognized her now. Yes, she had changed since their shared childhood. But was it enough that he drew absolutely no comparison between the girl he spent nearly every day with and the woman standing in front of him now? He certainly wasn't that different. Curious caramel eyes and an impish grin still lurked beneath the shy, skittish exterior he now donned. What had remained, if not intensified, was his placement—perpetually balanced somewhere in between his two older brothers. The arms that held the scales of their respective good and evil—though Rhea couldn't say who was which.

"Let's not dally, my Lady." Brander said and stepped between them, breaking the spell.

"Right. Of course." Her eyes slid to Kasper once more, trying to reconcile the boy she knew with the young man before her. She cleared her throat, put her mask of indifference back on, and breathed, "Thank you…?"

"Kasper. Or Kas."

Rhea clasped her hands in front of herself and nodded, putting on the pretense that this was their first introduction.

"Kasper. Thank you."

Kasper offered a tentative smile and stepped to the side.

Brander's shadow fell over Rhea and he dipped his head down to her ear. "You need to be careful, Princess. I don't trust these conmen."

"I know," she replied under her breath, "but I am certain this is the only way to save my people. My father will do nothing. I cannot sit idly by and watch them waste away." She gave him another quick smile before brushing past him and heading back into the ramshackle tent. Readying herself for the negotiations ahead, Rhea braced for the nauseating scent of perfume that clung to the inside of the tent. The smell was far too reminiscent of the palace for her liking, and the attempt at extravagance read as desperate more than anything.

She took the seat that Brander had occupied earlier, facing off with Kai. Kasper trailed in after them, taking a position to Kai's left, his expression clouded and vague. But Rhea was working much harder on keeping her gaze from the figure looming to Kai's right, leaning against one of the far support beams.

Her eyes betrayed her resolve, and she snuck a peek.

Instantly, she regretted it.

Cal's focus was on Kai, but that didn't stop Rhea from feeling the weight of his presence. He had grown into himself since she had last seen him. He wore his hair the same, and he still donned an all-black attire, but gone was the lean softness of a boy, replaced with the hardness and sharpness of a man. Perhaps the most unsettling aspect was the lack of light in his features. His brown eyes were dim and hollow.

Rhea hated how the sight of it made her chest ache.

Briefly, she wondered if he recognized her. She doubted it, and prayed that he wouldn't—but a small, foolish part of her also wished he would. Rhea shook her head slightly, pulling her mind back into focus.

There wasn't enough time to think about the past—too much was at stake. She cleared her throat. "So have you and," Rhea waved to the other two brothers, "your associates decided your terms?"

Kai smiled. "We have."

The Princess gave a curt nod. "Let's hear it, then."

Kai tilted his head, his smile never faltering. "I will help locate the item you seek and my brothers will assist in the journey; in return, you also allow my brothers to take whatever they wish from the Cave."

Beneath the table, Rhea twisted her ring around her finger as she considered their request. She hadn't anticipated taking anyone but Kai with them, but if he thought they were necessary then she wasn't in a place to refute him. Even if it would continually put her on edge to have all of the Nader men shadowing her.

She prayed she wouldn't slip up and reveal her identity to them. If they hadn't recognized her yet, then she doubted they would come to that conclusion on their own. After a few moments, Rhea nodded and said, "As long as it does not interfere with or impede what I require."

"I foresee no conflict." Kai reached out his hand. "Do we have a deal?"

The Princess lifted her own, but paused and drew back.

"And what of *your* price?"

A feline smile replaced the friendly one on Kai's face.

"Clever girl."

Rhea narrowed her eyes and lifted her chin. "I do not take kindly to your attempt to deceive me. Either name your price plainly, or the deal is off." The command in her voice was that of a queen's. The queen she would one day become—if they didn't fail in their task.

Kai rapped his knuckles against the worn wood table. "We may survive yet." He laughed hoarsely and added, "I ask only to be returned what was once mine."

Rhea raised an eyebrow. "Which is?"

The Seer's eyes gleamed with delight—or perhaps they saw something beyond them. "I want my position at court. I want to be absolved, made a full citizen, and restored. I want my life back."

"No." Rhea's response was immediate and concise.

Something flickered on Kai's face. Was that surprise? Had he not anticipated her response?

The wood creaked as Kai leaned back, watching her. "No?"

Princess Rhea tilted her chin higher. "I am not in a position to promise you that."

A corner of the Seer's mouth tilted up.

"You aren't?"

It was a question, but something lingered beneath the surface: Did Kai know who he truly spoke to? Rhea tried to keep her face clear of anything that would reveal her. It had been a calculated risk to come to Kai at all, but she had prayed to any god that would listen that he would be willing to help whether he knew her identity or not. And if not from kindness, then for the promise of wealth. But if he could be bought another way…

Kai gave a boisterous sigh.

"Oh, I suppose not. You are, of course, only a Ladies maid? No, no, much too poised for that, you are nobility, certainly. A Lady-in-Waiting perhaps?"

Rhea sat silently, her fingers itching to reach for her pendant, but she refused to give him the satisfaction of seeing her unnerved. He could toy with her all he liked. If he wanted to sit in the sweltering heat and contradict himself for the sake of drama, then she would permit it. She would even allow him to be the star of his own show, performing for each and every one of them to see.

"Yes, that's likely it," he hummed, "you certainly can't speak to the King, lest he smite you for the impertinence. No, I suspect only his heir, the Princess—well, I assume she's still the Heir. As far as I'm aware he still hasn't produced a son, much to his chagrin. Though I doubt even she could speak to him without consequences, but even perhaps—"

"Enough." Rhea finally snapped, exhausted by his games. "I... will put in a good word. Her Highness is amenable, so I'm sure some arrangement can be had."

A bright smile formed on Kai's lips as he spread his arms, bracelets tinkling and shifting. "That is all I can ask." His hand shot out once more. "Do we have a deal?"

Rhea had the sinking suspicion that she was signing their death certificate as she slid her hand into Kai's awaiting one.

All the air left the room as Rhea said sternly, "We have a deal."

Chapter Six

C al's tense gaze was trained on the threadbare rug that stood in as a makeshift floor, but he was no less aware of the woman and her escort. The shadows whispered and curled around Cal's ear, telling him of the tense set of the guard's shoulder and the anxious fidgeting of the woman. His rage was a storm on the sea, thrashing and relentless, but he had to quell it—at least until he got what he wanted. No, *needed* from these people.

Cal lifted his eyes to see the guard watching him intently. A smirk rose to his lips. The guard narrowed his eyes, his hand still in reach of his sword.

Good, thought Cal, *you're going to need it.*

The woman looked resolved as she reached for Kai's hand. Kai was smiling like a madman, but even his outlandish performance hadn't swayed what the woman had come here to do. The woman was a fool for trusting the Princess–and Kai for that matter–regardless of what the Princess was after. The woman released Kai's hand, returning it to her lap. Her gaze trailed from Kai's face, colliding with Cal's stare. Her eyes widened almost imperceptibly, and her breath caught. Something like recognition flashed in her expression, but she shook her head and returned her gaze to Kai. Cal narrowed his own eyes, taking in her features with renewed interest.

She was beautiful, with warm brown skin and dark ebony hair, but it was her swollen, lacerated lip that caught his eye. Had the Princess struck her? Her guard or a lover? Cal flexed his hand, his shadows rising in accordance with his anger. But he stopped. He shook his head, forcing his mind to focus on what mattered.

Did she know him? She likely bore witness to his power and wrath if she had been at court while Cal resided there. The woman looked to be in her early twenties, making her a few years younger than him. If their paths did cross at some point, Cal didn't remember, though it wasn't important. He hadn't even bothered to learn her or the guard's names—and didn't care to.

She was a means to an end.

She had the funds and information about the Cave of Splendors that Cal had spent the better part of a decade looking for—and he would stop at nothing to have it. Cal pushed off the pole he leaned against, drawing everyone but Kai's attention. The woman's guard palmed his sword and glared at Cal. Cal held his stare, silently daring him, begging him to draw. It had been a while since Cal had felt blood on his hands.

"Now, Lady Hera," Kai clicked his tongue, "this partnership will never work if your guard dog constantly threatens my brothers."

Cal's smirk widened into a sneer, and he let out a rough bark. Kasper choked on a laugh, and delight glimmered in Kai's eyes. The guard dog's nostrils flared, and he stepped forward. The woman placed a hand on his chest, halting him.

"We need them, Brander. Put your sword away."

The guard dog, *Brander*, held Cal's gaze, a challenge dancing there. Cal's blood was practically vibrating with the need to put the palace mutt back in his place. But a moment later, the man straightened and resheathed his sword.

"Good dog." Cal muttered, raising his chin in a challenge.

The woman suddenly turned her eyes on him, blazing with fury. "Do not speak to him in that manner."

Cal raised a brow. He summoned the darkness, allowing the shadows to ripple around him. He leaned down toward her, bracing his arms on the table. To her credit, she didn't shrink back, not even when Cal said in an icy voice, "I'm not one of your pets. I don't take orders from you, so I suggest you keep your commands to yourself."

The guard dog moved to grab Cal, but he froze halfway, his hand suspended in midair. Black shadows danced around his wrist, coiling and wending their way up his arm until they encircled his throat.

"Don't think for a moment that your dog could take me." Cal held the woman's gaze as he spoke. "My brother may have struck a deal with you, but I am here for myself. The success of your insignificant task is of no consequence to me. You'll do good to remember that I owe you nothing." Cal stepped back, and the shadows dissipated; the guard dog staggered as he regained his footing.

"You're as wretched as I remember." the woman said, more to herself than anyone, but that didn't stop Kai from raising his brow or Kasper from taking a rekindled interest in the conversation.

Cal didn't care. He meant what he said. He was only going along with his brother's plan to get the item he sought; whatever happened to the woman was not his concern. But something tugged at him, goading him into responding. Maybe it was her insolence or defiance. Whatever it was, it urged him to answer.

Against his better judgment, Cal turned and beheld the woman again. He took in her plain—but still fine quality—clothing and jewelry. It wasn't overstated like Kai's, but still indicated wealth. Cal had spent enough time at court to spot the truly wealthy. Their dress wasn't extravagant because there was no need for it. Their wealth spoke for itself. And that's exactly what this woman exhibited, from her haughty composure to the lithe in her speech. None of that mattered, not when Cal's entire goal was obtaining a treasure that had nothing to do with the petulant woman before him. Cal let his darkness—his *wretchedness*, as the woman had so kindly put it—shine through.

"If you think I was terrible before, you have no idea what you have gotten yourself into."

The light in the tent gutted. Voices whispered and taunted. Wind tore through the space, ripping at their clothes and hair. Shouts of protest rang out, but Cal paid them no mind, not as he honed in on the rhythmic pounding of the woman's heart. It kicked up faintly but held there, not rising despite the rapidly dropping temperature and the increasing intensity of the wind. No, it remained constant when even the guard dog's pulse thrummed faster and faster.

"Caliban." a voice sang out. It was persistent and lovely, a light in the dark. It beckoned to him, pleading with him to follow into the inky nothingness. For a moment, Cal considered following, and months ago he almost had, but that pesky, nagging sliver of hope kept him from tumbling off the edge. Cal called back the wind and darkness, reined in the voice, and returned the temperature to normal. Everyone stood in the same place as before. Kasper's eyes were wide and his knuckles were white against the black stone he clutched in his hand. Cal resisted rolling his eyes at his brother's fear. At the ridiculous notion that his crystals were a match against what Cal could conjure.

The woman still had a fierce look about her, despite her now disheveled appearance. "Is that all you have?" she spat at him. "Parlor tricks meant to terrorize and torment? I would have thought you would have grown out of such petty actions in ten years."

A dark chuckle fell from Cal's lips. "That was just a taste of my power, Lady Hera." he drawled, her name becoming a sneer against his mouth. "Parlor tricks indeed in comparison to what I am capable of."

Lady Hera raised her chin in defiance. Cal smirked in response before he turned to Kai, who was rearranging his clothes and fluffing his hair. He turned his warm, amber eyes to Cal and gave an impertinent smile. The grin tempted Cal to show the true extent of his power. Instead, he flexed a muscle in his jaw and asked, "When are we departing?"

Kai's eyes fluttered, and he looked at Lady Hera. "When would you like to leave?"

Cal cut his eyes in time to see her gaze shift from him to Kai. She cleared her throat and replied, "As soon as possible. Time is of the essence."

Kai nodded absentmindedly. "It is indeed." Kai clapped, startling Kasper, who still stroked the ebony crystal in his hand. "Well, let us gather the necessities, and we shall depart at sunset."

Kai stood dramatically, swishing his cape. It brushed against Cal's leg, and he defied the urge to rip the ridiculous thing from his brother's shoulders. Lady Hera stood, her mutt coming to her side once more.

"Wonderful. Brander and I will return with food provisions."

"That would be greatly appreciated." Kai added without looking back at her. She glanced at Cal, but quickly looked away. Cal smirked to himself. He was glad she was finally catching on to the monster that lurked just beneath the surface.

Ignoring him, Lady Hera turned her attention to Kasper, asking, "What markets will still be open?"

Kasper's nervous eyes darted around the room before he replied in an unsure voice, "Oh, well. Um, the bakery at the city edge stays open late. They should have some hard bread. And the butcher up the block from there will have dried meat."

Lady Hera nodded tersely. "Thank you. We will return shortly." She glanced at her guard dog. "Come, Brander."

The mutt sent one more menacing look in Cal's direction. Cal couldn't stop himself as he made whimpering sounds. "Run along now, doggy. We wouldn't want your master to leave you."

A muscle ticked in the guard dog's jaw before he turned and left the tent after Lady Hera. Cal smiled to himself as he turned to go back to his room.

"You shouldn't antagonize them like that." Kasper said quietly. Cal stopped dead in his tracks. He turned his icy gaze on his brother. Kasper—eclipse save him—still held onto the onyx stone.

"I beg your pardon, *little* brother?" Cal seethed.

Kasper's throat bobbed a moment, his eyes flicking to Kai, but Cal quickly stepped in front of his gaze. His little brother would find no ally in Malakai; this was between them.

"I mean that neither she nor her guard has done anything to us. There's no reason to be hostile or make an enemy of them."

Cal closed the distance between them in an instant. The surprise of his speed was evident on Kasper's face. "I need no reason for what I do, Kas." he spat. "But even if I did, *they*," he said, pointing toward the tent's entrance, "are an extension of *him*. If I want to exercise my ire on them, then I will do so. You can either be on my side, or get out of my way."

Kasper blinked slowly, but nodded his understanding.

Cal stepped away, and Kasper slumped in response. A twinge of guilt passed through Cal, but he shook it off. He couldn't afford weakness, and neither could Kasper. He had been too young to fully understand everything that had happened at the palace, and maybe Cal was envious of that. Maybe Kasper's innocence and naivety were too much for Cal's bitterness. Cal did not want to dwell on his shortcomings or regrets any longer. He turned from his brothers and stalked through the short breezeway connecting the tent sections. There were items and supplies he needed to gather—things he would need to keep them alive on this journey.

Judging by the aftermath of that initial meeting, Cal knew it would undoubtedly end in at least one death.

Chapter Seven

"What an absolutely pathetic excuse for a person." Rhea muttered. She lifted the sack of hard bread and ship biscuits higher, carefully examining the bag. Though, truthfully, she had no idea what she was looking for. Rhea had never prepared her own food, let alone shopped for it.

Even in the past week traveling with Brander, he had taken the lead on securing them provisions. It mostly came in the form of ordering from whatever inn they stayed in, but that was still more than she would have been able to manage on her own. Rhea subtly pondered what skills she did have and what value she brought to their journey—save for funding it. And even that wasn't *her* money, not really.

She had nothing that was her own.

Sighing, she let the sack fall back to the floor. She should have asked how they planned to travel, but she had been so angry, so caught off-guard by Caliban, that it hadn't crossed her mind. Brander shifted beside her, surveying the store, though he didn't offer any thoughts on what they should purchase. But by the tense set of his jaw, it was clear that he was still upset about their encounter with the Master of Fate and his siblings.

"I warned you that they may not be as you remembered them, my Lady."

Rhea sighed through her nose. "I know. I just hoped that they would be more receptive. If not to my ask, then at least the riches they would be paid." Rhea inspected another bag, her finger running over the ink printed on the outside of the bags. "Spiced with cinnamon and cloves," Rhea read to herself.

She wondered which the Nader men preferred.

"Agh." Rhea groaned and shook her head. Why did she care what they would like? Kai meant to provoke and unsettle her. Caliban antagonized her, and Kasper, well, he hadn't done anything but watch her. Every time she found him his gaze was already fixed on her. She'd wondered and worried over what he had thought when he first saw her. She had never expected Cal or Kai to remember her—she had been newly eleven when they were exiled—but a small part of her thought Kasper would.

Once again, she told herself it was a good thing that he didn't. Isn't that what she wanted? It would certainly make this journey all the easier. And maybe it was her vanity speaking, but even now she was tormented by the fact that her closest childhood friend did not recognize her.

"We need to leave soon, my Lady. The sun is setting, and I don't want to be caught out in the city after dark." Brander murmured, lifting the bag of spiced ship biscuits and the dried meat from the butcher's.

Rhea nodded. "We just need to finish up here, and then we can go."

The counter she approached was worn and non-descript, as nearly everything was this far from the wealth of Mirador's center. Brander sat their goods on it—two ten-pound bags of hard bread. Rhea had no idea how long their journey would take. The books she had read gave conflicting reports about the location of the Cave of Splendors. Even the one that she brought with her focused more on the legends of the Cave rather than where it resided, but she surmised that if they had to stop for supplies, they simply would.

The shopkeeper muttered their fee and Rhea deftly handed over more than twice the sum in gold, careful not to let her gaze linger on the face minted in the metal. She barely registered the look of surprise on the clerk's face as he quickly gave Rhea her change back.

"I'm sorry, I don't have enough to give you back what you are owed." the clerk's palms were upraised and his mouth drawn tight.

"It's alright." Rhea gave a quick smile and took what change was offered. "Thank you."

The clerk gestured to the other goods available. "Please take whatever you like, it's only right."

Rhea snuck a glance at Brander, his face impassive.

"Well, if you insist."

Rhea reached for the fresh baked goods, taking the ghraybeh from the shelf. Her sweet tooth was insatiable, and the aroma had drawn her attention from the moment they stepped foot in the shop. However, she managed to show enough restraint not to shove the warm cookie into her mouth immediately. She gave her thanks once more before exiting the store. Brander was in tow, carrying their supplies. Glancing up at the sky, she noted the rays of red and orange that the sun now cast across it.

"We need to hurry." Brander said gruffly.

Rhea turned to find that he stared out beyond them. There were more people out on the streets than before they had arrived at the butcher's. Some seemed to have just roused from an afternoon nap, while others seemed wary. Their eyes shifted about the streets, looking, searching for something—or *someone*. An uneasiness settled over Rhea, instinctively she stepped closer to Brander.

"Just keep your eyes down and your other senses alert. And if I tell you to run, you *run*." he said, punctuating the last word with force.

Rhea didn't want to know what terrible scenarios his mind had conjured. She had lived her entire life behind the safety of the palace walls, but she wasn't ignorant to the dangers that persisted beyond. They walked briskly down the street, the breeze stirring the dust and the remaining fragrances of shops readying to close for the evening. They weren't in a residential district, so the lights and lanterns of the shops around them were being extinguished as the sun descended to the horizon. Rhea continued to scan the streets, her eyes tripping over the characters milling about.

"Keep your eyes down. And pull your scarf up." Brander growled. Rhea wasn't one for taking orders, but Brander never spoke with force unless he thought it imperative. Rhea did as she was commanded, securing her maroon scarf tighter around her head.

They walked on for several minutes without incident. The only sounds were the conversations of the people they passed by and the scuffing of their boots against the limestone streets, which tapered off to dusty paths as they moved away from the city. The buildings shifted from towering structures to ramshackle hovels, the streets becoming more crowded with vagrants.

"And where are you headed, pretty?" A voice beckoned as Rhea and Brander passed by.

"Dangerous to be out at this time of night," another cooed, "it's not safe for a sweet thing like you."

Rhea's heart hammered in her chest. She fought the urge to lift her eyes and meet the male who dared speak to her in such a manner. Brander would protect her, that much she had faith in, but she was heir to the mightiest kingdom on the continent, and she would not let some degenerate cow her.

Another half mile, and they would be at the edge of the city. Rhea raised her gaze to see the sun winking out at the edge of the desert, giving its last light to illuminate the tents that billowed and swayed in the evening breeze. She shifted her gaze to the city around her; males trailed them. Rhea tried to keep her breathing even and prayed they would have the good sense to leave them be. Daring a look over her shoulder, she caught the eyes of one. He sent her a wicked smile that chilled Rhea to the bone—her steps faltering. Too late, she realized her mistake.

There was a scuffle of feet behind her, and she turned to see Brander—his sword out. Supplies thudded to the ground, forgotten. Four men faced off with him. They all smiled wickedly, varying amounts of rotting ivory teeth and golden false ones.

"You should have known better than to be here." one said before he spit a wad of phlegm on the ground. Another chuckled and shifted his stance. The third and fourth traded vile grins as they crept closer, curved swords and daggers in hand.

Sweat gathered along Rhea's temples and nape. The violence that their sneers and leering eyes promised reminded her far too much of her father. Her eyes darted to and from the men surrounding them and Brander. His jaw was tense as he shifted into a defensive stance.

"Run when I tell you." He murmured softly.

She barely heard him over the roar of blood in her ears. Brander moved, positioning Rhea behind him, and all four men in front.

"Enough of this." hissed the second man. He launched forward, his sword angled for Brander's chest. But Brander was ready. He parried his attack with enough force that the man went flailing backward. The others charged. Their weapons raised—murder gleamed in their hollow eyes.

Rhea stumbled backward, her foot catching on the sacks of food. She threw her hands back in an attempt to break her fall; the packed earth of the streets did little to ease her descent. She scrambled away, dirt and rocks digging into her palms as she tried to keep one eye on the fight in front of her and the other on the streets ahead. The clash of metal drew her attention back to Brander and the assailants. Brander swung, catching the blade of the first man, and twisted, shoving him into the other two. The third man lay on the ground, unmoving. Brander turned, reaching toward where she trembled on the ground and grabbed for her.

His fingers dug into the flesh of her upper arm as he hauled her up and gave a shove before shouting, "GO!"

The force of his shove and her own momentum nearly sent her to the ground again. She didn't want to abandon Brander. He was still outnumbered, but what good was she in a fight? No, she would be more help if she got away, and then he could focus on disarming the other three.

Rhea finally got her feet back under her and ran, not sparing another glance at Brander. She just needed to make it back to the caravan, then she could get Cal and Kasper to help. Yes, they would help her. She just needed to find them.

Rhea cursed her long skirts as she tripped through the city streets, drawing more unnecessary attention. More people shouted things and sent leering looks, but Rhea kept running. Her lungs and limbs burned like she never experienced. Her foot caught on her skirt and she careened forward. Curses tumbled from her lips as her palms smacked into the earth and pain shot up her arms. She scrambled up, wiping her hands on her skirt as she tried to get up. Finding Cal or Kasper was no longer an option. She wasn't going to make it that far. She saw an alley to her left and turned, ducking into the darkening corridor.

She just needed a moment to catch her breath. Rhea pressed her body against the warm bricks, sweat trickling down her spine. The breeze dancing through the alley did nothing to cool her. Rhea closed her eyes and tried to remember her purpose. The need to save her people. She had to stop the prophecy from coming true, and the only way to do that was to find Izor's Lamp. Rhea took deep breaths, though her lungs protested and her legs shook as if her bones and muscles had been replaced with jelly. She turned and pressed her forehead to the wall, her pulse thumping dizzily. This journey was always going to be arduous and dangerous, Rhea knew that, but she was quickly realizing that knowledge and experience were two vastly different things.

Rhea was unsure of how much time had passed before the throbbing in her skull abated enough that she could hear something other than its pulsating.

The breeze—and the shuffling of feet.

Her eyes flew open, but it was too late. A thick hand clamped down on her mouth.

"Be quiet, and this will be over quick, girl."

Raucous fumes washed over Rhea, souring her stomach.

She lurched sideways, but the force of the man yanked her to him, twisted her, and slammed her into the wall. Stars burst in her sight as her head cracked against the wall.

Panic rose in her chest.

She couldn't move. Couldn't fight. She was helpless. So stupidly helpless to save herself. She had been a fool to think that she could actually find the Cave of Splendors or survive the arduous journey. All of her reading on magic, strategy, and diplomacy were useless. She was going to die at the hands of some common criminal, and her kingdom would fall to destruction. She was a woefully ill-equipped fool.

The man's hateful gaze raked down her body, trailed by his other hand. Bile rose in Rhea's throat, burning as it threatened to appear.

The man opened his mouth to speak—but the words were cut off. His eyes widened, and then his hand went slack over her mouth. It took Rhea all of one second to push the man away from her. He tumbled to the ground, a jeweled dagger protruding from the base of his neck. Rhea lifted her eyes to find Kasper standing a foot away, the dead man between them. Kasper's gaze was hard and unyielding. His posture rigid and his face devoid of everything but death. He was wrath incarnate—and he looked so much like Cal.

The trembling that wracked her body was unstoppable. She lunged for Kasper. She needed to touch someone to replace the suffocating feel of the man's hand on her skin. Her arms locked around his body, and she pressed her face into his chest, savoring the faint scent of incense that clung to his clothes. Kasper stiffened beneath her touch but quickly slid his arms around her. She held him till the shaking subsided and her pulse returned to normal. She stepped out of Kasper's embrace, careful of the dead man at her feet.

She was dimly aware that to Kasper she was effectively a stranger, and perhaps she should have felt embarrassed, but all she could see in him at the moment was the boy she used to know. A faint blush stained Kasper's cheeks as his gaze flitted from Rhea to the body cooling in the streets. Already, blood pooled beneath, turning the dirt a rusty shade of brown. Kasper bent down and pulled the dagger from the man's neck. Rhea turned, pressing a hand to her stomach. She had no desire to see blood gush from the wound. Something wet leaked onto Rhea's neck. Instinctively, she reached for it, wincing as her fingers touched the back of her head.

"You're bleeding." Kasper whispered.

Rhea examined her fingers, her voice breathy and far away as she said, "The skin must have broken when he…" her voice trailed off, not eager to put words to the man's actions.

"Here." Kasper said, as he reached for the hem of his shirt and yanked, ripping a strip from the fabric.

Rhea opened her mouth to protest, but Kasper was already wiping her blood from her fingers. She smiled sheepishly and said jokingly, "Now if only healing my injury were as simple."

Kasper knitted his brows, and then they shot up, wrinkling his forehead. He looked down, his hands burrowing into the pockets of his threadbare breeches.

"What are you—"

A purple rock appeared in his hand. No, not a rock, a crystal.

A memory of a small boy with golden-brown curls and a missing front tooth flashed in Rhea's mind.

Kasper cradled the gem tenderly and looked at her, his eyes wide and searching. He lifted the crystal and gestured toward her head. "Can I?"

Rhea blinked once. Twice. And then nodded her head.

"Oh! Yes, of course." She turned, putting her back to him so he could reach her wound.

The air shifted as Kasper's breath skated over her ear and his fingers brushed against her head, drawing a shiver from her.

"Sorry, it'll be just another moment."

Rhea held still as death, even as her scalp began to tingle and itch where Kasper's fingers touched her. And then it was over. The sensation dissipated and Kasper's presence shifted to her side. Rhea started to turn and thank him, but a hand slid around her elbow and pulled her away, back to the main street.

"We should go before someone discovers the body. Cal and your guard should be heading back this way."

Rhea barely had enough time to register Kasper's words, or process that he had healed her, when Cal and Brander appeared before them. There was a shallow gash across Brander's shoulder, his chest rose rapidly, and there was a fervent but controlled look in his eyes. Cal looked indifferent, his gaze roving over Rhea in a way that made her want to pull her scarf tighter around her.

"Prin–" Rhea tensed at Brander's near slip, shaking her head quickly. "Lady Hera, are you alright?"

"Yes, I'm alright. Kasper got to me before…" she swallowed, uninterested in reliving the recent events so soon. She licked her lips and added, "Before anything unfortunate could happen."

Brander's eyes scanned her face and then further down, snagging on where Kasper still touched her arm.

"Take your hands off her." Brander all but growled.

Kasper narrowed his gaze.

"Brander, that isn't necessary. Kasper saved me."

Brander ignored her and instead repeated, "Remove your hand."

Kasper held Brander's gaze for another moment before looking to Rhea, who was unable to tear her stare from Brander. Heat burned in her cheeks at Brander's protectiveness. Rhea opened her mouth to tell Brander to back down, but Cal cut in before the words could come out.

"Easy there, boy. No reason to get rabid on us."

Rhea narrowed her eyes and stared at Cal.

He only smirked. Slowly, Kasper's fingers left her elbow, and she immediately mourned their absence. Kasper may not remember who they were to one another, but Rhea did, and she was grateful that his kindness and compassion had lasted into adulthood.

Rhea cleared her throat and returned her gaze to Brander. She lifted her chin and said sternly, "Thank you for saving me, Brander, which is exactly what Kasper did. I also appreciate your care and concern, but I do not need you to decide who can touch me."

Rhea saw her statement register on Brander's face. Like a physical blow. But to his credit, he merely nodded and said, "I apologize, my Lady."

Rhea knew she would need to discuss it further with him, but now was not the time. They needed to get out of the city before someone found the body and started asking too many questions. Rhea glanced at each of them, careful not to let her gaze linger on any one of them for too long. "We need to get moving before soldiers show up to investigate."

Cal chuckled.

Rhea narrowed her eyes at him. "Is something humorous to you?"

"Around these parts, people settle things themselves," Cal lifted an eyebrow, "we don't bother calling in palace dogs to handle our disputes."

Rhea crossed her arms. "People died tonight. That won't go unnoticed."

"I never said it would."

"What did you mean, then?"

"That the people that die here are of no consequence to people like you."

Rhea recoiled. "That's not true. The governor will want answers, which means an investigation. I can't afford to get caught up in a murder. My mission is too important. We need to move. Now." Rhea refrained from adding that the imperial soldiers were likely already on high alert because of her disappearance from the palace. Her father might be indifferent to her, but he would abhor not having her close enough to control and torment.

Cal's laughter splintered Rhea's thoughts. He turned and stalked away, sheathing the dagger Rhea hadn't noticed him holding before. "If you're done scolding the dog and pretending that you care about something other than your manicure, then I guess we can head back."

Rhea bit her cheek to keep her retort in check. He was working to get under her skin, and she wouldn't give him the satisfaction. Cal didn't look back once to see if anyone had followed.

Rhea knew he wouldn't, but she followed after him anyway.

Chapter Eight

Boredom was going to be the death of Malakai. He absentmindedly turned the sand in the miniature hourglass end over end. The sand tumbled over and over, filling and emptying itself. The grains of sand blended, shifting from respective particles to the whole of a collective.

It amused him. To watch the individuality of the sand fade into nothing, swallowed entirely by the similarities of the grains around it.

But after the third or fourth turn, the hourglass and its sand had lost its novelty. When Caliban and Kasper had departed, Malakai attempted to occupy himself by packing their things. But that had taken barely a half hour, and they still had not returned. Though, if the trouble Malakai had seen had come to pass, then it wasn't entirely surprising that they still hadn't returned. He knew they would be fine. A little bruised, perhaps, but intact.

Malakai stood, officially tired of his sand.

That was always the problem. Tedium and moods came and went too swiftly. Too quick for Malakai to adjust and be content. His sights settled on his favorite item, his chaise. He had found it abandoned not long after they had fled the palace and since then it went wherever he went. He ran a loving finger along the side before he flopped into the awaiting chaise. Dust clouded around him, relocating to the pristine white of his tunic. Malakai struggled to care. The tent was too quiet, giving too much space for his thoughts. Or, more specifically, the memories.

Malakai stood again, his fingers and mind itching for a distraction.

Entertainment.

Amusement.

Something.

Anything.

He moved his and Kasper's belongings closer to the entrance. And then rearranged them from biggest to smallest. Then newest to oldest. But nothing eased the restlessnesses. A swift departure was expected, given the trouble Malakai had seen. But that still hadn't taken very long, and idleness had quickly set in.

Malakai brushed his hands over his lute, covered in an inch of dust and propped in the corner of the tent. Perhaps he would resume his lessons. He struck a chord. Off-kilter and dull. Fitting. Sighing, he returned the lute to its resting place.

Finally, voices murmured from outside the tent, accompanied by the scuffle of boots. Malakai's heart leapt at the arrival of his siblings and the Princess—excited to finally start on their journey. He couldn't remember the last time he had felt genuine jubilance for anything other than new jewelry or more shisha, but here he was, practically bursting with giddiness. Malakai brushed his hands down his breeches and pasted on a brilliant smile.

The tent's flaps flew open. Caliban blew in like a tempest, not bothering to speak to or even acknowledge Malakai. His shadows curled around him as he disappeared through the back.

"Please be ready to leave in five minutes." Malakai called after him.

Caliban grumbled, but Malakai had already turned his attention back to the others who had filtered in and stood awkwardly in the space. Kasper's eyes were trained on the ground. His dagger's orange and amber hilt was glowing and clutched tightly in his fist. Malakai let his eyes trail over to the Princess and her guard, rage painted on both their features, though he wasn't sure who it was directed at. And honestly, it didn't matter. Malakai shook his head and smiled softly to himself. This journey would be eventful regardless of what they encountered on their way.

Wanting to dispel the tension, Malakai lifted his hands and clapped loudly. Everyone jumped and lifted their eyes toward him, as expected. "Now that we are all together again and in one piece, perhaps we can begin our adventure," Malakai said as he winked toward the Princess. Her guard bared his teeth in response, and Malakai clucked his tongue. "If you don't want to be referred to as a dog, I might suggest not acting like one."

Kasper snorted and then coughed to cover his laughter. Malakai merely smiled, ignoring the Princess's rueful gaze as it bore into his face. Caliban emerged from the back, boots pounding into the ground. He had a large burlap sack slung over his shoulder, likely loaded with unholy spells and curses. Malakai hadn't dared to touch his twin's things—lest they be spelled with something wretched.

His dark eyes marked each of them before he went to the tent entrance and gruffly said, "Let's get a move on."

The Princess's face was still blazing, her eyes tracking Caliban as she turned on her heel after him.

Oh, that would be trouble, indeed.

Kasper watched after them, his face feigning indifference, but something else simmered there, too. Malakai tilted his head, visions swimming in his mind. If Kasper hadn't recognized the Princess before, Malakai suspected his long-laid plans still held, but if not...Malakai shook his head and turned his attention back to the possible paths and potential outcomes. None were clear save for one: they all needed each other to even think of reaching the Cave of Splendors.

"Are we ready to depart?"

Kasper said nothing as he grabbed the bags Malakai had packed. The items inside clinked and clacked against themselves as he lifted them from the ground. He moved wordlessly through the tent and gave the guard a wide berth as he exited. The guard allowed Kasper the time to leave before he left himself.

Malakai let his smile fall, and he turned to survey the small tent. The hastily erected shelves were bare once more, and the caravan would take away the meager furniture they had collected. Malakai believed that what was lost would come back in time. He gave his temporary home one last look, his eyes lingering on his most treasured item—his chaise—before leaving the tent. The dry desert air ruffled Malakai's hair, and he inhaled the sand and earth scent of the breeze. He missed the jasmine and lily scent of the palace gardens, but the desert had grown on him in the last few years.

Malakai turned to find Caliban tightening the straps on a midnight mare. Four other horses—two dapple grays, a piebald, and a brown one—stood nearby, all ready to be mounted. There were also two mules, their supplies already strapped down to the creatures. Malakai connected to the piebald immediately and stepped forward, brushing his hand down its muzzle.

Kasper cautiously approached the brown mare, who nickered and nayed softly. Malakai smirked and said, "It's a sweet-tempered creature, Kasper. You'll be fine."

Kasper cut his eyes and blew out a breath before sticking his foot in the stirrup and hoisting himself up on the mare. He adjusted himself, his features becoming puzzled.

"What?" Malakai inquired.

The furrow in Kasper's brows remained even as he shook his head and said, "I don't remember learning to ride a horse, but…"

A breathy laugh pushed past Malakai's lips. "I've told you how fickle the mind is. Some things are just muscle memory. Even I don't actively remember when I learned to ride, but my body remembers."

"Still—"

"Worry no more about it. We have bigger things ahead of us," Malakai assured, his tone nonchalant. But with the Princess's arrival and Cal's presence, Malakai worried—

No.

Nothing was unraveling. Everything would be fine.

Malakai turned his attention from his brother and pressed a kiss into his horse's muzzle. He whispered kind words to the animal, then he moved around to the side and lifted himself up into the mount. Malakai gripped the reins, turned his mare, and watched the Princess and the guard. The guard inspected the mount and horse before he eased the Princess up, and then he took up his own mount.

Malakai, never content to not cause trouble, asked, "And where did you get these fine specimens, dear Caliban?" There was a beat of silence, only the horses and the shifting of sand between them. They set out, moving further from the city and caravan into the desert—toward the coast.

"A local stable was looking to offload some equestrian cargo." Caliban finally said, indifferently. "They were quite accommodating to our price range."

Malakai smiled at the sounds of dismay from the others, but said nothing. He chuckled to himself as he flicked the reins on his mare and urged her forward.

This was going to be an eventful journey, indeed.

* * * *

As darkness fell over them, Malakai had fallen to the back of the group, content to watch the others lead. The Princess and her guard stayed close to one another, not far behind Caliban, who had taken the lead. He knew where they needed to go, even if he hadn't bothered to tell the others. Malakai's eyes drifted over to Kasper, who was quieter than usual since he returned with the Princess. Something had transpired between them. The mare beneath Malakai obeyed as he brought it closer to Kasper, who cut his eyes to him, but said nothing.

Several minutes passed before Kasper's shoulders relaxed in the moonlight. Then, Malakai asked, "What happened with the Lady?"

The tension sprang through his body again, and he replied in a tight voice, "Nothing. She was in trouble, and I helped her. That's it."

A half smile formed on Malakai's lips. "Shall I divine the truth, brother?" Malakai was treading on dangerous ground, but he had to know if Kasper had guessed the truth about the lady. Kasper cut his eyes once more, his grip tightening on the reins of his horse. Malakai saw the contemplation on his features—ride ahead and draw the attention of the Princess, or stay back and endure Malakai's questions.

A heartbeat passed, and Kasper sighed with resignation.

"After I eliminated the threat, she hugged me." He muttered under his breath. Malakai raised a brow, but Kasper interjected quickly, "It was nothing, honestly. She was in shock or something akin to that. But her companion nearly tore my throat out because I was steadying her. I saved her and my reward was almost getting gutted." Kasper rolled his eyes, and his lip curled.

Malakai let out an entirely inappropriate laugh. The heads of the Princess and guard whipped in their direction, but Malakai paid them no mind. No, his attention was focused solely on the disdain rolling off Kasper in waves.

Gentle, sweet, unassuming Kasper was angry with someone.

Suddenly, Malakai's vision was clouded with images of children playing. The thudding of footsteps echoed through his mind, his chest filled with laughter that split his face into a grin, his heart lifted at the shared camaraderie of child-like secrets—

Malakai jerked, his horse braying and kicking in response.

"Kai, what's wrong? What did you see?" Kasper's bent brows and caramel eyes bore into Malakai. Malakai shook his head, dispelling the smoke from his vision.

It was a vision of the past. As Malakai looked harder into who the children were, he saw those familiar caramel eyes again. But instead of looking at him, they looked at the fierce and bright eyes of the Princess. Malakai released a shaky breath and willed a smile to his face. He reached out to grip Kasper's bicep and gave it a gentle squeeze. "I am well, just flashes of a long-forgotten memory."

Kasper's brows remained furrowed, but nothing was hiding in those eyes. Nothing suspicious of the truth. Malakai released his brother and sighed, this one much more forlorn. Kasper had no idea the Princess from his childhood was the woman he had saved earlier. He was wholly unaware hat the girl from his dreams and fractured memories was a mere fifteen feet away.

Malakai intended to keep it that way.

He fell back, giving his brother more space, and turned his attention to the stars that winked above. The heavens and cosmos spun and twirled around them, aligning for this moment to occur—that much Malakai was convinced of. Malakai wouldn't consider himself devout by any measure. Religion was so often just a means to control others, but there was something beyond ordered chaos. Whether it was the Forgotten gods or Fates or Destiny—names of any specific beings had been lost to the centuries of conquest and revision of history—Malakai didn't know, but there was too much falling into place for it to be mere coincidence.

He let the surety of his visions, of the dreams that had chased and followed him since before their exile, comfort him. If he was wrong, if his visions led them astray, then Malakai would be risking more than a chance at the life he was robbed of—the price would likely be one of their lives. For as wicked as it made him, Malakai was willing to accept the sacrifice.

Chapter Nine

Brander strained his eyes in the dark. The shadow summoner insisted that it was safer not to use a lantern, but Brander didn't trust him. He didn't trust any of them. Even if the Seer had sent the Necromancer and the boy to help them.

Part of Brander resented it, but his pride wasn't too great to acknowledge that without their help, he may not have gotten to the Princess in time. And if any harm had befallen her…no, Brander denied his thoughts from going there. There was no question how the story would end if Brander's fear got the best of him, and he had no interest in repeating that tale. Princess Rhea was the future–Desmorda's future–and he would not let her down.

Gripping the reins on his stallion tighter, Brander dared to spare a glance at the Princess. The moon offered little light, but the Princess's shoulders drooped, and her body jostled with the movement of her mare. Brander moved closer, bringing his stallion nearer, just in case. Abruptly, the Princess's hand released the reins, and she listed sideways, away from Brander. Brander reached out, blindly grasping for her shoulder, but it was futile.

"Lady!"

"Ah!" Princess Rhea exclaimed as she tumbled toward the ground–

But she didn't hit the earth. The youngest of them, Kasper, was there. His mare huffed and nickered beside the princess, but Kasper held on to her.

Brander dismounted swiftly and came round her horse. Fury and fear roared through his blood, banishing every rational thought. Brander shoved between Kasper and the Princess, ignoring the sounds of objection. Brander slid his arms under the Princess, pulling her from the saddle and setting her on the ground. If she were sick or injured—

"I'm fine, Brander, really. My eyes are just heavy." Princess Rhea insisted, but Brander wasn't convinced. She had mentioned that she had hit her head in the alley, but she had no signs of an injury when he checked before. He lightly brushed his hands over her shoulders and arms, his eyes scanning and searching for any sign of harm.

Princess Rhea huffed and stepped away from Brander. The Seer and Kasper now stood behind her, watching the scene unfold. "I told you," her tone, sharp and edged with irritation, "I am *fine*."

Brander held her furious gaze for a moment before he nodded and stepped back from the Princess. The Necromancer came round on his midnight mare. The ebony beast brayed, indicating that she, too, was irritated with the hindrance.

"What's all this?"

Brander opened his mouth to interject but thought better of it and remained silent.

The Seer slid off his mare and said, "I believe we have reached the limits of our ability to travel for the night. Perhaps we should retire for a few hours and begin again at dawn?" His words gave the impression of a question seeking permission, but his actions were certain as he gestured to the boy to begin unpacking the mule linked to his mare.

The Necromancer gave an annoyed sigh before he also dismounted. "We'll rest for a few hours." He reached for a pack and tossed it at Brander, who caught it deftly. "You take the first watch," the Necromancer added before he unfurled his own roll.

Brander didn't argue. He planned on staying up anyway. There was no world in which he put the Princess's life in their hands. At least no more than he had to. Brander wordlessly moved his horse to where Kasper had produced two wooden stakes with notches and was slipping the horse's reins through them.

Silence was Brander's companion as he handed over the reins and walked away. The sand of the desert slid and whispered around his feet, covering the soft nickering of the horses. He took up a position less than ten feet from the others. Close enough to step in if something went wrong, but he wanted to give Princess Rhea her space. He knew he was being more protective than he had been in the palace, but surely she saw how much danger they were in? How, at any moment, her life could become forfeit. Already they had encountered men that were prepared and eager to take what they wanted from her—and they had almost succeeded.

Brander would have been too late.

She would have lost her virtue and likely her life had Kasper not found her in time, but she was behaving as though it had been nothing. This was her first time away from the palace and, despite her extensive education, she clearly had no earthly idea how much more danger awaited them. In the morning, he would speak with her. He would try to make her understand that he wasn't trying to stifle or coddle her, but that her life meant everything. He attempted to let the tension in his body dissipate as he scanned the horizon for threats.

But every breath of wind across the desert stirred his fear and rage.

* * * *

"Here."

Brander looked up at Kasper, who held out one of the biscuits the Princess had bought earlier. Brander took in Kasper's own weary gaze, but accepted the food nonetheless. Tentatively, he took a bite and turned back to thank him, but Kasper had already walked away. Brander couldn't blame him. He had been hostile toward him since they had met. He felt a bit of remorse for his aggression, but it was heavily outweighed by his sense of duty to the Princess. Maybe one day, if they all survived this, then Brander could make his amends...but for now, he had no choice but to keep everyone at arm's length.

Brander sighed and returned to eating his second-rate dinner. The Princess still hadn't spoken to him; again, he couldn't blame her. She was woefully out of her depth, but from her apparent nonchalance he had to assume that she didn't grasp the severity of their situation. She was young and sheltered, and even with the abuse she had suffered at the hands of her father, she clearly still didn't think evil persisted in the world—or perhaps she chose to ignore it.

He shifted and watched the Princess finish off the last of her food. She removed her scarf and folded it neatly before laying down. Brander wasn't sure why, but he was certain she was purposely avoiding his gaze.

"You love her."

Brander jumped and reached for his sword. The Seer sat next to him, happily munching on his stale bread as though it was shawarma. The frayed edges of the saddle blanket peeked out from beneath his crossed legs. Brander resettled himself, mildly concerned as to exactly how the Seer had snuck up on him. But he remained there and sent sidelong glances at the Seer. Love in Brander's profession–his life–was a ridiculous notion. Being conscripted as a child made it certain that love would never be in the cards for him.

"I am charged with protecting her."

The Seer tilted his head, "Yes, but you also love her."

Brander turned to face the Seer fully. "No, I don't."

"It's alright," Malakai took another bite, "and I didn't mean romantic love, although I'm sure that's what you assumed. Everyone does when the concept is brought up. I sense more of a familial connection–parental even."

"I suggest you keep your thoughts to yourself." Brander said, his voice dripping with malice.

The Seer held his gaze for another moment before shrugging his shoulders. He popped another sliver of dried meat into his mouth. The breaking of the meat against his teeth rubbed against Brander's already raw nerves. It was only his extensive training that allowed him to maintain his composure.

The wind ruffled Brander's clothes and brushed sand against his skin. The cool desert air reminded him of the years he spent training with the other orphans from his village and those nearby. The King had conquered Brander's country, and the soldiers had moved in. Swift and brutal. Any hope of resistance or rebellion was snuffed out when the village leaders were put to the sword. Swear fidelity or die. Many young men and boys had been rounded up and sent to another part of the empire to be trained–broken, really–and rebuilt in the King's image.

"Sometimes, secretively, of course, I am grateful that my exile has allowed me another perspective of the world." the Seer said, shattering Brander's thoughts. Brander turned to find the Seer staring off in the distance, eyes seeing, but not. A faint smile graced his lips. "Being taken to the palace so young made me think that there was no other way to live, but in the years since, I've seen so much—changed so much."

Brander couldn't stop the snort that erupted from his lips.

The Seer returned his gaze to Brander's. He expected to find anger or indignation at Brander's offense, but there was nothing in his features save for that odd sense that he saw beyond the exterior—all the way to one's soul.

Brander didn't understand why, but he was incapable of stopping himself from saying, "You act nothing like the commoners. Your actions, dress, and speech are still that of the nobility. You are still as removed from commoners as when you lavished behind the palace walls. Aside from that, you wish to return to that life—to wealth and comfort." There was a bite to his words, an anger he worked hard to keep controlled. Years of being told to forget his family, to forget his life from before, came rushing back with a force that nearly took the breath from his lungs.

An infuriating chortle bubbled from the Seer. "I can experience something without wishing it to be my circumstances in perpetuity. If I have the opportunity to return to ease and excess, why would I not seize that?"

Blood and fury pumped through Brander. This man-child was treating what so many in Desmorda experienced for the entirety of their miserable lives like it was a leisurely trip. As if it was a lesson to widen his perspective and not the harsh reality of well over half of the kingdom.

Brander stood up abruptly. He wasn't sure where he needed to go, only that he needed to move. He turned his eyes, catching on the Seer, who still looked at him with that open but assessing gaze. Emotion flickered in his eyes.

Pity.

Brander would have none of it, especially not from the likes of him. He clenched his jaw and hissed, "I don't know what kind of spell or enchantment you're trying to work over me, but it ends now."

The Seer raised an eyebrow. His nonchalance tipped the boiling pot of rage in Brander. There was no stopping the hand that reached out and grabbed the Seer by the front of his tunic. Not once did the Seer's expression change, not even as he glanced down at the hand fisting his shirt.

Brander relished in it.

The snap on his control was tangible—real. And he *loved* it. Years of repression in the name of the King leaked out into Brander, lending him more strength. The man, this foolish, ignorant, self-important man had no idea what real suffering was. But Brander would show him. He wanted it. He wanted more. Feral delight burned—

The cool bite of metal pressed into his neck.

"Release my brother." growled Kasper. Moonlight illuminated the quicksilver blade.

Brander's rapidly moving pulse pushed against the blade, teetering on the precipice of death.

"Brander!" The Princess's voice cut through his blinding fury, sending him tumbling back to earth. Brander kept his eyes trained on the Seer, not daring to look away.

"It's alright." the Seer said blandly.

"Stand down, Brander." the Princess's voice was pure command. The obedience that followed had been beaten and whipped into Brander nearly four decades ago.

He extrapolated his fingers from the Seer's tunic, the fabric crumpled and smudged with grime. The blade at his throat remained for another moment before it too was removed. Brander took slow, deliberate breaths in an attempt to calm his pulse.

He glanced at the Seer, who cocked his head and said, "There's more to you than meets the eye."

Brander shoved down the urge to grab the Seer once more and give him the beating he was entitled to, but he decided he wasn't worth it. Wasn't worth incurring the Princess's rage any more than he already had. Brander glanced at Kasper, who still held his dagger in his hand, distrust blazing in his eyes. Brander clenched his jaw and turned away. His feet carried him further from the others, from the inquisitive gaze of the Seer, the distrustful look of Kasper, and the embarrassed glare of the Princess.

The Seer had done *something*. Seen *something*. And Brander had no interest in hearing what the Seer thought of his past or future. He walked until he didn't feel the press of their gazes upon his skin. He walked until the stress of keeping the Princess alive and the horrors of all he had done since being taken from his village–from his family–floated away on the midnight desert breeze. He dropped to his knees. The weight of his choices, or lack thereof, crushing him. He stared down at his scar-flecked hands. What had his life become? Who had he become? What would his mother think of him?

Once, he dreamed of danger and adventure. Both had come to him, though not in the manner he would have ever wished. A single tear tracked down his cheek. That was all the self-pity he would allow himself. He looked up, staring out at the desert that stretched on endlessly until it blended with the star-studded sky.

"Brander." Princess Rhea spoke from behind him.

He quickly reached up, wiping away the evidence of his anguish. Rising from the ground on unsteady legs, he slipped the mask of an imperial soldier back into place.

"Yes, Princess?"

Her throat bobbed and she crossed her arms—her gaze refusing to meet his. The disappointment and ire on her face were deserved. He had let his anger get the best of him and embarrassed her. Brander folded his arms behind his back and stared up at the moon glimmering in the heavens, awaiting his reprimand.

"Do you think I will make a good queen?"

Brander's gaze crashed back down to the earth and he furrowed his brow. "Of course I do. Why would you ask that?"

"Because I clearly don't command respect. I don't exude any type of authority. Despite the studying I've done to try and compensate for my lack of experience, I am obviously out of my depth."

Brander shook his head. "That's not true."

"It is."

"No, it—"

Princess Rhea whirled. "It is Brander. I can't even get you to respect my authority, how am I supposed to get an entire country to accept my claim? What's stopping the nobles from passing me over and selecting my uncle instead?"

Brander stepped closer. "You are the rightful ruler. You left the protection of the only home you have ever known and are risking your life to find salvation for your people."

The Princess threw up her hands. "Even if all of that is true, that doesn't mean I know how to lead."

"I can help you learn."

"How?"

The words stuck in Brander's throat. He didn't talk about his life much before his reassignment to the palace. "I used to lead men, and I can help you find your voice. But true leadership is not something that can be learned," He paused, pointing to his heart. "It's something that already exists within you. You just have to trust yourself."

Rhea hugged herself. Her brows were still bent, and her mouth was drawn tight. She looked younger in the moonlight. The years of abuse and self-doubt were harder to see. Brander had never learned why the King was violent toward his own child, though rumors suggested it hadn't always been that way. Many whispered that the Queen Hala's death had changed something–broke something–in him, but Rhea had never spoken to Brander about it.

"My father…is volatile and capricious. Once, years ago, I think he cared about his people's needs. He considered the taxes they were burdened with and their access to food, but now…" Princess Rhea took her bottom lip between her teeth, the wince from her split flesh barely registering on her face. She released it after a moment and heaved a sigh. "I just want to be good, Brander, and despite all of the wicked things he has done, I still want to make him proud."

The King would never appreciate his daughter, nor would she ever get the approval she clearly desired. The Seer's words about familial love came back to Brander, but they didn't evoke his fury this time, just sorrow. Brander cleared his throat, and Princess Rhea looked at him, tears shining. For a moment, he allowed his stern features to soften.

"You are not going to be a perfect queen, but," he said, a slight smile forming in his lips at the indignation flashing in her eyes, "you will rule. You will grow and learn to be better. You will become a queen worthy of her people."

Princess Rhea pressed her lips together and nodded. "Thank you," she whispered, her voice thick with emotion. Brander contemplated reaching out to her and offering comfort, but thought better of it.

The Princess gave him another solemn nod and said, "I think it's best we head back now. I wouldn't put it past the Nader men to abandon us out here." Her tone was light, joking even, but Brander saw the flicker of anxiety on her face.

"I will protect you at any cost."

Princess Rhea offered him a tentative smile. "Thank you. But we do have to work with them, so perhaps we should ease off on the threats."

Brander flexed his fingers and said, "I will try to be less hostile, but only so it doesn't appear as though I am undermining you. Again."

A soft laugh emanated from Princess Rhea and she gestured back to their makeshift camp. "Let us try to get some rest tonight."

Princess Rhea began walking, but Brander hesitated. He turned back to the open expanse of the desert once more. They were only a day's ride from his village. And for the first time since he last saw it, the thought of going home didn't make his stomach burn with shame.

Chapter Ten

asper had never taken a life. The altercation in the alley–Lady Hera's terror–burned in his mind. Every time he blinked, the scene blazed there, haunting him. Never had he experienced the hot spray of blood soaking into his clothes, clinging to his skin. Nor had he heard the sharp intake of air—witnessed the fleeting moment of understanding before consciousness slipped away entirely. The acrid tang of fear and death had never so wholly smothered his senses. And never had he watched the light dim in a man's eyes.

It turned him sick.

His guilt was a stone in his gut, dragging him further beneath the tide of self-loathing that threatened to sweep him under. No matter how much he thrashed and kicked against the shame, there was no escaping the horrors of what he had done. And now, that was all Kasper felt.

Smelled.

Saw.

Sometimes, he was certain the metallic flavor coated his tongue and slid down his throat—until he choked on it. Like the man had when Kasper had shoved his dagger into the base of his neck.

But it had been to save her. To prevent that monster from taking what wasn't his, what he had no right to. Kasper would never forget the terror and revulsion painted on her face with the man's weight pushed into her body. Nor would he forget the relief that softened her features when her gaze collided with his, and she reached for him. He was unsure of the draw to her. She was beautiful. More beautiful than any woman Kasper had ever met, but that wasn't the whole of it.

Something nagged at him.

A memory or a dream that was always just out of reach—just beyond his comprehension. Kasper cursed himself for what had to be the thousandth time over the last decade. If only he could *remember*. Kai had said it was his mind protecting him from the pain he likely endured at the palace, but Kasper desperately wished his mind would release his memories. If he could remember, then he might understand why he couldn't keep his eyes off of her, or why he was wholly fixated on the need to touch her again. He wanted to understand wh—

"It is alright, Kasper. You can put your blade away; he will not harm me."

The words jarred Kasper. He blinked, looking at his hand, realizing he was still clutching his jeweled dagger in his fist. The dagger that minutes before had been pressed to Brander's throat. He shook his head and said with more bite than he intended, "He's a palace guard, Kai. They're trained killers. He cares nothing for us, and even if none of that was the case, he just attempted to kill you."

A half smile formed on Kai's lips. "He may have a bit of a temper, but I assure you his anger toward me is a reflection of himself."

Kasper clenched his jaw. He hated when his brother spoke in riddles. Normally, Kai's pretty and convoluted words were saved for customers, but lately they had bled into his normal conversations. Kasper moved to take a step back or to take a breath, but Kai's fingers were still wrapped around his wrist—the dagger somehow in Kai's other hand.

"Don't fret, brother. The sins staining your soul will be absolved."

Kasper flinched, retracting from Kai's grip.

Kai was unfazed, even as Kasper shook his head and stalked away. He remembered why he spent an inordinate amount of time scoping out potential clients rather than in Kai's presence. And he was beginning to understand more and more why Cal had disappeared for years.

Determined not to let his anguish show, Kasper kept his steps steady as he walked past Lady Hera, though her gaze was fixed on Brander. The tight set of her mouth and the way she picked at her cuticles said all it needed to about her feelings toward her guard. Kasper had the passing thought that he should apologize, but for what? He wasn't sorry for stepping in, and she didn't seem to be in the mood for solace. No, Kasper need not delude himself with further entanglements. He was here to keep an eye on Kai and nothing more. At least that's what he would tell himself, even if he did catch himself glancing to see if she would acknowledge his passing.

Desperate for some solace, Kasper let his hand drift to the smooth jasper stone in his pocket, letting the stone's serenity and nurturing properties wash over him. He lifted the stone to his lips and closed his eyes. A pulse of power washed over him, soothing his ragged nerves. His magic was paltry in comparison to his brothers. Despite that, it was comforting to know that when he held his various gems, he could enhance their specific properties. He could even use them to mitigate some of the effects of nerves or small injuries.

"Licking rocks won't solve your problems, brother."

Kasper sent a glare Cal's way. He was stretched out on a bedroll, still swathed in his midnight attire, one boot ankle crossed over his knee as he stared at the night sky.

"Piss off, Cal."

Cal's gaze turned in his direction and Kasper immediately regretted his words. "Has my baby brother finally grown teeth?" Cal dropped his knee and sat up; his attention now focused entirely on Kasper. Cal clucked his tongue. "No, it couldn't be that. Perhaps defending your lady love was simply too taxing and all common sense has left you."

"Shut it." Kasper all but growled.

Cal raised an infuriating brow but laid back down and resumed his position, once again enthralled by the night sky. Kasper clenched his fist, the jasper stone's effect no longer working. He closed his eyes, forcing his mind away from his present environment. He longed for the crowded heat of the city; at least there, he could get lost amongst the masses. At least there, no one bothered to torment him. He was a nobody to them. A face to be seen and immediately forgotten. It didn't matter that half of his life was lost to him, or that he would only ever be Kai's lackey. He could pretend, for at least a moment, that there might be more out there. Kasper's feet shuffled through the sand once more.

"It'll get easier." Cal said, barely above a whisper.

"What?" Kasper asked, his irritation flaring once more.

"The killing. It gets easier."

Kasper stared at his brother. Nightmare made flesh. Death incarnate. And marveled at the tenderness of his words. At the vulnerability hidden between the pauses.

But Kasper shook his head. "No, I don't think it will."

A heartbeat passed, and Cal whispered, "Maybe not. Maybe you just get used to it."

"I don't think that's it, either."

Cal gave a rough laugh. "Perhaps not. Perhaps you just lose enough pieces of yourself that you can't be bothered to care anymore."

"If that's the cost, then it's not worth it," Kasper retorted.

"Then be prepared to lose more than you already have, brother. She would have died without you. Or would you have preferred to watch her bleed out in front of you? To watch her suffer and panic as that villain took and took and—"

"Enough." Kasper said, turning away from Cal. Despite the cool desert air, his face burned. He crossed his arms and clenched his jaw to keep his tears at bay.

A dark, humorless laugh issued from Cal's lips. "Typical. You always act all tough until you're faced with the truth."

The condescension leaching from Cal's voice made Kasper stiffen. "And what have you ever lost? Or sacrificed for someone other than yourself?"

The desert air around Kasper plummeted. Frost crackled on his skin, freezing his hair. Cal was before him in an instant as though he had traveled through the shadows. Frigid fury flickered in Cal's eyes, gutting Kasper.

Cal leaned forward, his breath a white cloud in front of Kasper. "More than you could *ever* know." Cal stormed away from Kasper and the camp, not giving Kasper time to respond or fully absorb his words. Kasper had no desire to go after him. He certainly didn't acknowledge the unending pain that had raked down his skin at Cal's words.

Had something happened when they were younger that Kasper simply couldn't remember? Did it have to do with their parents, or their banishment? Kasper bit the inside of his cheek until the metallic tang of blood flooded his mouth—the taste evoking the memory of the man he had murdered.

Kasper stayed stone still and took deep breaths for several minutes, the air around him finally returning to normal. He managed to get his stiff limbs moving and bent down on his bed roll. Despite the exhausting events of the day, sleep would not claim him. Not as he stared up at the fathomless stars and wondered what Cal had lost.

* * * *

"Come on, Kai. We have to get going."

"Mmm, five more minutes."

"We need to get a move on."

Kai pulled his scarf up over his eyes. "Cataclysmic dangers are in store for those who rush toward the shore."

Kasper rolled his eyes and prodded Kai with his foot. "Somehow I doubt that's the case."

Kai groaned again. "A sandstorm is imminent."

"Let me guess, it'll pass in five minutes?"

Kai pulled his scarf down and cracked open one eye. "Yes?"

Releasing a sigh, Kasper nudged Kai's elbows with his boot. Kai mumbled something else and rolled over, face-first into the sand. Kasper suppressed his laughter as Kai realized where he was and sputtered, trying to dislodge the sand from his hair and skin. Climbing to his feet, Kai swiped furiously at his clothes, brushing away the desert sand from his once-white robes. Kasper crossed his arms and walked away, allowing his brother time to collect himself. Kasper surveyed the others, noting the shadows that clung to Cal, while more were smudged under Lady Hera's eyes. Brander didn't appear to be faring much better as he yawned and scrubbed his face. It seemed no one had slept well, Kasper included.

The man he had killed had haunted his nightmares. His blood seeped into every pore, choking and blinding him until there was nothing but the suffocating feel of it.

He hadn't slept much after that.

Now, hours later, after they had broken camp, Lady Hera made a point to not look in Kasper's direction, let alone speak to him. Or maybe it was just his guilt gnawing at him. Either way, an odd tension had settled over them all. Only Kai seemed unperturbed by the events of the last twenty-four hours. Kasper chewed his cheek until the raw place he had bit the evening before reopened and blood filled his mouth. How did he explain to her that he struggled to keep himself together between his guilt and Cal's condemnation? That every decision he made pushed him further from the person he thought he was—the person he wanted to be. And that deep down, his mind gave voice to a fear that had haunted him from the moment he had shoved the blade into the man's neck.

He was becoming like Cal.

Kasper shook his head. Cal was ruthless. Cal had abandoned him and Kai. He had left them to fend for themselves, forcing Kasper to forfeit what innocence he had left—to use the despicable part of his magic that called up cursed gems from the earth. No, Kasper would *not* continue down this path if the outcome was Cal.

Kasper glanced at Kai, who had a soft smile painted on his face as he gently rubbed his mare's neck. If nothing else, perhaps this was all a reminder–a lesson even–that he needed to be more grateful to Kai for raising him. Kasper shifted, his gaze sliding to Cal. Yes, Kai might be oblivious and frivolous, but at least he wasn't callous and wicked. Dwelling on that, though, would not solve his current problems, like how the wind continued to blow the sand across the dunes. Or how the sun bore down into his clothes and skin. Sweat slicked his nape and brow, and his cracked lips begged for a sip of water, but Kasper would not waste it. He had traveled with the caravan enough to know that rationing one's water was essential to survival.

However, Kasper could better ascertain how much water he could drink if he had any idea where they were headed. As if summoned by his wayward thoughts, and Kasper hadn't ruled that out entirely, Kai trotted beside him. He was beaming like the sun personified.

"Good afternoon, brother."

Kasper spared him a wary glance. "Kai."

"Would you mind riding to the front and asking Caliban how much further he believes we will travel before arriving at our destination?"

Kasper raised an eyebrow. "Aren't you the one that's supposed to lead us to the Cave?"

"Yes."

Kasper paused, waiting for Kai to elaborate, but he remained silent. Still smiling. "So, wouldn't you know how long it will take us to get there?"

Kai shook his head, his feather earrings dancing with the movement. "Oh, no. The Cave is not here. It's across the sea."

Kasper whipped his head in his brother's direction.

"Across the sea?"

"Across the sea." Kai repeated.

Kasper stared at his brother, unblinking. He began to wonder if taking a second life would truly be that awful. "Are we to take a ship? How are we to pay for it? And what of the horses? Malakai, have you considered any of this?" Kasper said, his words coming out in a rush.

"Fret not, brother. All will be handled. But I would like to know how much longer I am expected to bobble back and forth in this saddle with this smelly, albeit sweet, creature fastened to me."

Kasper started and stopped half a dozen sentences, all of them dying on his tongue. He turned his head back forward, unable to look at his brother for another second. Arguing with Kai was futile. Brooding or getting mad was also pointless, as Kai was clueless to most negative emotions. Besides, Kasper found that hiding Kai's jewelry was a far more effective way to get back at him.

Kasper shook his head and kicked his heels into the side of his mare, sending her into a brisk trot. Kasper approached Cal's midnight mare, slowing his own horse. Cal cut his eyes, barely acknowledging Kasper's presence. Once, that might have hurt Kasper, but he had learned that Cal treated everyone with disdain, so it wasn't personal.

At least that's what Kasper kept telling himself.

Kasper squinted against the blazing sun but wasn't uncomfortable in the heat. Briefly, he wondered if Cal was actively cooling the air around him. Pity he wouldn't extend that courtesy to the rest of the group.

"Kai wants to know how much longer 'til we make it to the coast."

Cal slid his gaze to Kasper, but remained silent.

Kasper rolled his eyes. "Please spare me the brooding, Cal. I know you don't want me around you and I will gladly return to my post once I have what Kai wants."

Cal scoffed. "Always Kai's lackey." Condescension dripped from his voice.

Kasper bristled. "Someone has to look out for him. We both know good and well that you won't."

Kasper braced himself for the all-encompassing darkness or the plummeting temperature. But nothing came. Cal stared straight ahead. The only indication that he had heard Kasper was his white-knuckle grip on his mare's reins.

"We'll be there before sundown." Cal responded, his voice like a knife scraping over ice.

Kasper didn't linger and instead jerked his mare's reins, turning for the back. Kai remained there. Still smiling. A heavy sigh fell from Kasper as he returned to his brother's side, where he'd stayed since their exile.

Where he would be until his death.

Chapter Eleven

Cal flexed his fingers, over and over and over, trying to melt the ice solidifying in his veins. He had spent years—burgeoning on two decades—attempting to temper his rage, only for it to rise to the surface the moment he was around his brothers.

Their stories were identical in their origins. They had all been abandoned on the palace steps, per the King's decree that all children be examined for magical aptitude. The slight deviations came in the form of suffering they experienced. But even that had not been enough to foster a kindred spirit amongst them, let alone brotherly affection. It hadn't been any of their faults, at least not initially, but now too much time—too much hurt—had passed for Cal to look at them, Kai in particular, with anything but disdain. The King was undoubtedly at the core of all of Cal's suffering, but Kai was no innocent. Kai had cost him just as much, and Cal would exact his price against his brother and the King. No matter what he lost in the process. In truth, there wasn't much else that mattered to him these days.

Cal rolled his neck in an effort to dislodge the tension that had settled into his muscles after his conversation with Kasper. It wasn't Kasper's fault. Cal knew that, but the vitriol he spewed was obviously encouraged by Kai, if not outright supplied. It had to be. Cal hadn't seen Kasper since he was a child, and even then, Kasper hadn't recognized him, so who else would teach Kasper to hate him?

The wind suddenly shifted, the smell of salt and sea replacing the dry, earthy scent of the desert for a moment. Cal's anger toward his brothers faded from his mind—temporarily. An involuntary smile formed on his lips as the breeze ruffled his dark hair, floating the loose strands around his face. The onyx mare beneath him shook her mane, reveling in the wind as well. Cal reached down and patted her thick neck. The worst of her journey was behind her.

Unfortunately, the same could not be said for Cal.

Giving a slight tug on the reins, Cal slowed his mare. The sand sloped downward toward the docks, and the ground was notorious for shifting unexpectedly. The others wordlessly followed his lead. Cal appreciated the blind obedience, but he had a feeling that their submission was temporary. They continued, working their way closer to the docks teeming with life. Fishmongers and vendors peddling their wares, trying to lure in the late evening crowd or draw crews from their ships. Most of what they sold was rubbish, but for those who spent months at sea, a change in scenery or trinket could soothe the more jagged edges of one's sea-weary soul. After several minutes of carefully picking their way down the sliding sand, Cal's mare brayed once more, saying, *I'm tired and ready for a snack.*

Chuckling darkly, he whispered, "We'll get you something good, girl. Nothing fattening, but something tasty." She nickered again in agreement, and Cal gave her a firm pat on her neck.

"Are we boarding a ship?" An impertinent voice queried.

Cal's brief smile faded as *the woman* came into view. The look on her face was nearly as haughty as her tone. Cal spared her a glance, but stayed silent. He returned his gaze to the open sea and the ships, varying in size and function, docking and departing from the harbor. This was one of the few harbors along the coast that was naturally deep enough for the ships to dock without having to be anchored further out at sea.

"Yes, we are." Kai chimed in cheerily.

Cal didn't bother acknowledging his brother or responding to the woman's protests. He flicked the reins, urging his mare down the last stretch of sand until it gave way to clay streets. Gulls and the crashing of waves hummed like music to the cries and shouts of merchants along the streets and docks.

Cal slowed up again, allowing the others to catch up once more. Glancing at the others, Cal marked their faces, ranging from skepticism to suspicion—all but Kai, who grinned broadly.

The woman narrowed her eyes and scanned the horizon, attempting to glean which ship she would be expected to board. Cal assumed she had never been on a proper, sea-worthy vessel. In fact, she had probably never been on a boat at all. A prophecy Kai had issued not even three years into their time at the palace, flashed in Cal's mind. It claimed that the King would meet his end if his line ever crossed the sea. Cal never knew if that meant the King and his descendants, or the King's empire. Either way, the King had never pushed it—but had made it clear to Kai that any future prophecies pertaining to his rule were to be issued in private, or preferably, not at all.

Kasper came up beside Kai, his eyes jumping from the woman to the ships in the harbor. The years had added lines of wariness around his eyes and mouth. Next to Kai, Kasper appeared to be the older sibling. It seemed even exile couldn't dim the bright, optimistic light that was Kai, and for some reason, that made the frigid place inside Cal even colder.

The guard dog settled in his place next to Lady Hera. A condescending smile played on his lips, and he snorted. "I thought you gypsy types only traveled in covered wagons pulled by camels."

It seemed that the tongue lashing the Lady had given him hadn't taken, or perhaps he was feeling bold. At the guard dog's insult, frost crackled over Cal's skin, but he kept his face a mask of cool indifference. The opinions of a palace lap dog mattered little to him. Besides, the dog was quickly going to understand the pecking order of things. Cal swung a leg down from his mare, black clothes rippling with the motion. He moved soundlessly, shadows clinging to him as the sun dipped in its descent over the horizon. The sun beams scattered, painting the sky in shades of red and orange. A sailor's saying came to mind: *red in the morning, a sailor's warning, red at night, a sailor's delight.*

Cal didn't trust such beliefs when he knew what lay ahead in their journey.

"I am not boarding a ship until someone explains why that is necessary." Lady Hera proclaimed, her jaw set with impudence.

Cal was powerless to stop the retort that fell from his mouth, nor the biting tone he employed. "Because, *woman*, if you want to please your mistress and retrieve what she has asked of you, then you need to leave this pitiful excuse of a country and venture beyond the narrow worldview you hold. I know that's hard for you noble types."

To her credit, Lady Hera didn't recoil at the venom Cal spewed. But her guard dog gripped the hilt of his sword, his knuckles white with the effort.

Cal smirked. "Didn't learn your lesson last time?" The smile on his face grew wider, more vindictive. He willed the shadows to curl at the edges of his body, to nip and swirl, ravenous in their desire to consume. "Please, tell me you need a refresher." Cal pleaded, barely above a whisper.

"Cal." Kasper reprimanded.

Cal flicked his gaze to his brother. He half expected to find his bloodstone dagger clutched in his hand, but found nothing save for his mistrustful gaze. Cal raised a brow, but commanded the shadows to dissipate. The tension lessened in Lady Hera's shoulders, so Cal added, "My brother holds no sway over me. No mortal does. And I care not if you board the ship. Either way, I will be departing in an hour, with or without any of you. So, you can take that haughty attitude and find some other form of passage if you think you're too good to board the ship I select." He held her gaze for a heartbeat, daring her to respond, but she didn't.

Though he wasn't sure why, her silence left an ache in his chest.

Cal clenched his jaw and turned away from Lady Hera to find two figures emerging from the boarding plank of an ebony wood ship. A genuine smile found its way to Cal's lips as he strode toward them, his mare in tow.

"Which ship?" Someone uttered behind him. But he didn't care, not when the seawater spray on his skin was refreshing like water hadn't been in months. More of his stress melted away as the two newcomers approached. Their haggard appearances were a welcomed sight. Cal relished and savored the thud of his boots on the weather-worn wooden pier. The sea called to him, a song for his soul, a siren to his blood. A welcome to the only place that had ever truly felt like home.

Finally, the pair of ruffians stopped in front of Cal, grinning like fiends. The shorter of the pair, a woman in her late twenties, removed her three-cornered hat and swept into a low bow. The other, a male closer to his fifties, remained upright until the woman knocked an elbow into his side, and he doubled over. A chuckle pushed its way out of Cal's lips as he beheld the pair before him.

Cal heard boots and hooves behind him, but he refused to tear his attention from the man and woman in front of him. "Finnley." Cal said, addressing the woman. She lifted her head and gave him a toothy grin. Cal then nodded to the man, "Galen, looking as unkempt as ever." Cal made a tsking sound and turned back to Finnley. "As interim captain, I would have thought you would take better care of your crew."

Finnley laughed heartily. "It's hard enough to keep the Umbra in decent shape. Galen has to learn to care for himself." Finnley reached forward and clapped Cal on the shoulder.

Kasper, who stood just a few feet behind Cal, inhaled sharply.

Finnley paid him no mind as she smiled broadly up at Cal.

"The Umbra and her crew are pleased to have you back, Captain."

Chapter Twelve

He was a bloody privateer.

Rhea knew that employing Kai risked her father's wrath and a verbal beating. Allowing Caliban on their quest was putting her dangerously close to the edge of what would earn her several lashes. If the details as to how exactly she obtained Izor's Lamp ever came to light, her father might finally make good on his threat to disinherit her. But privateers? That was another matter entirely.

The King had outlawed piracy nearly two decades ago, and was delighted when news was brought of another pirate ship falling prey to the warships that patrolled his waters. She was already in enough trouble for sneaking off, but if she boarded a pirate ship–the ill-famed Umbra, no less–he would have her executed himself. And that was, of course, if no one discovered her identity and decided to take revenge against the King first. Given the number of predatory and raptorial eyes that roved over her–picking her out as the weakest among them– she feared that was the most likely outcome.

Brander's gaze fixed on Rhea's face, but she was determined not to show her panic. She forced her features into indifference and looked to the others to gauge their surprise and fear. Kasper's eyes were narrowed and darted from Cal to the others—Galen and Finnley.

Kai smiled softly, his expression distinctly unpuzzled. So, the Seer knew, but Kasper had no idea that their brother was a pirate.

Interesting.

An unburdened, pleasant smile lit up Cal's face as he turned back to them. His eyes collided with Rhea's, and she lifted her chin.

"So, you are a privateer?" She asked.

Cal lifted an eyebrow, and Finnley chuckled, throaty and unfeminine. "We're pirates, lass. We raid and pillage from whoever dares to cross our path. I know Cal here isn't much to look at, but he's been on the Umbra for some years and has proven himself a worthy captain."

Finnley cocked her head, appraising Rhea. Rhea fought the urge to squirm beneath the pirate's assessing stare. If Rhea were going to survive this journey, she needed to stop appearing to be a liability or a weakness. She swallowed her apprehension and remained stalwart.

Finnley's eyes glittered with amusement and something else— intrigue, or curiosity? "Yous look to be noble stock, but I wager even yous heard of us," Finnley added.

Rhea continued to hold Finnley's gaze. Oh yes, she had certainly heard of the Umbra. The ship and crew were infamous for their vicious and brutal tactics. Merchants and nobles often came to court begging for the King to dispatch the Umbra, but even with all his resources and power, her father had proven fruitless against the villains that terrorized the coast. Rhea slid her gaze to Cal—now she understood why. A look, perhaps the closest Cal would ever come to looking bashful, passed over his face. But it vanished as quickly as it appeared.

Cal cleared his throat and shifted his eyes to his brothers. "I have been known to engage in operations that were of...disputatious legality." Another smile came to his lips as he continued, "We leave within the hour. I suggest one of you get the horses sold off or put somewhere safe." Cal turned, heading down the dock toward the large, black ship looming in the distance.

Rhea was not unaccustomed to opulence and extravagance. She grew up in a palace that claimed to touch the heavens, but the ominous presence of the Umbra made her stomach flop.

"I believe it is best if we go ahead and board, Lady Hera." Kai said merrily. "Cal was not joking about leaving any of us." Rhea wanted to argue. She wanted to stomp her feet and refuse to go along with another command of the Nader men, but for all her pride, she wasn't stupid. In the short time they had been at the docks, she had already seen three patrols of imperial soldiers. She wagered it was only a matter of time before they got curious and came to investigate the Umbra. If the soldiers found Cal and Kai, that would be troublesome enough, but if they exposed her...she would be better off drowning herself at sea.

Kai handed over the reins of his horse to Kasper, who already held his own and Cal's.

Rhea glanced at Brander, whose eyes were pleading with her not to utter the command, but she lifted her chin and said, "Take our horses and go with Kasper."

Kai pulled Rhea away by looping his arm through her's and gently steering them toward the Umbra.

"Being on a ship is not too terrible."

Rhea smiled and swallowed her dread. "Oh, you've been on the seas?"

"No." he added glibly.

Rhea's smile faded as the shadow of the Umbra fell over them. Silence clung to the ship as though even the gulls and waves were afraid of drawing its ire. "Did you know he was a pirate?" She asked, her voice tinny to her own ears. From his earlier reaction, she had already guessed at the truth, but making conversation would help distract her from the terror that was attempting to choke her.

"I had my suspicions about his employment, but it wasn't until I had a vision about him a few months back that I knew for certain."

"I take it you all didn't stay together after the exile?"

Kai shook his head. "Too dangerous for us all to remain together. But perhaps this adventure will change that."

Rhea pursed her lips. Her chest ached at the thought of the brothers being forced to go their separate ways. But Rhea kept her thoughts to herself, knowing no good would come from expressing them. She reached for her pendant, and her boots thudded dully on the gangplank. She and Kai rose up the gradual incline onto the deck. Rhea licked her lips, dry and cracked from the harsh desert air. She wagered her skin would be in much worse shape when they returned home from the Cave.

If they returned home at all.

Rhea and Kai took the final step from the gangplank onto the ship. Officially off dry land for the foreseeable future. She glanced around and found several more crew members milling about. Checking ropes and pulleys, muttering passing remarks. She tried not to fixate on any one person for too long for fear that they would look back. There was no telling where in the empire they hailed from and if they would recognize her.

Rhea opened her mouth to ask to be shown to her quarters when Kai appeared in front of her and whispered, "I know who you are, *Princess Rhea.*"

Rhea's heart fell to her feet.

For a moment, she lost all sense of her body. Her hearing went fuzzy, and her vision dimmed. But she blinked, and Kai was still staring at her like the cat who got the cream. Rhea shoved down her horror and refused to let the panic show on her face. She crossed her arms and said cooly, "I haven't a clue what you're talking about."

Kai clucked his tongue, and his hand shot out quicker than she thought possible.

"If you plan to stick to that story, I highly recommend hiding this."

Rhea didn't have to look down to see what Kai held in his hand.

Her necklace—unremarkable to most, but a dead giveaway if one knew what they were looking at. And Kai, of all people, would certainly recognize her family emblem. Rhea reached up and snatched the pendant back.

Kai smiled widely. "Lucky for you, my brothers aren't very perceptive, but I would recognize the Abadi family crest anywhere." Rhea tucked the pendant away beneath the neckline of her tunic. "Yes, that would be most wise."

"Why bring this to my attention now? Why not expose me as soon as you realized?" Rhea said sternly as she crossed her arms.

Kai absentmindedly twirled a curl around his finger and shrugged his shoulders. "I saw no benefit."

Rhea raised a brow. "And you do now?"

"Not particularly, but the people aboard this ship who are not as loyal to my brother as the individuals you met earlier would not hesitate to sell you out—especially given the bounty your father put upon their heads."

"So, is this a threat or a warning?"

Kai bobbed his head back and forth. "A bit of both, I suppose, but mostly a warning."

Rhea uncrossed her arms and placed them behind her back. "I suppose you want to negotiate now." A warm smile spread across Kai's lips as he moved to loop his arm back through Rhea's. She allowed it, if only because refusing might attract too much attention.

"I only want what I asked for originally, which you and I both know you can give me."

Rhea bit down on the inside of her cheek. She had no desire to concede, but her options were limited. She didn't have the authority to reappoint him as Court Seer—not that her father would allow it even if she did. Perhaps she could grant him a pardon, but that meant getting her father's approval as well—or, at the very least, stealing his personal seal to stamp the documents.

They walked until they approached the far side of the ship. She stared out over the water, its color no longer a cerulean blue but a mosaic of pinks and purples. Rhea removed her arm from Kai's and gripped the ledge of the ship. Leaning over the railings, she peered into the water below, curious as to how deep it was. After several minutes, she righted herself and squared her shoulders.

"Alright. I'll do what I can to secure a pardon, but you can't breathe a word of this to anyone. What you know stays between us. And—" she paused, preparing herself for the consequences of what she dared to promise, "I'll reappoint you Court Seer when I ascend the throne." It was a gamble, but again, her options were limited. This at least bought her some time to find something else to entice Kai with.

Kai gave her an impish grin and a dramatic bow. "You have my word," he lifted his head and winked at her, "*Lady Hera.*"

Rhea fought the urge to roll her eyes at Kai's over-the-top behavior, but she should have known what she was getting herself into when she hired the Master of Fate. He was certainly more congenial than he had been while residing in the palace, but she wasn't surprised. Her father's presence had a way of making people diminish themselves.

Kai righted himself and turned, leaning against the ship's railing. His warm brown eyes danced with delight at all he beheld. Rhea wondered what it would be like to be so self-assured. To be confident in one's own abilities and not wonder if they were ill-suited for the life bestowed upon them.

"You know," Kai said, shattering her thoughts, "you read people almost as well as I do."

Rhea's forehead scrunched. "I'm sure I don't know what you mean."

Offering a gentle smile, Kai waved toward the ship. "I've been observing you—as I do with most people—and you examine them. Scrutinize and catalog their reactions and behaviors. It's a most interesting skill for a noblewoman to have."

Resisting the urge to roll her eyes for the hundredth time in the span of a simple conversation, Rhea curled and uncurled her hands. "Is that so?"

"Oh, yes. Most royals are hardly concerned with anything that doesn't directly affect them, so they have no need to pay attention to others. That's what advisors and councilmen are for, but you," he said, drawing back and running his eyes up and down the length of her, "are unique in that regard." He tucked an arm across his chest and raised his hand to his jaw, supporting it. "I do so wonder why that is."

Pain echoed in her skull from how tightly she clenched her jaw. She had her suspicions about why she was hyper-aware of the people around her. Why she was constantly watching their faces and noting their tone. And she hated the conclusion that her mind came to.

Another gift from her father, she supposed.

Kai laughed again and shook his head. The bemused gaze fixed to his face remained on her as he reached for her hand. He pressed a quick, chaste kiss to her knuckles and said, "I'll spare you the joys of my company for a time. Enjoy your first night aboard the Umbra, Lady."

Kai turned to leave, but Rhea reached out, halting him. "One last thing." She swallowed, searching for the courage to voice the words.

"Yes?" Kai said with an arched brow and a mischievous smile.

"Why doesn't Kas remember me?"

Kai's smile faltered, and he blinked. He shook his head and said hurriedly, "Trauma. He doesn't have any of his memories from his childhood—and it would only hurt him to try and remind him."

Rhea nodded, catching the meaning of his words. She licked her lips. "And Cal?"

Kai chuckled. "If my twin recognized you, you'd already be dead."

"Right." Rhea said, and she released Kai. "Thank you."

With a dip of his chin, Kai turned, disappearing into the fray of the crew. Rhea blew out a breath and pressed her forehead into her arms. Already, so many things had gone awry; what else would go wrong? Their journey was always going to be dangerous, but Rhea hadn't considered just how quickly things would start to go sideways.

Rhea lifted her head. The sun eclipsed the horizon, sending out the last of its light over the ocean, washing everything in shafts of golden rays. Rhea had never been to the sea. She had spent her entire life sequestered behind palace walls, especially after it became clear that she was the sole heir to her father's empire. Her uncle was technically an option, but he had been banished from court before Rhea had been born. He had only been permitted to return at her birth and her mother's funeral. She had no surviving siblings, though her father–up until three years ago–had a harem dedicated to trying to provide him a son.

No children had survived.

Making Rhea the only living child the King could boast.

No one would risk her being lost to the dangers beyond the palace grounds—though Rhea would have argued that remaining in her father's presence was even more perilous. But now, at twenty-one, she was old enough that the council could not stop her. And her father couldn't be bothered to intervene—most of the time.

"The horses have been taken care of." Brander said, coming up beside Rhea. She remained still, not turning to meet his gaze, opting to stare at the slowly sinking sun.

"Good. No reason for them to suffer whatever it is we are to face." Rhea sighed. She glanced back to the harbor, noting the soldiers that had still not paid the Umbra any mind. "Odd," she murmured.

"What?" Brander asked.

"The soldiers. I would have thought—"

"That they would have raided the ship?" He supplied.

She nodded.

"That's because the people of this harbor practice a level of discretion not found in many places in the empire."

Rhea whirled to find Cal smirking at her. He cut an imposing figure in his midnight brocade and a tri-corner hat that gobbled up the fading light. She forced herself to focus on his words rather than his rugged features. Narrowing her eyes, she said, "Didn't anyone ever teach you it's rude to eavesdrop?"

"Sorry, Lady. I was too busy being exploited. Besides, it's my ship," Cal retorted, stepping closer, "in fact, this entire harbor is mine, and," he glanced to the shore, "those soldiers are mine."

"Then why do they wear imperial regalia?"

Cal's smirk widened, displaying his gleaming teeth. Rubbing his chin, he said, "Well, technically, they are employed by your King... but they are, uh, monetarily encouraged to look the other way at my comings and goings," Rhea's eyes flared, but before she could refute Cal's claim, he added, "so if you thought to turn to them and betray us, I would think again."

Rhea pressed her lips together. She had no interest in drawing the guard's attention to her or Cal. She had made sure to lay low, but there was always an outside chance that she was seen—or worse, recognized. Even if she would delight at seeing Cal humbled–and bound in chains– it wouldn't help her get to the Cave of Splendors. Glancing to the port once more, her curiosity getting the better of her and—

Movement there caught her eye. A smile curled on her lips as she looked back at Cal. She lifted her chin and said, "I wasn't planning on it. However, you may want to ensure that the King's men are still in your pocket. Because from the looks of it, it seems like some have decided that your payment isn't sufficient."

Rhea's words registered on Cal's face, and he turned. Imperial soldiers were gathering in the harbor and pointing toward the Umbra. A string of curses fell from his lips and he took off, his jacket billowing behind him. He began shouting commands to the crew, urging them to hurry before the guards could reach the ship. Rhea briefly wondered why Cal didn't employ his shadows, but she decided it wasn't worth her time, not when there were other pressing issues. Turning back toward Brander, taking advantage of the chaos, she said, "I need you to promise me that if something happens to me, you will finish the quest."

Brander's gaze seared into the side of Rhea's face, but she still wouldn't look at him.

"What we have set out to do is too important." She added.

"Not more than you."

Rhea finally turned to him. Her breath caught at the anguish that pleaded with her in his eyes. But she persevered and said, "Yes, it is. My father could decide to try to have another heir with one of his concubines. Or he could reinstate his brother as a prince and pass the throne to him, but it won't make a difference if there's nothing to inherit."

Rhea reached out and took Brander's hands into her own; they were cool and clammy. "Promise me that you will do this. For our people. So that no more children are orphaned or mothers widowed. Please, Brander, promise that you will see this through."

The muscles in his cheek rippled, and he held her gaze. "Don't make me." Brander whispered. "There won't be a kingdom worth saving if you're not leading it. You are the first ruler in a century who has thought beyond their own wishes."

Rhea clenched her jaw against the tears that threatened to overtake her. A single tear escaped, and she raised her hand to swipe it away. "There are other good people who can lead. But the Kingdom needs this."

Brander held her gaze and gripped the hand he still held tightly.

"I will put your life before mine, always."

"Brander—"

"But," he interrupted and took a deep breath, "if something happens and I cannot save you, then I will finish this journey."

Rhea loosed a breath and gave an unsteady smile. "Thank you."

Brander said nothing else. He dropped Rhea's hand and stepped away, his face distant and his color paling slightly. He paused and said softly, "I don't think your father realizes what kind of daughter he raised."

Rhea lifted her chin, Brander's subtle praise lightening some of the burden on her soul. "I must have learned it from you." she replied, and she meant it. Brander was younger than her father by nearly fifteen years and had only become her personal guard in the last three, but he was a parental figure all the same. She swallowed against the emotion building in her throat, suddenly grateful for his immense loyalty to her. And it was to her. Not her father, the crown, or the kingdom.

She couldn't think of another soul that had chosen her over everything else.

Rhea turned toward the sea, the ship finally casting off away from the soldiers pounding their way down the dock and toward the Umbra. A measure of the tension in her shoulders released as the shouts of her father's imperial guards faded—gobbled up by the call of the open sea.

They were leaving the only home she had ever known—heading into uncharted, and certainly dangerous, territory. Breathing deeply, she took in the salty air, and reminded herself of all the people who were counting on her.

She could not and would not fail.

Chapter Thirteen

))) hen Malakai arrived in the harbor, he was quite disappointed with what he found.

The sea was nothing like what Malakai had imagined. In the days leading up to Princess Rhea's arrival, Kai had dreamed of the coast. The sea spray misted his skin, the sun baked him like a loaf of bread, and he inhaled the smell of the salt as if he were really there. But that came as no surprise. Many of his dreams and visions were so vivid that he hardly distinguished fact from fiction.

His senses were assaulted with the rotting stench of fish, their flesh baking in the summer sun for hours on end. Replacing the tranquil lapping of the waves along the shore was the screeching of gulls and the hollers of merchants packed tightly along the streets. Instead of finding ornate and delicate shells, Malakai was bombarded with the spoiled guts of the morning's catch. The festering seaweed that washed up and tangled into masses along the sand mingled with the rot, making his stomach twist with disgust. Needless to say, Malakai was nettled with his surroundings. Perhaps he had spent too many years cocooned by luxury to appreciate the mundane beauty of a seaside town or any of the ramshackle villages the caravan had visited in the last decade. Whatever the case, he fought against the wave of revulsion that threatened to overcome him.

Malakai's eyes drifted over commoners exchanging coins for bread, fish, or clams. Nothing unusual or interesting to stave off his boredom—

Until the imperial soldiers began gathering, their attention wholly fixed on the Umbra.

Shouts and clamoring rang out around him as the ship erupted into chaos. Malakai knew he shouldn't have found the prospect of being chased or—Forgotten forbid—being captured so intriguing, but he had spent so much of the last few years just *waiting*. Waiting for a vision that showed him the way back to his former life. Waiting for a pardon from the King. Waiting for anything worthwhile to happen to correct the wrongs he continually suffered. Now, something was *really* happening, and he was utterly transfixed by it all. But the shift in Caliban's demeanor was even more interesting as the ship began to sail out of the port—the imperial soldiers shouting and pointing as they attempted to get themselves organized enough to pursue the Umbra. The stiffness in his brother's jaw and the rigidity in his shoulders had lessened significantly. Even the shadows that normally clung to him had vanished entirely. Though, his skulking had persisted. Malakai smiled to himself at the ebony broadcloth jacket and linen pants Caliban now donned. He had tied a burgundy sash around his waist, and adjusted a three-cornered hat to his head.

He looked at home.

Caliban looked around—even amidst his ship's mayhem, the corner of his mouth lifted in a half smile. Until his gaze landed on Malakai. Instantly, his eyes narrowed, and tension bracketed his mouth.

Malakai brightened his grin and strolled forward to his brother.

Caliban cast his eyes, perhaps looking for a way out of the pending conversation.

"Brother!" Malakai said jovially.

A muscle feathered in Caliban's jaw. "Kai."

Malakai spread his arms wide. "What a lovely ship you have here."

Remaining silent, Cal turned his gaze to the shrinking harbor.

Malakai continued. "And what an eclectic group of privateers you have assembled. Tell me, Caliban, do they know where you come from? What master you served?"

Caliban turned on Malakai, crystalline rage crackling in his eyes. "I serve no one but myself. The men and women aboard this vessel know what they need to know of me. That I am ruthless and relentless in obtaining what I want."

Malakai stepped away and raised his hands placatingly. "I simply wanted to know where you stood with them so I knew how freely I could speak."

"You are not to speak with any of them. You are to enter the hull, find an unoccupied room, and remain there until we dock at our destination." Cal dropped his voice to barely above a whisper. "They are wary of magic wielders, especially—"

"Especially one whose particular brand of magic is outlawed? Or, in my case, heavily restricted?" Malakai suggested.

Cal narrowed his eyes. "Precisely. So, keep what you know of my magic to yourself. And tell the others to do the same. If you want to expose your own, then that's your choice."

"Noted. And what if you need me? Perhaps I can determine a safer course than the one you plan."

Caliban sneered. "You may have the run of your small world, Kai, but I command the high seas. There is nothing you could foretell that would surprise me. I can read the weather just fine, and I assure you, no other ship will dare engage us."

Malakai raised his brows and nodded. Clearly, the soldiers in the harbor had not unsettled Caliban. "I see. Well, if you do need me, I suppose you can send our brother to retrieve me."

A humorless chuckle fell from Caliban's lips. "Yes, I will dispatch your errand boy if necessary."

Another smile formed on Malakai's lips. "Well, then I shall take my leave of you, *Captain*."

Malakai twisted away, flourishing his cape behind him. The chaos aboard the Umbra had abated, and several crewmates shifted their gaze to Malakai—he smiled wider. Once upon a time, he shied away from the attention. He would even avert his eyes when he noticed the stares of others. Palace life had stripped him of that privilege.

"Kai."

Malakai slowed his steps, and Kasper appeared in front of him. His eyes shifted around him, and the muscles in his neck tensed. Malakai closed the distance between them and clapped him on the shoulder.

"Come, brother, let's find our accommodations for the duration of this trip."

"I need to speak with Cal."

Malakai waved dismissively. "I already have. He's just as unpleasant as I remember. He said if he needs me, he'll send word by you."

A muscle flexed in Kasper's jaw, and his hands hung loosely near his waist and weapons. "So, I am to be the go-between." It wasn't a question, and Malakai didn't answer. Kasper defaulted to the position when Caliban returned after years of being gone. They continued walking, taking in the sights and sounds of the Umbra, the place that had been their brother's home and profession for the past nine years.

"Is this really where he was all this time?" Kasper's voice was low, barely a murmur above the humming and droning of life on the ship.

"It would seem so."

Kasper shook his head, his dark golden-brown curls trembling in response. "I don't understand him. I know I can't remember what happened before the exile, but what kept him there? What was the purpose of remaining in the palace if this is the life he has always desired?"

Malakai pursed his lips. "Perhaps you can ask Caliban that one day."

A snort was issued from Kasper. "Fat chance of that happening. He's just as likely to skin me alive as answer my question. You know he's never been able to stand me."

Malakai stopped and Kasper did too. Malakai repressed the overwhelming anguish in his chest as he peered into Kasper's eyes. His and Caliban's eyes.

"You're seventeen, correct?"

A crease formed between Kasper's brows. "Eighteen."

Nodding, Malakai replied, "Ah, right." He resumed walking, Kasper in tow. They approached a raised area of the ship that held a door leading down into the ship's hull. Malakai paused, uninterested in descending into the vessel's bowels. Malakai watched his brother and, for the first time, contemplated revealing the truth. The truth of what had transpired all those years ago. Such anger, rage, and heartache limned Kasper's features, even in the dim lighting. Easing that burden wouldn't be difficult if he wasn't such a coward. Malakai opened his mouth, the words he had buried within himself for nearly a decade poised on his tongue—

"Oi! You two," a voice broke in. Malakai turned his gaze to his right and plastered on a smile.

"First mate, Finnley. How can we be of service?"

An auburn brow lifted, and Finnley's gaze dipped from Malakai's curls and feathered earrings to his sand-covered sandals. Malakai contemplated sending the young woman a flirtatious wink. However, something about the nonplussed expression in her eyes and the thick, jagged scar that sliced through her brow and down through her cheek suppressed the urge.

Finnley glanced toward Kasper, but he wasn't looking at her; his gaze was firmly trained on Malakai. His eyes narrowed, and his mouth pressed into a tight line.

Caliban's first mate rested her scar-flecked hand on the hilt of her sword, and she cleared her throat. A terrible guttural sound issued from her. She turned her head, hocking a thick wad of spit onto the deck.

Malakai's eyes fluttered. "Lovely."

Finnley wiped her mouth on the back of her hand and said, "Cap'n said to take you lot down in the hull to find your quarters. Galen's already down there, waitin'."

"Oh, how kind." Malakai said as he turned to find Princess Rhea and her guard. Malakai smiled and stepped aside, sweeping his arm in front of him. "Ladies first."

Princess Rhea's chin rose, keeping the invisible crown from tipping, and strolled forward. Malakai kept his poise, even as Brander glowered by. The guard looked a bit peaked, but he hurried down the stairs after the Princess. Kasper remained silent, but rolled his eyes and stormed down, leaving Malakai and Finnley alone.

The first mate gave him another once over and said, "Kitschy bunch, you lot are. What brought you all together, eh? Though I 'pose you and the other must be kin with the Cap'n, giv'n the similarities."

Malakai twisted the ring on his finger, peering into the hazel eyes of the woman before him. Despite her disheveled appearance, oversized jacket, and weather-beaten skin, she still held a semblance of beauty. He gave her a polite smile and started around her, his arm brushing against her.

Flashes of a small child dragging a threadbare doll across a clay floor crashed into Malakai. The scene shifted, and a woman lay on the ground panting. Ruby-red blood stained the arm of her turquoise dress. Her chest moved up and down in rapid pants, and she pressed her hand to her bleeding arm. "Mama!" cried out a small voice. The woman turned, her eyes wide and face wet with tears.

Fear and panic slammed into Malakai with such force his knees locked before they gave out and knocked into the Umbra's deck.

"Oi, you alright?"

Malakai gagged on the terror choking his throat—suffocating him.

The girl with the rag doll stood before the woman, trembling.

"Run, Anna, get out of here!"

The girl turned.

Too late.

Her hazel eyes were wide with confusion and fright.

Pain seared down Malakai's face, and he grabbed blindly at his cheek, a scream frozen in his throat. He fell to his side, unable to keep the vision from paralyzing him. His lungs seized, trapping whatever breath he had attempted to draw in. Malakai's vision went black, and the oil lantern blotted out instantly, but he hadn't lost consciousness. Swearing rang out around him, and the darkness descended upon him like a blanket, comforting and reassuring.

Hands slipped under his tense, twitching form.

The composition of the air changed, thickening and sweltering with humidity and stench. The reek of wherever Malakai was being transported would have further gagged him if his senses weren't slowly fading out. He was close to passing out, even as the darkness dissipated.

"What happened?" Hissed a familiar voice.

"A vision, I presume, and a violent one at that."

"He needs the tonic."

The rattling of bottles and shifting fabrics, itchy ones, filled the room as Malakai's body rested on a bed. He groaned and rolled onto his side but didn't dare close his eyes. Not until the elixir was forced down his throat. Hands came back under him, propping him up, and a bottle was pushed to his lips.

The earthy and bitter scent stuffed up his nose, and his eyes watered.

"Come on now, Kai. You need to drink this." Kasper's voice trembled, and his bent brows came into frame, the bottle clutched between his fingers.

Hot tears leaked down Malakai's cheeks at the tenderness in Kasper's voice—at the gentle caress of his hand along his jaw as the bottle trickled its contents down Malakai's throat. Another heartbeat passed, and the bottle was empty–forgotten–discarded. Malakai lay back down, Kasper coming with him this time.

Sleep tugged at the corners of Malakai's mind, urging him to tumble into its depths. He had just enough awareness left to reach out a hand and mumble something incomprehensible. A soft smile graced Kasper's lips, and even softer words were murmured before Malakai fell into the chasm of oblivion.

Chapter Fourteen

The narrow corridor was swaying slightly as Brander slipped back into it. He watched as the Necromancer carried the Seer into a room and hastily shut the door. Brander pressed a hand to his rolling stomach and paused for a moment longer, listening to the hushed whispers from the above stairs.

"Cap'n looked right worried about the pretty fellow—and I'm almost sure they're kin. Something about the eyes is the same."

"Hush up, Galen. The Cap'n wouldn't want us messing about in his business."

"Right, I know. But the shadows—"

"I already told you to shut it. Speak another word, and I'll have you swabbing the deck."

Boots thudded against the wood, retreating further from the steps. A few heartbeats passed before another set of boots withdrew from the stairwell. The door opposite Brander opened, and the Princess's head appeared in the opening. Her eyes darted down the hall and then landed on Brander. He stood at attention.

"Is there something you need, my Lady?"

Princess Rhea's slender fingers gripped the edge of the door, and she chewed her bottom lip. She looked almost girlish, innocent even. Sometimes, Brander forgot she was newly twenty-one.

"No, I'm alright. I just heard some shouting."

"I believe the Seer collapsed or became ill."

Her eyes widened, and her brows shot up. She moved further into the hall. "Well, is he alright?"

Brander shoved down the queasy sensation that washed over him and shook his head. "I do not know, my Lady. The Necromancer brought him down the steps and carried him into a room." Brander gestured toward a closed door, two down from where they stood.

The Princess stood fully in the hallway, clutching her robe tightly. "We have to see if he is well." Princess Rhea moved toward the door—

Brander stuck his arm out, blocking the Princess's path.

Fury flared in her eyes, and she crossed her arms. "Let me pass, Brander; that is an order."

Something in Brander snapped. He wasn't sure if it was the Princess's tone or the complete disregard for her own safety that did it, but whatever the case, Brander couldn't stop the words that tumbled from his mouth.

"Have you no sense at all?"

Princess Rhea recoiled as though his words were a physical blow struck.

Brander leaned closer. "You are a woman, a noblewoman at that. You cannot enter the quarters of a man without an escort—and I will not act as one. You may have no regard for your reputation, but I can assure you that if the wrong person sees you with one of them," he growled—the anger in his voice harder to maintain with his growing discomfort—and pointed down the hall, "they will not hesitate to sell you out. I will not allow you to put yourself in a precarious position. You entrusted me with your safety; please let me ensure that."

The Princess's throat bobbed once. Twice. She finally gave a hesitant nod, and Brander loosed the breath he had been holding. He half expected the Princess to launch into another lecture about Brander undermining her, but she remained silent.

Brander dropped his arms but didn't retreat. "If it will give you peace, then I will speak with them...but, Princess," he murmured. Her eyes refocused on him, an intensity in them he hadn't seen in a while. Brander swallowed against the pulse of fear. She looked like the King. Brander shook himself of his stupor and continued, "you cannot put yourself at risk for these men. They are just as likely to sell you out as help you. I am the only one you can trust."

The Princess's conflicted gaze held Brander's for another moment and said, "Alright. Please speak with them."

Brander's scar-flecked hand rose out of muscle memory and landed over his heart. "As you command."

The Princess gave a quick smile and pulled her door closed, disappearing behind it once more. Brander rolled his shoulders, endeavoring to alleviate the tension and discomfort settling there, but it was futile. If it wasn't the Princess's insistence on putting herself in harm's way, then it was the antics of the rest of the party. It also was unhelpful that the subtle swaying of the ship was not sitting well with Brander. He pressed a hand to his abdomen and prayed the unease he was feeling would subside. He lingered for another moment and then closed the distance between him and the room where the Seer was taken into.

His knuckles echoed dully as he rapped them against the wood and waited.

Nothing.

He knocked again, and again.

Silence greeted him.

Brander rolled his eyes and said in a low voice, "It's Brander, the Lady's guard." The creaking of wood and shifting of fabric could be heard on the other side of the door, but again, there was no reply. Brander considered bashing the door down. The thought of splintering the wood and seeing the perturbed expressions of those on the other side would lighten his spirits, but he refrained. He had to keep reminding himself what was at stake here. His personal feelings blinded him before, and it had cost him. Not only with the Princess, but before his reassignment to palace guard duty—when he led the King's armies.

Brander shook away the memories, determined not to let them surface now. Swallowing his agitation, he knocked again, and said, "The Lady has inquired after your well-being."

Shifting, the groaning of wood, and shadows flickering beyond the door.

"Who is it again?"

Brander sighed. "Brander, the Lady's guard."

"Hmm. I don't know anyone by that name," mused the Necromancer from behind the door. The voice sounded further away as he said, "Kas, do you know anyone by that name?"

"Leave it alone, Cal." said Kasper, weariness permeating his voice.

Brander could practically hear the Necromancer roll his eyes as he said, "You really are no fun." Light seeped into the narrow corridor as the door opened, filling the space with Cal's bemused features.

Brander crossed his arms and willed his irritation to dissipate.

"Can I help you, guard dog?" Cal raised an insufferable brow.

"The Lady heard the disruption and wanted to know if the Seer is well." Brander said through gritted teeth.

The Necromancer waved dismissively. "Oh, he's fine. Hazard of the profession and all." Cal moved to pull the door closed, but Brander grabbed the door and halted it.

"What do you mean 'hazard of the profession'?"

The light behind the Necromancer guttered, the flames dancing in the lanterns sputtering.

"Cal," Kasper called out in warning.

As Cal turned, and Brander glanced around him.

The Seer looked terrible. His skin was pallid, and there was a concerning sheen to it. His chest moved slowly, too slowly. The other brother, Kasper, wasn't faring much better. The shadows beneath his eyes were more prominent, and lines bracketed his mouth. Brander gripped the door, widening it and pushing into the room. Cal whipped back around, murder swirling in his eyes. Brander didn't care. Didn't care if the Necromancer lashed out with shadows and death. He stepped further into the room.

Darkness eddied at the edges of Cal's tense form.

Brander sneered. "Summon all the shadows you like, but Lady Hera has employed you all to do a job. A job that can't be completed if the Seer is sick or dead. So, I'll ask once more, is he alright?"

Kasper sat up, his weary expression tinged with annoyance. "He's fine. He had a particularly intense vision, and it was hard on his body." Kasper returned to the Seer and brushed a damp cloth over his brow. "Tell your Lady that he'll be better in a few hours. He just needed a tonic." He shot a look at his other brother and said, "Put the shadows away, Cal."

The Necromancer did no such thing until another form appeared in the doorway. Cal shifted his attention. "Yes, Finnley?"

"We're ready for you to address the crew, Cap'n."

Cal nodded and straightened his jacket. "I'll be up in a minute."

"Yes, Cap'n."

Finnley retreated, and Cal waited until her footfalls vanished before he stomped toward the door. He paused, his knuckles turning white against the threshold. Casting a vicious glance over his shoulder, he whispered, "My brother may have agreed to your Lady's terms, but you are on my ship, and you will regard me with the respect I am due on my vessel."

Brander smirked, though it lacked the bite he intended. The unease in his stomach was worsening with each passing minute, but he pushed past it and remarked, "Demanding respect seems beneath you, don't you think? Especially from a guard dog, like myself."

A sinister smile spread across the Necromancer's face. "My brothers take issue with my desire to put you in your place physically, so I have to resort to verbal threats. But make no mistake, if it comes down to it, my brothers' wishes won't be able to save you."

Brander bared his teeth. "I look forward to it."

The Necromancer laughed darkly. "I wondered if a man was still in there beneath all the palace conditioning. Nice to see the King didn't break your spirit entirely. You'll need that where we're headed."

Cal didn't linger, leaving Brander alone with Kasper and the Seer.

"Sorry about Cal. He's difficult on his best days, insufferable on his worst." Kasper ensured. Brander figured it was the closest he would get to an apology, not that he needed one. He was raised to be a soldier. There wasn't any malice that he wasn't capable of handling.

Kasper kept his attention trained on the Seer, who still hadn't moved, though his color had improved marginally.

Brander cleared his throat and pressed his hand to his abdomen to abate the nausea that cramped his stomach. Bile burned up his throat, but he held his breath, forcing the acid back down. He inhaled sharply and bit out, "I will inform Lady Hera of your brother's health."

He turned on his heel, desperate to escape the conmen, and returned to the Princess's room. It only took one knock for Princess Rhea to come to the door with large eyes and bent brows.

"The Seer is fine. His brothers believe it is a common symptom of using his abilities."

The worry remained in her features. "Common? I don't remember that happening in the palace. What if this happens when we are in the midst of danger?"

Brander shook his head. "They claim to have an antidote."

Indignation flared in her eyes. "That is not a solution."

"I know, but this is one of those risks that we must contend with. Unless you would like to return home now." Brander held his hope at bay. He knew it was unlikely, but perhaps if the Princess continued to be betrayed by the conmen, then she would come to her senses.

Sweat gathered on Brander's nape. His skin grew warmer, but a chill wracked him as his stomach cramped again. He leaned against the wall, attempting to give himself a reprieve while the Princess deliberated.

The Princess's unbound hair gently swayed. "No, we must persevere, but I will speak at length with the Seer once he is well enough to see me."

Suddenly, Brander doubled over, clutching his abdomen. Pain flashed through him like lightning splitting the sky. Had he eaten something? Was it poison? His mind raced with the possibilities, but the sickness was too great for him to think much past the pain.

The Princess's hand came down on his shoulder. "Brander, what's wrong?"

Brander was preoccupied with the sickness roiling through his body. The burning of bile worked its way up his throat.

"Looks like he's a wee seasick dearie. Might ought to get him in a room before he blows chunks all about the walls," clucked a passing pirate. Their heinous laughter followed Brander into his room, the Princess guiding him. Briefly, Brander appreciated having separate rooms. Whatever illness or affliction had befallen him, hopefully it would not infect the Princess.

Tears stung his eyes. His muscles quaked as he tried to keep his food down. He fumbled blindly in the low light. His vision was swimming, but he found a chamber pot just in time, his knees cracking as they smacked into the floor. Brander retched with enough force to make his vision double, over and over. The sickness subsided long enough for Brander to lean against the side of the bed, his skin clammy and sticky. An ache throbbed through his head in time with his thready heartbeat. His breathing was shallow, but every inhale burned against his ravaged throat.

The floor creaked. "Brander, are you alright?"

Brander raised a hand and waved weakly. "I'm fine, my Lady. Please return to your own cabin."

"I'm not sure I should leave you. You don't look well."

Another wave of nausea overtook Brander, and he frantically reached for the bowl.

"Aye, he'll be alright, dearie. I look after him." Brander recognized the voice as the same crewmate from before, but he had no energy to turn and look.

"I can stay with him..." Princess Rhea responded hesitantly. Brander couldn't blame her for not wanting to be in the room with him. She was royalty, witnessing her guard lose his lunch.

"I promise, dearie, I'll keep an eye on him. Besides, I know the tricks to get him back in sailing shape."

The floor creaked behind him again, and a tentative hand came down on his back. "Brander, will you be alright?"

He nodded weakly—it was all he could manage.

"I don't know what I can do to help, but I'll check on you every little bit. Alright?"

Brander nodded again, his throat too sore to form words.

The Princess's hand disappeared, and the wood shifted as she moved away from him. "Thank you," she muttered softly. The door snicked shut behind her, and Brander was helpless to stop the disappointment that settled in his bones.

Hands slid under his arms, urging him up from the floor.

"Come now, love, can't have you lying on the ground."

It took several minutes, but the crewmate finally got Brander onto the bed. He couldn't say it was much different from the floor. He also got his first look at his newest companion. A large, toothy grin made mostly of gold and silver greeted him, as did a threadbare tunic and leather eye patch. The nausea in Brander's stomach had eased some, but the sight before him sent another wave careening through him.

Brander was still aware enough to make heads or tails if the person before him was male or female, but he supposed it didn't matter. Not as they pressed a small brown bottle to his lips and said, "Here now, love, take a sip."

The concern of it being poison flitted through his mind, but the sickness plaguing him now was too dire to ignore. Silently, he prayed that if the Forgotten still listened, they would keep watch over the Princess. He held no trust for the brothers or the crew, but Brander would be useless if he succumbed to his sickness. He was out of options. Against all of the training and instinct in Brander, he drank the liquid.

The elixir was thick and bitter, but it soothed his raw throat, and he managed to keep it down. The crewmate sat at the edge of the bed and monitored him with a watchful brown eye. Several moments passed, and the intense rolling in Brander's gut lessened. His muscles began to relax, and his eyes became heavy. Alarm rang through Brander, but it was too late; the drug was already running its course.

"Relax, love. It's a light sedative to keep you calm." the crewmate said, their gold and silver teeth gleaming in the dim light. "Enjoy your nap!" They called out as they rose and left the room.

Everything was covered in a haze, and Brander couldn't see through it. Panic rose in his chest, but it was squashed by the sedative just as quickly. His breathing deepened.

His grip on his consciousness slipped from him, like sand through his fingers.

Chapter Fifteen

K ai's chest rose and fell too slowly. Kasper's eyes tracked it, up and down.

Up. Down.

Up. Down.

Up. Down.

Kai's skin was sallow and waxy; the stench of sweat permeated the air, turning Kasper's stomach. He knew he should have gotten more of the elixir back in Mirador, but he had barely been able to secure this one. And it had cost him.

A blood ruby had been handed over to the merchant without a moment of hesitation because to go without the elixir was not an option. But he hadn't expected to be setting off on a journey after a mythical treasure, and now he was left without any more tonic for Kai. Kasper leaned back on the bed, resting his head against the cabin wall, and exhaled noisily. He scanned the cramped room. The walls were nondescript, and the rest of the cabin was equally unremarkable. It was bare of anything but the essentials: a bed, dresser, and chair.

A chair that Cal had occupied for all of five minutes before Brander had intruded.

Kasper shook his head, unable to fully comprehend that he was aboard a ship bound for the Cave of Splendors. A location that was entirely unknown to Kasper, though it seemed there were several things that Kasper didn't know. Like how his brother was apparently a pirate. But not just any pirate, no, the *Captain*. The wanted posters in the merchants shop flashed in his mind. Kasper had never seriously considered turning in Cal for his magic, but the rewards for information on pirates had been tempting. Perhaps it was a good thing that the caravan had never traveled close enough to the coast that running into pirates would have been commonplace. Maybe the Forgotten had granted Kasper the small mercy of not being in a position to unknowingly betray his brother. Kasper's soul was already stained enough; he didn't think he could withstand adding *traitor* to the list.

But even that conclusion did little to ease the anger simmering in Kasper's chest. He crossed his ankles and arms. He supposed this was where Cal had been for the past nine and a half years. Though he wasn't sure why, that realization didn't assuage the anger roiling through his veins. Cal clearly had connections—he was the captain of the dreaded and infamous Umbra—he could have easily provided for them. If Cal had shared his wealth, then Kasper likely wouldn't have ever had to hand over the first cursed gem, and Kai would have enough antidote to ward off the negative effects of a vision. But no, Cal had left them behind without a second thought.

Abandoned.

Cal had abandoned him and Kai, and for what? Wealth? Fame? Kasper didn't care. He realized it didn't matter, either. Cal was selfish, always had been—well, as far as Kasper remembered—but at least Kasper now had proof of his low character. Kasper nodded quietly to himself. At least when this was all over, he would well and truly be rid of Cal. For years, Kasper held a foolish hope that Cal would return and repair their fractured relationship—what an asinine hope that had been. Since their banishment, it had been him and Kai against the world, with hardly a whisper from Cal.

Well, now he understood where he ranked in importance to his brother. Kasper's blood burned, forcing him to his feet. Perhaps he would tell him that now. Maybe he would tell Cal what he thought of him and the negligence of his family and his responsibilities. Kasper clenched his jaw. He would. He would berate his older brother in front of his precious crew. The people whose arrival lit up Cal's face more than Kasper or Kai ever could. He turned to grab the lightweight cloak he had discarded on the bed, but froze.

Heavy, weak brown eyes peered up at Kasper from the bed. A feeble smile graced Kai's cracked lips. "Kasper," he rasped out.

All of Kasper's anger fled his body as he dropped back down toward the bed, the mattress dipping under his weight. "Can I get you anything?" he asked softly.

Kai blinked slowly and waved a hand dismissively. "I'm fine, just tired."

Kasper nodded and took a seat beside his brother. Reaching out, he brushed a sticky curl from his temple. He swallowed and said through a tight throat, "I'm sorry."

A crease formed between Kai's brow. "For what?"

"For not seeing this coming. For not getting more of the elixir."

Kai's brow rose. "Ah," he said, cautiously reaching for Kasper's hand. Kasper didn't hesitate as he gripped Kai's clammy fingers. "It's not your fault, Kasper."

Kasper shook his head. "I should have gone back to the market and looked for more. I had a few more gems on me to use." Kasper cursed himself for not thinking ahead. He should have anticipated this, or at least prepared for the worst.

"I shouldn't have ever let you use the first one."

Kasper whipped his head toward Kai. It wasn't his words that startled him, but rather the utter anguish that echoed in his voice. Kasper stared into Kai's caramel-brown eyes, trying to decipher the origin of his despair. "We had no choice. It was that or starve." Glancing around, Kasper added, "Though given Cal's position, I don't think it necessarily had to be that way."

Kai's tongue darted out to wet his lips. He shifted, scooting himself further up the bed and into a sitting position. Kasper tensed, furrowing his brows.

Kai's frail shoulders curved slightly as he turned from Kasper, avoiding his gaze. "What do you remember of our time in the palace?"

Shrugging, Kasper said, "Nothing. I guess your theory about my mind protecting me by burying my memories is true. Though, sometimes, I think my dreams are glimpses of my past. A dark-haired little girl, a beautiful blonde woman, you—I can't really make sense of anything." A faint smile graced his lips. "Why?"

A wet, sputtering cough broke from Kai's lips and Kasper reached for a cloth lying on the dresser. Kai took it and wiped at his mouth. His eyes went wide at the sight of blood, but he quickly tucked the rag away.

"Because what you understand about our situation, Caliban's involvement in your life—has been skewed slightly."

Kasper furrowed his brow but stayed silent.

"When we lived in the palace, Caliban protected you and saw to your needs. He demanded that you be educated with the other children—leveraged the King's need for his particular abilities to get him to agree—and when we were exiled, he was the one who got you out of the palace."

A prickling sensation lifted the hairs along Kasper's neck. "What do you mean?"

Kai gave a long-suffering sigh and said, "I mean there were things that happened while we lived at court, things that displeased the King, and after I gave the prophecy...things got much worse." Kai shook his head. "You were too young to understand the full extent of what was happening, but when Caliban found out what had happened to Soline—"

"Wait, who's Soline?" The name triggered something in his mind, but it vanished when he pushed for it.

Licking his lips once more, Kai continued. "The plan had never been for me or you to leave, at least not initially, but Caliban's rage—what he had lost—" Kai shook his head, clearing away the memories.

Kasper didn't understand. He was unable to reconcile what Kai was telling him with what little he remembered. He closed his eyes and forced himself to recall those murky memories. A girl's laughter echoed in his ears, a nobleman's glare seared into his skin, starched clothes itched his neck, warm soup soothed his throat—but Cal was nowhere to be seen. Not even the events that Kai had just shared struck anything with Kasper.

Kasper opened his eyes and found Kai staring blankly at him. Nothing was in his gaze, not the mischief that normally gleamed there or even the hint of humor that usually lifted the corners of his eyes. Kai's dour appearance sat like a stone in Kasper's stomach. In all their years, even the lean ones, he never lost the light within him.

"I know none of this makes sense, Kasper, at least not right now, but I have spent too long letting you believe a lie. One that has caused you and Caliban tremendous hurt."

Kasper pulled away from his brother, the disappointment registering on his wan features. "Why are you defending him?" Kasper spat. He stood and gestured to the room around them and beyond. "This is what he left us for. This. He chose to abandon us after we were exiled." Kasper was mildly disgusted at the hurt in his own voice, but he couldn't stop it. Couldn't stop the burning in his throat as he fought against the tears.

Kai reached for him, grabbing Kasper's wrist, but he stepped out of Kai's reach and shook his head.

"There are things you simply don't know or understand, Kasper, and I am attempting to right that."

Kasper flung his hands up. "What could I possibly need to know that I don't already understand. You say Cal was the one who made sure I was educated and fed in the palace. Fine, I'll accept that, but you were the one who stayed with me. You cared for me when things got hard. Meanwhile, he was off gallivanting across the open seas. There is nothing you can tell me that will change how angry I am at him for leaving me." Kasper's voice broke despite his efforts to keep it level. And he realized for the first time that it was a deep-seated anger, not just some passing frustration, that burned in his chest every time he looked at Cal.

Taking a shaky breath, Kai pressed a hand to his chest. "Caliban wanted to take you with him."

Kasper froze. "What?"

Pressing his lips together, Kai added, "When we fled the palace, Caliban wanted you to go with him. He was going to take you on the run, but I...prevented it. I told him it was irresponsible to make a criminal of such a young child and that you would remain with me. He agreed, although begrudgingly."

Kasper's hearing went fuzzy. He was unable to comprehend the words he was hearing and the truth that Kai was revealing. Part of him wanted to reject it and accuse Kai of trying to repair the tattered relationship between Cal and Kasper with lies. But Kasper was incapable of bringing himself to say those words because, in his bones, he knew Kai wasn't lying.

Kai took another labored breath and said, "He came back three years after being away, and he was different. More ruthless than I remembered, but when he saw you—"

"I remember the first time he came back," Kasper cut in, his voice hoarse, the memories racing back to him as though Kai's words had unearthed them, "I...He startled me in an alleyway. I thought he was someone who wanted revenge for the gems I traded. I didn't recognize him at first, but then I did. I hated him. I hated that he left us."

Kai pressed his lips together and nodded. "Caliban came to me later and threatened me. He was angry I had wasted the money he sent and refused to give me more. I knew he was right, especially since I had encouraged you to use the gems you conjured to ease our financial burdens." Kai said with a nod.

"Your burdens." Kasper spat, remembering the money Kai would flippantly spend on his wardrobe and trinkets when food was scarce.

Kai winced, but nodded again. "Yes, mine."

A broken and disbelieving scoff fell from Kasper's lips as he stepped away. His hands went into his hair and remained there as he paced back and forth. All these years, Kasper had resented Cal and was so certain that his brother had chosen to stay away. In the nine and a half years he had been gone, Kai had never corrected Kasper in his assumptions.

Kasper raised his eyes to his brother. Kai took his bottom lip between his teeth, his body looking frail and weaker than Kasper had ever seen. Kasper exhaled sharply and said, "So, you mean...that after all this time, Cal didn't abandon us."

A heavy and thick silence blanketed the room. Only the groaning of the Umbra and Kai's wheezing could be heard. Kasper held his own breath. Waiting. Refusing to give Kai a way out of his admissions.

Kai's bottom lip quivered slightly as he held Kasper's unrelenting stare. "No, he didn't." Kai finally said, the word barely above a whisper.

A humorless chuckle broke from Kasper's lips. "All this time. All this time, you let me believe that Cal didn't want me around. And not only that, but you made me use the gems, even knowing the repercussions."

Kasper's breathing had turned shallow, his vision doubling. His pacing renewed as his mind turned, desperate to make sense of everything, but his reality was slipping away. The foundation that he had erected beneath himself was crumbling. What other truths were being hidden from him? What other lies had he been fed? Kasper stopped in front of Kai and looked at his brother. He really looked at him. And perhaps, for the first time, *really* saw him. Large brown eyes bore into his own, and cracked lips trembled as they awaited Kasper's response.

But he had nothing to say.

He shook his head in disgust and turned for the door.

"Where are you going?"

Kasper didn't stop or answer as he flung open the latch and stepped into the narrow corridor. Night was just beginning to fall, but the halls of the Umbra were already bathed in darkness. He could hardly distinguish where the night began and the Umbra stopped. Kasper was beyond caring. He stomped down the hall, pulled open the door to his room, and stepped inside. He shut the door behind him and let his pulse thrum in time with the lapping of the waves against the hull.

Another minute passed, and Kasper's feet went out from under him, his back knocking into the door and his body thudding against the floor. Hot tears of bitterness, betrayal, and wrath streamed down his face, soaking the front of his tunic. He shoved a fist into his mouth, stifling the sounds of his sobs. His knees curled up into his chest and remained there for minutes, hours, days.

He wasn't sure.

He knew nothing anymore, except that his brothers had lied to him. They had deemed him too unworthy, weak, or childish to handle the truth. Perhaps he *was* weak—too sensitive for the criminal life that both of his brothers seemed to flourish in. Every life impacted by his cursed gems weighed on him and made him sick for days.

Funny, he thought.

He wasn't old enough or mature enough to know the truth about himself, but old enough to use cursed crystals to condemn others to misfortune. Yes, he was weak, but maybe that was preferable to his siblings' cold, calculating minds. Maybe one day, he would be free of their machinations and no longer have to compromise his integrity for their schemes.

A dream to be had.

Kasper remained on the floor until his anger and hurt finally got the better of him. As he saw it, there were two choices in front of him: Stew in his anguish, or drown it. Kasper took all of one heartbeat to decide what he preferred, and then, he was out the door.

Chapter Sixteen

The ship's galley was as rowdy and rambunctious as any tavern Kasper had dared enter on the continent. Men cursed and drank, their beer and rum sloshing over the rims of their mugs. The liquid splattered the floor until the room stank of yeast and sugar, the dark wood sticky with their carelessness. Their tawdry ballads of fair-haired maidens and nightly adventures when they dared to dock in port were descriptive enough to turn Kasper's ears red.

He loved every moment of it.

The louder and drunker the crew grew, the more at ease Kasper became. He was mindful to avoid the unsteady gaits of the more inebriated men. Unlike Cal, fighting was not his preferred method for venting his frustration. He made careful work of finding the jars of rum and an empty cup. He poured it about half full and gingerly took a sip.

Immediately, the sugar–light and nectarine–enveloped his mouth. There were undercurrents of other flavors and spices, but their names were unknown to him. It didn't matter. All Kasper was concerned with were the effects. He never drank more than a few sips of wine or mead back on land, but even from the little taste of the rum he had consumed he already knew that it far surpassed anything else. He had no desire to wake up with a throbbing head, but he needed to take the edge off.

Maneuvering through the room, he looked for something to occupy his mind. Ordinarily, he had to remain sharp and aware to ensure that no one harmed Kai, but now…

Kasper tipped back his cup, letting its sweet and sugary contents wash away his anger. It coated his hurt in a saccharine glaze, making everything look fuzzier and less threatening. The haze of the rum even persuaded Kasper to claim a seat at a table occupied by three other people, all holding time-worn playing cards between their grimy fingers. Kasper was still aware enough to recognize two members at the table, Finnley and Galen, the two pirates that had greeted them before they boarded the ship. Kasper didn't know them, but they didn't run him off, so he took it as a sign that he was welcome to stay.

Galen leaned over, gave Kasper a broad smile, and said, "You're right on time. We were looking to start another game and needed a fourth."

The other pirate, an older, crude-looking man with sunspots and wrinkles, dealt the cards. While the deck was dispersed, Galen attempted to explain the rules of the game, but Kasper was unable to follow. If he had ever known how to play the game he was now a part of–or any card game, for that matter–he didn't recall learning it. Perhaps it was another of his lost memories. But he wasn't all that concerned with the rules anyway. He was too focused on making sure he stayed on this side of drunk—which was proving more challenging than Kasper expected. He had no idea how much alcohol was truly present in the rum, but it was more than he had anticipated. His reactions turned sluggish, and his anger was steadily bleeding away.

Finnley laid a card, and Galen followed. He looked at Kasper expectantly, and Kasper laid one of his own. A look passed between the three pirates, and Kasper had the distinct impression he had done something wrong, but his mind buzzed too much to be concerned.

"Ye have to put up to play that card."

"Pardon?" Kasper replied, though he was certain his speech was more slurred than even his ears detected.

Finnley rolled her eyes and threw her cards face down; Galen merely smiled and turned to Kasper. "Ye need something to bet with, like gold, jewels, or gems."

Kasper knew that word. Nodding, he reached into his pocket. He fished around until his fingers closed around the desired item. From his pocket, he produced an amethyst crystal. It glowed faintly between his fingers, and he felt its desire to rectify the effects of the alcohol in his system.

He would have none of that.

Kasper tossed the gem onto the table. It clattered noisily against the large gold coins piled next to the older man—his previous winnings.

"Will that do?" Kasper asked with a degree of smugness that he had never employed before.

Galen's eyes grew wide as he lifted them from where the gem rested and then up to Finnley's cold stare. Finnley remained impassive as she gave a curt nod. "Aye, it'll do."

Kasper smiled and watched the game with renewed interest. He had plenty of crystals he had no issue parting with. These he had come by honestly, which meant they wouldn't bring whoever possessed them a terrible fortune.

The next hour passed without incident. They played six hands before the man who had won prior to Kasper's joining had lost all he earned and then some. Kasper wasn't terribly concerned with losing, and instead relished the levity that the games and rum brought him.

Finnley sat back, her auburn hair glowing like rubies in the lantern light, not even bothering to acknowledge that she had all but run the table. The older pirate finally threw his cards down and stormed away. Finnley let the barest of smiles grace her lips before she glanced up and found Kasper watching her. Her smile vanished, and she rocked forward, the front legs of her chair clattering as they slammed back down on the floor. She rested her cards on the table face up—another winning hand. Kasper was almost entirely out of gems to play with, the sum now firmly in Finnley's possession. Finnley leaned forward and braced her elbows on the table. A wicked and terrible look gleamed in her eye that nearly turned the alcohol warming Kasper's belly sour.

"How is it ye came into possession of all these here rocks?"

Kasper lifted the cup to his lips but found it empty. He glanced long-ingly at the bottle Finnley had commandeered, but from the proprietary grip she had on the neck of the bottle, he didn't think she was interest-ed in relinquishing control.

Kasper placed his cup back on the table. "I bought them."

"Aye, I suspect that's true, but why do they glow?"

Kasper shrugged and said, "They do that sometimes." Then he reached for the bottle, undeterred by the consequences.

Finnley pulled the bottle away, just out of reach.

Kasper sighed, leaned back in his chair, and crossed his arms over his chest. He was dimly aware that antagonizing Finnley would likely result in some sort of recompense, but he was beyond caring. Finnley sneered at him, her scar turning crueler in the lowlight, and uncorked the bottle. The rum, a rich shade of amber, spilled from the bottle into her cup and then Galen's. Kasper ground his teeth, trying not to let his annoyance get the best of him, but he was burgeoning on being drunk and wanted more. Galen cautiously sipped from his cup; it was clear he had previously been privy to Finnley's interrogation routine. Meanwhile, Finnley swirled the rum in her cup, content to watch Kasper fume.

Finnley kept her voice low, barely audibly over the boisterous con-versations and sharp music as she said, "Me thinks that since ye brother is in the magic way, yous might be too. So, I'll ask again: why do they glow?" Finnley lost the pretense of being uneducated, and her features shifted to deathly calm.

Kasper wasn't sure if it was the alcohol making his tongue loose or if he had genuinely given up on caring what happened to him. Still, he tilted his head and said, "I can channel through gems and crystals. Almost all naturally occurring crystals have properties, whether it's healing or protection. My abilities allow me to amplify that, which is why they glow. The purple ones," he said, pointing to the three ame-thyst crystals piled next to the coins, "promote physical healing; the whitish ones repel negative energy. Now," Kasper added, sliding his cup toward Finnley, "If you want to know anything else, you're going to have to supply me with more rum."

A genuine smile formed on Finnley's lips for the first time all night. She lifted the bottle and tipped it toward his cup.

"It would be my pleasure."

Kasper grinned as the rum flowed from the bottle to his cup to his mouth—loosening him up more than was advisable. But Kasper didn't care. He was tired of being the responsible one. He was tired of making sure that Kai was safe and happy. He was tired of being treated like a child. Kasper was tired of it all.

He played more hands of cards than he dared try to keep up with. The fourth seat at their table became a revolving door of different crew members all looking to try and usurp Finnley, who was apparently a card hustler when she was in the right mood. Kasper continued to guzzle rum until someone replaced it with beer, which was watery and stale, but would do the job of continuing his descent into drunkenness. He could have sworn he saw Lady Hera—a smile ghosting her lips and a keenness to her eyes that was so *familiar* it sent a pang through his chest. But he wasn't entirely sure because his vision had doubled.

Eventually, he found his way to a bed—his, he hoped. Still, he wasn't terribly concerned as sweet oblivion tugged at his mind, drawing him under the thrashing current.

Chapter Seventeen

The walls and floor of Brander's cabin did little to muffle the swearing and merriment happening beneath them. Rhea wondered if that was why this room was selected for him. But even as she watched Brander's chest rise and fall with the steady rhythm that only a sedative brought, she couldn't stop her mind from *wandering*.

Her father had forbidden her from attending any festivities that weren't religious. Still, sometimes, she would sneak out and watch from afar just to feel like she was a part of the fun. But now, nothing was preventing her from joining the revelry. Rhea kept her eyes on Brander's sleeping form as she slowly slipped her feet from where they were tucked underneath her in the chair adjacent to Brander's bed. She pressed her lips together as she gently rose to the floor, careful not to do anything that would possibly rouse Brander. She stood still for a heartbeat and then turned, reaching for the latch on the door. Her hand paused, hovering over the handle.

This was a bad idea.

Any number of things might go awry. She might get hurt or drink too much. Her identity might become known, or one of the crew could try to assault her.

Rhea glanced back at Brander. He would be enraged if he knew she was even considering leaving the room, let alone joining the festivities. He would lock her in her quarters until they arrived at the Cave of Splendors, and even then, he probably wouldn't let her out.

But the thoughts of what it might be like to speak freely for once or simply enjoy a hand of cards dominated all other rational thoughts. She might never get the chance again. Rhea bit her bottom lip, chewing it until the tang of her blood filled her mouth, the split lip her father had given her reopening. She should return to her cabin and turn in for the night. There was no telling what horrors awaited them once they got out onto the open ocean. And she would need her rest if she was going to survive Caliban and his brothers—especially since Kai knew her identity.

Yes, she should go to bed.

That was the mantra Rhea repeated to herself as she stepped out in the corridor and headed toward her room, but the words lost their meaning as she continued past her door, following the forbidden echoes of fun.

* * * *

The pungent reek of too-close bodies mingled with the sugar of the alcohol and the brine of the sea. In any other circumstances, Rhea would cover her nose and try not to gag from the stench, but tonight…

Tonight, it was the most remarkable smell she had ever encountered. Tonight, it smelt like freedom.

Rhea pressed herself against the wall, her senses devouring everything. Men and women alike clung to cups and goblets that sloshed and splashed with liquid ranging from the yellowish tint of ale to the maroon hue of wine. They smiled and chortled with a carelessness that sent a bolt of jealousy through her chest. Some stumbled, blindly grappling for whatever purchase they could find, while others danced and sang with such fervor that Rhea wasn't convinced they weren't having a religious experience.

She ached to be a part of it.

Splaying her hands flat to the wall, she inched along it, making her way to the lone bottle of rum that rested on a surprisingly unoccupied table. Most of the crew were gathered around a few tables to the front of the room, their backs to her. She was thankful for that small mercy. As much as she wanted to be a part of their drinking songs and debauchery, she dared not push her luck. Swiping a bottle of rum and remaining undetected was the best course of action.

A noise struck up from the crowd of bodies—someone had found a fiddle—and Rhea paused. The song was nothing of note, just a few verses about a boy pining after his lost love and wreaking havoc to get her back, but the melody—even on a slightly out-of-tune fiddle—was haunting.

Rhea had always been drawn to music. She was forbidden from learning an instrument, but she would sit in court and listen to the musicians for hours. Rhea rose on her toes, intrigued to see who was playing, but the crush of bodies was too thick. She swayed slightly, letting the music wash over her and transport her back to the incense-filled rooms of her father's palace. Closing her eyes, she remembered the plush silk pillows she lazed on for so long that the embroidery would imprint her skin. Her eyes burned from the perfumes as she tried to keep them open. A dull throb would develop in her temples from the constant playing, but Rhea never complained—and only left once a governess dragged her away.

"Enjoying yerself, lass?"

Rhea's eyes flew open, and she rocked back on her heels, knocking into the wall slightly. A man, a few years older than herself, stood before her. He held the bottle of rum she had been eyeing before the music had taken over. Rhea blinked, and the man tilted his head, a smile forming on his face. A face that was surprisingly handsome, given the rough and worn appearances of most of the crew she had encountered—save for Cal. The newcomer's hair was a rich brown that curled along his ears and nape, offset by light brown skin and warm brown eyes. He had the common features and coloring of most people from Desmorda, but that didn't diminish their attractiveness.

Pushing past his appeal for a moment, she forced it not to cloud her judgment. She was in a room full of people, eyes, and witnesses everywhere, and the man in front of her was still smiling.

A smile of her own formed on her lips. There would be nothing between them. There *could* be nothing between them, but Rhea wasn't opposed to a bit of flirtation. None of the nobles' sons dared engage her after a debacle with a governor's son, which ended with him and his father both getting flogged. The rich iron of their blood as it leaked from their ruined backs still clung to her nose. The haggard screams of the governor's wife begging for mercy on behalf of her husband and son still reverberated through Rhea's mind. The King's cruelty knew no bounds and spared none—not even his own daughter.

Rhea glanced at the bottle still clasped in the man's hands. The man tracked her eyes and said, "Would ye like a sip?"

"I would," she said coyly. She had come here for a bit of fun and freedom, had she not? Surely, there was no harm in enjoying some spirits and company—at least for a few minutes.

The man's smile grew wider, and he turned and gave an ear-splitting whistle. A boy, no more than fifteen, came rushing over. The music and singing had grown loud enough that the man's words to the boy were swallowed up. The boy spared Rhea a glance before hustling off, disappearing back into the crowd.

"Just a moment, love. Sammy-boy is fetching us some cups." he said with a wink. "I'm Cade, by the way." he added, looking back at the other pirates.

Rhea had to fight the urge to roll her eyes, but his blatant good looks masked some of his less desirable qualities. A moment later, the boy—Sammy—reappeared with two metal goblets in his hands. Cade took the goblets, balancing them deftly between his fingers as he uncorked the bottle with his teeth and poured the dark amber liquid. Not a drop spilled as he handed Rhea's drink to her, grinning wickedly.

Rhea kept her eyes trained on the drink as she inhaled it. Although she was interested in detecting the specific scents and spices, she was far more eager to taste them. She lifted the goblet to her lips and took a sip.

Immediately, she wanted more.

Nothing had ever tasted so good. So lush. So decadent. What little wine she had been allowed in the palace was always watered down, but this rum was vibrant and full. She wanted to down the entire cup, but allowed herself one more sip before pulling the cup from her lips. Already, she wanted another taste.

"It's good, right? We raided some islands a few years back, and they had the best rum any of us had ever tasted. This is one of the last bottles. We planned to go back, but then Cap'n showed up, and now we're headed to some other island, but..." his words trailed off as he took a long sip from his drink, his eyes roaming over her body, drinking it in, too.

Rhea couldn't help but blush under his gaze, averting her own and taking a swig from her cup. The rum warmed her body as it trickled down her throat, and she finally found her words.

"But what?"

"But," Cade said, taking a step closer. Rhea noted the scars peppering his skin and the hint of gold in his otherwise soil-brown eyes. Cade licked his lips, "now you're here, and you look like you'd taste even better than the rum."

Rhea went wholly still at Cade's unabashed interest and brazen comment. She cleared her throat and drank from her cup again. It would have been wise to slow down and pace herself, but the rum made her feel good and it was a shield from Cade. Shaking her head and forcing a smile to her face, she said, "You're awfully forward."

Cade laughed, the sound was a deep rumble that skittered along Rhea's spine. "No reason to act shy about the things I want." He took another drink, still watching her over the rim of the goblet.

Rhea shifted her weight. The music and merriment were losing some of its intrigue. She was balancing on a precipice that, if she wasn't careful, she would be pushed over without another thought for what *she* wanted. And what *did* she want? A night of fun, free from Brander's scrutinizing gaze? A chance to be someone other than a Princess or a Lady?

Rhea wasn't entirely sure, but she knew that her coquetting with Cade needed to end. Rhea lifted her chin, finished the remnants of her rum and then set her goblet down gently on the table next to them. Cade's eyes glittered with something more wicked than amusement, and it chilled Rhea's blood. His intensity dared to extinguish the playfulness coursing through her.

"I think it's time I retired, but thank you for the rum." Rhea smiled politely and moved to step around Cade.

"Well, no reason to rush off." he said, reaching for her arm. "The music's just getting started. Why don't ye join me for a dance?" Cade tugged at her. Between the rum and Cade's insistence, Rhea stumbled slightly. Blindly, she grabbed for the table, steadied herself, and extracted her arm from Cade's grip.

"Not tonight, I'm afraid. Too much excitement has worn me out," Rhea claimed, giving a halfhearted laugh and pushing past Cade.

"Oh come on, now. Ye want to have a bit of fun." Cade cooed.

Rhea hesitated. It was a bad idea—for a number of reasons. But...

"Alright," she conceded, "one dance."

A broad and hungry smile spread across Cade's face as he reached for her and pulled her flush to him. The song and steps were foreign to Rhea, but it didn't matter as Cade took the lead. Pushing her to and fro, swinging her all around the room until her head spun and her stomach twisted painfully. But the alcohol in her system blurred the pain, bleeding it away to nothing. Slowly, she began to understand the rhythm. Her feet moved in time with the music and Cade became the steady and assured presence that guided her. The tension in her shoulders and jaw dissolved into nothingness, stealing away whatever apprehension had remained.

Why had she been anxious in the first place?

Cade's strong and sturdy touch held her in place, whisking her about the room at a dizzying but delightful pace. They whirled and stumbled, further from the entrance of the room and closer to the musicians. The song, an impossibly long one, finally came to an end. Her feet slowed their tempo, but the rest of her body struggled to adjust. Rhea's pulse thumped painfully in her temples and her breath came in short pants. All around her, the room buzzed with spirits and merriment. Licking her lips and briefly tasting the sugary rum that still coated them, Rhea began to pull herself from Cade's hold. But his fingers pressed into her wrists. Pain shot through her joints as the bones were crushed and compressed.

"Where ye tryin' to go? The funs just started!" Cade called over the music as another song kicked up and he pulled her tight once more.

The rum had cast her thoughts in a haze, and she was struggling to remember why she should leave. Unsure of her motives, Rhea gave in to Cade, who's features were glazed with lust. Rhea swallowed down her lingering trepidation. What was the harm with a little bit more dancing? Wasn't she enjoying herself? Honestly, when was the last time that she let herself relax and lean into a bit of impulsivity? Cade yanked and swung, her joints loose and taut at the same time. Her head spun, and she whirled around and around and around—

Her gaze collided with Cal.

Rhea's feet stuttered at the frigid violence limning his features.

Cade appeared in her line of vision, the desire in his expression quickly becoming deprivation. Seeing Cal had sobered her enough that she understood the peril she had stupidly placed herself in. Rhea blinked and shook her head. Her feet remained rooted to the floor even as Cade tugged on her.

"I'm suddenly very tired. I think I will retire now." Rhea announced as she managed to jerk herself free of Cade's grip.

"But—"

"I'm sorry," she called out as she hurried away. As she maneuvered through the room, her gaze caught on Kasper—who looked to all the world as drunk as a polecat. The sight would have been humorous if Rhea hadn't felt Cade's sinful gaze—and Cal's rueful one—searing into her spine.

Rhea's head swam as she hurried through the crowd, aiming for the door. The room's off-key singing, heat, and stench threatened to make her nauseous. Still, she was determined to make it to the deck before allowing herself to give in to her sickness.

She should have stayed in her room. A moment of fun and liberty was not worth the price of her safety or the quest. She knew better, but let her immaturity get the best of her. Maybe her father was right when he questioned her ability to be queen.

The air in the hull was thick and clung to her skin, even as she hurried up the hall and the two short flights of stairs before bursting onto the ship's deck. She gulped down the fresh air, working to inflate her lungs as much as possible to quell her rising panic. She padded over to the ship's railing, still taking deep breaths through her nose and exhaling out her mouth. The sea breeze cooled her heated skin. The air attempted to dry the perspiration pooling along her collarbone and nape.

She braced her forearms on the railing and leaned over the edge, trying to glimpse the water below. The sun was falling beneath the horizon, nearly gone, but it cast the sea—churning far beneath her—in an array of gold and orange. The gilded water concealed whatever beasts lurked beneath the subdued waves, but Rhea didn't doubt their existence. The book she had brought briefly covered some sea creatures that fishermen and privateers claimed lived in the waters, though the tales were murky at best. She had tried not to fixate on the dangers the book spoke of and instead read and reread the pithy passages that focused on the Cave of Splendors. Though, truthfully, even those had not inspired much confidence. But it was all she had. Other tomes dismissed the Cave's existence altogether. She had to hope that this one was right.

Another wave of nausea washed over her, and she closed her eyes against the discomfort. She shouldn't have drank so much. Her alcohol intake had always been limited and often watered down, and the rum she drank tonight certainly wasn't diluted. She pressed her forehead to the railing, relishing the bite of the wood into her skin. It grounded her and kept the wave of nausea at bay—at least for the moment. Sweat rolled down her neck, soaking into the fabric of her dress and sticking it to her skin.

"Not feeling well, love?"

Rhea whirled to find Cade standing behind her, the bottle of rum in his hand. A wicked grin on his face. A nervous laugh rattled out of Rhea as she glanced around the deck, hoping to see a passing crew-member. But there was no one and nothing but the shadows. Rhea turned her attention back to Cade and swallowed down her apprehension. She balled her fists at her sides and prayed to whatever god would listen that she would walk away from this encounter unscathed.

"I was disappointed that you left before we really got to know one another. I stopped by your room to see if you wanted to continue our, ah, conversation," Cade prowled forward, "but you weren't there."

Rhea laughed nervously again. "Yes, I wanted to see the sunset and get some fresh air before I turned in for the night—alone."

Cade was within a foot of her, the alcohol on his breath wafting into her face. The sickly-sweet scent of rum and lust. Rhea went still as the dead as Cade reached for her, lifting a curl and twirling it around his finger. He was drunk, that much she knew, but she had no interest in learning what his threshold for cruelty was.

"You speak like a highborn lass." he remarked, his gaze fixed on the dark strand of hair he twisted around his fingers. "Drink like one, too."

Rhea's eyes darted away from him. She needed to dislodge herself from his grip and get away. But to where? Her room was clearly unsafe if Cade knew which it was. And Brander was unconscious and would be of no use. Maybe if she could get to Cal's...

No. That wasn't an option, either. Her best hope was to get to her room and bar the door.

Rhea's spine pressed into the side of the Umbra as Cade stepped closer and took more of her hair into his hand. In an effort to fight against the trembling, Rhea clenched her fists and locked her knees.

She would not be a victim today.

Cade's mouth came close to her face, and she fought the grimace that his stench beckoned. "I've never had a noble girl before," he whispered. The words settled like a stone in Rhea's stomach. "I wonder if you feel different."

The encounter with the man in the alley flashed in Rhea's mind. The panic she experienced in that moment when it was clear that she was helpless locked her spine. When she knew without a doubt that no one was coming, she prayed that someone–anyone–would come anyway. She had no skills, no training to ward off an attack, but she would not go down without a fight and would not wait for someone to rescue her. She had no one but herself to rely on. Rhea set her jaw and straightened her spine, determined not to cower in the face of the monster before her. Cade's eyes narrowed, and his grip on her hair tightened. The pain lancing through her skull made her gasp and she stumbled forward. Cade shoved against her. He used his superior strength to turn her away from him and crushed her arms between her and the railing of the ship.

Cade's voice was rough and gravelly as he leaned down next to her ear and whispered, "I would say don't fight, but that makes it twice as fun."

Rhea took his words to heart and began thrashing. The darkness of the night was closing in around her, blotting out the sun as it finally disappeared beneath the water. Panic threatened to consume her, to drag her into the shadows and make her cower. It threatened to strip everything she was and leave her raw for the taking.

No.

Rhea threw her weight backward.

She would *not* be a victim today.

Pain reverberated through the back of her head as she connected with Cade's face. There was a sickening crunch, and the pressure behind her lessened. Rhea capitalized on the distraction, and she pushed away from the railing. Her blood thrummed through her, and her breath was like shards of glass in her chest. Cade reeled backward.

His eyes closed as he clutched his face in his hands, blood streaming between them.

Rhea would not consider herself a coward, but she knew when to run. Lifting her skirts, she sprinted away. Cade yelled something, but his voice was abruptly cut off, and the darkness swallowed his threats. She didn't stop or slow her pace until she was in her cabin, the chest of drawers and her bedside table shoved against the door. Her limbs and chest ached as she placed her feet against the drawers and her back to the bed frame. She extinguished the lantern next to her, plunging the room into darkness. The shadows sat with her, monitoring her every breath and movement. She was thankful for the company—even if it was just her imagination.

She rested her head against the bedframe, her eyes heavy, but her mind too frazzled to sleep. She had no plans to sleep anyway. The night slipped by, but Rhea stayed up. She kept vigil over her door until the wee hours of daylight began to shine through her window.

If Cade hadn't sought her out by now, he had likely lost interest or passed out—if she was lucky. Rhea would be sure to speak to Finnley about the man and make sure he kept his distance, but she didn't have much hope for what that would accomplish. Men like Cade rarely responded to commands and were only kept in check by violence.

Slowly, Rhea stretched her stiff, aching limbs and climbed off the floor. She didn't bother changing out of her dress and boots. Crawling over the threadbare blanket, she curled up on the bed and fell into a fitful sleep.

Chapter Eighteen

ade's body was still twitching when Cal planted his boot in his side and a crack splintered the night air.

He wasn't twitching after that.

Cal bent down to where Cade lay, his blood leaking onto the deck of the Umbra. Not dead—not yet, anyway. Cal wrung a thick rope in his hands, and his shadows twined around his body, hungry and incessant—waiting for the command to end Cade's life.

Soon, Cal thought. But first, a message needed to be sent to any other would-be assailants aboard the Umbra. A message that would ring loud and clear for the duration of the crew's life. Cal made quick work of looping the rope around Cade's ankles. He gave no thought to the fibers slicing into his own skin as he gave them one final yank and secured them. He relished in the pain; it was the only thing keeping him from ending Cade's life right then and there. It gave him something else, other than his blinding rage, to focus on.

Cal looped the rope around his hand once before tugging on it and dragging Cade into the belly of the ship. Cade's body made a satisfying thump as they went down the stairs. When Cal had witnessed Cade trying to assault the Lady earlier that night, his blood pulsed in his ears.

Thump.

Thump.

Thump.

With each smack of Cade's skull on the wood, some of his anger rippled away. He had to keep his shadows contained in case he passed any of the crew who weren't rip-roaring drunk. But as he passed the Lady's room, he could not stop them from unfurling and slithering inside—simply checking her quarters. They were an extension of his will, a manifestation of his innate desires. The shadows had simply always been, and they were eager to do his bidding. It was wholly different from his necromancy—a magic that consumed and ravaged him. A muscle feathered in Cal's jaw at the memories of the years that the King commanded he raise the dead. Swallowing, Cal shook off those thoughts and focused on his current mission.

The darkness within the room responded to him, stirring slightly, and…there she was. Cal smiled to himself at the Lady's ingenuity. She had placed her dresser in front of the door and had her legs braced against that. A perpetrator would have to exert tremendous force to try and get in. The shadows around her swirled, brushing against her skin, and she relaxed a fraction as though she, too, found comfort in the darkness.

Cal jerked his attention away from her room, forcing the petrified yet determined look on her face out of his mind. She should have never been in the galley. When she slipped into the room, transfixed by the chaos, he had almost gone to her and drug her back to her room by her braid. But then she had started conversing with Cade, and well, she was an adult. If she wanted to consort with the likes of him, then who was Cal to interfere?

He hadn't meant to keep watching her.

His plan had been to get drunk enough that the dead and night-mares would leave him be, but then she started *dancing*. Tendrils of her hair had broken free of her braid, a smile—a wholly unperturbed smile—bloomed on her face and—she looked like Soline. They were polar opposites in their coloring, but *something* about the way she spun and moved unearthed his long-forgotten memories.

Cal had been content to let her enjoy herself—or at least he was attempting to convince himself that he was—when their eyes slammed into one another. He had spoken—hadn't moved—he simply stared. But apparently, that had been enough to jar Lady Hera back to reality.

When Lady Hera had left the galley, Cal truly thought that was going to be the end of it. But then Cade had followed, and Cal didn't need the insight of his shadows to guess what Cade intended to do.

There was no remorse in Cal as he dragged Cade's still unconscious body down the last flight of stairs and into the galley, where the music and mischief were still going steady. Not a soul there had a clue what had just transpired above them. Frankly, this was unnecessary, but Cal couldn't stop himself as he put his index finger and thumb into his mouth and let out an ear-splitting whistle. Finnley was already on her feet, her face fixed in the same grim expression she had worn when Cal had left the galley to go after Cade earlier—like she knew what he planned to do. Cal gave no acknowledgment. He didn't let the hard mask he sported slip an inch. Mustering every ounce of strength he had–and subtly commanding his shadows to support Cade's limp body as well–Cal lifted Cade by the rope still encircling his ankles. The galley was dim enough and the crew was drunk enough that no one would know or suspect his use of magic.

The crew's faces shifted from drunken bliss to rueful understanding. Cal saw it in their eyes as they noted the swelling on Cade's face and the bruises blooming in an array of blues, purples, and blacks under his skin. They marked the blood–some dried and some still leaking–from the various lacerations on his body. Cal wanted them to see it and truly understand what the message was. Cal used the last of his strength to throw Cade forward, his body crashing to the ground—but the crew paid no mind to Cade and instead kept their gazes trained on Cal.

"I have never been ignorant to the things that some of you do when we raid or pillage. I have never condoned it, but punishing every one of you would leave me without much of a crew. But," Cal said, slowly drawing his sword free from its scabbard at his side, "some crimes are inexcusable, and it ends today."

Then he jerked his chin toward the freshwater barrel in the corner of the room.

"Wake him up."

Two pirates rushed, one reaching for a barrel and the other for a bucket. They made quick work of dumping the collected water on

Cade's head. Cade gasped and raised up. He lifted his head, trying to get his bearings and struggling against the restraints around his ankles. His dusty brown curls were dark and plastered to his head, obscuring his vision. Water dripped to the floor and splattered on Cal's boots as he stalked forward, sword in hand.

Cade flung his head back, exposing his face and finally allowing him to see the crew gathered before him. "Wh–what's goin' on? What happened?"

No one answered him. The crew's faces were a mix of indifferent and callous, but not an ounce of empathy was to be found. Cal continued forward until his shadow fell over Cade, who shifted on the ground and raised his face skyward. Cade's chest rose and fell in rapid succession. His eyes–well, the one that wasn't swollen shut–were wide and frantic, looking into Cal's stony features for the answers he wanted.

"You. Th–the shadows. They grr–grabbed me…" his words trailed off as he finally noted the sword gripped tightly in Cal's fist. Cade's throat bobbed, and he went still as death—a death that would be greeting him soon. Not a soul breathed or dared move as Cal grabbed Cade by the hair and yanked him back into his chest. Cade started to thrash and fight, but Cal calmly placed his blade at the base of his throat.

Cade's squirming ceased.

"You can't kill me." Cade seethed, his voice a desperate scream. "It violates every sacred pirate code!"

"Pirate code doesn't protect your crimes. Besides, you broke it first when you tried to assault Lady Hera." Cal growled. If the crew had been surprised at what Cade stood accused of, their faces didn't show it. Nor did they show an ounce of pity.

"The Lady dealt you the first blow, but now I shall deal you your last as Captain Caliban of the Umbra. May your body bloat and rot before the scavengers deem it worthy of eating."

Cade renewed his struggle, the blade against his throat at last drawing blood. "This won't stand. They won't stay on! They'll mutiny once they know what you are. You—"

But Cade's words became a gurgle as Cal dragged his sword against his neck. Cade toppled forward, unable to staunch the bleeding or break his fall as he collided with the floor. No one made a move to help him or give him the mercy of a quick death. Cade twitched for several more seconds, his body thumping obscenely on the floor before it finally stilled. Cal wiped the blood from his sword on Cade's back.

"The Lady is to remain untouched. You do not speak to or engage with her unless she speaks to you first, and even then, you keep it brief and civil." Cal waltzed calmly around the room, his eyes finding contact with each and every sailor that surrounded him, one by one. "You are not to go near her quarters. There is not to be a word of this breathed to anyone outside this room. There will be no exceptions, and if I find out you have disobeyed, then I will flay you alive and strap you to the bow, making what happened here tonight look like a mercy."

Many of the crew winced and recoiled at Cal's threat. The humiliation alone would be enough to make someone want to die, but to have the salt from the sea spraying against their open wounds until they succumbed to their injuries was especially cruel.

"Throw *this*," Cal said, stepping over Cade's body, "overboard and clean up the mess. I want it gone within the hour." Cal didn't wait to see how the crew reacted to his command. He was ready to be away from everyone for a moment. The darkness called to him, and he was prepared to oblige it. He stepped out into the corridor, already relishing in the thought of stripping off his blood-flecked clothes, when someone grabbed his arm.

Cal did his best to tamp down on his rage because no one other than Finnley would dare to touch him—not even Galen.

"What?" he ground out, avoiding her gaze.

"Why?"

Cal didn't have to ask what she meant; they had known one another long enough. "Because he hurt a woman."

Cade also saw Cal use his magic and certainly would have told the crew if he was allowed to live—but Finnley didn't need to know that.

She might have known about his magic, but Cal didn't make a habit of discussing it.

"Hurt a woman or hurt Lady Hera?" There was no teasing smile or smirk, just her cold, hard stare. "Saving her won't bring Soline back." Finnley said in a barely audible voice, shaking her head softly at him.

Cal pulled out of Finnley's grasp and took a step away, the darkness converging on them. "I know that, but—" Cal's words faltered.

Was Finnley right?

Cal had never stopped his crew when they committed heinous acts before, so why was this instance different? Cal attempted to convince himself that it was because she was on *his* ship, but deep down, he wasn't sure if that was the truth either.

Even in the dark, Cal saw the disappointment and trepidation lining Finnley's face. "If you start down this path, Cal, I don't know that there's any coming back from it."

Cal laughed humorlessly and turned away from Finnley, not wanting to see her dismay for a moment longer. His steps echoed down the hall, and he said quietly, "I've been headed down this road for a long time."

"There's still time to change course. To let it all go—Soline, your revenge, all of it." Finnley said, her voice hollow in the empty corridor.

Cal paused and looked back at her for a moment. "I don't think that was ever an option for me."

Finnley took a deep breath, her shoulders lifting and then falling. She walked toward him, her face indifferent now—resigned. "Well, if you're determined to do this, then I suppose there's nothing left for me to do. Except—"

"Except what?" For a heartbeat, Cal feared the worst. Finnley had the crew's support if she decided to mutiny against him. She had been with them, acting as interim captain for the last few months while Cal took time to reassess his life. And if there were any crewmates on the fence with their loyalty, once Finnley exposed his magic–his illegal,

Necromancer abilities—well, they wouldn't hesitate to throw him from the Umbra.

"Except, follow your command and be the best first mate this gods-forsaken ship has ever seen."

Cal laughed again, earnestly this time, and began walking, Finnley in tow. "I couldn't ask for a better one."

"And one day, when you've decided you've had enough of pirates and pillaging, I'll be here to take the Umbra over."

If everything went according to plan at the Cave of Splendors, then that day wouldn't be so far off. Cal loved the open seas, but he had run from his past for long enough. Keeping that to himself, Cal instead said, "There's not another soul I would trust her with."

Cal paused when he arrived at his quarters, and Finnley continued on past her own, claiming she slept better in the crow's nest anyway. Cal watched her disappear up the hall before he turned and kept walking. Even through the ordeal of the evening, Cal couldn't stop his mind from returning to *her*.

So, he wasn't astounded when he found himself standing outside Lady Hera's door, listening for her breathing. He summoned the shadows inside, and they leapt at his call like they were waiting for him. They stirred, and he found that the Lady was precisely where he had last seen—well, felt—her. She was still alert, listening and waiting for any sign that Cade might return. Cal considered knocking on the door to let her know the situation was handled, but…that would raise too many questions.

She might take him at his word if she were any other vapid noble girl, but this woman was too keen. She saw too much and forgot nothing. There was something different about her that continued to give him pause. Perhaps she was even closer to the Princess than she let on, or she knew more than she claimed. Cal chewed his lip, trying to determine what it was specifically about her that was preventing him from pretending she didn't exist. Shaking his head, Cal decided now was not the time to waste on worrying about what secrets Lady Hera might be harboring. He needed to leave her alone and let the events of this night fade from his memory. It would be better for all of them if he let her come to her own conclusions about what happened and kept his distance.

Even as Cal stepped away from her door, his shadows lingered. They brushed against her cheek, subtly moving the hair out of her face. Cal clenched his fist, reeling the shadows back in, but they resisted—only for a moment, but...

The hesitation was there.

They had done that earlier when he had stopped by the Lady's room to check on her the first time. He called the shadows back to him and examined them, aiming to decipher why they were inexplicably going awry. Nothing was different or out of the ordinary, save for the Lady's presence. Cal glanced at her door.

Surely, she didn't have some sort of influence over them. Cal was the only known necromancer in the entire kingdom—likely the whole continent—and if this woman had possessed the gift...well, she certainly wouldn't have been allowed out of the palace—let alone be allowed to serve the Princess. Cal's mind flashed back to his years under the King's command and the tasks he was forced to carry out, imagining Lady Hera in his place. He immediately shut down the thought, unable to envision anyone else withstanding it.

No, it had to be something else.

Something about the woman called to the shadows as though they *liked* her. Even now, they tugged from him, desiring to be closer to her again. Cal scoffed and turned on his heel. His shadows may have their own sentience, but they answered to him. At least, that's what Cal told himself as he stormed back to his quarters, dragging the shadows along behind him.

Chapter Nineteen

"**B**rander! Dinner time!" his mother's voice called out, echoing off of the clay buildings of his village. The lithe in her tone stirred something within him, but Brander couldn't comprehend how he was hearing her or how he was back in his home village. He glanced around, noting the red clay homes and the sun descending toward the mountains, casting the sky in brilliant shades of orange and maroon. Its heat was still fierce, but as it slowly slipped from the sky, it became more bearable.

The last thing he remembered was boarding a ship, though he couldn't remember why. Brander shook his head, urging his mind to reconcile what he knew to be true and what his senses were taking in. Perhaps he had died, and the Forgotten had taken pity on him by allowing him to experience one of his last good days with his family.

"Brander! It's time to come home!" His mother shouted again, and this time, he rose from his hiding place, deciding that if this was what his mind wanted him to relive, then who was he to protest? Brander recalled that earlier in the day, he and the other children played by the river, artfully dodging their mothers' swatting fronds and the occasional fishing boat coming in from their venture. Once the banks became too crowded and the heat too sweltering for even the water to protect them, the children retreated to the shaded reprieve of the cluster of palm trees near the end of his street.

Brander, newly seven, had already developed a distaste for schooling and the repetitiveness of its nature. The droning of the village teacher, a man whose wrinkles vastly outnumbered the children under his care, was enough to make Brander's mind wander. Brander smiled, remembering his dreams of adventure.

Not the mundane fishmongering that employed most of the males in his village, but fantasies of fighting monsters and protecting innocents. But even as a young child, Brander knew that was a lofty ambition—a dream that meant leaving his home and family, and his mom's honey cake.

The memory of honey cake spurred Brander into action. He was still dimly aware that this was a hallucination or some lucid dream, but whatever the case, he followed his instincts. He left the security of his hiding place—the game of hide and seek forgotten in favor of dinner—and ventured out into the dusty cart path, careful of the vendors packing away their wares for the evening. There wasn't much crime in his village, save for the occasional theft of food or clothes, but lately, more and more refugees from Desmorda were arriving. They all had weary eyes and slumped shoulders as they moved through the town. Most left after a few days, but Brander's father warned that their arrival meant nothing good. Brander winced, thinking of what would come and how right his father was.

Brander willed his short legs to lift him up the single step to the stoop of his home—his mother's humming floating on the brackish breeze. Pressing his chubby hand against the thatched door, he inhaled the sweet scent of yeast before hurrying to the table to claim his place amongst his family.

"New people always spell trouble." Brander's father said, his eyes glancing out the open window of their small house.

"That's no way to act, Adnan. They are wanderers." his mother said, spooning rice onto his father's plate.

Adnan shook his head, muttering a curse under his breath. "They spell trouble, Hazine. The King and his imperial army will be here before we know it."

Hazine clicked her tongue. "Habibi, you worry too much." she said. She winked at Brander and gave him an extra spoonful of rice. Brander smiled at his mother, despite his missing front teeth. He ran his tongue over the gaps, remembering that one had fallen out naturally, the other lost in a scuffle with a village boy.

Dinner passed in murmurs of conversation, with Brander's mother asking him about his day. Brander attempted to recount his exploits and his lesson with the instructor, but much of it was hazy. It didn't matter, though, because his and his mother's attention fell on his father, whose eyes continued to drift to the window. The air had shifted, turning cool, warranting the shutters closing. Then—and only then—did Brander's father leave his vigil at the window and join his family in their after-supper rituals. They cleared the table, wrapped up the extra rice—breakfast for the morning—and settled in front of the hearth. Brander aimed to contain himself as he found his way into his mother's lap while she sang a comforting melody that made his eyes heavy.

His father was in his chair, reading silently to himself, but occasionally, he would glance toward the closed window. His eyes hung as if he could see past the sand-eroded wood shutters to the world beyond that. A yawn escaped Brander's lips, and he snuggled closer to his mother. He relished her soft warmth and the scent of naan and honey that always seemed to cling to her. His mother's singing turned softer, more of a hum, lulling Brander further into sleep. He wasn't sure how much time had passed, or if he was even experiencing time like real life, but then he was weightless. The cool kiss of his linen sheets embraced him. Sleepiness tugged at Brander, but he didn't want to give in just yet—he didn't want this dream to come to an end. He rolled over, glimpsing the moonlight that slanted through the gaps in his shuttered window, though it wasn't closed entirely. His parents stood in front of it—at the foot of his bed—the moonbeams casting shadows over their taut features, his mother's back pressed to his father's chest. It was an embrace he had seen between them a thousand times, but the way his mother chewed her bottom lip gave him pause.

"There's smoke on the horizon, Adnan." Brander's mother said, her voice making Brander's pulse flare before she turned, facing her husband. "I'm afraid they will soon consume us." she whispered, her voice wobbling slightly.

Brander's father took his eyes from the window and looked at his wife. And though he himself spent the evening consumed with the terrors just beyond their door, he rubbed up and down his wife's arms and said, "Worry not, my love. I will do whatever it takes to keep us safe."

Brander's mother gave a sharp nod before she buried her face in her husband's chest. Brander's father ran his hands over his wife's spine. Brander blinked slowly, his exhaustion and his father's assurance finally pulling him under. He wanted to fight the tide of sleepiness—he didn't want to lose his parents again—but he was helpless as it dragged him from his peace.

* * * *

Brander threw off the covers and doubled over in pain, lurching to the side as the meager contents of his stomach threatened to expel themselves from his body. Cold sweat coated every inch of him, soaking through his clothes and the sheets of his childhood bed. But he wasn't in his parent's home. His parents were dead—slaughtered by the King's insatiable hunger for conquest and control.

Brander lifted his head in an effort to look around, but the world slanted, sliding out from underneath him and forcing him to close his eyes against the pain. He searched around, failing to make sense of his surroundings. Sweaty fingers drug across wood grain, and he cracked an eye open long enough to glimpse a wooden bed frame. A bed far nicer than he had slept on for years—not since he was a child.

The memories of the last several days came flooding back to him.

Princess Rhea.

The conmen.

Pirates.

Sickness.

He unfortunately understood why he was currently fighting for his life in a wooden box that was supposed to resemble a room.

Another wave of nausea, unrelated to his seasickness, cramped his stomach. Brander needed to get up and find the Princess. He refused to allow his weakness to put her in further jeopardy. Bracing himself, he pushed to his feet and swayed. His breath came in sharp pants, his chest rising and falling rapidly. Brander gritted his teeth and took a step forward, but another wave of nausea gripped him, and he fell backward, collapsing onto the bed. He leaned back, desperate for the room to stop spinning and for his sicknesses dissipate, but there was nothing to be done. Brander had never stepped foot on a ship before; he had never even seen the ocean, and now he was paying the price. He prayed to the Forgotten gods that the Princess would remain safe until he was well enough to protect her, but he had little faith. The gods hadn't done anything to protect his mother from the King's imperial march when its shadow descended upon his village.

He doubted they would heed his requests now.

Brander forced himself to breathe slowly through his nose, not making any unnecessary movements that would worsen his nausea. He stayed where he was until the moonlight in his room changed to watery sunlight, but all it brought in its wake was a throbbing headache. He wasn't sure if it was from the sickness or the dreams and nightmares that were plaguing him these days. Whatever the case, there was no relief to be found. His door creaked open and the person who had administered his first dose of medicine–the one that had rendered him unconscious–came ambling toward him, another dose in tow. The urge to fight back rose up in him, but at this point, he wasn't sure if he would survive the sickness and nightmares. If he had to pick, he would choose to relive his past.

"Another dose or two, dearie, and you'll be right as rain." the person cackled as they fed Brander the medicine and then toddled off, leaving Brander slowly succumbing to the concoction's effects. Brander's mind began to tumble back through his history, tripping over thoughts of his mother and his time in the King's army. Absentmindedly, he wondered what he would decide to fixate on this time. He prayed it was something good. But then again, he had so few happy memories to pick from, and the gods were not known for their kindness.

Chapter Twenty

Rhea's limbs were still sore when she dared to leave her quarters the following afternoon. Though she had rested some, the uneasiness of the fallout from her choices kept her from finding real rest.

Her stupid, ignorant choices.

Rhea should have known better. She should have known better than to put herself in the type of situation that would result in her nearly being assaulted. But her willful nature—the desire to have a moment of freedom—had won out. The King had claimed that her rebellious streak would be her ruin one day, and it almost had. He, of course, was referring to her running in the halls or not respecting his court, but the principle still stood. She was out of her depth. The encounter back in Mirador and now her altercation with Cade all but confirmed that she was more likely to get herself killed than save her people.

But Rhea resolved not to succumb to her base nature. She would only make rational, responsible choices from now on. It was enough of a risk leaving the comfort of her palace to find Izor's Lamp in the Cave of Splendors. There was no reason to seek out more thrills.

Rhea took care arranging her hair, her scalp still tender. Using her head to knock Cade back was reckless, but her options had been limited. She had paid the price of a pulsing headache, but thankfully, no other symptoms of a head injury were apparent.

The crunch of Cade's nose and the blood she had glimpsed as she fled were injuries that certainly weren't going to vanish overnight, but perhaps that worked in her favor. She would easily point him out to Finnley, and the first mate could address the situation—if there was even anything to be done about it.

Cal would have been the obvious choice to dole out punishment, but she had no interest in being ridiculed and humiliated by him for her foolishness. Finnley was second in command and had the respect of the ship—and she was a woman. Rhea assumed that, as a woman living a life of piracy, she may have experienced something similar and would be able to sympathize. There was also a chance that she would laugh at the entire thing and call Rhea thoughtless for having been in the galley in the first place…and then going to the deck at night, unescorted. Rhea wouldn't blame her, but she would still rest easier knowing that at least one other person on the ship knew what kind of person Cade was—even if nothing came of it.

Tugging at the collar of her dress, she loosed a breath. The fabric was breathable, but Rhea suspected anything would be restrictive at the moment. She smoothed her hands down over the skirts, steadying herself. There was a good chance she would see Cade once she left her room, but remaining confined to her quarters indefinitely was not an option. She wouldn't allow him to cower her so. Rhea stepped up to the chest of drawers, braced her hands on the side, and shoved every ounce of her strength into sliding them out from in front of the door. They slowly began to budge and inch away from the threshold. Rhea gave one final push against the chest as it finally allowed enough space for her to slip out the opening. She paused to compose herself, wiping away lingering sweat and smoothing an errant hair. However, that was likely futile, given the wind constantly blowing over the sea.

For a moment, she feared that Cade might be outside her door. It was unlikely, given the time that had passed and the lack of activity that had taken place outside her room. But she reached for the oil lantern, gripping it tightly just in case. Rhea stood straight and rolled her shoulders back before reaching for the latch and stepping out into the corridor. She waited for a moment. Waited for hands to grab her or for Cade's disfigured face to fill the space in front of her—but she saw nothing and no one. Exhaling, she returned the lantern to her room.

Her heart hammered with every step, and she did her best not to let her gaze linger on anyone she passed for too long. She wanted Cade confronted, but was not eager to do it herself in close quarters. Mercifully, she made it up the stairs and onto the deck without incident, the relief at that small victory washing over her. Now came the hard part: tracking down Finnley—before Cade found her. In the short time that Rhea had spent around the woman, she seemed to never be where you expected and constantly popped up when unprepared. Despite that, Rhea liked her. Her unpredictable nature was enviable and inspirational, and Rhea wished she could be more like her. Rhea scanned the deck, looking for the auburn hair that was a dead giveaway, and then—

There.

Standing at the mast was Finnley.

She was glaring down at a sickly-looking Kasper—it seemed the rum had gotten someone else into trouble, too—and tossed something at his feet. Rhea stifled a laugh at Kasper's bootless and sock-clad feet.

Finnley only remained long enough to see Kasper start to put his boots on, then she turned, her gaze sweeping over the deck, briefly snagging on Rhea before continuing on her path toward some rigging on the ship's side. Rhea pursed her lips and attempted to steel her nerves. Finnley might laugh at her, ridicule, or admonish her, but Rhea was doing the right thing. If Cade was willing to do something like that to her in full view of the deck, there was no telling what other despicable things he would get up to. Tucking away her cowardice, she willed her feet to carry her over to Finnley. Finnley was occupied with looping some rope and inspecting it. What purpose it served, Rhea couldn't begin to guess.

"I need to speak to you." Rhea said, clearing her throat. She started to reach for her pendant but refrained, remembering Kai's words. Instead, she nervously picked at her cuticles, awaiting Finnely's response.

Finnley's hands remained busy with her task, and she did not spare Rhea a glance as she continued to fiddle with the ropes.

Rhea dropped her hands and stepped further into Finnley's line of sight. "Now, if you don't mind."

"Yer talkin' now, ain't ya?" Finnley retorted, still fixated on the ropes.

Rhea lifted her chin. "Fine, it's about an incident that occurred last night." Rhea fought to keep her tone level. She would not be ashamed of what happened. It might have been reckless, but she had defended herself and would not allow someone to make her feel disgraced for that.

Finnley's fingers moved deftly over the ropes before she dropped them to the deck and moved on to the next set. Rhea followed, resolved to have this conversation now, whether Finnley wanted to or not. Rhea glanced around and then exhaled, sending the last of her trepidation out with the breath.

"One of the men aboard this ship endeavored to harm me. He was unsuccessful, but—"

"It's been taken care of."

Rhea stilled and then furrowed her brow. A hundred questions buzzed in her mind. How did she know what Rhea was referencing? Had someone seen them? Had Cade been found? Rhea started and stopped every question she had. Finally, she composed herself enough to ask, "What do you mean?"

Finnley waved dismissively. "It's been handled."

Rhea's anger got the better of her, and she grabbed Finnley's arm—which was likely near the top of the list of poor decisions she had made lately. Finnley's eyes were pinned to the spot where Rhea touched her before they slowly trailed their way up to her face. Rhea's senses returned, and she quickly removed her hand and took a step back for good measure.

Finnley held her stare for a moment longer before returning to her work, grumbling, "If you want specifics, you're going to have to talk to Cap'n."

Chills erupted across Rhea's flesh like the wind had abruptly turned cold. Talking to Cal about Cade was easily the last thing she wanted to do. Once, she might not have assumed the worst about him and his cruelty, but the years had changed him. She had little hope that he would have compassion or empathy for her. Had Cal punished Cade for his actions? Or merely warned him against doing it again?

Rhea had no clue, but she wasn't optimistic about the outcome.

Glancing around the deck, she searched for him. It took all of one heartbeat for her eyes to find him. Rhea considered going back to her room and forgoing the entire thing. But her curiosity was already getting the better of her as her feet moved toward where Caliban perched against the railing. A smirk formed on Cal's lips before Rhea ever made it to him, but she refused to back down now. She kept her shoulders squared and stopped in front of the Necromancer. Cal's gaze lazily drifted from her feet to her face.

"And to what do I owe this pleasure?"

Rhea narrowed her eyes at him. "Finnley said you would have more details on the incident from last night."

Cal's demeanor shifted. Gone was the teasing, aloof facade, replaced with the cold, calculating pirate Rhea was becoming accustomed to.

"It was taken care of."

"So, I was told," Rhea crossed her arms, "but I want to know what happened to him."

Cal arched an eyebrow and then pushed off from the railing, closing the distance between them. He towered over her, his height and his demeanor both overtaking her smaller frame, but Rhea wouldn't back down. It was always like this with Cal, a battle for dominance, and Rhea was in no mood to give him an inch.

Shadows stretched across the deck, making Cal's face look even more severe and handsome than normal. Rhea swallowed, shoving down any base attraction she may have toward Cal. Under different circumstances, she would be willing to acknowledge the appeal of his full lips and straight nose, but she forced her traitorous body to stand down. Cal's eyes studied her face, heat rising wherever they deigned to look. She fought the urge to reach for her pendant, once again remembering Kai's warning.

Cal tilted his head, still assessing her like a wolf with his prey. "Do you really want to know that?" Cal spoke in a low voice, one that threatened to send shivers up her spine. "Are you sure you want to know how his bones sounded when they splintered and shattered beneath my boots and fists? How he cried out in agony when his lungs were punctured and his organs ruptured?"

Rhea clenched her muscles against the rush of heat coursing through her as Cal's depthless eyes pinned her to the spot. There was nothing kind or romantic in Cal's words or gaze, but they made her pulse thrum and stomach flutter all the same. Some small–logical–part of her knew she should be horrified–scared, even–by Cal's admission, but…she wasn't.

He had beat Cade for her. Not only that, but he seemed to *enjoy* it. He had relished in destroying Cade's body on her behalf. Rhea swallowed, attempting to find some semblance of composure in the face of Cal's cruelty—and protection.

"Or maybe," Cal took a step so close to her that Rhea had to yield an inch despite her desire to hold her ground. His chest vibrated against hers as he delivered his final blow. "you want to know how he squealed when I slit his throat."

Rhea's traitorous eyes widened, just for a moment, at Cal's revelation.

Cade was dead. Cal had killed him.

She swallowed the emotions clogging her throat. "Why did you do it?" Her voice was barely a whisper.

"Because I'm the captain, and it's my responsibility to dole out any punishment." No remorse showed on Cal's face as he spoke.

"But why? Given his behavior last night, I highly doubt this was his first time attempting something like that." Rhea insisted.

Cal had killed Cade *for her*.

And she wanted him to admit it.

A muscle ticked in Cal's jaw. He retreated a step and turned away from her. A wounded animal caught in a trap, but refusing to accept its fate. "It doesn't matter why, only that Cade is gone, and nothing else like that will happen while you're with—" Cal's rage was tangible, seeping from him in waves that dared to capsize her composure and drag her down with him. "While you're aboard the Umbra." he clarified.

"Can you truly ensure that your questionable crew can control themselves?" Rhea didn't mean for her words to be an accusation, but she was hardly in control of herself. She knew she should shut her mouth and return to her room, but she was powerless to stop from smarting off to Cal.

Cal balled his hands into fists and unfurled them.

Once.

Twice.

He looked at her over his shoulder—hatred burning in his eyes.

Rhea's mouth went dry as he spat, "You dare question me?" He whirled on her—was inches from her face in a heartbeat. "I am in charge here, not you. You don't question my command. I don't care if you are nobility and a member of the royal household. Challenge me again, and I will have you thrown in the brig for the remainder of this journey." he sneered. An unholy, wicked light filled his eyes, and he continued, "Perhaps, I'll do that anyway."

Rhea stiffened, unable to make her voice work, but it didn't matter because Cal added, as his eyes dipped to her mouth, "Just so I don't have to look upon your haughty features and hear that conceited voice chase me from my rest. Now," he breathed, retreating a step and putting some blessed distance between them, "get off my deck before I have to clean up another one of your messes."

The apprehension in her bled away—the heat boiling her blood shifted from attraction to rage. "I didn't ask for any of this." she hissed at him, though she wasn't entirely sure she was just speaking about her altercation with Cade. She added, "I didn't ask you to kill him."

Cal spread his hands. "And, yet, you left me with no choice. You're foolish and childish if you really thought you wouldn't have to answer for your poor choices. Maybe next time you'll think a bit more before you go parading into a room of dangerous outlaws."

Red filled her vision. "You have no right—"

Cal laughed—the sound wicked and wild. "I have every right in the world. You have been pampered and cared for your entire life. You have no clue about the real world, which is precisely why you thought going into the galley would be a *fun adventure*." Cal spread his arms and added, "And now a man is dead. And you can live with that."

Rhea's entire body trembled with fury. Tears prickled in her eyes, but she would not give him the satisfaction of seeing her cry. A muscle in Cal's jaw flexed, and something flickered over his vicious features— but he turned, stalking away from her. Rhea's feet moved of their own accord—toward Cal—but the rigid set of his shoulders told her what any further attempts at pushing the conversation would get her. She didn't doubt for one second that he would make good on his threat. Rhea curled her hands into fists and imagined pummeling Cal's back until he gave her the answers she wanted.

Her fantasy did little to assuage the fire still burning in her chest, nor did it quell the intrigue at his reaction to her. He was either taciturn or downright cruel to everyone else, but with her there seemed to be some other reaction. Something that bordered on loathing, but wasn't quite so malicious.

Shaking her head, she turned on her heel, leaving Cal to his brooding. She had no interest in wasting her time wondering what the proper adjective was for Cal's feelings toward her. They weren't relevant in the slightest. Rhea had dealt with so many dismal, angry men in her lifetime that she was unwilling to put up with another. If Cal wanted to be difficult and confounding, then she would let him. She had her country to think about—her people, Izor's Lamp, and Brander's recovery to focus her energy on.

Cal and his moodiness didn't make the list. Or at least that's what Rhea kept repeating to herself as she descended back into the hull and pushed into Brander's room to find him, mercifully, asleep. She flopped down into the chair adjacent to his bed and stared at him. Looking, but not quite seeing. Cal had not changed one bit from the sullen boy he had been when he lived in the palace. He was just as arrogant and indifferent to anyone who wasn't deemed worthy of his time—which had only ever been Soline and Kasper. He cared for no one but himself, and if it appeared he did, it was only because it served his own interests.

Needing to move and work off her anger, Rhea stood. She paced back and forth in front of Brander's bed, half hoping he would wake up so she would have someone to talk to, but he remained woefully unconscious. Maybe that was for the best. Brander was, for the most part, level-headed and rational. But there was no world in which he wouldn't react poorly to her foolish decisions. Rhea turned and left, not wanting to remain in Brander's quarters any longer, aiming for her own room. Cal may have assured her she was safe while on the Umbra, but she was in no mood to be around people. She quickly closed the door behind her, but hesitated to shove the dresser in front of the door. Despite Cal's less desirable qualities, she never took him for a liar.

Rhea left the dresser in its place, backed away from the door, and heaved herself onto the bed. Her thoughts raced, and there was no chance she would rest, but the heaviness of her eyes said otherwise. She kicked off her slippers before climbing under the threadbare blanket and curling up on the mattress. Perhaps a good night of sleep was all she needed to feel more like herself. As she drifted off, her mind wandered back to the hatred in Cal's eyes as he recited all the horrible things he'd done to Cade. Her final thought before sleep claimed her was that, in some odd way, Caliban reminded her of her father.

That realization dragged her from her present worries and into the horrors of her past.

Chapter Twenty One

Kasper was never drinking again.

Specifically, he was never drinking pirate rum again.

The stagnant, alcohol-soaked stench of his room was making his nausea worsen and, in turn, the throbbing in his head was unrelenting. The smell was comparable to the overcrowded slums that existed in the most desolate corners of every city on the continent. Another whiff of himself transported him back to the putrid reek of too-close bodies and human excrement. It mingled with the cloying perfume that merchants claimed covered the stink, but the gagging that Kasper had to fight every time he wandered through the slums was a clear indication that their fragrances were insufficient. Aside from that, he wasn't entirely sure how he had made it back to his cabin. Nor was he sure where his boots had gone—but what he *did* know was that he needed fresh air.

Getting out of his cabin became his top priority.

The morning had come and gone, and Kasper had barely been able to pull himself from the bed to relieve himself. The sunlight streaming in from his window was far too bright for Kasper to even contemplate going out onto the deck, and the thought of eating food made him want to crawl further under the shabby blanket. No, he wanted to crawl under the *bed*. He wanted to find the darkest known corner, curl up into a ball, and perish like an alley cat sensing its own impending death.

But staying in his quarters was no longer viable—even if he had slowly become accustomed to the stench over the hours of lying in a hangover-induced stupor. The sun had slipped low enough into the sky and the alcohol had left his system enough that Kasper decided he could finally withstand leaving the confines of his room. He sighed and glanced down at his shoeless feet, lamenting the loss of his only pair of boots.

Kai had extras…

No.

Kasper would go barefoot for the rest of their journey before he dared ask Kai for anything else. He pulled his spare shirt over his head–thankful for it, as the one he had worn yesterday was flecked with his own vomit–and strode for the door.

* * * *

Kasper immediately regretted leaving his room.

His eyes burned until they watered as he emerged from the hull onto the deck. Mercifully, the deck of the Umbra was worn, so no stray splinters caught on his socks. Kasper moved across the deck, aiming for the shadows cast by the mast to get a reprieve from the blazing orange sun. Despite the intense pain burning in his eyes, the sea-salt air did seem to ease some of the nausea still turning in his stomach. Kasper loosed out a shaky breath as he leaned against the mast and braced his hands on his knees. Unexpectedly, a heavy hand fell across Kasper's shoulder, sending him lurching forward.

"First time drinking rum, boy?"

Kasper managed to look up and found Galen grinning down at him. Memories of losing cards and laughter clanged through him, but before he mustered a response, boots–his boots–thunked to the floor in front of him.

Raising his eyes, Kasper was greeted by Finnley's unflinching stare. "Ye threw up all over them last night—well, this mornin'. Had 'em cleaned for ya."

Kasper hesitated to reach for them. He couldn't remember the last time someone had cared to look after him, let alone bother to take care of his things. Looking up with a thank you forming on his lips—

"Needn't thank me, just didn't want them rottin' away on the ship."

Kasper pursed his lips and swallowed down his gratitude. Finnley clearly wasn't interested, so he cautiously reached for his boots and slipped them on. He straightened, already feeling more like himself as he wiggled his toes in the worn, supple leather. Finnley grunted once at Kasper before she strode away from him, leaving a grinning Galen still hovering over him.

When Galen gestured after Finnley, Kasper glanced at him, unsure why he was still standing there.

"Don't mind her. She's mighty rough around the edges and hateful as a dog, but she means well. Most of the time."

Offering a nervous laugh, Kasper recalled how Finnley had interrogated him over his crystals. He absentmindedly wondered about the gems, where they had ended up, and whether Finnley had kept them or traded them away for something she found of greater value. The answer came a moment later when he scanned across the deck and found her standing with Lady Hera by some rigging at the ship's far side. As Kasper watched her, he saw—or rather, felt—the pulse of the amethyst that resided in her pocket.

"She'd never admit it, but she felt bad for takin' all yer rocks."

Kasper looked to Galen, who was still smiling, and noted the heavy lines creasing his face and his red, weather-worn skin. Kasper suddenly had the feeling that Galen would make a good father. The assessment surprised Kasper, as he had never had an actual father figure—at least as far as he remembered—let alone known his own father. But Galen had a kindness about him and a calmness that put Kasper at ease.

"Thank you." Kasper said, waving toward his boots. "Not just for my shoes, but for taking care of me last night." Kasper thought it was safe to assume that if Finnley was willing to take care of his boots, then she also got him to his room.

Galen shrugged, his smile never faltering. "You're the Cap'n's kin, at least that's what Fin-girl said. And beyond that, you're a kid. Fin and I have always looked out for the youngins that come aboard the Umbra."

Kasper bristled at being called a kid. Cal and Kai certainly treated him like a child, but he got the impression that Galen's sentiment wasn't derogatory.

"How long have you been a pirate?" Kasper asked, clearing his throat.

Galen turned his gaze to Kasper, his gray brow furrowing and his mouth moving silently. "I reckon it's been nearly three decades since I joined the Umbra."

Kasper's eyes widened as he saw the man before him with new eyes. He noted the thick wrinkles creasing his forehead and crinkling around his eyes. His skin was splotchy, varying shades of pink and red, but his eyes were a gentle blue. His wizened features were in contrast with nearly everyone else on the Umbra, and Kasper suspected that the arduous demands of a pirate's profession significantly shortened one's life expectancy. Yet, here Galen stood.

"Did you always want to be a pirate?" Though, Kasper wasn't sure why he was asking Galen these questions. Maybe it was a need for connection or Galen's disarming nature, but whatever the case, Galen obliged him.

Galen shook his head and turned toward the horizon, his features bathed in the fading orange light, further highlighting the deep-set wrinkles on his face. Galen was quiet for a while, long enough that Kasper was certain he had unintentionally crossed a boundary. He opened his mouth to apologize and leave Galen to his thoughts when the older pirate spoke pensively.

"I had a wife. We were young, too young," he said with a slight smile, "but we loved each other and thought that was all ya needed to make it. Anyway, we got married, and then Shula said she was pregnant, and I'll admit it," Galen said, glancing at Kasper with a conspiratorial look and continued, "I was terrified. Me own father was nothin' to write home about, and I feared letting Shula and the babe down, but when I held her, oh," Galen shook his head again, his voice quivering, "but when I held her, I knew I would do anything for her. So, I took some odd jobs here and there to make ends meet. But it wasn't enough, so I started going on some long fishing trips. I was gone for days and then weeks. Shula understood, knew I was doing it all for them, but then…"

The words out of Galen's mouth faltered, and Kasper guessed how the story ended. It was the ending of a lot of people's stories that lived within the ever-expanding borders of Desmorda. Kasper started to tell Galen he didn't need to say anymore, but the older man wiped his face and continued, "It happened while I was gone. The army came through, and Shula did as they instructed; she housed and fed them until they left, and she survived them, which is more than most can say. But shortly after they left, Shula fell ill, and so did the baby."

The pirate's lip wobbled, and then his tears fell in earnest. He went quiet. Hot tears sprang into Kasper's eyes at the sheer devastation that ghosted Galen's face. To lose your wife and child in one fell swoop, and to be completely helpless to do anything to prevent it…

Kasper could hardly bear to hear the end of the poor sailor's tale.

"It was a fever that followed the soldiers. A common occurrence, they said–one that most people survived–but Shula was still weak from the birth, and the babe was so young, just four months old then."A thick, curled finger brushed against Galen's cheek. He composed himself, and features shifted to stony resignation. "Anyway, when I got back, the villagers had already buried them. After that, I didn't know what else to do. I had nothing else to live for. I was barely nineteen, but I felt like my life was over, so I joined a crew and threw myself into a pirate's life. I was here and there for a few years until I found the Umbra, and the rest is history."

Tears threatened to spill down Kasper's face, he had to clench his jaw to keep them at bay. Kasper had spent the last decade with Kai, who he wasn't sure had experienced any genuine emotions save for levity and indifference. To see someone so moved by the loss of another made Kasper's chest ache. He reached for Galen, and the man gave no hesitation as he leaned into Kasper, accepting the hug. It briefly occurred to Kasper that neither of his brothers would have offered comfort. Kai often withdrew when his clients displayed strong emotion, obviously overcome with it from whatever vision Kai had shared. And Cal...

Cal didn't allow himself to be close enough to someone to ever give sympathy.

Kasper's headache and nausea had faded sometime before, but the new ache in his chest was far worse. Though, he would have gladly taken ten more hangovers if it meant Galen's grief was assuaged.

Several minutes passed, and Galen finally lifted his head, wiping his eyes on his shirt sleeve. "Ah, I apologize for me tears. She's been gone longer than she was ever alive, but sometimes I feel the loss like it was yesterday."

Kasper nodded. He remembered a line from a poem Kai had read to him once. "I think grief is the evidence of love still lingering, but that doesn't mean it doesn't hurt."

Galen laughed and scrubbed his face once more. The sun had finally sunk beneath the water. The moonlight and the glow of lanterns were taking over the illumination of the deck, casting long shadows over Galen's weathered face.

"I think you might be wise beyond your years, kid."

Kasper suppressed a smile. "I'm not sure if that's a compliment."

A wistfulness settled over Galen's features as he looked at Kasper. The sorrow in his eyes said he saw more of Kasper than anyone else ever had. "I'm not sure it is, either."

Kasper swallowed and looked away. He didn't know what else to say to Galen. He wasn't unaccustomed to seeing people have emotional reactions. He was just unaccustomed to caring about them. He and Kai had moved around so much in the last decade that he hadn't bothered forming any actual connections with people other than Kai, but even

Kai only needed him for material things, never emotional support. Kasper wondered if this connection between him and Galen—if this reciprocity—was what it was like to be an actual family. Maybe Kasper wouldn't resent being called a child if he had been able to be one.

"Galen!" A voice—Finnley—called out, dispelling Kasper's thoughts.

"Yes, Fin?" Galen replied, and any remnants of his earlier grief vanished from his voice.

"I need some help getting these crates secured."

"Yes, Fin." Galen's signature smile replaced his despondent features. He turned and winked at Kasper. "I'll see ya around, kid."

Kasper tried to return the smile as he said, "Likewise."

Galen strolled off, trailing after Finnley's unforgiving glare. Releasing a breath, Kasper closed his eyes and leaned against the mast again. He relished in the slightly cooler temperature that twilight had brought. Though his stomach rumbled in hunger, he wasn't ready to brave the ship's hull again—fearing its stench would trigger his nausea, and he would hate to ruin his freshly cleaned shoes.

"How's the hangover?"

Kasper opened his eyes and found Caliban smirking at him, the moonlight making his features look sharper than usual. Kasper attempted to dredge up an ounce of irritation, but was too exhausted to manage it. "What do you want, Cal?"

Cal dared to feign innocence as he said, "I can't inquire about my little brother's health after his first time blacking out?"

With a roll of his eyes, Kasper righted himself and pushed off from the mast. He had no interest in being the subject of his brother's ridicule, and besides, he needed to eat something lest he lose what little strength he still had after his especially rough night.

"Have you been by to see Kai today?" Cal asked, his tone not quite teasing.

Ignoring Cal crossed Kasper's mind, but instead he paused, looked back at Cal, and said, "No."

"Do you plan to?"

Kasper crossed his arms. "What are you playing at?"

Cal held up his hands in surrender. "I just thought since you're his little helper, you would be at his bedside, watching each breath. I was quite surprised to find you in my galley last night. You and Kai didn't have a little spat, did you?"

Kasper clenched his fist and forced himself to keep from connecting it with his brother's jaw. He had no interest in explaining to Cal what Kai had revealed; besides, Cal knew the truth of who Kai was and what he had done.

And he had still done nothing.

Anger washed over Kasper. As much as he wanted to confront Cal about his lies, he was not interested in doing it tonight. Kasper turned from his brother.

"Have a good night, Cal."

Cal laughed darkly. "Not likely."

A heavy sigh exhaled from Kasper. He allowed himself a singular moment of anguish for the irrevocable damage his relationships with his brothers had suffered and the fact that he never knew his parents. He might have once thought that was the preferred option over the immense grief that someone like Galen experienced, but was never knowing love really better than losing it?

Kasper wasn't so sure anymore.

But he refused to dwell on the thought any longer, either, so as he entered the galley and took a bowl of stew, he grabbed another bottle of rum and washed away his regrets.

Chapter Twenty Two

C al glowered over the courtyard from the shadows of the mezzanine. His tutors had forced him to come out of his rooms. They claimed he needed sunlight and fresh air, but Cal knew it was all an excuse to distance themselves from him.

He heard the whispers and hushed words they spoke whenever they thought he wasn't listening, or more specifically, that the shadows weren't listening. They thought him a demon or devil sent to terrorize the people of Desmorda. They claimed that there was a reason necromancy and shadow work were heavily restricted and only done under the careful watch of the King. He considered sending a shadow or two after them, if only to watch them scurry away and smell their fear as it permeated the air, but he resisted. Cal shifted his weight, leaning against the pillar. If only they knew it was their precious King they should truly fear.

For now, anyway.

Cal sighed. He was annoyed by the heat, the chattering of the noble boys sitting at the fountain, and the droning insects. He turned, preparing to leave the sweltering heat for the dank comfort of his underground rooms. But a glint of gold caught his eye, giving him pause. He turned back to the courtyard and went wholly still. Leaning over the fountain, with a curtain of golden silk tumbling over her shoulder, gently stroking the petals of a water lily was her.

There was no proof that it was the same girl that he had seen in the halls three years ago. She had haunted his dreams, and though he didn't know her name he knew it was her all the same.

Cal's chest ached from not breathing, but his mind was too scattered, too untethered to think about anything but the girl in front of him. It was as though she had descended from the heavens. The light illuminated the strands of her hair and glimmered atop the water, spilling and rippling in the fountain. As they had years ago, Cal's feet moved of their own accord, like they knew she was his other half—the light to his dark, his savior from the shadows. The sunlight warmed Cal's cheeks like the fire smoldering in the hearth. His heart hammered in his chest. He was finally going to know the name of his—

Something wet smacked into his face and Cal flinched. He stumbled back a step and lifted his fingers to his cheek, coming away with a goopy, sticky liquid that smelled distinctly of honey.

Cal turned toward the five noble boys sitting on the fountain's edge, sweet buns oozing between their fingers. Their smirks and looks of triumph sent ice skittering over Cal's skin. Shadows gathered at his back—even in the broad daylight.

They would call him Night Incarnate. The boys' smiles faded as darkness fell over their faces, blanketing their amusement with fear. One boy dropped his sweet treat to the ground, another began trembling, and the third had a dark stain spreading across the front of his breeches. Cal didn't care. He was a nightmare, and they should fear him. Cal prowled closer, relishing in the terror that rooted them to the spot. There would be ramifications for his actions, but they would be nothing compared to the elation he would feel as his shadows slipped around their—

"Your name is Caliban, yes?"

Cal froze. No one used his full name—save for Kai, but they saw so little of each other that the sound of his name was foreign to his ears. He turned and looked at the girl. Sunshine Incarnate, with her flowing golden hair and clear cerulean eyes. Cal blinked, sure that he must be dreaming because why would she deign to speak to him otherwise?

The girl tilted her head, her hair sliding with the motion in the most hypnotic manner.

"Let's go!" The boys hissed to one another, but Cal hardly heard it and certainly didn't care.

"It's you."

The girl smiled at him, and if that wasn't the most beautiful thing Cal had ever seen.

"Do we know each other?" She said, reaching up to twirl the ends of her hair.

Cal attempted to shake himself of his stupor. "You were in the alcove that day. You made sunlight."

The girl laughed, the sound pealing like a bell through Cal, waking something in him that had slumbered for longer than he knew. The girl then lifted her hand, twirling her fingers in the air. The light around them shimmered, turning hazy and refracting until it scattered into a rainbow.

She dropped her hand and clasped them in front of her. "Technically, I can only manipulate light that already exists."

Cal remained staring at the empty space where the rainbow was moments before. Cal had always felt alone in the world, the only known necromancer in all of Desmorda, but for whatever reason, looking at the girl who commanded light—his near opposite—Cal didn't feel so lonely anymore.

The girl stuck out her hand, warm and sun-kissed skin with a smattering of freckles greeted him. Cal took her hand and shook it, earning another chuckle from the girl. Heat singed Cal's cheeks as it occurred to him that she meant for him to kiss her hand.

"Soline," the girl introduced herself with a shy smile.

Soline.

A name more perfect than he could have imagined.

A smile graced his lips as he replied, "Caliban." He swallowed and added confidently, "It's a pleasure to finally meet the girl of my dreams."

A blush crept across Soline's cheeks, and her smile turned more sincere. Cal's heart clenched at the sight of it, and he realized he would do whatever it took to keep it there.

"Necromancer!"

Cal turned toward the summoning. His eyes fell on the King as he stormed through the courtyard. Cal dropped to a knee on instinct, lifting his fist and placing it over his heart.

"Rise," the King commanded.

Cal rose, clasped his arms behind his back, and stared ahead. Soline was still behind him, staying quiet and still. Any warmth Soline had brought to him had vanished, and he prayed to every dark god that the King would pay her no mind. But the King's gaze slipped from Cal to Soline, and Cal was helpless to stop the ice that cracked through his blood.

The King's eyes traveled down her body and then back up to her face.

Cal wanted to scream that she was too young. She couldn't have been a year or two older than him, but an adolescent nonetheless.

"Who is your father, Lady…?"

"Count Mehra, Your Majesty. I am his second eldest daughter, Soline."

Cal clenched his jaw tightly to stop from scolding her—though no one could refuse the King.

"Hmm," the King replied, turning his attention back to Cal. "I have a job for you, Necromancer. Meet me in the dungeons." The King turned, storming off back in the direction he came from. All of the air went out of Cal, and he relaxed his muscles, giving them a slight shake.

"Wow." Soline said softly.

"Yeah,." he replied, unable to form a more coherent response. Even at thirteen, Cal was thoroughly feared at court, but the King's presence was another thing entirely.

Thoroughly dreading what the King had in store for him, Cal scrubbed at his face. He dropped his hand and opened his mouth to give his apologies, but Soline was already there, her slender, perfect hand brushing strands of his hair out of his face.

Cal froze as she tucked the hair behind his ear and said, "I take it you have somewhere to be?"

Cal pressed his lips into a thin line. "Unfortunately." Cal hesitated, waiting for Soline to understand what his magic must entail and what the King demanded of him. He prepared himself for her to reject and dismiss him—like everyone else had.

"Where will you be when you finish?" Soline asked, her hands clasping in front of her.

Cal blinked. "I'll need to go collect my little brother from the governess."

"Can I come with you?"

"Of course."

"We can meet back here? Or maybe where we first met?" A secretive smile spread on her face, and Cal could not stop his own from forming.

"I'll meet you here in two hours."

Soline tilted her head and nodded. "I'll be waiting."

Cal reached for her hand and, this time, pressed a kiss to her knuckles. He lingered for a moment longer than necessary. When he finally released her, he smiled at the faint blush staining her cheeks. Before he turned and headed for the dungeon, he dropped into a quick bow. He had no desire to get there, but he would already be incurring the King's wrath by being late—he had no interest in keeping him waiting.

By the time Cal had made it to the dungeon, all of the light and peace Soline had imparted on him had fallen away. The cold, indifferent mask of the terrifying Court Necromancer slid back into place.

"Ah, thank you for finally joining us, Necromancer," the King said, his voice echoing off of the dark stone walls.

Cal's footfalls were his answer. He continued down the corridor, ignoring the moans and clanking of chains from the prisoners in the cells he passed. As he slowed his stalking gait, the hall gave way to a room that held a singular table, the King, and a dead man. He reached for his sleeves, rolling them up in an effort to keep them clean of whatever fluids were expelled during this impromptu torture session.

Because that's what this was, if not for the man lying on the table, then for Cal. He took one final, steadying breath before fully emerging into the room and stopped in front of the table, staring at the King across the corpse. The King's wicked smile gleamed in the dim firelight. A spiderwalk chill crept down Cal's spine as he worked to keep his composure.

The King's eyes flicked down to the body, "This man was a suspected spy for a rebellion in a province in the south. But unfortunately, he drank a poison before we could extract the information that we needed." The King lifted his eyes, and a shiver coursed through Cal at the lifelessness in the King's black gaze.

"Resurrect him."

Cal clenched his fist and held the King's stare for a moment before looking at the body. It was still fresh. Death-stiff hadn't set in yet, which would make calling the spirit back easier. Cal was not just any necromancer—he was the only one in the known world, and completely at the disposal of the King of Desmorda. Cal didn't waste any more time; the King's patience was far from infinite.

Exhaling, he closed his eyes and dug into his magic.

The power over life and death resided in Cal, far deeper than his shadow-work, though they were somewhat connected. He breathed through the effort it took to summon a soul back from the other side of the veil. Cal opened his eyes. He stretched his fingers out over the body and pressed them into the corpse's cold chest. He fought back his revulsion at the feel of the rubbery skin beneath his hands as he willed the body to rise—to host the soul for a few more minutes. Anything more would require a ritual and blood, but Cal had grown strong enough to summon a spirit for a minute or two without the aid of spell work.

Abruptly, the body on the table spasmed and sucked in a ragged breath.

"Excellent," the King hissed as he moved closer, his hungry expression hovering over the body.

Cal had to remain in contact with the body to keep the soul present, so the King would have to lead the interrogation. The corpse's eyes flitted and darted around in confusion, but the King wasted no time. He grabbed the corpse's chin, resting control of its roaming gaze.

"Who is the leader of the rebellion? Where are they hiding? Who's supplying them?" He demanded. Cal blocked out the questions. They meant nothing to him, and he had to keep his focus on holding the spirit in the body. He counted his breaths, using them as a measure of how long he would be able to retain the connection.

Forty-five…

Sixty…

Ninety…

Sweat trickled down his temples and beaded along his forearms. But he tightened his grip on the body and centered himself.

One hundred fifteen…

One hundred forty…

Cal's hands trembled, threatening to spasm. He glanced up at the King and licked his lips. The King's fingers dug into the corpse's face so hard that bruises bloomed under the skin.

One hundred sixty…

"Your Majesty," Cal breathed, working to keep his tone level. His fingers twitched—fire burned in his muscles.

The King gave no acknowledgment that he heard Cal but continued his questioning. "Who are your contacts? Who has…"

One hundred ninety…

Blood roared in Cal's ears. Black spots dotted his vision. Vessels and veins burst in his lungs, the metallic taste filling his mouth.

Two hundred twenty…

Cal wheezed and attempted to beg the King to end this, but his words failed him, and Cal lost his grip on the body—severing the connection. Cal tumbled backward. His shoulder smacked into the stone floor, his head swimming. Aiming to get control of his faculties again, Cal panted, but then the King's face appeared above him, sneering.

"I didn't get everything I needed. Get up and reestablish the connection."

"I...I...can't." Cal said between ragged breaths.

The King narrowed his ebony eyes and bared his teeth. "Pathetic." He punctuated his disappointment with a swift kick into Cal's ribs. The air went out of him. Pain rippled through his chest as he rolled away and choked on nothing.

"I should have used your brother instead. He's far less dramatic than you." The King planted another kick in Cal's spine, and he arched in response, still gasping for air. "Stay down here until you figure out how to master yourself. And if I find out you've seen a healer after you crawl out of this pit, my next blow will be to that pitiful younger brother of yours." the King threatened before storming down the hall, leaving Cal alone with the dead.

Cal lay there until his pulse stopped throbbing in his skull, and every breath didn't feel like razors in his lungs. But for the first time since coming under the King's control, Cal didn't despair that he let down the King—because Soline was waiting for him.

Chapter Twenty Three

Flames danced and flickered against the ebony night. The smoke curled and floated on the breeze blowing through the sails, pushing them further from the coast and closer to the Cave of Splendors—the Isle Oum.

Cal braced his hands on the railing, staring across the churning sea. He closed his eyes and inhaled deeply, letting the mingling scent of brine and sulfur wash over him and fill his chest. This was the one place that was peaceful, the one place where the demons of his past and the dead didn't haunt him relentlessly. He opened his eyes and tilted his head up to the moon. The light bathed the world around him in sparkling silver, providing just enough illumination to make the lanterns hanging from the mast unnecessary. But even as the moonbeams cascading from the night sky brightened the deck, darkness clung to Cal. It slithered over his skin and pooled in the hollows of his soul, stroking his mind. Usually, he welcomed the darkness, embracing its silence and comfort, but tonight, it was *different*.

There was a hunger to it—an urgency that made Cal uneasy. Glancing around, he looked for a threat or a cause for the disturbance. His eyes tripped over the crew members who monitored the sails and murmured softly amongst themselves—unbothered. He scanned up the mast and noted Finnley in the crow's nest. Her auburn braid whipped in the wind, her legs dangled over the railing, and her arms folded behind her head.

His stomach flopped at the height and her apparent ease at being perched up there. Dropping his gaze, he turned back to the sea, finding no cause for his trepidation, but it lingered nonetheless.

He hadn't summoned creatures of the night or the dead in so long that he wondered if they were now seeking him out. If they were angry at him for not wielding them. Or resentful that he instead relied on parlor tricks with shadows to do most of the work. Cal turned his hand over, shadows slipping through his fingers like water. The shadows came easily enough, requiring very little of him. But the greater magic, the more dangerous, demanded a price that Cal hadn't been willing to pay in many years. Still, the discomfort and unease remained with him, as if it was waiting for Cal to stop looking at it and forget what haunted him. Cal shook his head and turned his thoughts from the ambivalence that stalked him. Instead, he decided to focus on something that filled him with anger.

Lady Hera.

Her haughty attitude and arrogance rivaled his own, and not in a way he found endearing. The way she regarded him with disdain sent frost down his spine, giving his resentment a razor-sharp edge. He cared not that the fire burning within her intrigued him because it was contrary to everything Cal stood for. She was a handmaiden of the Princess, who, if Cal remembered correctly, was nearly as impertinent as her Lady. Perhaps that was precisely why she had selected her for this quest. Cal wasn't sure that a typical noblewoman–demure and submissive–would have survived a day outside of the palace, let alone weeks amongst the Umbra.

Lady Hera behaved as though she knew Cal and had a reason to greatly dislike him. And perhaps she did. There was a good chance that the King had wielded Cal against her family, as he so often did—threatening them to keep them all in line. Whatever the case was, Cal found himself unable to stop his retorts when she smarted off. Something about her called to him in a way that was equal parts infuriating and intriguing. He couldn't pinpoint precisely what it was about her that made his blood boil, but whatever it was, it clouded his judgment. Already, he had spoken to her and her guard dog more than he had ever intended to, but when she opened her mouth and spewed her condescension, well, Cal couldn't help but respond in like.

He never should have intervened with Cade like he did, but he was helpless to stop himself. But then she questioned him and refused to back down. No other woman had ever dared challenge him the way Lady Hera had, save for…

Inexplicably, the breeze stilled, pausing its caress on his skin.

Cal's eyes flew open. Ice settled into his veins, and he detected it then. The shift, the digging of the darkness as it latched into his muscles, seizing his soul.

"Caliban."

Cal stiffened. He willed his body to become as unmoving as a corpse, unyielding to the presence behind him. There was no need for him to turn in order to know who his mind had summoned, who had lurked in his shadow from the moment they had sent off in search of the Cave of Splendors.

A hand, delicate and distinctly female, slid over Cal's tense shoulder. It slipped down, gliding over his chest, and came to a halt over his abdomen. Cal clenched his jaw, fighting the urge to look—acknowledging it would only serve to feed the spector further.

"Look at me." it whispered in a lover's voice.

Cal did no such thing. Even as the night rippled from him, indicating that he was losing his grip on his power—on the ghosts that hunted him.

The moonlight and stars winked out as shadows swarmed him, enveloping him. The wraith holding him slithered, adjusted, and placed herself right under Cal's chin. Still, he did not tear his gaze away from the blackness before him. Though his vision was obstructed, his other senses remained. The brine of the sea and the swaying of the ship persisted, attempting to ground him—but his resolve was rapidly faltering.

"Please, love. I need you."

The muscle under Cal's eye twitched. Her body, somewhere between corporeal and ineffable, pressed against his chest, begging him to embrace her. But he refused. Not yet, not until he had the Alakhira.

Cal sighed and gripped the hands that pushed into his chest. He was toeing the line of what was safe, but he was unable to resist her—he never could. From his peripheral vision, he glimpsed the top of her head, the golden hair that he knew cascaded down her back and pooled like spun sunlight.

"Soline, I can't. I want nothing more than to be with you, but it's not the right time."

The temperature around them dropped several degrees. Soline's elegantly manicured nails turned to talons and pierced Cal's flesh. Pain tore through his body, but he remained steadfast.

"*You can't look at me, but you can fantasize about another?*" Soline hissed, further digging her claws into his body, ripping into muscle and tendon.

Cal clamped down on her arms and shook her. "I only need her for the information that she has." Cal proclaimed. Kai mentioned that the Lady had a book with her that contained knowledge about the Cave and its contents. If he could get that book, he could prepare for what awaited them.

"*Liar.*" Soline hissed again.

"Be gone, wraith. Be gone and do not return." Cal commanded, releasing Soline. Her form flickered, and Cal detected the hatred, rage, and anguish pouring off of Soline in waves. It was equal parts overwhelming and alarming, but Cal held his ground. He proceeded with reciting the spell that would banish her, not permanently, but hopefully long enough for him to get to the Cave of Splendors and retrieve the Alakhira. Once he had the book–the one he had spent years searching for–they would be reunited. Soline bared her teeth, but Cal continued staring at the nothingness. His mouth and voice worked of their own accord even as Soline screamed and lunged for Cal.

Her talons never made contact.

Cal continued to say the words until the shadows dissipated and the twinkling stars returned to their place in the inky sky. Moonlight once more bathed the ship's deck and glinted off the sea like glass. Cal gulped down the ocean air, relishing in its saltiness. He leaned forward, gripping the ship's rail, allowing it to bear most of his weight. He pressed down, trying to stop the shaking that coursed through his body. He worked to slow his breathing by taking deep inhales and holding them. There was no danger; nothing would harm him. Over and over, he took deep breaths and paused, letting his body catch up with what his mind had already come to terms with.

He was safe.

Soline was gone and would not be back for some time, but that didn't stop her memory from creeping back in. The trembling in Cal's arms and legs finally subsided enough for him to release the railing and turn, facing the rest of the ship. Most of the crew had cleared out. He glanced up to the crow's nest, but Finnley's body had relaxed—a sparrow asleep in her roost.

Good.

He didn't need Finnley, Galen, or anyone else butting into his business. It wouldn't impact his ability to captain the ship, so they needn't concern themselves with it. Exhaling a final deep breath, he scanned the ship once more. He would need to turn in soon. They would all be as good as dead if he wasn't well rested before what he expected they would encounter. Cal rolled his shoulders and pushed off from the railing, aiming for the door that led down into the ship's hull and his quarters beyond. But movement caught his eye. He cut his eyes to his left and noted the figure huddled against the rail, face upturned to the moon. His body halted, drinking in the sight.

Onyx hair soaked in the moonlight, gobbling up any sliver that dared to cross her path. Her eyes were closed, her mouth parted as if caught in the throes of ecstasy. Cal was helpless to drag himself away, his rest forgotten. Before he thought better of it, his feet moved of their own accord, heading directly for Lady Hera.

Chapter Twenty Four

$\mathcal{T}$ he limestone of the palace walls blinded Rhea. She raised a hand to shield her eyes as she squinted against the glare of the blazing sun. The smack of flesh resounded in her ears, and the sting of pain radiated from her calves. Dropping her hand, she turned, grabbing for her smarting skin with a hiss.

"Princesses do not raise their hands to block the sun. If you didn't want it in your eyes or speckling your skin, then you should have brought a sunshade." scolded Rhea's governess, returning her reed cane to the ground. Rhea bit her tongue, even as angry red welts formed on the back of her legs. She didn't want to also receive a smack to the face for talking back.

Rhea spoke softly, swallowing her bitterness, "Yes, governess. My apologies."

The governess stayed silent, but the sneer etched into her wrinkled features was proof enough that she wasn't convinced of Rhea's contrition. They continued on their walk about the palace grounds, admiring the various flowers that were in bloom. Other ladies trailed Rhea, their lithe, gossiping voices trilling over her, buzzing in her ears like the bees to the blooms.

Rhea cared nothing for flowers—could hardly identify one from another—but she was expected to be soft, feminine, and interested in the varying flora. Keeping with the presumed facade, Rhea bent toward a bloom, inhaling its fragrance. It was sweet, almost sickeningly so, just like the last flower she feigned interest in, but she attempted to keep her revulsion from her face as she righted herself.

A lady, one that Rhea hadn't bothered to learn the name of, came sauntering toward her. Rhea admired her confidence, but she had learned many years ago that these women were not her friends, and they were not to be trusted. The Lady bent toward the same flower Rhea had moments ago, and Rhea's eyes tracked the woman's movement. She was exceptionally beautiful, with thick mahogany hair plaited and resting over her shoulder. Her frame was slender and petite. Her skin was fair and free of blemish, indicative of a life spent indoors—a life of comfort and ease.

"They are beautiful, Your Highness." The woman lifted her head, a demure smile painted on her full, rosy lips. "Perhaps we should cut some and take them to your mother while she's resting in her confinement?"

Rhea ground her back teeth but flashed a smile. It was too toothy for it to read as friendly, but Rhea didn't care. "Yes. I suppose we could take some to my father's concubine while she awaits the arrival of her child."

The Lady's eyes widened almost imperceptibly.

Almost.

"My apologies, Your Highness. I meant no disrespect." She murmured, raising a hand to her mouth to cover her shame. Her tone was nearly convincing, but the slight curl of her lips and tilt of her eyes gave her away. But so was the game. The never-ending match of snide remarks and slights that abounded in court.

A softer, more understanding smile spread across Rhea's face. "It is fine, an easy mistake to make." Rhea turned, intent on leaving the conversation there, but a slender arm slipped through Rhea's. Rhea fought the urge to shove the woman off, sending her tumbling into the nearby fountain. Instead, she continued her pace, hoping they would arrive at the garden doors before the woman said anything to further anger Rhea.

"It's such a shame that the King has been unable to sire a son, at least one that has survived through infancy."

Rhea clenched her jaw. So, it was to be that *sort of conversation. If Rhea hadn't already been in a sour mood, she might have been able to entertain the woman's comments. But the morning's lessons with the tutor had been tedious, and Rhea's governess was being extra liberal with her physical correction.*

The woman sighed as she reached out and brushed her fingers over the petal of a lily, or perhaps an orchid; Rhea wasn't sure.

"But I am happy to know a babe is on the way. Hopefully, the empire will finally have an heir. Though, if this one turns out to be a girl or infirm, perhaps the King will look for another maid." the woman smirked, throwing a sidelong glance at Rhea.

Rhea broke. Her patience worn thin.

She turned on the woman, digging her nails into the Lady's arm. "The empire already has an heir." Rhea whispered, leaning into the woman's face. "I will rule better than any males my father's whores may spawn, especially if they were to come from the likes of you."

The woman had the good sense to look terrified, her eyes wide and her throat bobbing with the effort to hold back her tears. Rhea sneered at her before extracting her arm and giving her a light shove. The sneer transformed into a delectable smirk as the woman tumbled backward, tripping on the train of her skirts. A guard rushed forward, grabbing her before she could fully fall into the fountain.

Pity, *thought Rhea.*

She turned on her heel, not waiting to receive the beating that the governess would most certainly dole out for Rhea's insolence. She was beyond caring. She was done being belittled and disrespected in her own home. Done with the court treating her position as heir as a placeholder until one of her father's consorts produced a male child. Intent on escaping the ridicule and condemnation of the court that reviled her for nothing more than the fact that she was female, Rhea stormed through the courtyard. Barely sixteen and already despised by the men who thought her unfit to rule.

She would show them. Show everyone that she led just as well as any man, if not better.

Rhea's hands slammed into the warm glass doors of the Grand Hall, but instead of finding the airy corridor, she tripped downward into black nothingness. Her hands and knees collided with an unforgiving marble floor, her joints barking in response.

Her breath came in hard pants. Daring to lift her head, her eyes darted around the room, aiming to make sense of the sudden shift in the environment. A cool breeze tickled the exposed skin of her back—her dress slipping down around her—and ruffled her unbound hair.

Something whistled through the air, and Rhea turned in time to catch a glimpse of a slender leather strap hurtling toward her. She raised her hands in defense, but it was futile as the whip made contact with the bare skin of her back. Blinding hot pain radiated from the point of impact. Rhea fell down on her face, a scream of agony breaking from her lips. She heaved, drawing air through gritted teeth as she tried to understand what was happening.

What utter fool had the audacity to strike her?

Where was her father?

Surely, he would not allow his only child to be stripped bare and brutalized. She lifted herself onto her hands and knees again and raised her head. Another whistle was the only warning she received before the whip sliced into her skin again, forcing her to the ground once more. Her scream was guttural and primal. More animal than human, but she was powerless to stop it.

Another.

Another.

Another.

Tears and bile burned in Rhea's throat, but the wave of pain was too much, too intense for her to do anything but lay prostrate on the marble floor.

"That's enough, Bilah."

Heavy, booted footsteps receded, but Rhea was helpless to stop her trembling or think past the horrific pain pulsing through the torn flesh of her back.

"Look at me." said a chillingly familiar voice, as pristine leather sandals appeared before Rhea, stopping mere inches from her face. She was incapable of lifting her head. Her stinging, watery eyes focused on the intricate straps crisscrossing over the man's feet.

Rough, thick fingers jerked her chin, forcing her eyes up. She fought back her horror as she beheld the enraged face of her father, King of Desmorda and the Conquered Nations.

Rhea supposed he was once a handsome man, with his strong brow and deep-set eyes, before the years of cruelty and disappointment wiped away any joy or love that once existed. The man before her may have sired her, but he was no more her father than the women he bedded were her mother.

Her father pulled on her chin, raising her up until she rested on her knees. Her dress fluttered around her, and she had the clarity to cross her arms over her chest, preventing it from slipping further. Malice and loathing burned in the King's black eyes as he peered down at his daughter. His only living child. His Heir. His fingers dug deeper into her chin, the thick, metal rings he donned bruising down to her bones—but the pain was inconsequential to her ravaged, searing flesh.

"You embarrassed me today. Assaulting a lady, calling my harem whores. You are a daughter of the blood and the future of the nation. For now." he growled with such intensity that spit flew from his lips, smattering across her cheeks.

So, that's what this was about. Rhea jutted out her chin, determined not to let her frustration and fear show.

"You claim to be able to lead like a man, then I will treat you like a son." he sneered, sinful delight dancing in his ebony eyes. "Which means receiving lashings when you step out of line. Still think you want to be my heir?" His voice was taunting, dripping with disdain and absolute hate.

Rhea swallowed, searching for her voice. "I am the blood of your blood. The one true daughter of Queen Hala, your one true wife. Until one of your concubines brings forth another child, I am all you have."

The King released Rhea's chin with a rough shove, hard enough that she careened backward. She threw out a hand to brace herself, but it slipped in something wet. She stared blankly at her hand as she brought it in front of her.

Blood.

Her *blood*.

Royal blood that her father had ordered a guard to draw forth by whipping her, repeatedly.

The King turned from his daughter, stalking back to his porcelain throne. Rhea took the moment to assess the damage further. The edges of her dress were visible to about her waist, and the fabric was torn. She hadn't even been afforded the decency of disrobing; her clothes were rented from her like a criminal. Rhea shouldered the dress in an effort to cover more of herself. But she froze when her father dropped onto his throne and fixed his stare on her again.

There was no hint of remorse or regret for his actions, but Rhea expected none. His jeweled fingers impatiently tapped the arm of his throne as if deciding what to do with her. Rhea lifted her chin, unwilling to let him break her.

"Rise, daughter." he commanded.

Rhea rose on unsteady feet and took a deep breath, still clutching her ruined dress around her. The King gave her a once-over before waving his hand in dismissal. Rhea turned, careful not to move the muscles in her back more than necessary.

"Next time you step out of line, you will receive more than fifteen lashings, and I will disown you." her father's voice boomed. She stilled at his words, her mind whirling to comprehend the threats he slung at her like knives. "Heir or not—there are others that I could name. Other capable men."

As she continued from the throne room, she willed her body to show no reaction. She forced her features into a mask of cool indifference. She didn't look at or acknowledge a soul as she limped toward her chambers. She would wear it proudly if her father wished to teach her a lesson and attempt to humiliate her. For it was not her shame she bore, but his. Let his court witness his cruelty to his own child and wonder not if, but when they would be on the receiving end of his ire.

Rhea lifted her chin until she saw her room's familiar burgundy doors. She reached out a hand to push through—

Rhea sat up in an unfamiliar bed, sweat pooling beneath her nightgown and her breath coming out in hard pants. Her eyes darted around the dark cabin, taking in the wood-paneled walls illuminated by the watery moonlight filtering in through the dingy window. Rough linen sheets grated against her skin, and the lingering scent of salt–the sea and her sweat–stuffed up her nose. Pain flared in her back, and she winced, reaching for it. The shift she wore was soaked with perspiration, but she ran her fingers along her back anyway, feeling for the raised flesh there.

Her fingers connected with the scar tissue, and she twisted, bringing her knees to her chest and placing her head in her hands. Slowly, she rocked herself back and forth, clenching against the slight tremble that threatened to overtake her body entirely.

It was only a nightmare.

Though it wasn't, not really.

She had truly lived out the terrifying ordeal, and on more than one occasion. But she reminded herself that she was not sixteen anymore and that she was hundreds of miles away from her barbaric father.

He couldn't hurt her here.

But she couldn't stay in her cabin any longer.

The room was too small, the walls too close to her, pressing in, in, in. Her breath seized in her chest—catching in her throat.

She wrenched the covers—the rough fabric unbearable for a moment longer on her sticky legs. The wood was cool against her feet but not enough to sate the burning of her flesh. She grimaced at the pain still lancing in her back—the ghosts of the whip searing into her skin with each movement.

She needed fresh air. She needed space.

She grabbed the thin dressing robe she had brought and made for the door, not bothering with shoes. She just had to get out.

Get out, get out, get out, get out.

She swung open the door, not bothering to be careful. A twinge of guilt–for deliberately avoiding Brander–coursed through her, but sometimes his nearness was suffocating. It reminded her too much of the palace—of her father.

Gods, her *father.*

Every time she blinked, she saw his shining black eyes. Those dark pits overflowing with loathing as he beheld her—his disappointment of a descendant. Or maybe that was just her self-loathing reflecting back at her from beneath her eyelids.

Forcing her unsteady feet to pause for just one moment, she listened for any movement behind the thick, wooden door to Brander's cabin. There was nothing, save for the creaking and swaying of the ship and the wind whistling through the rigging. The sound mimicked the high-pitched whine of the leather whip as it descended upon her again, again, and again.

Rhea wasted no more time as she scurried up the steps leading to the deck, taking them two at a time as she raced to escape her memories. She swung open the door and momentarily sagged against the threshold, white knuckles gripping the frame so hard she feared it might splinter. The entirety of the deck was illuminated in shafts of moonlight, encasing the sails, the mast, and the swaying ropes in a silvery glow. Rhea stepped further out onto the deck and heaved in the salty sea air. It tugged at her braid, ripping free strands of her hair. It pulled at her robe, urging her to take flight.

Her feet carried her to the railing, where she grasped the rail as if she were clinging to the edge of a cliff face. She peered over, unable to glean anything from the inky waves below—grateful that the water was too far down and much too turbulent to reflect what she was certain was a haggard face. She lifted her chin to the sky once more and commanded her traitorous lungs to suck in a shaky breath. She delighted in the cool air that settled into her bones and quelled the fire that singed her soul. Closing her eyes, she let the moonlight wash over her, its halo of luminescence a comfort from the nightmares that chased her from sleep.

"Something about being adrift at sea at night just soothes the soul."

Rhea jumped, her eyes flying open. She turned to the owner of the voice and beheld Death Incarnate—hovering not three feet from her. In the silvery light he looked younger, lighter—friendlier even. She narrowed her eyes before clutching her robe tighter and lifting her eyes back to the sky, resolute to ignore him and continue to bask in the solace of the night. His earlier words still stung, but her anger at them had largely faded.

The nightmares of her past had a way of putting things, especially petty arguments, into perspective.

A dark chuckle emanated from Cal as he shifted closer to her. Despite her apprehension of him, she didn't move away. She wouldn't give him the satisfaction of scaring her off.

Not this time.

She sent a sidelong glance at him, marveling at the way his midnight clothes rippled in the breeze. His shoulder-length hair also stirred around his face. He was five—nearly six—years older than her, but swathed in night and illuminated by the moon, he hardly looked older than twenty. She couldn't stop the question as it formed on her lips.

"Why did you become a privateer?"

Cal cut his eyes to her, mischief swirling in them. "Pirate." he corrected.

Rolling her eyes, Rhea turned her attention back to the sea. Though she had regained some semblance of control over her panicked mind, she was in no mood to cope with his vexations. "Never mind." she muttered and shook her head. Regret ricocheted through her at her foolishness. Attempting to engage him was futile. Sighing, she hoped he would take the hint and go sulk off somewhere—

Cal laughed again.

Rhea could hardly believe it. She struggled to recall if she had ever witnessed him laughing when he lived in the palace. Momentarily, she was in awe at the way his face transformed with the action. The rigidity that normally accompanied his features softened markedly, and she had no power over the errant thought that popped into her brain—that it suited him.

"I had to get out of Desmorda, and the stories I read of pirates always fascinated me."

"Interesting. I wasn't aware you could read anything other than sorcery." The words were out of her mouth before she thought to stop them. Rhea raised a hand to her lips, heat burning in her cheeks and neck. She dared to glance at Cal, who–to her surprise–still had a small smile gracing his lips. Rhea was taken aback by how relaxed Cal appeared, when just hours ago he had been insufferably boorish and short-tempered.

Perhaps the sea did soothe the soul.

"Yes, shocking, I know." Cal spoke, his voice pulling Rhea from her stupor. "But reading drab spell books and the like can get tiresome, so it's nice to read something meant to entertain once in a while. Stories of the high seas were always the most captivating." Cal arched a brow in her direction. "I believe we have that in common." Rhea flinched and opened her mouth to refute his claim, but Cal continued, "Kai mentioned you brought a book with you."

Pursing her lips, she said, "Yes. I wanted to know as much about the Cave of Splendors as possible."

A corner of Cal's mouth lifted, and he shifted a hair closer to her. "You wouldn't be interested in sharing that knowledge with me, would you?" His voice was a low, sensual rumble that heated Rhea's cheeks.

She cleared her throat. "No, I would not."

An emotion flickered in Cal's eyes. "And why not?"

Rhea narrowed her eyes. "And give you what little leverage I have? I think not."

Cal had the audacity to pout as he said, "Pity. But you can't blame a man for trying. I suppose I'll just have to entertain myself with the same old tales that I possess about the Cave. Certainly is a shame that we can't compare notes."

Rhea turned from him. She wanted to change the subject or, at the very least, stop talking about herself. She cleared her throat and said, "And what would the masses think if they discovered that the Nightmare made Flesh has a penchant for fairytales? Or that you left it all behind for pillaging and drinking?" She attempted to force some levity into her voice and smiled. She just wanted him to stop looking at her like that.

"I care not what others think of me."

Rhea barked out a laugh. Silence filled the space between them, and she hesitantly ventured another look at Cal. The amusement was gone from his features. His mouth was set in a hard line, and his jaw was tight.

"Surely, you jest." Rhea quipped.

Cal raised a brow.

Rhea dared to laugh again and peered back out at the sea, unable to take his intense gaze. "I rem–I heard stories about you at court. How you sulked around and terrified everyone who deigned to speak to you."

Well, not everyone, Rhea thought, but she wasn't in the mood to revisit those particular memories.

She cleared her throat and, against her better judgment, continued. "You care very much what others think of you. Otherwise, you wouldn't have made such efforts to hide your true self from those around you." Rhea could have sworn the stars winked out, and the moon vanished for a heartbeat. But she was not a coward, and she wouldn't let Cal, of all people, bully her into submission. She turned and faced him. The icy rage in his eyes made her heart trip over itself, but she held her ground. Lifting her chin, she delivered her final blow, "You are so afraid of letting others see you that you would rather keep everyone at arm's length."

The ice in Cal's eyes settled into her very being. Goosebumps erupted over her arms, her thin gown doing nothing to prevent the chill of his gaze from settling over her entire body. He stepped forward, barely six inches between them now. All signs of the carefree man from before were gone. In his place was Darkness given form.

Rhea fought the urge to hold her breath and shrink back as she gaped at him. Briefly, she wondered how his demeanor had shifted from a lighthearted and unfettered man to this entity of frosty rage within mere seconds. Her pulse thumped a steady, intoxicating beat in her ears, but she would not falter.

"And you think you see me, Lady Hera?" Cal whispered, his voice like sand across the stone. His scent—clove, cedar, and...were those lilies?—enveloped her, but she stood firm, clenching her fist against the trembling that threatened to overtake her. Kai's earlier words about her being able to read people came back to her. She had known the truth of them then, and she knew them now. But from the frigid fury frosting his features, she understood that perhaps now was not the time to voice her observations.

Cal's eyes dipped to her mouth, raking slowly over the curves of her lips. Her breath hitched in her chest as his eyes returned to her own. Something warm dared to undermine his chilled gaze. It was the same alluring look that had transfixed her all those years ago, and even earlier that day when she didn't quite understand what she was seeing or feeling. Nearly ten years later, she was close to identifying that mystery sensation thrumming in her blood.

She stared into those frigid brown eyes, lifted her brows in a silent challenge, and declared, "I know I do."

Something passed over Cal's face, the subtlest shift in his demeanor. He tore his eyes from hers and stepped away, his back now facing her. Rhea could have sworn all the warmth in her body was being ripped away from her, but that was ridiculous. Rhea pulled her robe tighter against her, not realizing that she had let it fall open, exposing her barely concealed body to the entire ship. A quick glance around confirmed that there was no one present—no one to witness whatever was brewing between her and Cal. Shame—and something else that Rhea refused to name—burned in her chest. She averted her eyes from Cal, searching for some way out of their battle for dominance.

"You need to go back to your cabin. And don't let me catch you out here again." Cal growled at her, his voice rough and full of command.

Indignation replaced Rhea's shame. "You have no dominion over me. I will go where I please, when I please." She spat out, the queen within her rising to the surface at his orders.

Cal turned. He was in her face in an instant.

"This is *my* ship," Rhea barely had time to blink before he all but growled at her, "whatever authority you wield over your guard dog or back home in your gilded cage has no bearings here. You'd be wise to learn that."

Rhea jabbed a finger in Cal's chest and bared her teeth. "You're just as hateful as you were nearly a decade ago. Glad to know that some things never change."

Rhea realized her mistake too late.

She went hot and cold all over. She began praying that Cal was too distracted to truly understand the meaning behind her words. Cal grabbed Rhea's wrist and pulled her flush to him; she didn't bother to fight his grip or grab for her robe that had fallen open, still terrified that he might have found her out.

There was wickedness in his eyes, nothing but pure depravity as he breathed out, "They call me the Demon Prince for a reason, Lady, and if you've heard stories about me and my power, you should remember exactly why." His smile widened, and a thrill shot through Rhea like lightning through an iron rod. "Or perhaps you would like a reminder?" Cal seethed.

Rhea clenched her jaw. Her father had gone to great lengths to keep the specifics of Cal's power a secret, but his abilities with shadows were known well enough. She remembered as clear as day one of the last times that he summoned his shadows in her father's throne room. His inky darkness gathered in a tidal wave that threatened to smother everyone and everything. Even then, she understood that Cal would never come to heel the way her father demanded all of his subjects to—especially his arsenal of magic wielders—and it would only be a matter of time before one of them pushed the other too far.

It seemed she had inherited that particular trait from her father with the reckless way she persistently pushed back against Cal. She yanked her wrist free and took several steps away, desperate for the space. Cal watched her with predatory intent—a wolf tracking its prey. Rhea's mouth curled into disgust. Why had she ever thought that the boy she had known at the palace still existed within the monster before her?

"Maybe you're right." Rhea said haughtily, holding her robe tight against her. "Maybe there is nothing left in you but despair and darkness." She swallowed and worked to keep her voice level as she turned from him, pausing to give him one last disdainful glare. "I hope you find whatever it is you're seeking on this journey…perhaps it might save you from yourself."

Cal issued a rough, terrible laugh. "How typical."

Rhea's lips curled into a snarl. "What's typical?"

Darkness swirled and tumbled around Cal as he peered down at her. "How you nobles act. There's always an air of superiority, and I guess I shouldn't be surprised since it was your *master* who made the enslavement of magic wielders legal."

"He doesn't enslave them." Rhea countered.

"No? Funny, I distinctly remember being turned over for a mandatory examination as a *child* and then handed over to the King to serve him. I don't recall being asked what I wanted."

"But—"

"And don't you dare tell me we could leave," Cal continued, rage liming his features, "it was made very clear that the education and upkeep we were provided came at a cost—one that was expected to be paid back."

Rhea ground her teeth. Of course, she knew that her father recruited magic wielders to serve him, but she hadn't known that they were essentially his slaves. Rhea shook her head, trying to clear away her ignorance at the extent of her father's cruelty, and replied, "The Princess will not continue the practice."

An unkind smile spread over Caliban's face as he leaned closer and whispered, "You're even more of a fool than I thought if you think your precious Princess won't keep to the same laws."

Heat stung Rhea's cheeks. "She won't. She's different. She wants to change things."

"Is that right? So, you mean to tell me she's the first royal that doesn't covet power? She'll be the first not to succumb to the allure of unchecked and unfettered strength? Somehow, I doubt that."

Rhea lifted her chin. "You know nothing about her. You're just applying the prejudices you hold for others against her—and you're wrong."

"Is that so? Then why is she seeking out the Cave? Why not gather support from the council and overthrow her father? Why not present him with reforms to make life easier for the empire? Why not marry a foreign prince and muster an army? Why is it that the only route she considered was to send an out-of-her-depth Lady to retrieve some magical item that likely promises its wielder immense power?"

Rhea clenched her jaw to stop from spewing more vitriol—but more accurately, to stop her tears. She would never admit to him that she hadn't considered some of the options he had suggested, nor would she admit how close to the truth he was about what she sought.

Rhea slowly loosened her jaw and said, "You may throw all the condemnation and accusations you like at me and my mistress, but that will never change the fact that you have taken lives and tortured people."

"At your King's behest." Cal retorted.

"And what of the years since you left his service? Surely, you dare not claim innocence. Not when your ship and crew are ill-famed and notorious all throughout Desmorda."

Cal leaned impossibly closer, his breath skating over her cheeks. "I know precisely what kind of monster I am, Lady, but never mistake my wickedness for that of the Abadi regime. And if you ever compare me to that worm of a man again," the starlight around them guttered once more, "I will give you every reason to believe the awful stories you've heard about me."

Rhea's eyes went wide at his blatant threat. She raised her hands between them and shoved him away. "You are wretched." she seethed.

"Forget my earlier kindness, Necromancer. I pray to every Forgotten god that you get *everything* you deserve in this life. That every terrible and evil thing you have done to others comes back on you tenfold."

Rhea turned away and didn't stop to hear if Cal responded, but she did cross her arms more tightly as the temperature plummeted behind her.

Let Cal be the creator of his own misery.

Rhea would not follow him down that path.

There was too much for her to think about, too many other people to consider. She didn't have time to unravel the horrors that Cal seemed content to wallow in. She would leave him to his own devices and ignore her treacherous heart, which begged her to reconsider.

Chapter Twenty Five

Malakai's tongue was a lead weight in his mouth. It attempted to prod the inside of his cheeks and teeth, but the effort to lift it was beyond his current capabilities. His limbs and joints were useless, too. The signals were sent by his mind, urging his muscles to contract and expand, to heave his parched and famished body from the maudlin bed he had rotted in for only the Forgotten knew how long.

He knew he had been in and out of consciousness for a while, but that could have occurred over the course of several hours or several days. His memory was spotty at best, with only glimpses of faces and voices echoing through his mind. He sighed exasperatedly; nothing in his memories was complete or coherent. There was no telling what he may have said or done since he passed out.

The effort of turning his head—that simple movement alone—sent a jolt of pain ricocheting through his skull. Orbs danced in his vision, temporarily blinding him. He took several deep breaths, pushing through the pain and allowing his body to adjust to the movement. Bright light streamed through the dilapidated window. At least a night had passed since Malakai had succumbed to the visions. He fought against the shame and embarrassment that attempted to burn its way up his throat. But he had nothing to be ashamed about. His blackout was simply a liability of his magic. It had happened before and would potentially happen again.

He assumed that Kasper had administered the elixir, which was unfortunate as he knew they now had none left. He would have to be more careful when conjuring visions until Kasper was able to procure him more. At least, that's what Malakai repeated to himself as he waited for someone to come tend to him. Malakai was giving up hope of being cared for when an unfamiliar crew member popped their head in, smiling.

"Yer up!"

Malakai attempted to return the smile, but it was simply too much effort.

"Was start'n to think ye wasn't gonna wake." The pirate joked, pushing into the room and hobbling over to Malakai's bedside. The pirate smiled as they leaned over Malakai's limp frame, pressing their grimy hand to his forehead. Malakai was powerless to stop his flinch as the pirate's clammy fingers made contact with his hot skin.

"Where's my brother?" Malakai inquired, his voice horrifically hoarse.

"Don't know, don't care." they chirped as they stepped away and smiled a horribly toothy grin. "Well, yer rite as the rain, so I's won't be back." The pirate turned on their heel and strolled out the door, pulling it closed and leaving Malakai in silence once more.

Sighing, he reclined against his bed, certain that Kasper would eventually show.

But he didn't.

A current of concern flitted through Malakai.

Perhaps danger had befallen him, or he had become ill himself. Was it possible Malakai had done something while in a trance? He had never harmed anyone during a vision, but it wasn't unheard of, especially if an antidote wasn't dispensed appropriately.

That must have been the case. Kasper was ill or hurt—bedridden somewhere himself. That was the only fathomable reason Malakai could come up with as to why his beloved sibling wouldn't have seen to Malakai's recovery. Malakai picked at a loose thread on his sleeve and watched the sun slip from his narrow view of the world. With the knowledge that he had awakened and managed to stay conscious for several hours—and with the pirate's paltry examination, Malakai assumed he was through the worst of it.

Malakai tried not to let his disappointment get the better of him, but he was truly baffled by the lack of visitors. He hadn't expected Caliban or any of the crew to check up on him, but it was concerning that Kasper hadn't bothered to stop by in the hours since Malakai had awoken. It was possible that he had simply missed his brother. Perhaps Kasper was there mere minutes before Malakai awoke, but as darkness descended over the cabin, that seemed less likely. He took a deep breath and willed his legs to rise.

The stiffness in his limbs made him wince, but he was not overcome with excruciating pain, so he persisted. Sweat beaded along his hairline, soaking what had to be a matted mess of curls, but he finally placed both feet firmly on the creaky wooden floor. Malakai paused to rest and get his bearings. His chest ached, and his legs trembled like they were made of jelly. He wasn't sure if he would even leave the room at this rate.

Taking a moment to glance around, he found no shoes or slippers.

Wonderful, he thought.

Malakai rolled his shoulders and gathered what little strength was available to him. If he didn't leave his room now and find something to eat and drink, he would likely give out from a lack of sustenance.

On terrifically shaky legs, Malakai stood and shuffled toward the door. The weathered wood mercifully had few jagged edges, though he did worry that a splinter was a possibility as he shuffled across the floor. His entire being felt heavy as if he had been dipped and coated in thick, hindering mud. But he trudged onward, ignoring the screams of his body begging him to stop. He ignored it and only paused at the threshold for a moment.

His journey up the rickety stairs to the main level of the ship was arduous, to say the least. But after several minutes of straining to lift his legs up one over the other, he finally managed to crest the last step and emerge on the landing.

And he had only taken six breaks—a glorious testament to his fierce determination and conquering will.

Malakai's feeble hands connected with the worn wood of the door—really, couldn't they do something about the quality of timber on this ship? He pushed forward, eager to be welcomed back into the presence of the others with open arms and delighted smiles. Immediately, his senses were assaulted with the yelling of commands, the incessant whipping of wind across his face, and the relentless scent of salt. He grimaced against the onslaught of sounds and sensations, but was grateful to be free of his dank quarters, if only for a few hours. Malakai stepped further onto the deck, dragging himself to a quiet section undisturbed by a pirate ship's ruckus and chaos. Scanning, he looked for Kasper, but found only the hardened and weathered expressions of Captain Caliban's crew.

Malakai sighed and waited. He hadn't decided yet for what or whom, but he was confident he would know when the moment was right. Until then, he was content to lean against the raised cabin of the ship. His eyes trailed over the ship's occupants, and he wondered about their lives. What had happened that led them to a life of piracy? Or were they fulfilling a lifelong dream of pillaging on the high seas?

But Malakai had to be careful, though.

If his attention lingered too long on any one person, he was at risk of enduring another harrowing vision. One brought on by accident so soon after his last episode could be detrimental to his health. So, he kept his eyes drifting and dancing through the crew. Never focusing more than a minute or two on any particular individual. But, for some reason, he was powerless to stop his gaze from finding his brother's second-in-command, Finnley. Malakai had learned from his vision–the one that prompted this sick spell–that Finnley wasn't her given name, but rather one she had adopted when she fled from her former life. What he had glimpsed the other day only gave him an inkling into what had led her to the Umbra, but Malakai knew more lurked beneath her scarred exterior.

Malakai remained on the deck for another hour, possibly two, before the murmurs of the crew about their growling stomachs registered with him.

Food.

He had completely forgotten about his need for nourishment! He was far too focused on gleaning interesting details from his brother's crewmates to notice the hunger that steadily gnawed at his stomach.

That would have to be rectified.

Slipping back into the hull and exhaustion nagging at his bones, Malakai trodden on, past his room and down deeper into the belly of the ship—adamant about finding the origin of the somewhat appealing aroma of food. It didn't really matter *what* he found to eat at this point. He just needed to fill his angry stomach with *something* before he could crawl back into his uncomfortable, piddling bed. Then, he could continue to fight off the after-effects of the vision that still plagued him.

The warmth emanating from the galley wrapped around Malakai, soothing the weariness in his soul. The cook took pity on him, ladled a stew into a hollowed-out wooden bowl, and pushed it into his quivering hands. The cook also set down a cup of water, which Malakai drank greedily, unable to ignore his mouth's cracked and dry state any longer. Malakai had dined in the palace for close to two decades during his servitude, tasting delectable meals made by the finest chefs on this side of the continent, but nothing had ever tasted so good as the rainwater and soup that sat before him now. Malakai spooned the meaty liquid into his mouth, barely pausing long enough to breathe. The stew was gone much too quickly, and his stomach still grumbled audibly. With his newfound strength, he stood and approached the cook once more, his bowl held out sheepishly. By some miracle or lapse in character, the stalwart cook allowed Malakai to take a second bowl.

He slurped it down, though not nearly as fast as the first, choosing to savor the warm broth and tender–albeit somewhat bland–vegetables this time before returning the bowl and departing, intent on returning to his room. Fatigue still clung to his body, and it wouldn't do him any good to push his limits. A few hours of rest would be enough for him to recharge. Then, he could return to the world above tomorrow.

Perhaps Kasper would visit him during that time as well.

Malakai heaved a great sigh as he marked his door, pushed inside, and found the cabin undisturbed. Exactly as he had left it hours ago. He ambled to the bed and fell into it, unfettered by the flimsy mattress or the threadbare linens. Sleep claimed Malakai, swift and unchecked. He was glad for it, even if it brought visions of monsters, danger, and death.

* * * *

"I see a tremendous joy coming into your life——"

"Gold?"

A hint of a smile played on Malakai's lips as he shook his head. "No, something much more precious than gold."

"Jewels?" The boy asked.

The young man whose hand Malakai held squirmed, his eyes wide and innocent. He wasn't a day over sixteen, and Malakai had to wonder what he was doing aboard the Umbra. But he didn't pry. The young man had asked for his future to be read, not his past, so Malakai focused his energies on that. Malakai suppressed his chuckle and gently squeezed the boy's hands, drawing his focus back to the reading. The boy pressed his lips together and stilled himself, a slight blush coming over his neck and face.

"It's not jewels, either." Malakai closed his eyes. That part wasn't necessary, but it was easier to focus when he couldn't see everyone staring at him. Plus, it gave him an air of mystery.

Malakai blew out a breath. He saw a woman, her abdomen great with child. Blood, tears, and the cries of a new life emerging into the world.

The smile on Malakai's face widened as he opened his eyes. The young man stared at him intently as Malakai said, "There is to be a child."

All color and humor drained from the boy's face. A hand clapped the boy on the shoulder, and he jerked forward.

"Ha! I didn't think you had it in you, Sammy. Though I guess you'll hafta to go back for that poor lass." guffawed Finnley. The others gathered broke into laughter, but the boy–Sammy–had gone stone still.

Malakai leaned forward and gripped Sammy's shoulder tightly. There was a slight quiver in the boy's bottom lip, and Malakai almost felt bad for him.

"I'm not ready to be a father." he whispered.

"I know, Sammy," Malakai said gently, "which is why it is great news that you are not the father."

Sammy's brows bunched slightly. "But you said—"

"I know what I said, but I wasn't finished, it—"

Finnley interrupted, "Sammy, it's Hannah!"

Sammy whipped his head around, his mouth gaping like a fish. "I'm going to be an uncle?" He turned back to Malakai, who beamed at him, confirming his suspicion. Sammy flew to his feet and turned to face his fellow crewmates; Malakai was forgotten on the floor.

"I'm going to be an uncle!" he hollered from the top of his lungs. The rest of the crew embraced him and broke out a bawdy tune that had everyone joining in on the merriment. Everyone but Finnley, who had hung back while the others paraded up and down the deck, sharing the good news. Malakai stood, aware that his fortune-telling session had concluded. Finnley fell in step beside him, giving him pause. Her smile stretched the mangled tissue of her scar as she glanced at him.

Still smiling brightly, she turned her attention back to Malakai. "Hannah's nearly a decade older than Sammy. Practically raised him after their mother died when he was two. She's the only mother he's ever known." Malakai kept his gaze focused ahead, uneager to cause another episode by looking too long at Finnley. "She got married about five years ago and, of course, was expected to start having children right away. She already had Sammy, but her husband wanted children of their own." Finnley's voice had lost its edge. She had also dropped the thick accent she normally put on. Malakai had to assume she feigned it in order to appear lower-born to the rest of the crew, but she had no reason to perform for him. He had already seen through all of her guises the day of his vision.

"It was hard on her. On all of them after she lost that first one—"

"Yes, I–I saw that." Malakai said softly. He wasn't eager to relive the flashes of Sammy's past that had come to him without warning. Finnley shook her head; the auburn braid swayed with the movement. Tendrils of hair breezed around her face, making her look almost girlish—if it wasn't for the horrific scar.

"I keep forgetting you can see people's pasts." she chuckled, but there was no humor in her voice. Finnley turned and faced Malakai, still smiling, but all remnants of joy were gone. She held out her hands and said, "Read my fortune. Tell me what exciting adventures await me."

The bite in her tone told Malakai all he needed to know about what she really wanted. But even if that hadn't been the case, he had no desire to see more of what he brushed the surface of days ago. He didn't want to relive her trauma or better understand what drove her to change her name and become a pirate. Malakai took a step back and dared to look away from Finnley. He hoped Kasper or Lady Hera would walk by, giving him an excuse to escape Finnley.

But apparently, luck was not on his side this time.

Hands still out in sinister supplication, Finnley continued forward. She finally dropped the empty smile and allowed a sneer to find her lips. Malakai retreated further, his back knocking into the railing of the ship. He ventured a look over the edge to find the swirling blue-green sea beneath. Turning back, he found Finnley with her teeth bared not six inches from his throat.

"Leave my crew alone. We don't tempt fate here with readin' bones and stones. We certainly ain't gonna let no Seer go poking about in our minds knowing our fears only to exploit them."

Malakai had the good sense to stay quiet and give the barest of nods. Finnley remained in Malakai's face for a moment longer before stepping back. She brushed her hands across his chest, wiping away some invisible dirt or debris. Malakai flinched, not from fear of her harming him—though that wasn't out of the realm of possibility—but in fear of a vision overtaking him at her touch. Thankfully, whatever god or force gave Malakai his ability must have felt benevolent because nothing happened as her fingers slid over his chest.

"Good. 'Cause I would hate to have to throw the Capt'n's kin overboard for a simple misunderstanding." Finnley added, her tone light—playful, even—but the threat in her words was just as evident.

Malakai didn't let his surprise register on his face. He and Cal were identical twins, so people would note the commonalities in their appearances. But as far as he knew, Cal hadn't bothered to address their familial connection with the crew.

"Of course. I apologize for the disruption. It won't happen again."

"That's what I like to hear." Finnley's smile returned, bright and cheery—and in complete juxtaposition with the cruel disfigurement on her cheek. "Have a pleasant day."

Finnley tipped her hat in Malakai's direction and turned on her heel, weaving into the throng of the crew. In a paltry attempt to still his wildly beating heart, Malakai pressed a hand to his chest. His body was still weak from the vision, and he noted its lingering effects in every breath. He leaned against the rail for several minutes, calming himself and observing the crew. Against the railing of the Umbra, observing the crew, was where Malakai remained until Caliban stalked by—a storm personified.

Malakai extracted himself from the railing and, against his better judgment, followed after his brother, in need of a word with him. His dreams, more warnings than anything, still swirled in his mind. He hadn't been able to make sense of the fragments, but maybe Caliban would have some insight.

Caliban came to a stop at the helm of the ship, his gaze fixed on the horizon.

Swallowing down his apprehension, Malakai saddled up next to his twin.

Caliban spared him a momentary glance before returning his eyes to what lay beyond them. From the intensity of his stare, Malakai wondered if his brother didn't have some prophetic vision of his own.

"There's something we need to discuss."

Chapter Twenty Six

Sweat coated every inch of Brander's skin, sliding down in rivulets on his still-forming muscles. The linen material of his breeches was soaked with perspiration, and the dust that settled on his pants was turning to mud. There was no reprieve from the scorching sun, slowly baking the earth and searing the exposed skin of his shoulders, neck, and back.

Brander dared to raise his arm to wipe the sweat from his eyes as he squinted across the barren training yard. His arm shook violently from the minimal exertion, but after hours of running and training, the limits of what he was able to withstand had been reached—and then surpassed.

A small, weak part of him hoped he perished beneath the unrelenting sun and suffocating heat. The part of him that wished he had died that day in the village—that wished he hadn't been a coward that hid when the King's army terrorized his village. But he hadn't died, and instead marched hundreds of miles from the only home he had ever known. Until he arrived at this vast expanse of desert seemingly fixated on killing him.

Ironic.

Lowering his hand, Brander sighed, and stared at the other recruits. He wondered if they, too, despised what they were becoming. If they had to fight to keep their meager rations down at night when the memories of their families and friends being indiscriminately slaughtered in the name of conquest came rushing back. He pondered if the guilt that washed over him every time he got stronger or learned a new maneuver haunted the other boys in the same way.

They were all to be the soldiers of the man who had burned down their homes and stolen them away in the night. But there was nothing left of Brander's old life, so perhaps it was time to make the best of a terrible situation.

"Hariri! Get moving!" An officer bellowed at Brander.

Brander obeyed, grabbing up the sword he had stuck in the ground, wincing with the movement. He was still sore from the last beating he had received for helping one of the other boys when he had nearly given out from exhaustion. The King's army would suffer no weakness, and unfortunately, Brander had a stronger constitution than most. Brander stepped forward, but suddenly, the world listed sideways, and he tumbled toward the ground. He braced for the impact of the dry earth—

But it never came. He still had the sensation of falling.

Falling.

Falling.

Falling.

Brander jolted upright in his bed. He grimaced and flinched against the pain that clawed at his stomach and throbbed in his skull. Groaning, he fell back against his mattress, dust motes and straw flying up in response. Despite the pain behind his eyes, Brander kept them open, trying to understand where he was. Black, wooden boards hovered overhead. He had the sense he was moving, but he was clearly in a room of sorts.

Then the memories came flooding back.

The Princess, shadows and light, a ship, and sickness.

Was the Princess safe? Had one of the pirates or brothers tried to harm her? Had she been smart and stayed in her rooms? Had he prepared her adequately to be vigilant of the dangers? If something happened to her, it was squarely on his shoulders. Brander closed his eyes and groaned again, desperate for some relief from his sickness and his mind.

Beyond needing to get out of the room to check on the Princess, the space's tightness was also wearing on him. He had never done well with small rooms or enclosed spaces, and unfortunately, the pirate ship had both. Brander needed to see the Princess and ensure she was well. That was his top priority—which meant getting out of this room. He opened his eyes, set his jaw, and willed his body to move.

"Tsk-tsk-tsk," came from the foot of the bed. Brander's chest seized for a moment before his eyes focused. He recognized the figure staring back at him. He remembered being forced to consume some sort of antidote for the sickness, and then nothing. Just moments of pain between the nightmares that plagued him.

"My, my, my." they replied before rising and moving to come up beside Brander. He had the good sense to recoil away from the person. Their eyes roved over Brander before they nodded their head once and said, "Looks like yer finally feelin' better. But we best keep yous calm for a bit longer."

Brander started to scramble away.

He was done taking medicine.

He would rather be sick than continue to relive his youth. But the person reached out and grabbed his jaw. Either they were much stronger than they appeared or Brander was quite weak because they forced open his jaw and slipped a vial between his lips. He sputtered and gagged on the liquid, but he still swallowed more than he wished.

"There we are now." The pirate stood and smiled their silver and gold smile. "Sweet dreams!" They strode out of the room without another word. Brander's fury was palpable, but he was determined to get out of bed and get up on the deck. He had no idea how many days he had been unconscious, and he couldn't afford to spend any more time not performing his duty. The Princess had brought him to protect her, but he could not do that from his bed.

What if they reached their destination and Brander was still fighting his nightmares? He had spent far too much of his life regretting his choices and believing himself to be worthless, but this mission–this journey–was his chance at redemption. There was no way he was going to allow his weaknesses to stop him from fulfilling his purpose.

He would help the Princess save their country.

He rose on his elbows, but his head was already swimming with fuzziness—his grip on consciousness loosening. He tried to push through it–to hold on–but just as before, the tonic took him. It swept him under and deposited him back in his nightmares.

Chapter Twenty Seven

It had taken Kasper a full day to leave his cabin after his second bout with rum. He thought it might give him the courage to face Kai and Cal, or forget them altogether. But his feet failed him every time he decided to confront Cal or question Kai further. He stood in front of his door, hand on the latch for nearly two hours, frozen with indecision.

The incessant grumbling of his stomach was finally what pulled him from his paralysis. Somehow, he found his way to the galley and took whatever was offered. He wasn't sure he even tasted the food. It didn't matter, though, because Kai had lied to him. Had allowed him to believe the worst about Cal, never daring to contradict the narrative that Kasper wholeheartedly believed. The longer Kasper thought about what Kai had told him, the less devastated Kasper became. Instead, a pit of rage opened up in him, gnawing and hungry for recompense.

That unrelenting anger carried Kasper up the stairs without pausing in front of Kai's door, and deposited him on the deck. Kasper shouldn't have been surprised that Kai had deceived him. Of course, Kai would take advantage of Kasper's memory loss and use it to benefit himself. It made Kasper wonder about every moment of the last nine years.

Was any of it genuine?

Did Kai even love Kasper, or was it all a ruse to keep him quiet and compliant?

A part of Kasper urged him to see reason and not assume the worst of his brothers, but how could he not? Kai had outright lied for his own personal gain, manipulating and betraying him. Cal had just let it happen. If what Kai claimed was true and Cal had actually cared for Kasper when they lived at the palace, it must have been out of obligation. There was obviously no love lost at their estrangement.

The sea breeze ruffled his hair and caressed his skin, an apology and comfort for the years of falsehoods perpetuated by Kai. Kasper let his feet carry him across the deck with no particular destination in mind; he just needed open space. For too many years, Kasper had been forced to make himself small, cloistered in the shadow of Kai.

No more.

Kasper turned his face into the breeze that propelled the sails. He tossed a disparaging look at the canvas as it flapped ceaselessly against the air currents. He disliked their submission to the wind–how the sails were completely at the wind's mercy–and how they reminded him far too much of himself. A device to further the plans of others, never thought of beyond their usefulness. Shaking off his pity and closing his eyes, Kasper inhaled deeply.

Kasper decided then that it was time to reinvent himself. To no longer be known as Kai's companion or compliant little helper. He would forge his own identity, separate from his brothers. Perhaps he would try to hone his magic and use his crystals for healing, or become a jeweler. He opened his eyes and smiled at the horizon and its possibilities. He made that promise to himself, the sea, and whatever forces governed it.

That had been four days ago.

Four days of refusing to check on Kai, even as his anger banked and his guilt threatened to inch its way in. But Kasper had remained firm in his convictions. He hadn't spoken to or engaged with another, intent on keeping his promise to himself. He focused on his plans for his future and what he would do with his newfound freedom—but he also thought of Lady Hera.

Kasper was certain there was something between them, and he was desperate to know what it was. If she had known him from the palace, wouldn't she have said as much? Or maybe the attraction he felt for her led him to perceive he'd known her longer than he truly had. Either way, didn't he have the right to know if it was all one-sided?

But his thoughts—and his resolve—had come to a screeching halt when Kai emerged from the hull, his skin waxy and his eyes weak.

Kasper had almost gone to him.

He had nearly given in to the shame and guilt coating every inch of his skin. But the wind blew, nipping at Kasper's cheeks, reminding him of his vow. So, Kasper remained at the bow, refusing to go to his brother's aid. Kasper remained stalwart, even as Kai set up shop and curious crewmates ventured nearby. It had begun simple enough: reading people's palms and divining a few fortunes, but after the young man—Sammy—stood and proclaimed his good news, Kasper fought the smile that tugged at his lips.

The boy's eyes were alight with a fervor that Kai's clients normally exuded when their futures held good news. The boy and his fellow crewmates celebrated and hollered as they walked around the deck, in case anyone hadn't heard of his blessings. Kasper was powerless to stop his eyes from slipping to his brother, who stood bright-eyed and cheery next to Finnley. But Kasper noted the gleam in Finnley's eye, the unease and hatred that resided there. He had seen it enough in the last nine years to know where this encounter was headed.

His breath caught in his throat as the first mate turned on Kai, and his features shifted, coming to understand what Kasper had gleaned moments before. Kasper bared his teeth and clenched his fists. Kai was an adult, and he could more than fight his own battles. There was no reason that Kasper needed to intervene. Unable to watch the scene unfold before him, Kasper turned away.

Whatever love or loyalty Kasper held for his brother was quickly fraying his resolve to stay impartial.

Kasper urged his tight muscles to carry him away. Away from it all. He owed his brother nothing. Kai had lied to him repeatedly. Kasper gave his brother everything. He had sacrificed his innocence—his childhood and his soul–for him, and all he received in return were Kai's deception and excuses.

Kasper owed him nothing.

He murmured the words aloud as if they would better convince him of their truth. A mantra to keep him from protecting his brother. No, Kai was undeserving of Kasper's protection. He was capable of taking care of himself. Kasper paced back and forth along the ship's side, certain he would eventually wear a hole in the dark wooden planks, but he persisted nonetheless.

"Are you alright?"

Kasper halted, stopping dead in his tracks.

Lady Hera stood before him, a concerned crease forming between her brows. Her full mouth was pursed, and she hugged her arms over her chest. The dark red dress she wore fluttered in the breeze, and tendrils of her ebony hair floated about her face. Her eyes darted around Kasper, trepidation filling them as the moments passed. Kasper shook his head in an effort to relieve himself of his stupor. He aimed for an easy smile, but he knew the corners of his mouth didn't quite reach his eyes.

"I'm fine." Kasper should have left it at that, but the words continued to spill from his mouth for some reason. "I learned some, uh, distressing news and I'm still processing it, I guess."

Lady Hera's features softened, her mouth and eyes relaxing. Pity. She felt sorry for him. She took a step forward, her hand extended, but Kasper took one back.

Turning toward the railing, he braced his hands on it. "I'm fine, really." he assured, avoiding her sympathetic stare.

Lady Hera hesitated, but then dropped her hand and stepped back, nodding softly. Her gaze burned into him, and whatever male pride he had loathed the sensation.

Kasper cleared his throat, intending to change the subject.

"Where's your guard? Brander, was it?" Kasper allowed a sidelong glance at the Lady and noted the tightness to her features had returned. The pair's dynamic was still a mystery to him. Clearly, the guard cared for Lady Hera beyond what was expected of a hired sentry, but he was somehow positive that it wasn't romantic. The guard was at least two decades older than her, so perhaps the guard viewed himself as her father? Perhaps the man was of some true relation. Kasper had no real knowledge of the Lady, save for what little she had shared.

Obviously, Kasper wasn't privy to the specifics of either of their lives, but he had spent enough time reading people—to try and get them to receive a reading from Kai—and he knew Brander's devotion went beyond mere duty. He had nothing else to base his suspicions on save for that lingering—and nagging—sensation that he *knew* her.

"He's in his cabin. Not long after we boarded, he came down with a terrible case of seasickness."

The muscles in Kasper's face twitched with the effort of holding in his laughter. For all of the guard dog's bravado, he was taken down by the rocking of a ship. "I'm sorry to hear that." Kasper coughed, attempting to hide his laugh.

Lady Hera sent a pointed look in his direction. "Yes, your concern for him is overwhelming."

Kasper turned his palms outward. He tried and failed to fix his features. The sly smile on the Lady's face said that she wasn't buying it.

Another cough broke from Kasper's mouth, but his smile broke through. "I assure you that I am sincere in my sympathy. Being continually nauseous sounds positively horrific—" Kasper's laughter overtook him. He doubled over and clutched his side. Tears leaked at the corners of his eyes. It wasn't even that the guard's illness was *that* funny, but it had been so long since Kasper had laughed that he was helpless to contain it.

"You are utterly ridiculous." Lady Hera muttered and turned to walk away.

Kasper managed to catch his breath and reached for her. He grasped her hand. Her skin was smooth, her touch warm and inviting.

She paused, turning to face him.

Momentarily, he was taken aback by her beauty. Of course, he had thought she was beautiful when he first saw her and in every moment since, but there was something about the fierceness in her eyes, the determination and intelligence that gleamed there. The wind howled around them, but she was unmoved. Solid and steady in the face of whatever was thrown at her.

It was so *familiar*.

She blinked, and Kasper returned to the present, realizing that he was still holding her hand.

He should let go.

He should bid her farewell and return to his brooding, but her unrelenting gaze pinned him to the spot. Words were foreign to him, something he didn't have the capacity to form. Not when he was thrown back into the memory of the night he had killed that brute. The night she had hugged him and thanked him. The feel of her pressed against him was so *familiar* that it stole his breath.

Kasper peered harder into her features, desperate to glean anything from them. Something that would explain this *draw* he had to her against his better judgment. Her throat bobbed. Her breathing hitched, but she remained still. Not even bothering to dislodge the wisps of hair now caught in her eyelashes. Kasper's blood heated to an uncomfortable level—his mind racing. Something was linking them. A memory that Kasper was dangerously close to unearthing.

He stepped closer, less than a foot between them now. Kasper licked his lips and whispered, "How–How do I know you?"

It was more a plea than a question.

Lady Hera sucked in her bottom lip. Kasper's attention zeroed in on the action. It had finally healed enough that she didn't wince.

Though his palms were slick with sweat, he didn't dare release her hand, even as the wind picked up and the sun proceeded to disappear behind thick clouds. Shouts from the crew were swallowed up by the wind's howls as it tore through the ship, swaying and rocking it with more fervor.

Lady Hera's large brown eyes, the color of smoky quartz, glittered with an emotion that Kasper failed to name. Shadows passed over her delicate features. The high cheekbones and full lips—the sunlight utterly blotted out by the clouds above.

Perhaps a storm was brewing.

Her lips parted, but Kasper struggled to make out her words. The wind had turned deafening, and Kasper, against his desire, lifted his eyes from Lady Hera's face. The pleasant, warm feeling coursing through his blood stopped cold at the sight of the sky. Kasper's mouth went dry as his mind tried to make sense of it all.

Large, rolling black clouds hurtled toward them. It was unlike anything Kasper had ever seen. They consumed any bit of sunlight that dared to breach their surface. They moved with a sentience that chilled Kasper's blood. When he glanced toward the horizon, he saw nothing but inky blackness, swirling and thrashing.

They were headed directly into it.

Lady Hera twisted and cast her eyes upon the sky as well. Her hand, still gripping Kasper's, went slack, sweat collecting on their conjoined palms. As she turned back, Kasper met her gaze.

"Oh gods..." she said, her voice trailing over him.

Oh gods, indeed.

Kasper needed to find Cal, and despite his still simmering anger toward Kai, find him as well. Tightening his grip on Lady Hera's hand, Kasper pulled her along behind him.

"I'm taking you below deck." he yelled back to her.

A yank at his hand drew his attention.

"No!" She bellowed above the turret of wind. "I need to know what is happening."

216

Kasper debated for a heartbeat. Debated throwing her over his shoulder and forcing her down into the hull, but that fierceness and tenacity shone through once more. Groaning, he retook her hand, leading her to the front of the Umbra. She blinked, apparently surprised that he didn't put up more of a fight, and then flashed a brief smile.

They wound through the crew, who were pulling at ropes, drawing in the sails, and battening down the hatches. Anything not already secured was quickly being tied down, and what was previously latched was being reinforced. Kasper spared a glance ahead and nearly blanched at the sight. An inky wave of night was set to descend upon them—the sun vanishing, and flashes of lightning providing brief moments of illumination.

They likely only had minutes before it encompassed them entirely.

The wind pushed and grabbed at Kasper, urging him to shelter from the darkness beyond. He had to squint against it, tears obscuring his vision. He stumbled forward, still holding onto Lady Hera, when he finally spotted Cal at the ship's helm, staring into the obscured horizon. He was a speck of night, nearly blending in with the shadows roiling ahead of him.

Kasper ground his teeth as he fought against the wind, clamoring up the last few steps until he was able to drag Lady Hera around in front of him. Crewmates continued to scurry about, but Cal's gaze remained fixed on the horizon. Kai was nowhere to be seen. Maybe he had the sense to seek shelter, something that Kasper and Hera *should* be doing. Instead, he twisted, placed his back on the rail, and pulled Hera close to his chest in an attempt to shield her from the fierce wind. Kasper called to his brother, yelling out his name above the gales that howled around them. Cal flicked his gaze to Kasper—something wild and untethered dancing in his eyes.

"What is happening, Cal?" Kasper bellowed over the booms of thunder and thrashing sea.

Chilled seawater sprayed as white-capped waves crashed into the side of the ship, dousing Kasper's back. He flinched, eager to move away, but there was nowhere else to go as the ship careened with the force of the waves. The sunlight was still being gobbled up by the thick blanket of clouds that billowed and flashed with lightning.

"What is that?" Terror racked Kasper's body, and he was not too prideful to admit that his trembling was not entirely from the wind and the cold sea spray. Lady Hera had remained silent the entire way, but her gaze had turned stony—determined and composed.

At least one of them was holding it together.

Kasper and Rhea lifted their faces in unison as Cal laughed, the sound equally as terrifying as the storm. Standing with his hands braced against the helm, steering the Umbra directly into the swirling tempest before them, he looked every bit the Demon Prince that people feared. Cal turned to face Kasper, a feral grin spreading across his face, his eyes like glittering obsidian. Wicked and unholy delight gleamed in Cal's expression as he faced Kasper, his voice filling with lilting insanity as he answered.

"The Ether."

Part Two:
The Ether

Chapter Twenty Eight

The thrashing wind tore tears from Cal's eyes as he stared at the wave of darkness. It swirled and tumbled, as foreboding and ominous as the King's imperial army when it swept across the battlefield. A lightning bolt ripped through the inky mass, swiftly followed by a deafening crack of thunder.

Cal's very being was vibrating.

Whatever this storm–The Ether, as it was so affectionately called– was crafted from beckoned to Cal. It sang to him, the melody dark and lovely. *Like calls to like*, Kai would claim. And perhaps that was the case. Perhaps whatever had created The Ether had made Cal—and this was his homecoming.

Terrible, unholy things awaited them. Monsters and beasts that were only rumored to exist prowled these waters, lurking in the shadowy depths. There were very few accounts of what The Ether actually was—mostly stories from older fishermen who had wandered too close to the ever-brewing thunderheads. Cal briefly wondered if the Lady's book contained any information about The Ether. It would have been nice to view the text himself, but based on their last encounter, he knew that would never happen.

None of that mattered now. As far as he knew, no one had braved the swirling, cataclysmic storm and lived to tell the tale.

Cal intended to be the first.

He inhaled deeply. The sharp scent of ozone washed over him, a smile forming on his lips. Leaning forward, he gripped the wheel harder. Shadows writhed under his skin, clawing and scraping to be released—to join The Ether. Cal pushed against the urge, demanding them to stand down; he needed to remain in control.

All around him, the wood groaned and shuddered. Cal turned to find his brother and the Lady still crouched against the ship's side. Cal tried to suppress a smirk. They had a right to be unnerved. Terrified even, of what was coming. But the ship's helm was not the place to cower. Cal opened his mouth to tell them to take cover when a shout rang out above the blaring cacophony of The Ether.

"Cap'n!" hollered Finnley, her voice laced with the slightest hint of panic. Her auburn hair was a torrent around her face. She gripped her hat tight to her chest, lest The Ether claim it.

"Get below deck!" Cal roared over his shoulder at his brother and Lady Hera. He left them crouching at the helm, at the mercy of the storm, and headed for Finnley.

Finnley's teeth were bared as she fell in step beside Cal. His eyes roved over the deck, searching for whatever complication Finnley was preparing to alert him to.

"She can't take the wind, Captain. We need to change course and find another way around."

Cal shook his head. "No, we stay the course."

A voice called out, followed by an ear-splitting snap.

Cal whirled toward the noise—a piece of the running rigging that had come untethered. Finnley grabbed him, barely pulling him below the wild thrashing of the frayed rope before it connected with his head. Finnley cursed soundly and rose back to her feet, her lips curled in a snarl.

"You might have been made to weather this kind of storm, Captain, but The Umbra wasn't." She gestured to the crew, scrambling to regain control of the rigging and secure it in place again. A soul-shaking groan emanated from the mast. "She will be smashed to smithereens if we don't turn around, *right now*."

A muscle flexed in Cal's jaw. He hadn't told the crew, not even Finnley or Galen, what specifically they were after, only that they were headed to an island in search of treasure. It wasn't necessary. They had never questioned him before, and he wasn't in the mood to be doubted now. Turning, he braved the blazing rage that burned in Finnley's eyes. Her fire was half the reason he had picked her as his second-in-command.

"We stay the course. Tell the others." Cal demanded, leaving no room for an argument. He turned, intent on checking the rigging himself and preparing for any manner of beast or creature that dared to breach his ship.

"Caliban."

Cal stopped and looked at Finnley once more. Her hair whipped around her haggard face like ribbons of burnished gold.

"Please," she whispered.

Not once in their nine years had Finnley ever gone against his orders—nor had Cal ever heard her plead for anything. It gave him pause. He peered into her face and saw her plea in every line. Cal clenched his fists and slowly tore his gaze from Finnley's face. That was the only answer he'd give her. Her shoulders fell, but she lifted her chin.

"You'll be responsible for any who perish, Cal," Finnley spoke, her voice grave, as though she were already planning the funerals, "and you'll write the letters."

Cal rolled his shoulders and turned from his first mate.

"I always do." he muttered, barely above the storm.

Finnley lingered for a moment, a bastion in the tempest—though one of equal destruction brewed in her eyes. Then, she turned, aiming for the helm of the ship and shouting commands as she went.

Cal couldn't let the others' fears obstruct his plans. If some lives were lost while retrieving the treasure he had searched relentlessly for, then so be it. All would be right in the end if he could obtain the Alakhira.

Then he could fix everything.

Cal threw himself into helping his crew maintain control of the ship. The woman and his brother were nowhere to be seen. If they were smart, they would do as he bade and find cover below deck, but he didn't let their whereabouts distract him. Finnley would handle dispensing orders at the ship's helm. Cal would be of use elsewhere until he needed to take up his command.

What they were to face was unknown, and Cal wanted to be as hands-on as possible to limit the chances of something going wrong.

Seawater stung his eyes as he assisted the crew in repairing the rigging. He clung to the water-slick rope and yanked hard, his skin tearing across the course fibers. The cuts smarted sharply as the tang of his blood mingled with brine. Gritting his teeth, he held firm, keeping the line in place while the others bolted it down.

"Got it!" Galen shouted, and Cal released the rope, not sparing a second glance at his torn flesh. There would be time to assess wounds after they made it through The Ether.

If they made it through.

Cal shook his head. Thinking like that wouldn't do anyone any good. He stormed toward the quarterdeck where Finnley manned the wheel. Lightning flashed, and the wind screamed and squalled in Cal's ears—warning him to turn back before it was too late. But he knew that the Cave of Splendors resided beyond the storm—that the unnatural black tempest concealed the fabled Isle Oum. Fabled because no one had ever stepped foot on it, at least no one he had come in contact with or read about. That was precisely why Cal and Kai both believed it was the location of the Cave and all the treasures it concealed. Cal, again, clenched his teeth at the Lady's refusal to let him examine her tome. There was much that was unknown about the journey ahead, but he could at least prepare if he had that book.

He promised himself that he would get that book at any cost once they made it through The Ether.

The Umbra creaked and listed violently to the side, throwing him off-balance. Cal reached out to the railing, subtly using his shadows to steady himself. One of his crew–Sammy–came careening toward him, his footing lost against the sea-slicked boards. Sammy stumbled backward into the rail. Cal blindly reached out, his fingers hooking in the boy's collar and hauling him back from the churning depths below.

"Thank you, Captain." Sammy said breathlessly as Cal grabbed his shoulders and pushed him back toward the deck.

"Watch yourself, or I'll put you in the galley!" Cal called over the wind, setting off once again toward Finnley and the helm. He didn't linger to hear Sammy's retort, but he glimpsed the rigidness that set into the young boy's shoulders as he stormed away.

Finnley bellowed and raged against The Ether. Her arms quaked with the effort of keeping the wheel from spinning out of control. A string of curses that would make most men blush fell from her lips in quick succession. Pride swelled in his chest at the sight of her bravely battling the storm despite her earlier hesitation. He was confident she could handle herself, so he continued on. Cal was nearing the bow when an abrupt chill slithered down his spine, slowing his steps.

The wind still raged around him, but an unearthly silence filled Cal's mind. He came to a halt amid the Umbra, scanning for the source of his unease. Airy, feminine laughter trilled through his mind. Instantly, his gaze narrowed on the billowing waves of blond hair disappearing around the mast and rigging.

Cal froze.

It was impossible. He had banished her spirit. It couldn't be—

His very blood halted its flow through his body. His heart misfired—reluctant to believe that he was truly hearing *that* voice. But there was another bout of gentle laughter—his skepticism fading.

Finnley and The Ether were forgotten. Cal followed, his feet carried him while his eyes fixed on the blond curls that seemed just out of reach. He still had the impression of the rain and saltwater on his face. He felt the slide of his worn leather boots against the soaked deck, and he heard his crew calling for him. But Cal was helpless to pull his gaze from the woman evading him. For nearly a decade, her voice had haunted him—tormented him—but now she felt real.

It couldn't be *her*.

Cal rounded more rigging. He practically flung himself from rope to rope as he followed the apparition toward the ship's stern. The wind tore at his clothes, and the salt relentlessly ripped at his skin, but he had to know. He had to know if it was a dream, a delusion, or some nefarious trick of The Ether.

Blond hair bobbed and swayed in the breeze, wholly unaffected by the storm raging around them. Cal closed the distance in a haze—the scent of honeysuckle and amber reaching him before he could make the final steps toward her.

He took a sharp inhale.

She turned, and the devastating beauty in those eyes hit him square in the gut. All the air was stolen from his lungs. He clutched his chest as though that would stop the ice that was filling his veins.

"Soline." he breathed.

The blond turned, a secretive smile painted on her lips. She was exactly as he remembered. Full lips, a pert nose, and golden-blond curls cascading over slender shoulders.

It was really her.

She was on the Umbra—not as a wraith or apparition—but actually, physically with him.

"Caliban." she replied, her mouth twisted, inviting Cal to taste it. Soline stepped closer, her soft body pressing against his. Tipping her eyes up to him, she extended the invitation of her lips. Cal leaned forward, clenching his jaw against the desire that raged in his body.

This couldn't be real—this *wasn't* real. He knew that. But there was nothing his mind could tell him that would override his instincts—not when it came to her. Fingers curled around his bicep, tugging insistently.

"I've missed you, Caliban. Why did you leave me?"

Closing his eyes and sucking in his bottom lip, Cal said, "I'm so sorry, my love. I never wanted to leave you, but I had no choice."

Soline clicked her tongue. "All is well now, love. I have found a way to be together forever."

Cal licked his lips. Every moment they had shared together–every moment they had lost–burning through his mind like fire. "Hm?"

Soline slipped her hand down his arm. Her feather-light touch ignited his skin, and she laced her fingers between Cal's. Cal opened his eyes and didn't resist as Soline led him toward the stern. The wind quieted to a dull roar in his ears, and the seawater was no more than mist on his skin.

Soline climbed onto the edge of the ship, her bare feet peeking from the bottom of her pink dress as she lifted the hem to step onto the railing. The murky waters churned angrily beneath her, and she stood out starkly against the darkness. An internal, unearthly light emanated from her, intoxicating and hypnotic. Soline released his hand and lifted her head to the swirling void above. Even the clouds seemed to reach toward her. They were as captivated as he was, evident by the way they eddied and swayed in tantalizing currents. Turning, she beamed at him.

She was sunlight made flesh.

Her pearlescent smile gleamed as she spoke in her saccharine voice, "Do you love me, Caliban?"

"Of course I do." There was nothing and no one that he loved more. Everything he had done–everything he was going to do–was for her. She was his reason for living.

Soline took another step up, perching on the rain and sea-slicked railing. The dusty pink gown she wore and her golden locks billowed in the gentle breeze—wholly indifferent to The Ether.

"Do you trust me?"

Cal all but fell to his knees. "More than anything."

That demure smile returned to her lips, and she held out her hand again. "Then take my hand."

There was only a moment of hesitation.

A singular pause in Cal's thinking, perhaps the last of his sanity, begging him to look more closely at what beckoned him. The wind nipped at him, and the ship's rocking tugged at his balance. He dared to tear his gaze away from Soline and to the wall of darkness beyond, only faintly illuminated by the lanterns and the sporadic flash of lightning.

Something was not right.

"Caliban?"

Cal returned his gaze to Soline, her tentative tone drawing him back from his thoughts. Another bolt of lightning tore across the sky, casting light upon the crease that formed between her perfect brows and her downturned lips.

His heart shattered at the sight of it.

What was he waiting for?

Cal slid his hand into hers and delighted in the light that returned to her eyes. Hungry and lovely. He stepped onto the railing, the storm nagging at his clothes, but Soline remained unmoved.

"Everything we've ever wanted is down there." Soline said softly, her eyes dipping toward the water. "Join me, Caliban."

Gods, did he want to—to be with her and leave behind his wretchedness and rage. He wanted to be Soline's once more. He wanted to be seen again the way she had seen him. Someone worthy of love and care. He stared into Soline's crystalline eyes and saw the future they had promised each other. The future that had been stolen from him. She was the only reason why he was on the godsforsaken ship, the only reason he was risking the lives of his crew to retrieve the Alakhira.

It could all end here. His decade-long plans for vengeance, his rage, and his current path. All the pain and hurt and devastation would be behind him.

Without Soline...what was the point of continuing?

Cal lifted his foot. It was foolish, ardently so, but he couldn't lose her again. Whatever this was, a vision or trick or something more sinister—Cal didn't care. His boot was suspended over the water, his weight shifting—

Stars burst behind his eyes.

He stumbled, thankfully, toward the ship. His shoulder and side collided with the deck of the Umbra. Cal cradled his head, his fingers slipping over his soaked hair—the metallic tang of blood filled his nose, mingling with the ever-present scent of salt. Opening his eyes, he found the world tilted around him. His vision blurred as he struggled to make sense of his surroundings, and of the *thing* that now haunted the space that Soline had occupied only moments before.

"Cal!"

Someone yelled at him, their voice echoing through the haze that still fogged his senses. Sturdy hands gripped him beneath his arms, dragging him away from the edge of the ship, but the world was still cloaked in darkness and clouded by seawater, rain, and blood.

"Get up!"

But Cal couldn't move. Couldn't tear his eyes away from the creature slinking along the railing.

"Where's Soline?" Cal's tongue was heavy in his mouth, his words coming out thick and strangled.

"Soline? Who is Soline?"

"She was right there."

A figure came into view. Kasper's frantic face filled the still hazy space in front of Cal. "Never mind that. You gotta get up, Cal. Now."

Kasper's face disappeared once more, and the tugging behind Cal resumed. The deck vanished beneath him before his legs and feet smacked into it once more. He was vaguely aware that he was being dragged down the steps, his boots thudding against each stair as Kasper hauled him away from where he had stood with Soline.

Soline.

Where was Soline?

Cal's head lolled; all control of his faculties was lost to him. His body was utterly limp in Kasper's grasp. He was still sliding against the deck, unable to offer Kasper any assistance while the creature, with its fish-like features, peered at him intently.

Narrow slits for nostrils flared, and bulging yellow eyes dominated its face. Flat, seaweed-like hair sprouted from patches at the top of a grotesquely angular head, and beads of water dripped from the ends onto its jaunt collarbones. A flat chest covered in sickly shades of molted blue and gray mimicked the bloated underbelly of a rotten fish. Torn and frayed frills fluttered around gills that were situated along its scaled sides, the flesh there squelching with each shuddering exhale. Its body tapered at the waist, an elongated torso giving way to split trunk fins that flopped and secreted a slimy, milky white liquid that pooled beneath it on the deck.

Cal's heart stuttered in his chest, his body going hot and cold all over. The tingling of his senses was slowly giving way to numbness. But even as his body gave over to his exhaustion and trepidation, his mind did not. His eyes roamed over the monstrosity, trying and failing to make sense of it. Even without the throbbing in his head, he would have struggled to form words for how repulsive—how utterly repugnant—the beast before him was.

And he had almost gone with it, tipping over the edge of the Umbra and into the murky, unforgiving depths below.

Cal was comfortable with death. It had been his constant companion for longer than he could remember. He dealt with Death and its cruelty on a daily basis, constantly toeing the line between the living and the spirit worlds. He had manipulated the forces that governed the beyond, using his powers to breathe life back into swollen, stiff corpses.

Cal had never feared dying.

Until now.

He shuddered at how close he had come to facing his own demise—the acrid tang of his own fear flooding his mouth. He had been moments away from meeting the Forgotten, or whatever governed the world, and the realization rattled his very bones.

Cal had captained the Umbra through some of their world's most treacherous and uninhabitable waters. He had witnessed—and conquered—more unthinkable horrors than he bothered to count. People had died under his command and at his orders. He had held fast as the life faded from their eyes and they fell prey to the horrors of ocean beasts or rival crews who vied for the same riches Cal sought. They had fought and evaded the Royal Imperial Navy more times than he cared to remember.

He was no stranger to the impossible.

And yet, the monster before him was unlike anything Cal had ever seen in his nine years on the sea.

They were in The Ether now, and it seemed the nightmares had come to play.

Chapter Twenty Nine

"*Good, Your Highness. Now, take the total of ten and subtr—*"

The doors to the tutor's chambers swung open. There was only a moment of quiet before the wood doors collided with the limestone walls, and the King's footfalls echoed through the room.

The tutor gave a long-suffering sigh—the only sign of impertinence that Rhea had ever witnessed from the scholar—before he shut the arithmetic text in front of him. He turned his annoyed gaze on Rhea and said, "We will continue this lesson tomorrow. Or whenever His Majesty permits it."

Rhea smiled, eager to be done for the day, but even more eager to see her father. She buried her face in his tunic, which smelt vaguely of ash and salt, but she was simply pleased that he had finally returned home. He pulled back and surveyed her for a heartbeat before he said, "Come, daughter. I have something I want to show you."

The smile on Rhea's face widened as she slipped her hand into her father's. The tutor muttered something about all of her progress being lost due to the interruption, but she didn't care as she bounded out of the room.

The King wordlessly led them through the winding halls of the palace. He didn't pause or acknowledge the nobility they passed, even as many sought his attention. No, he was single-minded in his path, resolute to reach his destination before it was too late.

He only turned back to look at Rhea once, and she was nearly undone by the love and admiration that shone in his hazel eyes.

"Just a bit further, pet."

He tugged on her tiny hand, pulling her further down the hall, her short legs struggling to keep up. It had been so long since she had seen him. Nearly six moons had passed since he had left on his latest campaign, his never-ending pursuit of conquering the continent. But he had returned, and immediately sought out his only and beloved child. Her chest warmed, and her skin tingled at the realization—he had chosen her above his court and duties.

He loved her.

Rhea's breath came in quick pants. Her short, spindly legs struggled to keep pace with her father's long strides. A whimper escaped her lips as she nearly tumbled toward the ground. Strong hands appeared around her ribs and hauled her up with immense ease.

"I've got you, dear."

Rhea's father swung her up and over until her legs rested on either side of his head, and the world around her bobbed about with a new perspective. Rhea shrieked and hugged her father's head at the sudden change. An unfettered laugh echoed against the pristine halls, and her father's shoulders shook with the effort. The King and Rhea bounced along for another few minutes before the never-ending hall gave way to a mezzanine that overlooked the gardens spilling out from four levels below. Rhea's father slowed his pace, stopping at the railing.

Swallowing the lump in her throat, Rhea leaned back away from the edge. She closed her eyes and squeezed her father tightly. Her stomach flopped at the sight of the ground looming below. The King tilted his head up and lifted his hand to his daughter. He ran a soothing hand down her arm. The panic threatening to overwhelm her lessened marginally, but she didn't dare open her eyes.

"Look, pet. Look out over the palace walls, not down."

Rhea hesitated.

Fear clammed up her insides. She was too scared to chance it.

Her father reached up once more and squeezed gently. "Come on, dear. Just look."

Rhea wanted to. She took several breaths and counted, promising to open her eyes when she reached ten.

"Open your eyes, Rhea. Join me in viewing the stars. Then we can go to bed, and I'll read you a story." Guilt tore through Rhea. She wanted nothing more than to have this moment with her father. She only needed to conquer her fear and open her eyes. A simple, uncomplicated ask. One that, in comparison to the lessons and watchful eyes of the court, was easy.

Rhea took one more steadying breath and started to open her eyes. Her lashes fluttered and—

Pain shattered the world.

Rhea tumbled from her father's shoulders.

Down

Down

Down

Her shoulders slammed into the ground. Rhea winced and tried to breathe, but her lungs seized around the air already trapped in her chest. Finally, she opened her eyes—though it wasn't falling stars that greeted her, but rather a canvas of eternal and endless night.

Rhea gasped in the air and fought to get her bearings. Finnley stood over her, steel glinting in her hand. Her auburn hair was plastered to her face. The grim expression she wore and the scar along her cheek were made more severe by the lanterns and lightning flashing around them. Following Finnley's line of sight, she found a creature birthed from nightmares and the deep sea.

Oversized yellow eyes, serrated scales, and flapping gills glared at Finnley. A sinister smile graced its slimy lips.

"Get back, ye sea-beast!" Finnley called over the torrent of wind. She lunged toward the creature, and the thing hissed and slithered out of her reach. Finnley stepped forward, maneuvering herself between Rhea and the monster.

"Immune to my charms, it seems." crooned the monster. Its voice was like thousands speaking at once, overlapping one another. It was somehow melodious and horrible at the same time. Ancient and young, beautiful and terrible, enchanting and horrifying. The creature continued to slide along the deck on its two trunks for legs, its attention split between Rhea and Finnley.

Finnley laughed humorlessly. "There's nothing from me past I wish to see."

The sea beast tilted its vile head, seaweed-like strands of hair limply falling with the movement. Pus-colored eyes assessed and tracked Finnley with unnerving clarity.

The pain in Rhea's chest subsided enough for her to think more clearly. She scrambled backward, pushing herself away from Finnley and away from that...*thing*. The creature that was currently eyeing her with renewed interest. Its tongue, black as tar, slipped from its mouth and flickered—scenting the air.

"Oh, *yesss*. Your dreams were delicious." the creature hissed, that inky tongue oscillating as it continued to savor her scent. "My sisters will be so envious when I rip into your throat."

Rhea blanched and planted her hands, desperate to get her feet under her. She should have listened when Kasper told her to go below deck. She shouldn't have let her pride almost get her killed—again. Rhea dared to glance around. She was at the bow where Kasper had left her to go after Cal. She remembered staying low to the deck and trying to avoid the worst of the tumultuous waves and thrashing wind. When *something* had whispered to her. Had urged her to leave her hiding spot and come out on the deck.

And then...nothing.

She had been utterly transfixed. Hypnotized into a vision of her past. She remembered nothing else before the moment she'd opened her eyes, in pain and lying on the deck.

The creature's large, yellow eyes bore into Rhea, still watching her with amused, ravenous intent. Rhea staggered backward until she hit solid wood. Her tongue was a lead weight in her mouth, but she managed to get it working enough to sputter out a few words.

"Wh–what are you?" Rhea didn't even care that her voice shook.

The creature smiled, bearing needle-like teeth that gleamed like obsidian in the low light.

"We are children of the Forgotten, born of The Ether and the magic that shrouds the Isle. We sing the song of cherished dreams and deepest desires. We feed the deep with the blood of our prey. And your blood, my pretty, I shall savor feasting upon."

With that, it lunged for Rhea with bloodlust-filled eyes. Webbed hands that converged into curved talons ripped through the air, aiming for Rhea's unprotected throat. Rhea froze, unable to even lift her hands in defense.

Her eyes snapped closed.

She was too much of a coward to embrace her death. She let the happy memories, what few there were, pass through her mind. She thought of the brief moments in her childhood when she and her mother were all that mattered to her father—when he was willing to lay the world at their feet. Those thoughts washed over her as she waited for the pain of shredded flesh before the darkness–or whatever came after death–claimed her.

It never came.

There was the singing of metal through the wind—then the sickening thud of flesh being severed. Something warm and wet splashed across her face and hands, and she flinched against it, an uncontrollable whimper escaping her lips. The putrid stench of spoiled fish replaced the ever-present scent of the sea.

Rhea cracked open an eye.

Once again, the Umbra greeted her, still rocking in the endless storm of The Ether. Finnley stood a foot away, her eyes steely as she stared at the space in front of Rhea, her sword extended. Rhea dared to look down.

Laying at her feet was the severed corpse of the creature. Its eyes stared up at her, unseeing. A pungent, inky liquid—the monster's blood, presumably—leaked from the stump that was once its neck. Had Rhea been raised by a different man, had she not been privy to years of executions and beheadings, she might have balked at the sight. But, as fate would have it, she was woefully familiar with death and its remnants, so she merely lifted her head and met Finnley's stern gaze.

Finnley dropped the sword and wiped the creature's ichor on her pant leg. "Are ye alright?" she asked, assessing Rhea.

Rhea nodded quickly. She was fine—or at least she would pretend to be until the nightmare was over. If there *was* an end to it. In truth, she hadn't felt alright since they'd embarked on this idiotic quest. No matter what Rhea attempted to claim, she was useless. In less than two weeks, she had faced death thrice. And thrice, *someone else* had saved her.

A burden, that's all she was on this journey. Everyone would have been better off if she had just handed over *Legends of the Cave of Splendors* and paid the brothers to retrieve the treasure for her instead of insisting that she come along. Despite the chill of the seawater, heat burned in her face and she desperately wanted to turn away from Finnley's gaze.

But Finnley didn't give her the chance. She flipped the sword, catching the blade deftly, and held the hilt out to Rhea. "Take it, lass, there's more of these devils aboard."

Rhea swallowed the bile, burning her throat. A refusal hung on her lips, but that wasn't an option. With trembling fingers, she reached out and took the blade. She had no idea how to wield it, but she wasn't about to tell Finnley that. She also didn't want to dwell on what the creature said and the implications of its threats. Rhea needed to make herself busy to block out what the monster had unearthed.

The quaking in her hands persisted as she gripped the sword more tightly. The blade wasn't too heavy, and the grip was worn. She could do this.

She could do *something* other than wait around for someone else to save her. It was likely that she would fail miserably, but she was still a princess. She still had people to protect and a future to safeguard. An image to uphold and wrongs to rectify. Blowing out a shaky breath, she nodded her head once more. "I'll follow your lead."

Finnley nodded in return and stalked away from Rhea. The pure fire in the pirate's gait ignited something inside Rhea's chest.

"Let's go take the Umbra back."

Chapter Thirty

Thick, malodorous blood sprayed across the side of the Umbra as Cal cut down another creature. Sirens, Cal suspected. Tales of them had been recorded, but, like many of the stories surrounding The Ether and the Caves of Splendors, they were varied and conflicting. One thing was certain——these sirens were bewitching with their songs.

But it was hard to enrapture someone if the creatures didn't have a head.

A sickeningly satisfying thud echoed in Cal's ears as the siren's head tumbled to the deck. The monster's black blood coated his hands and dripped from his sword. It mingled with the sea and rain water splattering and splashing upon the black boards of the Umbra. He swung around to find another creature slithering toward him, its teeth bared in a duplicitous smile. Its tongue slipped through its moss green, needle-like teeth and flicked in the air.

"I smell the magic in your blood, human. So similar to the Master's. It will be a delicacy to sip the marrow from your bones."

Cal didn't let the image of the siren feasting on him shake his resolve. Lifting his sword again, Cal ignored the blood on his skin. His own had clotted and began crusting over on the side of his face. His shoulder gave a bark of pain, but he disregarded it. He eyed the curved talons that tipped the siren's three fingers. He had learned the hard way how sharp they were. If it hadn't been for Kasper guarding his back, he likely would have been gutted minutes ago. Whatever magic or ability the sirens possessed still rang in Cal's ears, and it took nearly all of his effort not to succumb once another began their haunting tune.

"Come and get it." Cal taunted, flexing his fingers.

The creature flashed its teeth and lunged, claws aiming for Cal's face. Gritting his teeth, Cal sidestepped the attack. The air beside his head hissed as the siren's talons shredded it. It growled and whirled, and slashed out again.

Fool, thought Cal. As he stepped back and brought his sword down.

A howl of pain and frustration echoed in Cal's ears as his blade separated muscle and tendon. Bone snapped, and blood sprayed from the stump of the siren's arm. The monster careened backward, spewing what Cal assumed were profanities in its native tongue.

Cal laughed harshly and said, "I'm sorry, I don't speak fish."

"Demon." the siren hissed.

Cal flashed a wicked smile. "Now, *that* I understand."

He lurched forward and finished the job. Another head fell and thudded to the deck. The cutlass blade sang as Cal whirled from his latest conquest. Everywhere he looked, more and more of the sirens–and other nightmarish creatures–crawled over the sides of the Umbra and slunk on the deck. Cutting them down one at a time wasn't working. Again, he wished he had the Lady's godsforsaken book. Even if there was only an outside chance that it had some information on the creatures, well, that was better than nothing. But no, Cal had let his anger get the best of him, and now he was steadily losing his crew and ship to the monsters.

There were too many, and some of Cal's crew had *already vanished.* He needed to employ more than steel. Cursing his choices, Finnley's words came rushing back to him. If he somehow made it through the fight, what would be left of his crew?

He had condemned them to this death.

"Cal, look out!" Kasper shouted somewhere to Cal's left. He turned and raised his blade just in time to block the slash of talons. Sparks skittered down his sword. Large, leering eyes, ravenous and full of rage, hovered inches from Cal's face.

A relentless, ageless, and endless hunger swirled in the siren's eyes. Its skin was slick from the sea, and some sort of mucus the creature produced. The siren reeked nearly as bad as it did when its blood was spilled. It gnashed its needle-like teeth and lunged again—desperate to sink its teeth into Cal's flesh. He didn't want to ponder too long about the other siren's words. That his magic was reminiscent of the *Master's*—whoever that was.

Cal had never met any other magic wielder who commanded shadows and communed with the dead. There were still those who worshiped the Forgotten—though the gods' individual names had been lost to the centuries—and believed magic was a gift from them. But Cal had never put much stock into that theory. He had always chalked his particular abilities up to being born under a double eclipse, but what if it was something else?

Cal's focus slipped—his strength wavered. The siren pounced on the momentary weakness and surged forward, knocking Cal to the ground. His sword clattered to the deck, out of reach, and his hope vanished with it. He tumbled with the siren to the deck. The monster was a whirlwind of talons and teeth, all looking to rip him apart. Cal summoned the reserves of his strength and rolled the siren. He pushed, knocking the beast onto his back and pinning it beneath him.

The siren lifted its head and hissed, but Cal didn't budge. He slammed his forearm into its neck, choking out its gasping breath. His sword was lost in the struggle, but Cal was not without his options. His fingers deftly reached for the dagger concealed at his side and grabbed for it—

Suddenly, the world shifted, and pain seared through his ribs as his own blade was jammed into his side.

Serpentine hissing resounded in his ears as he was thrown from the siren he had pinned beneath him. His own weightlessness made his stomach flop, but the sensation was quickly replaced with blinding pain. He had only a heartbeat to register where he was hurtling to before he crashed into the side of the Umbra.

A different siren, this one bigger and covered in mostly green scales, threw itself at Cal.

Stars burst in Cal's vision, and he blinked furiously to clear them away. Instinctively, he threw out his hand, dredging up the magic that slumbered in his veins. His blood loss, disorientation, and fatigue were working against him.

In the nine years he had been aboard the Umbra, he had never used his magic openly. Necromancy and shadow-work were illegal—the penalty for using them was death. Beyond that, pirates tended to be distrustful of magic wielders. Only Finnley and Galen knew of his abilities; even that reveal had not been voluntary. No, he had gone to great lengths to keep his magic hidden lest the crew mutiny—but he was running out of options now. He was also unsure how his powers would react in The Ether. Would his magic be effective at fighting off the monsters, or if it would be a beacon for the creatures? At least if they were drawn to him, then he might spare the crew. There would be no going back once he revealed what coursed through his veins. If he didn't do *something*, there wouldn't be anyone left to despise him anyway.

Cal didn't spare another thought as he rallied his magic. It arced out from his body with no form or grace. A blind burst of desire born from a desperate and intense need–no, *want*–to live. The siren flew backward, flailing as it plummeted over the ship's edge, returning to the churning water below. Cal rose on unsteady feet and ripped the dagger free from his side. Pain bleated from his ribs, but he ignored it.

The other siren still hadn't recovered, and Cal wouldn't allow it the chance. He angled the dagger for the space above where he assumed its heart resided. He dropped down, plunging the knife–sinking it to the hilt. Bone cracked, and cartilage separated. The siren's eyes went wide, and it gasped again—for the last time. Its dark blood leaked and oozed from the fatal wound. Spasms wracked its body, but Cal was unrelenting. He pressed harder and twisted, using his flagging strength to end the miserable monster. Its oversized, yellow eyes rolled back in its head, the fight gone from its worthless body.

For good measure, he twisted the knife once more.

His lungs burned with the exertion. He had lost too much blood and had wasted so much energy fighting these things in hand-to-hand combat. He wouldn't survive this battle if he didn't use his magic— none of them would. Yanking his dagger free, Cal stood. He wiped the beast's blood on his pants and took one heartbeat to gather himself. But there was no time to relish in his victory as another shout rang out from his left. Cal whirled to find a siren with its dagger-sharp teeth clamped around one of his crew's necks. His blood froze for a heartbeat.

Too long.

"No!" Cal flung out a hand, his shadows darting forth. The darkness speared toward the monster and pierced through its scaled hide. The siren's jaw slackened around the man's neck as it reared back and let out a bone-shattering roar.

The siren fell back, dropping the man, and slumped to the ship.

Dead.

Cal willed his legs to work, to move him closer to his fallen sailor, but the damage had been done. His throat burned, and his eyes stung as he stood there, The Ether raging mercilessly.

The man twitched and choked. Deep gashes, glistening red with the blood pouring from his neck. Cal fell to his knees and pressed his hands against the wounds, a futile effort to staunch the bleeding. The man– Alby–grabbed for his own throat, his eyes wide and frantic with the fear of what hovered just beyond.

"Greet the darkness with courage, Alby." Cal whispered, certain his words were stolen by the wind and thunder. But Alby's eyes stopped wandering. They settled on Cal's face, and his nails ceased digging into Cal's hands. "I will be with you all the way."

Cal commanded his shadows to settle over Alby, giving him an easier path into what awaited beyond this world. Alby's blood flow slowed. His chest eased its pace at which it rose and fell. Cal's heart hammered in his chest, and fingers twitched with his utter uselessness. This was his fault. He should have heeded Finnley's words. He should have—

The terror in Alby's eyes lessened, and the stiffness of his body gave way. Cal moved his hand from Alby's throat and gripped his hand instead. "I'll see you on the other side," Cal said softly, as the light receded from Alby's eyes and his body fell slack.

A singular moment of mourning was all Cal allowed himself. One heartbeat of anguish for his fallen crew member—one breath of rage for Alby's death.

Cal folded Alby's hands over his chest and closed his eyes. Collecting his forgotten sword, Cal stood, surveying what other loss of life the Umbra may suffer before reaching their destination. There were more screams and shouts. The metallic tang of human blood mixed with the reek of the monsters and the ceaseless brine. The sharp scent of the ozone burning as lightning tore through the turbulent air made it worse.

Cal rolled his shoulders.

He had wasted enough time trying to be honorable, but they were beyond that. Exhaling, Cal set about clearing his ship of the demons that dared to haunt and wreak havoc upon it. The Ether and its creatures thought themselves the worst things imaginable—the type of monstrosities that grown men quaked before, or soiled themselves at the mere thought of encountering them. But Cal was a monster and a nightmare in his own right.

It was time he unleashed himself on the world.

Chapter Thirty One

hea was no longer able to distinguish between blood and water. The world beyond the end of her trembling sword and the spasming hand that gripped it was obscured. Her arms, stomach, and legs burned with the effort of warding off the monsters that continued to pour over the edges of the ship. More of the same kind of beast that enraptured Rhea earlier, but others, too. Beings crafted from craggy rocks and seawater. Others were more fish-like in their appearance, but still possessed humanoid features.

Rhea was a coward.

Every muscle in her body contracted, hungry for fresh air and a reprieve from the waking nightmare, but neither was to be found. Rhea flinched every time something slithered past her hiding place among the crates and barrels. Inching further between them, she prayed to the Forgotten that she went unnoticed. She was a fool, a weakling, and stupid. So very, very, *very* stupid for thinking she could find Izor's Lamp. She should have listened to her father. She should have stayed in the palace. She should have—

A scream pulled Rhea from her spiral. It was cut off in a strangled cry and choking gasp, quickly replaced by the satisfied snarls of one of the beasts. Rhea pressed further against the crates and ropes that concealed her from view. She tucked her sword against her legs. It clung to the wet fabric of her dress, the cool metal biting into her flesh beneath the soaked material.

She shivered so hard that her teeth clacked against one another. Her skin prickled with cold and fear as the wind continued to squall, and the sails snapped in the ferocity of the storm. She prayed to the Forgotten gods—if there even were any. Given the nightmare she was currently living in, she wasn't sure they had ever existed, yet she prayed anyway. Begging them to listen, hoping they would soon be out of The Ether, or that Cal and the rest of the crew would rid the ship of the monsters.

How would she face the others who hadn't cowered if she survived this? They hadn't held their breath when fins and scaled trunks slithered by. Rhea was heir to a mighty, indomitable throne, yet here she sat, huddled against the crates in an effort to go unseen. This memory would haunt her forever. It would creep back into her mind when she wondered if she was truly as strong and capable as she had convinced herself she was. Gritting her teeth, she blew out a shaky breath. Rhea would not be timid and fearful. She would not allow others to suffer—to bear the cost—while she sat idly by, waiting to claim victory.

She would not be her father.

Rhea pressed her lips together. Slowly, she unfurled her stiff, waterlogged limbs. Reaching out with her left hand, she pushed aside the thick ropes obscuring her view of the ship beyond, and rose on unsteady legs. Her fingers were swollen and tight from gripping the sword, the hilt slick with water. She had no plan, no training on how to wield a blade or otherwise. The King had made sure of that. Now, that deficit was likely going to get her killed—but she'd rather die trying to save the people aboard the Umbra than hiding away.

The dark world beyond her hiding place greeted her with its gnashing teeth of lightning and screams of ferocious wind. It ripped and clawed at her, pulling free her hair and sending her tumbling, even as she fought to remain upright. Rhea struggled to make out her surroundings in the dim light of the swaying lanterns and the sporadic flickering of lightning across the dark expanse of sky and sea. Finnley was nowhere to be found, nor was Cal or Kasper. Shouts, the clash of metal, and the rendering of flesh rang out from the stern of the ship.

Rhea swallowed and urged her legs forward. She needed to help them. What if Finnley or one of the men had fallen under the spell of the monsters? What if they had gone overboard, putting the entire quest in jeopardy?

Another step, aided by the wind insisting she join the fight. She continued forward until a voice molded from broken glass and smoke rang out, "Ah, the Great Masters have granted us a plaything."

Rhea froze. Not even the persistent wind moved her as she twisted to look behind her.

A nightmare.

That's what loomed behind her. It was unnaturally tall, towering at least two feet over Rhea. It had long, spindly arms covered in molten skin in varying shades of yellow, gray, and green. There was no fabric on its body to hide the bones that protruded from its emaciated figure as if it had never eaten—never know what it meant to be sated. A long tongue pocked with small circular discs, terrifyingly similar to that of an octopus, pushed through the cracked and jagged stumps of teeth that lined its too-wide mouth. Long, bony fingers, tipped with claws that glistened a sickly shade of green, curled and flexed in anticipation of the meal it had ensnared. It was all lean muscle and sinew as it leered at Rhea, a soulless, depthless gaze that Rhea felt traveling the length of her body. Its entire appearance was only made more horrific by the eyes that Rhea finally glimpsed.

Orbs, as white as porcelain, stared at her. They swirled like smoke trapped in glass, but Rhea knew innately that the creature saw as well as any other.

Its tentacle tongue continued exploring the air between them. Bits of mold and moss fell away from its broken teeth, and Rhea fought the acid that burned in her throat. Rhea clamped down on her icy fear as it writhed within her, begging and pleading for her to hide once more. But it wouldn't matter where she went now. This creature would hunt and haunt her until one of them drew their last breath.

Rhea lifted her chin.

She would be the one to walk away from this encounter.

She took a steadying breath and summoned what little courage she had mustered. She ignored the putrid smell emanating from the monster before her. If this encounter was the price of saving her Kingdom and her people, she would face it. Arms fatigued, she raised the sword at the ready, unsure of her grip or stance. Oh, how she wished she had been more insistent that she learn how to defend herself. But that remained her father's last barrier, the last hindrance that he would not allow her to overcome. Rhea had only once allowed herself to consider why her father denied her training, and the conclusion she had come to wasn't pleasant.

For if she could wield a blade with efficiency and prowess, then what was to stop her from slitting his throat?

The creature smiled wider and garbled, "Your bravery is admirable. Foolish, but admirable."

Rhea refused to let its words hit home. She wouldn't give them an inch. Not as she lunged forward and prayed to every god that would listen that she hadn't just signed her own death certificate.

The creature was quick—even on its emaciated appearing legs—moving deftly around Rhea. Rhea spun, keeping the beast in front of her. She angled the sword at the monster's chest, even as her sopping skirts tangled around her legs. She lifted her other hand to support the sword. It wasn't large enough to warrant needing two hands, but it felt too heavy, too cumbersome in her hands for her to wield correctly. Her muscles, weak and pitiable, protested every movement, no matter how miniscule. Already, a slight tremble was working its way through her forearms—her wrists screamed with the effort of holding the blade aloft. Blood—from the exertion of her lungs—coated her tongue, sending a wave of nausea through her. And though she knew nothing of the proper stance, she knew her's was certainly wrong.

The creature loosed a rasping laugh as Rhea's arms dipped, the end of the sword drooping with it.

"This will be quicker than I thought."

Righteous indignation burned through Rhea. In the creature's laugh and cruel smile, she heard the jeering of the court. She saw the callousness of her father's malicious gaze. She saw every nobleman and councilman who doubted her ability to be anything other than an ornament—a pawn to be married off and controlled.

She was *not* a means to an end.

Rhea dug deep within herself, looking for the girl who defied her father. The one that studied politics and strategy against his commands. The one that took the zealous beatings he doled out when the mood hit him. That girl was forged in the fires of rage and wrath, and she would not die at this monster's hand. Taking a deep breath, Rhea stabilized herself. She knew nothing of swordplay, but, like everyone in her life, this creature underestimated her—that was her advantage.

The quiver in her arm deepened. The exhaustion and fear she held at bay shone through in her features. Her eyes fluttered, and she staggered, the wind aiding her along.

The creature's tentacle tongue flicked out in anticipation.

"Tasty indeed," the monster said as it stepped closer. Rhea backed up, keenly aware of the crates behind her. They continued, the monster closing the distance and Rhea becoming more and more distraught. Her eyes flitted back and forth as she tried to escape the monster. Coarse ropes and crates brushed against her back—the end of the line. The creature was close enough that its rancid breath warmed her cheeks, so at odds with the frigid rain that assaulted her.

Rhea focused on her pulse, using it to steady herself. The plan in her mind was clear—her one reckless chance at escaping this creature.

The tentacle tongue pulsed out, foamy saliva dripping from its suction. A world forged from mist and smoke swirled in the monster's eyes as he leaned closer and hissed, "Let us have a taste."

Its tongue flicked out toward her face—

Rhea launched into action. Lifting the sword, she swiped for the creature. She shoved it forward, knocking it off balance. The monster hissed and screamed as Rhea's blade made contact with flesh—cutting clean through *something*. Another terrible scream skittered along her bones as something heavy, wet, and writhing flopped to the deck. Rhea didn't look to see, but her mind knew what was convulsing on the floor.

"Yuve shregbs," the creature sputtered, its words unintelligible. Green blood oozed from the wriggling stump that had once been its tongue. Rhea didn't try to stop the smile of satisfaction that pulsed through her at the small triumph.

The creature launched toward her wildly—glistening green claws aimed at her neck. Rhea's body reacted without thought, and she ducked beneath it.

Not low enough.

White-hot fire burned along her skin where the monster grazed her with its claws.

Rhea heaved at the wave of nausea knocking into her. Whether it was from the pain or a reaction to whatever coated the beast's talons, she didn't know. And she wasn't sure it mattered as her vision doubled and slanted. If it was poison, she likely only had minutes before she went unconscious, or worse.

She lifted the sword once more, but her fingers splayed inexplicably. The sword clattered to the ground, and a horrific trembling overtook her muscles. Her spine and neck snapped straight, and her mind ached and pounded like her father's war drums. The creature prowled toward her, lifting its arms. Rhea's arms raised in response, and her feet rose from the deck. More pain burst in her shoulder and shot down her arm—stretching her—

A guttural, primal scream tore from her throat.

The creature's smile widened.

Rhea was helpless. Hot tears streaked down her face, mingling with seawater. Whatever magic or wickedness this monster possessed allowed it to control a person if its poison infected them. Green blood still seeped from the creature's mouth, leaking down his face and neck, but it didn't seem to mind anymore. It tilted its head and regarded Rhea with preternatural interest. She closed her eyes, no longer caring if it made her a coward.

She didn't want to see the delight dancing in the mist that churned in the creature's eyes as it beheld its next meal.

Rhea prayed that the poison would kill her before the beast fed on her. From the sluggishness of her pulse, she figured there was a good chance of that. A thick fog was settling over her mind, making it harder and harder to remember why she was ever fighting in the first place. Why she had ever left her home and breached The Ether. She waited for more slashes to her skin or the slimy sensation of its sinewy fingers on her—

"Hera!" A voice cut through the gloom and despair, settling into the space between Rhea's slowing heartbeats. Her mind turned over, working to place the voice. It tugged at a memory in her mind, but she was *so* tired.

So very tired.

A terrible cry–cut short–rang out in front of Rhea. She opened her eyes. When had she shut them? *Why* had she?

She was weightless for a moment—

Stars exploded in her vision. Blinding pain followed as her head smacked into the deck, and her full weight came crashing down.

Down.

Down.

Down.

She was always falling.

More pain flashed in her temple—

But it was nothing compared to the wildfire burning in her veins. Heat licked and worked hard to stop the insistent beating of her heart.

A face came into view, hazy but familiar.

Large, worried honey-brown eyes peered down at her. Calloused hands slipped under her body and lifted her as though she was made of nothing but shadows and stars. His anguish was so vivid–so visceral–that she wondered if it was her hollowness reflecting back at her, or if he was truly this devastated by her impending demise—but who cared that much about her?

The rigid set of his jaw and the impertinence in his brow finally came into focus.

"Caliban," she said sleepily, her trepidation floating away like dust. Despite their physical similarities, she knew it wasn't Kai or Kasper.

It had only ever been Cal for her.

Black spots danced in her vision. Her eyes moved of their own accord, rolling away, but then she was shaken, drawing her attention back to Cal.

"Stay with me, Hera. I've got you now. I'm here." The desperation in his voice would have been concerning if the words hadn't made warmth spread through Rhea's chest. A warmth so different from the fire still burning in her limbs—gnawing away at her mind and soul.

A smile formed on Rhea's lips. Through the veil of death that loomed so close, she whispered, "I always knew you'd come back for me."

The stormy sky above finally stopped thrashing and flickering with lightning, The Ether ceasing its destruction. Rhea relinquished her tenuous hold on consciousness, succumbing to the comforting darkness that awaited her.

Chapter Thirty Two

Cal thought he knew terror.

Having trafficked in it for nearly his whole life—torturing men the King claimed to be spies, raising the dead just to suck the life back out of them again, losing Soline and then condemning her to a half-life existence—he thought he understood what it meant to regret one's choices.

Then he saw Hera's pale, prostrate form levitating in the air above the deck. Suspended and stretched—her body threatening to splinter, just like Cal's soul.

All other thoughts eddied from Cal's mind. His body moved on instinct. He thrust and sliced, the head of the siren he engaged falling to the wayside, but he was gone before it thunked to the ground. He leapt over corpses and carcasses. He saw nothing but her and the fright that was quickly becoming acceptance etched into her face.

"Hera!" he bellowed, his strides rapidly eating up the distance between them. But not fast enough.

Not nearly fast enough.

Magic was not an option. He was too depleted and erratic to trust himself not to accidentally strike Hera. Steel would have to do.

The creature, a horrid, humanoid figure made of leathery skin and bones, was transfixed—and distracted.

Gripping his sword, he vaulted over turned-over barrels and bodies. He planted his foot on the deck and raised his sword. Every ounce of strength he had rained down on the creature.

The creature turned just in time to see Cal's blade, the metal reflecting in its clouded eyes. It screamed, and—

Hera crashed into the deck, limp and nearly lifeless.

Dropping his sword, he fell to his knees and gathered her into his arms. Her head lolled to the side, her face so pale that her freckles and the flecks of blood dotting her cheeks were obscene.

Her body spasmed and trembled. It wasn't from the chill of the rain. He frantically grasped at her, pulling her sagging form into his chest. A soft smile tugged at her lips. Her eyes remained vacant, her gaze already far away.

"Caliban."

Cal froze.

He'd never heard her use his full name—wasn't even sure if she knew it. But there it was, passing through her wan lips—for the last time if he didn't *do* something. His pulse roared in his body, making it hard to make sense of anything else, but he forced himself to stay focused—even as everything in him screamed to save her.

Her fragile grasp on consciousness faded, her eyes rolling back into her head, and her lashes fluttering closed. He gave her body a solid shake, his trembling hand grasping at her face, forcing her eyes back to him.

"Stay with me, Hera. I've got you now. I'm here." he said, his voice shaking slightly as he scanned her for injuries. His eyes snagged on the torn fabric of her dress and the deep gash along her bicep. The injury alone—even with blood loss—was not enough to kill her, but the sticky green poison coating it certainly was.

Cal couldn't breathe.

He couldn't tear his eyes away from the sickly, oozing gash. Horror blasted through him as the skin around the laceration bloomed with decay, turning to mottled black, purple, and gray.

He couldn't fight this. He was one of the most formidable magic wielders on the continent, but his shadows had no power against whatever potent venom coursed through Hera's veins. Even his necromancy couldn't save her. The Alakhira was necessary to keep her on this side of death. His fingers trailed over her skin as panic and bile rose in the back of his throat.

He couldn't fight this.

He couldn't save her.

Hera made a breathy noise, so close to a laugh that it drew Cal's attention back to her face for a moment. His heart ached, threatening to split in half at the soft smile still plastered onto her lips. Perpetually stubborn, that defiance holding out against death—smiling in its presence—even as the color continued to drain from her face. Her pallid figure was in stark contrast against the black fabric of his clothing, her usual warmth completely depleted.

"I always knew you'd come back for me."

Cal's heart finished splintering.

It rented in two and bled out.

A tide of darkness and desperation engulfed him, and Cal lifted his eyes to the cursed heavens and screamed.

And screamed.

And screamed.

The storm—The Ether—halted.

Cal panted. His thoughts raced in time with his panicked heart. Because Hera was dying. *Hera* was dying.

Death perched nearby, patiently waiting, and the only thing holding it at bay was Cal's magic. It pulsed around him, ebbing out and out and out until there was nothing but blackness—nothing but pain.

Never had he reached this depth of his power before, he didn't even know it was possible to delve so deep within his darkness, and it was killing him—it was killing Cal. Burning through him. Consuming him. Threatening to detonate—to turn his body to ash and dust and take out the entirety of The Ether with him. But if he stopped, if he relented, Hera would die.

His shadows throbbed and thrummed.

A shield formed around them so strong that not even the Forgotten—or whatever existed in their world—could dare breach it.

"Give her to me, Cal."

Cal whirled, the action more searing and demanding than he thought possible. Kasper stood there, arms outstretched, his face contorted and pleading.

Cal couldn't release her.

No. He wouldn't release her. To give her up meant conceding to death and, for whatever unknown reason, Cal didn't think he would survive her perishing. His magic continued to surge around them, continued to take and take and take—from him. Drawing on his own life force—a substitution for his own. Magic demanded balance. A life for a life.

There was no end—no reprieve or rest for him.

Then someone, or something, latched onto Cal's shoulders. It jerked him, hauling him back from the precipice he was so willingly hurtling toward.

"Let him take her, Caliban. He can help her. Your crew needs you to lead them—we need you." Kai said from behind him. Cal resisted. He moved to throw off Kai's touch, but Kasper reached up to his own neck, removed something—a gem strung on a cord—and slipped it over Cal's head.

Kasper's power, faint in comparison to the thundering of Cal's magic, hummed and glowed in the red-orange stone. Tiger's eye. Grounding, protection, healing. All things Cal needed, but they wouldn't be enough to save him.

Nothing would be now.

"She's dying, Cal. Give her up. Kasper can save her."

Unsure if it was Kasper's magic amplifying the stone or Cal's own depleted magic burning through him, he shifted imperceptibly toward Kasper. The last vestiges of his rational mind urging him to do the right thing. Kasper's arms slid under Hera, and in the next breath, he was hurrying away with her.

Cal let go, then.

It no longer mattered if he survived—only that she did.

His magic surged, dragging him under and wresting control over his body. Shadows gathered, and the dead whispered as Cal rose, no longer wholly in command of himself.

Forgotten help whoever crossed his path.

Chapter Thirty Three

Kasper adjusted Hera against his body and hurried for the stairs that led below deck. Kai said something, but the words were lost to Kasper's blood thundering in his ears. He didn't acknowledge the few crewmates who eyed him and the encroaching storm, nor did he look back at his brothers. Kasper knew what kind of power his brothers wielded, and he knew that if they unleashed themselves on The Ether, nothing would be safe from their wrath. The best thing Kasper could do was to help Hera.

The green sheen on her skin had worsened.

"Hold, Lady," Kasper whispered as he raised a booted foot and slammed into the door to the hull. Ebony wood splintered and cracked under the force. Hustling down the steps, he did his best not to jostle Hera more than necessary. He landed in the hall with a thud, the reverberating pain in his legs secondary to his terror.

He hurried, aiming for his room. His quarters were cramped, but they would do. Rushing toward the bed, he gently lowered Lady Hera to the dilapidated mattress. A violent tremor coursed through Kasper as he pressed his fingers to the inside of her wrist, desperate to find a pulse.

There it was.

Weak and thready, but there.

A wave of relief knocked into Kasper, his knees nearly buckling.

She wasn't gone—yet. She likely only had minutes if Kasper didn't hurry. Swallowing down his rising panic, he looked her over for any other wounds. There were only tiny cuts along her arms and face, likely from the salt and wind, leaving the gash on her shoulder as the source of her condition. Clenching his jaw, Kasper fought the terror threatening to root him to the floor.

He darted over to the small chest in the corner of the room. He undid the latch, ignoring the quaking in his hands, and raised the lid. Gems and crystals of every kind and color glittered and gleamed in the crate. Crystals were conduits and bastions of power if one had the ability to unlock them. They radiated power—beckoning to him. He knew the stones he needed, the ones that would give Hera a fighting chance at surviving. He was not a Healer, not by a long shot, but they were out of options—and time.

Grabbing several stones, he ignored the biting pain of their sharp edges. As he returned to the bed, he arranged the gems. He placed lepidolite near the wound, then, brushing the loose hair away from Hera's chest, set bloodstone over her heart. He put an obsidian stone over her lungs and placed clear quartz at the base of her throat. Lady Hera's chest rose and fell far too slowly, the poison doing its work.

He wasted no more time as he gripped the raw amethyst he held and dragged it against his palm. Blazing pain tore through his hand, and Kasper gritted his teeth. Blood welled along the cut, and he held his bleeding fist out over Hera. Ruby-red blood dripped onto the lepidolite, bloodstone, obsidian, and quartz. A faint light glowed from within the gems, growing stronger until beams of light formed between them, connecting them.

Kasper almost recoiled at the strength of the poison. Had the cut been deeper or gotten into her bloodstream faster, she would have been dead before she made it to the hull. His throat was thick with the realization. But she was still breathing, still fighting.

Kasper dug deeper.

He went beyond the oily feeling of the poison and reached out for the power of the crystals. They hummed, coming to life under his command, bending to his will. He urged the lepidolite to clear the poison and infection. He compelled the bloodstone to purify her blood and the obsidian to cleanse her muscles of the toxin. Amplifying their strength with the quartz and amethyst, he drew on their enhancing abilities.

He gave himself over to the power of the crystals, allowing them to fulfill their purpose. *His* purpose. So often, his abilities only brought death, but in this instance, he harnessed his cursed magic for something good. After several minutes, the only sounds in the cabin came from the hum of the crystals and the storm raging outside. Kasper swayed on his feet, the world listing around him. He didn't have much more energy left in him, but the poison was still there, and Hera wasn't awake yet. Clenching the amethyst tighter in his palm, Kasper dove further into his magic. If saving her took all of him, his magic—his life—then so be it.

The crystals on Hera flickered and brightened, their efforts doubling. Kasper's vision narrowed, blurring at the edges. His reserves were depleted—his limits becoming evident. Not once in his eighteen years had Kasper wished for the burden of the nearly fathomless depths of his brothers' magic. But he did now—if only to save her.

Kasper swayed again. His legs buckled. The world tipped, and he lost his grip on the crystals. Pain flared through him as his shoulder connected with the cabin's floor. The crystals flickered, growing dimmer as Kasper's vision also darkened.

No.

No.

This couldn't be all he had. He clawed at his hold on his consciousness, but it slipped out of his grip. All his failures, his regrets and shortcomings slammed into him. He would never get the chance to understand why Kai had betrayed him, or find out why Cal hadn't come back for him. He would die, never understanding who he was.

But even with that realization, Kasper's last, fleeting thought was of his failure to save Hera.

Chapter Thirty Four

It didn't take long for Brander to realize that the screams surrounding him were not a product of his drugging, but evidence that the Umbra was under attack.

He was unsure of how many days had passed since he last saw the sky above from something other than the miserly porthole in his cabin, but it no longer mattered. His mission was to protect the Princess—everything else was collateral. Weakness from the seasickness still clung to his body. His mind was still heavy from the drugs he had been fed, but he fought through his discomfort.

Brander had to secure Princess Rhea.

His stomach cramped painfully as he shoved his boots on and reached for his bandelier. Trembles wracked his muscles as he slipped the leather over his head and moved to stand. Pain flashed behind his eyes and stabbed through his skull, but Brander pressed on. Clenching his jaw, he carefully made his way to his door, achingly aware of the ships swaying and the roiling of his stomach.

Blowing out a breath, he pushed out of his room. The air in the narrow hall was sharp and charged, a storm brewing about them. Brander forced his legs to work and his mind to stay focused on his mission. He didn't give the nightmares that had haunted him the last several days an inch. Fear would not be permitted, not when peril was hovering so dangerously close.

He glanced toward the Princess's door; mercifully, it was closed. Stumbling toward it, he slammed a heavy hand against it.

"Lady? Are you safe?"

Silence answered him.

Brander struck the door again. "Lady!" he bellowed, but still no reply. Brander cursed. Cursed himself for being weak and pitiable. And cursed the Princess for being stubborn and reckless. If they survived this, he was going to give her a tongue-lashing for the danger she constantly put herself in. His breath came in labored pants as he clambered up the steps that separated the hull from the deck. Narrowing his eyes, he prepared for the streaming sunlight. He stepped out from the hull—

Swirling storm clouds and streaks of lightning illuminated the darkness greeting him. Stumbling forward, he struggled to get his bearings—the shadows looming all around were far too reminiscent of his nightmares. In the swirling clouds, he saw the smoke of his village burning under the King's command. In the booms of thunder, he heard the warhorses trampling through the streets. In the blood that coated the deck of the ship, he smelled the murder of innocents.

Brander swallowed, but his throat was dry as sand, and his mind was still so heavy. He turned, looking for someone who would explain what had happened in the days since his confinement—but there was no one. Screams and shouts surged above the storm's thrashing, but they sounded leagues away. In the brief moments when the world was light enough to see something, Brander finally spotted someone. He lurched forward, desperate for some explanation of what was happening. Crossing the deck, he fumbled in the dark toward the person hunched against the ship's rail. Brander reached out to the person, but their back was still to him. With the next bolt of lightning that tore across the sky, Brander realized that the man in front of him was no man at all, but some monstrosity birthed from nightmares.

Brander stumbled back, the storm compounding his instability and confusion. Was he still enthralled in his nightmares? No, he was certain he was awake. And he was certain that the Umbra was under attack. But it was no normal assault—there were literal monsters aboard.

Brander's instincts and years of training were the only things that kept him from being gutted as the creature turned and swept out with a dagger. No, not a dagger, but claws that protruded from its fingers.

The beast hissed and slithered toward him. The lightning that ripped across the sky highlighted the blood and gore stuck between the monster's teeth. The understanding of what Brander beheld was enough to shake the last of the fog clinging to his mind's recesses. He withdrew the curved dagger from his bandelier and shifted his stance. The beast snarled at him and lunged, but Brander was ready this time. He ducked under its talons and sliced upward, catching the monster under its arm. Hot liquid splashed against his skin, but Brander quickly raised up and stepped toward the beast, driving his knife into the base of its neck. A broken scream issued from the beast's lips as Brander twisted the blade and yanked it sideways, freeing it from its throat.

If the Princess was up here amongst these monsters with no one to protect her…

Wiping the blade on his pant leg, he continued toward the front of the ship, his heart a war drum in his chest. His eyes frantically scanned the faces of the passing crew, desperately seeking out the Princess. Maybe she had gone deeper into the ship. Brander should have checked there first. But it would be a waste to turn back now. He hurried past crewmates engaged in combat with the same kind of creature that he had slaughtered. The part of him that hadn't turned indifferent by serving in the King's army wanted to help those outmatched or wounded, but he needed to ensure the survival of the conmen first.

Otherwise, this was all for nothing.

Brander slowed as he approached a raised portion of the deck that overlooked the bow. He drew up short, his breath catching in his throat.

The Necromancer battled against two creatures that must have been crafted from the darkness itself. Long, spindly limbs tipped with claws slashed and sliced at the Necromancer, aiming to kill him. The Necromancer dodged and fled their assaults, all the while with a broad, feral grin. But it was the Necromancer's eyes that gave Brander pause. The sockets in his skull mirrored the swirling storm overhead, and there was nothing kind or human in his features. His skin had thinned, displaying the darkness and shadows that lurked beneath.

If Brander hadn't already thought the Necromancer was a demon, this exhibition confirmed it. He had half a mind to take the chance to kill the Necromancer himself. No one would question a blade gutting him, given the claws of the monsters he battled—but he needed to find the Princess first. The Necromancer threw out his hand, but he wielded no weapon. Unearthly power—midnight shadows shaped into a stream-lined beam—arced out from the Necromancer. The shadows barrelled toward them, aiming for their chests, and slammed into the creatures. Above the waves and thunder, their bones snapped and splintered. They flew backward into the ship's side, its force rocking the entire vessel. Nothing survived that kind of devastation. But against all logic, the creatures rose, their exposed gray bones re-knitting themselves.

"What in the Forgotten?" Brander breathed. Never in all his years had he witnessed something so unnatural. He had to find the Princess. He had to beg her to reconsider this quest. Surely, if this was on the way to the Cave of Splendors, then the Cave itself would hold more horrors. They had to get off of this ship. They had to go back—

"Brander!" A voice called out above the noise. Turning, he dared to take his eyes off the creatures advancing on the Necromancer once more. The Seer approached him, his cream and alabaster clothing almost offensive in all the darkness and chaos.

"What is going on? Where is Lady Hera?" Brander cried out.

The Seer reached him and Brander noticed that, while his hair and clothes were not immune to the torrent of wind and rain, there wasn't a speck of blood on him—human or otherwise. Brander ground his teeth at the Seer's pacifical nature.

"We entered The Ether!" Malakai called above the noise. There was a subduedness to him that Brander had not glimpsed before—this place was dulling the brightness he seemed to exude. "These creatures, sirens and other monstrosities, climbed aboard not long after. We've been under attack since."

Brander set his jaw. So, it was a fight for survival, then. "How do we clear the ship of them?"

The Seer shook his head. "You can't, but Caliban and I can."

Brander glanced back at the Necromancer. One of the creatures was cornered, but the other skittered behind and dug its talons into his shoulder. The Necromancer bellowed and whirled with his magic, knocking the creature aside. But he was losing. No matter what he did, his magic would not keep the monsters down. Brander considered helping him or occupying one monster long enough to let the Necromancer recover, but he hesitated. He needed to find the Princess.

"Where's the Lady?" Brander's eyes still scanned the deck, searching for her. He turned, pinning his gaze back on Malakai.

The Seer's smile faltered.

"Where is my Lady?" Brander repeated, his tone deepening an octave as he took in the Seer's grave expression.

Malakai swallowed, his eyes blinking rapidly as he opened his mouth to speak. "She tried to help—"

"*WHERE?*" Brander bellowed, his anger becoming a storm of its own as he raged at the Seer. He should have never allowed the Princess to come on this infernal mission. He should have never allowed her to place her faith in these sorcerers and thieves.

"The hull!"

Brander's head went hollow, empty of anything other than terror at the Seer's statement. His one purpose was to ensure her safety, but his weakness had prevented that, and now her life was in danger. He was useless. Brander swore that if the Princess was permanently harmed, he would surrender himself to The Ether and whatever horrors it held.

"She's in good—"

Brander didn't hear the rest of what the Seer said, and he didn't want to. His shoulder roughly knocked into the smaller man, and he sprinted back to the hull.

Chapter Thirty Five

The various paths and potential outcomes split in Malakai's mind. They ripped at his tenuous hold on reality, rendering any hope of helping his brother next to impossible. But Malakai gritted his teeth, dug his hands into the soaked wood of the Umbra, and forced his magic to submit. It thrashed and clawed, still splintering into all the possible conclusions, but he ignored them all, save for one.

The one that didn't spell their doom.

Malakai slowed his breathing and centered himself. Leaning into the quietness of his soul, he waded past the unruliness of his power. Reluctantly, the visions and burning light in his chest subsided enough for him to wrest control. His magic, which only ever displayed as visions and prophecies, was thrashing in his blood—eager to be more. Malakai hesitated, unsure what would happen if he gave into the blazing light within. The burn of it was stronger, more potent, than he had ever felt. Perhaps it was an effect of The Ether, or his magic responding to his intense need. Whatever the case, he remained reluctant.

When he opened his eyes, the futures he saw were fading, giving way to the carnage before him. Crew and creatures in various states of dismemberment, laying around the ship. Some had fire in their eyes and determination in their jaws, even as their lives seeped from the gashes along their bodies. Malakai knew that some of their lives were already forfeit, if not from the pallor of their skin, then from the certainty of his visions.

Malakai couldn't dally any longer. Despite his reservations over what would happen if he dove into the fire blazing in his chest, he was out of options. He rallied his power, summoning the light that blazed from within. Raising his palms, it blasted from him, a searing heat rivaling the desert's hot seasons. He had little control over how his magic manifested and had never used it defensively, but desperate times, right?

He squinted against the brightness, the light obscene in the utter darkness. The white-hot magic connected with the creatures, disintegrating them immediately. There was hardly a moment of shock that registered on their faces before the wind carried off what remained of them. The pirates who were too close to the creatures met the same fate. But where the monsters were enraged, understanding and thanks passed over the pirates' features before they became dust in the air.

Malakai stumbled a step, catching himself on the railing. A tremor rocked his body, but he remained upright, exertion weighing on him. He stared down at his hands, though he wasn't sure what he expected to find. Despite the effectiveness of this new facet of his magic, there was no way he could do that again. Not without killing himself or inadvertently harming others.

He needed a way to channel his magic.

The storm paused for a heartbeat. Another tremor coursed through Malakai, but this was different. It was born from blind rage and raw power. Instantly, he knew from whom it had originated. He straightened his spine and willed his unsteady feet to carry him to Caliban.

Caliban cradled the Princess's body, clutching her to his chest with fervor. His magic swirled around them, shadows writhing and thrashing, enveloping the group in a hurricane of darkness. Malakai caught a glimpse of his brother's anguished face, his pupils like black holes in a starry night. Dark bruises settled under Cal's eyes, and Malakai understood that his brother was no longer in control of his magic, but rather at its mercy.

Which meant they all were.

Kasper was there, struggling to extract the lady from Malakai's twin's grasp. Malakai pleaded with his twin as Kasper reached for their brother. This was the only way to save them all.

Caliban's icy eyes fell on Malakai—seeing, but not. Malakai remained stalwart. There was no other choice, no other option, but this one. Finally Caliban conceded, relinquishing control.

"Take her below deck, Kasper." Malakai said into his brother's ear. "We'll handle this." he assured, but Kasper ignored him as he barreled past, the Princess lifeless in his hold.

Visions splintered in Malakai's head again, and he faltered, falling away from Caliban, who had risen from the deck—not looking at all like himself. Pressing his back into the ship's side, he tried and failed to get his bearings. A hundred different versions of the scene before him flashed in his mind. Of Caliban banishing the creatures but losing himself in the process. Or all the ways Caliban would expend himself and be caught unawares, meeting a terrible fate. Malakai saw his own death—gruesome and violent.

The only path that ended in them surviving The Ether required them to work together—something they hadn't done in over a decade. Malakai steeled himself for what was certain to be an impossible task, but there would be no chance for survival if it didn't happen now. Malakai panted through clenched teeth. He strained to regain dominance over his visions, to remind himself that he was in control—he was the master of himself. Too often, Malakai was subjected to the whims of his magic, to the demands of his clients, to the command of a King. But he would not allow his mind and heart to succumb to the tortuous call of his power.

Malakai righted himself and pushed off from the railing once more. His eyes locked on the battle Caliban was engaged in. Two creatures hewn from darkness and blood swiped and sneered at him. Already, Malakai saw Caliban's strength flagging, his attacks becoming sloppy and imprecise. He was a whirlwind of steel and shadows, but neither were at his command.

Heavy footfall drew Malakai's attention from his brother. Brander stood nearby, gaping at Caliban as he beheld the horrors The Ether had wrought and Caliban's futile attempt at stopping them. Malakai told Brander as much, plastering a reassuring smile onto his face and urging him to leave the fighting to him and Caliban. Brander was clearly conflicted. The soldier within and the desire to protect those who couldn't defend themselves warred with the understanding that his blade was useless against the horde.

Concern was etched into the guard's face as he finally turned from the melee and asked, "Where is the Lady?"

Malakai's smile fell a bit as the guard eyed him with growing apprehension. Rhea's pallid face, her head hanging limping in Kasper's arms—flashed in his mind.

"Where is my Lady?" Brander repeated, and Malakai flinched at the pure venom in his tone.

"She tried to help—" Malakai spoke with genuine disquiet, his words cut off by the outburst of the soldier before him.

"*WHERE*?" Brander demanded, his face blanching despite the rage radiating from him in waves.

"The hull!" Malakai cried, watching helplessly as Brander's features went slack with terror. "She's in good hands!" He attempted to call out, but his words fell on deaf ears as the guard whirled away, nearly knocking Malakai over as he stormed toward the hull.

Malakai turned back to the fight below him. Swallowing his discontent, he put aside thoughts about the Princess and her well-being. He could not be distracted by other paths—he knew his place was on the deck with Caliban, and that only the two of them would be able to save the Umbra. Malakai withdrew the short, slender blade he kept tucked along his waistband. Unlike everything else Malakai owned, it was unadorned with gems or jewels. It was fitted with a simple leather hilt and an unremarkable steel blade. He had never used it in battle in the fifteen years he had carried it. That was still his plan, but he would do what was necessary to survive The Ether.

The dizziness and unease of his last vision had finally subsided enough for Malakai to move again; this time, he showed no hesitation.

Caliban had knocked back both beasts, but their bones had already started to repair themselves.

Again.

He held his breath as Caliban bared his teeth and palmed his dagger—murderous intent flashing in his dark eyes.

"Caliban!" Malakai called out. It was a risk to divert his brother's attention away from the creatures, but a necessary one.

Caliban spared a glance in his direction, the shadows that darkened his eyes fading. That was all the opening that Malakai needed. Closing the distance between them, he gripped the hilt of his knife tightly, and slashed out. The blade made contact, and the metallic and earthy scent of Caliban's blood filled the air, stronger than before. Ruby-red blood welled up, and Caliban cursed, his mouth curling into a snarl and his eyes flaring with rage. Malakai moved quicker, dragging the blade across his own flesh before blindly grabbing for his brother's bleeding palm.

He regretted the path he was putting his brother on, but the Umbra would be overrun with monsters if he didn't do *something*. Everything they had worked for—everything they had sacrificed—would have been for nothing. Malakai prayed to Fate, or the Forgotten, or whatever was master over the cosmos that he wasn't making the ultimate mistake.

Malakai's spine locked. His blood buzzed with power that no mortal should ever wield. He clenched his jaw, but he was certain that the cracking sound reverberating through his skull was his teeth breaking. Trying to breathe through the tidal wave of power that loomed over him, he said, "Take my magic."

"What?" Caliban retorted.

"Take. My. Magic," Malakai ground out, the power in his veins searing like the lightning still sizzling around them. "Use it!"

Caliban stared, his eyes searching Malakai's face—not for confirmation, but for betrayal. Even with the world crumbling around them, the sky cracking apart, and demons destroying everything they held dear, there was no trust between them.

Malakai couldn't blame him.

He also couldn't afford to care.

Malakai poured all of his focus into not succumbing to Caliban's might. His entire body sang and shook against the pure onslaught of his brother's power as it burned through him.

"It's the only way." Malakai said through bared teeth. His hold on his brother's hand grew weaker by the second—his grasp on consciousness even more so. "*Use my magic.*"

Caliban kept his gaze locked on Malakai for a heartbeat longer, then turned and threw out his free hand. Searing white light–tinged with strains of black–beamed from Cal's palm, knocking into one of the sinewy creatures and blasting it apart on impact. The other screeched, and Caliban turned his attention to it.

It was there and gone in a blink.

Caliban whirled, tugging Malakai with him, and it was all Malakai could do to keep his footing. How Caliban was able to stand, much less think and maneuver through his ship, while siphoning Malakai's power was terrifying. But Malakai couldn't dwell on that as Caliban dragged him down from the ship's bow and across the deck.

Malakai's consciousness ebbed each time Caliban rallied their magic. There was an odd sense of relief in the release, though—as if this was what Malakai's power was crafted for. The divination was a mere consequence or side effect of the pent-up energy. It made Malakai wonder more about his brother's magic. He questioned if it, too, had urges to be unleashed and consume, or if his careful control all these years had honed it into something much more disciplined—and deadlier. That must have been the case, seeing how Caliban cleared the ship with brutal efficiency. Targeting the sirens and other creatures that screeched and squawked before the light pouring from the brothers incinerated the monsters.

By the time they reached the stern of the Umbra, the screaming and wails of the beasts had quieted, leaving the moaning and cries of the injured in their wake. Malakai was stumbling, his grip on Caliban's hand tenuous, but Caliban kept firm. He stopped at the ship's edge, overlooking the path they had cut through The Ether. Malakai had no idea how long they had been in The Ether or how much longer they had to go, but from the set of Caliban's jaw and the shadows simmering in his eyes, he wagered they were not done with their mission just yet.

With intense purpose, Caliban marched on. He still drew on Malakai's magic, but a quick glance at Malakai's haggard appearance must have enlightened him to his brother's slipping consciousness. Caliban dragged Malakai over to some crates secured along the ship's side and propped him up against them. The overwhelming anguish that had consumed Malakai's body since he joined hands with Caliban abated to a throbbing ache in his skull and palm.

"Rest here for a moment." Caliban said, with all the tenderness of an executioner.

Malakai slunk down against the crates, ready to be done with it all. Still holding firm to his hand, Caliban was clearly not ready to release the power he now had access to.

Caliban's face was all hard lines and determination as he bent down to his brother and said, "I've never felt power like that. Not even when we broke out of the palace. What I felt flowing between us...Kai, it felt nearly endless."

There was a hunger in his eyes that made Malakai's insides quiver. Caliban clearly hadn't known before what they were capable of once joined, and now that he did, would he enslave Malakai—like the King had enslaved them?

"We could get revenge, you know? For all of it. We wouldn't need whatever awaits in the Cave of Splendors. Together, we could do it."

Malakai's earlier fear flooded his mind—flashes of a bleak, desolate future. Malakai attempted to swallow, but his throat was a desert.

"It's not our destiny," he managed to reply, though the words felt like sandpaper against his tongue.

"Destiny. Fate. Providence," Caliban scoffed, staring out at the awaiting darkness. "I care nothing for what others have determined for me. I forge my own path."

Pity filled Malakai's chest.

Oh, how he wished that was the truth.

Glancing at Malakai, Caliban read the sympathy that lay there. He cut his eyes away and stood abruptly, his face painted with disdain.

"The world will know me, Malakai. Once I have the Alakhira and I've set things right with Soline, they will hear my name and know to tremble. And if I decide to come for him, there will be no mistaking who took *everything* he holds dear."

Malakai rose up.

Caliban's path, the one he had been set on a decade ago, would only lead to death and destruction. Malakai opened his mouth, but the words were stolen from him as Caliban raised his hand and aimed for The Ether.

Chapter Thirty Six

A groan tore from Kasper's lips as he blinked against the dim light of his cabin. He rose up on his elbows and shook his head—trying to dislodge the fog from his mind and struggling to make sense of his surroundings. What was he doing on the floor? A throb emanating from Kasper's palm nearly stole his breath. Shoving aside his pain, he slowly climbed to his feet. Had he cut himself when he fell, or had that come before?

Kasper sucked in a breath as he stood on shaky legs, and everything came flooding back to him.

Lady Hera lay unconscious on his bed, blood and crystals covering her. Kasper's heart missed a beat as he dove toward the bed. He crashed next to her and hovered his ear over the top of her too-still chest. Holding his breath, he prayed to whatever power or deities would listen that she was still alive. Slowly, her chest rose and fell, and relief flooded Kasper. Leaning back against the cabin wall, he exhaled, attempting to gain control over himself. He was alive, and so was Lady Hera. That was all that mattered for the moment. Closing his eyes, he took a cleansing breath. He should get up, return to the deck and help the others, but his legs wouldn't move. Kasper's abilities with a blade were average at best, and his magic was useless in a fight.

Perhaps he was more useful watching over Lady Hera.

Sheets rustled, and a crystal clattered to the floor, rousing Kasper. He pushed up from the wall and tentatively reached out for Lady Hera. Her skin was slick with sweat and had lost its normal olive complexion, but she was awake. Her eyes darted wildly around the room, and she moved to sit up.

"It's alright. You're safe and…" Kasper's words faltered. He was hesitant to say cured. He had no idea if what he had done had worked or if it was merely a temporary fix. Kasper had little experience with poisons, particularly those of a magical nature. Never had he attempted to heal more than a cut, so his confidence in his abilities was next to none.

Easing to his knees beside Lady Hera, Kasper brushed a reassuring hand along her still-damp hair. She jolted at his touch, her frantic gaze finally settling on his face. Heat warmed Kasper's cheeks at the intensity–and familiarity–of her stare. He licked his lips and said, "I'm here. You're safe."

Her brows furrowed, and she said in a raspy voice, "Kasper?"

The warmth in Kasper's face flooded the rest of his body.

"Yes," he breathed.

The fear in her face softened a fraction, and she whispered, "I never thought I'd see you again."

The breath caught in his chest. Kasper knew the feelings Lady Hera evoked in him, but he hadn't dared to think she might have felt the same way.

Her eyes fluttered, and some of her color started to return to her cheeks. Kasper glanced at the wound on her shoulder. The sickly green color had receded, and the gash didn't look nearly as deep. Still, he would need to monitor it. Moving, he aimed for the bandages and salve he had brought, when cold, clammy fingers slipped around his wrist. He paused and stared down at Lady Hera.

"I've missed you, Kas. After everything, with the exile, I thought I would never see you again. But the Forgotten have been kind," Lady Hera said with a complacent smile and sleepy eyes. Her fingers rubbed idly along his skin, but it felt like fire was dancing in her wake.

That feeling Kasper had experienced earlier on the deck came barreling back to his mind. The sensation of knowing her from somewhere. Kasper peered into her unobstructed face.

"So, we do know each other? I haven't been imagining this…attraction?" He whispered.

Unfettered laughter burst from Lady Hera's lips. "We've known each other for ages, Kas."

Kasper's mind was a whirlwind. For not the first time in the last two weeks, Kasper wished he remembered anything from his childhood. Or that he had Kai's ability to See so he could put to rest the lingering sensation that he and the Lady had a history. It had haunted him from the moment he laid eyes on her, but she had obfuscated whenever Kasper tried to question her.

They must have known each other—unless she believed him to be someone else. Maybe she was just supplanting her memories with the closest person available.While that was a possibility, he knew deep down that there was more to it. And if they did know each other, why did she lie about knowing him before? What was the benefit of pretending to be strangers? Something linked them, and Kasper was close to figuring it out. If he could set aside his hurt and anger with Kai, he would ask him to try reading his past again.

He sank down beside Lady Hera and slipped his fingers between hers. She didn't register the contact. Her sleep-heavy eyelids fluttered again, but she continued to smile softly. Pulling gently on her hand, he dragged her attention to him.

"Lady Hera."

"Who?"

"Lady Hera." he said more forcefully.

Lady Hera turned to him, her brows scrunched and mouth twisted in agitation. "I don't know her." she yawned and turned away from Kasper. "I'm so tired."

Kasper opened his mouth, ready to beg her to stay awake and explain what she meant. But his plea was halted by the door banging open. Lady Hera and Kasper both jumped at the intrusion. Kasper's surprise was quickly replaced with annoyance as Brander filled the entryway.

"Who's there? Leave, before I call my guards!" Lady Hera commanded with the force of a queen. Kasper felt compelled to lower his eyes but kept his gaze trained on Brander.

Hurrying into the room, Brander was undeterred by Lady Hera's demands. He reached for her, but she drew back, scurrying up to the top of the bed.

Kasper's brows creased, but he was unsure how to ease her anxiety.

"Be gone from here! My father will have your head for this intrusion! Send him away, Kas." She raged, crawling further up on the bed.

Brander halted—his face a blend of agony and confusion.

The Lady didn't look much better. The ease that slipped into her features earlier was replaced with blatant terror.

"Lady, it's me. Brander, your guard," he urged with more tenderness than Kasper would have thought him capable.

Lady Hera's face scrunched in contemplation. Clearly, she was trying to make sense of what Brander insisted, but her mind simply would not allow the connection to be made. "I–I don't know you. Kas, who is he? Did my father send him?"

Kasper was speechless. Obviously, Hera was experiencing some memory loss–something he could certainly sympathize with–but he didn't want to agitate her further. "Yes, I believe he did. He's to be your new guard."

Hera's eyes darted back and forth, but tension slipped from her shoulders and face. With apprehension, she slid back down in the bed, releasing the blanket she had gathered around her face. "Alright, if you say so."

"I do." he said gently. "You lay back down and get some rest."

Nodding slowly, Hera tucked herself back underneath the blanket.

"Can I speak with you for a moment?" Kasper said softly, turning to Brander. To Brander's credit, he complied. He retreated and walked toward the door, pausing at the threshold.

Kasper rose, but Lady Hera reached for him. Her fingers pressed firmly into his skin and muscles. The effort of extrapolating her fingers from grasp fractured his heart.

"I'll be just a minute, I promise." he assured in a soothing voice. Lady Hera's creased brow eased slightly and rested back against the bed, but her eyes never left Kasper. Giving her a tentative smile, Kasper turned, heading for where Brander waited, his arms crossed tightly over his chest.

Brander's jaw and neck muscles were taut as he spat out, "What's the matter with her?"

Employing every ounce of restraint and patience Kasper had, he said gingerly, "She suffered an attack. When I found her, she was already unconscious, but there was poison or venom around the wound, so I brought her down to try and treat it."

"Try?" Brander seethed, more veins becoming prominent along his throat.

"Yes, try. I am not proficient in poisons—"

Brander's eyes were wide. He bared his teeth, and a vein running along his temple bulged. "So, you thought you'd just experiment on her? She's nobility, you gutter rat. I ought to slit your—"

Closing the distance between them, Kasper angled his obsidian knife, pressing it to the soft spot beneath Brander's ribs. The guard sucked in a sharp breath but held his tongue.

"She would have died if it weren't for me and my brothers." Kasper hissed. "I did the best I could with what limited information I had. The sheen from the poison is gone, and the wound appears to be closing. She is awake and talking. I think you should be grateful for that rather than threatening me, seeing how you were nowhere to be found when she was injured."

Brander's nostrils flared, but Kasper's words had found their mark if the slight curve of the guard's shoulders were to be believed. Brander ground his teeth and said, "I just want to know if she's alright."

Kasper tilted his head. "I didn't hear a thank you."

Brander narrowed his eyes. "Thank. You."

A corner of Kasper's mouth lifted, and he withdrew his knife. "You're welcome." He didn't let himself dwell on how easily the cruelty had come to him or who he shared that particular trait with.

He jerked his chin toward Lady Hera, who had sunk back down in the sheets and was drifting off once more. "I passed out when I tried to draw the poison out. She came to not long after I did. I don't think much time has passed, but I don't know." Kasper scratched the back of his neck and considered keeping the rest to himself, but he knew the guard still had questions, so he continued, "She seemed to know who I was, but I think she might have confused me with someone from her past. And from how she reacted to you, it seems pretty clear that she doesn't have all her memories."

Kasper wanted to ask if Brander knew much about Lady Hera's past. If she had always lived at the palace, or if there was any chance that she and Kasper had a history. But from Brander's pained expression, now wasn't the right time.

"She needs to rest—"

"I can watch over her."

"No."

Murder danced in Brander's eyes. Kasper wondered if anger was the only emotion he was capable of processing. Raising an eyebrow, Kasper said in a low voice, "She was clearly agitated by your presence. So, you cannot stay with her until she remembers you; otherwise, she'll never rest." An idea came to Kasper, and he added, "But if it would give you more peace of mind, then by all means, stand guard outside her door."

Working his jaw, Brander stared at Lady Hera's sleeping form through the cracked door. Several moments passed before he said begrudgingly, "Fine. But I want a detailed report of how she's doing every half hour, and the minute she asks for me, you get me."

Kasper snorted. "I'll give you a brief report at the end of the day, and I promise the moment she asks for your company, I will be more than happy to retrieve her guard dog," Kasper sneered, allowing more of that cruelty to infect his tone. Kasper wasn't sure where it was coming from or why he was resorting to it, but he had to admit it was effective.

Brander shifted his weight from one foot to the other and then sighed. He looked defeated and fatigued as he said, "Just take care of her, please. Her survival means more than anything."

Kasper let the gravity of Brander's words sink in, and for the first time in days, he felt sympathy for the man. "I can tell. And clearly, this poison took its toll on her." Kasper again wanted to ask about the comments she had made. She was forthright and congenial with him— like friends reconnecting, but he had no memories and thus no basis for his assumptions. He needed to know more. Kasper opened his mouth to ask, but a blinding white light shone through the small window, distracting him. Squinting, he raised his hand to shield against the unexpected brightness.

"What in the Forgotten is that?" Brander bellowed, as he too covered his eyes from the light.

Kasper couldn't venture a look, and wasn't sure he wanted to. Blistering heat seared from outside the window, making the room uncomfortably warm. Had something happened? Surely, they hadn't escaped The Ether already. But Kasper had no clue what would emanate such a powerful light amid the storm.

Minutes passed, but neither could do anything as the light blinded them. Then, inexplicably, the light was gone, stealing the heat with it. Tentatively, Kasper lowered his hand, expecting to see the storm still roiling outside, but the sight he was greeted with was almost more concerning.

"Is that…?"

"Yeah, I think so." Kasper finished. He glanced at Lady Hera, who, mercifully, hadn't stirred. He turned to Brander and said, "Go on deck and find out what irrevocable damage my brothers have done."

Brander must have been just as disturbed as Kasper was because he didn't argue. Turning on his heel, he disappeared down the corridor. Taking cautious, measured steps, Kasper stepped further into the room, moving closer to the window above the bed. Lady Hera's breaths came in even and slow, but Kasper was still careful as he leaned over her and stared at the clear, cerulean sky.

Chapter Thirty Seven

Brander lamented leaving the Princess. She was hurt and scared, and he wanted to do nothing more than assure her that he was there—even if he hadn't been there to keep her safe. Even if he wasn't sure if he would ever recover from the shame and guilt that failure brought him. Kasper was right. His presence only served to bother her, and that was the last thing he wanted to do.

He hustled toward the stairs, his long strides eating up the distance. If Kasper hadn't been present when the blue sky had revealed itself, Brander would have thought it was a dream or hallucination. He had enough of those lately. Landing on the last step, he pushed open the door. He closed his eyes and held his breath, waiting for the unrelenting stench of blood and brine to greet him…but it was gone. Not entirely, but muted enough that he wasn't overwhelmed.

He cracked open an eye.

The Ether was gone. A turquoise sky and still waters replaced the continuous flashing of lightning and roiling waves.

Brander couldn't believe it. He glanced around and was greeted by the crew milling about, staring at the sky. Brander pressed forward and stepped out on the midnight deck. His eyes scanned for the Seer and the Necromancer. He searched the front of the ship, but only found remnants of the creatures. Flies crawled over their glazed eyes, and their seawater-slicked scales baked in the sun's heat. Crew members stood over the bodies, trading weary looks and hushed words. Others were lifting the carcasses and heaving them over the side of the ship.

Brander moved on, uninterested in watching the corpses bloat or splash in the water below.

Shouting resounded from the back of the ship, and Brander followed the noise. Finnley's voice rose above the creaking wood and thudding of boots, calling out orders to her subordinates.

"Bring the sails out!"

"Get these bodies overboard and clean up this blood before it stains the wood!"

Brander was impressed with her ability to command the others. They obeyed without question; men and women moved to carry out their orders. He looked around where she stood and found his mark. The Seer was slumped, unconscious, against some crates. His twin—their resemblance still uncanny to Brander—stood with his back to him, staring off at the sea beyond. Brander sighed, preparing himself for the hostility that the Necromancer would greet him with.

Brander passed by the Seer and noted that his chest rose and fell in a steady rhythm. He was still breathing, but his color was concerning. His skin, normally a warm olive shade, was wan. Purple smudges glared from beneath the Seer's eyes, and there was a bloodstained rag wound around his palm.

"What happened?" Brander breathed.

"I happened." Cal responded, his tone steady and smug.

"What did you do?" Brander rasped as he recoiled a step away.

A corner of Cal's mouth lifted, and he shrugged. "I destroyed The Ether."

Annoyance at Cal's short answers flared in Brander, but he tamped it down. It would be foolish to incur his wrath. Brander crossed his arms and asked sternly, "And what was the price?"

The Necromancer's eyes flicked to his brother's unconscious form. "I don't know yet." he replied indifferently.

Brander wanted to be angry. He wanted to condemn the Necromancer for his carelessness, but…he would have done whatever was necessary to protect the Princess. Still, he asked, "You truly risked his life without concern for the consequences?"

Cal's features hardened, and he squared his shoulders. "Kai offered himself–his magic–to me. Sharing magic is not illegal, at least not by any laws I observe, but it is risky. I never thought that his was the kind that could be shared, but I assumed he knew what he was doing. Besides," Cal threw Brander a conspiratorial look, "I wasn't really in a position to refuse."

Brander ground his teeth. If the Seer was permanently injured or didn't recover, then Brander was unsure how that changed their plans. The Princess had never provided Brander with the specifics. Malakai had been the one to give the prophecy, so she surmised he would be the best chance to find Izor's Lamp. But if the Seer was too weak or power-less, what would they do? Going back empty-handed wasn't an option. He had no idea what would happen to the Princess if she returned to her father without a solution. Brander didn't want to even think about the punishment she would face for leaving the palace. Finding the trea-sure was likely the only way that the Princess's life wouldn't be forfeit upon returning.

"How is she?"

Brander's thoughts shattered at the question. He shook his head at the Necromancer and furrowed his brow.

"The woman, Hera. She got hurt." Cal swallowed, and shadows momentarily curled around him. "I caught her before she collapsed, but I don't remember anything else."

Brander paused. Cal's fingers tapped against his bicep impatiently. Surely, he didn't care more for a woman he just met than his twin? Unless…unless something had changed in the days that Brander was unconscious. Terror crawled up his spine. Aside from her being the Princess and Cal a demon, he was worldly and despicable; she was still so young and naïve to the horrors of life. Brander was her protector, but there was only so much he could save her from if she sought out the

Necromancer. Brander was not her father, and he had no place to tell her what to do, but…

Narrowing his eyes, Brander said, "Why do you care?"

The Necromancer gave a dry, humorless laugh. "If she dies, then I imagine her mistress would inquire after her, and I have no interest in being blamed for a noblewoman's death."

Despite Brander's skepticism of the Necromancer's claim, it wasn't worth arguing. He jerked his chin to the motionless heap that was the Seer and said, "He should probably be looked at by someone. It would be a shame to lose a brother to negligence."

Cal guffawed. "If you say so. Finnley!"

Brander turned. The scarred second-in-command whipped her in their direction.

"Sir?"

"Get someone to take Kai below deck."

Tendrils of her reddish-brown hair floated around her face as she flicked her gaze to the Seer and back to Cal. Her throat bobbed once. Twice. "He doesn't look good, Captain."

Rolling his eyes, Cal said, "I didn't ask for an assessment of his well-being. Just get him in the hull." Cal turned on a boot heel, leaving Finnley staring at the space he occupied. A muscle jumped in her cheek, but she shook her head and moved toward the Seer.

Brander stepped back, reluctant to find himself in her path. But when she ducked down to the Seer and slipped her arm under his shoulder, Brander lurched forward. He didn't think as he positioned himself to catch the Seer's unoccupied side. The Seer's limp body hung between Brander and Finnley, his slight frame surprisingly solid.

Finnley cut her eyes to Brander and ground out, "I don't need your help."

Brander bit back his retort. He was trying to keep his promise to Princess Rhea and be less hostile toward the others, but their insolence made that increasingly difficult. Instead, he blew out a breath and said, "The Seer clearly needs help. He can get that quicker if we work together."

Finnley grumbled something, but it was too low for Brander to hear. They began to move, half carrying, half dragging the Seer back toward the hull entrance. Brander focused more on the state of the crew and ship now than when he emerged from below. New gouges and chips were cut into the ebony wood, and overturned barrels and fraying ropes littered the deck. The Umbra had taken a beating during the attack, nearly as much as the crew had.

Men and women moved about in various states. Some looked whole, but Brander recognized the haunted look in their eyes. The shadows that clung to them. He had seen it many times after quelling a rebellion in a city or village from which one of his men had come. He recognized it in himself after he lost nearly his entire platoon. Several of them sported new injuries. Some were more minor, a gash or laceration— others were entire limbs. But perhaps the most harrowing was the number of bodies that were unmoving. Lifeless, glazed eyes stared at the crystal-clear sky, no longer seeing anything. Once, the sight of those mangled bodies and corpses made Brander sick. But not anymore.

Grunting beside him, Finnley shifted the Seer's weight and adjusted herself. Brander scanned her, noting that she was covered in the green-ish-black blood of the creatures, but very little human—in fact, there weren't any visible cuts or blemishes on her.

Noting Brander's attention, Finnley narrowed her eyes at him. "If yer a fan of those eyes, I suggest you turn them back forward."

Brander didn't flinch. Threats were the only currency aboard the Umbra.

"Why didn't you listen to your Captain?"

A muscle ticked in Finnley's jaw. "I did."

Brander shook his head. "No, he told you to get one of the others to take the Seer below deck."

Finnley grunted again and shifted the Seer's weight once more. With a wince, she faltered, briefly pushing the Seer on Brander, but quickly recovered. She jolted, and Brander's eyes darted to her ankle.

"You're hurt."

"I'm fine."

"You're not bearing weight on your left ankle."

"I said I'm fine." she ground out and grimaced again.

Brander scoffed but adjusted the Seer's weight, bearing more of it. They walked on in silence, their progress slow as they picked over injured crew, corpses, and overturned cargo. Brander didn't comment on Finnley's limp again or the state of her crew, but he understood the pain in her eyes—it had stared back at him several times over Brander's life. Of all the people Brander had interacted with aboard the Umbra—save for the Princess–Finnley was the only one he felt a kinship to.

It hadn't occurred to him how much he missed that sense of camaraderie. The feeling that someone had your back as much as you had theirs. That sense of brotherhood wasn't present in the palace amongst the guards—no, the King made sure that no one, save for him, had the loyalty of his guards. Finnley's self-assuredness and grit reminded him of the men he had served with in the King's army.

They approached the door leading to the hull, and Finnley slowed. She eyed the door, working out the best way to get the Seer down without aggravating her injury or dropping Malakai down the narrow stairs.

Clearing his throat, Brander said, "You can take his feet and guide him down, and I'll bring him down by his shoulders." Finnley flexed her jaw and regarded him for a moment before she gave him a terse nod. Brander returned the gesture, and they shifted the Seer between them.

Carefully, they moved down the stairs, taking the steps one at a time. They stopped before the Seer's door, and Finnley said, "Here," as she pushed Malakai into Brander's arms. Then she raised a booted foot–the one not injured–and slammed it into the wood. The door shuddered, and Brander suppressed a grin.

Yes, he definitely liked Finnley.

They moved into the room and gently laid Malakai on the bed. The Seer was still unconscious, but his color had improved marginally. Brander was no Healer, but he had seen enough battle to know the signs of fatigue. He made a mental note to tell Kasper, or the pirate that had tended to Brander, to check on the Seer. Brander stood back and surveyed Malakai, unsure if he should leave. Finnley stood stone still, her hands balled up and jaw tight.

"I've been on the Umbra for nearly a decade. I've seen good men and women die, but what I saw today…"

Brander nodded and said, "It was brutal. I've served in the King's army for nearly thirty years, but those creatures and the storm, it—"

"No," Finnley cut him off, shaking her head, "no, it wasn't that. I've worked under Cal for the last six years and seen some truly horrifying things, but witnessing him like that…I don't think I'll ever be able to unsee it."

Brander nodded. He had only glimpsed Cal, but the shadows he wielded and his vacant expression had been terrifying. Brander knew that Finnley would not take kindly to physical contact, even in the name of comfort, so he just stayed. He remembered the days when all he wanted was someone to be there—not necessarily speak or offer support, but just *be*.

He and Finnley remained quiet for several more minutes. The only sounds between them were their breathing and the scuffle of boots overhead.

Shaking her head, Finnley said, "He's always been…flippant. About the crews' lives, mine included, but never this careless. Never this reckless." Finnley twisted, gazing at Brander. He was hit with everything she felt in her bright eyes, wide with fury—and anguish. "I hope whatever your *Lady* is after is worth everyone's lives because that will be the cost." She jerked her chin to the Seer. "I don't have to have the gift of prophecy to know that."

Brander swallowed down the urge to tell Finnley the truth.

To explain that so many more lives were at stake if the Princess *didn't* get the treasure she sought. But he knew that, even if he did, it wouldn't change how Finnley felt.

It hadn't changed how he felt when Brander was told that the lives of his platoon were secondary to the King's cause.

Finnley stayed silent as she turned on her heel and swept from the room, leaving Brander staring at the limp form of the person who had put them all on this path a decade ago.

Chapter Thirty Eight

Cal's blood still roared in his ears. Hours after he had released Kai, his blood still thrummed with the power—still ached for more. Though, he was loath to admit how difficult it had been to release his brother. The sheer amount of magic between them was unfathomable. If he had known about their connection and the depthless abilities between them, Soline would still be alive...and the King of Desmorda?

The King would be dead.

Cal shook his head, trying to clear away his agitation. He turned away from the aqua-colored sky and the water shimmering beneath the bright afternoon sun and back to the Umbra. It took a fair amount of effort to stop staring at the absence of the storm, especially when he was the one who had dispelled it.

Legends would be written about him. Tales of his heroics and immense strength. He had conquered The Ether, and all that was left to do was claim his prize. Once he had the Alakhira, he wouldn't need anything else to take his vengeance—though, having Kai by his side might expedite things. But he wouldn't bank on that.

Not yet, anyway.

The Umbra, though battered and donning new scars, gleamed beneath the gore and death that coated nearly every inch. Despite the ship remaining intact, Cal couldn't ignore the death that glared at him from every angle. The crew roamed about, clearing away the debris of shattered crates and broken barrels—and bodies, monster and human alike, that littered its surface. Death was an old friend of Cal's, but he wasn't fond of it when it visited his ship.

Cal sighed. He set about rolling up his sleeves and stepped down from his perch at the bow of the ship. It would take several more hours to clear away the corpses of the sirens and other monsters. Then, the rites needed to be conducted for the fallen crew. Flexing his shoulders, he winced at the tension in his muscles.

It was going to be a long night.

Continuing down from the bow, Cal landed on the main deck. The crew flinched as he drew near, and wary looks passed between them. Avoiding their gazes, he reached for the nearest overturned barrel and pushed it upright with the crew's help. He moved silently through the ship, painfully aware that his presence was eliciting more disdain than anything. It was important to him that the crew see him as a member of the vessel rather than just its captain—but no matter how many bodies he disposed of or how much cargo he cleaned up, they managed to keep their distance.

Cal set his jaw and retreated to a vacant part of the ship, empty save for a siren's carcass and one of the sinewy creatures. He was interested in what they were and what, if any, magic remained in their bones and tissues. There were ordinary people who robbed the graves of well-known and powerful magic wielders to steal their remains. It was a common belief that they held remnants of their abilities, but Cal had never allowed himself to cross that line. He already spent too much time with the dead; he wasn't interested in desecrating their resting places. But these beasts were different, not human at all, but clearly preternatural. Dissecting and examining them wouldn't break any of Cal's morals—what was left of them, anyway.

Two pirates passed by, speaking in low voices, and Cal held out his arm. "You, two. Take these creatures below to my quarters."

The crew's faces blanched as they glanced from Cal to the monsters. They were still and unresponsive, wholly ignoring Cal's command. Irritation flared in him, and he snapped. "Are you two daft or dimwitted? I gave you an order."

The two men recoiled at Cal's tone, but quickly fell into step. One moved to take the feet of the siren, and the other slipped their hands beneath the webbed underarms of the beast. They grimaced, but didn't otherwise complain, slowly taking the creature away.

Cal stepped away from the corpses for a moment, clenching and unclenching his hands. Shadows curled under his skin, bleating against the too-sunny sky. Gripping the railing, he squeezed his eyes shut. He was eager for a minute of peace, but the moment he shut down the thoughts of conquest and carnage, his mind barreled toward thoughts of *her*.

The wood of the railing groaned beneath his hands as he tried and failed to forget the chilled sensation of her skin or the vacant look in her eyes. He worked to not fixate on that tug between them. That unnerving pull to her had him abandoning his crew to answer her call.

But he had *felt* it.

But even thinking of the Lady couldn't stop the reality of what he had revealed to the crew from sinking in. He had made the deliberate choice not to ever show his abilities to his crew, only summoning them when alone or in the dead of night. Besides the fact that necromancy and shadow-work were outlawed, Cal knew how his type of magic affected people. He was more interested in earning their respect because of his merits as a captain and pirate. If Cal were simply a Seer, or wielded elemental magic, they might have seen past it. They might have even forgiven him for keeping his magic a secret, but his kind—shadows and death—were illegal and fully cemented their distrust of him. Now, his crew had seen what he was capable of. It was only a matter of time before they turned on him.

"Captain."

Cal turned and found Finnley standing behind him. Her posture was rigid, with her back ramrod straight and hands clasped behind her.

"Finnley," he responded.

"May I have a word with you?"

Cal raised an eyebrow, but nodded. It must be serious if she was dropping the pretense of being uneducated. As he beheld her tight features, he was reminded that Finnley knew the death and carnage surrounding them now was the likely outcome of trying to breach The Ether. She had warned him–begged him–to change course. The destruction wrought was of his own making.

Stepping forward, Finnley filled the place beside Cal. She leaned out on her elbows, staring out over the water. Her scar looked more haggard, and her shoulders sagged in exhaustion. They were quiet for a while. They stared out over the water, watching it gently rock the ship toward the fabled Cave of Splendors.

"We lost Galen." Finnley said, breaking the silence. A single tear slipped down her cheek. Cal had never seen her cry, and watching that solitary tear roll down her face cracked open his chest.

Cal flexed his jaw and nodded his acknowledgment, unable to make his voice work. The losses were obvious; he had seen them himself. Even with that blatant truth, Cal had convinced himself that seeing Finnley through the worst of it meant the toll hadn't been too great.

Clearly, that hope was folly.

Finnley raised a hand and swiped at her nose. "The crew is going to hold a memorial for everyone tonight at sunset—if there is a sunset in this place."

Clearing his throat, Cal said, "I'll make sure everything is cleared before then and that the bodies are prepared for their last rites."

Finnley waved dismissively. "I've already seen to everything."

"Fine, then I'll perform the rites."

Pressing her lips into a thin line, Finnley's throat bobbed.

Tensing, Cal sensed something unspoken hanging between them. Cal clenched the wood railing. Finnley was not one to mince words, so why was she hesitating?

"Speak, Finnley." Cal commanded.

Finnley worked her jaw and then turned, facing Cal. He saw it then. The toll the fight had taken on her. It was in the shadows under her eyes and the hollowness in her gaze. She carried the deaths as though she had caused them. But where he noted her anguish, he also saw the set of her jaw and her shoulders squaring. The look of a captain trying to keep their composure and strength for their crew.

"They don't want you to." she said plainly.

Cal furrowed his brows, unsure if he had heard her correctly. But Finnley said nothing else and offered no other explanation. Rolling his shoulders, he said, "And what reason did they give? I am their captain, after all." Cal said the words, but they sounded hollow to his ears. He wasn't sure he had been their captain since he had chosen to leave several months ago.

Finnley sighed. "Many of them don't know you, and after," she gestured to the sky above, "your display...they're wary of you, Caliban."

Cal flinched at the use of his full name. Perhaps that showed how far he had fallen in her eyes. Turning, he pressed harder against the railing. The part of him that made the Umbra his home rebelled at the idea of relinquishing that control, but what had been his plan after retrieving the Alakhira? His plans had always been to resurrect Soline and eventually take his vengeance against those who harmed her, but where did the Umbra fit into that?

Cal cursed himself. He had gotten too comfortable playing at being a pirate in the last decade and lost sight of his true purpose. He was never just a pirate. He couldn't separate the necromancy and shadow-work from himself any more than he could change his blood or eye color—it was an integral part of him. Perhaps it was time to hand over command of the Umbra to someone else.

Exhaling, he turned back to Finnley. She lifted her chin as though awaiting a scolding, or possibly a beating.

Cal would dole out neither. He merely nodded and said, "I kept my magic concealed for a multitude of reasons, ones I'm sure you could guess at. Chief among them was so I could earn the respect of my crew through my merits, not fear. It seems that is no longer an option. I will stay away from the ceremony, if that is what they wish." Swallowing, he ignored the stinging in his eyes, "And after we complete our journey, I will relinquish control of the Umbra to you."

To Finnley's credit, she showed no emotion. She dipped her chin and quietly said, "It has been a pleasure to serve alongside you, Captain." She moved to step away, but Cal couldn't help himself. He reached out and grabbed her shoulder. She paused and stared at him with that unrelenting gaze.

"I have one last request," Cal said, the words sticking in his throat. He swallowed and continued, "I would like to say my farewells to Galen."

Finnley's throat bobbed once. "I think he would appreciate that." she replied, her voice cracking.

The ship creaked as Finnley left Cal to make the arrangements, giving him this last gift of saying farewell to their brother.

* * * *

Galen's lifeless gaze stared up at the ebony boards of the Umbra. Finnley had done a good job of cleaning him and sewing up the gashes along his neck where a siren had struck the fatal blow. Cal glanced at the clothes that adorned him, worn and threadbare, but clean. Finnley must have taken a set from his pack to replace his blood-soaked clothes. She even attempted to comb the thinning hair atop his head. The other pirates that perished were left on the deck before their burial. Only Galen had received the honor of being brought into the hull to have his body prepared—it was his right as the longest-serving crew member.

But Cal's eyes snagged on his wan face.

Never again would a smile grace his lips, nor would his chortling laughter echo through the galley. Cal clenched against the turmoil that brewed within. Galen was aboard the Umbra for over fifteen years before Cal or Finnley joined. He had taken pity on them, showing them the ropes and tricks of staying alive on a ruthless pirate ship.

And now he was dead.

Cal sighed and reached forward, brushing his fingertips over Galen's eyes, closing them for the last time.

Suddenly, an awareness prickled along Cal's skin, and he tensed. His magic rose up, ready to strike the unseen force. Glancing around the small room, Cal assessed what had tipped him off. He peered into the dark, his eyes traveling over the barrels of salt, hard biscuits, and freshwater, but there was nothing. Still, the hairs on his neck stood on end. Cal only felt this way when she was about to make an appearance. Soline tended to materialize when Cal's emotions were raw and unfettered, but it was far too soon for her to be showing up again. He had made sure that he completed the banishment, but perhaps being near the source of The Ether changed things. Still, Soline had never taken this long to show herself. Turning in a slow circle, Cal looked around, not daring to blink. He subtly rallied his magic, shadows curling around his fingertips.

"Cap'n?"

Cal whirled back to Galen's body, half expecting to see him sitting upright on the waist-high table. But he lay as still as before.

"What's going on?" the voice asked from behind Cal. He turned again, but found empty air. Frustration burned up in his chest, and he turned back to Galen's body. Cal thrust his hand into his jacket pocket and fished out two gold coins—Galen's payment to the afterlife. If Galen were being buried on land, Cal would place them on his eyes, but a sea burial was different. A cloth, weighed down by stones, would be placed over his body, sending him to the depths.

Moving closer to Galen's body, Cal intended to slip the coins into his pants pocket and be done with it. As he reached toward the body, his hand froze in mid-air. His eyes snagged on a shimmering figure hovering at the head of the table.

Slowly, Cal lifted his eyes and found Galen staring down at himself. Well, Galen's spirit, anyway. Cal straightened and narrowed his eyes at the spector, not entirely understanding what he was looking at. The dead had always spoken to Cal when *he* summoned them; only Soline had ever just appeared at will. But sure as The Ether was gone, Galen stood there, his head tilted, a funny look on his face.

"I knew me hair was thin'n, but it's near gone!"

"What are you doing here?' Cal breathed out.

Galen lifted his head, fixing his eyes on Cal. A goofy smile broke across his face. His form wavered for a moment, but it came back into focus. He lifted his hand in greeting and said, "Hi-ya, Cap'n."

Cal was helpless to stop the smile that overcame him. "Hi, Galen."

Galen moved around the table and stood beside Cal, still glancing at his body.

"Am I dead?" There was no fear or contempt in his voice, just genuine curiosity. He reached for his neck, toward the jagged laceration. His translucent fingers brushed against the ruined flesh but dissipated as he tried to make contact.

"Yes," Cal swallowed, before continuing in a tight voice, "not long after we entered The Ether, the ship came under attack. These monsters, sirens, came aboard—"

"I remember." Galen said, straightening and bringing his hand to his throat. "Shula was lyin' in our bed, sing'n our little girl to sleep, and I couldn't help meself. I had to be with them. Just once more." Galen's smile was soft, and his voice was barely above a whisper.

Something wet dripped down Cal's cheek. He surreptitiously wiped his face—tears.

He had never known that Galen had a family; he just assumed, like Finnley and himself, that he found the pirate life preferable to life on land. He never considered that Galen might have had a complete other life before the Umbra. Galen had never spoken of it, and seemed content to swab the deck and pillage for treasure. Shame slid over Cal's skin like oil. He found that looking at Galen–corpse or spirit–was next to impossible. But he forced himself to look at the apparition and uttered, "I am sorry that I couldn't save you."

Lifting his eyes, Galen gave Cal a half smile before gently shaking his head. "I don't hold ye responsible, Cap'n. A pirate's life is hardly ever long, and I've lived a good one."

Even with Galen's reassurance, Cal's guilt was a stone settling in his stomach. He wondered if Finnley knew about Galen's past. She probably did and kept it to herself, deeming it something Cal wouldn't need to know. Cal cleared his throat and said, "Is there anyone I need to contact or write—"

Galen cut him off with a shake of his head. "No. The only people I love are dead or here." Galen flickered, and Cal wondered how much longer he had before the other realm came to collect. "But, tell Fin-girl that she's the best of them, and it was a delight watching her become a leader."

"I will." He would pass along Galen's message because he was right.

With a nod and a smile, Galen said, "It was an hon'r servin' with you too, Cap'n. You and Fin brought some light back to my life. So did yer littlest brother. Reminds me a bit of you."

Cal clenched his jaw so hard he feared his teeth would crack, but he knew the tears stinging his eyes would escape if he did nothing. He had come here to say his farewells, not break down.

Galen flickered again, and this time, he lifted his hands and watched them disappear and reform before him. "I s'pose it's time for me to get goin'."

Cal nodded.

There was still much Cal didn't know about spirits, but he understood that if a soul found peace, they would cross soon after their death.

Blowing out a breath, Cal rubbed the gold coins between his fingers, warm from being clenched in his fist. He finished what he had started earlier and slipped the coins into Galen's jacket pocket. He turned and faced Galen, who watched with a contented look.

His form wavered and thinned again, and Galen said, "Thank you, Cap'n."

Cal's voice failed.

Perhaps that was for the best because as soon as Galen vanished from the room, Cal's knees hit the floor, and his sorrow flowed freely.

Chapter Thirty Nine

asper wiped his nose and eyes as Finnley and the other pirates stood over Galen's body.

Finnley's lips moved, but Kasper was too far to hear the words. He didn't need to, though; he had his farewell, which he wished to impart to Galen. Though he hadn't known the man long, he felt a kinship to him all the same. Galen had been one of the few to show compassion to Kasper, and even from their brief conversation, Kasper knew that Galen was the kindest person that Kasper knew—or at least remembered knowing. He hadn't belittled Kasper or treated his youth as something to be scorned or reviled. He accepted Kasper and shared a piece of himself—and for that, Kasper would be forever grateful.

A tear rolled down Kasper's cheek, and he let it fall. He let his sorrow gather in his eyes and spill down his face, splattering on the ebony deck. Blood and gore had covered the wood hours ago, and now it was all gone—along with a third of the crew.

Kasper issued a heavy sigh as Finnley's lips stilled, and she stepped away from Galen's body—her tears illuminated in the silvery moonlight. Other pirates, their faces portraits of sobriety and despondence, took up positions around Galen's body. They began covering him with the canvas that he laid upon.

Kasper pushed off the railing he leaned against. He had no desire to see Galen go overboard. He turned, but drew up short as his gaze fell on his brother.

Cal stood, swathed in rippling shadows, his eyes swollen and his mouth tight as he stared at his crew. They lifted their fallen comrade and carried him toward the skiff—ready to be lowered to the water below.

Stillness settled into Kasper's bones, not wanting to impede on what was clearly a private moment, but he couldn't tear his eyes from Cal either. His eyes remained fixed on Cal's anguished face, watching the tears stream down his cheeks—falling in earnest as Galen was loaded onto the skiff and lowered to the sea. Kasper cursed himself for the ugly jealousy that rippled through him at Cal's sorrow for Galen—something he never would have shown for Kasper.

Suddenly, Cal jerked as though he knew the precise moment that Galen's body was eased into the water, sinking beneath the tranquil waves. Cal sniffled and then turned, presumably to leave. He halted, though, his eyes snagged on Kasper.

Kasper sucked in a breath. He prepared for a reprimanding or plummeting temperatures—but it never came.

For a heartbeat, Cal held his gaze. Then, he gave him a terse nod and turned—leaving Kasper alone once more.

All of the tension went out of Kasper's shoulders, and he sagged against the railing. His exhaustion was palpable and looming, but there was still much to do. There was much to resolve, but none of that had to happen tonight.

Kasper shoved off of the railing once more and headed for the galley.

Chapter Forty

R hea kept her eyes pressed together, desperate to keep them
closed. She had no desire to move or think. And she wasn't
particularly interested in taking another breath, but her lungs
betrayed her, inhaling a ragged gasp. Her eyelids fluttered against her
will, and she grimaced against the candlelight illuminating her room.

Much to her own chagrin, she finally peered around the room—but
it wasn't her belongings cluttering the small space.

Because this wasn't her room.

Memories came flooding back in rapid succession. Pain burned
through her arm, stealing her breath. She winced and cursed at the pull
in her skin. Baring her teeth, she reached up with her right hand, trying
to assess the damage.

"Finnley came in and sewed it up."

Rhea jerked her head toward the voice. Despite the mind-numbing
pain in her arm, she remained tense as her eyes adjusted to the darkness clinging to the corner. Her heart skipped a beat for a moment,
thinking that perhaps Cal had come to see her. She held her breath as
the figure rose from the shadows. However, her excitement faltered a bit
as she beheld inquisitive–yet, perpetually sad–features, and she knew it
was Kasper. Despite all the brothers' similarities, Cal and Kai especially, Rhea could easily tell them apart. Kai had an ease to him that was
disarming, while Cal remained stern, sharp. Kasper was somewhere
between them. Kind and understanding, but bitter and wrathful. Rhea

sighed and shook her head. The characteristics of the Nader men were not her priority. She readjusted herself and settled into the thin, but numerous, blankets surrounding her.

Kasper came forward–the fruity scent of rum wafting from him–but he hesitated. His eyes moved over Rhea's face as if he were apprehensive about something. Rhea offered him a smile to diffuse their subtle tension, but Kasper did not reciprocate. Instead, he shifted closer to the side of the bed. He scanned over her body, his eyes catching on her arm. She followed his eyes. The skin of her shoulder was exposed, bearing a five-inch-long gash from her shoulder down her upper arm. The skin was sealed shut with black thread. There was the barest hint of pink around where her skin was previously lacerated.

"It looks like it's healing nicely. Might not even scar."

"It wouldn't matter if it did." Rhea said without thinking. Immediately, she winced, realizing her mistake too late. She was masquerading as a Lady-in-Waiting—noblewomen weren't supposed to be marred or have blemishes. But his statement eased her subtle worry that her back had been exposed at some point during the melee.

She flicked her eyes to Kasper. He didn't react, and for that, Rhea was grateful. She considered yawning and feigning sleep to avoid saying anything else that would compromise her identity, but before she could, Kasper said, "How much do you remember? From the attack."

Rhea pursed her lips. Her instinct was to deflect, but something about the openness of Kasper's gaze made her answer honestly. "Not much. I remember being on the deck and being soaked with rain and seawater. I remember deciding that I didn't want to die a coward, so I tried to fight back." Rhea swallowed against the emotion welling in her throat. She recoiled at the memory of the creature that nearly ended her. Shaking her head, she continued. "I cut off its tongue and ducked under its arm, but it was still too quick, and it got me. The pain…the pain was unbearable, and I suppose I would have died on the deck if C—your brother hadn't saved me."

Kasper nodded, clearly lost in his own thoughts. He moved closer to the head of the bed, something clutched between his fingers that he rubbed absentmindedly. "When the storm paused, I found you in Cal's arms. You were so pale." Kasper's stare was far off—vacant, but he continued. "The poison was moving too fast. I brought you down here and did everything I could." his voice broke, and he shook his head. "I didn't know if you were going to survive."

She really was lucky she hadn't died. That knowledge did little to change her perspective or her plans. If anything, it reaffirmed that she needed to find the Cave of Splendors and save her kingdom. She wouldn't be around forever, and she needed to secure its longevity for when she was gone.

Licking her lips, Rhea was instantly aware of the dryness of her mouth. Kasper's intense gaze was fixed on her. He quickly moved toward a wooden tankard and cup on the small table next to the bed. He hastily poured a cup, sloshing some over the sides, before he twisted and pushed it toward Rhea. She took the cup, her grip shaky. She had no idea how long she had been out or when she last ate, but she was aware of the fatigue in her limbs and mind. She set her jaw and pushed through it.

She took several slow but long sips, savoring the cool splash of liquid on her ravaged throat. After a few minutes, she lowered the cup from her lips, rested against the pillow once more, and closed her eyes. Sleep crept into the recesses of her mind, and she was tempted to give in to it, but Kasper cleared his throat. She felt obliged to acknowledge him since he had saved her life—again.

Her eyes fluttered open, and she found Kasper still looming above her. He worried the object between his fingers, which had a slight glow emanating from it.

"How did you heal me?" Rhea, of course, knew of Kasper's abilities. He had already used his magic to heal her once, but she was eager to get his attention focused on something else.

Kasper frowned.

He dropped his hands, slipped the object—a purple stone—into his pocket, and flopped into the seat next to her bed. He scrubbed his face, looking more haggard than she had ever seen him. His bottom lip was tucked between his teeth, and he stared off into the gloomy dark of the cabin—then exhaled loudly.

Rhea remained silent. She was unsure if he would speak, or merely reminisce on whatever memories Rhea had unearthed.

The purple stone appeared again, but Kasper was staring at it more intently now. "Gems and crystals possess certain properties."

Rhea nodded. It was common knowledge that specific stones held specific abilities. Healing, wealth, protection, love, and other things. The purple gem in Kasper's hands flared a warm light.

Rhea gasped as he reached out and placed the stone in her hand. She trusted him–she always had–so she didn't hesitate as she gripped the stone, warm from his hands, tightly in her fist. Waves of tranquility washed over her, pulsing from the glowing gem in her hand and over her body.

"I can sort of amplify and channel a gem or crystal's ability."

Glancing around the room, Rhea took in the various gems and rocks with new eyes. She knew all about Kasper's abilities. But keeping up the facade of their past was vital, so she turned back to Kasper and whispered, "You used the properties of the crystals."

Kasper ducked his gaze, a faint blush coloring his cheeks. "I didn't know if it would work, but I had to try. Your heartbeat was so painfully slow, and your color was gone. I had to try."

Swallowing, Rhea reached out to Kasper. She slipped her fingers over his hand, and his eyes lifted to hers, tears shining.

"I'm grateful you did." she said softly, a smile ghosting her lips.

"I was so scared I was too late."

Rhea squeezed his hand. "Everything is all right now."

"Is it?" he said dejectedly.

Rhea furrowed her brows, unsure what he meant.

Kasper noted her confusion and pressed his lips into a thin line, staring down at the floor. There was something else. Something he wasn't sharing. Rhea's mind immediately went to the worst. They had been blown far off course, or someone else was hurt. Someone was dead. The only thing keeping Rhea from spiraling was the purple gem still glowing faintly in her closed fist.

"What is it, Kasper? What has happened?"

Lifting his head, Kasper read the concern on her face and in her voice. He leaned forward and cupped her hand into his, giving it a reassuring squeeze. "Nothing. Everyone is fine—well, everyone that matters to you."

Rhea flinched, but there was no malice in Kasper's tone, just truth.

Exhaling again, Kasper said, "Is there anything else you remember? Anything after the attack?"

Frowning, Rhea attempted to recall the last few days. The Ether and the attack were clear and vivid, but beyond that was murky and fragmented. Pieces of memories and feelings, but nothing concrete. Rhea tentatively shook her head and said, "No. Nothing but flashes, and even those are hazy at best."

Kasper nodded and released her hand. He moved to stand, and confusion washed over Rhea. She pushed up in the bed, even as the wound along her arm protested.

"What is it, Kasper?"

He shook his head and waved her off. "It's nothing, I promise."

"No, it certainly isn't 'nothing'. You've been looking at me like you expect me to know something I have no recollection of and are upset that I don't. So just tell me what I'm supposed to remember." Rhea's tone bordered on demanding, but she didn't care. She was tired, sore, and sleepy. She just wanted some straight answers.

"Fine," Kasper said, turning and placing his hands on his hips, "after I healed you, you woke up and said some...stuff."

Dread, so intense that even the gem in her palm failed to quell it, settled into her gut. Rhea fluttered her eyes. "Like what?" She waved and laughed dismissively. "It was likely all nonsense. I have no memory of it, so it couldn't have been that important."

Kasper's eyes were wide and insistent, like a child's. He looked so much like he did when they made up stories and ran around the castle that Rhea's heart stammered in her chest.

"'Like you *knew* me. As though we had a past—a history. And," Kasper dropped down beside her bed and took her hand once more. The purple stone gave a quick pulse at his touch. "I have felt this tug to you since you stepped into my brother's tent. There is something between us, Hera, and I know you know what it is."

Rhea stayed perfectly still.

There was such intensity and desperation in his eyes that she almost broke.

Almost. But there was too much at stake. Too much risk lay in revealing the truth of who she was and what they had meant to each other when they were children. That connection was *real*, born of a shared childhood love and experiences. Rhea set her jaw and promised herself that once she had secured the treasure she sought, she would tell him the truth. He might never forgive her, but at least he would have his answers.

Rhea forced her voice to work as she choked out, "I don't know, Kasper. I'm sorry I can't be of more help."

Kasper held her gaze for a heartbeat and then released her. He dropped her hand and rose from the floor. The wooden beams creaked mournfully as he stepped toward the door. But he paused, his hand hovering over the latch, and whispered, "You should get some more rest. I'll be by later to check on you." With that, he left, and Rhea didn't try to stop him this time.

Hot, stinging tears rolled down her cheek as she rolled on her side. She brought the purple stone up to her face, examining it for the first time. It was beautiful in the way only crystals and gems were. Veins of varying shades of purple mingled, forming what she could only assume to be amethyst. Her favorite gem as a child. Rhea turned her face into her pillow to muffle her cries. She had no idea how much time had passed before sleep mercifully claimed her once more and swept her under a tidal wave of guilt and regret.

* * * *

Rhea woke to find her cabin–Kasper's cabin–illuminated with bright sunlight. That was confusing for a number of reasons, but the more pressing issue at the moment was why Finnley was slumped in the chair next to the bed. Her feet were propped up on the foot of the bed, and her hat was drawn low over her brow—her face wholly obscured. As if roused by Rhea's attention, Finnley lifted her head and dropped her feet, her boots thudding against the ebony floor.

"Good, yer awake." she remarked as she stepped over to the table at her bedside. Rhea's eyes tracked her movement as she lifted a small tray heaped with dried meat and hard biscuits. On cue, Rhea's stomach grumbled at the sight of the food. Unfortunately, it was so utterly unappetizing that she had to keep herself from scrunching her nose in disdain. After a few weeks away from the palace, she would have thought she would have become accustomed to eating for the sake of survival, but she still longed for more savory food.

Pushing herself into an upright position, Rhea was careful of her still-healing arm. Finnley set the tray in her lap before returning to her chair and throwing her legs on the bed again.

Rhea took a tentative bite of the dried meat, her mouth watering at its sheer saltiness. She knew the biscuit would be no better, so she gnawed on the meat as best as she was able. Several minutes passed in silence; the only sound Rhea's chewing and swallowing. A million questions rattled through her mind, but she kept quiet, unsure why Finnley was present but positive she would find out soon.

Finnley nodded, seemingly satisfied after Rhea had choked down three pieces of dried meat. She regarded Rhea once more and said, "I'm sure ye have questions."

Nodding and swallowing she said, "A few."

"Right. Well, first thing. The storm is gone. Cap'n scattered it not long after ye were hurt."

Rhea twisted toward the small window above the bed. Bright blue skies and sunlight streamed through the pane. She turned back and said, "Is it gone for good?" She had many more questions: How did he dispel it? What had it cost him? Why was she in his arms during the fighting? What—

"As far as we can tell. Cap'n ain't said nothin' else 'bout it. So, we think so." The skin around Finnley's scar seemed to stretch and pull tight as if she wasn't interested in discussing this latest development.

"Is everyone alright?" Rhea asked softly. Kasper didn't share who specifically hadn't made it.

The tension in Finnley's face grew as she worked her jaw and then said in a tight voice, "Everyone in your party made it out. Your guard and the Seer are fine."

"What about the crew?"

Something—sorrow, regret, guilt—flared in Finnley's eyes. She quickly looked away and said, "Most, but not all."

Rhea pursed her lips and said gently, "I'm sorry. They were good people—most of them. Of course, I didn't know them well, but I could tell they were good people."

"Aye, they were."

Silence blossomed between them once more. Rhea was unsure what else to say. The amethyst stone rolled between her fingers. She focused on the smooth texture rather than Finnley, who was clearly still processing the loss of her crewmates.

Suddenly, the weight on the bed shifted, and Finnley stood, looking like she was ready to take flight. However, she stopped and stared down at Rhea.

Rhea froze, anticipating a scolding. Memories of her father, governesses, and tutors burned in her mind. The tongue-lashings–and beatings–that left her flushed and wanting to disappear flashed as well.

"It took courage to try and fight like you did. When I gave you that blade, I didn't know if I would find it stuck in a beast, or you." Pride swelled in Rhea at Finnley's comment, but it quickly faded as she continued, "But, you nearly died and almost got others killed in the process. If you want to fight, or at least not be a liability to those around you, you must learn how to defend yourself. Don't let that noble blood preclude you from protecting yourself. Because when those idiotic brothers or your guard die doing something stupid, which they will, there won't be anyone left to save you except for you."

Finnley didn't wait for Rhea to reply; she turned on her heel and stormed out of the room. Rhea's cheeks burned with shame and embarrassment because Finnley was right. She had allowed her father to keep her helpless and relied on the men around her to ensure her safety. She should have fought harder to be taught to defend herself when she was at the palace. Not only was she risking her own life by placing it in the hands of others, but she risked theirs, too.

Rhea leaned back against the pillows. She was still so weak from the poison and blood loss, but she was on the mend. And as soon as she was well enough, she would learn how to fight.

Chapter Forty One

Malakai pressed the heels of his palms into his temples, forcing the fractured pieces of his mind back together. Pain flashed and sizzled like meat in hot oil, destroying his focus and forcing him to lie back on the worn mattress.

Four days since he'd given up his magic.

Three days since he could summon a vision.

When Malakai awoke, finding himself in his cabin relatively unharmed–save for the gash along his palm–he relaxed a fraction. But it wasn't long before he realized that he had no recollection of his dreams in spite of him being unconscious for hours. Not once in his life was there a time when he wasn't instantly overwhelmed with the flashes of his subconscious. At first, he thought nothing of it, merely a consequence of exerting so much magic so quickly. But then night fell, and no dreams came to him. Nor did they the next night.

Nausea cramped his stomach, but it had nothing to do with sickness. Never, in the nearly quarter century that Malakai had known about and used his magic, had it ever abandoned him. But now, it lingered in the recesses of his mind—just out of reach. Taunting and mocking him.

That simply would not do.

Forcing a vision became his only option. He gulped down the remnants of a stimulant he had brought—to no avail. His power remained dormant in his body.

He was nothing without his magic. Nothing more than what everyone had always accused him of being—a charlatan, a fake, a phony. He had always taken comfort in the knowledge that he *did* have power. That the future, however precarious, was always within his reach. When there was something to be divined, he was the one people sought out, even if they first believed him to be a conman. But now, there was nothing. No glimpses or flashes of things to come or things that had passed.

He was nothing more than an empty vessel. A waste of space. The dreams of returning home to the palace, to a life of ease, excess, and comfort, flitted away. He had asked the Princess for his position as court Seer, but she would have no need for him if he couldn't do the one thing he was made for.

Malakai released his head and sighed. A solitary tear slipped from the corner of his eye and down his face. The pain ebbed from his skull and pooled in his chest, but it never abated. Malakai rolled on his side and brought his hand up to his face. Dragging his nail across a scab, he tore off the loose flecks of clotted skin and blood. He cursed himself. He cursed the gods.

He never should have handed Cal his magic.

Sharing magic was frowned upon—illegal in some places—and considered risky for a reason, but Malakai thought he would be immune to the consequences. He should have looked further into the vision and understood that this future resulted in him losing his power. But *lost* still wasn't the fitting descriptor. It was there, hovering and waiting, but for what Malakai couldn't say. He had never lost that connection, and now, he hadn't the faintest idea of how to restore it.

What he did know was that as soon as his brothers, or anyone for that matter, discovered he could no longer divine the future…Malakai didn't want to spend too long thinking about what they might do.

Malakai dropped his hand and stared blankly at the bare wall before him. Knocks echoed against his door, but he ignored them. Or he feigned being asleep if someone came in. He had no desire to face them, but his window for wallowing was quickly closing. He needed to get up and rejoin the crew. There was still much of their journey left, and though he didn't have access to his vision, Malakai still knew plenty about their path ahead. He also knew plenty of his companions' secrets—secrets he would leverage to maintain his value on this quest if necessary. There was also Princess Rhea's book…

Another heartbeat passed before he pushed himself up from the bed and planted his feet on the floor. He glanced down at his body and grimaced. He hadn't bothered to change or clean himself since Caliban had cleared away The Ether. Malakai might not feel like himself, but he still had appearances to maintain.

He rose from the bed, swaying as black spots momentarily danced in his field of vision. A growl rumbled up his spine, and he pressed a hand to his stomach—he would also need to find something to eat. After his vision cleared, Malakai padded over to the chipped wardrobe and pulled open the door. He was greeted with the familiar scent of his incense, and he breathed, letting the memories of better days wash over him. Foolishly, he hoped that something he associated with his magic would awaken his abilities, but nothing stirred within him. Malakai released a heavy sigh and reached for his spare clothing.

* * * *

One sponge bath, a clothing change, and a hearty breakfast of stale bread later, Malakai stood on the deck of the Umbra, squinting at the late evening sun. He stared longer than was advisable, but he wanted a good look at what had cost him his magic. Finally, he dropped his hand and glanced around at the crew. Even if Malakai hadn't been present for most of the fighting, he could pinpoint the ship's new scars and the crew's haggard looks that spoke to their latest trauma.

Malakai knew that without his sacrifice, they would likely all be dead. Their bodies would've been a feast for the monsters. The Umbra resigned to a watery grave—joining other ships claimed by The Ether. But even with that knowledge, Malakai wasn't sure he would have gone through with it had he known the outcome was the loss of his magic. He worried his bottom lip between his teeth while considering the cost of life and the loss of his abilities. He finally concluded that the death of his magic and literal death were equal in their devastation—but at least this way, there was a chance he could recover his magic. In theory, anyway.

"I didn't get a chance to thank you." A voice announced behind him. Malakai turned to find Finnley staring at him—her arms crossed and her scar stark in the blinding light.

Malakai stumbled back a step.

Never would he forget the vision that had rendered him unconscious the last time he had touched her. "Finnley," he cooed and took another step back. His eyes darted around the ship, desperate for someone–literally anyone–to rescue him, but there was no one there. Finnley took a step forward, her gaze still locked on Malakai. He didn't need his powers to know there was no escaping her. If she wanted an audience with someone, she would have it. Smiling, he twisted his gilded ring around his finger, "to what do I owe the pleasure?"

Finnley's face revealed nothing as she said, "I wanted to thank you for what you did. It was no small thing, giving yourself over to your brother like that. That took courage—or immense desperation."

Malakai's smile wavered. Guilt crashed down on him. He had only given his magic to Caliban to save himself and the future he was so desperate for. Malakai swallowed the lump in his throat and pasted on a brilliant smile. "It was the least I could do."

Raising an eyebrow, Finnley made a noise of agreement in her throat. Malakai hoped this was the end of their exchange and started to bid Finnley farewell when she asked, "What did it cost you?"

"I beg your pardon?" He questioned, his voice quivering.

"That display. It drained you of your energy while Cap'n seemed fine. Refreshed even. I was just wondering what it cost you to surrender a part of yourself to him." Finnley stepped closer, cutting the distance between them to mere inches. Something sharp and unyielding gleamed in her eyes as she whispered, "Especially when you take such pains to appear in control of yourself and the world around you. But you know what I think?" A cruel smile graced her lips, tugging at the ruined flesh of her face. "I think it's all an illusion. A farce. An attempt to exert your influence on the world when, in reality, you are just as blind and helpless as the rest of us. So, I'll ask again, 'What did it cost you?'"

"Everything." The word was out before Malakai could think of trying to stop them. Something about this woman unnerved him like no one else ever had. She saw through his veneer of eccentric tendencies and flamboyant behavior. She saw all the way down to the fear that ruled him and the terror now forcing its way to the surface. Tears burned in Malakai's eyes as he tried and failed to keep himself together. Never had he shown such weakness in front of others. But here he was, crumbling over some carefully placed words. He was a fool for letting himself unravel so easily, and yet there was nothing he was able to do to cease it.

Malakai braced for Finnley's sneer at or mocking words, but the insults never came. Instead, she took a single step away and clenched her jaw before whispering, "That's how you made me feel that first night when you unearthed those memories. That out-of-control, reckless feeling? You caused that after you decided to go digging in my memories. It only serves you right that you experience a modicum of the anguish you wrought on your victims."

Frustration–at being misunderstood and accused–rose up in Malakai's chest, and he blurted out, "I don't control the visions."

Finnley's stern expression hardened further. "What?"

Malakai took a deep breath and released it. "I don't *always* control the visions. Whether I see the past or future is chance at first. Sometimes, they happen if I simply touch someone or something, or even meet someone."

"Is that what happened to me?"

Nodding, Malakai replied, "They aren't normally that intense, but when we interacted, I got a glimpse of your past. I never intended to do that."

A muscle flexed in Finnley's jaw. Her eyes cut away at a passing pirate before returning to his face. "Did you tell anyone about it?" she bit out.

Malakai's curls swayed as he shook his head. "Never. What I witness is private. I never share what I see with anyone other than who it pertains to, especially if it was an unprompted vision or memory."

Almost imperceptibly, some of the tension in her shoulders was released. Malakai knew the peace between them was tenuous and likely temporary, but he was helpless to stop himself as he asked, "Is that why you've been so hostile toward me?"

Shrugging, Finnley looked away. "Partly. I also didn't trust you based on what Cap'n shared about you."

Malakai was unsure whether to be offended or flattered that Caliban had bothered to speak about him at all. Malakai rubbed his chin and recognized that he needed to capitalize on this momentary truce. He thrust out his hand, the red slash across his skin vulgar in the sunlight. Wariness danced in Finnley's eyes as she regarded him.

Aiming to keep his voice level, Malakai said, "I think we both understand one another now, and I think, moving forward, we can make better use of our time rather than quarreling."

Finnley's arms remained crossed over her chest. A gull cried out from overhead. A pair of crew members passed by, conversing quietly. A second passed, or it could have been an eternity; Malakai wasn't sure. Finally, Finnley sighed and uncrossed her arms. Malakai saw the hesitation swirling in her eyes, but she eventually reached out her hand, clasping Malakai's.

A vision flashed through Malakai's mind.

Images of an island, lush and vibrant, teeming with life. Large, ancient, undisturbed structures gleamed with an internal light hidden deep within the earth. Treasure, more than any man should ever possess, glittered and sparkled beneath an unseeing statute. But lingering there, in the shadows of the vision, was danger. Waiting and watching to see what they would do.

Malakai's lungs seized, and he sucked in a sharp breath. He released and stumbled away from Finnley—whose features had returned to their distrustful nature. Malakai doubled over as the last vision receded from his sight, but the memory of it burned into his mind.

"What's going on?"

Malakai struggled to find the words. A laugh bubbled up in his throat and frothed on his lips. He straightened and cast his face toward the sun, the light searing into his eyes. He didn't care because he could See again. Finnley was still staring at him, but he paid her no mind. As he tilted his head back down, his grin nearly split his face. Malakai put the suspicious look in Finnley's eyes out of his mind and spoke jovially.

"I've had a vision."

Chapter Forty Two

Malakai was practically vibrating.

His visions were *back*.

The setting sun blazed into his skin, but it was inconsequential. His visions were back! Dropping his face back down, he was greeted by Finnley's skepticism.

Her arched brow stood starkly against her scar as she said flatly, "I thought you had those all the time."

Malakai shook his head. He considered telling Finnley the truth, but surmised it wouldn't matter either way. As long as he didn't read her or the crew, she didn't seem interested in what he did. "I need to go speak with my brothers. Do you know where they are?"

Finnley rolled her eyes but raised a weathered hand and pointed over Malakai's shoulder. He turned, glimpsing Kasper. Twisting back toward Finnley, he opened his mouth to thank her, but she was gone—the wind swirled in her place. Malakai smiled to himself and then turned once more, preparing to face his younger brother.

Kasper didn't look at Malakai as he approached. Despite the elation of having access to his magic once more, his standard, self-assured nature waned. Why was Kasper avoiding him? Malakai's affliction and the descending of The Ether upon the Umbra had consumed much of his energy and focus. How long ago had they boarded the ship? A week? Longer? Malakai shook his head, attempting to convince himself that it didn't matter. Whatever–if anything–was between him and Kasper, a conversation would surely remedy it.

Even with that conclusion, his feet still stuttered as he approached. Malakai latched onto his resolve. He lifted his chin and forced levity into his voice as he said, "Dearest Kasper, how are you?"

Tension was etched into Kasper's weary features as he slid his eyes to Malakai. A muscle ticked in Kasper's jaw, and he looked away from Malakai once more.

What was Kasper's issue? Perhaps the nature of his spell had been particularly alarming, or maybe Malakai had done something to him without remembering it. Maybe it had nothing to do with Malakai at all. He considered inquiring, but there were more pressing matters at hand. Besides, Kasper tended to be very forgiving, so it was just a matter of time until he moved past whatever was bothering him. Instead of prodding him on his sour disposition, Malakai glanced to where Kasper's eyes were trained; a subtle smile spread over his lips.

Princess Rhea's arm was looped through Brander's as they took slow, measured steps along the deck. Malakai surmised from the tense, pained look on Kasper's face that he wished it was him beside the Princess instead. Though Malakai was unconscious for longer than the Princess was, he had overheard enough passing conversations to know that his brother had not left her side since the attack—even after Kasper had taken the Princess to his rooms.

Malakai couldn't help the twinge of envy that flared in his chest. Since their exile, it had always been him that Kasper fussed over and protected. Malakai was not ignorant to the fact that *he* should have been looking after and caring for Kasper, but it wasn't in his nature. He lacked the fundamental traits that made a person selfless and nurturing, allowing them to set aside their desires to care for another. Besides, Malakai's abilities had kept them afloat—mostly. But, now, looking back on the near decade that Malakai had spent simply expecting Kasper to care for him, he might see how he was a burden for his younger brother.

Malakai swallowed down his regret—it wouldn't do any good now. Wetting his lips, he summoned up the sun-shiny facade that had served him so well for years, and said, "I've had a vision." He paused, waiting for Kasper to turn and acknowledge him again.

But he never did.

Kasper's eyes tracked the Princess's slow progress, never leaving her. Malakai considered stepping into Kasper's line of sight to get his attention. He refrained. Even he wasn't *that* pathetic, though his brother's blatant disregard did sting.

The sun was heating his cheeks to an uncomfortable level—or maybe that was Kasper's rejection? Either way, Malakai persisted. "I saw the Isle, well, flashes of it." He laughed nervously. "It wasn't a complete vision like normal, although I think I gleaned enough, but, um…" Why was he rambling? Malakai may not always feel confident, but he made an effort to appear that way. Maybe it was his visions leaving him for so long, the guilt over his earlier cowardice, or the heat simmering in Kasper's eyes that made Malakai lose his words. Malakai rolled his shoulders and began again. But before the words could leave his mouth, Kasper turned on him, his rage rolling off of him in waves.

"Tell it to someone who cares, Kai." Kasper said as he stepped around Malakai. Kasper's shoulder clipped Malakai, sending him careening toward the railing. He threw a hand to brace himself, but flashes of a vision—

No, a *memory* tore through his mind.

It was of him, but from Kasper's perspective.

His chest ached, caving in on itself. Tears stung his eyes, and his throat burned with the effort of keeping his volatile emotions at bay.

Malakai remembered then.

He had told Kasper—not the whole truth—but enough that Kasper couldn't stand to be in the same room as him, let alone speak to him.

Malakai gasped and cursed himself for being so forthcoming. Even if he had no personal recollection of making that choice. He almost would have preferred to topple overboard than deal with the lingering embarrassment of Kasper's dismissal. But, as callous as it sounded,

Kasper's feelings were irrelevant—at least at the moment. When Kasper calmed down and allowed Malakai to explain why he had done it, then everything would be right again. Kasper just needed time.

Right?

He took a moment to shake off his disappointment and regret. Finding Caliban was still his priority. Kasper might not be interested in hearing what Malakai had to say, but he knew Caliban would—if only because it was about the Cave of Splendors. The Cave held Caliban's only chance at restoring Soline and whatever else he believed necessary to redeem—or further condemn—himself. Mustering up what fragments of his ego remained, Malakai forced himself to scan the ship for his twin. The sun was steadily slipping out of the sky. It descended to the glittering water below, casting the Umbra in gold, red, and orange shades. He might have taken a few more moments to appreciate the beauty of the rolling waves and sky, but time was of the essence. Besides, there was no telling what kind of mood Caliban would be in.

Malakai's slippers whispered against the ebony deck, his eyes straining in the fading light to locate his brother. There was the familiar tug in his gut, that nauseating connection that he always had with his twin. Malakai had never met another set of twins, so he couldn't say if their connection was a product of their magic or their birth. Whatever the case, Malakai followed the sensation down into the hull, passing through the long corridor of cabins. He went down another set of stairs until he came to a halt in a storeroom of sorts, Caliban's back facing Malakai.

Caliban's arms were braced on either side of a table that was suspiciously clear of items, save for a dark stain in the worn wood.

"What do you want, Kai?" There were notes of annoyance, disdain, and...exhaustion? The first two were to be expected, but the exhaustion was surprising, to say the least. According to Finnley, Caliban had been reinvigorated and restored after he had used Malakai's power. Perhaps it wasn't physical fatigue. In the dim lighting of the room, he made out the tense lines of Caliban's back. His jaw was also flexed as he turned and glanced at Malakai over his shoulder.

"I had a vision." Malakai said cheerily.

Caliban arched an eyebrow. "Isn't that what you do?"

A strained laugh escaped Malakai's lips. He shifted his weight from one foot to the other. "Well, yes. Ordinarily."

"Ordinarily?" Caliban asked as he turned to face Malakai, leaning his back against the table.

"Well, they went away after you used my magic to dispel the storm, but they are back now." he assured, his voice lifting.

Caliban turned to face Malakai more fully.

Instinctively, Malakai reached for the familiar but false countenance. It was the only thing that kept him from balking every time Caliban set his withering gaze upon him. He swallowed and squared his shoulders, determined not to cower.

"What do you mean 'they're back now'?"

"They...left me. After I lent you my magic." Malakai struggled to find the right words. It didn't matter, though, because Caliban narrowed his eyes on his twin. A muscle twitched in his jaw. Malakai continued, "I saw the Isle and some of what is to come, though none of it was particularly clear. I saw treasure, but there was a sense of foreboding."

Caliban crossed his arms. "What good does that do me?"

Frowning, Malakai shifted his weight again. "Well, I thought you would want to know since this affects all of us."

"Does it? Because the way I see it, if you've lost the one thing that makes you useful, then there's no reason to bother including you in anything."

"I haven't lost it." Malakai said indignantly. "It was just gone for a few days. Likely a side effect of you *stealing* my magic."

Caliban chuckled darkly and pushed off from the table. His long strides eating up the distance between them. "Funny, I remember you quite willingly–desperately, even–handing over your magic. But, if you haven't lost it, then read me. Tell me what's to come."

Malakai swallowed thickly as his brother shoved his sleeves up and exposed his forearms. He wanted to refuse, but Caliban wouldn't allow him to leave this place until he proved one of them wrong. Gripping Caliban's scarred wrists, he inhaled through his nose—bracing for the vision.

But…it never came. Malakai pressed, reaching for the familiar white light of his magic, but there was nothing.

Dropping his wrist, Caliban sneered. "That's what I thought." He moved to step around him, but paused. "You know, you've only ever been as useful to me as your visions were relevant. I hope for your sake that you're right and this is a fluke, but something tells me that this vision is the anomaly and that your luck has finally run out."

Malakai went stone still at the venom in Caliban's words. But as Caliban stepped around him, he reached out, catching Caliban's shoulder. "I hope for both our sakes that you're wrong because I am the only chance we have at surviving what's to come."

A corner of Caliban's mouth lifted. "We shall see, won't we? Oh, well…you might not." He shrugged off Malakai's touch and disappeared into the dark, shadows clinging to him.

Silence enveloped him again, smothering his fleeting hope that his magic wasn't leaving him. But he hadn't missed the flicker of apprehension that showed in Caliban's eyes. There was a brief moment of fear when Malakai shared that his visions were inconsistent, or perhaps gone altogether. Sighing, Malakai rubbed his hands up and down his arms. He needed to know for certain whether his magic was truly gone. He turned from the small, dank room and hurried from the sentient gloom.

Chapter Forty Three

Shadows curled around Cal's fingers. They wove in and out, writhing and wriggling in time with *their* pulse as Cal stared out over her sleeping form. Cal wasn't sure how or why he chose to enter her room, but after what Kai had shared, he needed to be somewhere else. Ever since Hera's life teetered on the precipice of death, Cal was keenly aware of the thrum of her heartbeat. Even days after the attack on the Umbra, days since Kas had healed her—a thread still tied them together. Cal wondered if it was solely a result of his magic, or if the desperate plea he uttered in the moments he held her had inexplicably linked them.

Shifting in his chair, Cal leaned in closer to Hera. The draw to her before was inconveniently annoying, but now it was unbearable. Nearly every thought he had was about her. What she was doing, how she felt, and what she thought of him. He knew it was foolish and unproductive, but that hadn't stopped him from entering her rooms in the dead of night.

Voices echoed down the hall—just outside the door.

Cal halted his obsessing to hear them better. He stilled his shadows and held his breath, but then the voices retreated, their conversation muffled by the thick wood of the cabin walls. He relaxed his shoulders and released his breath. With a flex of his fingers, the shadows resumed their roaming.

Hera had been moved back to her quarters a day earlier, but he wouldn't put it past her guard dog to slip into her room while she slept—clearly, that idea had already occurred to Cal. Glancing toward the small window just above the bed, he noted the moonlight that poured in, illuminating the contents of the small cabin. Hera's dresses and scarves were discarded atop the small chest of drawers, the rich silks and jewel-toned velvets in sharp contrast to the scratched wood grain. Rings and necklaces were strewn haphazardly over the worn bedside table, a plate of half-eaten dry biscuits and meat also rested there. Next to it was the book, *Legends of the Cave of Splendors.*

Cal considered taking it. Given the state of the room, he doubted Hera would even notice—at least initially. And even if she did realize it was gone, how would she know it was him? Besides, once he got the information he needed, he could always put it back. But even as the book sat there, ripe for the taking, Cal hesitated. Whatever ridiculous morals he clung to prevented it. He cursed himself. Hera would never willingly give over the book, but stealing it from her–while she slept, no less–didn't sit well with him. Cal released a long-suffering sigh and let his anger go.

Finally, Cal let his eyes slip back to Hera. Her chest moved slowly but steadily; she was well and truly asleep. Her ebony waves were splayed around her like a dark star erupting across the dusk-colored sky at twilight. Impossibly long and thick eyelashes fluttered against her warm olive cheeks, which were dotted with a smattering of brown freckles that covered the narrow expanse of her nose. With her features relaxed, the crease between her brows was gone, and the rigid set of her jaw was diminished. She looked younger. But the closer he peered, the more apparent the nearly invisible white scars marring a handful of places around her exposed face and arms became. Her split lip had healed, but that didn't stop the rage that throbbed in Cal's skull at the memory of it. Cal couldn't understand how a woman like her–fierce and uncompromising–served the Abadi family, or how she tolerated the subtle abuses she had clearly been objected to. Surely, she knew of the atrocities committed at the King's hand. However, if she were in a similar position to Soline, there would never be a choice.

Cal clenched his fist at the thought of the King and the havoc he had wreaked on Cal's life. His shadows grew more insistent at his rage. The King owed Cal a debt. And Cal would collect on it.

Eventually.

Voices reverberated around Cal again, but he didn't question their origin this time. The night around him thickened, and his shadows pulsed in response. Cal leaned back in his chair and sighed through his nose. It was getting harder and harder to keep the dead at bay. Whatever magic created The Ether and was tied to where the Cave resided—the Isle Oum, Cal recalled—was tampering with his magic. The shadows grew darker, moving to blot out the moonlight, but Cal resisted. His fingers dug into the arms of the chair, the wood giving a soft groan in reply. He was the master of his magic, not the other way around. Even if his magic was being meddled with. Or perhaps amplified beyond his control.

He would not give in so easily.

The voices around him intensified, becoming more insistent. They plead with him to do their bidding. To help them cross back or seek revenge. Cal would do no such thing. Gradually, one voice rose above the rest. It beckoned to him, and his resolve slipped—only by a fraction, but it was enough. Shadows engulfed him. They snuffed out what light had remained.

Cal's heart jolted. He clenched tighter against the chair arms and pressed his feet firmly against the floor, desperate to keep himself grounded in reality. It only took a heartbeat for a cold, moon-white hand to slip over Cal's shoulders and trail its fingernails down his arm. He stared unblinkingly into the inky darkness. He noted the shift in the space. The subtle way the command of the darkness was tumbling away from him terrified him.

Soline came around in front of Cal with a lovely, coy smile. Her skin glowed with an unearthly light, bright enough that Cal had to squint against it. Cal blanched as Soline sat down on his lap. She was more corporeal than she had ever appeared before—like she was really with him. Cal's fingers spasmed. They ached with the desire to hold her, to give in to the demand that her large cerulean eyes held. She looked almost as good as she had in the vision the sirens had conjured up—almost.

"Oh, how I've missed you, Caliban." Soline murmured as she dropped her head to his and ghosted a kiss over his cheek. Cal's breathing went shallow, and he closed his eyes. He poured every ounce of self-control he had into not encouraging Soline. She was a beacon in the dark, a boon of safety and love. She was all Cal had ever wanted—and he had lost her. His inadequacies and shortcomings had cost Cal her life once, but now, he was close to rectifying that.

"Have you missed me?"

"Every day." he answered and opened his eyes.

"Awww," Soline purred, stroking a manicured nail along his jaw. She brushed another kiss and then sat up abruptly. The sky-blue of her eyes darkened, and her soft, angelic features sharpened into something wicked. "I can't see how that's the truth, Caliban, when you're in another woman's bedroom." she hissed.

The oddly solid presence of Soline vanished, leaving Cal feeling hollow and ragged. He blinked, expecting to find Soline's sneering face inches from his, but only darkness greeted him.

Cal sprang to his feet.

He scanned the swirling shadows, looking for any sign of Soline. She was still in the room—that much he knew. Like the draw he felt for Hera, he was always acutely aware when Soline was nearby. Reaching forward, he twisted his wrist, willing the shadows to part...but nothing happened. He yanked more forcefully, but again, they didn't budge. Trepidation tripped in Cal's chest, but he tamped down on it. Darkness fed on fear, and he would not give it an inch.

Slowing his breathing, Cal took a step forward. The gentle swaying of the ship and the scent of worn wood, salt, and a light hint of lillies confirmed that he was still in Hera's room, even if his sight was hindered. If the shadows would not answer him, he would simply have to resort to other methods. Cal whispered a spell, a simple one that allowed temporary vision in darkness. Unlike most magic wielders, Cal didn't revile the use of spells. It might have been the main avenue of power for witches and warlocks with little natural ability, but Cal saw no reason why he couldn't use it when necessary. Besides, how were spells and blood magic any different from conduits like Kasper's crystals, which allowed him to harness his magic better? The magic of Isle Oum was clearly more potent than even Cal—he would take any advantage available to him.

Briefly, Cal wished Kai were with him. He wouldn't have to bother with spells. He could simply dispel the darkness with Kai's light...but then he risked harming Soline or Hera. Sighing noisily through his nose, Cal blinked as the spell slid into place. The room was still murky, but he made out the outline of Hera's bed and the chest of drawers against the wall. He scanned, looking for Soline's wraith-like form, and stopped dead in his tracks.

She hovered over Hera's unconscious body, peering down at her with unnerving interest. Cal cursed silently. He should have known from the moment that Soline appeared that she would go after Hera. A spirit Soline may be, but she clearly held more sway here in the reach of the Isle than Cal was accustomed to.

The Umbra creaked beneath Cal's measured steps, but Soline paid him no mind. Reaching out, she trailed a finger along Hera's cheek. One might have mistaken it for a loving gesture had it not been for the rage rippling off of Soline in waves. Dropping her hand away from Hera, Soline finally turned to look at Cal. Her features had grown more gaunt and hollow. Her cheekbones and clavicle angles were sharper, protruding painfully from her skin. Once full and vivacious, her lips were wan and stretched tight over her exposed teeth.

"Is this what interests you, Caliban? A girl no more than twenty-one, alone and vulnerable? Utterly ignorant to your true nature?" she sneered at him. She crossed her arms over her sunken chest, her nails tapping impatiently against her too-thin arms.

Licking his lips, Cal assured, "It's not like that, Soline. She's a means to an end. Once I get what I need from her, I will finish what I started a decade ago."

"Liar! You *want* her." Soline seethed, her eyes burning with envy and hatred. Cal swallowed. Spirits sensed lies, but Cal had no other option, not when the truth was something he hadn't even dared to face himself.

He shook his head. "I don't, I promise. Whatever you think I feel for her, I assure you it is merely misplaced affection I hold for you. I am doing all of this for you—for us." Cal pleaded.

Soline tilted her head, and her eyes narrowed into slits. She still stood so close to Hera, and Cal didn't doubt for one moment that Soline would lash out at her. Cal prayed to whatever wicked god favored him that Hera would remain asleep. Soline was still staring at him, and Cal quickly glanced at Hera.

A bitter scream reverberated from Soline.

She flew forward, her nails aiming for Cal's eyes. "I knew it! You care for her. You *desire* her!"

Cal turned and sidestepped Soline. She was solid enough that her momentum carried past her him, but she whirled and swiped at him. Her nails slashed the flesh of his cheek. Pain seared through his torn skin. Usually, the pain was a figment of his psyche, but he knew immediately that she had really cut him this time. Blindedly, Cal reached toward her, his fingers grasping her rail-thin wrist. Applying pressure, he yanked, dragging her against his chest. Fury lined her angular features. Where her cerulean eyes had once been were now replaced with dark pits of hate. The skin covering her face had gone taut, cheekbones jutting out from beneath it. Her nails were razors—jagged and broken, but horrifically sharp.

"Cease this foolishness, Soline." Cal hissed. "Everything I have done, everything I have risked, has been for you. You have been with me, haunting my every move. You *know* that this is all for you. Please, my love, stop this."

Soline railed against him. Though she appeared frail, she leveraged a surprising amount of strength. Cal released her out of fear she would somehow further harm herself, despite the worst having already happened to her. But perhaps whatever this was, this suspended state of being, this never-ending limbo, was true hell. Death would be a blessing compared to the bitterness and sorrow that vibrated from every inch of Soline. If only he had never cast that spell. He was too weak and inexperienced to do it properly, and now…

Whatever price the spell required, it had clearly exacted it on Soline, leaving her a shell of her former self, with nothing but anguish and spite to fuel her.

Soline flitted away from him, going back toward Hera. Cal launched at them, but was met with a wall of energy. The wraith's eyes glowed with magic as she raised her hand toward Cal. His muscles locked up instantly, rendering him incapacitated.

"I picked up a few tricks from the dead littering the waters around the Isle. They taught me how to tap into your magic." she said with a wicked grin, her gaze still fixed on Cal. "There's still so much of your magic you don't know about, Caliban. But I can show you," turning, she looked down at Hera again, her gaze shifting to hunger, "I just need a body–a real body–to do it. Then, we can set everything right, Caliban. All you have to do is trust me." She twisted her head and stared at him. The fullness of her features had returned, as had the love in her eyes. "You trust me, don't you, Caliban?"

Cal struggled beneath her hold on him. His throat burned with the words he couldn't say. Soline cocked her head, her gaze examining him.

"No, I don't suppose you do." Shaking her head, she looked back at Hera. "I trusted you once. Look where that got us. I guess it's only fair then that I take what you covet."

Understanding dawned on Cal. He thrashed in earnest, trying to burn through whatever magic Soline employed, but it was futile. Panic seized Cal's lungs as Soline reached forward and plunged her hand into Hera's chest.

Chapter Forty Four

The wind ruffled the dark strands of Cal's hair, tugging them from the knot he had secured them in at the base of his neck. He lifted a pale, scar-flecked hand to the sky, squinting beneath the blazing sun. Spending time in the sun or the gardens was of little interest to him. He much preferred the chilled rooms in the underground vaults beneath the palace. But Soline had asked, so Cal had obliged.

He glanced sidelong at Soline, drinking in her exquisite form. Long, slender limbs supported her as she leaned back in the grass, her face tilted toward the sun. Her eyes were closed, but a soft, blissful smile graced her lips. Shimmering golden hair floated in the breeze, not even daring to snag in her impossibly long eyelashes. Cal's heart stuttered in his chest as she turned and looked at him. Large, cerulean eyes pinned him to the spot—Cal nearly forgot how to breathe. She was easily the loveliest girl at court, and Cal was the lucky fool she had taken an interest in. Every time she asked him to this grassy knoll, Cal was sure it was to break things off with him. Why would a gentle, kind, and exceptional woman give him the time of day, let alone pursue him?

Soline's smile widened. She shifted, fully facing Cal and tucking her knees under herself. Cal turned too, and resisted the urge to reach out and catch a strand of her golden hair and slide it between his fingers.

"What are you thinking about?" Soline asked.

"You. Always you." Cal breathed. Only around Soline had he ever allowed himself to be that vulnerable.

A blush crept on Soline's face, and Cal was helpless to restrain himself. He reached for her, and she met him halfway. Slipping his hands over her ribs, he lifted her from the ground, depositing her in his lap. A fit of giggles broke out in Soline—the most beautiful sound in the world. He bent toward her, his body blotting out the sun, and pressed his lips to hers. She met him with the same intensity that coursed through him, and he was reminded that she wanted him as much as he wanted her.

He thoroughly explored her lips, neck, and face, paying special attention to her freckles. When he glimpsed the heat glazing her eyes he considered going further, but a voice broke through the haze.

Lifting her head, Soline twisted out of Cal's lap. Immediately, he lamented the loss, but quickly shoved aside his disappointment as he spotted Kasper climbing up the small hill—his tag-a-long in tow.

"Kaspie!" Soline called out, her arms stretched wide. Kasper fumbled up the hill, his short legs struggling to close the distance as fast as his mind wanted—but so were the hardships of a seven-year-old. Finally reaching them, Kasper all but fell into Soline's waiting arms. Soline tumbled back, and Cal caught her, pulling her back into his chest. The aroma of honeysuckle and amber filled his nose as he buried his face in her hair and inhaled deeply. Their combined laughter rose up on the wind and was carried away. After a few minutes, Kasper disentangled himself from Soline and began picking blades of grass to try and make it whistle.

"Come on, Rhea. I'll show you how Cal showed me."

The girl, Rhea, stood hesitantly a few feet away, observing them all. Her mouth was drawn into a tight line, and her hands were clasped behind her back. Rhea's gaze drifted from Kasper to Cal, and he was struck by how much worry permeated her very being. Her eyes widened when she saw that Cal was already watching her, and she quickly looked away.

"I don't think my governess would approve." she said wistfully.

"Who cares what that old bat thinks." Kasper replied, still focusing his attention on the blade of grass between his fingers.

"My father—"

"He's not home."

"Someone will tell him."

Soline stood abruptly, dragging Cal's attention away from the worrisome little girl. Reaching toward her, Soline said, "The King will not hear a word of this, I swear it. And if he does, then we will defend your honor." Soline turned and cast a glance at Cal, "Won't we, Caliban?"

Cal smiled and gave a dip of his chin. "With my life."

Rhea's eyes went wide once more. She sucked in her bottom lip, but still did not take Soline's hand. Soline gave Rhea another easy, kind smile and bent down to eye level with Rhea. Leaning in closer, Soline's hair brushed by Rhea's, the strands of gold and ebony mingling. Soline's voice was a murmur, but wind and distance stole the words. Leaning back, Soline rested on her haunches, and Rhea gave her a quick nod. Smiling, Soline took Rhea by the hand, leading her back to where Cal sat.

Easing back to the ground, Soline sat behind the girl. Sinking her fingers into Rhea's hair, Soline braided it into plaits, weaving in small flowers that Rhea plucked and handed her. Cal was content to watch Soline braid and then unravel Rhea's hair repeatedly while Kasper roamed the hill, looking for the perfect blade of grass. The pure joy that radiated from Soline was infectious. Cal couldn't help but think about how wonderful a mother she would make. Her ease with Kasper and Rhea, her gentleness and kindness with him. Leaning over, Cal brushed a kiss over her cheek, her skin warm from the sun finally descending from the sky. Soline didn't pause her task, but slid her gaze to Cal.

Rhea glanced back and said, "That's not proper!"

"Oh, it's perfectly proper if you're in love, Rhea." Soline responded as she leaned into Cal's kiss.

Rhea squinted her eyes, clearly conveying that she wasn't convinced, but she turned back around and said nothing more.

'What was that for?" Soline asked.

A corner of Cal's mouth lifted, and he said, "Nothing. I just wanted to."

Soline feigned exasperation, but a genuine smile spread over her face. They remained there for another hour or two, the sun dropping toward the horizon and the pangs of hunger making themselves known. Rhea got up to play with Kasper, who was now trying to collect sticks and stones to make a fort.

Soline situated herself between Cal's legs, her head resting against his chest under his chin. Their eyes were on the children, but Cal's mind was elsewhere, especially as Soline traced the white scars on his hands and the lines on his palm. This was peace, life, and happiness. With Soline and Kasper in his arms, nothing else mattered. The world could collapse around him, but as long as he had them, then he didn't care. Cal didn't need his brother's gift of prophecy to know what his future held. He saw it clear enough.

Cal shifted and kissed Soline's head, infusing it with every thought and feeling of love he held for her.

Sighing in contentment, Soline whispered, her gaze still fixed on Kasper and Rhea, "What are you thinking about?"

"The future." Cal replied, "Our future."

Soline went still for a moment and then twisted in Cal's arms, facing him. Those sky-blue eyes bore into him with such intensity and love that Cal struggled to remember his own name. Moisture gathered in the corners of Soline's eyes as she lifted her hand to Cal's cheek and whispered, "I love you, Caliban."

Cal opened his mouth, the words falling from his lips—

Fanfare blared in the distance, drawing everyone's focus to the palace gates. The King marched through—triumphant from his latest conquest, no doubt.

Soline turned back to Cal and pressed a quick kiss to his cheek before she rose and held out a hand. "We should get the children back. The King won't be pleased to find his daughter's skirts covered in mud." She said with a laugh. "Besides, my ladies told me I was expected to attend court when he returned from battle."

Cal rolled his eyes. "Doesn't he have enough simpering courtiers to keep him entertained? He already has a harem. What does he need from you?"

Shrugging, Soline said, "I'm just trying to keep my father happy."

"I hope that won't be the case forever."

"It won't." Soline assured. She leaned down and pressed a searing kiss to his lips. Cal considered pulling her back down to the ground with him, but she broke the kiss and smiled. "Come along, now."

Feigning annoyance, Cal reached up and took her hand—a hand he planned to hold for the rest of his life.

He would destroy anyone who dared to intervene.

* * * *

Cal bellowed and raged against the shadows restraining him, but he was helpless. Utterly *useless* to try and stop Soline from killing Hera.

"Get away from her." Cal growled and thrashed. Soline's hand had disappeared into Hera's chest, but still, Hera did not rouse. Cal briefly wondered if only he could be physically harmed by Soline. If their connection allowed her to interact with him. Soline shoved further into Hera's body, a hungry, vengeful look on her wan features.

"Be still, love, I am almost done."

Fear pulsed at the base of Cal's neck, but he wouldn't succumb. Cal leveled his breathing and searched deep within himself to the yawning pit of rage, bitterness, and power. He rallied it to the surface, dragging up every wisp he could manage, and then he unleashed himself.

The shadows encircling him dissipated without another thought.

Whirling her head in his direction, Soline hissed. It didn't matter, though, as he surged forward, his arms outstretched. His hands connected with Soline's shoulders, sending them careening into the wall. Pain lanced in Cal's shoulder as it connected to the bedside table and slammed into the floor.

Cal hoped and prayed that no one would come running, and that Hera would remain asleep. He didn't even want to begin to think how he would explain this to her.

Soline's nails sunk into Cal's flesh. It was only his years of torture and torment at the hands of the King that kept Cal from bellowing in pain. Gripping her more tightly, he shook, attempting to dislodge her from him.

"End this, Soline, or I will." Cal growled.

"No! I can fix this!" She howled and continued to thrash beneath his grip. Whatever strength The Ether granted Soline wasn't enough to fend off Cal. He pushed harder, pinning her beneath him. Righteous rage burned in him. He wanted to punish and destroy her for what she dared do to Hera. Only the memories of their shared history, of the love he still held for her, made Cal relent.

"Stop this, now. That woman does not deserve to die."

Soline's eyes went wide, some of their sky-blue hue returning. "I wasn't trying to kill her." she said softly, her voice light—like the wind winding through the tall grasses.

"What did you think possessing her body would do?" He begged, his fingers loosening on her shoulders.

Soline leaned up. Her full, lush lips were just inches from his. The resolve Cal had amassed was crumbling. Being blown away like sand in a storm.

"Don't you want us to be together again? We can have everything we want—it won't matter whose body I inhabit." she said fervently.

Cal was ashamed that not long after Soline died, he considered doing the same for her. But there hadn't been another he could bear to look at and love like they were Soline. Cal's fingers loosened further; the fight leaving him almost entirely. Soline settled back against the ground, conceding her plans and the fight.

Cal relaxed, grateful that she could be reasoned with even as a wraith. But then Soline tensed—the hungry light returned to her eyes, and her lips thinned once more. Cal tensed again, frantically grasping at her shoulders.

Too late.

Talons extended, Soline surged forward with newfound strength.

Cal toppled backward—his head cracking against the floor.

Soline's nails scraped and sank into the wood as she crawled toward Hera. "I'm doing this for us, Caliban. Just another moment, and then you'll see!" She pulled herself up to the bed—Cal reacted before he thought.

Shadows shot out from his hand and slipped around Soline's outstretched wrist. Cal willed the shadows to go taut—

The snapping of Soline's wrist sent out a sickening crack.

Thin, cracked lips peeled back, revealing pointed teeth as she released a howl of anguish. Pain flared in Cal's chest at the thought of hurting Soline, and he reminded himself that this was not the woman he fell in love with but a shadow of what remained. This was a wraith that fed on pain and rage. It would not be sated until it had consumed the entire world. Once he had the Alakhira, he could restore her.

He could fix everything.

With a flick of his wrist, another shadow wrapped around Soline's unbroken arm. Then, he pinned her to the cabin wall. Soline bellowed and thrashed, but she was no match for him, not even with the help of The Ether.

"I will never forgive you for this, Caliban." she spat. "Never."

Cal didn't let his heartache and despair read on his face as he rose from the floor and moved to stand before Soline. A shell of the woman he loved, that was all this *thing* in front of him was.

"I love you, Soline. Soon, everything will be right."

Soline bared her teeth and snapped them at Cal, but he proceeded with the spell to banish her. It took longer than it ever had before, but Soline's form finally began to fade, shifting from corporeal to ghost-like. Then, she was gone, and silence descended over the cabin once more.

Cal's breathing was labored, and his skin still stung where Soline's nails had cut into him. He glanced at Hera, who still had not stirred.

Whatever granted Soline the knowledge of how to access his magic must have kept Hera asleep and the noise contained to the cabin. Sighing, Cal thrust his hands into his hair and looked out the small window at the cloudless night sky. If the dead were getting stronger, then there was no telling what they would face once they reached the Isle.

Once again, his eyes slid to the book that remained undisturbed on the table. The only known account of what might exist in the Cave of Splendors. Calloused fingers twitched at his side. No one would ever know—except for him. Cal's teeth ached from the force of clenching his jaw. He turned away. He needed to be away from this woman before he did something truly regrettable.

"Wh–who's there? Cal, is—"

Cal called the darkness to him, wrapping the lingering shadows around him. He remained still as death, not daring to breathe too hard.

Hera's mouth was drawn, her eyes wide as they darted around her room. She reached toward her neck—clasping the golden pendant that rested there. Staring out into the shadows of her cabin, she watched intently, but after several moments, she leaned back against her pillows. The heel of her palm pressed into her eyes and she scrubbed with fervor.

Cal wanted to linger, but this might be his only chance to slip out without being noticed. Pressing the shadows closer to himself, he crept backward toward the door, never taking his eyes off Hera. He would need to watch her closely for the next several days to ensure that nothing Soline did had lasting effects. Or at least that's what Cal told himself as he reached for her door and quickly darted through the opening. He pressed his hands to the wood and gently closed the door, praying that Hera would still be too disoriented to notice. Leaning against the threshold, he listened for any movement. When he heard nothing, he sagged against the worn wood.

Relief and exhaustion washed over him.

Cal was a fool to go to Hera's room. He knew better than to allow himself to get close to her, to wonder at their connection. Soline had already been jealous and spiteful; now, there was no telling what she would do.

Sighing, he pinched the bridge of his nose, applying enough pressure to abate the throbbing in his skull. A temporary relief from his poor choices and headache. Regrettably, it wouldn't last. Cal would have to face the damage he caused, but that would be a problem for tomorrow. In the morning, he would be better equipped to consider why he had gone to Hera's room and incurred Soline's wrath against her. Had he just taken the book, he could have at least claimed that was the reason why. But now, all he had done was make her a bigger target for his dead lover and further complicate their tenuous relationship.

Dropping his head, Cal pushed away from Hera's door—the action took more effort than Cal cared to acknowledge. Part of it was physical fatigue, but the rest...no, he couldn't think about it now.

The pulsing in Cal's head returned, but he ignored it as he followed the corridor away from Hera's room and to his own. Dawn was at least two hours off, which meant he could get some rest before he needed to captain his ship. While it was still *his* ship, anyway. He needed to consider and address so much, but he simply did not have the energy to fix it all. So, he pushed into his room, spared a moment to kick his boots off, and fell onto his bed. Sleep was already prodding the edge of his mind, and for once, Cal didn't resist the call of his dreams.

Chapter Forty Five

An ache pulsed in Kasper's temple, throbbing into his jaw. He wasn't sure if it was the lack of sleep, or the newly returned sunlight that blinded him every time he emerged from his cabin. Fatigue still clung to his body, wholly worn out from exerting so much magic to heal Lady Hera—and hungover from the rum.

He still wasn't entirely sure how he had managed it. The process—the magical properties of the gems and crystals, and his affinity for them—he understood, but he had never attempted something so large. Had never been able to. But maybe whatever magic protected the Cave of Splendors emitted some kind of charge or signal that was amplifying his abilities. He considered asking Cal or Kai if they had felt anything different. Surely they had, given what Cal had done to the storm and the monsters in it. Either way, when he coupled that with constantly watching Lady Hera and checking on her, he was utterly run-ragged. But he would do it all again to save her. Even if she never expressed her thanks—which, selfishly, he hoped she did—he didn't regret his choice.

She was back in her own room and largely taking care of herself, but Kasper couldn't stop his mind from ceaselessly worrying about her. He kept waiting for her to scream in agony. Or turn that sickening shade of green again. But day after day passed, and she continued to appear perfectly fine—for the most part.

Shadows purpled under her eyes, and her shoulders sagged almost imperceptibly. Kasper wondered if it was from a lack of sleep, or if she had been affected by the sirens. He hadn't asked, but he knew many people, Cal included, had been.

Sighing, Kasper raised up off the railing of the Umbra, the wood groaning slightly at the change of pressure. He turned and squinted out over the deck—his eyes tracking Lady Hera and Brander. The guard was marginally less insufferable since their last confrontation. Kasper forced himself to imagine the situation from Brander's perspective and consider how he would have felt if it was Kai. Well, before the truth had come out. The over-protectiveness and hostility that Brander wore like a cloak was understandable, so Kasper decided to let go of some of his animosity and be kinder. Surprisingly, it worked. Brander glared at him less and didn't reach for his sword nearly as much. Kasper wondered if Brander could actually grow to tolerate him, but that wasn't his most pressing concern. Especially not as Cal stalked toward him, effectively cutting off his view of Lady Hera.

Kasper reached for the cool indifference he had learned worked best when dealing with Cal—but hesitated.

Kai was the one responsible for their rift, well, mostly anyway. Cal had chosen to go along, but did he know the truth of Kai's lies? Kasper didn't know. Frankly, he did not have the energy to do the mental speculation to figure it out. Still, Kasper crossed his arms and stared at his brother, hoping his features read as nonchalant. Most of the time Cal's emotions were leashed and hardly discernible, but Kasper marked the frustration etched into the lines of his face and the tension of his shoulders. His boots thudded hollowly against the deck, slowing as he filled Kasper's field of vision.

Kasper leaned back against the railing and braced against it. Facing the tranquil waters, Cal took up the space beside him. Kasper fixed his gaze on Lady Hera once more. Her steps were assured and steady as she and Brander made another pass around the mast. It was clear that Cal was waiting for Kasper to speak. Crewmates passed by, sparing glances in their direction. Their conversations faltered for a moment, but picked back up as they moved away.

Kasper opened his mouth to feign needing to rest. It wasn't a lie, but Cal spoke.

"I wanted to thank you."

A stillness settled over Kasper, and he narrowed his eyes. Before he could speak, Cal reached toward his neck. He removed a necklace and passed it back over to Kasper. Kasper examined it, trying to place the gem—

"I know that I haven't always taken an interest in you and often disregarded your magic, but—" Cal's voice broke off, and he shook his head. He cleared his throat and said, "Thank you for saving her—and me."

Slipping the red stone into his pocket, Kasper said in a thick voice, "You don't have to lie. I know that you've had a greater hand in my upbringing than I previously believed." Kasper didn't acknowledge Cal's gratitude; he couldn't breach what the emotion limning Cal's features meant.

"I take it Kai told you the truth."

It wasn't a question, but Kasper turned toward his brother and stared at him—waiting.

All hints of anguish vanquished from Cal's face as he arched an eyebrow. "That he's a pathetic liar?"

Pressing his lips together, Kasper pulled back the defense that fought to escape. Kai *was* a liar, but it was hard to undo years of habit.

A corner of Cal's mouth lifted, and he turned back to the open water. "I see that old ways die hard."

Kasper rolled his eyes and turned back to the deck. Lady Hera and Brander had vanished from his line of sight. "You can say whatever you want about him. I don't care anymore."

Clicking his tongue, Cal said, "Doesn't sound that way."

Heat burned in his chest at the accusation. He didn't care about Kai—or at least he was trying not to. Still, he set his jaw and said, "I don't care how it sounds to you."

"Clearly."

Kasper jerked his head toward his brother. "Why are you here, Cal?"

"On this ship?"

"Talking to me. You haven't bothered to have a real conversation with me for over a decade." Kasper snapped, the last bit of his restraint burning up like stubble.

Cal feigned innocence and said, "I'm not allowed to speak with my little brother?"

Kasper's nostrils flared, and he clenched his hands. He channeled every ounce of self-control into not slamming his fist into Cal's jaw. Cal's unperturbed gaze held onto him, having gone wide with anticipation. Faint amusement replaced the pain Kasper had gleaned earlier.

He was enjoying this.

Of course, he was. Cal was practically a sadist in the way he delighted in others' pain. Kasper resolved himself not to give Cal any further satisfaction. He flexed his hand and let the tension out of his jaw, imagining his anger ebbing away until it was nothing to him anymore.

Another moment passed, and Kasper crossed his arms. "Just say what you came here to say and leave me alone."

Cal had the audacity to pout, but his features quickly shifted back to the hardened, distant brother that Kasper was more accustomed to. Kasper cursed silently. Everything was a joke to Cal—even Kasper's obvious anguish.

"Did you know?" Kasper asked. "Did you know the extent of what he did?"

Clearing his throat, Cal said, "How did you find out? I can't imagine Kai willingly parting with his deceptions after so long."

Sighing, Kasper looked once again at Lady Hera and Brander, who had rounded the deck and now walked toward them. Lady Hera's gaze slipped to them for the first time since she had emerged onto the deck over an hour ago.

Against his better judgment, Kasper told Cal how Kai had revealed the truth to him.

"And you aren't taking it very well, I see." Cal glanced at Kasper and sighed, "I knew he was keeping the truth from you for a while."

Kasper shifted his weight and shoved down the bitter burn of his hurt. His jaw flexed, the memory of Kai's betrayal as fresh as it was over two weeks ago. But it wasn't just Kai who was at fault. The accusation burned in Kasper's throat, begging to be unleashed. He wasn't sure his voice would work, but he tried anyway.

"You *left* me."

Nodding slowly, Cal's gaze shifted back to the horizon. "I did." There was no regret or remorse in his voice—just acknowledgment.

Kasper dropped his arms to his sides and curled his hands into fists. "That's all you have to say? After everything, that's it?"

A muscle ticked in Cal's jaw. "What do you want me to say, Kas? That I'm sorry? That I should have taken you with me? Because I won't." Cal didn't relent, even as Kasper flinched. "I may not have liked it, but for all of Kai's lies and hypocrisy, he was right about you staying behind. The Umbra was not a kind place when I joined at seventeen. It certainly was no place for a child."

Kasper slammed his fist into the railing. "I wasn't a child when you came back—Kai made sure of that."

Cal's eyes slid over Kasper, but he gave no reaction. "No, you weren't, but you hated me, and I didn't think it was worth fighting about."

"You mean I wasn't worth fighting for."

Cal shrugged.

Desperate to keep the stinging tears of rejection at bay, Kasper clenched his jaw so tightly he thought his teeth would crack. "Right, well, thank you for enlightening me about where I rank in importance as your brother." he spat before turning on his heel, desperate to maintain a shred of dignity.

"Kasper," Cal called out.

Pausing, Kasper turned his head, looking at him over his shoulder. Lines were etched into Cal's face, making him look older, more haggard—and less like Kai. He pursed his lips and then opened them as though he wanted to say something, but he closed them again and glanced away. Kasper rolled his eyes and turned away once more.

"You should forgive him, Kas. Kai is deeply flawed, but he is your brother."

Turning slowly, Kasper said callously, "And what about you?"

A crease formed between Cal's brows. "What about me?"

"Have you forgiven him? For everything he's done to you—for all the ways he's failed you, used you? Or, how about this: should I forgive *you*?"

Cal was stone still, save for his fingers twitching at his side.

Lifting his chin, Kasper questioned, "Well?"

"No." Cal said definitively, though Kasper didn't know which question he answered.

Kasper nodded tersely. "Don't tell me to do something you aren't willing to do yourself."

The sea breeze lifted strands of Cal's hair. "You're better than me, Kas. Better than both of us, always have been."

Kasper lifted a shoulder. "Maybe I'm not as good as you thought. Maybe I'm exactly what you both made me." Kasper turned to leave, and this time, he well and truly did. His feet carried him further and further. He wandered the deck, not paying much attention to his surroundings. He only put in a modicum of effort not to get in the crews' way as they made repairs.

Their commonplace conversations grated against Kasper.

Didn't they comprehend that his entire understanding of his brothers, his past, and himself had been wholly upended? Kasper knew it wasn't fair to place that anger on them; they had done nothing. But to know that there wasn't a soul aboard the ship, not even his brothers, who understood him only served to stoke the fires of his rage. It turned his thoughts bitter and malicious.

Cal spoke of Kai's hypocrisy and lies as though he were somehow exempt from such judgments. But that was the crux of it all, wasn't it? Kai had deceived and used Kasper for nearly a decade, and Cal had let him. Both would argue that they were doing it for Kasper's benefit, but he saw more clearly now. They saw him as a child who was expected to heed their commands without question. They could make decisions on his behalf with no consideration for what he wanted.

He understood there was an ugly selfishness in them all. Kasper had done his best never to give in to it; his brothers reveled in it. They put themselves and their desires before anyone else and didn't care who was harmed in the process.

The end justifies the means.

Kasper finally came to a stop at the stern of the ship. The blazing sun had finally settled into the horizon, fracturing the sky and water in the various hues of red, pink, orange, and just a hint of purple. It was beautiful–breathtaking, even–but the sight of it did little to assuage the burning ire that Kasper felt for nearly everyone in his life. Parents who didn't want him, brothers who only used him, and a woman who he was *certain* he knew but she fervently denied any connection. No, it was more than just some connection; it was a bond that ran deeper than Kasper understood. She may continue to refute it, but Kasper knew the truth of it in his bones—and he was resolute to prove it.

His harsh, broken laugh shattered the serenity of the sunset, but Kasper didn't care. He was tired of being a good brother and friend, always doing the right thing and putting others first. He was only on this godforsaken ship heading to certain death because of his love for his brother.

Plans of a future–far from his brothers–took shape in his mind.

Perhaps he would put his magic to good use and become a Healer after all. It was an honest, respectable living that he wouldn't have thought possible months ago. But now…

Kasper stared at the sinking sun, the orange orb burning his eyes, and made a vow. He would look out for his own interest for once, starting now. If his selfishness got them killed in the Cave, then so be it.

It was *precisely* what they all deserved.

Chapter Forty Six

Brander's gaze roved over Rhea. He examined her gait. How she shifted her weight, and how she held her jaw when she moved. For nearly three years he had watched her, and he knew her tells. He knew when she was masking torn flesh or bruised ribs. Or when it was something deeper than physical pain.

Despite what people had whispered at the palace, there had never been a romantic undercurrent to his attention. Yes, he cared for her and was very protective, but he was nearly two decades older than her. The Seer's words came back to him. He did love the Princess, but like a parent loves their child. Brander had no children of his own, and the Princess had a living father. But the King had never been that for her—at least as far as Brander knew.

And as much as Brander didn't want it to matter what people thought, it did. At least it did if they felt that Princess Rhea returned the affection in any way. The sneering courtiers were always looking for some reason to discredit her. An inappropriate relationship with a common guard would undoubtedly do the trick. But here, out in the middle of nowhere, where not a soul on board–save for the Seer–knew them...he was finally able to give her the help and attention she had needed back at the palace.

The kind of attention her father was supposed to provide.

Rhea bent down toward her boots, her arms extended, muscles drawn tight. Her recovery was going well, but Brander wanted to ensure she was well enough not to be constantly monitored by him or Kasper. She held the stretch for a count of five before she righted herself and looked at Brander expectantly. Color flushed her cheeks, and her brown eyes glittered in the mid-morning light.

"Well, are we ready for our daily walk?" Her voice and her features were tight.

Resisting the urge to roll his eyes, Brander said, "I wouldn't have to watch you like a hawk if I could trust you to take care of yourself." Rhea fixed her hands on her hips and opened her mouth to argue, but snapped it closed a moment later. With a smile and a nod he said, "That's what I thought."

He could scarcely count the number of times she had gotten into some sort of scrape or danger while at the palace. She would sneak off to the Healers to avoid a scolding by a governess or, worse, her father.

Sighing with exasperation, Rhea stomped toward the door. She started to brush by Brander, but he caught her arm. It was a break in protocol and propriety, but with everything at stake, Brander wasn't sure any of that mattered anymore. Out here, in the middle of the sea, the only thing that *did* matter was her safety. Rhea paused, her large brown eyes swept up to his and held there. Brander scanned the lines of her face, looking for any sign of pain or discomfort. She set her jaw and stared at him, unrelenting.

"How are you, really?" He said softly.

Momentarily, her features shifted. A soft smile graced her lips. "Better than I've been in years." It was a passing platitude, not meant to be taken too seriously, but Brander knew better. He knew what Rhea had endured, the treatment she had suffered at the hands of her father and those he allowed to harm her. He wouldn't say he had much in common with the Princess, but her strength and resilience were something he understood.

Nodding, Brander released Rhea's arm. He expected her to follow him and continue through the door and to the deck, but she didn't. Instead, she looped her arm through his and said, "Why don't we enjoy the sunshine that comes at such a high cost?"

Brander hesitated. They still had a mission to complete, and the Princess had already made it clear what lengths she would go to in order to save her people. Brander had been like that once. Now, he had seen too much death and destruction to hope for a better world—but for her sake, he would try.

"As you wish." he whispered, and they left for the deck.

* * * *

Brander filled his lungs, appreciating the air no longer tinged with electricity and blood. He and the Princess walked in comfortable silence, as they had for the past four days. The routine and predictability of it was nice, though he knew it wouldn't last much longer. They had to be getting closer to the Cave, which meant putting themselves in danger once more. But Brander decided not to fixate on that. Time would pass either way, so why not enjoy the peace while it existed?

"I need to learn to wield a blade."

The tenuous peace shattered. Brander slowed and turned, looking at the Princess. Her eyes were fixed in the distance, but her bottom lip was drawn between her teeth. Brander's mind raced with every reason why her request was bad. It was his job to protect her, and if he had done it better, she would have never raised this interest.

Reaching for Princess Rhea's hand, Brander dropped his voice so no passing crew would overhear. "I will do better, Princess, be better. I promise."

Princess Rhea knit her brows, her perturbed gaze finding Brander's. "Brander, that's not what I meant. I—"

"You wouldn't need to learn self-defense if I had protected you better." His eyes fell, shame burning in his cheeks. "If I hadn't been so weak." His mind wandered back to the endless days he spent sequestered in his cabin, unable to leave or do anything other than dream of his past and the things that haunted him. Whatever elixir or brew that was administered was potent, but effective. He hadn't suffered the effects of sea sickness since, but the time spent ill had nearly cost him everything.

Princess Rhea lifted her hand. She reached for Brander's cheek and forced his eyes to meet hers. Reluctantly, he looked at her.

"I do not blame you. For any of it."

Brander set his jaw. "But if I had been there, then—"

"Then what? You would have died?"

"That would be better than harm befalling you." he insisted.

Pursing her lips, Princess Rhea said, "My life does not inherently hold more value than yours."

Brander gave an exasperated sigh. "You know that's not true, and not a single other person who knew the truth would agree with you."

A side of the Princess's mouth kicked up in a grin. "I think our esteemed Captain would disagree with you."

A muscle ticked in Brander's jaw, and he growled, "That's the last person whose opinion I care anything about."

Offering him a tight smile, she said, "I agree, but never mind that. Back to what I said before. I want to learn to wield a blade." Brander started to pull away, but Princess Rhea held firm, forcing him to look at her. "And I want you to be the one to teach me."

Giving her an annoyed look, Brander said, "It wouldn't be right."

Princess Rhea's eyes widened, and she gave a humorless laugh. "It wouldn't be right? Brander, I think we're well past propriety. Besides, this is about my safety. We can both better ensure my well-being if you know that I can protect myself—at least to some extent."

"Princess, please—"

She cut him off with her hand. "After everything I've endured, do you really think this would be the worst thing?"

Hating the anguished look in her eyes, Brander paused. He was loath to dwell on the abuse Princess Rhea had suffered, the way her father had tormented her. Perhaps she could have stopped it if she had learned how to use a weapon. And hadn't he broken many rules in the past several weeks? Doing things he would never have dared before? Things had changed, but did the benefits of the Princess learning to wield a blade outweigh the risks? He huffed and started to give his excuse when an infuriating voice cut in.

"Lovers' quarrel?" purred Cal as he sauntered up to them. The familiar anger that Brander experienced whenever he was near the Necromancer flared to life in his chest.

Brander tensed and turned, but Princess Rhea slipped her hand down to his forearm, halting him. "Brander."

Pausing, he stepped back, clenching his jaw. As much as he wanted to strike the Captain, it would do him no good.

Cal laughed and made a whimpering sound in his throat. "Poor guard dog's leash being yanked on."

"Enough, Cal." Princess Rhea said with a glare. Releasing Brander, she took a subtle step away from him and crossed her arms over her chest. Brander aimed to ignore the slight.

"You seem to be healing well."

Brander paused at the Necromancer's words. They were wrapped in derision, but there was an undercurrent of something else.

Lifting her chin, Princess Rhea said, "I am."

"Good. That's good to hear." he said, still smirking.

Brander wanted to run Cal off, but he refrained. This was the Princess's fight, not his.

Her throat bobbed and she glanced away. "Don't you have somewhere more pressing to be? Some poor underling that needs to be harassed?"

Cal regarded her, his eyes trailing down her body. Then, back up to her face. Princess Rhea tensed under his examination, her cheeks flushing.

Smirking, Cal chuckled. "Fine. I'll leave you to your, uh, little spat."

The flush already staining her cheeks spread to her neck. Cal merely winked, turned on his heel, and whistled as he walked away. Brander watched his retreating form, the anger burning in his chest hotter with each passing moment. Then, he turned back to the Princess.

"Disregard what I said earlier. I'll teach you."

Princess Rhea's gaze flew back to Brander's, strands of her hair flitting in the breeze.

"Truly?" she asked, her tone filled with delight.

"Truly, but," he paused and pointed to where Cal lingered, resting against the ship's railing, "you have to promise to use it against him."

A grin split Princess Rhea's face. "Deal."

Brander smiled then, too. He would teach the Princess and give her the basics to protect and defend herself. She would need at least that much to survive what was ahead of them. Then, perhaps she would take her blade and run it through her father. Ridding the continent once and for all of his wickedness.

Chapter Forty Seven

"Squat. Hold that. Now stand upright. Squat again." Kasper circled around Rhea, his eyes assessing her. His gaze was intense, but it differed from how Cal looked at her. She fought the shudder at the memory of the way his eyes had lingered on her body as though he were seeing into her. It had made her body tingle—not unpleasantly, but unnerving all the same. Kasper's gaze, and even Brander's, remained distant, clinical even.

She wasn't sure which she preferred.

Kasper made another pass and then stepped back. His caramel-colored eyes found hers, holding her gaze. Rhea sucked in a breath. She needed Kasper to clear her so her training would start. She wasn't entirely sure how much time they had left until they reached the Cave of Splendors, but she overheard the others trying to determine how much further they had to go. They were in uncharted waters; they might stumble upon the Cave tomorrow, or it might be another two weeks. It was hard to say either way. But however long they had, Rhea wanted to spend it getting stronger and learning to use a weapon.

"How do you feel?" Kasper asked.

Releasing a breath, Rhea smiled. "Good, great even. I don't have any discomfort."

"None at all? No fatigue on your walks or trouble sleeping?"

Rhea shrugged. "There's no discomfort after walking, and I have no more trouble sleeping than normal." Nightmares had plagued Rhea for longer than she remembered. Had they gotten worse since the attack? Perhaps. But wasn't that to be expected considering what she endured? She didn't think it had anything to do with her injury, save for showing her vulnerability.

Lately, her dreams included a beautiful blonde woman, who was oddly familiar, but her face was always obscured. They were so vivid that sometimes she awoke unsure of what was real. Sweat would dampen her hair, and her heart would beat so painfully that it would take several minutes before she recognized where she was. She chalked it up to stress and recovering from the attack, but a small part of her wondered if it was something more. If something happened to her in those minutes between Cal catching her and Kasper healing her, or maybe in the hours of dreamless sleep that followed.

Kasper arched an eyebrow.

Shaking her head, she tried to recover. "I'm well, I promise." She wanted to add that she was ready to stop being monitored like an invalid, but refrained.

Kasper held her stare for a moment longer, a hand covering his mouth. "I don't know how well I healed you." he admitted, taking a step back and dropping his hand. "I've never attempted anything like that." Kasper sighed, his gaze so intense as it roamed over her that Rhea was certain he was seeing into her very soul. Finally, he exhaled and met her eyes. "I can't see anything physically wrong, but you should still be cautious and keep an eye out for anything beyond the ordinary."

Forgetting herself for a moment, Rhea smiled and flew forward at Kasper. He tensed under her embrace, and she hastily retreated. A wave of emotion passed across his face, and he averted his eyes. Rhea's cheeks heated, remembering her and Kasper's last conversation. She hated lying to him. She hated that she was causing him further pain by insisting that what he was sure existed between them was a fabrication. But she had no choice. If he knew—gods, if *Cal* knew—they would never make it to the Cave.

And her life would be forfeit.

Clearing her throat, Rhea turned toward Brander, who stood idly by, watching. She was grateful that he had finally heeded her advice and made peace with the brothers—well, Kasper and Kai, anyway.

"Ready?" he asked.

Rhea nodded her head. She was eager to leave the awkward interaction with Kasper behind, but before she made it out of the door, Kasper called out.

"Wait."

Pausing, she turned back to him. Kasper chewed his bottom lip for a moment before reaching up and lifting a gem strung around his neck. He slipped from his head and held it out.

Rhea stood still, her mouth parted slightly and her brows drawn.

"Here." Kasper stepped closer and reached for her hand, pushing the gem into it. It was warm, startlingly so, but a sense of comfort enveloped it. She looked back up at Kasper and found him staring down at where she clutched the gem.

"What is this?"

"It's Tiger's Eye. It offers the wearer protection. Usually, it's only if an attack is of a psychic nature, but I've imbued it with my magic so it can help defend against more minor attacks." Kasper flicked his gaze up to hers, a blush creeping over his neck. "It's not much, but I thought it might—"

"Thank you, Kasper." She took the cord and slipped it over her head. She carefully tucked it under the collar of her dress, the gem resting against her pendant—her family sigil. "It is a kind gesture, truly."

The blush staining Kasper's face deepened, but he nodded and stepped back. Rhea smiled at him and then turned back to Brander once more. "Let's go get started, shall we?"

Brander's shoulders sagged with defeat, but he led her from the room all the same. Rhea barely contained her excitement as she stood a bit taller and lifted her chin.

358

She would finally learn how to properly use a sword. She would be able to fight. She wouldn't be helpless any longer.

She would become a warrior.

* * * *

Rhea was not going to be a warrior.

Sweat trickled down her spine, and her ankle-length linen dress clung to her damp skin, tangling around her legs. She spent an inordinate amount of time sweeping the loose tendrils of her hair out of her eyes and off her sticky face. But the heat and her discomfort were not her most significant obstacles. That distinction went to Brander, who was taking her through another mindless lesson on stance. She had yet to touch a blade, and when she inquired about it, Brander had dismissed her altogether.

"Your feet need to be further apart than that; otherwise, you'll be off balance and your attacker will make easy work of incapacitating you."

Rhea huffed, but slid her feet further apart.

"That's too far apart."

Whirling on Brander, Rhea said indignantly, "I'm not going to stand still in a fight, so why do I need to spend so much time on my stance?"

Brander gave her a soft smile, not a hint of frustration on his face—a credit to his time as an imperial general. He merely raised a brow, waiting for Rhea to return to position.

Rolling her eyes, she muttered, "Fine," then returned to her stance.

"Good," Brander praised, "now raise your arms like this." he said, and then demonstrated. Rhea followed his example, and they continued for the better part of two hours. He checked her stance, ensured her arms were in the right place, and monitored whether she was breathing right repeatedly—until Rhea's head was swimming with it all. Even though she had still not used a blade, she reminded herself that she could defend herself in other ways. She had fended off Cade without one, and with Brander's training, she could have used her body more effectively.

Leaning against the rail, she gratefully took Brander's flask. The late afternoon sun was baking into her back, intensifying the burning sensation along the ruined skin. Wincing, she shifted to subtly dislodge the fabric clinging to her scars, but it was fruitless.

Several minutes passed, and the gentle breeze drifting across the deck did little to assuage her discomfort. Still, she had no desire to go below deck. She returned the flask to Brander and stepped away from the railing, rolling her shoulders to work out the soreness that settled there. She turned back to Brander, who was watching her with that annoyingly perceptive stare.

He pushed off from the railing to join her. Rhea began to sink into her stance, but he set a hand on her shoulder. "I think we've made some good progress today. Let's get some rest and pick up tomorrow."

The air went out of Rhea. "But we haven't even gotten to weapons. All we did was stand."

"And that was enough for today. You're still recovering from a severe injury."

Rhea stammered, failing to find the right words. She would get nowhere if Brander planned to only work with her for an hour or two. No, she needed to learn how to handle a blade *now*. They had no idea what they would face at the Cave—

Metal clashed and reverberated behind her.

Twisting, she found Cal stripped down to his breeches hanging low on his hips. He held a long, broad sword against another, equally long but slightly slenderer blade—wielded by Finnley, who had a wicked grin across her face.

Cal withdrew, and Finnley spun away, just out of reach of Cal's blade. Sending winks and taunts, Cal tried and failed to goad Finnley into launching an attack. Finnley would be at a disadvantage if she tried to match Cal blow for blow. Cal's frame was wider, taller, and more muscled. Finnley would have to find another way to beat Cal.

Rhea marveled at their movements and their different approaches. Finnley moved like water, graceful and fluid, sliding through the motions and finding the path of least resistance.

Cal, on the other hand, was…vicious. Brutal, relentless attacks that made Rhea flinch every time his blade made contact with Finnley's. Rhea was sure that Finnley would eventually buckle under the weight of his assaults, but she held fast, deflecting when possible—evading when necessary. They went on for what might have been hours, one gaining ground and then losing it. Others had taken notice, too. Crewmates formed a loose ring, and coins slipped from one grimy hand to another. Looks of surprise and dismay were scattered, save for Kasper and Kai. Kasper watched on with anger and—wistfulness? Kai observed distractedly, as if he had already seen the match's outcome.

Finnley landed an impressive strike, going on the offensive for once and catching Cal unawares. Murmurs burned through the crowd. Rhea turned toward Brander, who also watched with a mix of intrigue and disgust.

"See? That's what I want to be able to do."

Brander cut his gaze to her. Lowering his voice, he said, "Princess, I don't think that will be feasible."

"What? Why not?" she replied with indignation.

Pointing a finger, Brander said, "That takes years of practice, and besides, you said you wanted to learn to defend yourself."

"I do," Rhea exclaimed, her voice rising, "I want to learn to defend myself with a sword. I can do that."

Brander gave her a look—pity—Rhea recognized, and she understood. He had only meant to show her the basics of hand-to-hand combat. A sword and perhaps a dagger were out of the question—at least for a long while. Rhea swallowed the lump in her throat and tried to push past the buzzing in her ears.

"I want to learn to fight, Brander. Please." She despised the slight shaking in her voice, but she was desperate. Never again did she want to feel as helpless as she had against the creature or the men who had attacked her. She would make the men who leered at her and fantasized about the horrid things they wanted to do to her pay for their vileness. She would not be weak or dependent on anyone else. If Brander wouldn't teach her, then—

"Aye, what's goin' on here?" Finnley's distinct voice cut through Rhea's spiral. She turned back to where she and Cal were fighting moments ago to find Finnley standing only a few feet away, glaring at her and Brander.

Rhea was powerless to stop her gaze as it traveled past Finnley to where Cal stood. Sweat slid down his muscled chest and abdomen, glistening in the sunlight. His arms were extended over his head, and his sword hung limply from the hand next to his head. Like some dark, long-forgotten god that sought to corrupt and take Rhea. She tried to swallow, but found her mouth to be dry.

She quickly pulled her eyes away—but not quick enough. Cal caught her and sent a smirk that burned her cheeks.

"It's nothing." Brander said, pulling Rhea's attention back to him.

Rhea clenched her jaw and crossed her arms. It certainly wasn't nothing, but this was not the time or place to have this conversation.

"Is that so? Didn't sound like nothin'." Finnley taunted. "Sounded to me like the lass wanted to learn to fight, and you aren't too keen on it."

"It doesn't concern you." Brander said through his teeth.

"No? Want to settle it, then? Like warriors?" Finnley grinned like a fiend, and Rhea had to tamp her rising fear. Whatever had happened to Finnley to make her the way she was must have been terrible.

Brander snorted and said dismissively, "I don't fight women."

Raising her arms, Finnley glanced around at the crowd. "I don't see no women challenging you."

"You're a man, then?"

Finnley laughed cruelly. "I'm your nightmare made flesh."

Rhea pressed her lips together, prohibiting a smile from appearing and stifling her laughter.

Brander shifted his weight from one foot to the other. "Still, I won't raise my sword to you."

"What about me, guard dog?" Cal called out, stalking closer. There was a frightening gleam in his eye as he smiled and said, "Am I worthy of your fighting prowess?"

Rhea wanted to disappear. She wanted to jump into the water and sink deep beneath the waves, but she wouldn't give Cal the satisfaction of seeing her run.

"What are you playing at, demon?" Brander growled.

Shrugging, Cal replied, "You think you're above meeting Finnley's challenge, so I want to know if it's cowardice or pride."

"Neither." Brander seethed and reached for the sword sheathed at his side.

Rhea's eyes went wide, and she stepped between Cal and Brander. "Brander," she bit out, "do not sink to his level. You are above such childish taunts."

"Is that what you think, Lady?" Cal mocked. "That because His Majesty employs him that he's anything other than village swine?"

The wicked edge to Cal's voice made Rhea's hair stand on end. But she wasn't afraid. Perhaps that was foolish, but she realized all she ever felt when she looked at him was anger and...want. But that wasn't right. No, she wasn't allowed to feel that, for anyone, but least of all *him*. Rhea straightened and met the challenge in his eyes, in the curve of his lips.

"Brander may not be nobility, but he has more honor than you could ever hope to have."

Cal raised his hand to his chest, feigning disbelief. "You wound me, Lady." he said, dropping his hand and rolling his eyes. "Or you would, if I cared for something as useless as honor. Honor won't get me to the Cave. It won't keep me alive, and it certainly won't help me get my vengeance. So, forgive me if I have no use for it."

Rhea narrowed her eyes. She began preparing her next attack, but a shadow passed over her—Brander stepped between her and Cal.

"Brander," she urged, but a storm was brewing in his eyes—one that spoke of retribution and death. Rhea trembled slightly. Would Brander force the issue and accept Cal's challenge?

A muscle flexed in Brander's jaw—then he retreated. "I will not fight you." he said, his voice barely more than a rasp. Rhea's shoulders sagged with relief, and she stepped away. All thoughts of continuing her training eddied from her mind. All she wanted now was a hot meal and her bed.

But Cal made a tsking sound and said, "I'm afraid that simply won't do." Metal sang as it zipped through the air. Rhea whirled in time to see Cal's blade coming down on Brander's unprotected neck.

She froze. The events flashed and unfolded so fast that she thought she might be having one of Kai's visions. But then Brander's sword was there, meeting the challenge. Gritting his teeth, Brander shoved Cal, who was smiling like a fiend even as he tumbled backward.

"I don't want this, demon."

Flipping his sword end over end, Cal said, "Yeah? Well, too bad. I do."

Rhea's stomach fell, and she cursed man's abominable pride. These stupid men were going to get each other killed before whatever lived in the Cave could. But Rhea's anger bled away into fear as Cal and Brander faced off.

Death was promised in both of their eyes.

Chapter Forty Eight

Rhea's skin went clammy, and her knees knocked together. The crew murmured amongst themselves, coins clanked as they traded hands and bets were placed on who would walk away from the encounter.

She had to stop them.

She willed her legs to move and prayed her voice would work. With her arms outstretched, she stumbled forward. Her fingers grappled for Cal's arm, gliding over his sweat-slicked skin. To his credit, Cal didn't shake her off, but glanced down at where they touched. Rhea swallowed against the dryness in her throat and croaked out.

"Don't."

Cal's brutal, relentless gaze softened. For a moment, Rhea thought he might reconsider, but whatever had changed in his expression vanished.

"He's made his choice."

"Cal, please." she begged. In the span of five minutes, she had begged two different men to heed her wishes. The realization left a bitter taste in Rhea's mouth. She was a princess and heir to the greatest power on the continent, yet she still lacked control over her life and those around her. But, as much as she wanted to rail against the dismissal, what had she done to earn that respect other than be born into a position of power? Brander and Cal knew what it meant to sacrifice and command others—Rhea didn't. She had no discernible skills or true value, it was no wonder she wasn't able to do anything right.

A muscle ticked in Cal's jaw, and shadows gathered in his eyes, clouding their grave-soil hue. His lips parted, then shut, and he looked away from Rhea.

Rhea's heart sank. Releasing him, she conceded the loss.

Cal stalked away, Brander following. The rest of the crew reformed their circle as more hushed words and money were exchanged. Rhea didn't imagine many were betting on Brander. Standing behind the crowd, her view of the impending fight was obstructed.

Rhea's stomach twisted painfully. Either she lost Brander, the man who had taken a chance on her—swore his sword and life to protect her—or Cal died. There was a preferable outcome, wasn't there? She should be praying to every god, their names lost to time, that Brander would come out the victor—but the words stuck in her throat.

Cal had saved her life. Though she still hadn't summoned the courage to inquire why, she couldn't ignore it. And even with the years of denying the truth, she had a pull to him. It wasn't affection; it couldn't be. Cal was heartless, vile, and irredeemable. No, any lingering attraction or empathy she held for him had vanished when he left the palace a decade ago; what she felt now was an echo of it. A memory. Or, at least, she would keep telling herself that until her heart conceded its foolishness. Cal obviously had no feelings for her, save for believing her a means to an end. He had saved her because her death would complicate things. The looks and teasing remarks were to rile her up and distract her—nothing more. But if he knew who she really was…it was unthinkable. Rhea was positive whatever treasure lay at the end of their journey didn't rival the prize that she would be for Cal. The King's daughter, Heir to the throne, in his clutches.

The rapturous sound of swords clashing reverberated through Rhea and shook her out of her stupor.

If neither of them would listen to her, maybe someone else could talk sense into them. Scanning the crowd, she found Finnley sitting atop the deck's upper level. She watched the duel with mild interest and dug the grime out from under her nails with a short knife. Rhea shoved through the crowd, ignoring the curses and shouts of protest.

Stopping just under the woman, Rhea shouted, "Finnley!"

Cal's second spared her a glance and paused her cleaning.

Rhea gestured to the fight. "Stop this. Make Cal see reason."

Finnley lifted an eyebrow and heaved a sigh. She slowly put her knife away and returned her gaze to the fight. Rhea refused to look. The shouts, clanging, and creaking wood were enough to keep her from wanting to see what happened. She wouldn't survive the fallout of either of their deaths.

"Finnley." Rhea repeated with more emphasis.

Finnley's auburn braid swayed as she shook her head. "There's nothing to be done. A challenge was issued, and your guard accepted."

"He only accepted because Cal almost killed him."

Finnley lifted a noncommittal shoulder. Rhea reigned in a scream. She turned on her heel and spotted Kai standing among the crew; Kasper wasn't far from him.

Good. Two birds with one stone.

Rhea marched over, again pushing others out of her way. In her peripheral vision, she saw Cal and Brander. Cal was backing up, crimson blood dripping from his arm. Brander was sweating but otherwise unharmed. Brander was a professionally trained soldier–a general–with thirty years of military experience. Cal might be younger and wield magic, but Brander was bigger, stronger, and more disciplined.

Why didn't that realization ease the knots in Rhea's stomach?

Reaching Kai, she grabbed him by the arm, dragging him over to Kasper. He gave no protest, but Kasper's eyes flared at the sight of Rhea, then narrowed when he saw Kai. There was clearly something amiss between them, but Rhea wasn't concerned with that at the moment.

She stopped in front of Kasper and commanded, "Stop it."

Kasper's brows knitted together. "Stop what?"

Rhea flung her arms wide and pointed. As if to punctuate her point, a cry rang out as metal sliced through the air.

Crossing his arms, Kasper said, "Why would I do that?"

"Because your brother might die!"

Scrubbing his chin, Kasper glanced at Kai and retorted, "I don't know if that would be the worst thing."

Rhea got the sense that Kasper wasn't speaking entirely about Cal. She knew the brothers had their differences, but they were family. Surely, Cal dying would bother them. Rhea turned to Kai, pleading with her eyes.

Kai's eyes danced nervously between Kasper and Rhea. "I don't know that intervening would do anything at this point. I'm sor—"

Rolling her eyes, she turned back to Kasper. "You should be ashamed of yourself, Kasper. Cal isn't perfect, but I suspect he's done more for you than you realize."

Kasper flinched and dropped Rhea's gaze.

"And you," she whirled on the Seer, "surely you saw this, predicted it? You must have known that their animosity would lead to this." Though Kai's eyes went wide, he clamped his mouth shut. Rhea failed to stop the vitriol falling from her lips. "What a waste of magic. Utterly useless."

Choking back a laugh, Kasper muttered, "Well, not entirely useless. He can always be used as a bad example. Bad example of a brother, a Seer, a person—really anything."

"A family trait." Rhea spat, and Kasper flinched again. She took a beat and composed herself before she said, "You're better than this."

Kasper didn't respond and instead turned away, disappearing into the throng. Rhea struggled to grasp what had changed in Kasper, making him cold and uncaring toward his siblings. What had he seen or done in the last nine years that had robbed him of his selfless spirit?

Rhea's fingers shook as she struggled to control her emotions. She turned away from Kai and Kasper's retreating form. But the rising shouts and distinct tang of blood froze her in her tracks. Her heart fell to her feet as she beheld the horrors of pride.

Cal was facing her, his sword gripped tightly in one hand, the other pressed against his abdomen—blood leaking from between his fingers. His lips curled back, exposing his teeth, baring them like an injured animal. He jolted back, narrowly avoiding a swipe of Brander's blade. Brander was toying with Cal, enjoying having him on the run. Rhea didn't need to see his face to know that Brander wasn't seeing Cal, but rather what Cal represented. The nobles and overseers of the world that trampled the weak and killed the soft—Brander saw her father.

But Cal wasn't her father. And for all of his snide comments and insults, Cal didn't harm innocents.

Brander cut the distance between him and Cal. Cal scrambled away, but he was too slow, or Brander was too quick. Brander brought the hilt of his sword down on Cal's wrist. He cried out. His fingers splayed, and his blade clattered to the ground.

Rhea gasped and jerked—sweat dripping down her temples. Her mind and heart were torn between who needed to survive this fight.

The gathered crew moved restlessly, eyes darting around. Everyone was trying to determine if they were going to witness their Captain be slaughtered. Brander's shadow fell over Cal's kneeling and panting form. Cal paid the guard no mind. He prodded the split in his swollen lip and then licked the blood away.

Rhea was rooted to the spot. She was unable to breathe, speak, or even comprehend that Cal was going to die.

Suddenly, Cal's features shifted. Cruelty shone in the hard lines and shadows under his skin.

Brander's eyes flared, and he unexpectedly gasped. His sword fell, his hands flying to his throat. Brander rose into the air while Cal climbed to his feet.

Rhea surged forward, breaking free of the crowd. "Release him!" she cried out.

Brander grappled at his throat, tearing at empty air, but it wasn't empty. Shadows encircled his neck.

The smile Cal sported was wild and wicked. His gaze fixed on Brander's flailing form, the sight chilling Rhea's blood. But she was her father's daughter, and one day, she would rule against the wishes of nearly every noble in her father's court. What hope did she have to lead an empire if she could not get one unruly, reckless man to heel?

She was moving before she thought better—grabbing Cal's forgotten blade.

"Release. Him." Rhea commanded, Cal's sword pressed to his own throat. She was close enough to smell the salt, sandalwood, and blood clinging to his skin.

His eyes darted to her. His throat bobbed, sliding against the sword. Brander was still suspended, still clawing, but he would not last much longer. Rhea pressed harder, and a thin line of blood appeared at Cal's neck. Cal's eyes went wide as he held her gaze. Rhea would *not* be the one to break, even if that meant—

Even if that meant taking Cal's life.

She would be Queen one day. She would control the lives of an entire nation and make hard decisions daily about who lived and who died.

Cal's lips twitched—

Brander went flying. Rhea's gaze snapped to where Brander's body crashed into the mast with a sickening crack. Her arms went slack, and she was moving again. But Brander wasn't. What had Cal done? What if he was dead? What if—

Calloused fingers wrapped around Rhea's arm and dragged her backward. Metal glinted in the corner of her eye, and then the sword was at her throat. Her chest heaved, but she remained still. Hot breath brushed the shell of her ear, further stilling Rhea.

"The next time you draw a blade on me, *Lady Hera*, you better be willing to use it."

Cal held her there for another heartbeat—both of their pulses throbbing. Then he withdrew the blade and gave her a slight shove.

Rhea tumbled forward but caught herself. Against her better judgment, she turned back to Cal. He dared to smirk at her. "If you want real lessons on defending yourself, come see me." He jerked his chin in Brander's direction. "The dog is holding you back. He doesn't see what I see."

"And what is it you think you see in me?" Rhea sneered.

"A survivor." Cal replied. He sketched a bow, then turned on his heel, limping back through the crowd. Rhea tamped down on the urge to pick up Brander's sword and skewer Cal with it. Instead, she turned and rushed over to Brander. Finnley was already there, her hands skimming along his body. Rhea crouched next to him, her heart crawling up into her throat.

"He may have a few broken ribs and a head injury, but he'll live."

Sighing, Rhea pressed her hand to her chest, trying to slow the rapid beating of her heart.

Finnley turned toward the crowd still milling about, coins making their final exchanges. "You two," she called out to a pair of young, wide-eyed boys who looked a few years younger than Rhea, "take the Lady's guard to his room and see that he gets water and food. And send for the Healer."

They did as told, lifting Brander between them and carrying him.

Fatigue settled into Rhea's bones, and she fought the urge to sag against the splintered mast. She moved to stand, but Finnley caught her arm. Rhea braced for another scolding or threat, but Finnley's eyes were weary as they beheld her.

"Cal was wrong, but he was also right. I told you before that you needed to learn to defend yourself, and now...well, now, I don't think you have a choice. Which means your clothing choices need to be more agreeable. After you get your guard settled, come see me."

Rhea's words died in her throat, so she simply nodded. Finnley released her, and Rhea didn't linger. She was foolish for thinking she could board a ship like the Umbra and come out unscathed.

It seemed now she had no choice but to embrace that reality.

Chapter Forty Nine

Cal hated Hera—no, he *loathed* her.

He hated her stubbornness and impertinence. He hated her ebony hair and unyielding stare—the one that dared him to rise to the occasion. He hated how she challenged him at every turn and made his soul burn like it hadn't in a decade. But most of all, he hated how much she reminded him of Soline in those moments. Physically they bore no resemblance, but their fierceness and compassion for others was uncanny.

Limping down the stairs that led into the hull, he ignored the stares and whispers from the crew. They were ready to be rid of him and his outlawed magic, but his little demonstration reminded them precisely what he was capable of when provoked. He grunted as he landed in the hall, the motion far more jarring than he cared to admit. He dared to pull his hand away from his side; even in the dim lantern light, the slick, coppery look of his blood was visible. Grimacing at the sight, he ventured to look at the still oozing wound along his abdomen.

The guard dog would have gutted him if Cal was a heartbeat slower. Thankfully, his guts had remained intact. Though, admittedly, his pride had taken a hit. Cal gritted his teeth through the pain as he pressed his hand back to his wound. He commanded himself to breathe through it as he forced his legs to carry him down the corridor. He just needed to get to his room and put the whole ordeal behind him. Then, he could stop thinking about the horror and hate that burned in Hera's eyes when he refused her demand to rescind the challenge. He knew she would despise their duel, but he hadn't expected her to draw a blade against him—*his* blade. He refused to admit what glimpsing that fire did to him—what it had stirred in him.

His door finally appeared at the end of the hall. He suppressed his sigh of relief as he leaned against the wood and it gave way beneath him. He stumbled slightly, his booted toe catching on the once ornate rug. Though he pressed his lips into a thin line, he groaned, his wound leaking more. He cursed as drops of his blood splattered onto the rug before he moved over to the basin in the corner of his room. Exhaustion weighed on his bones, but he continued past the bed—he needed to clean and sew up the gash first.

Easing into the mahogany chair at his dressing table, a string of curses fell from his lips. He leaned his head back against the chair and closed his eyes, remembering better times that didn't include stitching up his own flesh. He took several deep breaths before he cracked open his eyes and resigned himself to at least another hour or two of pain. After that, he would take some of his healing elixir—or get drunk enough that the pain and nightmares wouldn't plague him.

Cal glanced over to a bottle of spirits on the table, but his eyes snagged on the portrait of Soline. He quickly averted his eyes back to the liquor, giving it half a moment of consideration before he grabbed the bottle and tipped it back. The liquid burned on the way down and sent warmth flooding through his veins. It was stupid to imbibe before sticking a needle through his flesh, but he seemed to be on a streak of bad decisions, so what was one more? The Umbra and his crew didn't need him. He had already failed Kasper and Soline, so what was the point of thinking through his choices?

Taking another long pull from the bottle, he enjoyed the burn of the amber liquid before he reached for a sterile cloth next to a basin and pitcher of water. Splashing a healthy dose of the spirits on the fabric, he gritted his teeth and pressed the cloth to his wound.

Fire blazed along his skin.

It took everything in Cal not to stand up and kick his chair across the room. His breath came in hard pants, and only when the initial burning subsided did he work up the nerve to move the cloth along the rest of the laceration.

374

Sweat beaded along his skin, and he prayed to every dark god that it was from the exertion of his task and not the early signs of infection. The inferno around his wound finally dulled to a constant stinging—tremendously unpleasant, but bearable. Cal took another swig from the bottle and the buzz in his head turned pleasurable. Leaning back in his chair, he took a brief reprieve before he set about the objectively more painful portion of his evening.

Eyeing the wooden box next to the basin that he knew held the needle and thread, he dreaded using them. He would have given next to anything to have someone else do it, but no one had sewn him up since…

Cal's eyes caught on the thin, nearly invisible scar that bisected the edge of his eyebrow in the mirror. The scar was a remnant of Soline's work. He looked back to her portrait again. He had commissioned it a year and a half before her death—the youthful glow of sixteen glimmering in her eyes. Reaching toward the portrait, he put it facedown.

Though his throat burned, it wasn't from the liquor. Cal shook his head and then set his jaw. He had delayed the inevitable long enough. No one was coming to stitch him back together. Not now, not ever. Reaching for the box, he wasted no time threading the needle. He reclined in the chair, stretching out his leg, assessing the best angle to start. The gash originated just above his navel and slashed downward toward his left hip. It wasn't terribly deep or long—maybe four inches in total—but given the location, the wound would have difficulty healing, so stitching it up was necessary.

His eyes stung, and his hand shook slightly. From the spirits, he assured himself. But the voice deep within—the voice that sounded far too much like Kasper—begged to differ. Cal flexed his fingers and moved to thread the needle through his flesh—

A knock on the door resounded through the room. And then it was open, someone pushing on in. Cal opened his mouth, preparing to yell at the intruder, when—

Hera stood on the threshold.

She furrowed her brow in confusion. Then her eyes flared, and color stained her cheeks as her eyes dipped from his face to his abdomen. His naked abdomen. An image of Hera's fingers skating down his stomach–venturing lower–burned in Cal's mind. Gritting his teeth, he worked to keep a blush from appearing on his face. But her stare had the innate ability to expose all his nerves to the world.

"What?" Cal managed to ground out, but it sounded more pained than angry.

Hera blinked and then shook her head. She looked back into the hall as if expecting someone to appear and explain her intrusion, but then she turned back to him, her mouth opening and closing without making a sound.

"Hera." Cal said forcefully.

Her mouth snapped shut, and her blush spread to her neck. She lifted her chin, as if attempting to maintain some semblance of control, but cracks appeared in her stony exterior, exposing her vulnerability.

Cal sighed. She had just witnessed him fight her guard dog on the deck. She had fought against wicked men and the monsters in The Ether. And she had held a *blade* to his *neck*. Violence and bloodshed clearly didn't make her squeamish, so why did she seem so flustered now?

Clearing his throat, Cal said, "Is there something you need? From me, or otherwise?" He wasn't sure why he added that last part, or why he had softened his tone. Maybe it had something to do with how she toyed with the gold pendant hanging from the chain around her neck, or how her eyes kept darting to his exposed chest—and lower.

Cal had–begrudgingly–come to terms with his attraction to Hera, but was she also attracted to him? The way her gaze drifted and her posture remained rigid pointed to yes. Usually, Cal would allow a smirk to grace his lips and his posture to become more…inviting. But, whether it was the spirits or the peculiar nature of their relationship, Cal wasn't behaving as usual.

Hera glanced back into the corridor once more before she turned back to him and said, "I was looking for Finnley's room. She told me to come by and get some different clothes. Apparently, mine aren't suitable for learning swordplay."

"I'll say." Cal remarked, his eyes trailing her body with blatant interest.

Hera went wholly still. Her eyes widened slightly, and Cal realized what his statement and gaze implied. He opened his mouth to correct her assumption when Hera shook her head and said, "But, clearly, this is not her room, so I'll go."

She turned to leave.

Cal's heart skipped.

"Wait!" He called out, lurching forward—pain splintering through his abdomen. Curses fell from his lips, but he didn't look to assess what further damage he had done.

Hera paused, then turned back to face him. It was beyond foolish to ask her to stay. He may have saved her, and he may find her attractive, but they were not friends. But the thought of being alone made his heart clench in a way that he didn't think he would be able to dull, even with liquor.

Hera's eyes were open and searching. Brown, gold, and green melded together in a kaleidoscope. Cal was helpless to stop staring at them. He didn't want them to leave either, so he blurted out.

"I'm sorry."

Hera's brows rose, but she crossed her arms.

Swallowing, he continued, "I shouldn't have forced the challenge."

Cal wasn't sure why he said it. Maybe it was the liquor stripping away his inhibitions, or perhaps he was tired of keeping everyone at arm's length. Hera was infuriating and confounding on her best days, but she was also fiercely compassionate and kind. Cal was in short supply of kindness these days.

Hera chewed on her bottom lip, and Cal honed in on that action.

A heartbeat passed, and Cal was still watching her. Hera noted his attention, and she stopped at once. A muscle ticked in her jaw, and she pressed her lips together.

"He shouldn't have engaged you, either."

"Still," Cal added, "I shouldn't have put you at risk like that. I'm the Captain, and I knew better. It was reckless and stupid and unnecessary."

Hera averted her gaze, but waved dismissively. "I always knew things would come to a head between you two. It was only a matter of time. I'm thankful that you—or Brander—weren't too severely harmed."

"He's alright, then?"

"His ribs are bruised and he has a head injury. But if Kasper uses his crystals, then he should recover."

Cal nodded, and a tense but familiar silence fell between them. There was always tension between them. Before, Cal had thought it was born of disdain and distrust, but perhaps all of the stolen glances and snarky remarks indicated something else.

Longing and loneliness did not mix well with alcohol, Cal concluded as he shifted in his chair, aiming to dislodge the building discomfort burning in his blood. Hera's eyes drifted back to him, and he noted the heat smoldering in her gaze. It wasn't proper or very smart, but what if—just to release some of the tension—they—

"Did he cut you badly?"

Cal furrowed his brow, trying to understand Hera's words. Before he could shake off his stupor, Hera uncrossed her arms and gestured to Cal's abdomen.

A slight smile formed on her lips. "Your side. It's split open." she stifled a laugh with her hand. "There also seems to be a needle sticking out of it."

Cal looked down, astounded to find that there was indeed a needle jutting out from the ravaged flesh of his stomach.

"Oh, I had forgotten about that." he said impassively.

378

Hera pressed her hands to her face, further attempting to suppress the laugh that dared to escape. Cal must have been more drunk than he thought because it occurred to him that he would do whatever it took to hear that laugh again. Hera shifted her weight from her heels to her toes and then back again before she stepped forward, finally entering the room—and closing the distance between her and Cal. Slowly, she sank to her knees before him. Cal went wholly still, his brain malfunctioning at the sight before him.

She was *kneeling* before him—between his legs—in the privacy of his cabin. Certainly the thought of her had crossed his mind, but this—

Cal swallowed and shifted, aiming to dislodge his building discomfort. Cal had to call on every ounce of willpower to stop from reaching out to stroke her hair. Her eyes slid from his wound to the table where his liquor still resided. She sniffed once before wrinkling her nose.

"I take it you've imbibed a bit this evening."

Cal let out a dark chuckle and lifted a brow. "I had to do something to take off the edge."

"Brawling didn't do it?" Hera said with a hint of amusement.

Holding her gaze, Cal noted the slight hitch in her breathing. He spoke with absolute serosity.

"Not even close."

The blush in Hera's face returned with a vengeance. She averted her eyes and cleared her throat. Her hand darted out, grabbing for the bottle. Exhaling, she took a too-quick drink. Her face contorted, and she gave a sputtering cough. Cal's eyes remained fixed on her as she wiped her mouth on the back of her hand and set the bottle back on the table. His lips curled into a smile, and he managed to arch an eyebrow.

"Not much of a drinker?"

Coughing, Hera shook her head. "Not ordinarily. Ladies…of my station aren't permitted to drink very often," she gave another cough, "and certainly not any spirits *that* strong." Her brows were bent as she glanced at the bottle once more like she feared it would leap from the table.

"Why start now?" Cal asked, his curiosity getting the better of him.

"I needed the courage." she said, her voice steady and clear.

Nodding in agreement, Cal thought of everything he wished to say to her, but the last vestiges of his pride and dignity wouldn't permit it. A few more sips of the liquor would solve that. Cal refrained, though; it would only further complicate a delicate situation. He and Lady Hera would simply have to keep up their dance—until one finally faltered.

Rolling her shoulders, Hera reached for the needle, her hands trembling slightly. Cal slowed his breathing, fearing any sudden movements would scare her off. Though, given all they had endured, he suspected there wasn't much that would frighten her. Cal didn't allow himself to linger on the feelings that revelation evoked. Instead, he glanced around the room, desperate to have anything else to focus on in favor of the sensation of Hera sliding closer to him and moving herself deeper between his legs.

"I hope you know what you're doing." he muttered, still putting his gaze anywhere but on her.

Hera laughed. "I guess you'll find out one way or another."

"Forgotten, save me." he said, shaking his head.

The exhale of her breath caressed over his exposed skin as she laughed again. Staring at the ceiling, Cal counted the planks as Hera's breath skated over him and her fingers brushed his abdomen. He clenched his fist and curled his toes in his boots as she lifted the needle and began stitching up his skin. Now was not the time to give into his base nature—not when this was the kindest thing anyone had done for him in years. She made a pass, then another before Cal twitched, his muscles aching at her nearness and feather-light touch.

"Are you ticklish?"

Cal gave a long exhale through his nose and flexed his fingers, desperate for anything to distract him.

"Something like that." he choked out.

"Sorry, I'll try to be quick." Hera assured.

That was the last thing Cal wanted, but he refrained from expressing it. Instead, he said, "It's good to know that all those needlepoint lessons translate into something useful."

Hera exhaled, her brows furrowed in concentration but a smile on her lips. "Unfortunately, that wasn't where I learned to sew."

"No? Tapestries, then? No, let me guess: quilting." he teased, desperate to keep his mind off of her closeness to his waist.

"Nothing so domestic, I'm afraid."

"What was it then?"

Silence pulsed between them long enough that Cal assumed Hera wouldn't answer. But then, as she made one final tug at his laceration, she quietly said, "My own wounds."

Cal went still.

The alcohol was doing its best to cloud his mind, but he blinked past the haze to really *see* the woman before him. Hera remained on her knees between Cal's legs, not meeting his gaze. Again, his mind wandered, and the heat in his blood was nudging him closer to a precipice. He clenched his teeth, desperate to hold onto a scrap of his honor, and refocused on Hera's face. But it wasn't shame etched in her features—it was rage. Cal understood that feeling better than most. It had been his constant companion for as long as he could remember.

Hera clamped her lips together and then abruptly stood. Cal hadn't realized that he was leaning toward her until he had to reel backward to keep from colliding with her.

Shaking her head, Hera quickly glanced at the table, placing the used needle there. "Make sure to keep that clean and try not to get into any more fights before it's had a chance to heal." Turning, she aimed for the door, but Cal's hand flew out, slipping around her wrist. Hera glanced at him over her shoulder, moisture dampening her eyes.

Cal beheld all that was there: anger, frustration, hurt, loss, and longing. He saw all of it and was beginning to understand who Hera was. She wasn't some daft and pretentious noble girl. She was cunning and ambitious, and though he still questioned the story she supplied about her connection to the Princess, Cal didn't care. He knew the things that mattered. He opened his mouth to say it, to tell her that he understood her pain and ambition, that he knew–better than most–what it meant to be let down and hurt by the person who was supposed to protect them, but the words stuck in his throat.

Hera's shoulders dropped at the same time his did, and all he managed to utter was, "Thank you."

Then his fingers fell away from her wrist.

Nodding her acknowledgment, she headed for the door, her boots thundering across the floor. Reclining in his chair, Cal's hand absentmindedly reached for the liquor remnants. But as his hand hovered over the bottle–his eyes catching on the down-turned portrait once more–Hera paused momentarily, her fingers curling around the door frame.

Cal's heart kicked up in his chest.

Hera would falter first. She would be the one to acknowledge this *thing* between them. She turned, barely peeking over her shoulder at him for just a moment. Their eyes collided, stealing Cal's breath. His mouth fell open, his admission burning in his throat, and then—

She turned back and left—taking Cal's hope with her.

Exhaling slowly, Cal flexed his fingers until his throat was no longer clogged with the truth. He grabbed the bottle and tipped it up. He drank its contents and then fumbled for another in the cabinet across the room. He needed a minute. A reprieve from his all-consuming thoughts and desires.

A moment of peace from his unrelenting torment.

Chapter Fifty

Malakai stared at the space the Princess occupied before disappearing after Brander, her words still ringing in his ears. He was used to having his abilities questioned and being called a fraud. But for there to be truth to the accusation of being useless, well, to say that Malakai was taking it hard was an understatement.

But Malakai *did* have a vision that day with Finnley.

He knew it, so why couldn't he conjure one since? He considered that it was a fluke. Or perhaps a hallucination. But he knew what he had seen. He knew that the lush, verdant island with the treasure buried deep within was real and within their grasp. The salt-tinged air scratched against Malakai's skin, and he flexed his fingers to dispel his growing agitation. But the longer he lingered in the briny air, and the warmer his face grew, the harder it became to not give into his annoyance.

He *needed* to have a vision.

Turning from the deck, Malakai peered out over the water. He closed his eyes and breathed deeply. Perhaps he merely needed to clear his mind. His magic was an extension of him. It was at his command, so he simply needed to regain control of himself.

Malakai took several breaths through his nose and gently blew out his mouth over and over—until his pulse slowed and his skin cooled. The murmurs of conversation and thudding of feet faded into nothingness. He continued his breathing and emptied his mind—despite

Caliban's claim that one could not empty what was already hollow. He cleared his thoughts and focused on the gentle lapping of the water against the hull.

He stood perfectly still and concentrated on the water.

Back and forth.

Back and forth.

Back and forth.

Pressing his eyes closed, he breathed in the brine, and reached down into the light that dwelt within. He reached for the power that had been his constant companion before he even understood it. He glimpsed it, hovering just out of sight and reach. He surged forward, desperate to feel it again—

It vanished.

Malakai's eyes flew open, and he lurched forward, his hands flying out before him.

But there was nothing.

Nothing but clear blue skies and turquoise waters. Water that was quickly coming into focus as he tumbled toward it, his momentum sending him overboard. Grappling for the railing, he twisted and clamored for anything to stop him from falling into the sea below. The Ether may have dissipated, and the creatures may not have attacked them since, but Malakai held no faith that more horrors weren't waiting beneath the pristine waves.

His nails cracked, and wood splintered as he desperately tore at the ship for purchase, the world passing in a blur—

It stopped.

Pain howled through Malakai's wrist and shoulder, and the joints subluxated from the force of his body abruptly stopping its descent. He looked up and was greeted by Finnley's hard stare. Her calloused fingers dug into his wrist, scraping against his tender skin.

Malakai barely had time to blink before she bared her teeth in a grimace and yanked him up. Though he yelped, he tried not to squirm—lest Finnley drop him. She bellowed, and more hands appeared, grabbing Malakai's arms and clothes and hauling him over the railing. His hands took the brunt of the impact, his palms and knees screaming as they connected with the wood—and Finnley.

"Argh! Get off me, ye witch!" Finnley bellowed.

Despite his near-death experience, Malakai had to restrain a laugh. Of all the names he had been called, 'witch' was a first. He had far too much natural ability to resort to witchcraft—but if his Sight didn't come back, maybe he would be forced to.

Finnley bucked and flailed beneath him. He tried his best not to give her cause to whack him, but that was proving difficult as she continued to thrash. He gathered she didn't like to be touched, but her reaction seemed exaggerated—

Their skin touched, and Malakai went ramrod still.

Again, the island appeared to him, this time sharper—more vibrant. Large, waxy leaves flapped gently in an unseen wind; water droplets plunked on the damp soil beneath them. The vision shifted, and he was underground again, the air heavy and cool—a reprieve from the baking sun. A small room was dominated by a table covered with food so delectable that Malakai's mouth watered even within the vision. The vision warped, and he was in the vault of treasure once more. The treasure—even more ornate and luminous than before—was heaped before him, this time more than just gems and gold. A chill crept up Malakai's spine as he beheld the pale statute looming over the bounty. Its face was veiled, or perhaps worn smooth from eons of time—

But it saw.

It saw all, and was perhaps the beating heart of the island—the long-forgotten god that ruled over this place.

This was too much.

Too much.

Shaking his head, Malakai tried to end the vision, but then the statue looked. Its awareness surrounded him, snatching his breath and latching onto his soul. He did his best to tamp down the rising panic in his chest, but nothing had ever felt this real.

Malakai reeled backward, intent on wrenching himself free, when a voice, more ancient than time itself, wicked and wild and kind and dangerous, whispered to him:

The Isle always demands a price, and It does not bargain.

Then, he was tumbling backward, back into his body, his bones trembling with the effort to keep him upright. Calloused fingers dug into the delicate flesh of his arms, hauling him up and back. Malakai managed to pry his eyes open and was greeted with Finnley's indignant stare. Murder danced in her eyes as she advanced on him. Malakai had the good sense to take a step back. Or, at least, he tried. His progress was halted by a wall of muscle and the thick fingers of the crewmate behind him, gripping his biceps.

Finnley flung a scar-flecked finger in Malakai's face, close enough that his eyes went cross from looking at it, and said, "Ye better stay far away from me. I'm sick of yer shenanigans. Every time ye touch me, you go into one of yer fits."

A realization barreled into him, and he went utterly stiff.

"You're an amplifier."

Finnley's finger dropped, and she narrowed her eyes in suspicion. "What?" She questioned, her tone losing some of its anger and bravado.

Malakai moved to step forward, but Finnley's flared nostrils and the increasing pressure around his arms gave him pause. He shook his head, clearing away the racing thoughts.

"Every time I touch you, I have a vision. Caliban's and Kasper's magics have been stronger since boarding the ship. The common denominator in all of us is you."

Finnley's eyes darted to the pirates, who pretended not to listen and watch. But Malakai was beyond caring, not when the answer to the question he had been asking for days was finally answered.

"It's the magic of this place. The Isle and The Ether." Finnley countered.

Shaking his head, Malakai said, "You're the key, Finnley, to all of this. You can give us all the advantage against what awaits on the island."

Barking out a laugh, Finnley moved further away from Malakai, taking his visions with her. "That's the most foolish thing I have ever heard. I'm a plain and normal human, always have been."

But Malakai saw it. The shadow of doubt that clouded her eyes, pulling at the scar across her face. Finnley knew more than she was letting on, and Malakai was willing to bet that the past he had glimpsed of hers was directly tied to her innate hatred of him. She hated him, certainly, but that hatred was borne of *fear*.

Reaching for his sunshiny exterior, Malakai laughed good-naturedly. "Perhaps I was wrong. Caliban said before that he sensed the Isle had magic. Perhaps that is it."

Finnley didn't relax. If anything, her muscles were more tense, anxiety lining her limbs. But she flicked her stern gaze to the man still holding Malakai. She gave a quick jerk of her chin, and inexplicably, the ebony boards of the Umbra rose up to meet his face. Malakai threw out his hands at the last moment, his palms smarting as they connected with the worn wood. Boots thudded by, retreating from Malakai, leaving him alone on the deck. He stayed on the ground for a heartbeat longer, uninterested in catching Finnley's rueful glare again.

Finally, he leaned back, resting on his knees, and began scheming on how to get Finnley to agree to join them on the Isle.

* * * *

Malakai's arm ached as he held it up, hovering millimeters from Kasper's door. He wasn't sure if it was from the rough treatment he received from the crewmate earlier, or the fact that he was in the same position for nearly five minutes—attempting to work up the nerve to actually knock.

But Malakai needed to talk to someone about Finnley and the potential benefit she would provide if they brought her with them to the island. Admittedly, he should be having this conversation with Caliban, but locating him and having a productive conversation were arduous tasks—tasks he was not mentally prepared for.

Dropping his hand, Malakai prepared to accept his cowardice and return to stewing in his rooms. Something he had been at for hours since his revelation—

The door swung open.

Kasper's wide-eyed stare greeted him. His chest and abdomen exposed gleaming skin in the candlelight, and his damp hair curled around his ears and nape.

"You bathed." Malakai said with forced levity.

Kasper arched an eyebrow and pushed past Malakai, aiming for the narrow corridor.

Huffing a sigh, Malakai trailed after Kasper. The sting of rejection was sharp, but considering everything else, they would need to move past their differences. If Kasper's tensed muscles were any indication, he didn't share the sentiment.

Yet.

Malakai continued after Kasper, following him further into the ship's bowels. Kasper continued until he arrived at the galley, where the cook–a one-eyed, grimy-looking man–doled out a spoonful of some sort of white, lumpy substance. Malakai chose not to brave the cook's food, opting to snack on the dried meat and biscuits available instead. The memory of the food in the Cave flashed in his mind, strengthening his resolve to tell Kasper about the vision and Finnley.

Graciously, Kasper took the bowl from the cook, dipping his chin in acknowledgment. Malakai also flashed a winning smile, though it was not as well received as Kasper's recognition. The cook narrowed his remaining eye and curled his lip distastefully, but Malakai stayed steadfast.

Stalking to the far corner of the galley, Kasper took up residence at a small, dingy table. There were two chairs, which Malakai took as an invitation to join Kasper. Kasper's shoulders were tense, but he gave no acknowledgement to Malakai as he claimed the rickety seat across from him, placing his back to the rest of the galley. Kasper's attention remained on the gruel in front of him. The only sounds were his slurping and the constant bubbling of the pot that the cook manned.

Malakai took a moment to inspect his ruined nails. He had cleaned them up after his near fall off the side of the Umbra, but it still pained him to look at the cracked nail beds. They were now free of dried blood and splinters, but wrecked nonetheless. He gave a pointed sigh, folded his hands on the table, and watched Kasper diligently spoon his supper into his mouth.

The endless days at sea must have gotten to Malakai because, after another minute of slurping, he said, "Don't you want to know why I was standing outside your door?"

"No." Kasper replied resolutely.

Malakai scoffed. "Well, don't you want to know why I followed you down here?"

Kasper took a long time scooping up another spoonful, keeping his gaze fixed on the bowl.

"No."

Gritting his teeth, Malakai leaned forward, his patience worn thin. "You can't stay angry with me forever."

Kasper's eyes snapped to him, heat simmering there. "Can't I?"

But it wasn't anger burning in his eyes—well, it wasn't entirely anger blazing there. There was also hurt, anguish, and despair. Malakai's posture softened slightly, and he reeled back, sliding back into his seat.

"You're hurt." he said softly.

Lines bracketed Kasper's mouth. A muscle twitched in his jaw before he returned his eyes to his supper.

Crossing his arms, Malakai said, "Well, the least you can do is tell me why you've been avoiding me. I can't imagine what I've done to warrant such treatment." Malakai lied. He knew why. In a horrible moment of conscience, he saw himself revealing a portion of his subterfuge. But he wanted to see if Kasper would truly push the issue or simply let it go.

Kasper's spoon clanked against the side of the bowl and raised his gaze to Malakai once more. "You can't? Not a single thing that you've done or withheld from me in the last decade would possibly result in me being so angry that I want nothing to do with you."

Nodding, Malakai responded, "Ah, that."

Kasper gave a broken laugh and glared at his brother with malice. "You learn that I've become privy to your deception, and that's all you have to say?" Kasper shook his head, picked up his spoon, and resumed eating.

Malakai began working through ways to smooth things over with Kasper. He had taken advantage of Kasper and exploited his gifts for his own benefit, but hadn't he done it with the right intentions? They were destitute after the money Caliban had left them ran out, and every door was shut. Surely, Kasper knew that he wouldn't have taken such drastic measures had they not been necessary. Looking at the tension lining Kasper's shoulders and face, he wasn't sure he would agree. Malakai was content to let Kasper stew. If he refused to see reason, the only option was to wait for him to come around. Sooner or later, Kasper would; he was reasonable like that.

Scraping his spoon against the bottom of the wooden bowl, the last bit of the mystery supper passed between Kasper's lips. His skin had dried, and his hair had some as well; the ends were still curled, but they were lighter, closer to Malakai's color than Caliban's.

The spoon clattered against the bowl, and for the first time since Kasper sat down, he leaned back against the chair and surveyed Malakai. His eyes lingered on his face, taking in what Malakai hoped read as contrite and remorseful. Kasper's eyes traveled down, taking in Malakai's wardrobe, which was admittedly less elaborate than expected, but still more ornate than anyone aboard the Umbra.

Swallowing his pride, Malakai said softly, "You look well, all things considered." Kasper had expended much of his energy and magic on saving the Princess, though Malakai hadn't learned to what extent. He wanted to know. He wanted to speak and confide in Kasper like they had for years.

Kasper's rueful gaze softened, and he said, crossing his arms over his chest, "What do you want, Kai?"

Malakai leaned forward, opened his mouth, and then paused. He had so much to say, but where to start? Could he get back into Kasper's good graces in a single conversation? Or should he cut to the chase and simply tell him what he learned this afternoon. Slowly, Malakai sat back in his chair and glanced around. A few crew members were in the galley but seemed more interested in their food than Malakai's conversation.

"I had a vision today."

Rolling his eyes, Kasper moved to stand. "I don't have time for this, Kai." He reached for the bowl, but Malakai intercepted him, grabbing his wrist.

"Please." Malakai said, his eyes wide and pleading.

Kasper hesitated, his features shifting like he was fighting to hold fast to his convictions. Malakai prayed that they wouldn't win out. Finally, something like resignation passed over his face, and he returned to his seat. Malakai exhaled—Kasper's forgiveness was certainly forthcoming.

"Thank you." he said gently.

Kasper nodded, but wouldn't meet Malakai's gaze. Malakai suspected this was the best he would get, so he launched into his tale. He described his visions, the treasure, the statue, and the looming danger. He told of how his visions left him and how he had almost gone overboard. Kasper's expression never changed, remaining impassive as Malakai finished, "And that was when I realized that Finnley is an amplifier."

Kasper arched a brow, the only indication that he was listening. Malakai held his breath, waiting for Kasper to do or say something. Finally, Kasper sighed, rapped his nails against the table, and said, "Alright."

Furrowing his brow, he said, "Alright? That's all you have to say?" Malakai leaned forward, bracing his elbows on the table. "I've just given you insight into what we could face on the Isle and a way to make all of us more powerful. All you can say is 'alright'?"

Shrugging, Kasper said, "I don't know what you want me to say, Kai."

Malakai flung up his hands. "I want you to care. I want you to realize the gravity of our situation—of what is at stake here."

Kasper shot forward, closing the distance between them. "There is nothing at stake for me, Kai. I didn't agree to go on this journey. You did. Like always, you decided what was best for me without considering what I might want. So, whatever happens to you or to Cal is none of my concern."

"How can you say that?"

Kasper's eyes widened, and he stood up so quickly that his chair toppled over. "How can I say that? You lied to me for years, Kai. You used me, and you only owned up to your actions because you were delirious."

"That's not true!" He exclaimed, his voice rising to meet Kasper's.

A broken laugh rasped out of Kasper. "It's not? Then why did it take you passing out for the truth to come out? Why not be honest when Cal came back the first time?"

Malakai pursed his lips.

Nodding, Kasper added, "That's what I thought." Kasper withdrew from the table and took a step away.

Malakai didn't have it in him to stop his brother. But Kasper paused and said, "And you know what the worst part about all of it is, Kai?"

Looking at his brother's eyes, Malakai noted their red rim and glassy appearance. Something sharp speared through his chest, and he couldn't help the shame that coated his skin.

Kasper's lip wobbled only once as he said, "You never even apologized."

Kasper turned away from Malakai, leaving him and his regret in the galley alone.

Chapter Fifty One

Soline would have loved the high seas.

She would have loved the salt-scented air twining through her hair. She would have loved the seawater spray as the waves crested and sloshed against the weather-worn ebony boards of the Umbra. Soline wouldn't have even minded the hard days aboard the Umbra, as long as she ended them in Cal's arms.

Cal had even wondered how the crew would have received her. They were a motley crew, rough and crude on their best days, but Soline could make anyone like her—though, she rarely had to try.

The memory of their last time on the hill—one of his precious good memories with Soline—came rushing back to Cal, momentarily stealing his breath. He fought to clear his mind of it, to put off the anguish it brought—because thinking of that day subsequently brought up other memories. Turning away from the deck of the Umbra, Cal stared out over the tranquil sea. He quickly shut his eyes—even the shade of the water evoked memories of her. For years, she had haunted him, but now she clung to him like his shadows, always within reach. In the swirling darkness behind Cal's eyes, he saw her weeks after their afternoon on the hill. He hadn't known it then, but the changes—the shift in her—had already begun.

Soline rested her chin on her knees, her legs pulled tight against her chest. Cal sat beside her, reclined into the pile of pillows on the chaise in the foyer. His fingers drew idle shapes along her back, the pattern an amalgamation of runes he had read in a spell book earlier that day. Soline's back rose and fell in a steady rhythm, but Cal noted the tension in her muscles. The tautness of her shoulders and the lines bracketing her mouth. But Soline remained quiet. She claimed her head ached from the incessant chatter of the noble women and nauseating incense that the King demanded be burned at all hours of the day.

Cal asked about her time, but she simply shook her head and promised it wasn't interesting enough or worth retelling. So, they sat in silence. Cal was content to do so; just being in Soline's presence calmed him. Even his shadows and the darker things that plagued him took a respite when she was near. Cal's fingers made another pass along Soline's back, subtly swirling the tendrils of her hair in their wake. Suddenly, she stiffened and turned toward Cal. His hand froze, hovering in midair.

Soline's large eyes blinked once. Twice. "You'll love me no matter what."

A statement, not a question.

Cal sat up straighter and reached for her face. His hand dwarfed her cheek, and he loosened a breath as she relaxed into his touch.

"Always." he said, with a tenderness reserved only for Soline and Kasper.

A tear escaped down her cheek and her bottom lip quivered.

Cal crushed her against his chest. He prepared for the onslaught of tears, for the whole-body shakes and tremors that he had witnessed the night Soline's mother had passed. He readied the words and murmurs of comfort that had soothed her ragged soul when she returned from laying the lilies on the too-small coffin that rested next to her mother's.

But they never came.

Soline didn't shed another tear, but Cal held her all the same, gently stroking her golden hair. Cal was unsure how long they had stayed like that, but at some point, Soline had fallen asleep, and Cal had carried her to her chambers. The mattress dipped beneath him as he gingerly placed her on the bed, Soline's maids right behind him, pulling up the blanket to cover her. Cal mustered up every ounce of restraint in him so as not to press a kiss on her lips, but instead place it on her temples. Everyone in the palace may have known they were courting, but he would not have her propriety called into question.

Cal brushed his fingers along her jaw once before he righted himself and stepped back from the bed. Turning, he bowed to the maids. He was technically ranked higher than all of them, but he saw no point in treating them as less—he was far too familiar with the feeling.

"She is utterly exhausted from the excitement of the day." one of her maids said in a hushed tone.

"Excitement?" Cal asked.

The maid's eyes went wide, and she nodded her head fervently. "Oh, yes. The King had performers from a traveling caravan entertain, and he gave her the seat of honor. Paid special attention to her, too. Even had her give a small demonstration of her abilities."

Instantly, Cal's mood soured. Soline was beautiful and kind. She had caught the attention of other nobles before and never returned their affections, but if the King...

No, Cal wouldn't even give the thought credence.

He bowed to the maids and turned on his heel to leave, but the lingering thought of the King's eye turning toward Soline made him wary.

Cal's eyes flew open, and he turned away from the open sea. He clenched his jaw against the emotion searing in his face.

Soline was gone, and she was never coming back.

She was a wraith, cursed to wander this plane of existence because Cal had failed her once. More than once. He failed Soline by not saving her in life, and then again when he botched his attempt to revive her. He had made her into a monster. At the very least, he owed her rest and peace from her miserable state. Every day he lived with shame and regret that he hadn't protected her, or given her the tools to defend herself, and that would torment and haunt Cal for whatever remained of his wretched life.

A metal rattle drew Cal from his spiral, and his gaze snagged on the flutter of ebony hair—the shade nearly identical to the Umbra in its prime. Sweat darkened the fabric of the linen tunic Lady Hera wore—borrowed from Finnley, he suspected, as he had only seen her in long dresses until now. And try as he might, he was helpless to stop his gaze from dipping to her legs, now encased in breeches that allowed her to move more freely than the cumbersome skirts. Mercifully, other parts of her remained covered, but that didn't stop Cal's mind from *wandering*.

That's how it had been since she first entered his brother's tent. His eyes always drifted to her whenever she was in the vicinity. At first, Cal had chalked it up to annoyance and made sure she stayed out of his way. Then he reasoned it was just the acknowledgment of her beauty—but that wasn't the truth. There was an undeniable pull toward her, like the Earth's gravity had shifted, drawing him into her orbit. That night on the deck, when they argued and he further glimpsed the fire burning within her, had initiated the shift—even if he would have been loath to admit it then. But the attack on the Umbra and her impending death further skewed the balance. Cal had almost lost himself to his magic that day. Try as he might to convince himself that it was to ensure he got the information she was withholding, or to keep from drawing the ire of the Princess, neither of those things were the truth—at least not entirely. Yes, he wanted the book Hera was safeguarding, but he no longer saw a reason to take it by force. She would share the knowledge when she was ready. And as for the Princess, well, he could care less what she personally thought...but Lady Hera was important to her— and *she* was becoming important to Cal.

There was no longer any ignoring that whatever he felt for her went beyond surface-level interest or disdain. When she had appeared in his room, touched him, and tended to his wounds, his feelings for her had shifted from appreciation of her looks to wanting to know more—to wanting her. And now, even with memories of Soline plaguing him, with the plans nearly complete, he was still thinking about Hera.

Then, as though she had heard his thoughts, Lady Hera turned toward him. Annoyance—and something else—blazed in her eyes, illuminating the gold flecks and strands of emerald in her brown-hazel irises.

Cal was helpless to stop the smirk that worked its way to his lips; no more than he could stop himself from sketching a bow. Immediately he regretted it, as the motion pulled at the still-healing wound on his abdomen. The guard dog gave as good as he got—better if Cal was being honest—but Cal had the advantage of being younger and having access to a cache of healing elixirs. Despite his discomfort, his eyes never left her, allowing him to glimpse the way she stiffened and lifted her chin. She turned back to Finnley, wholly ignoring him.

Cal's smirk spread into a smile, and he leaned back against the railing, content to watch Hera train. She moved slowly through the maneuvers. Raising the sword up and sweeping it down in an arc. Over and over and over until she got the hang of it, and Finnley was—well, not *pleased*—but accepting of her progress. Aside from Cal's eventual vengeance on the King, this would be his recompense. If he could give Hera the chance to defend herself from whatever horrors awaited them on the island—and beyond, if they survived—then he would do it.

"Again." Finnley growled and shifted into position. Hera mirrored her stance and lifted her practice blade. The edges were too dull to cut, but would still bruise and sting if hit with it. Already, abrasions were blooming along Hera's arms, but from the determination lining her face, it was clear that a few injuries wouldn't deter her from learning to wield a blade.

Cal angled his head, attempting to understand how a girl—clearly of noble birth and in a position of influence—had become accustomed to pain. An oily pit opened up in Cal's stomach at the thought of Hera's motivation. Had her father harmed her? Cal never knew his parents, something he had always resented, but perhaps absent parents were preferred to abusive ones. Cal wanted to think that this woman, who was clearly the most trusted member of the Princess's household, would have been protected and off-limits to the King's proclivities. But he wasn't that naive.

Position and influence hadn't saved Soline.

Shifting her weight, Finnley feigned left, but changed course at the last second to attack Hera's unguarded side. Hera lunged, meaning to block Finnley's assault, but failed to anticipate the redirect. The flat of Finnley's blade smacked Hera's bicep. Hera hissed and swore. She whirled on Finnley, but Finnley was already out of reach. A muscle in Hera's jaw twitched, but she kept her sword up—refusing to concede.

Nodding toward Finnley, Hera said, "Again."

Finnley obliged.

Cal stood idly by for the next hour, watching Finnley strike a blow and smothering his laugh at Hera's swearing. But she never quit. After each blow, there was a lesson and an explanation for why Hera failed to see the attack coming. Finnley was going through another set of maneuvers, more complex than anything she had dared to show Hera. She whirled and executed a nasty combination that resulted in Hera losing her footing and tumbling toward the deck, with the help of Finnley's blade slamming into the middle of her back.

Hera had cried out, her back arching—

Cal was moving before he thought better of it. He reached out for Hera to whisk her away from the humiliation and pain of it all, but a blade gleaming dully with the late afternoon sun pressed against his chest. Lifting his eyes, Cal found Finnley's hard stare. His second-in-command shook her head once.

"She needs to learn this lesson here, or she dies out there." she said with a chin jerk toward the open water.

Flexing his hand, Cal considered the ramifications of blowing Finnley off and taking Hera away anyway—but he knew Finnley wouldn't hesitate to whack him with the flat of her blade.

He had nearly convinced himself that Finnley was taking their training too far when she slipped her fingers around his arm and said softly, "She's not Soline, Cal."

Cal jerked back and out of Finnley's grasp. His breath came in sharp pants, and he said through gritted teeth, "I know that."

Arching a scarred brow, Finnley crossed her arms. "Do you?"

A muscle feathered in Cal's cheek.

Shadows nipped at his clothes, begging to be unleashed.

Finnley didn't spare him another glance as she said, "If you can't control yourself, get off my deck."

Cal worked to dampen the anger that was steadily igniting within his chest. Blood throbbed in his ears as his eyes roamed beyond Finnely, toward the deck where Hera crawled onto all fours. Pain contorted her face as she gently flexed her back. Cal saw it then. The raised, ruined flesh peeking out from the top of her tunic. Scars from a whip, by the looks of it. They weren't new by any standards, but from the grimace Hera made, Cal knew they ran deep—the product of years of lashings.

Shadows erupted from Cal's body.

They blotted out the sun and enveloped him in darkness. Cries and swearing rang out all around him, but they fell on deaf ears as he slowly covered the distance to her and dropped to his knees in front of Hera. Her eyes widened, but she lifted her chin and clenched her hands against her trembling. She couldn't see him, her senses smothered by the shadows, but Cal saw her perfectly—more so than before.

A tremor shook his fingers as he raised his hands to her cheek and brushed away the tendrils of hair clinging to her damp skin. He murmured a spell that allowed her to see, and she blinked against the dark as he returned to focus. For a heartbeat longer than necessary, he let his fingers linger, but there was so much coursing through Cal's mind.

Anger, regret, shame, fear, and...*longing.*

Yes, that was the name for the emotion that Hera evoked in him every time he looked in her direction. Cal had refused to give it a name. Thought it a betrayal against Soline, but...Soline was gone. And even the wraith had understood what Cal had failed to. He *wanted* Hera. Seeing her–not as a means to an end or an inconvenience–but truly *seeing* her made those feelings that much clearer.

Cal's fingers made another pass over Hera's cheek, but she shifted away. Her tunic slid with it, exposing the tops of the scars on her back once more. His eyes narrowed on the ruined tissue, his body going hot and cold at the sight.

"Who did that to you?" Cal asked, his voice rough as gravel.

Hera followed his line of sight and stilled.

A moment passed, and she shrugged, moving the fabric to cover her back again.

"No one."

"Don't lie to me."

"It's none of your business." she snapped, her eyes burning with righteous anger.

Cal clenched his jaw to rein in his temper. Hera had proven she was not afraid to match Cal blow for blow. Taking a deep breath, he forced his anger away. Hera remained silent, her gaze fixed on the darkness around them—looking anywhere but directly at Cal.

Loosing another breath, he said, "Is that why you wanted to learn how to use a blade? To stop your abuser? Or perhaps even the King?" The buzzing, whispering quiet of the shadows filled the space. Cal guessed well enough who would dare strike a noble lady—and who would permit it. A sick, oily feeling settled over his stomach. "This won't happen again."

A broken, half-hearted laugh fell from her lips as she finally looked at him. "You can't promise that."

The hollowness in her eyes and voice stole Cal's breath. It reminded him so much of those last days with Soline.

Cal glanced at Soline's shoulders over the top of the spell book he was pretending to read. They were curled inward as she absentmindedly plunked the harpsichord, the sound hollow and wistful in the silence of her room. Cal flipped the page, still not absorbing any information, but he didn't want to leave her presence either.

Though Cal attempted to talk to her earlier about her week in the King's court, she refused. They hadn't seen each other, save for in passing, in nearly three weeks. The King demanded Soline's presence at all hours of the day, and Soline was in no position to refuse him—not until Cal could ask for leave from court and take Soline with him. Cal refused to let his mind assume the worst. The King had a harem that was well known, but he never took the daughters of titled men. Cal had to hope that being the daughter of a count would protect her until Cal got her out.

He glanced over at the untouched tray of food. He had encouraged her to eat the supper, but she had refused. Kasper had behaved similarly when he was ill, but according to the Court Healer—and from his own assessments—Soline was the portrait of health.

But something was wrong.

Closing the book, Cal dropped his feet to the floor. The suddenness of the sound startled Soline, and she turned to look at him. She sported a smile—one that failed to reach her eyes.

"What's wrong, my love?" Cal said softly as he strode toward her and sat on the divan beside her. Reaching for his hands, Soline traced the faint scars on his skin—avoiding his question.

Cal slid a finger under Soline's chin, gently raising her eyes to his.

Tears welled there, slipping down her cheeks.

They moved simultaneously, Soline reaching for Cal and Cal pulling her in. They held each other for what might have been hours—Cal's shirt growing more damp by the minute. Cal didn't care. Nothing but Soline and Kasper mattered in the world—and he would do everything in his power to protect them.

Finally, after Soline's sniffling subsided, she lifted her head from his chest, her eyes swollen and puffy.

"I'm s—so sor—sorry we haven't had ti—time for each other lately."

Pressing a kiss into Soline's hair, Cal inhaled the cloying scent of the King's preferred incense. Cal's mind spun with a hundred different possibilities. Had she been made to perform? Had the King promised her to some noble? Had he—no, Cal stopped himself before he lost his temper.

"There's nothing to forgive."

Another sob broke from Soline, and she leaned into him once more. "There's so much you don't know. So much I have done. You won't forgive me for it, I know it." she said, her voice muffled against his shoulder.

Worry continued to worm its way into his mind, and he murmured into her hair, "There's nothing you can do or say that would make me love you less."

"You don't know that."

"I do."

"Caliban—"

"Soline." he said with more force than he had ever used with her. "I love you. You and Kasper are my world. There's nothing we can't withstand."

Soline's lip quivered. Her eyes dropped from his, her hands resting on her abdomen. She shook her head, slowly at first, then more vigorously. "What I've done, Caliban, what's been asked of me. I can't—" her voice broke off in a sob once more, and Cal pulled her in more tightly. Whatever had happened to her, whatever they had made her do, was breaking her. Cal's heart raced. He needed to do something before he lost her entirely. He needed to get her out. He almost had enough money to buy his and Kasper's freedom, and then—

Then, they would be a proper family. Him, Soline, and Kasper. Like he had always dreamed.

He would go to the King in the morning and set everything right.

If only Cal had known what was coming. Cal had failed Soline. Had failed Kasper. Had failed Galen. He was tired of losing people that mattered to him. And now…

Reaching for Hera, Cal took her hands into his own—thankfully, she didn't pull away. He carefully lifted a hand to tuck a stray curl from her face. Callouses caught on the soft skin of her cheeks, her freckles stark against her wan skin.

"I will not let another innocent be harmed by the evils of this world."

Hera's bottom lip trembled, but she quickly clamped her mouth together to cease it. He took her hands into his own once more and stood, Hera rising with him. The shadows and darkness around him began to thin and dissipate. The bright light of the mid-morning sun broke through in shafts, illuminating the gold and green in Hera's eyes. Rising voices and the lapping of waves around them were nearly painful after several minutes of silence. But Hera remained firm, even as Cal released her and reached for the dagger he had concealed in his boot. Slipping the dagger from its hiding place, Cal flipped the blade, pointing the hilt toward Hera.

She glanced at him for only a moment before taking the dagger and inspecting it. Kasper, eyes wild and full of fear, appeared behind Hera—but he skidded to a stop when he beheld the scene before him.

Cal paid him no mind as he said in a low voice, "A sword is a great option for open combat, but I suspect that a dagger will be more effective for what you are going to face. Daggers are swift and silent. You aren't a warrior, and may never be, but you can still defend yourself. Use what you have to your advantage. You're cunning and quick—never forget that."

Hera raised her eyes to his and held his stare. There was no fear or trepidation in her eyes—only resolve.

"Thank you." she said, her voice barely audible over the breeze.

Offering her a slight dip of his chin, he turned. He needed to put some distance between them before he did something he couldn't take back. But he paused as slender fingers slipped around his wrist.

Looking back at Hera, he noted her throat bobbing before she said, "Not just for the blade, but for seeing me."

Cal scanned her face—painfully aware they had an audience who saw and heard everything. It didn't matter. He spent much of his time–far too much–denying himself the things he wanted. The people he wanted. Constantly living in the shadows, waiting and watching for the perfect opportunity to strike—for the *right* moment to act. But what if life wasn't about finding one singular good moment, but rather a collection of many?

As he turned back to face Hera more fully, his shadow fell over her. A single thought came to his mind, and while he had not realized it at the time, when the words tumbled from his lips he knew their meaning to be undeniably true.

"I've known who you are from the moment we met."

Impertinent. Stubborn. Haughty. Overbearing.

Obstinate. Steadfast. Passionate. Unyielding.

This Lady–this utter *force* of a woman–had been in front of him the entire time. He had simply been too blind, too engrossed in his own plots, to appreciate her for what she was. Hera's eyes went wide, and her breath hitched in her chest, but Cal wouldn't let her run away from the truth that he needed to lay bare. Stepping nearer to her, Cal closed the distance between them.

Cal loved Soline.

He loved her with everything in him, but she was gone, and he knew she wouldn't have wanted him to live a half-life, denying himself anything that might bring him joy. She was too good of a person to wish that on him. Could Cal love another and still execute his plans? Hera would understand his goals—his motives. They were the same in that regard. Pushing back the loose strands of Hera's ebony hair, he inhaled her lily and jasmine scent. He leaned down—her lips parting and her eyes slowly going closed at the inevitability of his destination. The full, lush lips he had wanted for—

The bellowing of a horn ripped Hera from his grasp. She stormed away from him toward the ship's bow, their moment forgotten. A cold, hollow space took residence in his presence, where she had been seconds before.

Cal began plotting the slow, agonizing demise of whoever had dared to intrude. But when he lifted his gaze to the horizon, his mouth went utterly dry.

Kasper fell in step beside him, eyes wide. "Is that—"

"Land."

Part Three:
The Isle

Chapter Fifty Two

Searing heat burned through Rhea's entire body, making it impossible to focus on anything. She attempted to convince herself that it was the exertion from her training with Finnley and not from what she had shared with Cal—or their almost kiss. But the way he had looked at her, and held her, and touched her, and—

Gods, what had she been thinking?

Everything was already complicated and confusing enough without adding *that* to it.

What had he meant, *I've known who you are from the moment we met*? Why had Cal covered her in darkness? Why had she sewn him up the other day? What did her scars matter to him? Rhea knew there was no way he had actually guessed at her identity. No, Cal meant something else entirely, something that went beyond earthly names and bloodlines.

And that terrified Rhea almost more than anything.

But as Rhea's boots—Finnley's really, and a size too small at that—stopped at the ship's railing, she found one other thing to be fearful of.

The Cave of Splendors.

Rhea's breath caught in her throat at the overwhelming beauty of the island. Lush, vibrant trees with large, flat fronds gently swayed in the distance. The greenery was interspersed with vibrant, flowering plants running from purple to red to orange. A waterfall emitting a spray of water refracted and scattered a rainbow of light across the trees, replacing the constant lapping of water against the hull of the Umbra. Further down, the jungle abruptly stopped, greeted by a white sandy shore with waves gingerly rolling against it. Briefly, she wondered how they had come upon the island so fast. Indeed, a scout would have seen the land off in the distance before it appeared just a few miles away. But, given everything else they had encountered, she decided that chalking it up to magic was as good an explanation as any.

Rhea gripped the railing, trying and failing to keep her pulse under control as she scanned the island for the Cave's entrance. Her book, *Legends of the Cave of Splendors*, had next to nothing on the particular layout of the Cave, but rather the rumors of why the Cave of Splendors existed, the treasures it held—and the monsters that guarded it. She knew that the time of her holding the contents of the book over the heads of the others was rapidly coming to a close, but she couldn't dwell on that right now. Chewing her bottom lip, she tried to think about something else. She was as close as ever to Izor's Lamp being in her grasp. With its magic–with its wishes–she would save her people.

"Beautiful."

Rhea jolted at Cal's voice and his sudden presence. Glancing at him apprehensively, she found him already staring at her.

Suddenly, her mind was back in the cocoon of darkness with him, where they were that only things in the world that mattered. There was no prophecy, abusive fathers, or banishment; there was only her, and Cal, and his gentle caress against her skin. Rhea had not realized how much she wanted that until the shadows vanished, and she was faced with reality again.

Rhea swallowed the lump in her throat as Cal stared at her. His gaze was intense, but not uncomfortable–like it had been when she had knelt between his legs–and she was helpless to look away. Maybe she should tell him the truth—if he didn't already know. It was clear that whatever existed between them extended beyond physical attraction or admiration, and maybe–just maybe–he could see past her origins.

Maybe, the emotions coursing between them would be enough for him to accept her—for *exactly* who she was.

The thought had Rhea opening her mouth, the truth bubbling up in her stomach until it perched precariously on her lips.

"Cal, there's something—"

"Finally! The blessed Isle of Oum!" Kai exclaimed as he joined them on the bow.

Rhea blinked fiercely—abruptly broken from whatever spell she had clearly been under. Her heart nearly dropped with the realization of what she had almost done. She backed away as Kai stepped between them, grateful for the space. Everything about Cal was too intense. His ardent words and glowing gaze had completely disarmed her—and wholly distracted her from her mission. As much as she craved his nearness—the feel of his hands on her skin, the embrace of his words on her heart—she knew she must deny herself of him. She needed to be fully committed to obtaining Izor's Lamp from the Cave of Splendors and using it to save her Kingdom. She hadn't dared breathe a word about what she sought for fear Kai or one of the others would try to take it for themselves, but now, when she was within reach of it, she let the hope of the treasure within the Cave of Splendors wash over her.

Taking a deep breath, Rhea turned toward the brothers and pasted on a bright smile. "I'm going to go ready, Brander. We depart for the island within the hour."

Then, she hurried past them, not sparing another moment for her mind or heart to question her cowardice.

* * * *

Rhea ran her pendant back and forth on its chain, watching intently while Kasper waved a glowing purple gem around Brander's head. He had knitted Brander's ribs together within an hour of them being broken three days prior, but his head had been a more delicate process.

Her foot tapped incessantly. It made the only noise in the room, aside from the creaking of the ship and the shifting of Kasper's clothes as he moved back and forth in front of Brander. Rhea dropped her hand from her neck and tapped her fingers against her leg, waiting for Kasper's assessment. The fear that Brander wouldn't be well enough to join her on the island surged, making her stomach flop and her hands clammy. She also couldn't stop the paranoid thought that Cal had intentionally harmed Brander to keep him on the ship. Without Brander protecting her, who could she rely on? Kasper would do what he could to protect her, but if danger arose and it came down to saving her or one of his brothers, would he really choose her?

What she endeavored to do was of greater importance than any one of them. She couldn't afford to take chances.

Rhea stepped forward and said, "Well?" Her voice was edged with impertinence.

Kasper dropped his hand from Brander's face, his expression revealing nothing as he slipped the now dim crystal into his pocket. Wiping his hands down his breeches, he sighed, "He's better, but I would be hesitant to recommend that he do anything strenuous. If there are any more injuries to his head, or any added stress on his psyche, it might cause permanent damage." Kasper's gaze dropped from Rhea, landing on the floor. "I, uh, wouldn't suggest that he go on the island."

Rhea clenched her fist, aiming to keep her disappointment—and her fear—from her face. Brander stood up so quickly that Kasper fell back a step, knocking into the chest of drawers.

"I'm not staying behind."

Righting himself, Kasper insisted, "I understand your frustration, Brander, but—"

"No. No 'buts'. I'm not leaving her with the likes of your brothers."

"I can protect her," Kasper said, gesturing to Rhea, "I will do that."

"She's too important. What she's come here to *do* is too important. I can't risk it." Brander said, shaking his head.

Rhea pursed her lips. She wanted to be annoyed that they were talking around her, but she was too focused on the guilt gnawing away at her like water against stone. She needed Brander with her, but asking him to join her was putting him at further risk for permanent injury—or worse.

Brander finally looked at Rhea and said, "If you will still have me, I will come."

Dread stuck in her throat. If she said yes, if she took him, then she was all but condemning him to lasting injury. But, if she journeyed to the island alone…

The King had mocked Rhea's soft heart and compassion many times in her life, citing it as the reason that she would fail as a ruler. Lifting her chin, Rhea stared into Brander's fierce eyes, noting the warrior he embodied at every turn. If only she had a fraction of that strength.

"I would have it no other way."

Nodding, Brander then turned to Kasper, whose eyes had gone weary and sad. Rhea clenched her jaw against the shame that she bore. Brander's blood was firmly on her hands, and when Kasper slid his gaze to hers, she knew that he knew it, too.

Kasper nodded once and said, "Well, I'll take my leave."

Rhea bit her tongue to stop herself from begging him to stay. But Kasper had given his opinion on Brander's condition, and there was nothing else he could offer, so Rhea stayed quiet as he slipped from Brander's room. She waited for the door to snick shut before she allowed the first tear to fall.

"Princess," Brander murmured as he stepped toward her.

Raising her hand, she warded him off, and he stopped—ever the soldier. He remained stone still until Rhea had wiped away the singular tear trailing down her cheek and released a shaky breath.

"You know I was angry with you for engaging in Caliban's challenge, though he left you little choice…but that is behind us now." She swallowed and continued, "We need to focus on our mission. We must be ready to depart for the island as soon as possible, so gather whatever you require and meet me on the deck to board the skiff."

Turning on her heel, she began moving towards the door, intent on entering her own room. She needed a moment to think, to breathe, to *grieve* the choices she was being forced to make—

Brander's hand came down on her own, effectively halting her spiral.

She turned halfway back to him, and tears welled up in her eyes again as he said, "I told you once that it would be an honor to give my life for yours. I mean it just as much now as I did then. The people of Desmorda need you, Princess. If I can look back and know that my pitiful excuse for an existence aided you in any way at all...then it will all be worth it. *You* are worth it."

Though her throat burned with effort to keep her tears contained, she nodded once. "Your family would have been proud of the man you've become, Brander. I know that I am proud to have you in my service, and to call you my—" Brander was more than a guard, or even a friend, but the words stuck in her throat. Shaking her head, she continued, "I'll see you within the hour."

Brander blinked his surprise once before he let her go, his grip on her hand falling away as she hurried out the door. She didn't slow until she found her cabin and slipped inside, firmly pressing her back against the rough wooden door. She sank to the floor, knees buckling under the weight of her choices. Then, and only then, did she let the tears fall.

Chapter Fifty Three

Kasper leaned on the railing of Umbra, staring out at the blinding white sand and ignoring the ache in his chest that told him to return to Hera and swear his fealty. She had been at the center of this since she walked into Kai's tent. Previously, he had thought his involvement was due to his desire to protect Kai and attempt to repair his family, but now he knew it was *her*. He was sure of it, and now, his instincts were telling him to go to the Isle.

Dropping his head, Kasper laughed dejectedly to himself; the image of Cal embracing Hera burned into his mind. Kasper was a fool to believe that Hera could have wanted him over Cal, though he shouldn't have been. He was constantly being overlooked in favor of his brothers; why would this instance be any different?

He lifted his eyes to the island once more. It didn't matter that she had chosen Cal, not really. Kasper wouldn't turn his back on Hera—and he was helpless to ignore that he still desired her. The vow he had issued earlier to Brander and Lady Hera still held; he would protect her with his life if necessary. He didn't have much else to live for these days, anyway. Pushing away from the railing, Kasper reached for the pack at his feet. He grimaced at the state of the bag and its meager contents. It only contained a spare set of clothes and any crystals that he thought might be helpful.

"Kas."

Kasper turned to find Cal waiting for him, and for once, there wasn't any amusement or disdain on his face. He seemed distracted and distant. His eyes kept slipping off Kasper as he refocused on the mythical island beyond.

Glancing over Cal's shoulder, Kasper took in the lush landscape once more. After a moment, his eyes found their way back to Cal, and he said, "It's hard to believe that it's actually real."

Cal shook his head. "I never doubted it."

"Really?"

"I scoured the seas for it not long after I became captain. I found The Ether, but I could never breach it. The storms were always too violent."

Kasper crossed his arms. "What made you think you'd get through this time?"

Shaking his head, Cal replied, "I don't know. I think, on some level, the Isle has to choose you. Maybe all those times before, it wasn't ready—or maybe I wasn't. But I'm here now, and that's all that matters."

Kasper was quiet. He wasn't sure why Cal had bothered to answer his questions. They had spent the last few weeks trading barbs and snide comments, and before that, there had hardly been any interaction between them—at least any he remembered.

The thudding of boots drew Kasper out of his stupor, and he looked toward the newcomers. Lady Hera, Brander, and Kai all came strolling upon them, each one wearing a different shade of apprehension. Kasper aimed to keep his face neutral. They would need to work together if they were going to make it to the Cave and back alive. But what value did Kasper offer? Before The Ether, he wouldn't have thought much at all, but now his magic—stronger than it had ever been—had helped. Had healed, even.

Cal looked at Kai and then jerked his chin toward the Isle. "Tell us what you've seen."

Kasper suppressed a smile at Cal's brusk tone with Kai. It seemed that, despite everything they had endured, there was to be no love lost between them. Kai's eyes darted to the island and then back to Cal. Kasper had been around Kai enough in the last decade to know when his visions weren't proving useful.

He looked that way now.

But Kai lifted his chin and said, "The island is sentient. It knows that we approach and that we seek its treasure. The makeup of the inside of the Cave is largely crystalline, and there are multiple rooms. We will have to descend deep into the Cave to find the treasure."

The description of the crystalline structure of the island piqued Kasper's interest, but he stayed quiet, tucking that information away.

"I figured that," Cal snapped, "I want to know the specifics. Where should we land? What path do we take? Are there any creatures that will attack us? Where in the Cave is the treasure? Tell me that, Kai."

"Well, there might be some, uh, creatures patrolling the Cave. Some beasts or other entities, so we'll have to be on our guard."

"That's all?" Lady Hera said.

Kai swung his gaze to her, his eye twitching slightly. "Well, you have a book on the Cave. I don't see you supplying any information."

Crossing her arms over her chest, Lady Hera added, "I'll be happy to share that with everyone—as we need it."

"What? That's not—"

"Leave it, Kai." Cal cut in. Kasper didn't miss the way the Cal was watching Hera, or how their eyes connected briefly as he came to her defense. "I want to know more about what you saw."

Kai's throat bobbed, and he gave a nervous laugh. "Well, you know how unpredictable my visions can be."

"Sure, but you also admitted that you lost the Sight." Kasper added with smug satisfaction.

Kai stiffened.

Lady Hera whirled. "Is that true?"

Raising his hands in surrender, Kai asserted, "They might have left me for a time, but I assure you everything is back to normal. I, uh, just—"

"That's not what you told me." Kasper remarked, stepping further from Kai. Kai's eyes finally settled on Kasper, and hope seemed to fill them for a moment.

Kasper arched a brow. He was uninterested in providing a rescue, and instead said, "You told me the other day that you can only have visions if you touch Finnley."

"Why is that?" Hera asked, her indignation rippling off her.

Narrowing his eyes, Kasper said, "Because she's an—"

"Amplifier." Cal finished for him.

Kasper whirled on his brother. "You knew?"

"A what?" Hera asked.

A muscle ticked in Cal's jaw, his eyes moving from each of them before finally landing on Kai. "You had no right."

Kai pressed a hand to his chest. "Me? I discovered it by accident. I didn't do anything."

With a shake of his head, Cal said, "She's worked hard to keep that piece of her concealed. She never wanted any part of this."

"What is an amplifier?" Lady Hera asked again, her tone far more insistent than before.

Turning toward her, Cal's face and voice softened immediately. Kasper wanted to look away because Cal's tenderness only confirmed what Kasper suspected. "An amplifier is what it sounds like. She enhances magical abilities. In Kai's case, she helps him have visions, which, from what he's told me and Kas, are gone without her assistance."

"Then she has to come with us." Hera stated.

Cal shook his head again, his eyes turning stony. "No, she has no role in this; she remains on the Umbra with the rest of the crew."

"If Finnley can help us on the island, she needs to come along." Hera insisted, stepping closer to Cal. "She might give us the advantage we need."

"I tried to explain that to Kasper the other evening." Kai chimed in.

"Shut up." Cal, Hera, and Kasper said in unison.

Kai withdrew a fraction, turning his attention to his cuticles.

Cal started to reach for Hera. "Hera—"

"No." she said and took a step away from Cal. "We need her. You can convince her to come with us. Or order her to. I don't know exactly why you came on this journey—whether it was for revenge, or for power—but whatever the case is, you thought it was worth risking everyone on this ship's lives. We need to see this through, and we need Finnley to do that."

Cal hesitated. He flexed his hands and worked his jaw. Kasper was surprised at the conflict that clearly weighed on his brother. Without Finnley, they would be going in blind, but if she went with them, she was in greater peril. After several moments, Cal finally dropped his head and said dejectedly, "Fine." He glanced at the island. "You all start boarding the skiff. I'll go get Finnley."

Lady Hera did an excellent job of not letting her triumph show on her face, or perhaps she truly was grieved at the idea of her demand putting Finnley directly in harm's way. Either way, if Lady Hera planned to say a thank you, Cal didn't wait to hear it; he strode off with the stern intent to find Finnley, shadows stirring in his wake.

Brander, who stayed quiet, caught Kasper's eye and gave him a terse nod. A truce had formed between them; some might even consider it a friendship. Kasper would have been loathed to admit it before, but there were similarities between Brander and himself. They both put the well-being and needs of others before themselves, and they were never cared for in the way they did for others. Brander was still not fully recovered from his fight with Cal, but here he was, putting himself in further danger, all out of duty and obligation to Lady Hera.

Reaching out for the Lady's few items, Kasper said, "I will load your things."

Three weeks ago, Brander would have refused and probably threatened Kasper. But instead, he allowed Kasper to take them and said, "Thank you. For all of it."

Kasper nodded, a warm feeling spreading through his chest. Once, he doubted his usefulness on this journey, but he had helped people and he would continue to do so. Turning to walk away, Kasper was acutely aware that Kai was trailing after him. Kasper said nothing as he deposited the packs into the skiff and leaned against the ship's side. There was no reason to climb aboard until everyone was ready to depart. The wind ruffled Kasper's hair, and again, there was that tug in his gut, urging him toward Isle Oum.

Kai came up beside him, unsure and sheepish. Kasper didn't acknowledge him; if he was lucky, he would get through the remainder of their journey without speaking directly to him.

"Kasper, we need to talk." Kai said.

Kasper sighed. Clearly, his brother had other ideas. Gripping the rail, he stared at the swaying palm trees in the distance. Maybe, when they recovered the treasure, Kasper would stay behind on the Isle—at least then he wouldn't have to worry about his siblings bothering him.

"Please," Kai murmured and stepped closer, even daring to place a hand on Kasper's arm.

Kasper jerked away and nearly knocked into Lady Hera and Brander. He attempted to look apologetic to them and then turned back to Kai. "I thought I made myself clear the other day. I have no interest in speaking with you then, now, or ever. Do your part to get us home alive and leave me out of it."

Kai reached for him again, but Cal interceded. "Leave it, Kai. You've done enough, don't you think?"

Dropping his eyes, Kai turned away.

Kasper wasted no time with a thank you, and instead turned to find Finnley storming toward them, a small pack in hand.

"You got her to agree?" Kasper said to Cal in a low voice.

Cal's face revealed nothing as he said, "I am her captain, and she is beholden to my command."

Giving all that had transpired, Kasper wasn't sure that was the whole truth of it. Blowing past them, Finnley swung over the railing and dropped into the boat. She situated herself in the skiff and then looked up at all of them peering down at her.

"Well? Ye all gonna dally around, or are we gonna find some treasure?" Finnley barked at them from below.

Kasper spared the others a glance. "Here goes nothing." he muttered, before hopping in the boat, landing beside Finnley with a thud. She didn't spare him a glance, and instead kept her fiery gaze fixed on the shore ahead.

"Whatever dark beast lurks on that island is going to swallow us whole."

Following her gaze, he spoke softly, "I fear you might be right."

The others filed into the boat and took their seats, an odd, somber sensation falling over them. Kasper couldn't help but think this was the last time they would all be together, whole and unharmed.

Chapter Fifty Four

The island was the most breathtaking thing Brander had ever seen. Life vibrated everywhere he looked. From the palm trees, heavy and plentiful with coconuts, to the colorful fish darting in the shallows around their skiff. Brander considered dipping his fingers into the water to see if they would come to him, but he refrained and gulped down the fresh air instead. For the first time in weeks, the air didn't smell of salt or sickness. He swore he smelt the fresh fruit and vegetation even before the skiff slid into the shore—his stomach grumbling in response.

The island reminded him so much of the places he would dream about as a child that a pang reverberated through his chest. Back when monsters only existed in his imagination, and he was equipped to slay them. He wasn't ignorant of the true monster that inevitably destroyed everything he held dear. But now he had faced monsters from myths, and was headed to what was likely their creator. It was enough to make anyone want to turn and run, but Brander had sworn on his mother's grave long ago that he would never run from his fear again.

Kasper heaved a great sigh, drawing Brander from his thoughts as the skiff rocked with the force of lodging itself in the surf. Wiping the sweat of his brow on his arm, Kasper looked relieved to be done with rowing. Brander would have helped him and Finnley, but there were only two sets of oars, and Kasper had given him a warning look that spoke of an argument if Brander pushed it. His head still ached, and if he was honest, his ribs were still sore. Taking a deep breath was difficult, and if he moved the wrong way, pain wrenched through him.

But Brander would keep that to himself.

Cal was the first out of the skiff, his boots splashing in the shallow water, his long black jacket fluttering in the breeze. Stepping toward the surf, he staggered in a daze. But he caught himself and turned back toward the skiff, his eyes alight with a new type of hunger. While they rowed over he had kept his attention primarily focused on the island, but every few minutes, Brander would catch Cal glancing at the Princess. Though Brander still had no idea what had transpired between them when he was incapacitated, whatever it was, it had the Princess keeping her eyes on the water.

It needed to be addressed. Any strife between the party needed to be put out in the air. If there was one thing he learned while he served in the King's army, it was that a distracted mind was dangerous. But this wasn't the imperial army, and these weren't his soldiers. He couldn't command them to sort out their differences. He would just have to pray to every god that would deign to listen that their disputes wouldn't lead to their deaths. But truthfully, Brander wasn't feeling very optimistic.

Returning to the boat, Cal held out a hand to Finnley. She gave him no acknowledgement, swung over the skiff, and splashed into the water. Droplets of seawater sprayed on Cal's face, and Brander braced for Finnley's smiting that was undoubtedly imminent. But, to his everlasting surprise, Cal calmly wiped the water from his face and stepped toward Rhea. He completely bypassed the Seer, who held his hand out, clearly waiting to be helped to shore.

The Seer blinked once, pressed his lips together, and nodded slowly. Brander didn't try to hide his smile as Kai carefully draped one leg over the edge of the skiff and then the other before he slowly slipped into the water, hardly making a ripple. Next to Kai, Kasper plopped down into the water, thoroughly soaking the Seer with the splash he created. Brander chuckled, and the Princess whirled on him, lightly smacking him on the arm. Brander shook his head and reached for their packs.

Despite Brander's wishes, he knew the Princess wouldn't allow him to carry her from the skiff. He started to suggest it anyway, but then Cal was there saying, "Let me take you to shore."

Stiffening, Brander's hackles rose—at least initially—and he looked to Princess Rhea. The Princess hesitated, her fingers stilling on the side of the skiff. She glanced from Cal to Brander and said, "I can manage."

Smirking, Cal replied, "I know you can, but I don't want your boots to get wet."

Princess Rhea smiled. "I appreciate it, really, but Brander has already offered to carry me across." The Princess turned to Brander, her eyes wide. "Haven't you?"

"Of course, my Lady." Brander replied. He quickly handed over their packs to Cal, who was still standing there, blinking away his surprise. Brander had been right to assume that there was something between the Princess and the Necromancer, but he knew it wasn't his place to stop the Princess. Though he would gladly be her buffer from the pirate, if she desired.

Dropping into the water, Brander held out his arms for the Princess. She quickly climbed into his arms and looped hers around his neck. Brander didn't miss how Cal's jaw flexed, or the taut lines of his face as he took the remaining packs and trudged toward the others gathering on the shore.

The Princess was quiet, but Brander shifted her closer to his mouth and said softly, "I'll never deny your request, but I would be interested to know why the Necromancer thought you would allow him to carry you."

Pursing her lips, Princess Rhea kept her gaze fixed on the shore. Brander's muscles burned slightly as he fought against the heavy, wet sand that sucked at his feet. He did his best to not jostle the Princess as he yanked his boots from the sand and stepped out of the surf. He went a few feet out of the tide before he deposited the Princess, lightly setting her down in the pristine, white sand. She brushed at her clothes and cleared her throat. She looked at him with tight features and said, "Thank you, Brander."

Brander pressed his lips into a thin smile and placed a fist over his heart. "Always."

Nodding, the Princess turned to join the others, but she stopped abruptly and reached for Brander, pulling him into a hug. Brander froze, thinking of how inappropriate this display of affection was and how everyone in court would frown upon it. But they weren't at court, and no one here cared. Wrapping his arms around the Princess, Brander briefly thought about what having a daughter would have been like—a daughter like Princess Rhea.

Princess Rhea pulled away and opened her mouth to speak, but Brander interrupted her and said, "I knew when I was conscripted into the army that I would never have children of my own. But if I did, I would hope they would be like you—brave, kind, intelligent. Any father would be lucky to have you as a daughter."

Princess Rhea's bottom lip wobbled. Tears started to pool in the corners of her eyes, threatening to slip over the edge. Reaching up to her face, he brushed away an errant tear. The Princess let out a shuddering breath and then lifted her chin. "I count you as a father in all the ways that matter, Brander, and it has been the greatest honor of my life to know you."

Brander had to clench his jaw to stop his own tears from welling. Sighing through his nose, Brander glanced at the others beyond, who were pretending not to pay attention to them. He was grateful for the others, even if he didn't wholly trust them. They had all played a part in getting the Princess to the island; none of this would have been possible without them. Brander looked back to Princess Rhea, a small smile forming at his lips.

"Let's go find your treasure."

The Princess's eyes lit up, and a grin broke out across her cheeks as they began walking toward the others. He was content with their silence—satisfied that he had said all he needed to say—but then the Princess spoke quietly.

"Thank you for always protecting and believing in me."

Brander said nothing, but silently prayed that he would live up to the Princess's expectations.

Chapter Fifty Five

The sand shifted beneath her borrowed boots, and the wind tugged at her braids and nipped at her raw, sunburnt skin. Rhea was exhausted and sore from her new training regimen, and her mind still spun with thoughts of Cal. But she was *finally* at the Cave of Splendors.

The Isle of Oum and all of the treasure that it held. The salvation of her crown and her people rested beneath her feet. And it was hers for the taking, assuming a horrible death didn't prevent her success. Slowing her pace, she looked at the looming palm trees and the colorful animals that chirped and fluttered from the limbs. The creatures looked similar to the exotic birds she had seen in the palace before, when menageries were brought in from all across the continent with the intent of impressing her father—though none ever did. She recalled when her father took a keen interest in one enormous bird, and then had it served for their supper.

"Lady Hera!" Kai called as he walked to her. She still found it remarkable that he managed to remain pristine. His white clothes, gold jewelry, and even his feather accents were blemish-free. His hair had grown out some, the sides beginning to catch up with the length from the middle section, but aside from that, he looked unchanged. She would have to inquire about his care routine, if they survived the Isle.

Slipping his arm through Rhea's, Kai led her away from Cal and the others. She noted the watchful gazes from everyone—everyone but Finnley, who was staring menacingly at the swaying palm trees and cawing birds. Rhea worked to keep her face neutral, even as her heart kicked up a beat.

"You almost told him."

Pressing her lips together, she feigned ignorance. "Told him what?" The *him* was a given. Everything revolved around Cal.

Kai raised a hand and pointed to bleached cliffs in the distance. An equally white pillar stood vigil there, and she briefly wondered what could have constructed the monument. "Who you really are."

Rhea pulled her eyes from the cliffs, cursing herself for just how close she had come to revealing her truth. She wanted to be honest with Cal, but now was simply not the time. She needed to remain focused until she had Izor's Lamp safely within her possession—she could not afford to spend precious energy attempting to tend to any budding relationship, especially when she didn't know how Cal would react to her news. But while she certainly had her own reasons for wanting to conceal her identity for a little longer, that didn't quell her curiosity as to why *Kai* wanted her to continue the ruse.

"Well, wouldn't that be advised that at this point, seeing that my lies only further complicate the tenuous peace amongst our party?" She prodded, eager to gain insight into his schemes.

Dropping his hand, he looked at her with cautious eyes. "Once, I might have thought it was appropriate, but now…"

"But now what?" Rhea implored.

"Now, there is too much at risk. His feelings about you have changed, I can see that without my gift, but if you tell him now, it'll only confirm his beliefs about the world. He hates your father, and you by proxy. If you tell him the truth, well, there's nothing he won't do to right any perceived wrongs."

No one at the palace would ever tell her the specifics of what had happened between the Nader men and her father—save for the prophecy. But if there was more, as Kai claimed there was, what would Cal do to exact his vengeance? Rhea pulled her arms from Kai's and crossed them over her chest.

"And you don't want that?"

Kai's face took on the most sincere and pensive look Rhea had seen from him thus far, making him look younger—and more convincing. "Despite what everyone thinks about me, I care for my brothers. And you," Kai shrugged noncommittally, "in my own way. And I've seen the future, Princess. Trust me on this one."

Pursing her lips, she mulled over Kai's words. She knew what his goals were. He longed for his old life—for comfort and luxury. She wasn't sure how Cal played into that, but she also didn't realize how deep Cal's hatred ran for her father. Rhea was hesitant to put her faith in the Seer, but something about his solemn gaze urged her to reconsider. If Kai was to be believed, then…

"Fine, I'll continue to keep our secret. For now."

All the tension left Kai's body. "Oh good, very good. Truly, you have no idea how good it is that you agree. It's just—"

"Good?" Rhea offered, amusement curling her lips.

Laughing, Kai replied, "Yes, good."

Rhea smiled, but his relief nagged at her even further. "Why does it matter so much to you, though?"

Kai's eyebrows rose, his face once again fixed with a calm, easy expression. "Nothing of importance. Just some personal matters."

Rhea's features shifted from amused to combative. She lowered her voice, peering at him from beneath her lashes. "You're not usually one to keep secrets, Kai."

"I'm not?" Kai responded, his own expression and tone shifting to match hers. Frustration flared in her chest.

Fine. She would continue to play his game.

Rhea began to walk away, but she turned to glance at him over a shoulder. "You better be careful, Kai. The future isn't yours to predict anymore, and it might just surprise you."

Rhea's steps carried her further from Kai, but not from the new questions she had. Had she wrongly assumed that Kai was only interested in returning to court? Or had his goals shifted after he lost his connection to his magic? She doubted that his desire for her silence lay in his concern for his brothers, and she was sure it had nothing to do with her well-being. Kai was just as likely to cast her off the cliffs as he was to pull her back from walking off them. Whatever the case, Rhea would need to keep a closer eye on the Seer. There was hardly a man more desperate than a man who'd lost everything.

"Are we ready to leave yet?" Finnley asked, her tone bordering on snide. Rhea noticed that her accent had shifted. Gone was the pirate slang and pretense of being uneducated, replaced with the dictation of a woman raised amongst tutors and scholars. Rhea made a mental note to learn more about Cal's second, but now was not the time—not when Izor's Lamp was within reach.

A bemused expression darkened Cal's face as he stuck his sword in the sandy earth, the ground shifting from white sand to dark, rich soil, rife and teeming with ferns and large, pink-orange blossoms. "Well," he said, casting his eyes to Kai, who appeared beside Rhea, beaming like the sun personified. "We were expecting that our resident Seer would enlighten us to the path, but seeing how he's broken—"

"I can still do it." Kai proclaimed. "I just need a bit of assistance from our dear Finnley." Everyone's gaze slid to Finnley, who narrowed her eyes, her expression guarded. Her scar seemed more prominent, harsher against the vibrancy of the island. Her mouth was set in a hard line, wisps of her auburn hair floating around her face. Rage rippled off her. Guilt and shame twinged through Rhea—it was at her insistence that Finnley join them. "Finnley, dear, may I borrow your arm?" Kai asked, reaching for her.

Rhea's insides were slick as oil as Finnley held her ground for a moment before she yanked up her sleeve, took two steps forward, and bared her arm to Kai. Kai smiled, his nimble fingers wrapping around her scar-flecked flesh. Rhea glanced around at the faces of the others. Kasper's eyes were downcast, refusing to acknowledge the entire ordeal. Brander was watching Finnley's face, likely coming to the same conclusion that Rhea had, but—like the soldier he was—he wasn't going to interfere. And Cal, well, Cal was watching Rhea. His attention was all-consuming–ravenous, even–and Rhea's breath caught in her throat. It seemed to be doing that a lot these days. Her tongue darted out to lick her lips, and she noted his eyes dipping to her mouth.

Heat rose in Rhea's face, and she quickly looked away, desperate to have her attention on anything but Cal. She landed on Kai's face, which was fixed in utter ecstasy. It felt like she was intruding on a private moment, with the way his white eyes rolled backward into his head—but then it was over in an instant. Kai released Finnley, and she stepped away hurriedly, tugging her sleeve back in place. Again, Rhea hated herself for her complicity in Finnley's assistance, but she knew she would have to make more uncouth decisions if she were to become queen. Though, that didn't mean it wouldn't leave a stain on her soul.

"Well?" Cal said, his voice devoid of any of the heat present in his gaze just moments ago.

Smiling, Kai turned and gestured toward the alabaster cliffs he had pointed out to her earlier, and then to the thick and vivacious jungle ahead of them. As Kai pointed, Rhea noticed a small opening in the dense jungle. "Through there. A path leads up to the cliffs. Then, a little ways past that, there is an entrance to the Cave of Splendors."

"Any danger?"

Kai shrugged. "Just the usual sort."

"Specifics would be nice, Kai." Kasper intoned.

Kai's eye twitched, and his smile faltered a fraction. "Specifics are… hard. I don't think the island wants to give up all of her secrets. But I've seen the path forward."

"Just nothing on it." Kasper said with a note of exasperation, his eyes glancing to the cliffs and snagging there.

Cal turned to Rhea, and she knew what he planned to ask before he opened his mouth. Twisting toward Brander, she held out her hands for the book he was in the midst of retrieving. She dipped her chin in thanks as her fingers slid over the worn, leather surface. Brushing her index finger down the spine, she savored–and feared–the last of her leverage slipping away. She said a silent prayer that she wasn't making a terrible mistake as she turned to face the others.

"I read this text and similar others numerous times before I set out to find Malakai." She swallowed, steeling herself as she flipped to the right section. "This book proved to be the most informative about the origins of the Cave, the items within, and what guarded it." Running her finger down the page, she stopped on a passage. "From what I've read, there are creatures roaming the island. Beasts that serve as sentinels. According to this, some are equipped with wings, and others have impenetrable flesh. But they are all intelligent and determined—and very hard to kill." she added, her voice thick with trepidation.

Cal's gaze was fixed on her face, but there was no fear there. "What else?" he said, his voice tender.

Rhea pressed her lips into a thin line, flipped ahead, and continued, "This text claims that the Cave is a nexus point, or a place of concentrated magic. Some theorize that it is a rift between worlds, and even the origin of the gods that call this world their home."

Looking up once more, she scanned everyone's face. She wasn't sure what she expected from them, but it was Cal who nodded and said, "So we need to tread lightly and be alert."

"This place is magic itself, so yes, I would advise caution." Rhea replied. She wanted to look away from Cal's intense gaze, but it pinned her to the spot. If breathing wasn't an automatic function, she wasn't sure that she would have been able to do it. Cal's mouth parted, Rhea's chest hitched—

"Well," Kasper said, shattering the spell, "I guess there's nothing left to do but start." Grabbing his bag, he slung it over his shoulder and headed into the jungle. Finnley followed wordlessly—Kai in tow. Brander hesitated, waiting for Rhea's cue. She gave him a nod, and he filed in behind the others. Rhea started to as well, but then rough fingers slid over her wrist, halting her. Rhea looked up into Cal's dark eyes, noting the gold flecks there.

"Did you bring the dagger?" he asked. Rhea nodded, her eyes never leaving Cal's as she reached for the blade she had secured in her boot.

She held it out before her, and Cal took it, giving it a once over. "I had planned to teach you how to use it before we got here, but some quick lessons will have to suffice."

Flipping the dagger, he pointed the hilt toward Rhea, and pressed the blade just under his ribs. With his free hand, he grabbed Rhea's and placed it on his side. Warmth fluttered through her at the feel of him against her palm, but she fought to maintain her composure and pay attention to Cal's lesson. Putting the dagger's hilt in her right hand, he said, "Aim here. Just under the ribs. You're guaranteed to hit something vital, and your blade won't get stuck."

Rhea nodded. "Thank you." she said softly. "I'll try not to stab myself in the meantime." she added, trying to add some levity.

Chuckling, Cal said, "Yes, please be careful. I'd hate to have to strip you down and stitch you back up." Rhea went wide-eyed, her heart stammering in her chest, as his tone suggested he would be glad to do the opposite. Cal stepped closer, and the air went out of her lungs. "Hera, what I said on the ship before—"

Her blood thumped so hard in her ears that his words were muted. She couldn't hear him out, not now. There were still too many lies, too many secrets between them.

"What was that, Brander?" Rhea turned from Cal, looking toward the others slowly entering the jungle. "I think Brander needs something, I should go see what it is."

She started to move, but Cal grabbed her again. "Make all the excuses you like, Lady Hera, but we will discuss this thing between us. Mark my words." Cal's fingers fell, and Rhea forced her gaze away.

She scurried off, her dagger still clutched in her hand. She was a coward. Avoiding Cal forever was not an option–the truth about her would eventually come out–but she wanted to prolong the inevitable for as long as possible. Was that selfish? Probably so. But, nonetheless, it became her resolve as she took her place next to Brander and ignored Cal's stare burning into her back.

Chapter Fifty Six

The lure of the island was bordering on unbearable. It was a lullaby, a scream, a melody, and a cry. It beckoned to him like nothing ever had before—it was stronger than the call of the sea, or even Soline. Cal's restraint was nearing its end, and it was taking everything he had not to give into the island song—the thrumming in his blood. If the others were experiencing anything similar, they were better at masking their discomfort. If Cal was being honest, he probably would have submitted to it already and abandoned the others in favor of soothing his ragged nerves, but *she* was there.

Every time he looked at her, touched her, the seduction of the Isle ceased—at least for the moment. If Cal's draw to Hera was in danger of wavering, the island quickly dispelled that notion. His feelings for her were not just simple attraction or lust. They were bound to each other in some way, a way that he had never felt before—not even with Soline.

Cal would never discount his relationship with Soline. He loved her, truly, but that had been adolescent love. The kind that was bright and simple. The kind that was effortless and easy, in only the ways that lovers who haven't faced the horrors of the real world had. Soline always worked to bring Cal out of the shadows and curb his inclinations to darker impulses, but Hera…she joined him in the shadows. She understood that the world didn't operate solely in the light, that sometimes—more often than people would care to admit—a person would have to get their hands dirty. He suspected that if Hera ever stopped using her guard as a buffer and confronted him, she would have to admit to what Cal was beginning to recognize.

He didn't dare give a name to it, but as he watched her hurry away, he knew it was only a matter of time—and he knew when he got off the island that resisting the pull to her would be impossible. They were cut from the same cloth and borne the same hardships; they understood each other, even when they didn't want to. Cal was content to wait for her—because what they were to each other was inevitable.

But even as Cal thought that, *believed* that, there were still whispers in his mind. The ones that warned him away from Hera. Those voices were louder here on the island. And they sounded distinctly like Soline. Cal kept his eyes peeled, his senses open. Kai was useless; yes, he pointed them in a direction, but Cal surmised he likely would have been able to determine that on his own. No, once again, when it really mattered, Kai's gift of foresight was worthless.

* * * *

"Something is wrong with her Malakai, I know it. She's been sick for weeks, and she won't let me see her." Cal said, pacing back and forth in Kai's chambers.

Kai sat cross-legged on an oversized white and gold pillow, his all-seeing gaze tracking Cal's movement. Kai pursed his lips and gestured with his hands, the movement causing the stacks of bracelets on both arms to slide and tinkle as they collided. Cal opted to only wear rings. The noise of bracelets and necklaces was far too reminiscent of bells that people placed on their pets—always aware of their location.

"I haven't seen anything, Caliban." Kai said softly.

Stopping abruptly, Cal yanked up the sleeve of his dark shirt, and thrust his arm toward Kai. "Read me again."

It wasn't a request, and Kai knew that. Kai held his brother's icy gaze for a heartbeat, conveying his impending regret.

Cal's impatience grew, and he shoved his arm forward. "Please, Kai. I never ask you for anything."

Shaking his head, Kai untucked his feet—the anklets there jingling—and slid forward. He took a deep breath and tentatively grabbed his brother's arm. He knew what he would see before the images flashed in his mind:

Soline lied in bed, pale and sweaty. Healers moved about the room with cold, damp rags. Others carried away bowls of water—tinged red. Priests and acolytes murmured prayers, their words quiet but fervent. A scream rented the air—terrible and earth-shattering. Soline tried to move and leave the bed, but the healers grabbed her, restraining her. They assured her all would be well soon.

She was blessed.

She was fruitful.

The Empire will worship her.

But they don't know, not even as they pull the blankets back and see the blood spilling from between her legs.

Hours passed, and still no progress. The whispers and prayers became more insistent. She's still bleeding, they whisper. She's too weak, they murmur.

Soline tried to leave again. She called out for Caliban, but he was nowhere to be found. He had abandoned her because of her deceit. Soline fell back into the damp pillows, exhausted and heartbroken.

The room's doors opened, and a man entered, bringing a tray of tools. Soline glimpsed them being arranged at the foot of her bed through her heavy lids, and she understood.

It's been too long, with no progress and no results. They mean to cut her open.

The King must have an Heir.

The Heir that resides in Soline's womb.

She thrashed and kicked—fighting off the midwives and servants, using up what little strength had remained in her.

Hysteria, they'll say, the labor was too much for her; she had to be sedated. But Soline thinks of him. Her Dark Prince, even as the opium starts to pull her under, and the pain along her abdomen scorches her.

Reeling backward from Cal, Kai's breath came too quickly. Sweat beaded along his scalp, and he tried to regain control of his racing heart.

"Well?" Cal demanded. His tone was harsh, but Kai knew that genuine concern—and fear—lay beneath it.

Shaking his head, Kai reached for the lie he had spun the last three times Cal had asked what was wrong with Soline. Cal knew how a woman found herself with child, though he and Soline had never lain together—he wanted to do right by her and wait until they were far from the palace.

Kai wondered how Cal hadn't come to the truth about Soline's condition— willful ignorance was the only conclusion Kai found. Kai was too much of a coward to shatter the illusion. "She has a sickness, but most survive."

"Specifics, Kai, please. Can it be cured? Can the symptoms be eased? Please, Kai," Cal said, dropping to his knees before Kai, "I'll do anything to help her. I love her."

Kai bit the inside of his cheek to keep from telling the truth. If Cal knew that the King had taken Soline's virtue and that she was now carrying the King's child—there would be no empire left. Kai was wise enough to fear the destruction that Cal would wreak if he so desired—if he were properly motivated. The King forcing himself on Soline would surely be motivation enough.

No, Cal could never know the truth.

Swallowing the blood flooding his mouth, Kai said, "There's nothing to be done for her. She'll be fine, Cal. Trust me."

Cal held Kai's gaze, the exhaustion and worry heavy on the Necromancer. But Cal sighed and nodded, "I do trust you, Kai. I just love her so much, and I worry for her."

Kai put all of his focus into maintaining the neutrality of his features as he nodded. "I know you do. But worrying yourself sick will change nothing." Kai glanced at the candle clock, noting the time. He took Cal's hands into his own and stood. "It's late. Go get some rest. Soline will likely feel better soon, and you'll want to be at your best for her."

Cal smiled. It failed to reach his eyes, but it was the most relaxed he had been since he entered Kai's chambers an hour ago.

Cal left Kai's chambers feeling lighter and hopeful about Soline's situation.

He wished that feeling had lasted longer.

* * * *

"Cap'n."

Shaking his head, Cal attempted to clear away the memories his wretched mind had drawn up. Cal focused on who spoke and found Finnley glaring at him. There was no point in asking for her forgiveness. He didn't deserve that, not after he forced her to join on the pains of exposing her gift to the crew. Finnley was no fool; she knew they would turn on her if they knew she wielded magic, even a passive gift.

"Yes, Finnley?"

Jerking her chin over her shoulder, she said gruffly, "The others want to stop and rest for a few minutes, replenish the water."

Cal furrowed his brows. They had disembarked the Umbra an hour ago at mid-morning. Cal opened his mouth to say as much, but he noted the glazed orange sky. Turning away from Finnley, he looked back the way he had come. Sure enough, the white sand shores were hardly more than a haze at the bottom of the incline that they steadily climbed. Whirling back around, he found Finnley staring at him with an arched brow. Where had the time gone? Cal recalled arriving on the island, interacting with Hera, and then...nothing. He had been sucked in a memory–a bad one at that–and now it was nearly nightfall.

"Are you alright, Cap'n?"

Cal shook his head again. "I just lost track of time, I guess. Are we making camp?"

"Briefly. Just long enough to find fresh water and branches suitable for torches."

"Right, well, thank you for letting me know, Finnley."

"Of course." Finnley said, and Cal moved around her, heading toward whether the others had stopped. Abruptly, she called out, "Cap'n?"

"Yes?" He said, more sharply than he intended, failing to keep his irritation out of his voice. None of this was Finnley's fault; she was undoubtedly the *last* person who deserved his ire.

Finnley glanced around, her eyes darting toward the jungle. "Be careful." she said softly, the edge gone from her voice, still looking around at the trees. "This place…I don't trust it. I have this feeling it's watching us, waiting for us to let our guard down before it strikes."

Cal was quiet for a long moment, his gaze catching on the Umbra, a black speck against the red-orange horizon. Finally, Cal looked at Finnley and spoke with deadly calm, "Finnley, I fear you're more right than you realize."

Cal hadn't thought about that night with Kai in years. To be frank, he chose not to think about it because every time he did, he was powerless to stop the rising, murderous tide within him that demanded he take retribution on his twin. And the island knew that. It had already gone prodding through his memories and was looking for the right one to use—the one that would turn Cal against the others.

Cal gritted his teeth.

He was his own master, and no island or god or whatever inhabited this wretched place was going to get the best of him.

Turning from Finnley, his footfalls were loud to his ears as he came upon the others already talking amongst themselves and sorting out their supplies. Cal dropped into a crouch and surveyed their provisions before he glanced at the faces of the others. He noted weariness and exhaustion, but no vacantness. Kai's mouth was pinched, and his eyes darted around, but otherwise, he seemed normal—well, normal for Kai. Cal did his best to shove down the anger rising from just looking at his brother. Kai's betrayal ran deep, and Cal had not forgiven him–and he never would–but now was not the time to give into his rage. That was what the island wanted, what it was betting on, and Cal would not give it the satisfaction.

Each of them had their own secrets—their own demons haunting them. Cal prayed–for the first time in a long time–that they, too, would master their minds and not let the island's magic destroy them. He contemplated telling them what he had experienced, but he wasn't quite sure he was able to put words to it, and besides, what good would it do? They were likely already aware that the island would test them, and if they weren't, then they were fools who should have remained on the Umbra. But, if Cal was being entirely honest, he was loathed to admit that the island had stolen several hours from him.

"I'm going to look for some branches." he said to no one in particular. No one replied, but Hera did look at him—acknowledge him. That was enough to tell him he wasn't enthralled by the island anymore. Maybe he just needed to stay close to her.

He wouldn't mind that.

Cal turned and headed back down the path. The sun was quickly disappearing, taking the light with it. Time was of the essence. He stepped off the worn path and into the jungle—not far, lest he lose his way. He may have been released from the island's hold on his memories, but he wasn't eager to experience any of its other tricks. He searched for a few minutes, found a few suitable branches, and cradled them to his chest.

A tingling sensation crept down his neck.

Cal wasn't unaccustomed to eerie feelings, given the nature of his magic, but this was different—it was older, more earthen, and muskier. Far too similar to the scent of a crypt or tomb that had been undisturbed for centuries. It clung to him, heavy like stones tied to his feet.

He turned in a circle but found nothing. He swept his gaze back and forth as he returned to the path, but the sensation remained.

A flash of metal caught his eye.

Finnley's sword—her family shortsword that she carried instead of a cutlass or typical curved blade—discarded on the ground. She would never have abandoned the messer blade, especially not with what it meant to her.

Their mission of finding the treasure within the Cave of Splendors was forgotten. Dropping the branches, Cal sprinted back to where the others had stopped, their location illuminated by an amber glow.

"Finnley's been taken." he said, his voice thin and frantic to his own ears. This was his fault. He had forced her to come, and now she was gone. She was the only person who had stood by him in the last decade, and he had all but sentenced her to death. He was stupid, selfish, foolish, wick—

"What?" Kasper said as he stood, his face going white as bleached bones. The others joined them, their faces conveying genuine concern—particularly Kai's.

Ugly, raucous hatred welled up in Cal. If Finnley was well and truly gone, Kai would be useless and his presence utterly obsolete. But even Kai's downfall was not reason enough to abandon Finnley.

"We're going after her. Get this cleaned up and get moving." Cal didn't wait to see if they did as he bade. He turned on his heel and returned to where Finnley's blade remained. Bending down, he studied the dirt for clues.

"Don't worry, Fin. I'll find you. I promise."

Cal hoped he hadn't just made himself a liar.

Chapter Fifty Seven

The calm exterior Malakai fronted was rapidly deteriorating. Seconds on the island stretched into minutes, which, in turn, stretched into hours. He knew, rationally, that they had only been on the island for a few hours, but for Malakai, it might as well have been an eternity.

In addition to that, the island didn't want him there. The buzzing in his ears and the oppressive heat began immediately after he had climbed out of the skiff. He wanted to complain about it. A paltry attempt at building camaraderie with his companions–who were indifferent to him at best, and outright despised him at worst–when it occurred to him that none of them were experiencing the island in quite the same way. Yes, sweat beaded along their skin. They swatted the occasionally errant insect, but they weren't feeling the island in the same way he did.

He did his best to look inconspicuous; the last thing Malakai wanted as someone who saw the future was for people to start questioning his sanity. *That* usually resulted in being burned, or chained to a wall until one perished. While Malakai was fairly certain it wouldn't come to all that, he wasn't eager to test it, either. So, he kept his fretting to a minimum and worked not to swat too often at the insects—which only seemed to be pestering and biting *him*. Still, he caught the odd glance from Kasper, a concerned look from the Princess, and a glare from Finnley.

Only Caliban and Princess Rhea's guard paid him no mind. The guard was likely indifferent to his suffering unless it would somehow spread to his charge. Caliban—well, Caliban appeared to be battling some sort of demons of his own. His expression was vacant and clouded. He was with them, but not. Malakai knew the expression well, as it had been his own often enough in his life.

Malakai perceived that he was doing rather well to keep his discontentment to himself. Even when small, angry, red welts formed on his exposed skin and the only relief he found was from digging his nails into them. The itching was made worse by the perspiration clinging to his skin and dampening his white linens. He quietly lamented the discoloration that was indeed occurring to his clothes. But Malakai resolved that he would not let the island drive him to the brink of insanity; despite what the others likely believed of him, he was strong enough to withstand.

And then the voices started.

They began as soft whispers. Indistinct and non-descript, but as they climbed up the steep hill, they grew louder and louder, slowly replacing the constant droning of insects and magic. He clenched his teeth against the discomfort, but his resolve was slipping. Every murmur grated him and pulled at his already fraying nerves.

Malakai was accustomed to voices when in the midst of a vision, but his mind stayed quiet outside of that. He was unique in that regard. Some of the other Seers and supposed prophets he had encountered over the years were driven insane by the incessant chatter of voices. When the King discovered that Malakai's gifts were not burdened with the ceaseless whispers, his interest had…intensified. Every other Court Seer seemed to have an expiration date, a limited amount of time that they could inquire about the future or consult the past before the gift claimed their minds. The price for knowing what was to come—but not Malakai. He never suffered the fits or bouts of insanity that so many others had succumbed to.

Had Malakai let that singularity go to his head? Perhaps. But that was in the past, and Malakai was all about looking toward the future.

Though, when whispers began to emanate from the suffocating jungle and no one else mentioned them, Malakai understood that he was being singled out. Usually, he would have been flattered at the attention, but in this particular situation, he recognized that–despite the alluring appearance–it was not a compliment to be set apart.

Get out

Stay

Leave this place

He wanted nothing more than to assure those voices that he would be happy to oblige, but he couldn't leave the Isle of Oum without the Princess securing her treasure. He had known the risk before undertaking this journey—more so than anyone, he understood it because he had *seen* it. But he also knew the life he had lived for the last decade was not one he was willing to turn back to. That wasn't living; it was survival, and Malakai was done with surviving—well after he survived this journey. He owed himself–oh, and Kasper–that much. But the longer he spent on the island, the less convinced Malakai was that he would outlast the machinations of the entity inhabiting it. Aside from that, there were no assurances that his gifts would return to him. He kept hoping and waiting—but nothing.

And now Finnley was gone.

Malakai was worried–effusively so–but he had to admit that it had nothing to do with Finnley and everything to do with her abilities. He knew, objectively, that he certainly *should* care about her well-being. Though she put on a hard exterior, Malakai had glimpsed her compassion—particularly toward his brothers. Maybe that was a contributing factor to Malakai's apathy. Despite taking a liking to Cal and Kasper, Finnley had despised him from their first encounter. Whatever the case, Malakai struggled to feel anything other than dread at the loss of his tenuous connection to his magic. Cal's tense expression and the haggard looks of the others did little to ease his concerns, either. And for the first time in Malakai's life, he felt genuinely useless.

What would he do if Finnley never came back?

Real fear crept up Malakai's throat, threatening to steal his breath. He sprung up from the ground, and the others turned their eyes on him with varying degrees of curiosity and concern.

Despair

Hope

Suffering

Whipping his head back and forth, Malakai narrowed his eyes in suspicion at the darkening jungle around them. He scanned the wide-leaf plants and thick trunks for the source of the voices. Rationally, he knew it was magic–some unseen force originating from the island–but logic had escaped Malakai some hours ago. He turned in a circle, the others to his back—

Weakling

Warrior

Coward

Caliban left them, disappearing back down the slope, presumably toward Finnley's last known location. The others, clearly not burdened by the same stupor that Malakai was, quickly collected their meager belongings. Standing idly by, Malakai was still staring out into the jungle, sure that he could make out the shape of something–or someone–staring back at him. His eyes burned with the effort of keeping them open, but blinking might make what stared back at him disappear–or worse–come closer.

Finnley was gone—taken, if Caliban was to be believed. Which meant there was *something* on the island other than them. The Princess had mentioned that creatures resided on the island, as well as theories about its origins. Malakai narrowed his eyes, straining in the darkness, not daring to blink lest he miss something.

Fool

Savant

Charlatan

Malakai's eyes watered and blurred with the effort of holding them open. The darkness was closing in, enveloping him, urging him to come closer. Every rational part of him begged him to run away, but the draw was far too appealing, too alluring, too—

"Kai!"

Blinking, Malakai stumbled forward. Something gripped his shoulder. He turned to find Kasper's amber gaze boring into him. Kasper tugged at him, dragging him back—Malakai glanced back to the jungle and realized he was nearly off the path and stepping into the brush. He swallowed down his trepidation. It seemed the island wasn't satisfied with simply luring him into madness; no, it wanted to *claim* him.

Like it had claimed Finnley.

Peering into the densely packed jungle, Malakai was positive that he would find some beast staring back at him…but there was nothing and no one. Some of the tension went out of Malakai, and he reached up to scrub a hand over his face. It did nothing to relieve the mounting pressure behind his eyes or in his temples. Kasper continued to pull him away from the darkness and back to the paltry light of their torches, which only served to illuminate the haggard and wearisome expressions of the Princess and her guard.

"Are you alright?" The Princess asked, but her tone had no sympathy, only cool indifference.

Malakai shook his head, unable to form a lie—not that one would be believable at this point. No, he knew that if his erratic behavior hadn't clued the others into his current mental state, then his disheveled appearance certainly would.

"Here." Kasper muttered while rummaging in his pack. A moment later, he produced a crystal, its details hard to make out in the waning light. It wasn't the opaque black of obsidian, nor did it have the red hue of bloodstone. "It's quartz, but it has trace amounts of metal present that make it appear like smoke is trapped within." Kasper said as he held the crystal up for a moment, noting the twining gray through the structure. Bringing the stone back down, he pressed it into Malakai's hands. "It has grounding properties and offers protection. I don't know how much good it'll do against whatever malevolent forces govern this place, but it's something."

Malakai sagged with relief. He had never given much thought or credence to Kasper's abilities—save for when he drew precious gems from the earth to support their livelihoods—but he could admit how lost he would be without them now.

"Thank you, Kasper, truly."

Kasper shrugged. "You're no good to us dead or half-crazed."

Pressing his lips together, Malakai gripped the gem more tightly in his fist. He wasn't sure if it was just his mind telling him that he was feeling better, or if the crystal was genuinely working. The fog around Malakai's mind seemed to lift a little, and the voices that still whispered hateful, vicious things seemed to quiet.

Kasper glanced at the Princess and her guard, who watched with closed expressions. "Let's go, before Cal decides we're not worth the trouble." He said, shouldering his pack as he headed down the hill after Cal. The Princess observed Malakai for another heartbeat before turning, her guard in tow—leaving Malakai alone once more. Malakai counted his breaths, appreciating the silence in his head now more than ever before. He brought the quartz up to his chest and started down the hill, indignation tugging at his heart. Malakai's only connection to his magic had been stolen, and this gods-forsaken island was intent on driving him insane.

Had Malakai truly led a life that warranted such cruelty?

He didn't think so.

Sure, he was manipulative. He often lied and occasionally cheated, but weren't there worse crimes? Worse people? Still, Malakai silently promised whatever entity was listening that he would try to be better—*if* he got his magic back.

Everything in life was conditional, including his morality.

He looked around once more to ensure he was alone before he said quietly, "You may have won this round, but I intend to win the next."

And come daylight, you'll have wished you had never allowed me on your shores."

Nothing moved or rustled in the trees or bushes, but Malakai knew the island was watching him, listening. As he made his way back down the slope, he still heard its muttering, though it was muffled and distant.

Liar

Savior

Betrayer

Malakai blocked out the memories those words conjured, but he couldn't help but fear what the island knew.

And what it would do with the truth.

Chapter Fifty Eight

At first glance, Kasper thought it was a pillar or statue to some long-forgotten god that ruled over the island. The details of it were lost to the distance, but it was clearly humanoid. His eyes continued to cling to the figure, even as the others paid it no mind. He wasn't sure why it interested him, but for whatever reason, his gaze kept drifting toward it.

Finally, he forced himself to look ahead and focus on the broad, ridged leaves of the trees that were thrice the size of his hand. He paid special attention to the vibrant and colorful birds that fluttered around the treetops. Their hues dragged forth a memory of his time in the palace, though it was hazy at best—and then it was gone. Kai had always said it was his mind protecting him from trauma—though he no longer knew if there was any merit to that.

Kasper had dropped his gaze and shook his head. More pressing matters were at hand than his foggy recollections or some ominous statue perched off in the distance. Besides, if his curiosity still lingered in the coming hours, he would likely be close enough to see it in detail if they continued to follow the winding trail to the cliffs above. But even as they pushed further into the jungle, the heat and humidity pressing in on him, the urge to ensure that the statue remained lifeless was impossible to resist. His eyes slipped to the bleached cliffs once more.

The statue was gone.

Kasper's steps faltered, and his eyes darted along the cliff edge, toward the spot where the clearing met the thick jungle. There it was, its arm now upraised in greeting—or perhaps warning.

The sweat dampening his skin and clothes turned cold, and his mouth went dry. Blinking, he attempted to will the figure back to its origin at the edge of the cliff. Maybe it indeed was a person, and they were in danger. But it remained unmoving, eerily still in a way no person was able to be, facing him in salutation.

Kasper stumbled forward as something—no, someone—collided with his shoulder. Strong hands clamped down on him, stopping him from crashing to the ground, but he still noted a pink worm the width of his pinkie inching through the damp soil. As he righted himself and met Finnley's stern gaze, he glanced at the cliffs once more.

The statue was gone again.

His eyes went wide, and cold chills erupted across his skin. Raising his hand, he pointed to the now empty space on the cliffs. "Did you see that?"

Finnley's narrowed eyes slid to where Kasper pointed. They lingered for a moment, and then she looked back at Kasper.

"No."

Dropping his hand, Kasper's chest moved rapidly. "Truly? You didn't see the stone figure earlier? The one that's now gone?"

Glancing back at the cliff with renewed interest, Finnley's eyes scanned. "There was a statue before..." she murmured softly.

Kasper's shoulders relaxed a fraction, grateful that he wasn't going insane. "Something is going on with this island. I felt it before we ever stepped foot on it." he said, remembering the tug he experienced on the ship before they departed. He thought it was his desire to impress Hera with his loyalty, but what if it was really something else?

Finnley didn't respond. Instead, she shouldered her pack and moved to step around Kasper. He let her go ahead, but quickly fell in step behind her, quietly whispering, "Doesn't that concern you? Shouldn't we tell the others?"

"Why? We knew there was evil lurking here before we broke through The Ether, no sense in pretending that's changed."

"But—"

"But nothing. Besides," she said, glancing over her shoulder to the others still making their way up the increasingly steep and narrow path, "they neglected to offer me a choice in the journey, so whatever befalls them is their own fault."

He opened his mouth to argue, but couldn't find the words.

Hadn't he sworn the same thing not too long ago? Hadn't he turned his back on his brothers for all their lies and deception?

Kasper held his tongue, but kept one eye on the vacant cliff.

Chapter Fifty Nine

Kasper knew what had taken Finnley—or at least suspected what had. He pressed his lips together to keep from blabbing his secret. But from the fervent gleam in Cal's eyes, Kasper wasn't sure if he would be able to stay quiet.

Cal's footfalls were abrasive in the soft rustling of the leaves and flapping of birds going to roost. His hands tore at the plants, ripping them—roots and all—from the ground for any sign or clue where Finnley had gone. There was another sword—Finnley's—hanging at Cal's side, dwarfed by Cal's dark blade.

Clutching his amazonite in his fist, he willed it to lend him some of its courage. Immediately, Kasper became more stalwart and confident. His jaw relaxed, and he rolled his shoulders back. His fears and timidity ebbed away like the rolling waves on the beach. Kasper yanked the amazonite from his pocket, inspecting it for any defect or abnormality. The turquoise and white stone was smooth from years of erosion, but was otherwise unblemished. Kasper knew the surge of courage was not of his own making—no, it certainly came from the gem—but he had never felt anything so potent in all his years of channeling through gems and crystals. He shook his head and pocketed the stone once more; his concerns over the efficacy of his magic would have to wait.

The zing of metal caught Kasper's attention. Cal had moved beyond shredding the plants with his bare hands and was now slashing at them with his blade. Even in the waning light, the shadows gathered at Cal's shoulders, winding and curling around him.

Finnley's life might very well be on the line. Any sane person would turn and head the other way, not daring to engage Cal when his rage was so visible, but Kasper's confidence was bolstered.

"Cal," Kasper called amid the torrent of hacked leaves and limbs. Cal paused only long enough to send a rueful glare Kasper's way, instantly diminishing his courage. But Kasper had already committed to telling his truth. "Cal." he called more firmly, and this time, Cal stopped. His withering stare was fixed wholly on Kasper. Lifting his chin, Kasper said, "I know what took Finnley."

"Who?" Cal barked.

"Not a who, per se, but a *what*. The statue on the cliffs. It moved. I saw it, and Finnley did too."

"You saw a person and didn't say anything?" Cal seethed, marching toward Kasper.

Kasper held his ground, undeterred. "It wasn't a person–at least not like you and I–it was made of stone. We all saw that."

"Yes, but only you saw it move."

"Finnley saw it, too." Kasper repeated with exasperation.

Cal stepped closer. "And where is she now, Kas? Huh? Where has she gone?"

The thudding of boots echoed behind them, but Kasper didn't turn to acknowledge them; they would be of no support anyhow. Brander and Hera had their own concerns, and Kai...well, Kai was apparently struggling with something that none of them could see. Kasper wished he could for reach the amazonite in his pocket. As though responding to his thoughts, the stone warmed in his pocket—its properties seeping into Kasper. Again, he wondered why the stone worked so well, but he wasted no time on it. He pushed back against Cal, sending him a few steps back.

"Fighting with me won't get her back, so you can either calm yourself or get out of the way."

Cal blinked, though Kasper wasn't sure if it was a momentary lapse from shock at Kasper's assertiveness or a temporary pause before he unleashed himself on Kasper. Cal's white-knuckled grip on his sword loosened, and he sheathed the blade. He stepped back into a bow, extending an arm and dropping his head in mock respect.

"Lead the way, little brother."

Kasper nodded, enjoying the newfound strength that his gems were lending him. Turning, he noted the expressions of the others, all displaying varying degrees of awe. "I know it sounds outlandish, but I saw the statue move, and Finnley did, too. I think it knew that and took her when she went off alone."

"How do we find her?" Lady Hera asked, her fierce gaze illuminated by the torchlight. "Kai's magic is obsolete without Finnley, so we can't divine her location."

"True, but..." Kasper's voice trailed off, an idea forming. He peered up toward the cliffs that were now lost to the darkness. Blowing out a breath, he closed his eyes, using a centering technique he had seen Kai employ hundreds of times. He quelled the thrumming of his blood and reached for the obsidian he kept around his neck.

Instantly, he was grounded. The noise and distractions around him melted away, and then—he felt it. The subtle thumping—the heartbeat of the island. Kai had mentioned there were crystal structures within the Cave. If Kasper could somehow connect to them...

Kasper opened his eyes and pointed just to the left of the cliffs, into the thick darkness of the jungle. "They went that way."

"How do you know?" Kai asked, his tone curious but edged with something else—something akin to jealousy.

"I feel movement."

"Assuming that's true," Cal growled, "how do you know it's not an animal. Or some trick by the isle?"

Shaking his head, Kasper refuted. "It's different. I was looking for her specifically—I felt *her* energy."

"She is an amplifier," Kai offered, "maybe her energy drew the statue to her, and now you're tapping into it."

Kasper didn't know, and as much as he didn't want Kai to be right, it was as good an explanation as any. He shrugged and said, "Maybe."

"Well, I don't care if it's energies, vibrations, or the godsforsaken rocks speaking to you. It's the best lead we got, so I say we follow it." Cal said, withdrawing his sword again.

Cal didn't bother waiting to hear if anyone was on board with the change of plans. Stepping toward the dense underbrush, he began hacking away again. Brander wasted no time drawing his blade, too, and assisting in cutting away the lush growth. Kasper pressed his lips together, suppressing a smile. Who knew it only took Finnley being abducted to bridge Cal and Brander's differences?

"We'll find her, I know it." Lady Hera said beside Kasper. Glancing down at her, he noted the tense set of her jaw and the pinched look of her brow. He doubted that she was truly speaking to him, but he reached for her hand anyway.

"We will."

Lady Hera looked at their joined hands and offered him a tight smile. Kasper returned a more emphatic one. Then, he looked ahead at the path that Brander and Cal were cutting through the jungle.

For once, Kasper believed in himself.

Chapter Sixty

If innley was not far from them now; Kasper knew it. Their progress through the jungle was steady, though made slower by the thick underbrush and dim lighting of the torches. Kasper and Hera had taken to holding the torches while Brander and Cal continued to cut a path through the foliage. Kai, mercifully, stayed silent behind them, but every few minutes Kasper would turn to look—just to make sure Kai remained with them, lest another member of their party go missing. Kasper wasn't sure that the loss of Kai would be all that demoralizing, but it *would* be an additional impediment that would slow them down even more.

Kai remained in sight; his fingers gripped tightly around the quartz that Kasper had gifted him. A pang of sympathy pulsed through Kasper at the sight of his brother's wide and anxious eyes. Clearly, Kai was still suffering from some unseen ailment, presumably caused by the island, but Kasper quickly averted his gaze and shoved down his compassion. Kai had done nothing to earn it. He deserved all the suffering that came his way.

Kasper breathed and centered himself, using the obsidian to aid him. Closing his eyes, he shifted his thoughts to Finnley—someone deserving of compassion and help. The island appeared in his mind, waves of energy pulsing across it. They rippled over the surface; the trees and animals were momentary blips as they continued out and over the isle. Kasper wasn't sure where the waves originated–whether this was some unexplored facet of his power or the if island choose to allow him to see it—but either way, he quickly found the vibrations that were stemming from Finnley.

The shock waves from her movements proved she was still alive and fighting against her captors. Kasper concentrated on her, ignoring the animals that scurried around her and the rushing water from a nearby stream. An ache throbbed in his temples, but he persisted, eager to know the extent of his abilities.

"Have you found her?" Hera said, pulling Kasper from his thoughts. The mental images of the thrumming island and Finnley fighting faded, and he opened his eyes to find Lady Hera peering up at him.

Kasper furrowed his brows. Had he always been that much taller than her? Had he somehow grown? No—he just was finally standing at his full height rather than blending into his surroundings. Hera still gazed up at him expectantly. Shaking his head, Kasper realized he hadn't fully heard her—too aware of his own musings.

"I'm sorry, what did you say?"

The corners of Hera's mouth tipped up in a restrained smile. The expression—and the fact that *he* had been the one to put it there—bolstered his confidence further.

"I asked if you had found her." Hera repeated.

Finnley's thrashing body flashed in his mind. The reminder of their grim reality moderately dampened his pride. "Oh, yes. Now that I've looked for her again, it's getting easier."

Some of the tension left Hera's face. She nodded and turned her attention back to Cal and Brander, who were still clearing a path to Finnley. "That's good. That ability might come in handy later."

Kasper lifted an eyebrow and said coyly, "Worried we'll get separated?"

The crimson stain on her cheeks was visible even in the scarce lighting. "Possibly. There's no telling what those caves and tunnels may look like."

Stepping closer, his arm brushed against Hera's. "Don't worry, I won't let you out of my sight."

A nervous laugh escaped Hera's lips, and her gaze quickly darted from Cal and Brander back to Kasper. "What has gotten into you?"

Kasper's bravado faltered for a moment as he noted the edge in her voice and the lines bracketing her mouth. "Did I say something wrong?"

Hera gave him a furtive glance and said, "No, you're just acting different."

Kasper opened his mouth to ask her if the change was bad, but Cal and Brander's swinging abruptly came to a halt. Instinctively, Kasper dove into his new power and saw in his mind the scene still several yards ahead of them. Finnley was on the ground. Her chest was still moving—thank the Forgotten—but she was bound and restrained. Kasper quickly opened his eyes, wanting to confirm what he had sensed.

His heart fell into his stomach, and the remnants of his courage—courtesy of the amazonite—faded away. Kasper could just make out Finnley's hunched figure on the ground. There were restraints around her arms, face, and legs. Beyond that, there were three stone figures surrounding her. They were even bigger up close, measuring well over two feet taller than Kasper. Kasper hoped that was the worst of it, but then the statues reached for Finnley, placing their marbled hands on her. Light flared beneath their palms, and Finnley's back arched and thrashed under their touch.

"Enough of this!" Cal growled. He leapt over the fallen trunk ahead of them, barreling toward the small clearing.

"Cal!" Hera and Kasper hissed simultaneously, staring after him.

Looking back at them, Brander jerked his head in the direction Cal ran. "Stay hidden, Lady." He murmured, gesturing with his hands for them to stop walking. Then, Brander leapt over the fallen trunk and hurried after Cal.

Kasper wanted to laugh.

Cal was the only known Necromancer and shadow-wielder born in the last century; what help could Brander—or any of them, for that matter—provide?

Lady Hera clearly didn't share Kasper's line of thinking, though, because she turned and shoved her torch into Kai's hands before sprinting after the others—blatantly disobeying Brander's command. Kasper released a frustrated sigh before thrusting his own torch into Kai's hands and taking off after her. They should have made a plan, or at least marginally prepared, but Cal never was one for waiting around—not when everything he wanted was so close.

Kasper tried to ignore the increasing hum of the island as he tore through the trees. The sound nearly drowned out any other thought, but he forced himself to remain focused. The oversized waxy leaves of the trees and plants slapped and stuck to his damp skin. The vines and flowering plants tugged and snagged at him, but any thoughts of himself emptied from his mind as he broke through the clearing.

Viscous and inky shadows rolled off of Cal, gathering at his fingertips and lashing out like a whip. They writhed and whirled, wholly at Cal's command. He twisted, and the shadows advanced, aiming for Finnley's captors. Some sharpened, forming arrows that honed in on the statues. The statues that Kasper now recognized were made of granite, marble, and quartz—constructed to be indestructible. They had faces, but they were smooth and devoid of distinct features, with only impressions of where a mouth, nose, and eyes would be. Kasper wanted to meet the being that carved the statues, as they were truly remarkable, but when Cal's shadow-arrows made contact with the structures, he braced for the impact of the shards…but it never came. Lowering his hands, Kasper expected to find the statues obliterated, but they remained intact—and advanced on Cal.

Kasper withdrew his dagger, unsure what good it would do. Glancing around, Kasper found Brander engaged in battle with the pure white marble figure. His sword clattered uselessly against the stone, and blood leaked from his lip. Lady Hera busied herself with freeing Finnley, and Kasper realized with horror that it wasn't ropes restraining Finnley, but stone bands.

A crashing sound rang out from behind Kasper, and he turned to find Kai tripping into the clearing. His eyes went wide as he beheld the losing battle that Cal and Brander were engaged in. Kasper clenched his fist, annoyed with Kai's ineptitude, and shouted, "Go help Hera!"

Kai gave a slight jump but then hurried over, dropping the torches to the ground as he reached for Finnley.

Tearing his attention from them, Kasper focused back on Cal. He moved closer, careful not to get in line of the shadows as they continued their assault on the quartz and granite statues. They were even more fascinating up close. They clearly operated with some sort of magic, but their movements were so fluid and dynamic that Kasper had difficulty not stopping and staring at them. He shook himself of his stupor and lifted his blade. It was a paltry defense against the stone figures, but Cal would have time to summon enough force to incapacitate one if Kasper distracted the other.

Swallowing his fear, Kasper charged for the back of the quartz figure. He stabbed toward its lower back, where its kidneys and other vital organs would be located. But as his blade made contact with the quartz exterior, it glanced off. Kasper grappled for his arm, hissing against the reverberation turning his bones to jelly. Stumbling away, he cradled his arm and tried not to drop his dagger, even as his fingers trembled and ached. Beyond nearly taking himself out of the fight, the quartz statue hadn't even noticed Kasper's attack.

Clearly, a direct assault was not going to be fruitful, and that was becoming more evident as the white marble figure's arm flew out and smacked Brander in the chest. Brander's sword went flying, as did he, right into a tree trunk with a stomach-turning thud. He crumpled to the ground—unmoving.

"Brander!" Lady Hera screamed out as the marble figure stalked toward his unprotected body.

Ignoring the remaining stinging in his hand, Kasper gripped his dagger tighter and vaulted himself across the clearing toward Brander. He had no plans. No particular moves in mind, save for one thought— keep Brander alive and buy Hera enough time to escape. This fight was unwinnable, not against the unbreakable stone creatures. Kasper had enough wherewithal to grab Brander's discarded sword and hoist it in front of him. He blocked the marble being from raining down an additional blow—one that surely would have been the end of Brander. Kasper's teeth, bones, and vision rattled and chattered with the effort of blocking the assault. He wished he had a crystal imbued with physical strength as he shoved with all his might, attempting to force the stone creature back.

But then, the statue did the most curious thing.

It tilted its head and *looked* at Kasper.

Blinking, Kasper attempted to understand how this being looked without eyes, or why it was staring at him like it found him of particular interest. Still, Kasper decided he wouldn't waste the blessed opportunity. Bolting forward, he swung his blade with absolutely no precision or grace. He had trained only with daggers and short blades. Brander's long sword was foreign and clumsy in his hands, but he needed the reach. A dagger was useless against these creatures, but the sword was long enough to keep them at bay.

Meanwhile, Cal whirled and slashed, a storm of steel and shadows. His fury was palpable as he continued his assault, but to no avail, as the statue persisted—wholly undeterred. Back toward the middle of the clearing, Lady Hera and Kai yanked and pulled at Finnley's restraints, but they made no progress. Their best bet would be to try and drag her away from the fight, but Kasper knew Hera would never leave Brander.

Kasper continued his assault; his arms had gone numb from the repeated vibrations that rang up and down his limbs. The marble figure did not fight back, only absorbing the blows with that curious expression still painted on its face—or lack thereof.

Lady Hera suddenly bolted from Finnley and crashed to the ground next to Brander. In the same breath, Kai stopped trying to pry the stone from Finnley's arms and instead clasped his hands on her shoulder. Kai's head fell back, and Kasper realized with shock and anger that he was forcing a vision. Rage rippled through Kasper, and he engaged the marble creature with renewed interest. He slashed and stabbed, every strike glancing off harmlessly. Red colored his vision as his thoughts narrowed to the creature in front of him.

He had to destroy the statue so he could kill his brother.

His selfish, opportunistic brother, who would stop at nothing to get what he wanted, even if that meant risking the lives of others. Kasper would punish his brother for wasting time and putting his interests above the safety of the group. He would—

"Touch it, Kasper!" Kai called out, having come out of his trance. "Touch the statues and pull the magic from them."

Kasper wanted to tell his brother to shut up. He wanted to ignore him, but Kai was a Seer and–unfortunately–Kasper had to listen to him now. Gritting his teeth, he dropped his sword and launched himself at the marble creature.

Chapter Sixty One

Rhea pulled at the loose thread on her gown, trying and failing to keep her eyes from finding Kasper's back again in the long line of children standing before the King. Each of them brought before their King for the magic that flowed through their veins. Each of them tested to see if their abilities were ones that Rhea's father would find valuable—and if he did, they would become his property.

Rhea often wondered if the King secretly despised her for her notable lack of magic. It never failed to escape her notice, the acute interest he gave the children he perceived to be beneficial to him—the gifts and praise he bestowed upon them. She wondered if her father did it to endear the magic wielders to him. So they wouldn't balk at their lack of autonomy when they were old enough to understand that they were his to command and use as he saw fit. For that reason alone, Rhea would never be jealous of them. In her short eight years, she understood that gaining the attention and favor of the King was not always a good thing.

Rhea's eyes cut to her father's right, where his Seer, Malakai, stood at attention. There wasn't a hair out of place in his coiffure, nor a speck of dust on his pristine alabaster attire. To all the world, he would appear to be a young man who held considerable influence and power in the King's court, but Rhea saw the torn cuticles and the weary set of his eyes. Her eyes moved of their own accord, searching for the Necromancer, Caliban. Rhea knew better, though. Caliban never came to these proceedings, but she thought...

Rhea straightened. Her gaze snagged on Caliban's dark figure cloaked in shadows, leaning against a pillar. His eyes were fixed on Kasper, now third in line from the King. Rhea chewed her bottom lip as she waited through the *agonizing minutes of the two children in front of Kasper. Their gifts were unremarkable; one stirred a breeze, and the other cooled the room by a degree or two. Perhaps, if they could be developed, they would be something more, but from the King's relaxed posture, Rhea knew he saw nothing of use—lucky souls. But as Kasper stepped up to the dais, his golden-brown curls still damp from his bath, the King sat up. He glanced at Malakai, who had gone as white as his robes.*

"Is this your kin, Seer?"

Malakai's gaze shifted to Kasper and then back to the empty space above the crowd. He nodded once. "Yes, Your Majesty."

The King leaned forward, his eyes glittering and roving over Kasper intently. "Interesting." The King's lips curled upward, and then he waved toward Kasper. "Well, get on with it then."

Kasper's thin shoulders rose and fell with a steadying breath. Then he reached into his pocket and produced a small purple crystal.

Rhea went wholly still, her breath catching in her throat.

Kasper cupped the crystal in his palms. Seconds passed, and Rhea knew the King would only allow a moment more before he dismissed Kasper and barred him from the palace. Rhea would lose her best friend. But if the King was too pleased with Kasper...

The gem in Kasper's hands glowed, emanating a soft purple light.

Rhea released a breath. The stone pulsed, the light ebbing like a heartbeat.

The King arched an eyebrow, his gaze flickering between Kasper and the gem in his hands. "Is that all? You make rocks glow?"

A smattering of laughter echoed through the court, and Rhea glanced at Caliban, but he was gone. Peering around frantically, she found him marching toward the dais. Rhea clenched her fist, unable to do anything to stop the events from unfolding in front of her.

Kasper's slight frame started to tremble, and he looked to Malakai. The Seer's eyes were still fixed on the room beyond—indifferent to his youngest brother's plight.

Sighing, the King twisted in his throne, looking toward Malakai. "I had expected more from your bloodline."

Malakai spared Kasper a glance, unsympathetic to Kasper's quaking. Then, he looked away and said coldly, "As did I."

Rhea flinched at the disregard in Malakai's voice. It was a risk to refute her father, but to dismiss Kasper outright—

The King chortled, the sound clanking through Rhea like an off-kilter bell.

"Enough." Caliban commanded, his hand coming down on Kasper's shoulder. Pulling Kasper behind him, Caliban put himself between his little brother and the King.

A wicked gleam formed in the King's eye as he spread his arms wide and declared, "Ah, the infamous Necromancer deigns to emerge from the dungeons to show himself to the court."

Rhea clenched her jaw so hard she was sure her teeth would crack. Her pulse thrummed through her, practically drowning out the tense conversation at the front of the throne room.

The King tapped against the arm of his throne as he stared down at Caliban, waiting to see if the Necromancer would balk. Even at thirteen, Caliban was headstrong and resistant. Rhea feared her father would be waiting a long time for him to concede.

Malakai shifted and raised his palms. "Your Majesty, perhaps—"

"Silence!" the King commanded, raising his hand. Obeying, Malakai returned his gaze to space above the gathered courtiers. "The boy shows no real talent aside from illuminating some rocks. Therefore, he serves no use in my court." The King waved an indolent hand, and the guards moved toward Kasper and Caliban.

"We had a deal." Caliban growled. Kasper hid behind Caliban and hugged him tightly. The shadows around the room gathered and thickened. They pooled, sliding and slipping until a sea of darkness covered the floor. Courtiers shouted and tripped over one another in a futile attempt to be spared from Caliban's wrath.

Rhea merely stood and watched. The way he commanded the darkness was intoxicating and mesmerizing. She was never fearful in Caliban's presence, but today, she understood why everyone else was—including her father. The King glanced around his throne room, taking note of the fear, panic, and hatred that his court sported. His fingers splayed out and flexed twice, before he lifted a hand to silence his devotees.

"Enough, enough. Call off your nightmares, Necromancer. The boy can stay."

Rhea almost fell to the floor with relief, but forced herself to stay upright.

Caliban took Kasper's small hand into his own and pointed off to the side of the room where Rhea knew Soline was waiting, even if she wasn't visible. Kasper's golden-brown curls disappeared through the crush of courtiers, who still stared at Caliban and the inky darkness curling around their calves.

Rhea took the opportunity to move through the crowd, carefully weaving between the distracted adults who paid her no mind. The lingering tension in her muscles eased at the sight of Lady Soline's warm smile and golden locks. Soline pushed the too-long curls from Kasper's eyes and gently patted his cheek, before taking him by the hand and leading him away from the throne room. Rhea trailed after, secretly wishing someone would care for her the way Kasper was doted on, but she was her father's daughter, and no one dared show her affection—lest they incur his wrath.

After a few moments, Rhea decided she was far enough from the throne room that she could call out after Kasper. Soline and Kasper turned, and Kasper's face split into a grin.

"Rhea!" He exclaimed and hurried back to meet her. They collided in a hug that practically knocked the wind from her lungs, but she didn't care—her best friend wasn't leaving her.

"I was so afraid he was going to send you away." she whispered into his neck. She withdrew and smiled, her two missing front teeth on display. "I thought you would have to show him what you can really do."

Kasper pulled out the purple stone and quietly said, "I did, too."

Keeping the specifics of Kasper's powers quiet and letting the King believe that he could only illuminate crystals was the best way to keep him safe. Rhea pulled Kasper in for another hug, grateful that at least one of his brothers cared enough to protect him from the King—and foolishly wished that someone would protect her, too.

* * * *

Rhea struggled to tear her eyes from Kasper as he gritted his teeth and pressed his hands into the featureless face of the stone creature. Light flared beneath his hands, so bright that Rhea threw up her own to block it. Despite the searing light, Rhea kept her eyes open—there was still so much danger circulating around them. The light dimmed, and Rhea dropped her hands, expecting to find Kasper dead, or at the very least, unconscious.

But he was unharmed.

Kasper stood, staring at his hands, which glowed faintly. A pile of rocks rested at his feet. Furrowing her brows, Rhea looked from the rocks to Kasper.

"Did you—"

"I don't know. I just touched it and—"

"Kasper, look out!" Kai called out from next to Finnley.

Kasper looked up in time to see the speckled rock statue barreling toward him. Rhea gasped—he had no defense, save for his hands and the magic within them. He threw them out once more as the statue grappled for him, catching him around the waist. The pair crashed to the ground, but Kasper managed to grab the statue's shoulders. This time, Rhea was ready for the light and squinted against it as it glared out. The light grew brighter and brighter, until there was nothing to see but the light itself—

And then it was gone.

Left in its place was Kasper, and a crumbling heap of rocks.

Rhea's jaw dropped, unable to comprehend what Kasper had done. She struggled to reconcile what she knew of Kasper's magic, what little he had demonstrated before landing on the isle, and what he was exhibiting now. It was unfathomable.

But one statue still remained.

Bellowing in rage as he summoned the shadows, Cal bent and twisted them to his desire. Rhea was mesmerized by it—by *him*—just as she had been that day so long ago in court. He lashed out at the crystalline statue—an assault that would have killed any ordinary being—but the statue was unaffected. The creature swatted away the semi-corporeal manifestations of the shadows as if they were flies—simply pestering the otherworldly being rather than attempting to kill it. Cal cursed as he narrowly avoided a backhanded blow from the statue. He dove for the ground and rolled, profanities still falling from his lips. Coming onto his knees, he twisted toward them and shouted over his shoulder.

"A little help would be nice!"

Rhea could do nothing but watch on in horror. Still under the pile of rocks, Kasper began to shake off his stupor and push to his feet. He wasted no time creeping up behind the crystal being, whose focus was wholly on Cal. Cal threw out another blast of shadows; this time, when the creature swung for Cal, Kasper caught it on the arm. Rhea raised her hands, bracing herself for the third and final burst of light.

But Kai exclaimed, "Don't deplete this one entirely!"

Rhea had no idea what Kai meant, but Kasper must have understood because just a few moments later, light began to shine from his hands. She gaped as Kasper's power illuminated the quartz, the glow flowing through its arm, up its shoulder, and across its wide chest until the entire figure was luminescent. The beauty of it almost stole her breath—the milky stone shining like bright opal as it was embued with Kasper's abilities. She almost mourned the loss as it slowly dimmed, and the crystal creature knelt on the ground.

Still sat in awestruck wonder, she turned to Kai and opened her mouth to ask if he had always known what Kasper was capable of. But Brander stirred beneath her, stealing the words from her tongue. Rhea snapped her attention back to Brander, gently slipping her hands under his shoulders to help him sit up.

"Careful, Brander. You were unconscious for a few moments."

Easing himself into an upright position, Brander blinked furiously at his surroundings. Rhea wondered how many more hits he could withstand before irreparable damage was done, but she knew Brander would never tell her. She could only hope that Kasper's healing would mitigate the harm. Rhea chewed the inside of her cheek, mimicking the anxiety gnawing at her insides. Lifting her eyes back to Kasper and the statue still kneeling at his feet, she endeavoured to form words.

"Kasper, can you–I mean, if you are able–could y—"

"Yes, I can examine him." He replied, letting go of the crystal statue but still staring at his hands—as if he, too, was utterly shocked by what he had done. Rhea loosed a breath, keeping one nervous eye trained on Brander as Cal moved to stand beside the statue. He had his shadows at the ready, though what good they would do now was anyone's guess.

Brander moved to stand. "I'm alright, My Lady. I promise—"

"Let him look you over." She commanded.

A muscle ticked in Brander's jaw, but he complied. Kasper moved quickly, his still glowing hands roving over Brander's body. Rhea tracked his every movement, awaiting Kasper's assessment and fearing the absolute worst. What if Brander had further damaged his ribs, or broken new bones? Kasper had warned her on the ship about the severity of Brander's head injury. What if he received another concussion? Rhea was certain that any additional harm to his brain would have lasting impacts on his memory, his ability to speak, his motor funct—

"He's fine now." Kasper muttered, dropping his hands.

Rhea blinked. "What do you mean?"

Pursing his lips, Kasper asserted, "I fixed the damage to his organs and the swelling around his brain."

Rhea went wholly still. Her mind whirred in an attempt to form a single coherent thought—to even *begin* to grasp what he was saying.

"What? Kasper, how did y—

"I don't know. The island, or maybe the magic I drew from the stone beings, has amplified my abilities. It was like I could *see* the damage done and correct it."

"Without using crystals?" Cal asked, a perplexed gaze pasted on his face. Even his shadows seemed puzzled, the tendrils curling backward into him like a dog slinking behind its owner's legs.

Kasper gave a solemn nod. "It would appear that way."

Rhea was at a loss for words. Kasper's magic had always been shrouded in mystery—although part of that was done intentionally to prevent her father from using him, *possessing* him. Still, he had always been limited to manipulating the energies that resided in crystals—Rhea had never seen him conjure anything on his own, but now...

Now, he was not beholden to the confines of what the crystals could do—he was the power source. With that kind of raw, limitless power, he would be unstoppable. And whoever Kasper was loyal to would be invincible. Rhea tried not to think too long about the ramifications of that knowledge. But if she went into her reign with a Seer, a Necromancer, and someone who had the power to manipulate the very energies of the world—no one would dare contest her claim, not even a brother or her uncle.

She would be untouchable.

Rhea's chest ached with elation. She would be able to help her people. She could provide care to the sick and injured. Her armies—

Shaking her head, Rhea cleared away that line of thinking. She was *not* her father. She did not conscript people to use and wield like weapons. Her reign would be just and fair, free from corruption and villainy. She would lead her people into a new era, and she would not start it by enslaving magically gifted people to do her bidding.

Standing, Rhea pulled Brander up along with her. She needed to get off of this island before more of her thoughts were perverted. She turned to find Kasper leaning down next to Finnley, his hand on her restraints. They splintered and cracked, falling away from her in an instant. Finnley wasted no time shaking off the pieces and standing to her feet. Rhea wanted to reach for her, to comfort her, but she knew well enough that Finnley would not appreciate the gesture–especially coming from her–so she refrained.

"Are you alright?"

Finnley paused, dusting off her clothes. "What do you think?"

Rhea pursed her lips, remorse settling in her gut. When they got off this island, she would find a way to make it up to Finnley. She would offer her a reward, or perhaps persuade her father to grant her a title—

"We need to get going." Cal added gruffly, his gaze deftly avoiding Finnley. At least Rhea was not alone in her guilt.

"Agreed," Rhea added quietly, before she pointed to the crystal structure still kneeling on the ground, "but what do we do with that?"

"It comes with us." Kai chirped. "Obviously."

Finnley turned on him, the utter fury in her glare making Rhea shrink back into her skin. "Those *things* nearly killed me. It dies just like the rest of them."

Kai didn't yield an inch, despite the fact that Finnley's anger loomed over him—her small stature secondary to the pure rage that radiated from her skin. "It can be of use to us."

"It is an abomination!" Finnley whirled, turning toward the creature with murder blazing in her eyes.

Stepping between them, Kasper set a placating hand on her shoulder. By some miracle, Finnley didn't immediately shrug it off. "Don't, Finnley. I can control it."

Rhea stepped closer to the trio, her curiosity officially winning out over her fear. "What do you mean, Kas?"

Kasper shook his head. "It's hard to explain, but I took enough of the magic from it that it can't operate without me. It's at my disposal."

Recoiling a bit, Rhea glanced at Cal. "Is that ethical?" Rhea blinked, hearing the words as they left her mouth. With everything she had done or allowed to happen, did it really matter what was ethical anymore? She wagered she would have to commit even more immoral acts before she secured the safety of her people.

Cal arched an eyebrow at her. "Who cares? It might give us a leg up on whatever else is on this island. I say we keep it."

"Agreed." Kai said enthusiastically.

Kasper nodded as well. Glancing at Brander, Rhea said, "It *would* be nice to have something fairly indestructible to protect us. Plus, we won't need torches, since it produces its own light."

"Yes, it would." Brander bobbed his head.

Finnley crossed her arms and spat, "I guess I shouldn't be surprised since you all decided long before now that my wishes weren't relevant."

"Finnley—" Rhea called out, but Finnley raised her hand, immediately halting her.

"Save it. Let's just get off this godsforsaken island."

"Excellent idea." Cal replied. Lifting his sword, he pointed into the gloom. "I say we head that way, toward the cliffs. And I think any further stopping from this point on should be limited."

Rhea nodded her agreement and attempted not to let her guilt and shame get the best of her. Finnley was right, and Rhea had no recourse for her choices—save that they were the ones most advantageous to her.

"Alright, then." Kasper said softly, motioning toward the crystal being still kneeling on the ground. It rose, and Rhea didn't miss that Finnley flinched away from it. She desperately wanted to ask her what had happened in the time Finnley had been missing, but she knew it would be futile. Finnley would likely never trust her again.

Kasper gave everyone a final, solemn glance, before uttering, "I guess I'll lead the way."

He then pointed, and the statue moved, marching toward the cliffs.

Chapter Sixty Two

Brander had never felt better. Perhaps when he was a teenager, before he broke his arm in a training exercise, but that was over three decades ago. Since then, he had fought in numerous battles and had suffered countless injuries. Pain had become his constant companion, always lingering when he pushed himself too hard or when the seasonal rains flooded the rivers. But now, as he strolled through the jungle, nothing bothered him.

Well, the crystal creature parading them through the wilderness was a touch concerning, as was the Princess's furrowed expression. But in truth, there was little Brander was able to do about either. That didn't stop him from attempting to help the latter.

Brander slowed his pace just slightly, and Princess Rhea followed his lead. He didn't want to put a tremendous amount of space between himself and the others for fear that other island inhabitants would take an interest in them. Already, he noted several pairs of eyes that tracked their progress, but they remained far enough from their path that Brander kept his blade sheathed—though he kept his hand close by.

"Are you well?" Brander asked softly, keeping his head forward, gaze sweeping the treeline.

A small laugh came from the Princess. "I'm almost certain I'm supposed to be asking you that." A beat of silence passed between them, and Brander started to push her into answering, but then Rhea continued. "I don't know, honestly. Bringing Finnley was the smart move, the most sensible move, but—"

"But it weighs on you." Brander finished, glancing toward her. Brander spent enough time with the Princess that he had learned the way she thought and her physical tells.

Princess Rhea pressed her lips into a thin line. "Precisely. And now Kasper has all this power and…" The Princess's words faded, and she shook her head.

Remaining quiet, Brander allowed her the time to process her feelings. He knew little of the brothers' time in the palace; they were banished five years prior to his arrival, and two years before he had been assigned to her charge, but the Princess had filled him in on the essential parts. She had mentioned that Kasper used gems for channeling, and Brander had observed that much. Kasper, nor the Princess, had indicated that he was capable of much more than that. But clearly, there was more to his magic than any of them—including Kasper himself—had realized.

"My father," Rhea ventured, her voice dropping so low Brander had to step closer to hear her, "wouldn't hesitate to use him."

Brander nodded. The King was known for essentially enslaving magic wielders—powerful ones, especially. Brander had never submitted for examination since he displayed no ability, but he knew being in the King's retinue was a different kind of conscription.

"If he had any idea what Kas could do, he—" Her words broke off as something crashed in the jungle nearby. Instinctually, Brander drew his sword and pulled the Princess behind him, his eyes peering into the awaiting darkness. More yellow eyes peered back at him, but he failed to make out their forms. He prayed that the gods, Forgotten or otherwise, would listen and that his party would make it out of the jungle unscathed. But he feared that his prayers would go unheard. Brander didn't dare look to his left, even as the light emanating from the crystal being grew brighter, illuminating more of their surroundings.

He wished it hadn't.

The light revealed the creature staring at him from the limbs of the trees. A pair of enormous yellow eyes dominated its otherwise black face. A single strip of red ran the length of its flat, broad nose. Thick, black fur covered every inch of its body, save for its face, hands, and feet—appendages that were wrapped around tree trunks and limbs, holding them aloft from the ground. Brander counted six of the creatures, and despite the alarm that their dexterity brought, his gaze lingered on their eyes. They were curious and far too intelligent for his liking—promising a painful death. He had seen something like them once in a book, but the name of the beasts escaped him.

"Monkeys." Princess Rhea breathed from behind him, and Brander knew it to be the truth. The light grew brighter once more, and the monkeys reeled backward out of the sphere of illumination, but not before Brander glimpsed the leathery wings at their backs and the yellow fangs crowding their mouths. Brander's mouth went dry at the sight. What kind of horrid island had they sought out? And which one of them would die in pursuit of its treasures?

"We need to keep moving." Cal ordered, though his words lacked their normal bite. Perhaps the pirate's haughty attitude was beginning to wear thin. Brander would have savored the moment if he wasn't so uneasy over the latest development.

"It's not much further," Kasper assured in a tight voice, "we're almost at the Cave entrance."

Brander wanted to inform him that his words did little to ease the knots forming in his stomach. Instead, he reached for the Princess and began walking, keeping tighter to the others. The earlier conversation between him and the Princess would have to wait.

An eerie silence fell over them as they trudged through the jungle. The monkeys were still lingering beyond the reaches of the light, their movements and chattering the only sound. Brander was further grateful for Kasper's healing as his muscles hardly ached, even with the tension he kept in them as they walked on. Finnley had fallen back to the rear of the pack, falling into place beside Brander. Ordinarily, he would demand that the Princess be closest to him, but putting her in the middle of them all was safest, especially since the brothers also had a vested interest in her safety.

Already gaunt and suspicious, Finnley's features had taken on an additional edge, making her scar more pronounced. Her fingers tapped incessantly against her knife—the one she had lost when she was taken. Her eyes moved back and forth, scanning and searching, presumably for the next threat. Brander couldn't blame her. She was forced on this journey and, so far, she had suffered the brunt of the harm. He didn't view her the same way he did the Princess—naive and inexperienced, and needing his protection. No, Finnley had more than proven herself, and even if he still wasn't wholly in agreement with her life choices, he did respect her as a fellow soldier. As such, he recognized the shell-shocked look in her eyes.

Clearing his throat softly, Brander said, "Your pulse will eventually settle. Once your body realizes you're no longer in danger."

Finnley gave a harsh laugh. "Is that right? And when will that be? When we go into that death trap of a cave? Or maybe when those beasts finally decide to rip us to shreds?"

"Fair point," he replied, watching a monkey perch on a nearby limb, "but your body can only exist in that state for so long. Ultimately, exhaustion will win out. You can either relax or succumb to it, but you will have to come down at some point."

It wasn't his intention for his words to be harsh, but it was the reality. Her jitteriness and irritation were evident, but Brander knew it wasn't from the threat of violence. Finnley was a seasoned pirate and had seen her fair share of skirmishes, so there was obviously another reason for her anxiety—and if she didn't get it under control soon, it would likely get her killed.

Finnley sighed, and her shoulders relaxed a fraction. She spared him a glance and said, "Thank you."

Brander dipped his chin in acknowledgment. "Soldiers have to look out for one another."

"Is that what I am? I distinctly remember you refusing to duel me just a few days ago." she said with a hint of amusement.

A faint smile formed on his lips. "That was an error of judgment on my part. You held your own against the Necromancer, and I suspect you would have likely beaten me. I let my prejudices get the best of me at that moment. I apologize for my mistake."

Shrugging, Finnley said, "It wasn't the first time someone had underestimated me. In truth, I'm used to it. I didn't have anything to prove that day for myself, but I wanted the Lady to see that she did deserve to learn how to fight."

Brander pursed his lips. He still wasn't sure that Princess Rhea should wield a blade for fear she would do more harm than good, but it was clear that present circumstances were forcing the alternative.

"I just want to keep her safe." Brander said, more to himself than to Finnley.

Nodding, she said, "I know, and that's admirable. She's lucky to have someone looking out for her, but you won't always be around." Finnley didn't have to elaborate; Brander understood well enough. Princess Rhea needed to be able to defend herself when Brander inevitably became too old, or died.

Brander cleared his throat. "If you want to talk about what happened, I'm here to listen."

Finnley remained quiet for several minutes. Brander resigned himself to her silence, but then she softly spoke. "I'll keep that in mind."

Solitude resumed, though it wasn't true quiet because more monkeys had joined the ranks. They were invisible to the eye, but Brander felt their presence. Their gazes trailed them, watching and waiting—for *what* Brander didn't know, and he wasn't eager to find out. Their chattering grew louder, and the limbs around them creaked and swayed, presumably with the addition of more monkeys. Brander kept his grip on the hilt of his sword, his eyes focused on his surroundings.

They weren't getting out of the jungle without a fight.

"It's just up ahead." Kasper said, the first words spoken in the last several minutes. Squinting, Brander noted the jungle thinning out, giving way to a clearing. Salt floated in the air, and water crashed against the shore. Brander knew that if he pushed past the others, he would find the cliffs they had spotted from the water hours ago.

His mind ran through all the possible scenarios as more monkeys whooped and clambered around them. The monkeys were equipped with wings, meaning their attack could come from the sky, and running them toward the cliffs would be pointless. Going back further into the jungle would be counterproductive. The monkeys were native to this place, and even with Kasper's abilities, he couldn't be everywhere at once. The cave entrance was their only option, but that meant entering a place they knew nothing about.

Or, they could simply fight the beasts outright.

Brander clenched his jaw, not particularly pleased with any of those options. And from the tense set of everyone else's shoulders, Brander surmised that they weren't thrilled with the conclusion they had arrived at, either. One thing he knew for certain was that he couldn't protect Rhea from all of the variables—she needed to get to the cave as quickly as possible. They all picked up their pace without the order being given, quickening from a steady walk to a light jog. It didn't go unnoticed by the beasts. Their wings beat in the air, the sound deafening as they took flight from limb to limb and bounded toward the clearing. They whooped and called to one another, their excitement reverberating through the jungle, forcing the trees and ground to tremble.

"Run!" Brander shouted, gripping his sword tighter as he broke out in a sprint. They had to get to the cave, it was their only chance of survival. They sprinted as the monkeys swooped down toward them, swiping out their claw-tipped hands.

"Hit the dirt!" Finnley yelled, diving for the ground.

Ignoring her order, Brander raised his blade, slicing toward a monkey as it dove for him. His blade cleaved the thick jungle air and sang as it connected with the beast's leathery wing, sending it screeching and spiraling back into the trees.

"Hurry!" Kasper called out, waving from the clearing. A monkey dove, coming precariously close to his head with its claws. At the last second, he ducked behind the statue, and the beast careened away from its unearthly light. "The cave is just up here!"

Gritting his teeth, Brander searched for the Princess, eyes roaming the clearing as the pack of monkeys continued to darken the sky. Their dark fur and wings consumed what little light shone from the night sky overhead, making it almost impossible to make out the faces of his companions. He could hardly tell the difference between man and monkey as he looked around frantically, skimming the shapes in front of him for her familiar dark hair, and then—there she was. A fraction of relief washed over him, though it was quickly dampened by the fear in her wide, terrified eyes.

"Go!" Brander barked at her, pointing in Kasper's direction.

For once, the Princess obeyed him without question. As she ran for Kasper, Brander spared a moment to assess his surroundings. Finnley was still prostrate on the ground, her knife white-knuckled gripped in her hand. Cal had his black blade in one hand, and shadows wreathed around the other. Kai was nowhere to be found—no surprise there—but Kasper's statue swung wildly at the monkeys. Its crystal fist connected with one of the monkeys flapping around its head, sending it careening toward the ground. The statue wasted no time lifting a foot and bringing it back down on the monkey's skull—a sickening crack filling the air. The monkey did not stir again.

There was some comfort in the knowledge that the beasts could at least be felled with brute force, but Brander was a man wielding a piece of steel—the odds of winning against the horde of monkeys whooping in the air and trees were slim. But he would not go down without a fight. So, he lifted his blade, set his feet, and made peace with his inevitable death.

Chapter Sixty Three

The scent of iron filled the air, effectively choking off the sea salt breeze blowing in from the cliffs and the sweet floral fragrance that wafted from the night-blooming flowers. Cal fought his revulsion as the monkeys descended upon them, blotting out what little light the moon had offered and blocking most of what Kasper's quartz puppet emanated.

Moving on instinct, he sliced and stabbed with brutal efficiency honed after years at sea, raiding, and plundering. He gave no thought to the beasts' lives—if they were mindless minions, then death was freedom. If they were willing participants, their lives were forfeit from the moment they appeared in the trees.

Cal willed his shadows to unfurl around him, spooling at his feet and preparing to strike—but they hesitated, resisted even. A muscle in his jaw flexed at the rising anger in his chest. They had fought his control earlier against the statues. There was something about this island—something that protested his magic. He thought that when they had entered The Ether it was like calling to like, but perhaps it was something more sinister than that. Whatever the case, Cal was sick and tired of fighting his own magic in addition to an external force.

He pressed onward, rallying his strength and infusing every bit of command he had into forcing the shadows to comply. Again, they balked, but their concession quickly followed—bending to his will. He curled his fist, and the darkness compressed, forming darts. A wicked smile crept to his lips as he flung his hand, sending the darts hurtling toward the monkeys. The monkeys let out a deafening shriek–confirmation that the shadows had found their mark–but Cal couldn't relish in his victory for long as one spiraled down from the sky, aiming for him. He threw a hand, sending a wave of suffocating darkness for it as he swung the blade in his other hand, slicing through the muscles and sinews of the monkey's meaty throat.

Its death cry was cut short, ending with a gurgling sound. Cal raised a booted foot and kicked out, sending the beast tumbling backward into the melee. Satisfaction coursed through Cal as the monkey's bodies fell around him, and he stepped over them, slowly clearing away the vermin. The island could send whatever manner of creatures it wanted, Cal would destroy them all. It could disrupt and interfere with his magic, but he was stronger. He was the master of himself. He smirked down at a monkey felled by his shadows, noting the gaping hole in its chest. He relished in his small victories and delighted in the glassy, lifeless gaze of the beast. Stepping over it, he left it to rot in the dirt.

Cal glanced around, the battle still raging around him. The quartz statue still swung its fist, swatting the monkeys from the sky like buzzing insects; the beasts' bones broke and cracked upon contact. Kasper, Kai, and Lady Hera were nowhere to be found, presumably taking shelter in the cave. Blood stained Brander's side, but he made no indication that it pained him as he thrust his blade out, piercing the abdomen of a monkey. But even his stamina was finite, and eventually, he would be overwhelmed. Finnley was finally up on her feet, dagger in hand and blood splattering her clothes. Cal gritted his teeth; he needed to end this now. Gripping his sword tighter, he rallied his shadows, and began toward Finnley.

Suddenly, pain rippled through his calf, tearing his focus. The monkey–the one Cal *knew* his shadows had slaughtered by the circular holes in its chest–buried its talons in his leg.

The beast had been felled—how was that possible?

Instinct kicked in. Cal swung his blade, severing the creature's arm at the elbow. It shrieked and fell backward, blood spurting from its wound. Swinging his blade again, he buried it into the monkey's neck. Cal's breath came in hard pants, his mind whirling and failing to comprehend how the monkey had come back from the dead. His eyes darted around and found that it was not an anomaly, but that all around him, the bodies of the dead monkeys were rising.

"What in the Forgotten?" Cal muttered in disbelief. Stumbling backward, he barely managed to keep his feet beneath him.

"They aren't staying dead!" Brander called out, coming to the same realization that Cal had. Neither steel nor magic was keeping the beasts down.

"What do we do?" Finnley demanded, her eyes wild and frantic in the dim lighting of the crystal creature.

Cal shook his head, still moving backward from the rising horde of the undead animals. His magic was useless, utterly *useless* against the forces operating on the isle. The trepidation that filled Cal in The Ether flooded him once more.

They wouldn't survive.

Cal would never put Soline to rest.

He would never be with Hera.

He would never make Kai pay.

Chapter Sixty Four

T urning, Cal took off, sprinting toward the cave.

"Where are you going?" Finnley bellowed.

Cal continued running until the Cave was within sight, his brother's once bone-white tunic glowing dully in the moonlight.

"Kai!" he yelled and withdrew a dagger at his side. Dragging it across his palm, the pain barely registered as his blood welled to the surface. Kai rose sheepishly, stepping out of the mouth of the cave.

Grabbing Kai, Cal slashed the blade across his brother's arm.

"Ahh!" Kai cried and tried to recoil away, but Cal held fast, waiting for his blood to rise. He quickly shifted his grip, placing his bleeding palm over Kai's wound.

Cal's mouth fell open at the surge of raw power coursing through him. His gums throbbed, and his very bones vibrated. He had craved this sensation for weeks, and now it was his again. With this kind of power at his disposal, he could resurrect Soline. He could—

"Caliban!" Lady Hera shouted.

Cal blinked once. Twice.

He attempted to understand why she was calling out to him. Her soil-brown eyes were fierce and commanding—a Queen amongst commoners. Her voice was nearly as assertive as she called out to him.

"Come back to me, Cal. Come back to me and finish this."

Her words pierced something in Cal, and he turned, dragging a limp Kai with him. He was *going* to finish this, and he was going to take this godsforsaken island down with him. Cal felt no urgency, save for wanting to return to Lady Hera, but he hurried all the same.

Return to Lady Hera.

End this.

Return to her.

End this.

Her.

That was Cal's mantra as he lifted his free hand, drawing from the power that flowed from Kai and into his very bones. It heated his blood, chasing out the darkness and depravity that lurked from within. The beasts, so simple and primitive, turned to face him—the statue, Brander, and Finnley forgotten. Smiling, Cal was pleased that the island and its minions finally recognized him as the threat that he was. Cal's smile grew as the beasts growled and descended upon him.

"Take cover." Cal said to no one in particular, and spared a singular heartbeat before the power blasted out from him. Light–hot and blinding–erupted from Cal, engulfing the monkeys as they raged, desperate to tear him apart. But they never got the chance.

The light consumed them. It incinerated them immediately—their cries snuffed out in an instant.

The magic washed over Cal, rippling and cascading in waves. He would never reach this level of strength on his own. No amount of training or amplification from Finnley matched what Kai offered him. This kind of power, this kind of magic, was wasted on Kai. He read fortunes of no consequence to appease the rich and swindle people out of their money. The possibilities of what Cal could accomplish were nearly limitless. Everything he wanted, everything he had *longed* for. It could all be Cal's. He could restore Soline. He could protect Hera.

He could kill the King.

"Let him go, Cal!" Kasper shouted from somewhere to Cal's left.

The light around him banked, dimming to that of a torchlight rather than a miniature star. Glancing down to where he still held onto Kai, Cal noted his waxen skin and the eyes that lolled within his skull. Cal tilted his head to examine the specimen withering away beneath him. He was faintly aware that the being was his brother, but the fraternal connection to him was barely a glimmer—especially in the face of all the power at his fingertips.

"Release him, Caliban. The beasts are gone. We're safe." Lady Hera commanded, appearing next to Kasper, a dagger in hand. *His* dagger. Lady Hera's throat bobbed once, and she repeated, "Release him."

The part of Cal that remained aware of the world around him and his connection to it yanked on his mind. His fingers spasmed, and Kai slumped to the ground. Cal's legs almost went out from under him at the sudden loss of power. An ache pulsed in his skull, and his mouth was filled with an acrid taste. Staggering backward, Cal fumbled for something to keep him upright. Hands slid under his arms, and he found Kasper supporting him from behind. Cal opened his mouth to protest, but Lady Hera cut his words off.

"Kai's out cold. We need to stop and rest for at least a few hours."

Shaking his head, Cal moved to stand, but Kasper gripped his arm tightly. "We need to rest, Cal. We can start again in a few hours."

Finnley and Brander came into view, looking worse for wear. Between them, they had an array of injuries that would have put an average person down. Cal swallowed the bitter taste on his tongue, but relented.

"Fine. We'll rest in the Cave, but we must be up before the sun."

No one answered him.

They slowly gathered themselves up and moved toward the mouth of the cave. Kasper released Cal and gestured toward the statue. It wordlessly reached for Kai and scooped him up—a lifeless doll in its arms. Lady Hera moved toward Finnley and Brander, supporting them as they limped toward the cave. They would all need some of Kasper's healing before the night was through.

Cal worked not to feel the sting of Lady Hera's neglect of him, but she was clearly avoiding his gaze. He had promised himself he would address the growing tension between them before it was all said and done, but this was not the time. A heavy silence settled over them, and Cal couldn't find it in himself to try and talk. In less than a day, they had all nearly died twice, and Cal had a growing fear that they had still not seen the worst that the island had to offer.

Chapter Sixty Five

Malakai clenched his fists at his sides, fighting the urge to tug at the high starch collar that itched and scratched his neck. His steps were soft and unhurried—indolent even. He was the picture of grace, elegance, and languidness. He was the envy of everyone in the court; from his dress to his position, everyone wanted what he had—or to be him.

But Malakai kept his attention on the back of the King's head, ignoring the courtiers' stares and whispers. This show of opulence meant nothing to the King; it was just a way to remind his subjects of all he owned and, more specifically, who he owned.

So, Malakai played his part, knowing what the King expected from him. He had to remain perfect.

Immaculate.

Flawless.

The procession finally stopped and Malakai took the familiar, well-rehearsed twenty-three paces to the right of the King—the place of honor. Releasing a slow breath as he came to a halt, Malakai turned to look at the court gathered beneath them. Malakai lifted his chin and bolstered himself against the onslaught of requests that were going to be unleashed.

A smile spread across the King's face, and Malakai knew the truth of the smile as the first petitioner came forward with a chest of gold. It was enough gold to keep Malakai in comfort for all his days, and this courtier handed it over without a second thought. If the nobility wanted their future told, they had to pay the King's price. Malakai was his possession, and Malakai gave *no visions or prophecies without the King's express permission—but even with that chest of gold, he still couldn't buy his freedom from the King's house.*

The nobleman bowed deeply at the waist and said, "Your Majesty. In all your wisdom and strength, I humbly beseech the services of your Seer."

The King absentmindedly drummed his fingers on the arm of his throne, weighing the merits of the lord's request. Malakai already knew that the King would permit him to give the lord a vision. He already knew what the lord would ask, and what he would tell the lord.

Malakai focused his efforts on keeping his face neutral—indifferent. If he stayed still enough, he could almost pretend none of this was happening, but then the King spoke, shattering the spell. Stepping forward on instinct, Malakai reached for the nobleman, who stared up at him greedily. Malakai fought the revulsion at having to touch the man.

He hated this part of it. He hated the lack of autonomy.

He hated the King.

He hated himself.

He hated—

"Kai. Wake up, Kai. You need to eat something."

"Mmhmm," Malakai replied.

Something or, more accurately, someone, gripped Malakai's shoulders and shook him. If Malakai had the strength, he would have thrown off their touch, but as it stood, he failed to find the energy to even open his eyes. He had little sense of his body save for the contact points between him—whoever was touching him and the ground.

The hands around his shoulders tightened and shook harder. "Come on, Kai, you need to wake up."

Malakai muttered, "Just five more minutes," though the words were more instinct than anything.

A moment later, the hands disappeared, and someone said, "It's no use; he's completely out of it."

"No, he's not. He's just being a child."

Boots scuffled against the damp ground, coming nearer to where he lay. Glass clinked, then the startling *pop* of a cork coming loose echoed around him. Malakai had no chance to prepare himself as he inhaled, and the sharp scent of stale urine–smelling salts–flooded his senses.

Malakai's eyes flew open, and he sat upright. His muscles contracted and spasmed as he gagged, attempting to expel the noxious fumes from his body. His nose and throat burned with onslaught of the chemicals. He fell forward on his hands and knees and was greeted with the cave's cool, slick, stone floor. Despite the heaving and coughing, nothing came up save for his spit. After a few moments, he managed to get his bearings and sat back against the wall of the cave.

He rested his head against the wall and stared at the ceiling, noting the glistening moisture and moss dappling the crevices. It took more effort than he cared to admit for him to lower his gaze and look around the rest of the cave. He was met with the haggard and weary stares of Brander and Finnley. Malakai aimed for a smile, but even that was too strenuous.

A flat, dry biscuit appeared in front of Malakai. "Here," Kasper said, shoving it closer to his face, "eat this."

Reluctantly, Malakai took the biscuit. He had no appetite–partly due to Kasper's ill-mannered wake-up call–but he couldn't afford to remain weak. He slipped the biscuit between his lips, content to let it dissolve in his mouth. Kasper stepped further away, leaning against the wall beside his still-glowing quartz statue on the cave floor. A canteen of water was placed next to Malakai by Rhea, who offered him a tight smile before returning to her place on the far wall next to Brander and Finnley. Caliban was nowhere to be seen, but Malakai knew he wouldn't be far, not with the Princess sitting there.

Malakai glanced away from them and down into the gloom of the cave beyond. A steady drip of water echoed from somewhere in the cave, mingling with their breathing and providing the only sound in the space.

Malakai couldn't stand it.

Turning back to the others, he swallowed down the sawdust biscuit and said, as jovially as he could muster, "So, how is everyone? I see all visible features are intact."

Drip. Drip. Drip.

Malakai sighed. He was perturbed that Caliban had taken his powers without consent, but he understood the situation had left him with little choice. "Well, I suppose I have been better, but it could be worse given the circumstances. I wouldn't mind taking a quick bath, but I might make do with a change of clothes. Though—"

"Shut up, Kai." Kasper growled.

Pressing his lips into a thin line, Malakai suppressed a smile. He clicked his tongue and said, "I'd apologize for disturbing your quiet, but we have had a distressing last few hours, and I thought that it might do everyone some good to—"

"Shut up, Kai." Caliban repeated, appearing out of the dark.

Malakai listened this time, remembering the harrowing feeling of his magic being ripped from him—again. His anger flared. Being at Caliban's mercy was nightmarish on its own, but living with the memory of what Caliban was capable of–and what he was willing to do–was an entirely different thing.

Caliban stopped in the center of the space, his eyes sharp and aware as he assessed them all. "The cave keeps going, slowly sloping downward into the earth. We can all rest here for an hour or two, then we need to get moving again."

"We're going to have to rest longer than that, Caliban." Kasper grumbled.

Caliban turned toward him. "We can't afford to waste that kind of time. We might be safe now, but given what we've encountered thus far, there's no guarantee that it will last."

Gesturing to Malakai, Kasper said, "He can't go anywhere until he regains some of his strength. He'll be more of a liability like this than he normally is."

Heat licked at Malakai's face. It wasn't *his* fault that he was so weak. He had just had his magic ripped away from him—*again*—in order to save the rest of the party. They would clearly be lost without him, so why was he the one being labeled as a liability?

Sighing, Caliban intoned, "Can't you just heal him?"

Kasper crossed his arms, but he wouldn't meet Malakai's gaze. "I tried already. Whatever you did to him can't be fixed with magic."

"Everything can be fixed with magic."

With a shake of his head, Kasper added, "Not this."

Malakai shifted at the conflict that coursed through him. He wanted to feel a modicum of gratitude that his brothers wanted him healed, but it was only so they could get on with their quest.

Pinching the bridge of his nose, Caliban was quiet for several moments. Finally, the Princess broke the silence, saying, "We all need the rest, Cal. We've been through a lot today."

Malakai stifled a laugh. He had lost his connection to his magic, arguably one of the worst things to happen to any of them, but he also marveled at Caliban's subtle softening toward the Princess. He watched as Cal dropped his hand, turning to look at her with gentle eyes.

"Fine, but someone has to stay on watch."

"I'll take the first one." Kasper offered.

Malakai waited for Brander or Caliban to refute the proposal, but they wordlessly moved into position on the floor to rest. The Princess settled between Brander and Finnley. Caliban sat next to Malakai, while

Kasper gestured to the statue, which then stood and moved deeper into the cave, presumably to stand guard.

Exhaustion seeped in, grabbing hold of Malakai's mind. He slid down further against the wall, taking advantage of the pack he was resting on before his abrupt awakening. Turning on his side, he faced his brother. Caliban had already closed his eyes and folded his hands over his chest—a dagger clutched in them. In the dim light of the cave, Caliban looked years younger, like he had in the days leading up to their exile. Or maybe Malakai was just feeling nostalgic, given the nature of his dreams and the taunts from the island.

Though Malakai's body wanted to rest, his mind churned, refusing to shut off. His restlessness was aided by the cacophony of snoring that echoed off the walls from the other side of the space. Malakai attempted to distract himself into sleep by watching Caliban's chest rise and fall in a steady rhythm. Counting the breaths, he watched for the twitching of his leg—the tell-tale sign that he was indeed asleep. Minutes passed, and his breathing remained constant, but the twitch never came.

Malakai opened his mouth—

"What do you want, Kai?"

"Do you remember our parents?"

Drip. Snore. Drip.

Sighing, Caliban opened his eyes and turned toward Malakai.

Malakai braced for Caliban's reprimand, but instead, his brother shook his head and said, "Not really. They're still alive. But I don't remember much beyond some vague figures."

"I saw them. Once. When they came to drop Kasper off."

Snore. Drip. Snore.

"And?"

Malakai shifted, the image of their parent's flashing in his mind. "We look like our mother. We have her eyes and mouth."

Caliban huffed, his face sharp in the gloom. "Why bring this up, Kai?"

In truth, Malakai wasn't entirely sure why he had mentioned it, but he opened his mouth and said, "I think we forget sometimes that we are brothers."

Caliban's soft chuckle was swallowed by the darkness. "I haven't forgotten, Kai. Nor could I ever."

"You say that, but the hostility—"

"You have earned it," Caliban said with lethal calm, "don't pretend otherwise."

Malakai swallowed against the lump in his throat, the effort of this conversation dragging on the reserves of his strength. He scooted closer to his brother, not wanting his voice to carry in the cave. "I know you think me the villain in your story, Caliban, but I—"

"Spare me, Kai. I have no interest in your false apologies."

Rising on his elbows, Malakai brought his face less than a foot from his brother's. "I wasn't going to offer you an apology. I know it wouldn't mean anything to you. I just…" Malakai's words trailed off, his strength and confidence waning as his fatigue set in.

The dripping of water and snoring resumed, and Malakai again resigned himself to the noise. He still wasn't sure what his intentions were with his attempt at a conversation with Caliban, but he was no more at ease now than he was several minutes ago. Flipping on his back, he stared at the cave ceiling, though he couldn't make anything out in the darkness. He shuddered to think of the things lurking there. The beasts slithering and crawling in the shadows, waiting for the moment to strike. He turned again, blowing out a frustrated breath. How he wished he were anywhere else but here. He wan—

"What were you going to say?"

Malakai's mind ceased spiraling for a heartbeat as he turned back to his brother, raising up onto his arm once more.

Gesturing toward him, Caliban continued, "Earlier. What were you going to say?"

Licking his lips, Malakai stared at his brother, trying to read Caliban's face in the darkness. Malakai only ever saw what their lives could have been had the King not taken them once. It was just a flash of a future that he struggled to remember now—but there had been a whole other life destined for them, one they would never know.

Malakai blinked once.

Twice.

Then said, "We were children when we were brought to the palace, and I can't help but think that if we had been afforded the chance at a normal childhood...if we had been raised by our parents, that we might have been—"

"Friends?" Caliban offered.

Malakai swallowed. "Precisely."

Nodding slowly, Caliban leaned back on the ground, his gaze fixed upward. Taking his cue, Malakai rested back on the pack, his eyes again finding the gloom lurking above. Sleepiness finally settled over him, slowly dragging him beneath the waves. But before sleep claimed him wholly, Caliban whispered into the dark.

"I think we might have even become true brothers."

Chapter Sixty Six

Brander's snoring was going to be the death of Kasper. He tried to remain close to the others, but the noise was deafening—echoing off the stone walls and burrowing into his tensed muscles. Kasper worked his jaw, attempting to loosen it, but to no avail. Keeping watch this close to the others was only serving to further his agitation, so he commanded the quartz statue—a being whose existence still perplexed him—to stay with Lady Hera until he returned. Kasper may have still harbored resentment over the half-truths that the Lady had given him, but he couldn't very well leave her unprotected, and it was clear that Cal's magic wasn't entirely effective on its own, so this was the alternative.

Flexing his fingers, he steadied his breathing as he moved further from the others. Ordinarily, it would be dangerous and ill-advised to wander off from the group, but he needed some distance from them. Besides, Kasper was more than capable of looking after himself. His magic was the only one that was reliable, and he could handle himself against whatever creature threatened him. His peace of mind was crucial, given he was now being bombarded with everyone else's emotions.

They may have thought they were doing a decent job of keeping their concerned—and somewhat frightened looks—to themselves, but Kasper felt their apprehension. Their emotions pulsed off them in waves, making a throb form in his temples. He blew out a breath and massaged the soreness. He needed mental clarity and strength if they were going to survive this, and distance seemed like the best way to achieve that. But worse than that was the way Lady Hera had looked at him. The trepidation, bordering on fear, had sobered him up quickly. It was almost enough to make Kasper throw his remaining crystals aside and refuse to use his magic again.

Almost.

But the sheer amount of power that Kasper now had at his finger-tips, the control and strength—there was no surrendering that. He had spent his life in the shadows of his brothers' magic, the nearly limitless well of their abilities that made them so feared and revered. Was it such a bad thing that Kasper was now experiencing just a fraction of their power? If Lady Hera's reaction to him was to be believed, then yes, but Kasper had to admit that the power coursing through him, the control and assuredness that it brought, was heady. His brothers might finally see him as an equal and not a child to be set aside and ignored.

The small part of him that still governed his morals warned against the allure of power. What if this influx of potency to his magic made his cursed gems more deadly? Would sacrificing his soul, and likely the love and respect of others, be worth the power?

Kasper wasn't sure he was ready to face that answer yet.

Ambling further into the gloom, he welcomed its silence and tran-quility. He liked that the only sounds were the shuffling of his feet and his steady breathing. He had no idea how long he traveled, but he wanted an escape from contemplating his own mortality, so he walked and walked and walked. Kasper's eyes slowly adjusted to the darkness surrounding him and he realized with a jolt that the cave walls had crystals embedded in them, dull and lifeless in the shadows. They dot-ted the ceiling, like lackluster stars in the sky, and continued down into the cave until Kasper's strained eyes could no longer detect their shapes in the darkness.

He stepped closer to the one encrusted in the wall immediately to his left. Lifting a hand, he brushed his fingers over its rough edges. Immediately, the crystal glowed a soft pink. Kasper staggered back a step, his heart kicking up in his chest. This island was full of traps and dangers, and Kasper was sure he had just triggered one. He waited for the floor and walls to start shaking, or for bolts to fly from hidden compartments, but everything remained still and as it was.

Glancing around, he allowed his pulse time to recover as he came to terms with the fact that nothing was amiss. Kasper swallowed against the dryness in his throat and mustered the courage to step back up to the wall, where the crystal still glowed faintly. He briefly looked down the tunnel he had walked, waiting for someone to be alerted to his actions, but again—nothing happened. Between Kasper's new awareness of the world around him and the quartz creature remaining on watch, he felt a modicum of comfort that everyone was alright. Kasper didn't waste another moment as he reached up and pressed his hand to another lifeless crystal.

It glowed instantly, emanating an emerald light. Pressing onward, he dragged his hand along the wall, lighting the crystals. It wasn't long before the cave was illuminated by the glittering gems, casting an array of colors around, ranging from pink to green to orange to blue—all beautiful, brilliant, and breathtaking. A faint hum filled the air, persistent enough that Kasper was compelled to walk further into the cave.

His concerns and worries began to fade away, slowly drowned out by the humming that grew louder with each step he took down the sloping tunnel. He refrained from touching any more crystals, but they lit up all the same. Kasper needed to know what was at the end of the cave and where it led. His pace grew more frantic as the crystals grew brighter, and the humming changed to a sing-songy melody that called to Kasper's soul. It was a song he had never heard, but it spoke to him nonetheless. The gems embedded in the walls and ceilings ebbed in their brightness, pulsing in time with his rapidly increasing pulse. Whatever was at the end of the cave, Kasper was meant to find it.

It was hidden away *for* him, and would only answer *to* him.

The singing had grown so loud that Kasper's footfalls and breathing were lost to it—swallowed up in the ethereal song.

The song that was the end and beginning of everything—the first and last breath, the sunrise and sunset, the birth and death of a thousand worlds. Kasper was utterly consumed with reckless abandon. Never had he been so free and yet so guided in his life. His purpose, his future, lay at the end of the cave. Hurrying, his feet moved of their own accord and only stopped when the singing ended and the light blazing from the gems suddenly winked out.

Kasper's hungry gaze swept around the room, unable to comprehend the world that had opened up around him.

Kasper never had a real home, not once in his life. But staring at the towering, glowing crystal cavern, he finally understood what that word meant. The echoing song of the cosmos around him, the unburdened weightlessness he wasn't sure he had ever felt, and the understanding that the universe was not some ambivalent, uncaring force—but the pulsing beat of life.

Kasper's mouth went dry. His blood pumped so quickly through him that his head swam, and his legs went boneless. Swaying and stumbling, he was drunk on the sheer amount of energy and power that vibrated through the cavern. His vision cleared for just a moment, and a crystal structure—a palace—took shape before him. His breath caught in his throat. His heart leapt—

The world went out from under him.

Chapter Sixty Seven

Brander's eyes flew open, blinking furiously in the cave's dim light. Years of training and instinct flooded his muscles, and he immediately shifted to an upright position. He looked around, eyes flitting toward the Princess and scanning the cavern for any sign of danger. The statue that Kasper commanded still stood in the center of them. Its glow was diminished from what it was before he had fallen asleep, but it still provided enough light that he made out the slumbering forms of the others.

The statue still kept vigil, its featureless face staring out into the gloom. Brander relaxed a fraction, leaning back against the wall. Going back to sleep wasn't an option; years of going days without rest were too ingrained in him to override. Besides, he wanted to be awake to keep watch. He may have overcome some of his distrust and prejudices toward the brothers, but that did not eliminate *all* of his reservations.

Brander prepared himself for the ache that was certain to have settled into his bones while sleeping on the unforgiving packed earth floor of the cave. But when he eased himself up from the ground, nothing hurt. His bones did not bark, nor did his joints protest. Brander further tested the waters by rolling his ankle, which he broke when he was twenty. Not a flicker of pain as he turned and stretched the bones that never healed quite right.

Standing, he was careful not to make too much noise as he surveyed the others. The Princess was curled on her side, facing Finnley. Their breathing synced as their chests rose and fell at a steady rate. Glancing at the twins, he noted that their backs were pressed against each other, and their breathing was also constant and heavy.

The statue remained, still producing a soft light that allowed Brander to see a few feet ahead. The darkness in the cave was so absolute that it rivaled The Ether. In that perpetual storm, there had at least been lightning that occasionally illuminated his surroundings, but here in the cave, there was nothing. The darkness seemed to breathe with them, rising and falling in an unvarying rhythm. Brander squinted against the dark, trying to determine where Kasper kept watch, but he gleaned nothing.

Moving further into the shadows, his hand hovered above the hilt of his blade. The opaque gloom rapidly gobbled the light from the statue, leaving Brander blind. Still, he persisted—he was a soldier trained by the greatest army on the continent, and he could master his apprehension. Kasper wouldn't have gone far from the others; Brander was sure of it, but as the darkness engulfed him, he lost all sense of direction. His confidence waned, but he continued walking. Time, if it even passed normally here, had lost all meaning. He persevered, but his eyes never adjusted, and the oppressive sensation of the darkness never abated. Brander's pace slowed to a crawl. Maybe Kasper had gone the other way, back toward the mouth of the cave. Perhaps he had gone to ensure the monkeys or some other horrid beast hadn't followed them. Brander came to a halt, his own breathing and heartbeat the only sound he discerned in the cave. His commanders had beat most of Brander's fears out of him long ago, but one had always remained. One that Brander had fought to keep under wraps, even while confined in the cramped cabin aboard the Umbra.

The undetectable walls around him began to close in, pushing tighter to Brander. The air in the cave, already damp and thick with the subtly sweet stench of rot, pressed in on him, stealing his breath. Twisting, Brander was eager to return to the light, where he would confirm that the cave walls weren't narrowing and he wouldn't be crushed to death. Kasper's magic allowed him to sense his surroundings, so he was likely fine. He didn't need Brander following after him. But if Brander didn't get air, light, or space, he wasn't sure *he* would be alright. Rocks skittered and echoed in his wake, but Brander couldn't be bothered to care, not when the walls were still steadily coming in.

In

In

In

How far had he gone? Had he somehow turned down another tunnel unwittingly? The Necromancer had said that the cave continued to slope downward, but he had not mentioned whether other paths branched off of the main one. Brander's breath caught in his throat. His pulse thrummed at a dizzying speed. Picking up his pace, he broke into a sprint.

In

In

In

The walls pressed further. The floor of the cave rose up. Brander flung out his hands, his skin catching and ripping on the rough ground. The sharp scent of iron filled the air. Something wet dripped from Brander's palms. His vision doubled. His chest was too tight, too constricted to suck in a proper breath. He willed himself to focus, and he managed to scramble back to his feet. If he could get to the light, he could assure himself that all would be well. If he could only see the space around him. If—

Suddenly, the light of the statue came into focus, and Brander nearly wept at the sight. His pace remained frantic until the blurry outlines of his companions appeared. He stumbled again, but managed to keep his footing as the light washed over him, chasing away the shadows that clung to him. His lungs burned with the effort, and a metallic taste filled his mouth. His vision blurred, and he fell to his hands and knees, desperate to regain control of himself. Pain flared in his hands, but it barely registered.

"Brander!" a voice called out to him, but it was muffled and far away. Black spots danced in his vision. A wave of nausea rolled through him—threatening to claim him.

Chapter Sixty Eight

"**B**rander!" Rhea screamed, her knees protesting as she fell to them before her guard. She pressed a shaking hand to his forehead, swearing under her breath.

"He's cold and clammy." Rhea turned toward the others as they skittered to a halt behind her and said, "Something's wrong—an infection, or poison. Where is Kasper?"

"He's gone." Cal said, sleep clinging to his voice in a way that made Rhea's stomach flop.

She shook her head, forcing herself to focus. "What do you mean he's gone?"

"I mean, he's not here." Cal said, crossing his arms over his chest.

Rhea froze. Her mind pulled her in a hundred different directions, but her body could not execute any of them. Blinking, she bit the inside of her cheek, forcing herself to take a course of action. Finally, she turned back to Brander, who was still far too pale and trembling.

"Brander, did something happen? Did something take Kasper?" Brander's pupils were blown wide, a vacant expression limned his features, but he managed a small shake of his head. Groaning, Rhea stood abruptly and hooked her hands behind her neck. "Just as soon as you think everything is calming down, it all gets ripped apart again."

She began pacing, needing to move—needing to do *something*.

"Just settle down. We'll find him." Cal said.

Whirling on him, Rhea narrowed her eyes. "Settle down? We have lost our only reliable guide on this island, and Brander is *sick*—"

"Brander is fine." Finnley cut in.

Turning toward her, Rhea's face was fixed in disbelief as she gestured toward her guard. "Does he *look* fine?"

Finnley tilted her head, her face impassive, her auburn braid sliding over her shoulder. "He's having a panic attack. It'll pass."

Brander made a grunting noise, and Rhea turned to find that he was easing himself back on his haunches.

"Panic attack?" She asked, her gaze wearily pinned on him like he was an insect, or a helpless animal.

"Crew would get them sometimes. Usually, they were brought on by something that frightened them."

Brander cut his eyes away from the Princess, his pallor being replaced with pink. Rhea stayed still as he managed to draw himself up to his feet, even as a tremor worked its way through his body. Brander glanced at them all, but his gaze settled on Finnley as he said quietly, "Tight spaces have always…unnerved me." His voice shook ever so slightly, but he pressed on. "I awoke to find that Kasper was gone, so I went further into the cave to try and find him, but I—" Brander shook his head and clenched his jaw.

"It's alright, Brander." Rhea said softly. She reached for him, but Brander stepped away, refusing to meet her eyes. Pressing her lips together, Rhea made no further attempt to comfort him—clearly, he didn't want it.

"We need to get moving. If something has happened to Kasper, then we can't afford to waste any more time." Cal said with indifference as he shouldered his pack.

Rhea wanted to protest. Brander was obviously still recovering from the episode as he clenched and unclenched his hands, but perhaps moving on and letting Brander sort it out on his own terms was the best course of action. Walking back to where her few items rested, she reached for them, the light of the statue remaining bright behind her. Her fingers moved deftly over her belongings as she made a mental checklist of her things. Turning, she noted that Kasper had not taken his own belongings. She tried to swallow past the apprehensive lump in her throat as she moved toward his items and began collecting them as well. Chewing her lip, she turned and stepped around the statue that kept vigil behind her.

"How will we find him, Cal? Kai's sight is not reliable enough."

Cal's eyes glittered with amusement. "Interesting," he murmured, leaning back against the cave wall. Planting one booted foot up and crossing his arms over his chest, the side of his mouth curled upward as he peered at her with unnerving attentiveness.

"What is?" Rhea asked, eyebrows raised in annoyance.

Still grinning, Cal pointed down the dark path before her. "Walk a few feet that way."

Narrowing her eyes, Rhea crossed her arms. "Why?"

"Humor me." Cal requested, his eyes traveling the length of her body. Rhea paused for a moment, silently debating whether she wanted to heed Cal's request. This was certainly not the time for games, and she had half a mind to remind him of that. But, knowing Cal, he wouldn't relent until she did what he asked, so she heaved a sigh and reluctantly did as he bade.

The statue followed her every step.

Whirling on her heel, Rhea stared wide-eyed at the crystal creature. Her eyes never left its blank face as she asked, "Why is it following me?"

Cal gave a dark chuckle as he approached Rhea, her toes curling in her boots in response. "My dear little brother is so chivalrous, leaving his crystalline companion to be your own personal guard."

Rhea's mouth fell open.

Breezing past her, Cal gestured to the awaiting gloom. "You control our light source, and I suspect you can even give it commands. Why don't you play Queen for us and give it an order?"

Rhea and Brander stilled at Cal's flippant words. There was no way he knew the truth, right? Surely, if he did, he would have made that known. Cal hid his true feelings well, for the most part, but something of that magnitude would certainly register. Rhea swallowed and lifted her chin, turning her attention back to the statue.

"Lead us to Kasper." The statue had no features to indicate that it had heard her demand, but the light in it flared once before it turned, marching off into the awaiting darkness.

Finnley gave a low whistle. "I had my doubts on whether that would actually work."

The statue disappeared down the path, its light reflecting faintly on the crystals embedded in the walls. Rhea, Cal, and Kai wasted no time stepping in behind the statue, but Finnley and Brander hung back.

"Are you alright?" Finnley murmured. Though Rhea didn't mean to eavesdrop, she was also invested in Brander's well-being, and he obviously wasn't keen on sharing it with her. Brander's answer was lost to their echoing footsteps and the water dripping in the cave, but Rhea heard Finnley reply, "I get it. I used to be afraid of water. For a while, I refused to take baths for fear that I would drown."

Rhea slowed her steps, ever-so-slightly.

Brander cleared his throat. "Then why become a pirate? Being comfortable around water seems to be a base-level requirement."

"Something else made it look like the safer option."

Rhea wanted to pause and lean in. She wanted to know more about Finnley's experiences. More specifically, she wanted to know what would scare Finnley so much that running away was the better choice.

Blowing out a breath, Brander said, "I take it you're telling me this to say that I can overcome my fear, conquer it even."

Rhea's ears strained in the reverberating cave.

"Fear like that ever truly leaves us."

Brander was silent, and Rhea released some of the tension in her shoulders—a product of trying to listen in on a conversation that was definitely not meant for her. Rhea blinked, focusing on the task at hand, but Finnley spoke again, drawing her attention once more.

"But," Finnley said softly, "I think it helps to know you're not the only one with fears. This life often forces us to pretend we're untouchable and infallible. Especially around the likes of those magic wielders, and that can be isolating. I've guessed at the life you've lived, and I just wanted you to know that your fear doesn't make you weak. It just makes you human."

"Being human might not be enough. It might get—"

A cough–Malakai's–drowned out Brander's words, and Rhea sent him a withering look, though her face was cloaked in shadows.

"—anyone that's made it out of this life alive." Finnley said resolutely. Brander's steps faltered, and Rhea's did too as she struggled to hear his reply.

"You're very wise. I hope you'll be comfortable enough to tell your story someday."

A ghost of a laugh echoed softly from Finnley. "You might be waiting a long time for that, guard dog."

A warmth spread through Rhea's chest—comforting at first, but then it slipped into her limbs, leaving them flushed and tingling. She wanted Brander to be safe and happy. She was glad he found someone to share his fears and hopes with, someone he could rely on to understand him given his particular life experiences—even if it wasn't Rhea. He saw her like a daughter—a child meant to be shielded from the worst of the world. She was grateful for that, but wished he would allow her to be there for him. But if Finnley provided that outlet, then Rhea would make her peace with it.

But she was powerless against the ache of rejection that burned in her chest.

Chapter Sixty Nine

hea stayed close to the crystal figure; she had no desire to eavesdrop further on Brander and Finnley. The creature's presence was a comfort, especially in the cave's oppressive darkness, easing some of the apprehension that lingered in her chest. Kasper had keyed the creature to her, and she suspected it would only get so far away from her. She had to remain close lest they waste any more time finding Kasper. It also happened to be a convenient excuse not to be next to Cal. The tunnel had narrowed enough that only two were able to walk beside one another comfortably, leaving her to pair off with the statue.

Despite the creature being made entirely of stone and nearly eight feet tall, it moved silently through the cave. Rhea wondered why Kasper would choose to leave the statue to her. She tried to convince herself that it was purely from a practical standpoint. He was angry with his brothers, and she was the reason they were on this island. Perhaps he thought it was wisest to protect her, lest they not get their reward for their work—but that wasn't the truth, and Rhea knew it.

It was precisely why she was avoiding Cal and his weighted looks. She did not have the time to field their affections. Nor the energy to untangle and unravel the complexities of their relationships. Once she chose, once she made it clear who her heart longed for, who it had always wanted—there was no going back. They had both tried to force the subject and attempted to wring an answer from her, but she had put them off. She cursed how single-minded men often were, especially concerning their hearts and desires. Surely, they saw the need to prioritize? That there was more at stake than just their wants?

A light breeze lifted the tendrils of her hair, momentarily stirring the stagnant, damp air of the cave. The darkness–thick and unrelenting shadows–stirred just beyond the reaches of the light. The darkness had always beckoned to her, called her. And now it sang the song of her desires. Maybe she—

No.

Rhea shook her head softly. She had to stay focused. If she allowed her wants to guide her, she would put everything at risk. Caliban may harbor affection for her now, but if he knew who she was...

It wasn't worth the risk.

Or maybe they *did* understand what was at stake, and that was why they were so intent on resolving it. If they could sort out how they felt about her, and she would be able to do the same, then perhaps their focus and efforts would be applied better elsewhere. If she had been able to be honest with them both, then maybe the unwanted tension would have stopped.

Or it would all blow up in her face.

Tell him, tell him, tell him, the darkness seemed to whisper.

Rhea forced herself to keep her pace even. She refused to let her inner war register with the others or slow their progress. The shadows around them pulsed—breathing in time with a certain someone. Rhea shook her head; she couldn't afford to get distracted. They needed to find Kasper and the treasure. After that, maybe she would address the ache that burned in her chest every time she looked at Kasper. Or how her breath caught in her throat when she looked at Caliban.

The shadows curled at the edge of the ring of light the statue produced, swirling more of the still air. She was certain they pressed closer, inching toward her, but that was ridiculous. Pursing her lips, she fought the urge to look back at him. What harm would it do to be honest? In truth, it would likely ease her burdens and allow her to better focus on securing Izor's Lamp. Rhea lifted her chin, confident in her resolve.

Tell him, tell him, tell him, the shadows beckoned.

She slowed her steps, aiming to take her place next to Caliban, but movement in the corner of her eye halted her. The shadows ebbed and flowed around her, caressing her and—

Whirling on Caliban, Rhea hissed, "Are you using your shadows on me?"

Amusement twinkled in Caliban's eyes, a corner of his mouth turned up. Shadows curled around him, temporarily obscuring his features.

"Why? Is it working?" Rhea balled her hand up into a fist and stepped toward Caliban. Feral delight darkened his face. "Come on, my Lady, give in to your base nature. Let those wanton desires loose. I know you have them."

Rhea sneered at him, hated him—hated that she *wanted* to give into them—and said, "Is that so?"

Caliban stepped closer, and Rhea was powerless to stop from inhaling his sandalwood, salt, and...lily scent. The sudden and unexpected smell of lilies startled her, and she moved to take a step back, but Caliban reached for her, halting her.

"It is, and you want to know why?" Caliban whispered, his face close enough to her that she saw the hints of gold in his brown eyes. "Because we're alike, you and I. Cut from the same dark, twisted cloth, no matter how much you protest it. That's why my shadows seek you out and why I..." his voice trailed off as his stare dropped from her eyes to her mouth. His tongue darted out from between his parted lips and wetted them.

Swallowing, she fought the urge to look away from the intensity of his gaze. She held her ground, refusing to give him any further satisfaction. She lifted her chin, and his eyes returned to hers. They held each other's unrelenting gaze.

"We are nothing alike." she ground out.

An infuriating smirk came to Caliban's lips. "I love when you do that."

Warmth licked up Rhea's spine at his words, at the heat in them, but she pushed back against the rising tide of lust and said through clenched teeth, "Release me."

Caliban narrowed his eyes. "I will. As soon as you admit that we are similar."

"I have nothing in common with a monster like you." Rhea snapped as she wrenched herself out of Caliban's grip. To his credit, he didn't fight her, even as she continued to glare daggers at him. Rhea had to remember herself and her mission. She had no time to get entangled with a man like Caliban—no matter how much she was drawn to him.

Flashing her a wicked smile, he said, "Keep lying to yourself, but eventually, the truth will come out."

The flames that Caliban had stoked within her banked at his words. He had no idea how close to the truth he actually was. No matter how much Caliban claimed to want her–to understand her–he had no idea who she really was.

And if he found out…

Pursing her lips, she scolded, "We need to stop wasting time and find Kasper." She turned on her heel and marched forward, the crystal statue keeping pace. Rhea kept her jaw clenched and her fist tight at her side. She needed to hold on to her anger, for it was a far better emotion than the mind-clouding desire that overtook her every time Caliban looked at her. Anger would keep her alert.

Anger would keep her alive.

* * * *

Being angry was exhausting.

Rhea's feet caught on the ground more times than she cared to admit. She rubbed her at eyes—the grains of sand that she was *certain* resided there remained.

The others weren't faring much better. Kai was muttering to himself and gripping the crystal Kasper had given him so tightly in his hands that blood dripped from between his fingers. Brander's wearisome eyes looked hollow as they continuously scanned the cave walls and floors as if he expected them to close in at any moment. Finnley, well, Finnley's sneer was a permanent fixture on her face, but from the slump of her shoulders, Rhea knew that fatigue loomed. Only Caliban seemed unperturbed by their circumstances. He walked with the same self-assured stride that he always did. There wasn't an ounce of fear or dread present in his expression. Rhea surmised that a creature born of nightmares and darkness must be at home on an island crafted of the same terrors. But Rhea did not concern herself with Caliban anymore. He may have gifted her a blade and aided her at times, but she owed him nothing and she couldn't afford to let him distract her.

Izor's Lamp was her priority.

Her throne was her priority.

Her *people* were her priority.

Not Caliban.

Lifting her chin, she repeated that to herself over and over and over again. Until there were no other thoughts in her mind. But the longer they walked, the more unsure of everything Rhea became. What if the statue only went this way because Rhea thought they should go this way? What if Kasper was gravely injured, or—Forgotten forbid–dead? The more worrisome Rhea's thoughts became, the quicker her pace grew. Or maybe it was just the ringing in her ears that was making her anxious. Whatever the case, she found herself nearly jogging, heading blindly into the awaiting darkness of the cave.

"Lady Hera, is something the matter?" Brander said, appearing at her elbow. Concern replaced the wariness that hung about his eyes.

Blinking, Rhea shook her head. She glanced down the tunnel into the gloom. "I don't know. I just–I thought—" She took a breath and shook her head. "No, let's just keep going." she said, her tone sharp.

"Yes, your Highness." Caliban called out from behind, the insolence in his tone digging into Rhea's bones. She didn't dignify his taunt with a response and instead squared her shoulders and pressed on.

She *was* going to be Queen one day. She had to build her resolve and rise above the goading and disrespect she would face once she ascended. They continued on in silence. She was *so* tired. So exhausted that she closed her eyes, just wanting to rest them for a moment. Shutting out the input of one of her senses gave her a modicum of peace as her feet continued to carry her forward. She took several deep breaths, inhaling and exhaling. She counted her heartbeats and thought of nothing but—

"Hera!" Caliban yelled from behind her.

Rhea's eyes flew open, and she stumbled over a precipice, falling straight down toward a crystal ravine. She flung out her arms in a futile attempt to stop herself from careening toward the ground. This couldn't be where she met her end. She had so much left to accomplish. She had to save her people and assume her birthright. She had to—

The world stopped streaming past her.

Her screams broke off abruptly as she began to float upward, the world moving in reverse. Jagged and unforgiving cliffside slid past her, but her mind struggled to make sense of it all. Her heart was beating so hard. Her stomach continued to tumble even as the edge she had stepped off of came back into view. Her legs shook with such violence that she collapsed before her feet even touched the ground. Bile burned in her throat, forcing its way up into her mouth. She fell onto her hands and knees as her stomach cramped and retched. Tears stung her eyes— nothing but water and stale bread coming up. She choked and gagged until her body was utterly spent, and nothing but saliva dripped from her mouth. She managed to draw herself up onto her knees as strong arms enveloped her. Rhea leaned into it, coming to terms with the fact that she had almost died.

Again.

Her mind buzzed, reprimanding her for her carelessness. She was too tired–too ragged–to take it all in. Sucking in a breath, her ravaged throat seized with the effort, sending another course of tremors through her. A chin pressed into the top of her head, a hand ran the length of her back, and a voice murmured softly into her hair.

"I've got you. You're safe now. I've got you."

Rhea didn't have to look to know that Caliban had saved her and now comforted her. She was so tired. Tired of walking. Tired of being scared. Tired of fighting—literally and metaphorically. She just wanted to put everything right in the world and rest.

Caliban held her for several minutes until her trembling had mostly subsided. When she finally retreated from his arms, she noted that the others–even Brander–had found other things to pay attention to, for which she was immensely grateful. Caliban held her gaze, a silent question in them.

Are you ready?

No, she wanted to say. She wanted to stay in his arms and forget that a nation depended on her, and that they still needed to find Kasper. Reluctantly, she climbed to her feet. Caliban's hands slipped from her back to under her arms—still supporting her. His eyes remained trained on her face even as she turned and looked toward the ledge she had blindly tumbled over. Heat licked at her cheeks, but her arms were alarmingly chilled.

She turned back to Caliban, expecting his concern and care to be supplanted with a teasing smile, but he wasn't looking at her anymore. Her brows furrowed as she glanced to where his eyes were fixed. Her mouth immediately fell open, and she went wholly still as she beheld the crystal palace.

Chapter Seventy

Kasper's blood buzzed with magic. It was like the song had been injected directly into his very soul. His boots hardly made a sound as he meandered down the rose-pink crystal corridors. His eyes drank up the sights, trying to catalog every fixture, archway, and wall.

Continuing on in silence, he was unsure what had called him to this place, but certain that he was meant to be there. He passed through the fifth archway he'd encountered so far, though they were all identical to one another. Kasper knew exactly where he was and how to return to the entrance if he so desired, but he had no such inclination, especially not as he approached the sixth archway, this one closed off by two large crystalline doors. He had no way of knowing that placing his hands on the doors would unlock them, but he knew it to be true all the same. The crystal warmed and flared with an internal light as he pressed against them. They gave way beneath him, swinging open to reveal—a throne room.

The breath in his chest left him in a whoosh, and he nearly fell to his knees. His magic rose, throbbing and pulsing—desperate to be unleashed in this place that seemed to be crafted specifically for him. Kasper managed to keep his feet beneath him as he ambled forward, aiming for the gleaming throne at the far side of the room. He wasted no time climbing the dais and sinking into the throne—*his* throne, he decided. Sighing, he surveyed his kingdom, and concluded that he wanted to remain here for all of his days.

Chapter Seventy One

Rhea was woefully familiar with opulence and excess. Her home was a palace that boasted over a thousand rooms and had enough riches to feed a thousand families for centuries. But even that knowledge could not have prepared her for the spellbinding grandeur that was the crystal palace. Rose-pink spires soared up so high that Rhea had to crane her head backward just to try and see the tops, but even then, they were lost to the shadowy reaches of the ceiling of the cavern. With its pink and pearlescent structures, the palace was sprawling, gobbling up any exposed terrain on the cavern floor. Rhea suspected that if she were to go inside the palace, she would find a labyrinth of rooms that rivaled—no, *surpassed*—her own.

She was certain Kasper was nearby. He had to be. Rhea looked around, searching for a way down from the cliff they perched on, save for the one she had already tried. Taking measured steps around the edge, she walked back and forth on the expanse, which was no more than five feet wide.

"Fin," Caliban called to his second in command, "toss me that rope from my pack."

Hope sparked in her chest as she turned toward Caliban. He caught a bundle of rope no thicker than an inch in diameter. He began unwinding it, foot after foot until it was unspooled on the ground.

"I fear that's not quite long enough." Brander said, peering over the cliff's edge.

Rhea's heart sank as she looked back at the rope and moved closer to the edge, standing next to Brander.

"Careful, Princess," he murmured in her ear, "that drop is nearly sixty feet." Rhea's stomach fell to her feet. She had almost fallen that far. If it hadn't been for Caliban and his shadows—

"Your shadows!" she exclaimed, turning back to Caliban, who was looping the rope around his elbow from his wrist.

Snapping his fingers, Cal nodded. "Good thinking, my Lady."

"What are we doing?" Kai asked. No one responded; instead, Brander and Caliban found a place to secure the rope. Kai came and stood beside Rhea and said, "What is the plan?"

Rhea restrained herself from making some glib remark about his inability to see the future. "They're—"

"What? Can't you just glean their plans from looking into the future?" Finnley asked, appearing beside Kai. She covered her mouth in feigned modesty. "Oh, I forgot. You can't do that anymore."

Dropping her head, Rhea stifled her smile. It was a low blow, certainly, but given everything Kai had done, it wasn't wholly undeserved. Rhea snuck a peek at Kai and found him unbothered by Finnley. Kai stared ahead, watching Brander, Caliban, and now Finnley working to secure the rope to a sturdy-looking rock.

"You get used to it." Kai said, breaking the silence.

"What?"

"The taunts. The jeering and snide comments. You get used to it."

"Still, doesn't it start to wear on you? Always being cajoled?"

Shrugging, Kai said, "I suppose it can be wearisome, but that's what happens when the King sets you apart from everyone else." He turned to look at her with that unnerving gaze he shared with his twin. The one that made her skin itch—like he was *seeing* her. "You'll know the feeling soon enough."

A muscle ticked in Rhea's jaw. "Is that a prophecy?"

Kai smiled. "No. Just an observation."

Rhea started to contest, but Brander called out, "We've got it. Now we decide who goes first."

"I will." Kai offered, a brilliant, over-the-top smile pasted on his face. He was already stepping to the edge, his hand waiting for the rope. Rhea watched the others exchange looks, before Caliban approached his brother and handed over the rope.

Crossing his arms, Brander asked, "Why?"

Kai's bright smile never wavered as he said, "I mean, I have no fighting skills, no healing abilities, and I've lost my powers. I'm the most expendable, right? That's certainly what everyone thinks, so who better to go down first than the least valuable."

Rhea's face heated with shame. She sometimes forgot that Kai wasn't stupid, or as oblivious as everyone treated him. One didn't survive in her father's court for as long as Kai did and be a simpleton. But no one protested Kai's claim, not even as he started climbing down the cliff face. Rhea got as close as she dared to watch his progress. Mercifully, the cliff face was conducive to climbing, allowing Kai to find footholds so he was able to use the rope to create tension for his descent. It wasn't long before the rope ended, and the ground loomed thirty feet below.

"Now what?" Kai called up, his voice echoing around the vast cavern until it doubled over itself.

Leaning over the edge, Caliban cupped his hands around his mouth and shouted, "Now you jump!"

Kai shifted so was perched on the wall. Pebbles and dust tumbled beneath him. "Funny, brother. An excellent jape, really, but, uh, what is the plan from this point?"

Caliban rolled his eyes and called out again, "Jump, Kai. I'll use my shadows to slow your fall."

Kai moved again, and more dirt cascaded in his wake. Glancing up, dirt and sweat streaked Kai's normally, kempt face and hair. "Are you sure you couldn't just float me down?"

Shaking his head, Caliban said, "The shadows aren't that sturdy. You'll just have to trust me."

Looking down once more, Kai muttered, "Yes, that's what I was afraid of."

Rhea licked her lips and shouted, "It's going to be alright, Kai. Just have faith."

Kai lifted his shoulders with a deep inhale. His muscles tensed, and he leapt from the wall, the rope fluttering behind him.

To Kai's credit, he didn't scream, not even as the ground came rushing toward him. Seconds passed, or maybe it was hours; either way, it felt far too long, and Caliban stood idly by, examining his nails—shadows still not summoned.

"Caliban." Rhea reprimanded, cutting her eyes toward him.

He slid his eyes to her and then rolled them. He raised an indolent hand. A tide of darkness rose up to meet Kai's plummeting body, a mere ten feet before he would have splattered on the ground.

Rhea turned back to Caliban and narrowed her eyes. "Cutting it a bit close, don't you think?"

Caliban shrugged. "I have to have a bit of fun, don't I?"

"I'll get you back for that!" Kai shouted from the cavern floor. "Just you wait!"

"Yeah, yeah, yeah..." Caliban said with a wave of his hand and a subtle smile.

"You have better gotten *that* out of your system." Finnley muttered as she took up the rope and began her descent. Though she followed the same path as Kai, she didn't hesitate when she reached the end of it. She flew from the wall, and Caliban's shadows greeted her much more quickly than they did for his brother, who stood at the bottom of the cave, watching with crossed arms and a tapping foot. Brander went next, and Rhea tracked his progress until he disappeared into the awaiting darkness.

"You're up next, my Lady."

Rhea nodded, her hands trembling slightly as she took the rope and positioned herself with her back to the palace. Even with the coolness in the cave, sweat coated her palms and nape. She blew out a shaky breath as she gripped the rope tighter.

"Hey," Caliban said, drawing her attention away from what she was certain was her imminent death. There was a vulnerability to his gaze that made Rhea feel stripped bare before him. "I've got you. I won't let you fall."

Rhea wasn't sure her voice would work, so she nodded instead.

Mirroring her, Caliban said, "Go ahead."

As Rhea took a tentative step down the cliff face, the earthy scent of dirt was overwhelming.

"Now, lean back just enough to create some tension in the rope so you can use that leverage to control your descent."

"Alright..." she replied, her voice as shaky as she was.

Her hands slid down the rope at the same time that a bead of sweat dripped down her temple. The rock and dirt of the cliff shifted beneath her foot, some of it coming loose as she adjusted her position. She made small movements until her upper body was a foot from the wall, with her feet braced against the cliff face. All her muscles burned while she held her body weight, and sweat continued to coat her hands.

"Good," Caliban said from above, "now you can start to push off from the wall and slowly make your way down."

Rhea nodded. She could do this. She was the Heir to the greatest power on earth. She had withstood her father's abuses. She had survived The Ether. She would survive this.

Cautiously, she lifted a foot from the wall and shifted her weight. She loosened her grip on the rope just enough that gravity would pull her down, and she moved a foot down the wall. She unconsciously glanced down and immediately regretted it. Closing her eyes, she hugged the rope tight to her body. The rope swayed with its force, swinging her into the rock. Pain shot through her ribs and shoulder at the impact, but she held tight. Images of her near fall flashed through her mind. The ground rushed toward her. The sensation of weightlessness and the feeling of nausea it evoked threatened to overwhelm her.

"Hera! Come on, Hera, you can do this."

Rhea shook her head. She couldn't do it.

She couldn't.

She *couldn't—*

"Look at me, Hera. Please."

It was the 'please' that caught her attention. She had never heard him utter the word genuinely, only ever to mock someone. Lifting her head, her eyes burned with the threat of tears.

"You're stronger than you realize. You can do this."

Clenching her jaw, she nodded her reply. She took a moment to collect herself before she eased back off the wall, placing her feet into crevices on the cliff face and putting tension back into the rope.

"That's my girl." Caliban said softly.

Rhea ignored what those words did to her. She poured all of her energy into getting off of the godsforsaken wall. Caliban continued to murmur encouragement and directions as she descended the cliff. Her arms trembled as she worked to keep herself up, but she would see this through. She was still a good forty feet from the bottom; Finnley, Brander, and Kai were still specks beneath her, but the majority of her panic had subsided.

Caliban was right; she was stronger than she knew.

Rhea took a moment to look up at him and found him grinning down at her. Not smirking or teasing, but a genuine, open smile—like he had worn back at the palace when they were just children. She could look at that smile for the rest of her life, and she was helpless to stop the smile that formed on her face in response.

Shifting, Rhea opened her mouth to speak, but the words were cut off by a quake that rocked through the cavern. Rhea's eyes widened as the cliff face began shaking violently. The rope gave a sudden, jarring jolt, and her heart plummeted into her gut. Dust and small rocks rained down from the ceiling, pelting her shoulders, her hands, her face.

Her foot slipped.

She scrambled for a purchase, for anything to stop the inevitable, but her limbs were at their limit, and the world was still shaking vigorously around her. Her hands spasmed, slick with sweat and blood from the coarse fibers of the rope—her grip lost.

"Hera!" Caliban screamed for her as the last of her resolve dissipated, and she flailed backward.

Rhea's only thought as she fell to her death was that she wished he had known her true name.

Chapter Seventy Two

C al didn't think as he dove over the cliff's edge after Hera.

The wind tore at his clothes, but he gave it no thought as he willed his body to go faster, to fall faster.

All of his thoughts were of her and how close to death they had all come in the last few weeks. He couldn't leave this life without knowing how she felt against his skin and tasted on his lips.

Cal did not hesitate as he used his shadows to propel himself toward her, pushing his body faster toward the quickly approaching ground.

Hera's screams—soul-shattering and guttural—were scarcely heard over the wind roaring in his ears. Petrified fear was etched into her lovely features, and her ebony curls flew around her head wildly. Her arms were flung wide, and Cal knew what he had to do, if not to save them both, then at least her.

He willed his shadows to give him another boost, and this one put him within reach of Hera. He stretched his arm forward, and she swung hers near enough for him to take hold. He poured every ounce of strength he had into pulling her toward him—it was a homecoming. Soft, warm, and welcoming.

All the things Cal had denied himself in the last decade.

Then he spun.

He forced her to his chest, placing his back to the ground.

The ground that was feet away.

Not enough time to break his fall with his shadows.

Not enough time to save them both.

Not enough time.

Not enough—

Cal rented the air with a scream, summoning every bit of his magic to slow their fall. His awareness of the world narrowed to the scent of jasmine and lilies.

Lilies, the scent of his shadows, but also the scent of *her*.

Cal was pleased he had made that connection before he smashed into the earth.

He let the feel of her body–her head at his chest, and the rest of her cradled against him so that his body took the brunt of the impact–and her heavenly smell envelope him as he collided with the ground—

The world went dark.

Chapter Seventy Three

ebris coated every inch of Malakai. His eyes burned, and he coughed and sputtered, trying and failing to expel the dust from his body. He doubled over and retched, his stomach cramping with the effort to rid himself of the irritant.

Saliva dripped from Malakai's mouth. Reluctantly, he wiped it on his arm, turning his once-white sleeve into a disheartening shade of brown. He frowned at it, but resigned himself to the fact that his outfit was a lost cause.

"*Caliban!*" Princess Rhea screamed.

Turning toward the sound, Malakai's heart crawled up into his throat. Caliban lay in a crater on the ground, unmoving. Princess Rhea was astride him, her ear pressed to his chest. Her face was turned from him, but he knew the agony that was fixed in her features. Finnley appeared at her side, slipping her arms under the Princess and dragging Rhea from Caliban's body.

"Get off me!" Rhea bellowed, thrashing against Finnley.

"Get her!" Finnley yelled, and Brander reached for her, pulling the Princess tight to his body. Finnley dropped down next to Caliban and began pressing down on his chest. Malakai had seen a process like it when he and Kasper traveled with the caravan. A man, a sword swallower, had collapsed during his performance. His wife, the caravan's Healer, had been called, and she started pushing on his chest. A maneuver to get his heart going, Malakai had later learned. But Malakai had already known the man's fate; he had seen it a week prior when the sword swallower had come to him asking to have his fortune read. What Malakai would give now for the assurance he had then. He had no idea if the future he had seen weeks ago remained intact or if the wants and desires of his companions had shifted the outcome. No one's life was guaranteed—not even Caliban's.

Finnley moved with brutal efficiency, her lithe body going in some rhythm only she was privy to. Malakai knew, distantly, that he should do something, but his feet were rooted to the spot. He was a watcher, an observer. That was his role, his nature—never to intervene or alter the course of actions, lest you bring some horrible recompense back on oneself. If only Kasper were here. He was the doer, the healer—perhaps Malakai was entirely expendable. But that was his brother.

His *twin* lying in the dirt—still and unmoving.

Finnley moved toward Caliban's head. Tipping his chin up, she pressed her lips to his, and blew. Once. Twice. And then returned to her compressions. But it was useless, and that became clearer to Malakai the longer Finnley pushed on Caliban's chest, and the Princess screamed in her guard's arms.

A plan. An idea. Malakai's feet moved before he registered it. He stopped in front of Rhea and grabbed her face. The fact that she didn't bite him, or her guard squash him, spoke to the direness of the situation. Malakai poured every ounce of his strength into holding her still and yelled.

"Listen to me!"

Her thrashing lessened, and her wailing subsided. Tears streamed down her face, but a moment of clarity passed over her features.

Malakai held tight as he said, "Call for the statue, now. Will it to come to us. It might save him."

Rhea's lip quivered, and more tears spilled down her face. "But he's—"

Malakai squeezed, holding her in place. "I know, but do it now." Malakai looked to Brander and nodded. Brander's face was a mask of cool indifference, a soldier's expression, as he slowly placed the Princess back on the ground.

Wiping at her face, Rhea cleared her throat. Looking back up the cliff she and Caliban had plummeted from, she shouted, "Come to me."

The words had barely left the Princess's mouth before the crystal creature appeared in the air above them, falling toward the ground. Brander grabbed Rhea, and Malakai fell toward Finnley, a poor attempt to protect her from the statue's impact. Malakai braced. A *boom* resounded across the cave floor, momentarily shaking the world once more. Malakai raised his head in time to see Rhea break away from Brander and sprint to the statue that had landed not even ten feet to the left of where Caliban lay.

"Save him." she commanded, her voice broken and raw. And just as with her last directive, the statue moved instantly, closing the distance between it and Caliban.

Finnley started to scramble backward, but Malakai grabbed her. "Wait. It's going to need you."

"Me?" She said with incredulity.

He nodded, his plan coming together. The statue knelt down on the other side of Caliban and reached for his body.

"Grab the statue, amplify its power."

Finnley's eyes were wide. "That's insane. You have no idea—"

"We don't have time. Do it!" Malakai shouted, exerting more authority than he had ever mustered. Finnley flinched away from Malakai, and flashbacks of the past–her past–he had glimpsed all those weeks ago roared back to him. But they didn't have time for that. Because his twin was dying, possibly already dead.

Despite the fear radiating from Finnley, she reached for the creature, placing her hands on it at the exact moment it touched Caliban.

Light flared.

Malakai raised his arm to shield his eyes and turned away. Staring down at the ground, he prayed earnestly to every god he had ever heard of or read about that his plan would work. It was a long shot, but to do nothing was not an option. Agonizing seconds passed, and Malakai stared at the damp earth. Brander's boots. The shimmering crystal—anything but his brother's rigid form.

The light banked, and Malakai was pushed aside, the ground rising up to meet him. He hit the earth with a thud, but for once, he didn't lament over his ruined clothes. Turning, he found the Princess leaning over Caliban, her hands cupping his face. She reached up, brushing loose strands of hair from his forehead, and softly murmured, "Come back to us. Come back to me."

Holding his breath, Malakai waited for something—anything to happen.

Caliban's eyes flew open.

The tension rushed out of Malakai's body. He fell back against the ground and stared up at the ceiling, his limbs limp with relief. He placed a hand over his racing heart, willing his pulse to slow as he silently thanked the gods above for their mercy and kindness. His plan had worked. He had failed his brother before–too many times to count, really–but now, in this instance, he had saved him.

"I'm alright." Caliban assured.

Princess Rhea's words erupted in a broken sob. "You were dead."

"Maybe a little."

"You saved me."

Finnley appeared over top of Malakai, drawing his attention away from his brother and the Princess, and held out a hand toward him. Malakai didn't hesitate as he took it, but Finnley pushed back, holding him down in the dirt.

"Don't do that again." Finnley seethed, her eyes hot with rage.

Malakai didn't have to ask what she meant; he simply nodded and said, "Noted."

After Finnley pulled him up, Malakai set about dusting himself off. He glanced to where Caliban and Rhea still lay. Next to them was a pile of shattered crystals, presumably what was left of the crystal creature. Briefly, he mourned the loss of the statue, but he wagered that even Caliban would weigh it as a fair trade. Malakai glanced at the pair; Rhea was still holding his face, and Caliban had his hand on her cheek, his thumb gently stroking her skin.

"I told you that I had you." he said softly, not breaking eye contact.

Rhea laughed and pressed her forehead to Caliban's. Turning away, Malakai allowed them their privacy—as much as possible given the circumstances. Malakai hummed quietly as he moved to stand next to Brander and Finnley, who were looking toward the crystal palace.

Sliding his gaze to Malakai, Brander said, "I don't suppose you two could conjure up a vision about where Kasper is?"

Malakai pursed his lips. "Unfortunately, not. But I would bet all of my worldly possessions that he's in there."

"What makes you think that?" Finnley asked, her tone unusually pleasant.

"For whatever reason, this island seems particularly interested in Kasper. It stands to reason that it would lead Kasper to a place like this." Malakai had tried not to be irritated by that revelation earlier, even as the island had ceased its whispering, but perhaps it would work in their favor.

Tipping his head back, Makakai stared at the ostentatious spires looming overhead. In truth, Malakai had no desire to enter the palace, but it was standing between him and his future.

And that simply would not do.

* * * *

Holding his breath, Malakai waited for a beast or monster to intercept them as they crossed the threshold of the palace. Nothing was locked or guarded—there hadn't even been a door. No traps or alarms had sprung as they meandered through the quartz halls. Nothing adorned the walls, floors, or ceilings. There were only endless expanses of pink and iridescent crystals from which everything was crafted from.

Malakai appreciated the dedication to the monotone interior design choices. He loved to be styled in an all-white ensemble, but even he would embellish and accessorize with hints of gold or lapis lazuli. He craned his head back as they passed under a chandelier made entirely of quartz with no flames flickering from it. Even the sconces mounted on the walls were bare, as though the entire palace was constructed by someone who admired human craftsmanship, but had no need for things so antiquated as fire.

Like the quartz creature, the palace emanated an internal light— glowing softly from within. Malakai couldn't help but wonder what powered this place. If it was a manifestation of the island's innate magic or some creation by the island's inhabitants. They had yet to meet an actual person, only beasts and creatures intent on harming or abducting them. Had they wandered into the home of whatever god or master governed this island? Had it taken Kasper to steal his magic, or to elevate him? Malakai chewed his lip and mulled over what the Isle Oum could possibly want with them all.

As they continued down the disorienting halls, Malakai led the way, but no one spoke. He wasn't sure how he had become the group's de facto leader, but it probably had something to do with no one caring for him. He would be lying if he said it didn't sting. Someone had been concerned with his well-being all his life, whether it was some courtier or Kasper; there had always been *someone* by his side, but now...

Turning left, he headed down a corridor resembling the one they had been in earlier. Malakai slowed and examined the hall, attempting to discern anything remarkable or distinct about it, but it was the same as the others.

"Do we have any idea where we are headed?" Finnley asked, her voice reverberating off of the crystal.

Pasting on a cheery smile, Malakai said, "Nope."

"Wonderful." she muttered.

Malakai turned to find Princess Rhea hovering closely to Caliban. Her eyes roved over him constantly, like he would disappear the instant she took her gaze off him. Caliban's eyes were weary, his face haggard. But given that his heart had stopped beating and several bones had been broken, including the ribs that cracked during Finnley's efforts to revive him, he looked well—and lucky to be alive. Whatever magic the statue had surrendered during the process had been enough to fix most of Caliban's injuries, but it had done nothing to wipe away the haunted look on his face. Malakai itched to know what his brother had seen and felt when he existed beyond this plane in those brief minutes. He surmised, though, that he would be the last person Caliban would divulge that information to.

Suddenly, a crashing sound brought Malakai back to the present. His hands flew to his ears, a futile attempt to block out the disturbance. Whirling toward the origin of the noise, he found Finnley standing at the wall, her blade wedged between the wall and a sconce. Her face was contorted as she jammed her dagger behind the sconce until it gave way and crashed to the ground. Malakai flinched again, having never been a person who did well with unexpected loud noises.

"What in the Forgottens' names are you doing?" Brander shouted in between the crashing of sconces to the floor.

Finnley moved to the third and began prying it away from the wall. "We have no idea where we are headed, and we are wasting time. Someone or something has put in a tremendous amount of effort to create this place. It stands to reason that if vandalism occurred, they might just show their faces." She shoved hard, and the sconce bounced once before it shattered against the floor.

"And you think bringing them here to us is the answer?" Caliban asked, his voice laced with incredulity.

"Yes." Finnley declared, her face flushed with exertion.

Caliban regarded her for a moment. Then he nodded, limped over to the wall, and set about prying the nearest sconces off. Brander and

Princess Rhea exchanged looks, and then they too selected a sconce and began destroying the palace. Malakai could do nothing except stand there and watch the madness. He winced and cringed every time a sconce was successfully removed from the wall, or a blade made a gash in the stone. It was horrifying to see such beauty razed.

Turning, Malakai looked down the hall. His eyes widened, and he staggered back a step before he twisted over his shoulder and shouted.

"Stop!"

The others, somehow hearing him over their own destruction, heeded his command. Six quartz statues, all the same shade of pink quartz as the palace, headed toward them. They looked identical to the statues that had kidnapped Finnley earlier, and moved in that same uncanny, eerie way. Finnley went white as she beheld the newcomers, but the others, even the Princess, lifted their blades—as if they would do anything against them.

Caliban was slowly making his way toward Malakai, and he lamented the prospect that his magic would be drained from him once more.

But the crystal creatures stopped about six feet away.

No one dared take their eyes off of them. Crystals statues they may be, but that did nothing to hinder their speed and agility. Then, one stepped forward. Everyone took a sharp inhale and braced for the fight. And though the statue was featureless, with no nose, eyes, or mouth, the statue spoke:

> Our master sends his greetings and asks that you follow us to meet with him. What you seek can be found there.

"What we seek?" The Princess repeated. "Wait, does it mean the treasure or Kasper?"

Malakai turned over the statue's statement in his own mind. Was it as simple as following the statues to the treasure room? He doubted it. The island was shifty and tricky. No, there was undoubtedly some *other* meaning. And who was the master they spoke of? Was that who lured Kasper away—or stole him?

Caliban shifted his weight out of a defensive stance. "Who is your master? What does he want with us?"

"Is he the one sending the monsters after us?" Finnley demanded.

Our master sends his greetings and asks that you follow us to meet with him. What you seek can be found there.

"Why is that all it's saying?" Brander asked no one in particular.

Pursing his lips, Malakai said, "I think that its master only gave it that one message, similar to—"

"A parrot." the Princess supplied.

"Yes, a parrot. A giant crystal parrot. It can only repeat what it's been told, not originate new thoughts or responses."

"So, what do we do now?" Brander asked.

Sighing, Caliban sheathed his blade. "I guess we follow it."

No one argued. How could they? They had no other leads or options, and the presence of the six quartz statues, even with their supposed docility, still threatened them.

"Well, no use wasting more time. Let's get to it." Malakai said with as much enthusiasm as he was able to muster, given they may very well be walking into a trap or certain death. But that was the reality all along, wasn't it? Malakai just bemoaned the fact that he wouldn't be able to see their demise coming.

He hated to think that he would go out looking unaware.

Chapter Seventy Four

al hated how much the throne room that the crystal statues paraded them into reminded him of the King's. Appearance-wise, there weren't many similarities; the King lavished himself with ornate fixtures and lush pillows, and in the crystal palace, everything was, well, crystal. It was the atmosphere that evoked Cal's worst memories. A vision–of Soline with the King–flashed in his mind, and Cal had to grind his teeth to stop from reacting. Soline was gone. She would rest soon—and when Cal was good and ready, he could seek his vengeance. They passed through the archway that led further into the throne room, and Cal's eyes honed in on the crystal throne at that far side of the expansive space.

Lounged atop it was Kasper.

Narrowing his eyes, Cal squinted to confirm that the scene before him was real. He struggled to understand what Kasper was doing there, and why he wasn't in any obvious trouble. "Kasper? What in Forgotten are you doing? Is this really where you've been?" Cal seethed as he hurried his approach.

With one leg draped over the arm of the throne, Kasper inspected a crystal when his gaze shifted to him, and he righted himself.

"There you all are! I was wondering if you would find this place," Kasper said, then laughed, "though I suppose it is hard to miss."

Cal could barely contain his rage. He had assumed that Kasper was in danger or, at the very least, that he had been abducted like Finnley had, but no. He was here, sprawled out on the crystal throne as if he were king of this place. Cal finally reached the dais, but two stone creatures stepped into his path before he had the chance to climb it. Baring his teeth, Cal reached for his blade, though he knew it wouldn't be helpful against these beings.

Kasper's face, full of delight and cheer, faltered. "Cal, why are you angry?" Kasper's gaze shifted to the others gathered a few paces behind Cal. "And why are you all covered in dirt?"

"Because we had to climb down a cliff to get here." Brander answered gruffly.

"Why didn't you use the stairs?" Kasper asked, pointing to his left, where a spiral staircase disappeared into the gloom above and presumably led to the tunnel they had come from.

They all turned, staring wide-eyed at the stairs.

Counting to ten, Cal attempted to calm his fury. He took a deep breath until his pulse was a dull drum beat in his ears. Ignoring Kasper's comment, Cal was grateful that Brander had left out the part about Lady Hera falling and Cal jumping like a madman to save her—and that he had died in the process. Something he still hadn't fully wrapped his mind around. He who had dominion over the dead and darkness had succumbed to it—at least for a few minutes. He hadn't been terribly surprised by what he had seen and encountered, but Soline's presence was notably absent. Rationally, he knew that she wouldn't be there. His botched attempt at resurrecting her had turned her into a wraith, something that existed outside of both the mortal plane and the spiritual one, but he had still hoped—foolishly.

"Have your guards stand down, Kas, so we can finish this."

Furrowing his brow, Kasper asked, "Finish what?"

Caliban tried to tamp down on his rising anger. "We have to find the treasure, Kas. I assume you don't have it here."

Kasper looked around and gestured to the room. "What more treasure could you ask for? We have safety and security here. I have never been more powerful. I have nearly indestructible quartz attendants at my command. What more could I want?"

"Sunlight, food, water, and fresh air, for starters," Cal retorted, "but also—"

"What? Revenge? Status? Wealth?" Kasper shook his head. "That's never been my desire, Cal."

"Then why did you come on this journey? Why come all this way and risk your life if you weren't even interested in the outcome?"

Waving a hand, Kasper dismissed the quartz beings, and stepped down the dais until he stood a step above Cal. "I came because I was loyal to Kai. I came because what else was I to do? I had no life outside of attending to him and providing for him, so logically, I came on this venture. But since then, some truths have come to light, and I no longer see the need in my taking care of him."

Cal smirked. "That's the smartest thing you've said in weeks."

Rolling his eyes, Kasper turned to go back to his throne. "You all may continue to search the cave for the treasure you seek, but I have no reason to look any longer."

"Kasper, wait..." Lady Hera pleaded, standing beside Cal. He longed to brush his lips to her neck and inhale her lilies and jasmine scent again, but he refrained. He needed to keep a clear head and remember why he had come to the Cave of Splendors.

Kasper paused before the throne and turned to face them again. Lady Hera swallowed, reached toward her neck, and fished out a gem strung on a leather cord. "You gave me this to protect me. You nearly killed yourself to heal me. You—" Hera caught herself, pressed her lips together for a moment, and then continued, "I know you're hurt by whatever it is that your brothers have done, but you don't want to hurt people, and you wouldn't want people to needlessly suffer."

Flexing his hands, Cal used the movement to stop himself from reaching for her. He couldn't imagine what kind of memories standing before a throne and begging its ruler conjured up for her. Seeing her so desperate renewed his desire to burn the King and his line. His primary goal was to put Soline to rest, but taking revenge on the King wasn't off the table.

Lady Hera took a deep breath and continued, "You speak of safety and security," she pressed her fist to her chest, Kasper's necklace still clutched in her hand, "that's all that I want—that the *Princess* wants for her people. Your brother's prophecy speaks of such terrible destruction for the Kingdom and its inhabitants—I owe it to all of them to try. I only seek to retrieve a treasure that can stop this. I need your help to find it. Help me save my people."

Kasper hesitated, his eyes lingering on Lady Hera's face. Cal saw it then, the true affection he held for her. Cal wanted to be enraged; he wanted to throw his brother down and reprimand him for even daring to feel that way about her, but he couldn't. Cal understood all too well the allure of the Lady. She had made him see the world and himself in a way he hadn't dared since Soline's death. So, no, he couldn't fault his brother for loving Lady Hera. But Kasper was still a boy, barely eighteen, and Cal wagered he had barely even *spoken* to any ladies—noble or otherwise. He might be infatuated with Hera, but he would never understand her the way Cal did.

Hera dropped her hand and lowered her head for a moment. She exhaled, then lifted her chin and rolled her shoulders back—her face utterly resolved. "Help me, and I will tell you about your past."

A crease formed in Cal's brow, and he glanced between Hera's determined expression and Kasper's flabbergasted one. Kasper blinked—realizing everyone was still watching him, and shook his head. Pressing his lips into a thin line, he cleared his throat.

"Fine, I'll help you retrieve the treasure."

The tension went out of Lady Hera's shoulders instantly. Surging forward, she embraced Kasper. He stiffened for a heartbeat and then returned her hug. As understanding as Cal wanted to be, he was still a man, so he turned from their embrace and stepped back down to the floor. He turned to see the pair disentangling themselves and walking down the dais.

"So, which way do we go from here?" Finnley asked, her tone indicating that she was bored with the proceedings.

Cal suppressed a smile and looked at his brother.

Kasper closed his eyes for a moment, a look of concentration passing over his features, and then he opened his eyes and pointed to his right. "There's a passageway beyond the throne room, hewn from the earth, that leads further into the cave. I sense a lot of rooms and paths splintering off from the main tunnel. That's the way we should head."

"Wonderful," Kai chirped, "let us be on our way once more."

No one responded to him, but they did take a collective breath before they trudged toward the doorway that Kasper had indicated, likely heading into even more danger.

* * * *

Cal welcomed the darkness of the earthen tunnel. The damp, cool air was similar to that of a crypt or tomb and, as a necromancer, the smell was a comfort to Cal. The shadows were thicker here, more corporeal than they had been since they had stepped foot on the island. Cal wasn't sure if that was a good omen. It was evident by the nervous glances of the others, their faces partially lit by the sparse gems embedded in the walls that Kasper illuminated by merely passing by them, that they were ill at ease in the tunnel. But Cal relished it. This was his domain, his seat of power, and the further they descended into the earth, the more comfortable he became.

"There's a bend in the tunnel up ahead. We just need to keep following it for a hundred feet or so." Kasper called back to the others. The tunnel was narrow enough that they had to continue single file, and the ceiling was so low that everyone except Lady Hera and Finnley had to duck.

"Then where do we head?" Lady Hera asked from behind Cal. He willed the shadows to gently brush against her neck. A reassuring gesture to remind her that, even in the dark, he was still with her. Their relationship—if one would even call it that—was in a precarious place. Ill-defined and shaky, but there was clearly something deeper than passing affection or lust between them. And Cal—as long as Hera desired it, too—was determined to explore it once he set his past wrongs right. He kept waiting for the guilt and shame of letting Soline go consume him, but it never did. Perhaps a decade of regret and pining was all a soul could take.

"There's a branch off the main path we need to take. It leads into a room, but that's all I can really tell at this point."

"Oh, don't tell me your magic is becoming unreliable, too." Finnley said dryly from behind Cal.

Kasper's expression was obscured, but Cal knew him well enough to surmise that he was bunching his brows and pressing them together into a hard line.

"No, it's not that," Kasper assured them, "the wrong path is duller and less defined than all other paths and rooms. The island lets me get a sense of our surroundings, but not the whole picture."

Blowing out a frustrated breath, Finnley said, "I cannot wait to be off this fickle and sentient island."

Cal chuckled softly and willed his shadows to caress Lady Hera's cheek. She gave a soft jolt, and Cal smiled at himself. It would be agony to wait to touch her again, but he made himself promise, after their near kiss on the Umbra, that he would do right by her. Court her properly, if that's what she wished, and they would live the remainder of their days away from the putrid court they had both been raised in, away from the vileness of the Abadi family. They would know peace and happiness—Cal would make sure of it.

"Alright, there's an opening to everyone's right, so just follow me AHH—"

"Kasper!" Cal yelled after him, as Kasper's golden-brown curls disappeared from view. The light in the tunnel had winked out, plunging them into total darkness. When Kasper didn't respond, Cal rallied his shadows and stormed into the opening that his little brother had vanished through—

Cal's feet went out from underneath him, and then he was falling.

Falling

Falling

Falling

The damp, compacted earth of the cave floor came rushing up to Cal so fast that he didn't have time to summon his shadows to break his fall. He collided with the ground, pain radiating up through his body. Groaning, Cal's mind was torn between his own pain and concern for Hera, but he hurried to move lest one of the others come tumbling down after him. He looked up to find Kasper standing two feet away, staring at a table laden with fresh fruits, cheeses, and meats. Caliban's stomach grumbled, and his mouth watered in response. It was the most delicious food he had seen in years. Not since he was at court had such a bounty been laid before him. The smells and sights alone were enough to sustain Cal, but he spied so many foods he hadn't eaten in a decade. He wanted nothing more than to sink his teeth into the plump, flavorful flesh of the plums he—

"Caliban!" someone called from above, dragging him from his stupor. He looked up and remembered himself.

"Kasper." he said sternly.

Kasper's body contorted, his shoulders and hips turning toward Cal first, his head then reluctantly following.

"We need to get the others down here safely."

Nodding and still a bit dazed, Kasper replied, "Of course."

"Caliban! Kasper! Are you both alright? Say something, please." Lady Hera called down to them.

"We're fine, Kasper just, uh…" Caliban threw his brother a furtive glance, "miscalculated. Jump down individually and I will catch you with my shadows."

"Alright," she replied, "I'm coming down now."

Stepping back, Cal willed his shadows to gather, creating a cushioned base for the other's fall. There was a sudden but short scream, and then Hera was there, enveloped in shadows. They held her until her feet touched the ground, and Cal reached for her. It was unnecessary contact, but he couldn't help himself. He slid his hand under her elbow, cupping it. Her eyes flew to his, heat sparking there. Even a touch as innocent as that ignited what burned between them.

Kasper coughed pointedly, and Cal fought the urge to roll his eyes, but he released her. They couldn't let themselves get carried away.

Not yet.

"Alright, we're ready for the next one." Cal called out.

The rest of the party came down, one after another, until they all stood around the table. The room itself was unremarkable. Its low ceiling was similar to the tunnel they had come from, but long enough to accommodate the ten-foot-long table and the chairs that inhabited it.

Finnley let out a long, low whistle. "This is a feast fit for a king." she said, walking around the table, inspecting it from all angles. "Is it real?"

"It's all organic matter." Kasper replied.

"Is that organic matter, too?" Brander asked, pointing toward the head of the table at the far end of the room.

Stepping back, Cal beheld the monster that sat at the feast. The creature was bone-white with folds of loose alabaster skin hanging from its emaciated form. Its belly was swollen, like that of a malnourished child's. Its hands, splayed flat against the table, were tipped with long onyx nails that curved wickedly and bore into the table's wood. The table obscured the lower half of its body, but its face was perhaps the most terrifying thing Cal had ever looked upon. A smooth white head with no eyes, only the sunken-in sockets where its eyes should have been and two thin slits, each two inches long in the place of its nose. Where its mouth was supposed to be was a thread, the color of blood, stitching its lips closed.

Cal's appetite soured immediately. Something was amiss. Why had the creature not attacked them when they first entered the chamber? How was all of this food here? The island was magic, but this was clearly some sort of trap.

"No one eat anything, don't even touch it." Cal commanded.

Everyone stepped away from the table, their apprehension as thick as the humidity clinging to the air. Cal scanned the room, accounting for everyone. He marked them each, Kasper, Lady Hera, Finnley, Brander, and...

Turning to his right, Cal looked toward the other side of the table.

"Kai, no!" He yelled, reaching out with his shadows, but it was too late. Kai's fingers slid around the greenest apple Cal had ever seen and lifted it from the table. Cal's shadows collided with Kai in the next breath, sending him flying into the far wall next to a door. The apple fell from his hand, thudding softly to the earthen floor.

A horrible screeching sound split the air. Cal fought the urge to flinch away from the noise and whirled to find the source instead. To his horror, the monster at the end of the table was moving. Its claws, previously burrowed in the wood, were wrenching themselves free. The table shrieked and splinted with the force of the pale monster ripping itself free of the table.

"Get back!" Cal yelled to the others and rallied his magic. He dared to glance at Kai and found him lying on the floor, dazed but conscious. He needed to get to his brother. If the past few encounters with beasts on this island were any indication, he would need his brother's magic. Everyone, even Lady Hera, unsheathed a blade and readied themselves for a fight. It was one against five; surely they could handle one emaciated monster. Finally, the being freed itself from the table and lifted its gnarled hands to its face. Cal hoped the horror would stop there, but then the creature turned its claws on itself—ripping at the seams holding its lips together.

"Holy gods." Lady Hera murmured, more to herself than anyone.

But Cal couldn't stop himself as he said, "I don't think there are any gods here."

Blood leaked from the tears in the creature's lips, dripping from its skin and the thread. Cal was frozen—unable to move or attack. The pale monster lifted its hands further and turned them outward, exposing its palms. In the center of its palms were the eyes that were absent from its face. Cal's blood went cold as the creature smiled, baring its long, jagged black teeth, and spoke.

"It has been too long since I dined with mortals."

Cal flinched at the monster's voice, which sounded like a thousand blades being scraped against stone. He forced himself to breathe past his revulsion, gripped the hilt of his blade tighter, and shifted his feet.

The eyes in the monster's palms blinked in unison, and it turned, scanning the room. "So much magic. So much power," the creature said as its ruby-red tongue slipped between its teeth and licked at its lips, tasting its own blood, "but even more tasty are the secrets each of you keep. I should like to drink them." The creature laughed like broken glass rattling in a bag. Its gaze swept the room once more before landing on Lady Hera. "Each must speak the Truth that another does not know. Once your secret has been shared, we may dine together as gods and heroes did in the days of Old."

"And what if we don't?" Finnley demanded, still sizing up the creature like she planned to launch herself at it at any given moment.

The pale monster turned toward her and tilted its head and hands, assessing her with those beady eyes. "Then I shall feast on you."

Finnley blanched at the monster's words, and Cal knew them to be true. There would only be one way out of this room, and despite the appearance of the pale creature, Cal didn't think it would be as easily felled as he previously thought.

"If we do this, if we play your game, you'll let us go?" Cal questioned, forcing more confidence into his voice that he felt.

The creature turned its horrid gaze upon him, its smile widening slightly. "I honor my word. If you all share your heart-of-heart secrets, then I shall let you pass to find the treasure you seek."

How the creature knew what they sought, despite the fact that none of them had said a word about it, Cal didn't know. And he decided not to linger on it. The monster leaned back in its chair, the wood groaning in protest.

"You're not far now. But my patience grows thin, and my appetite does not. I suggest you hurry before your secrets are no longer enough to sate me."

Cal hesitated for a moment before he reluctantly sheathed his blade and turned to the others. "Let's just get this over with and get out of here in one piece."

The creature chuckled and said, "Though that may be your wish, I fear the truths revealed will not be so kind."

Cal didn't dignify the monster's taunt with an answer, but from the vacant expressions of the others, he feared the pale creature was right.

Chapter Seventy Five

"**N**o food may be consumed until all have spoken." the monster told them as they sat at its table.

Cal sent a glare in Kai's direction, who, wisely, didn't meet his eyes. They moved wordlessly, no one daring to sit near the monster. Cal took the seat most opposite the creature, Kasper took the seat to his left, and Finnley to his right. Kai sat beside Finnley across from Brander, who claimed the seat between Kasper and Lady Hera.

Clearing his throat, Cal said, "Is there an order you prefer, or can that be left up to us?"

The monster smiled, "I shall leave it to you, Necromancer."

Cal narrowed his eyes and said, "Fine. Kai, go."

Kai's eyes went wide, and he pressed a hand on his chest. "Me? Surely someone else has a more interesting secret to share first—"

"Kai."

"Alright, uh, well, sometimes I re-wear outfits. I know it's shocking, and trust me, I am loath to admit it. But it's the truth." he said with a nervous laugh and glanced toward the pale monster.

The creature's smile vanished. "Insufficient!" it bellowed and pointed toward Finnley. Suddenly, vines burst out of the dirt wall behind her and encircled her. Finnley's scream was cut off by the vines smothering her face and strangling her throat.

"Insufficient!" the monster yelled again, and the vines tightened.

"Tell another truth, Kai!" Cal commanded as he took his dagger and began hacking at the vines. "A better one!" he added.

Kai was unresponsive, staring at Finnley's struggling form.

"Now, Kai!" Kasper screamed and reached across the table to smack him—hard. It was enough to drag Kai from his stupor. He threw up his hands and turned toward the monster.

"Fine! Fine! When we fled the palace, Kasper came with me, and I took him to a blood witch. She performed a spell on him that buried his memories, blocking him from accessing them. I did it so he wouldn't remember his life from before, at least not all of it. I didn't want him to remember Caliban, or how I didn't protect him. It was a chance for all of us to start over."

The vines surrounding Finnley vanished immediately. Finnley gasped and grabbed for her throat, attempting to gulp down air. She looked toward the monster and managed to ask, "Why me? Why not one of his brothers?"

The creature regarded her and said, "He cares the most about your well-being."

Panting, Cal glared at his brother, still processing what he had revealed. A torrent of emotions ripped through him—how dare he bespell Kasper? And with a blood witch, no less. If Kasper didn't kill Kai for his transgression, Cal might do them all the favor. He looked to Kasper and found his brother staring at Kai as well.

"All these years. All this time!" Kasper stood so fast his chair tipped over. "You said it was trauma—that I had lost the memories! But you *stole* them!"

Standing as well, Cal held out a hand to Kasper. "We can talk about this later. Right now, we need to get through this." Murder danced in Kasper's eyes, but after a moment, he righted his chair and returned to his seat. Kai never looked up, his eyes trained on the floor.

Cal returned to his seat and avoided the gaze of the monster. "Brander."

Lady Hera's guard had his hand folded in front of him on the table. His stare was fixed on the honeyed ham that glistened before him. The crystals in the walls cast shadows across his face, making him appear older than a man in his fourth decade.

"My village was raided by the King's army. Every man, woman, and child were put to the sword, save for the boys who were old enough to be conscripted. My parents died while I hid and watched my village be destroyed by the King's men." Brander said, his voice low and haunted. "Despite that, I trained hard. I rose through the ranks until I became a general in the King's army, one of the few that wasn't nobility. I had no former life to cling to, and no one knew me, so I put all my effort into being the best. It was an honor, and I treated it as such. I became an extension of the King's will, carrying out his orders and putting villages, like my own, to the sword." Brander paused, his throat working. His features turned even more somber as he continued, "I was the best. Until I returned to my village."

Lady Hera reached for Brander, her hand moving to cover his, but Brander dropped his hands into his lap. He lifted his chin, meeting the monster's gaze. "Everyone believes that the reason I snapped and killed everyone was because I was angry about what had happened to my village three decades before—but that wasn't it. I saw my father. The father that I thought had died, the father I had mourned. But there he was, with a woman that wasn't my mother and new children."

A muscle ticked in Brander's jaw. Cal fought the urge to avert his gaze from the guard.

Loosing a breath, Brander shook his head. His voice came out broken as he said, "I killed him. I killed everyone, and then I turned on my men when they dared to stop me. In total, I killed fifty people that day, which, of course, is nothing in comparison to the countless others I slaughtered in service to the King."

Everyone was silent as Brander finished his tale. Cal turned his gaze to the table, unsure what he had expected from the guard when he named him next. Perhaps some story about leading a rebellion or sneaking out to drink when he was on duty, but not that he was a *kinslayer*. Not the wholesale slaughter of innocents and his own men.

Slurping sounds came from the far side of the room. Reluctantly, Cal looked up to find the pale creature grinning with feral delight. "What a most delicious admission. Who's next?"

Cal opened his mouth to say that they were done with this—

"I'll go." Finnley offered. She looked at the others, waiting to see if anyone would object, but no one spoke. Finnley sucked in a breath and exhaled it. "I killed my father because he killed my mother."

Cal stayed silent, waiting for the rest. There was undoubtedly more to the story, but Finnley remained closed-lip. He slid his gaze to the monster, expecting it to be dissatisfied with her secret. Briefly, he wondered who Finnley cared the most about amongst them for the creature to target with its vines.

The pale monster just blinked and said, "Next."

Only three remained. Cal glanced at Lady Hera, noting the lack of color in her face and the way her eyes remained downcast. Curiosity and dread prickled along his neck. What secret could she have that was so terrible she refused to meet anyone's eyes? Cal pursed his lips but moved his attention to Kasper, who was still glaring at Kai, clearly not past what Kai had shared.

Nonetheless, he said, "I'll go." Kasper leaned forward in his chair, the only one among them who didn't look distraught or weary, and said, "I am more powerful than you," he looked to Cal, "both of you."

Cal tried not to let his skepticism show because there was clearly something off about Kasper. It was evident in the wildness of Kasper's eyes and his twitching fingers.

"It's true," Kasper continued, "when I left you all and found the crystal palace, I learned things about myself, about my power. Things that you all couldn't even begin to comprehend. I could take your powers, and Finnley's too, right now, and there would be nothing you could do about it." Leaning back in his chair, a smugness radiated from Kasper that made Cal want to roll his eyes. "In fact, I almost did take your power. The island wanted me to, and when you all were hurrying your way here, I was going to do it."

"Why?" Cal asked, his annoyance getting the better of him.

Kasper's wild gaze turned on him. "Why? Because I'm tired of being Kai's lackey. I'm tired of being disrespected by you. I'm tired of being treated like a child who's excluded from the adults' conversations. I'm tired of always being in both of your shadows, treated as less than because I can't see the future or commune with the dead. Well, you know what? I could take every bit of that from you."

"Why didn't you then?" Cal said, leaning forward on the table and bracing his arms on it. "Why not exact your revenge on us when you had the chance?"

Kasper's feral gaze darted toward Lady Hera and then back to Cal.

Cal smiled. "Ah. Love."

Narrowing his eyes, Kasper opened his mouth.

Raising a hand, Cal cut Kasper off. "I need no further explanation, Kas. I see it plainly. You are and have been in love with Lady Hera since the moment you laid eyes on her. I suppose that could have been the secret you revealed, if everyone hadn't already known it."

"Caliban." Lady Hera chided.

Kasper's face went bright red. "That's enough, Cal."

"I agree. Because even if you somehow managed to steal my power, it still wouldn't change the fact that she," he said, pointing to Lady Hera, "doesn't want you. She has picked me, and even if you kill me, she still won't want you. You know why, Kas?" Cal leaned forward once more and dropped his voice. "Because you'll still be weak. You'll still be a child, play-acting at being an adult."

"Stop it, Cal. Just tell your secret and be done with this." Finnley demanded from his right.

"I caused the earthquake." Kasper rushed out, his face flush with anger. His eyes flashed with the realization of the gravity of what he shared. He whirled toward Lady Hera. "I didn't mean to, of course, but I had already channeled into the island to take their powers, and then I felt you, your fear, your hope, and...I faltered. But the magic had already built up, so it had to be released. I didn't realize what it would do, that you were already climbing down. Hera, you have to understand how sorry I am—"

"It's fine, Kas. Let's just move on." Lady Hera said quietly, not meeting Kasper's gaze. Kasper clearly had more to say, but he refrained, slinking into his seat, his mouth agape and his eyes shining.

Keeping an irreverent smile on his face, Cal fell back against his chair again and peered down at the food in front of him. His family was destroyed. They would never look at one another the same, and there would never be a hope for trust between them again. Sighing, Cal slowly met the gazes of the others; only Finnley and Brander met his eyes. Cal nodded and looked down the table to the monster who demanded this sacrifice. Its skin wasn't as loose and gaunt as it was before. Muscle and fat now clung to its bones, and its swollen abdomen no longer looked distended, but rather full with sustenance—as though it truly was being fed with their secrets.

Shaking his head, Cal attempted to clear his thoughts and to get this farce over with. "I once was in love. Lady Soline was her name, though some of you already knew that. She died, and I tried–foolishly, selfishly–to resurrect her. Rather than her simply remaining dead, I managed to screw up just enough that she became a wraith. A creature that has haunted me for a decade, not truly dead but not alive, either—begging to be restored." Cal looked down at the table, but snuck a glance at Lady Hera; she still stared at her lap. "I came here seeking a way to do just that, but this journey has altered my plans slightly. Now, I simply want to put her to rest...for both our sakes."

Silence fell over the table. Cal kept his rage burning in his chest, refusing to acknowledge the vulnerability of what he had shared. Some of them knew of Soline, but none–save for Kai–knew of her true fate or what Cal had sought to do for her. But Hera had changed all that— and Cal wanted her to see that she had revived his black heart.

The monster made the slurping sound once more. "Delectable." He turned his attention to Lady Hera. "One left, and it may be the tastiest of them all."

The curiosity that had been piqued earlier came rushing back to Cal. He wished that Lady Hera had sat next to him so he could comfort her. Clearly, she was distressed, but something warned him against it.

Slowly, Lady Hera raised her head, tears already welling in her eyes, but she remained steadfast. She briefly looked across the table, catching Kai's gaze. Cal failed to mask his surprise. Surely, there was no love lost between them. Perhaps Kai had seen something in a vision about her past. Still, it was unlike Kai to offer encouragement in the face of anguish, yet he gave a subtle nod to the Lady before she turned toward the creature.

Lifting her chin, Hera said, "My mother died when I was young, and my father took it very hard. He began seeking out other wives and was very cruel to me, going so far as to be physically abusive at times."

Cal clenched his fist at the truth revealed, although he had guessed at some of it after seeing the scars on her back. He wanted to pull her against his chest and remind her that she was safe with him, that he would never let harm befall her again.

The monster clucked his tongue. "Insufficient."

Lady Hera stiffened, and Cal furrowed his brow. Her secret was on par with any of theirs.

"Try again." the creature commanded.

Lady Hera's eyes darted to Kai's once more, who looked more alarmed now than when he'd had to share his own truth.

Swallowing, Lady Hera stuttered, "I–I don't know——"

"Wrong answer." the monster snarled. Vines burst from the dirt wall, ensnaring Cal, Brander, and Kasper. Cal didn't have a chance to draw his blade before his arms were pinned to the chair, and his airway was cut off. He struggled and thrashed against the vines, trying to find a way to loosen their grip. Brander and Kasper weren't fairing much better, even as Lady Hera, Finnley, and Kai yanked at the vines.

"Just tell the truth!" Kai bellowed, his fingers getting caught under the vines which were trying to kill Kasper.

"Do it, Lady!" Finnley agreed.

Cal managed to glimpse Lady Hera's face amid the chaos. Her eyes were wide, and her fear struck him. Tears streamed down her cheeks. She was utterly terrified.

"It's alright, my—" Brander said before the vines cut off his air.

"Magic," Cal managed to gasp and lock eyes with Kai. "Use… magic."

"I think not." The monster snapped its fingers. Suddenly, a wall came crashing down on Cal's senses, and his magic fell out of reach.

Turning toward Lady Hera, Kai shouted, "Now, or we will all die!"

The creature at the end of the table was beginning to salivate and rise from its chair. "The bones of magic wielders are always the sweetest."

"NOW!" Finnley and Kai shouted in unison.

Lady Hera looked around frantically. Finally, she turned and faced Cal. Her features were swollen, red, and wet from her tears as she whispered, "Please forgive me."

Cal couldn't respond, as black dots were dancing in his vision, his pulse turning thready.

Turning toward the monster, Lady Hera choked out, "I am Princess Rhea Haliana Adamaris Abadi, Heir to the Kingdom of Desmorda." she turned to Cal, and the understanding of her words flickered within him like the black spots in his vision. "I am the King's daughter."

Chapter Seventy Six

The vines around Kasper vanished, the air returning to his lungs. Kasper pitched forward, his hands coming up to his throat as if that would ease the burning. He needed all the fresh air and blood flow possible to understand what Lady Hera—no, the *Princess*—had just proclaimed.

The pale monster chuckled, returning to his seat at the head of the table. "Now that you all have been truthful, we can break bread." It reached for a loaf of bread and cracked it, the scent of warm yeast floating through the room. "And what would bread be without spirits?" Wine and mead filled the crystal goblets beside each of their plates, the rich, fruity smell wafting up to meet Kasper. His stomach clenched painfully at the sights and smells before him, but all he managed to do was turn his head and look at Lady Hera.

But it wasn't Lady Hera anymore...

"Princess Rhea..." Cal breathed from the end of the table, his cold, furious, and conflicted gaze fixed on the Princess.

Princess Rhea trembled as she spoke. "I wanted to tell you. I almost did a few times, but I couldn't—I was too afraid, I–I..." Her words faltered, and she dropped her eyes. Reaching up to her chest, she lifted the pendant she always wore from under her clothes, and rubbed her thumb over its emblem.

The Abadi family crest. Kasper had just assumed that it represented the house she served as the Princess's Lady-in-Waiting, but now he understood.

Sniffling, Princess Rhea spoke. "I feared that if you knew the truth of who I was, you wouldn't help me, or you might…"

"Kill you." Cal finished, his voice devoid of emotion. There was nothing on his face either, at least nothing obvious, but Kasper saw the rage in the lines of his body—the taut and strained muscles of his exposed arms and neck.

Standing, Cal braced his hands on the table, narrowly avoiding the plate filling itself with food. Kasper flinched back on instinct, eager not to be in his line of sight. But he was helpless to look away from his brother's face, and there, he found death waiting.

Cal held the Princess's gaze, his voice icy as he leaned forward. "I should have taken you back to your gilded palace and slit your throat in front of your father for what he did to me. For what he took from me."

Brander moved to stand, but Princess Rhea placed her hand on his arm and halted him.

Kasper blinked back his shock as Cal stood upright, his pointed gaze landing on him, then Kai, and finally Finnley. "We're leaving now." Cal moved away from the table, but the creature at the other end snapped, and vines burst from the ground, snaking their way around Cal's legs.

Cal yanked at his restraints and bellowed, "Release me! We have done what you demanded."

The pale creature chuckled. "You have made the sacrifice; now you must partake in the meal. If you do not, you will rot in that chair, never to see daylight again." The monster gestured to Cal's chair, and more vines appeared, pulling him down until he was seated once more.

Cal continued to struggle and fight against the vines. The monster growled, the sound rumbling through the room and rattling the crystal plates and cups.

"Enough of that, Necromancer. As my guest, you will abide by my rules. You will eat and be grateful; when the time comes, you will leave together, and your magic will be restored."

Kasper's eyes widened, and he reached for the well of power he knew existed within him. It was still there, but a barrier of onyx stone had been erected, cutting off his access to it. Kasper turned toward his older brother.

"Do what he says, Cal. Just play along until we can leave this chamber."

Cal had stopped his thrashing, but murder still blazed in his eyes. He turned his glare on Rhea, just for a moment, and quickly looked away. A muscle ticked in his jaw, but he finally ground out, "Fine."

The monster smiled, and the vines vanished once more.

Some of the tension left Kasper, and he relaxed in his chair. Glancing across the table, Kasper found Finnley was the only one who dared to eat the food before her. She dug in with abandon, cutting and spearing her food before hastily shoving it in her mouth. Kasper watched with amazement, his eyes tracking her progress as if he had never seen someone eat.

Finnley finally looked up. Her fork froze in midair, a hunk of beef dripping with gravy just inches from her mouth. Her eyes darted around the table, and she proceeded to stuff the beef in her mouth and speak around it, "What? I haven't had my mother's pot roast since before she died."

Furrowing his brows, Kasper was curious as to how she knew it was her mother's cooking, but when he looked down at his own plate he found that it had been replaced with a crystal bowl and spoon. Instantly, Kasper knew it was his favorite dish, though he couldn't remember when he had ever eaten it. Gingerly, he lifted the spoon and scooped up some vegetables, meat, and broth. The liquid smelled distinctly of chicken. A terrible, breath-stealing pain lanced through his temple, and he almost dropped his spoon. He took a deep breath through his nose, lifted the soup—carrots, peas, and chicken—to his lips, and nearly melted.

It was like coming home. It was a hug at the end of a hard day, the comforting words of a loved one.

Kasper managed to retain some civility and not lift the bowl to his lips and slurp it all down in a single go. He forced himself to take measured spoonfuls. He was determined to savor this soup. He looked at the other's food between mouthfuls, attempting to discern what they ate. According to Finnley's assumptions, the plate–or bowl, in Kasper's case–was filled with that person's favorite meal.

Cal dined on roast chicken, placed atop flatbread, and drizzled with orange sauce. Kai had two fish stuffed and flavored with various berries and herbs. Kasper took another spoonful and found Brander eating some sort of syrupy cake that he treated with such reverence that Kasper was compelled to look away. His eyes wandered to the Princess's plate, expecting to find some exotic meal befitting a noble with immeasurable wealth, but instead, he saw a soup.

His soup.

The spoon fell out of Kasper's hand, clattering against the bowl. The noise drew everyone's attention, and the Princess's eyes rose to meet him. She glanced at his food, marked it, and said, "My governess, the only one I truly liked, used to make this for me–for us–when we were sick or hurt, or just longing for comfort. Even after all these years, it's still my favorite."

Kasper swallowed and nodded. "So, all those times I swore I knew you, I kept drawing up blanks, and you kept insisting that I was wrong. You were just playing me for a fool. Even when you were recovering from the poison and you," the realization hit Kasper fully, "you did know me then, but when you came out of it, you brushed me aside." Another falsehood. Another person who didn't see the value in telling him the truth.

"No, Kasper, I..." the Princess stopped, collecting herself. She took a quick inhale and continued, "I thought you might know me when we first saw each other, but when you didn't recognize me and your brother explained that you wouldn't, I didn't—"

"You knew." Kasper said, looking at Kai. There was no accusation or condemnation in his voice, just resolve. "You've known the truth the entire time."

Kai swallowed his mouthful of fish. He slowly dabbed at his mouth and set his napkin back in his lap. "It was in the quest's best interest that the Princess's identity remain secret. I never intended for any of this to come out."

"Well, of course you didn't, Kai." Cal intoned sardonically. "Then the game would be up, and you would have lost your most valuable piece." Cal laughed softly. "Always trying to be one step ahead of everyone. Always treating people as a means to an end."

"And you don't?" Kasper interjected.

Cal set down his flatware with a noisy thud. "Are you truly defending him?"

Narrowing his eyes, Kasper said, "No, but you're just as guilty. You're using everyone here to get what you want, so maybe don't get too high on your horse."

A wicked grin spread across Cal's face as he leaned toward his brother and said, "You want to know the difference, Kas? I've never pretended to be anything else than what I am. A villain. I don't hide behind a title or fancy clothes." He sent pointed looks in the direction of Kai and Princess Rhea. "I am wicked, and it's high time everyone here remembers that."

Abruptly, Cal stood. His chair toppled and he flung a blade out. The dagger sailed through the air, covering the length of the table, and struck true in the creature's throat.

The monster wailed, grabbing for the blade, but Cal was faster. He leapt onto the table, grabbed Kai, and yanked him up. Kai wasn't afforded the chance to protest as Cal took a knife from the table and slashed it across his arm. Food and drink were trampled and crushed underfoot, but Cal was single-minded in his pursuit. Cal's hand, already bleeding, clamped down on Kai's wound, and then he turned his attention to the pale monster still clamoring over the dagger protruding from its neck.

Cal held out his free hand, and Kasper had the good sense to look away as blinding white light filled the room. A terrible wailing echoed off the rock walls, and then—

Flesh sizzled like meat in hot oil, popping and bubbling with violence.

Magic surged up in Kasper, nearly overwhelming him. The crystals embedded in the walls and on the table glowed, and he quickly tamped down on his power—now fully restored.

"What did you do?" Brander growled from beside Kasper.

Cal turned toward them, dropping Kai, who slumped to the table in a heap. "I did what had to be done. I'm not going to be held hostage by some creature."

Wreathed in shadows, Cal dropped down from the table, and strolled toward the door Kai had fallen next to earlier. He turned toward everyone else still at the table and said, "I intend to finish what I came here to do. Kasper, Finnley, you're welcome to join me; everyone else," his eyes swept over the room, "stay out of my way." With that, he reached for the handle, opened the door, and disappeared through it.

Glancing at the others, Kasper tried to decipher their next move. Suddenly, a chair slid against the dirt floor, and Kasper looked to find the Princess standing. Gone were her tears and sorrow, replaced with the fierce woman who donned the name Lady Hera.

Princess Rhea rolled her shoulders and lifted her chin. "I'm not going to let some *man* tell me that I'm no longer entitled to the treasure I seek, purely because his feelings are bruised." She looked to her guard. "Come on, Brander. We're going after the treasure."

"Yes, Princess."

At that, Brander stood, as did Finnley, leaving only Kasper seated. Even Kai managed to drag himself off the table and prop himself against the wall.

Turning her attention to Kasper then, Princess Rhea's gaze softened slightly. "I know you're angry with me, your brothers, and likely the whole world, but Kasper, I am doing this for my people. I would be greatly indebted to you if you would be willing to set aside your hurt for long enough to help me. After that, I will leave you alone forever."

Kasper hesitated. He didn't know what he wanted anymore. He didn't even know who he was. But he did know that he was tired of his life being dictated to him by others.

Clasping her hands in front of her, Princess Rhea added, "But it is entirely your choice." She gave him a curt nod and turned to walk away from him. Before he could think better of it, Kasper's hand shot out and slipped around Princess Rhea's wrist, halting her.

Princess Rhea's eyes shone with something akin to hope.

"I will help on one condition."

Princess Rhea's brows lifted. "Name it."

Swallowing, Kasper said, "You keep your promise from before. Help me remember who I am."

A smile formed on Princess Rhea's lips and she said, "It would be my pleasure."

Kasper released the Princess, stood, and glanced at the others. He had no qualms with Finnley or Brander, but Kai was a different story. There were too many lies and abuses for him to simply let go. But Kasper turned away from his brother. His issues with Kai would have to wait until they obtained the treasure.

Nodding to the Princess, Kasper said, "We go at your command."

Chapter Seventy Seven

Brander was powerless to contain the smile of pride that spread across his face. His Princess was becoming a Queen, a ruler worthy of her people and throne. And all that stood between her and securing her birthright was finding Izor's Lamp.

Taking a deep breath, Princess Rhea said, "Right, well, we have no time to waste. We need to get to the treasure before Caliban does. Otherwise, we run the risk of a confrontation with him. He may not be after the *same* treasure, but I wouldn't put it past him to exercise his anger if he can."

"You think he'll attack us?" Kasper asked.

Princess Rhea pursed her lips.

Brander could only guess at what she was feeling. She had grown to care for the Necromancer, perhaps even love him. As much as it disturbed Brander, there was a kindred spirit between them, some darkness borne of cruelty that each of them harbored. The defining difference is that the Princess did not let the darkness rule or consume her the same way Cal did.

The Princess clasped her hands. "I think he won't hesitate to eliminate a threat. Real or perceived. He despises my father, and I suspect that if he can stop me from saving my Kingdom, then he will do just that. We can't take that chance," Princess Rhea looked at Kasper and continued, "but we have the advantage."

Kasper furrowed his brows for a moment, but then nodded. "Right. What are we looking for?"

Exhaling, the Princess said, "I'm looking for a lamp. Izor's Lamp, specifically. According to legend, it belonged to a wizard named Izor, who sought to increase his power, but was greedy and reckless. Now, the tale diverts on whether he accidentally turned himself into a jinn and trapped himself in the Lamp, or if the gods punished him for his greed by imprisoning him. Either way, all the legends agree that he resides in the Lamp, and whoever possesses the Lamp is granted three wishes."

Kasper arched a brow but didn't press further. "Okay, I'll scout ahead for any rooms that have gold...and try to avoid falling into any more rooms with monsters." he said with a tentative smile. He turned toward the door and stepped out into the darkness beyond.

Finnley's lips were curled in a half smile as she winked at Princess Rhea before filing out after Kasper. Then, the Seer appeared in front of Princess Rhea and reached for her hands. Brander fought the instinct to cut the Seer down where he stood. He was trained as a soldier, and setting aside years of lessons in just a few weeks was difficult.

"I am sorry that the truth came out like this," Kai said with more sincerity than Brander thought possible, "but perhaps it is a good thing. In my line of work, I've come to understand that events may not unfold as we foresee, but what was meant to happen almost always does." He gave Princess Rhea another smile that didn't quite reach his eyes.

Instantly, the Princess's shoulders dropped. Brander showed no hesitation as he moved, pulling the Princess in for a hug. She buried her face into his shoulder, and her tears began to spill. Brander held her tight and let her release everything she was holding. Her whole body shook and trembled with her crying, but Brander remained steadfast. They had all shared a piece of themselves, revealing a vulnerability that had unquestionably altered the course of their journeys, but perhaps none so much as the Princess's.

"I'm not sure I can do this." Princess Rhea uttered between sobs.

"You survived your father's cruelty, battled against mythical beasts, and faced off with the most feared Necromancer in the known world. You can do anything, and you will survive this."

Shaking her head, Princess Rhea said, "You saw how he looked at me, how his entire perception of me shifted—Kasper's, too. They hate me. They know me, know my *heart*, and they still hate me. How will my people ever accept me?"

Brander pulled back to look at the Princess. Her eyes were rimmed red and swollen. It made her look younger, perhaps closer to her true age. Brander tucked an errant strand of hair behind her ear and murmured, "Sometimes I forget how young you are. Barely twenty and one, and the world's weight has already been placed upon your shoulders."

"And I'm failing at every turn. Every choice I've made has been the wrong one, and it's costing more than I can afford."

"You're learning. That's what it means to be a young person, to make mistakes and learn from them."

"But—"

Brander gripped Princess Rhea's shoulders firmly. "You being here–on this island, risking your life to find a magic lamp–is already more than your father has ever done for his people. Your father is cruel, malicious, and fickle; that is all the Kingdom has known for decades. As someone who rose through the ranks of his army, I can promise you that the people are ready for a benevolent and consistent ruler. They are ready for you, Princess."

Princess Rhea's bottom lip trembled, tears still streaking her face. Brander wiped at them, slipped his fingers under her chin, and lifted her face.

"You are a Queen worthy of your people," he said with a soft smile, "now, let's go save them."

Princess Rhea gave an earnest smile, and the sting that had persisted in Brander's chest since his mother's honeyed cake appeared before him finally eased. Brander had spent years of his life resenting all the moments and circumstances that brought him to his current position.

But seeing the Princess smile and become the kind of person his mother would have loved made it all worth it. Even if he perished in the next breath, he could die knowing that he had the privilege of calling Rhea a daughter.

Wiping at her face, Princess Rhea finally spoke. "Thank you, Brander. You've always known exactly what I needed, even if I didn't." The Princess leaned in for one more hug, and Brander kissed the top of her head.

"Always." he said softly.

A moment later, they moved wordlessly back into the tunnel, but they had said everything that needed to be said between them. She was his Princess and, one day, his Queen, and he was her guard, willing to follow her to the ends of the earth.

Chapter Seventy Eight

A s Rhea emerged into the gloom of the tunnel, she immediately felt the difference of the darkness. Before, it had been comforting and warm, like falling asleep in the summer beneath the stars, but now…

Rhea shivered at the cold, damp air. She attempted to shake off the sensation of hollowness that clung to her. But she didn't dare acknowledge why the shadows were different to her and instead pressed on, determined to find Izor's Lamp and save her people. She hurried her pace as Kasper, Finnley, and Kai came into view. Thankfully, all the tunnels and rooms had crystals of varying sizes embedded in them, which Kasper made emit light. They all turned to face her, and she raised her chin before her eyes landed on Kasper.

"How close to the treasure are we?"

"If what I'm sensing is correct…" Kasper spoke tentatively, rubbing the back of his neck. "If we continue down this tunnel, there is a shoot branching off to the left—similar to the one that we jumped down to get into the dining room. That should deposit us in a treasure room."

"*A* treasure room?"

Kasper grimaced. "There seems to be several. Some have gems and other precious metals, tomes, and jars…others have artwork—statues and paintings. There is mix of everything, and it goes on for a while."

"Is there not another treasure that would work?" Finnley questioned, edging closer to Rhea. "A spell book or something? What do you specifically need the Lamp for?"

Rhea blew out a breath, partly relieved that the burden she had carried for the last several months was finally being shouldered. "I need the Lamp so I can save my Kingdom." Rhea swallowed, working up the courage for the next part. "Nearly a decade ago, Kai issued a prophecy that spelled doom for Desmorda. In the ten years since, my father has done nothing to try and prevent it, so two years ago, I started trying to find a way to stop the inevitable. I searched for months, trying to find any history of a prophecy being stopped, and I found nothing. But then, I learned about Izor's Lamp."

Finnely still stared at her with a confused look, and Rhea fought against the pang of insecurity in her chest. She always knew the Lamp was a long shot, but it was the only lead she had. She needed them to believe in it–to believe in *her*–the same way that she did.

Wetting her lips, Rhea stepped closer to the others. "According to legend, whoever possesses Izor Lamp's is granted three wishes. I plan to wish for the prophecy to be reversed, so that the people of Desmorda are protected. The prophecy is magic, so it stands to reason that something *else* magical could nullify it—or at least, I hope it will. This is the last chance I have to try and save them from whatever is coming."

Rhea's breath felt like razors in her chest, but her discomfort was secondary. This was her purpose, and this was what she came to do. Her issues with Caliban and her fractured friendship with Kasper didn't matter in the face of saving her Kingdom. She turned toward Brander and held out her hand. Wordlessly, he reached into his pocket and withdrew a folder—a weathered piece of parchment. Rhea took it greedily, desperate to look upon its contents once more. She unfolded the parchment and displayed it for the others.

"This is an illustration of the Lamp. I don't know how precise it is, but that's all we have to go on."

"May I?" Finnley asked.

Rhea handed over the paper and clasped her hands tightly to tamp down her anxiety. Examining the image, Finnley traced her fingers over the curve of the handle and the slope of the lid.

"It looks like any ordinary lamp, save for the ruby on the lid. If there's multiple, it might be hard to find." Finnley handed the paper back over to Rhea, and Rhea tried to hide her disappointment.

"I know." she said dejectedly.

"But," Finnley added, "we won't give up until we do. Right, fellas?" Finnley sported a feral grin and looked to the others. Kai smiled back, but Kasper had gone white.

"Kasper?" Rhea said, moving to place her hand on his arm. She recoiled at the touch of his skin. "He's cold as a corpse."

Kasper's mouth hung open, and his eyes appeared vacant. Rhea waved a hand in front of his face, snapping her fingers in order to gain some sort of reaction, but he didn't respond—he didn't even *blink*. She turned to Kai, worry seizing her.

"What's wrong with him?" she demanded.

Shaking his head, Kai stared at his brother's stiff form. "I have no idea. He's never done this before."

Rhea wouldn't accept that. She was too close to her people's salvation to let another mishap stop her from getting what she had worked so hard to find. Pushing past her discomfort, she reached for Kasper again, gripped his shoulders tightly, and shook hard. "Come back to us, Kas. We need you." Rhea dug her fingers into the flesh of his shoulders, knowing that her grip was bordering on painful. "Kasper, snap out of it!" she commanded, and gave another rough shake.

Finally, he blinked and stumbled backward.

Finnley was there to catch him, sliding her arms under his to support his weight. Stepping in, Brander grabbed hold of one side, Kasper suspended between them. Rhea placed her hands on Kasper's face, holding his head and peering into his vacant eyes.

"Kasper, what's going on? Has something happened?"

Kasper shook his head, his eyes still foggy and far away. "He's found a book."

"A book?" Rhea demanded, furrowing her brow. "What book?" In all of her research, she had never come across a book that could truly help her rectify her situation. Surely, she would have known something about it if a *book* was the key to stopping the prophecy. Her mind whirled with the possibility that she had somehow overlooked something so simple. She turned toward Kai, who wore an almost matching blank expression to his younger brother. "Kai, what on earth is he talking about?"

Kai stared at Kasper and swallowed. "The Alakhira."

"What does that mean?" Rhea asked, her patience running thin.

"We need to go, *now*." Kai said, reaching for Kasper and attempting to drag him back down the tunnel and away from the treasure rooms.

Rhea grabbed for him, digging her nails into the flesh of Kai's slender arm. "You will not leave," she commanded, "we are too close to finding the Lamp."

Kai laughed—a wild, maniacal laugh that startled Rhea, causing her to loosen her grip on him. The noise was obscene–bordering on frightening–but Kai was undeterred. No one moved or said a word; Rhea was dumbstruck at Kai's bizarre behavior. After a moment, she found her voice again and barked out an order.

"Stop that at once."

Kai's laughter turned into a cough, and he wiped away the tears leaking from his eyes. He righted himself, muttering, "My apologies, Princess, but can you not see that it's over? That there is nothing to be done now?"

"That is not true. I can still find the Lamp. I can still save my people. I can—"

"Are you truly so ignorant?" Kai sighed with exasperation. He closed his eyes and pressed his lips into a thin line. "Apologies, again. But if Caliban already has the Alakhira in hand, there is nothing we can do."

Stepping closer to Kai, Rhea questioned, "And why is that? What are you not telling me?"

"Princess—"

"Stop coddling me! Stop withholding information from me, or Forgotten help me, I will feed you to whatever hideous evil inhabits this mercurial island."

Kai shook his head and looked to the side before meeting Rhea's gaze again, heaving a sigh. "It's Caliban." he said with defeat, gesturing toward the treasure rooms waiting beyond. A sadness settled into his features, a despondence that made Rhea pause. "He is the doom that I spoke of in the prophecy. I thought if we got to the Lamp first, or if his affection for you changed his course, that things would end differently... but we're too late." Kai blew out a breath, his eyes turning to that eerie, milky white, and recited his prophecy:

> *"The days of this reign draw nigh in score minus half,*
>
> *The Long Night shall fall, smiting all in its grasp,*
>
> *Death is wrought by thine own hand,*
>
> *Thy Kingdom will fall as Destruction clears the land.*
>
> *When Hope seems lost and doom is spelled,*
>
> *The Power of Love will prevail."*

The crease between Rhea's brows deepened. "What do you mean? I–I don't understand."

"Caliban is the Long Night." Kai took a step closer to Rhea. "Have you ever wondered why he hates your father so? The true reason behind our banishment?"

"The prophecy." Rhea supplied, blinking fiercely.

Shaking his head, Kai took Rhea's hand into his own. "The prophecy I issued after Soline–Caliban's lover–found herself with child..." Kai paused, averting his gaze to her pendant, "with your father's child."

Staggering backward, Rhea's shoulder smacked into the dirt wall. She wanted to rebuke Kai's claim and deny that her father would do something so vile, but the words died in her throat. Her father was well known for his harem and his relentless pursuit of having a son, but—memories flooded her. She had only been ten when Soline had vanished from court. Not long after that, the brothers were banished. Rhea had cried for months, lamenting their loss, but no one had given her an explanation, save for her father revealing that Kai had received a prophecy. Rhea was powerless to stop the bile that burned in her throat as it forced its way up. She turned to the side and wretched until there was nothing left in her stomach. A warm, reassuring hand found its way to her back, but Rhea couldn't think far enough past her disgust and shame to be appreciative. She righted herself and wiped her mouth on the back of her hand.

"I know that the truth can be hard to hear, hard to believe—"

Lifting a hand, Rhea cut Kai off. "It's not. I–I remember Lady Soline." Lady Soline, beautiful and lovely. Adored and admired by all, but Rhea remembered that she only ever saw her with one man— Caliban. Until...

"My father..." she shook her head. "He is not worthy of the crown. My people do not deserve to suffer under him a moment longer. I will retrieve and use the Lamp to stop the doom you foresaw, whether it is truly Caliban or not." She met their eyes and released a shaky breath. "I will usher in a new era, free of corruption and evil. Will you all help me see that to its end?"

"Of course," Kasper said in the next breath, "I didn't abandon you before, and I won't now."

Finnley held her gaze a moment before she gave a terse nod. "This world needs more heroes."

Pressing her lips together into a small smile, Rhea locked eyes with each of her companions, resolved in her plans.

"Then let us save my people."

Chapter Seventy Nine

Cal was going to kill the King. He was going to *destroy* him. He was going to wreak havoc on every single thing the King loved. Everything he treasured and held dear would be obliterated and smashed to dust. The King would pay for taking his and his brothers' childhoods, for taking Soline, and for abusing Lady Hera.

Rhea.

Princess Rhea.

His *own* daughter.

Frigid, icy rage crackled over his skin, spearing through the room with preternatural speed. How dare the King raise a hand to his daughter? How *dare* he make her question her worth and degrade her. Water and spirits in nearby jugs froze and exploded into shards. Chalices and crystals fogged and fractured before they, too, erupted with Cal's fury. The fragments littered the treasure room floor, further breaking under his boots with a satisfying *crunch*.

Ignoring the other glittering treasures and dust-covered books in the room around him, he made his way to the front of the space, where a shrouded statue stood vigil. Cal gazed upon it for a moment, his eyes scanning the inscription on the pedestal.

Master of Mystics

God of Mysteries

Cal rolled his eyes, disinterested in the shrine to some forgotten god.

No, he was far more interested in the treasure laid at its feet, ripe for the taking. He plucked the human-skin-bound book from the trove, gripping it tightly as he ran his finger over the spine, exhaling his words:

"The Alakhira."

Wasting no time, he opened the text and began reciting from its unholy pages. The words flowed from his lips effortlessly. A song, a lullaby, a hymn that no being of this universe could name—but one they would know by heart. Cal's heart kicked up another beat in his chest, pounding hard and thrashing like a stallion in a storm. The words came faster and faster, swirling around him in a torrent. It was like being back in the thrill of The Ether, only safer and more assured.

Darkness ebbed around him, flowing from him and the book, meddling and fusing together. Shadows slithered out from the edges of the room, gathering around him and giving form to *her*. Black-tipped nails scraped over his white knuckles and up his arm. His flesh raised in response, but he disregarded it. There was too much at stake, too much to gain, for Cal to lose focus now.

"Yes..." Soline urged, slipping around to stand behind Cal. She rose up on her tiptoes and placed her claw-tipped hands beneath the collar of his shirt, dragging them against his chest. "Say the words, Cal, claim your power. Take our vengeance. Claim your birthright as Destroyer of Worlds." she whispered to him.

Cal faltered, the words slipping away from his lips, and his grip on the Alakhira loosened.

"What?" he breathed as he turned to look at Soline. For a moment, she was as she had once been. Shimmering hair spun from gold. Fair skin, sun-kissed with freckles. Cerulean eyes full of warmth and light. A bright smile that chased away the darkness.

She reached for him, and her hand—normal once more—brushed over his cheek. "Claim it, love," she said, reaching for the book, "the power held within these pages is beyond the magic of this world. The spells within will give you access to power that can *reshape* worlds. No one could challenge you." Soline gripped his chin and forced him to look at the statue again. "You would be a god."

Cal turned back toward her and hesitated, staring at Soline's perfect face. Her expression was so open, so earnest that, for a moment, he considered. He returned to the book and stared at the words again. The spell he read from now allowed him to raise the dead—for a time. He just needed enough power to exact his revenge on the King; he never had any plans to rule a nation, let alone the world. But if he did...

"Stop!"

Cal's head snapped up to find his brothers, Finnley, the guard dog, and the Princess hurrying toward him.

"Put the book down!" The Princess commanded, but drew up short when her eyes landed on Soline. Her eyes went wide, and her entire body tensed. Cal tensed, too, his gaze darting between Rhea and Soline.

A feline smile formed on Soline's lips as she slid around Cal and said, "So, you finally told the truth of who you are. I glimpsed it that night when I tried to take your body as my host, but Caliban banished me before I got the chance to tell him."

"What?" Rhea asked in disbelief.

"Soline..." Cal said, his voice laced with warning.

Soline turned to him, some of the wraith beginning to shine through once more. "Have you always loved her, Caliban? Even when she was a child? Just a precocious Princess and Kasper's little playmate?"

Gritting his teeth, Cal said, "Of course not. I loved you." He stepped closer to Soline and reached for her, but stopped.

Soline's feline smile turned into a sneer. "But you love her now. You have forgotten me, forgotten what her father did to me!" Soline turned, her hair gone white as bleached bones, her skin thinned, and her nails elongated into talons again. Her movements were jerky and volatile as she hurried away from Cal. "If you will not restore me," she screeched, "then I shall have her!"

"Princess!" Brander bellowed.

"Soline!" Cal yelled.

Moving, Brander stepped in front of the Princess. His blade was drawn, ready to defend his charge against any threat, but Cal was quicker. He flipped through the Alakhira, looking for the spell he had found earlier—the only one he had intended to use before he learned the truth about Lady Hera. His eyes skimmed over the words, their meaning coming to him with practiced ease. He had spent years searching the known world for tomes and scrolls to teach him the language so that he would be ready when he had the Alakhira in hand.

Closing his eyes, Cal allowed himself one more heartbeat of longing. One more breath to wish and want for a world where cruel men didn't hoard power. A world where he wasn't an out-of-depth Necromancer, who foolishly believed his immense power would be enough to resurrect the woman he had loved. He held his love for the person Soline had been and knew, deep down, that she would have abhorred what had become of her. He owed her the respite of death and the ability to pass beyond the plane of existence she currently suffered on. He was to blame for her tortured existence. His reckless love and ambition had destroyed what goodness remained—now it was time for her to rest.

Opening his eyes, Cal said softly, "I'm sorry." And then he began reading the spell.

Soline released a terrible screech as she raised a clawed hand and swiped down, aiming for Brander. Brander's sword was raised, but as Soline's hand came down, it passed through the blade like a shadow. With a hiss, Soline whirled, turning her full attention on Cal. The icy chill of her gaze on him was unbearable, but he remained steadfast. This creature–this shadow of Soline–was not her, and she deserved to be freed.

"How dare you!" Soline cried as she ambled toward him, her form becoming less and less corporeal with each word passed through Cal's lips. Something wet dripped onto Cal's cheek, but he continued to read.

Soline appeared in front of him, a portrait of wrath. "You will regret this," she seethed, her hate pouring off her in waves. Cal's gaze hit the last line of the spell, and his voice wavered for a beat.

With these words, Soline would cease to exist entirely.

"Don't do this, Caliban." Soline pleaded, her wraith features gone once more and replaced with the girl Cal had loved. Taking a deep breath, Cal lifted his eyes to meet Soline's, and uttered the final lines. A tear tracked down Soline's freckled cheek, and she reached out her hand, the wisps of her fingers brushing over Cal's cheek with a phantom touch.

Cal shuddered and beheld Soline's unfettered stare. "Forgive me." he begged. Her eyes shuttered and reopened, light glimmering in them as they had before her death. She gazed at him and mouthed, *thank you,* before closing her eyes.

Blinking away his tears, he reached for her—

But she was gone—forever.

The strength went out of Cal's legs, and he fell to the ground, his knees popping with the force. Tipping his head back, he looked up toward the ceiling of the cavern that twinkled with gemstones—a mockery of the stars in the night sky. Darkness swarmed him, and he let it as he released a guttural scream borne of his never-ending anguish.

Chapter Eighty

Kasper was grateful for the darkness that Cal summoned. It allowed him a moment to wipe his own tears away. Seeing Soline prodded at some memory buried deep within Kasper's mind. Kasper appreciated his missing memories for the first time since Kai's deception was revealed. Seeing Cal's pain had been enough to make Kasper's heart ache in his chest, but he had no interest in feeling the sensation himself.

The shadows began to thin, and the room became more visible to Kasper. The others still stood where they were before, all wearing expressions of remorse and pain. Lifting his eyes to where his brother knelt, he expected to find him in the worst state of all. But Cal's eyes were no longer lined with silver, but hard set and determined. His lips had ceased their wobbling and were now firm and expectant as he poured over the text in his hand.

The Alakhira.

Kasper's blood went cold. He looked at the others. Brander still guarded Rhea, but they were both crouching on the ground. Finnley and Kai were nowhere to be seen, presumably looking for the Lamp. None of them could take him on their own, and if Cal amassed more power, there would be no stopping him. Kasper might be the only one who had a chance to reason with him before things went too far. He had offered himself as the distraction while the others searched for the Lamp—or anything that would stop his brother.

Cal began chanting once more.

"Cal, what are you doing?" Kasper called out as shadows and wind swirled about the room, and whispers echoed off the walls. Kasper stayed low to the ground, but slowly moved toward Cal. The wind continued to howl, picking up speed with each foreign word Cal spoke. "End this, Cal! You put Soline to rest. There is nothing else to be done!" he yelled over the wind. Kasper crept closer until he was behind a large shelf of books blocking the worst of the wind.

Cal paused his chanting. "I am ending this, Kasper. I'm ending what was begun nearly a decade ago, or perhaps long before then."

"What are you talking about?" Kasper replied, before he darted out from behind the bookshelf and stepped in full view of Cal.

Giving him a pitying smile, Cal said, "I would tell you to ask our brother, but I know how fruitless that would be. So instead..." Cal removed his dagger from its sheath and dragged it across his palm, blood welling. Lifting his eyes to Kasper's, Cal spoke again in the foreign tongue.

Kasper went wholly still, and Cal approached slowly, like a predator playing with its prey. Kasper was frozen, stiff as a statue, as Cal replaced the dagger, took his lacerated hand, and pressed it to Kasper's forehead.

Holding Kasper's gaze, Cal said, "Remember."

And Kasper did.

Every memory that Kai had repressed came flooding back to Kasper. He fell to the ground, pain lancing in his temples, tearing at the fabric of his mind, ripping his soul apart at the seams.

Faces flashed by in a torrent.

Rhea, the King, Soline, Cal, Kai, and more were fleeting and names unknown to him.

Rhea ran, her curls unbound and reckless.

The sting of skinned knees and the scent of iron-rich blood welling.

Steam curling from a bowl of soup, already soothing his sore throat.

The King's disapproving glare and enormous shadow fell over them.

Soline and Cal put him to bed after a long day of lessons and playing.

Kasper failed to understand it all—not in the moment, not as it all came rushing back, filling in the places that were left hollow and vacant. Kasper writhed on the ground, struggling to breathe, think, and be.

"But it's not enough just to know who you are..." Cal said, stepping over Kasper, "but what you *can* be. And I think it's time you uncover that, brother."

Blood pounded in Kasper's ears, but he still had enough awareness to know that Cal had started chanting again. Kasper's body went hot and cold; his muscles contracted, and he arched off the ground. His blood boiled, and his mind fractured as something cracked within him. Something was released, but the oblivion of unconsciousness swept over him, winking out his awareness.

Chapter Eighty One

"**S**top it, Caliban, you're hurting him!" Rhea screamed from across the cavern. She rose from where she cowered, unwilling to take another moment to watch Cal's worst be unleashed on Kasper.

Brander reached for her, shouting, "No, Princess! We need to find the Lamp. Otherwise, we are no match for him."

She yanked out of his grasp. "Go look for it then! I've got to help Kasper." She left no room for discussion as she rose and squared her shoulders at Cal.

Cal gave a horrid, wicked laugh. "Come now, Princess, you know true pain. This..." he gestured toward Kasper, who was still twitching on the ground, though he didn't seem awake any longer—a small mercy. "This is nothing."

"He's your brother."

"Precisely. That's why I'm helping him. I'm giving him the power and strength to cripple and weaken those who would dare to stand against him."

Continuing to move closer to Cal, Rhea kept one eye on Kasper's limp form and one on Cal. "And if he were to rise against you?"

Cal laughed again. "Unlikely. See, I've given him his memories back——you know, the ones Kai stole? I suspect he'll be rather grateful to me once he wakes and realizes I've returned those *and* expanded his powers, even beyond what this pitiful island offered him."

His words chilled Rhea to the bone, but keeping him talking and distracted was vital. She had to give the others time to find the Lamp. "And what are your plans once you leave here? What do you plan to do with all this power?"

Arching an eyebrow, Cal said, "You haven't guessed yet?"

Rhea gave him a sarcastic smile. "Humor me."

Sighing, Cal leaned against an enormous, looming shelf of books. He looked down at Kasper and nudged him with the toe of his boot. Kasper's body had stopped twitching and his breathing turned deep and steady—still unconscious, but definitely alive. Rhea hoped that he would be alright, and that Finnley, Kai, or Brander would return with the Lamp soon.

Cal unsheathed his dagger.

Rhea flinched, but he didn't turn it on her. Inspecting his nails, he used the blade to clean them. He glanced up at her and said, "Well, since you've been so forthcoming with me on this journey, I suppose I can offer you the same courtesy."

The sarcasm didn't go unnoticed, but she took the verbal assault.

"After I finish up here, I will travel back to Desmorda. I will amass an army and march on your father's palace."

Rhea tried not to let her terror register on her face. Yes, she didn't want her father in power, but to *kill* him? And the lives that would be inevitably lost in the process...

Cal knew what effect his words would have on her. She continued to move closer, hyper-aware of the shrinking space between them. Hours ago, being close to Cal would have been all Rhea wanted, but now...

Now, there was an ocean between them.

Clearing her throat, Rhea lifted her chin. "And then?"

Cal made another pass at his nails and sheathed his dagger. His cold, piercing gaze met her, and her breath caught in her chest. "And then I'll kill your father."

"You wouldn't." she breathed.

Furrowing his brow, Cal stepped over Kasper's body, finally closing the distance between them. "Wouldn't I? What do I have to lose? He already killed Soline, stole my childhood, and abused—" Cal stepped away and shook his head. "You should want him dead as much as I do." Cal looked at her, an unsettling light illuminating his eyes. "You should *want* him dead. Join me, Rhea. Join me, and we can put an end to his cruelty."

Rhea hesitated. She hated what her father had done and was ashamed to share his blood and be a part of his legacy. But to murder him? Had it truly come to that?

"All you have to do is say yes, Rhea."

The hope in Cal's voice made her heart ache. Rhea couldn't stop herself as she reached for him—

"Princess! We have it! We have it!"

Turning toward the shouting, a rising hope swiftly replacing the despair writhing in her chest. But a commotion, a scuffle, stopped her. She turned to find Brander, teeth bared and eyes focused, jabbing his dagger into Cal's side.

"Brander, no!" She yelled, but it was too late.

Cal exclaimed and flung out an arm, sending Brander flying backward until he collided with the far wall. Dirt and stone fell from where he crashed—giving way to a passage that had been sealed shut. Brander collapsed to the floor, unmoving beneath the debris.

"Brander!" Rhea screamed, but it was of no use. She couldn't get to him. She couldn't heal him without Kasper, and he was still unconscious. Finnley and Kai were at the far side of the long room, picking their way over the mountains of treasures that littered the floor, leaving no clear path to her. She was helpless. Utterly powerless to save anyone.

The encounter in the alley, the monsters on the Umbra, and the monkeys on the island all came barreling back into her mind. They confirmed that, not for the first time, she was of no use to anyone.

Turning back to Cal, she found him reaching for his side, his hand coming away red and wet. He gave a tired, rasping laugh and looked at her. The hatred, rage, and…betrayal in his eyes made Rhea's heart crawl into her throat.

"A distraction, then. Keep me occupied until your guard dog could gut me. A dirty trick, but I guess I shouldn't have expected anything else from you. You are your father's daughter, after all."

Rhea tried not to let the sting of those words burn in her chest, but Cal knew the impact they would have. Finnley and Kai were still too far away with the Lamp, and it had to be in Rhea's possession for the wishes to be her own. Cal raised his hand, and shadow figures appeared before them. Finnley gritted her teeth and quickly pressed a dagger into Kai's hand moments before the shadows descended upon them.

Brander was hurt; she knew it, and Kasper was unconscious.

There was only her and Cal.

"Well, I better not waste any more time!" Cal bellowed as he opened the Alakhira anew and chanted in the hideous tongue. The wind through the chamber kicked up again, ripping at Rhea's clothes and knocking her from her feet. Darkness gathered in the room, opaque and suffocating. Rhea's breath was lost to her, her heart beating too fast for her to think of anything else.

The room shook and trembled fiercely, but Rhea would not let her fear master her. She drew upon her resolve and began to crawl toward Finnley and Kai, who had taken shelter behind another bookshelf on the far side of the room—still surrounded by the shadow figures. Cal continued to read from the book as he walked toward the exit that had appeared when Brander collided with the wall. He was unfeeling and relentless in his pursuit of vengeance, but Rhea knew his heart. She had seen the good in him, even if he no longer saw it himself.

Pausing, Rhea looked toward Finnley and Kai once more. She wouldn't reach them in time, and she couldn't fight off the shadow figures, either. Rhea had to do *something*. They had come too far and sacrificed too much not to try. She would not die a coward. Rhea gave a frustrated scream and rose to her feet, running blindly for Cal.

Someone yelled for her, probably Finnley, but she refused to heed it.

She had to stop him, if not with magic, then with whatever sway she still held over him. She tumbled and fell even as Cal walked, utterly unperturbed by the storm he had created. He was a bastion in the maelstrom, and even amidst his terrifying chanting and chaos, Rhea was still drawn to him.

"Caliban!" she called out to him, and Cal turned at the exact moment he spoke the last line from the text.

Rhea's eyes darted as the wind roared, carrying every shadow and scrap of darkness toward Cal. He tipped his chin up and stretched his arms wide as the darkness swarmed him, covering every inch of him until it seeped into his skin. Fighting the urge to scurry backward, she held her ground. But then the earth began to tremble, and a grin made of pure ecstasy spread across Cal's face.

For the first time, Rhea felt truly afraid of him.

Dropping his chin, Cal examined his hands, watching the shadows writhe and wriggle underneath his skin. The sight was utterly horrifying, but Rhea tamped down on her fear and said as confidently as she could manage, "You don't want to do this, Cal." She took a step forward. "You don't have to do this."

Cal tilted his head, like a wolf looking at a wounded deer. "This is what I was made to do." he said, his voice deep and rumbling. He turned from her, looking toward the exit.

Rhea was out of time.

Cal looked back at her, and for a moment, something akin to regret flashed in his eyes. But it was gone in an instant, his gaze hardening. "Don't try to follow me. If you do, I can't be held responsible for the harm that will befall you." Cal moved, heading for the exit quicker than Rhea would have thought humanly possible.

He raised his hand, shadows gathering at the cave ceiling, dirt and debris falling like rain. If Cal got away, everything she had worked for—everything she had *sacrificed*—would also be buried under the wreckage. She didn't think as she lunged for him, meaning to catch him or slow him down, but something—no, someone—knocked her aside as the cave ceiling came crashing to the ground.

Rhea hit the floor hard.

Her vision sparked with midnight stars.

The last thing she saw before she lost consciousness was a wall of rock and dirt—the ceiling of the cave—collapsing directly on Brander.

Chapter Eighty Two

As Cal stormed down the tunnel, there were no other thoughts in his mind save for ones of vengeance and death. Soline had been right about the spell in the Alakhira. Cal felt the changes of his magic—the darkness colder, wilder, more wicked. The new depthless well that even Kai's added magic didn't begin to touch was also an excellent addition.

Cal summoned the shadows.

They came more easily than ever, similar to fire in how they moved and writhed over his body, eagerly awaiting his command. His footfalls were nearly silent in the earthen tunnel as he smiled down at the power wreathing his fingers.

He was unstoppable.

Staring ahead, Cal saw the path toward his vengeance. The King had been left unchecked for too long, abusing his power and leaving a path of ruination in his wake. Cal smiled to himself. The King thought he knew power, but he was sorely mistaken. Glancing down at the shadows enveloping his hands, Cal's smile grew wider. He clenched his fist, snuffing out the shadow-flames. For now.

What the King thought he knew of power was a farce.

Cal would show him *exactly* what real power was.

The days of this reign draw nigh in score minus half,

The Long Night shall fall, smiting all in its grasp.

Acknowledgements

First and foremost I want to thank my Lord and Savior Jesus Christ for my eternal salvation. Without his unending love and mercy there would be no hope or reason to live out each day. While this story is a work of fiction and would never have been possible without God granting me the time and imagination to write it, it will never begin to breach the perfect and wholly true account of the King James Bible. "For God so loved the world that he gave his only begotten Son, and whosoever believeth in him shall not perish but have everlasting life." John 3:16 KJV. Though it is my sincerest wish that people enjoy my work and connect with the characters, it is my even greater hope that seeing what God has done with my life will enable them to seek Him out as their savior.

I owe a tremendous amount of gratitude to one of my very best friends, Reagan. Without you there would be no Masters. Thank you so much for being my sounding board and cheerleader in my writing. Thank you for the exquisite cover, map, and internal art that you created which further brought this story to life. I could never adequately express how much you mean to me. Thank you to Becker with Jones Novel Editing for helping me find the rhythm and provide me with the feedback to craft this story. Your advice and edits have been instrumental in bringing this book to life. Thank you to Jordan, Sydnee, Brooke and Courtney for being some of my first readers, and for giving me invaluable support.

Thank you to my family for allowing me to ramble on about the plot and characters incessantly for months on end. I extend a special thank you to my husband, Nicholas, for supporting me consistently throughout this process. You have been so understanding and reassuring, especially in the moments when I didn't think I had a story worth sharing. I will forever be grateful for everything that you've done to help me fulfill this dream.

Lastly, thank you, dear reader, for taking a chance on me. Writing and developing this story has meant the world to me. If even just one person out there has enjoyed it or found something that they could connect to, then it was all worth it.

I hope that you all will continue with me on this journey.

* * * *

About the Author

Samantha L. Dalton, a history educator from Virginia, has always had a passion for storytelling and disappearing into fictional worlds. Drawing on her love for both historical influences and the fantastical, she brings her debut novel *The Masters of Mystics* to life, blending rich world-building with compelling and complex characters. When she's not teaching, or writing, Samantha can be found immersed and enthralled in all things fantasy, from epic tales to magical realms. Her deep appreciation for history and mythology breathes life into her writing, making her work a thrilling journey for fans of the genre. *The Masters of Mystics* is just the beginning of what promises to be an exciting literary career.

Headshot by Reagan A. Reynolds.

read on for an excerpt from the next
installment in The Masters series:

the
Masters
of Ruin

Cal lifted a hand to ward off the sunlight that threatened to blind him after days underground. But it wasn't his *hand* blocking the golden light, instead it was the shadows he conjured. They were an opaque wall around him, effectively choking out anything that Cal wasn't interested in seeing. His power, magnified by the spell he read from the Alakhira, writhed under his skin. He marveled at the strength and increased tenacity of his shadows. Never again would he be weak. Never again would he suffer the stupidity and insolence of mere mortals. Never again would he bend the knee to an earthly king. A smile spread across Cal's face—everything was within reach.

Vengeance would be his.

Loose, dark soil gradually replaced the packed earth of the cave, giving way to the vibrant jungle. Some of the tension eased out of Cal's shoulders, dissipating with his shadows as his eyes began to adjust to his new surroundings. Thick, leafy fronds greeted him. They swayed in the gentle breeze, accompanied by the soothing chitter of animals and birds. Cal knew he hadn't exited the cave where they had entered some days ago, but it mattered not. The Isle of Oum was not terribly large, all he needed to do was make his way back to the shore and walk until he found the skiffs they left on the beach.

Continuing on his path, it slowly brought him up and out of the winding underground caves. He scanned the jungle for any beasts or monsters that dared to approach him, but everything was quiet. Cal remained alert nonetheless, his eyes continuing to scan and his shadows flickering around his form.

Keeping a steady but brisk pace, sweat gathered along his nape and rolled down his back, soaking into his grime and blood covered clothes. It wasn't long before the soil gave way to sand and the scent of the sea enveloped him. Taking a moment to inhale deeply, he let the ocean wash over him and seep into his bones. The sea had become a second home—a place that had tested his mettle and pushed him to his very limits, but also his refuge. The sand became darker and denser as he approached the surf, the crashing of waves drowning out everything else. The wind transitioned from a gentle tugging to a torrent that ripped at his clothes and hair. The salt and sand carried on the wind scratched his skin, making what was already sore and raw worse. But he paid it no mind. His discomfort was secondary to his mission.

Scanning the horizon, he searched for any sign of the Umbra. A ship of its size should be visible, even in the haze of a late afternoon sun. Cal followed the coastline as it continued to curve, his boots sinking into the wet sand, taking him back to where the skiffs would still be. Agitation flared in him, but he tamped down on it. It would serve him no purpose to let his looming frustrations get the best of him. He had collapsed the quickest exit from the cavern—there was no chance they had followed him. Even if Hera–*Rhea*–used Izor's lamp to clear the path, it would still take them a while to—

Cal's thoughts shattered, and he drew up short as his eyes snagged on something floating in the surf. The water around the island had been clear and free of debris when they had arrived and, given the horrors they had encountered, he doubted anyone else had appeared while they were underground. Stepping further into the surf, the saltwater seeped into his breeches as the waves surged and crashed into the shore. He squinted against the wind and sun glaring off the water. The sand and silt sucked at his feet, forcing him to pull his knees to his chest and yank his feet to make any progress. Cal still couldn't make out what floated in the surf, but he didn't let his mind wander to the worst or give into the fear that was building in his chest. He waded in further, the water reaching his waist. Surging forward, he stumbled, grabbing for the thing tumbling in the waves. His water-slicked fingers slipped around it and he pulled it toward him, staggering backward to the shore.

But then, the waves roared and came crashing down on him.

The world disappeared out from under him as Cal lost his footing. His weight, coupled with the weight of the object he had grabbed, sent him flailing backward, plunging into the tide. Cal had only a heartbeat to suck in a breath before the water slammed into him. Saltwater stung his eyes and shoved up his nose. He had no choice but to release whatever he had grabbed as the waves rolled him, sending him careening through the water.

Despite years at sea, panic still thrashed in Cal's chest at the disorienting, weightless sensation that the sea thrust upon him. Pain rocked through his shoulder as it collided with the seafloor. Wincing, he bucked upward, desperate to be out of the water.

Cal's head broke through the surf and he gasped for air, relishing the brief reprieve, before another wave crashed down on him. This time, Cal didn't fight the wave, and instead he loosed the tension in his limbs and let the water carry him back to land. Cal waited, holding his breath, until his back and boots scraped the sand. He threw his hands out, pushing himself up and out of the water. Cal's throat burned as he coughed and spurted, trying to dislodge the water from his lungs. He blinked away the salt stinging in his eyes as he shoved his hands into the sand and crawled further onto shore. Shaking his head, Cal sent droplets of water in all directions as he flipped onto his backside and drew his knees up to his chest. He watched in annoyance as the foamy waves lapped against his booted toes. He was a fool for even attempting to breach the tide. Nothing was worth nearly drowning, not when his vengeance was almost in hand.

Sighing, he pressed his forehead to his saltwater soaked knees, the fabric rough with salt and sand. He needed to stay focused. He couldn't afford to be hindered by his curiosity, or a half-witted sense of justice. Nothing would stop him from avenging the wrongs of his past.

Cal was drawn from his thoughts by something bumping lightly against his foot. Reluctantly, he lifted his head and found Sammy's glassy, lifeless eyes staring back at him. Cal reeled backward, scrambling away from Sammy's water-logged corpse. He couldn't understand. Couldn't comprehend the sight before him—what his eyes were trying to tell him.

Water sloshed over the body, pulling it out for a moment, and then gently pushing it back onto the sand.

It couldn't be true.

It couldn't be.

It couldn't—

Another body washed up a few feet away.

Then another.

And another.

Pushing to his feet, Cal tried and failed to wrap his mind around what could have happened. He operated on instinct, grabbing the bodies and dragging them further onto shore, out of the longing, relentless reach of the tide.

Ten in total.

Ten lives, lost—

Or stolen.

Cal summoned his magic, the effort took next to nothing. Suddenly, Sammy's lean, boyish form apparated in front of him.

"Woah..." Sammy said, his transparent form giving a subtle flicker before becoming corporeal.

Briefly, Cal marveled at his own strength. He hadn't summoned spirits often. They were too volatile, too unpredictable, and often had their own agendas. When Soline or Galen had appeared to him, they were only shadows of their former selves. Soline only became solid because of the island and whatever nefarious magic it trafficked in.

Sammy was inspecting his hands when Cal finally cleared his throat. Sammy's attention snapped to Cal, and he lifted his hand in a paltry salute.

"Capt'n!"

Cal clenched his jaw, doing his best to keep his face clear of any reaction. Shades and spirits fed off of strong human emotion, and he had no time or energy to fight with them.

"What happened, Sammy?" Cal said, his voice, mercifully, coming out level. "Who did this?"

Sammy reached for his throat, and Cal noted the gash that lingered there, even in death.

"They didn't want to stay. They said you were a monster, a demon, and that you would get us killed." Sammy glanced to the bodies littering the shore, his gaze lingered on his own. "Not all of us agreed."

Cal turned from Sammy. Flexing his fingers, Cal redirected his anger into them rather than blasting a hole in the island. Lifting his eyes to the water once more, he found the Umbra, hardly a speck on the horizon. Those cowards killed his men and stole the Umbra.

His ship.

Cal whirled back toward Sammy, his rage settling like ice in his veins. Stepping closer to his crewmate, Cal quietly lamented the boy's death. He was barely sixteen, a child with his entire life ahead of him.

And now he was dead.

"Do you want revenge?"

Sammy furrowed his brow. "Capt'n?"

"For your wrongful death. Ask me for vengeance and it's yours."

Cal's breath felt like shards of glass in his chest, but he remained still as Sammy's eyes shifted back to the other bodies littering the sand. His throat bobbed once. Twice.

"No..." Sammy said softly.

Confusion washed over Cal and he opened his mouth to question him, but Sammy interjected.

"I've never been the kind to hold a grudge. Besides, I've got my parents and some nieces or nephews waiting for me. But the others…" Sammy's words started to drift off.

Cal nodded. "No need to explain further, Sammy. Go find your family and your rest."

Sammy beamed at Cal. "Thank you, Capt'n." Sammy's form began to thin around the edges, becoming hazy and transparent. But before he vanished entirely, he called out, "Tell First Mate Finnley thanks for teaching me to play cards, and for staying with me those first nights aboard the Umbra!"

And then Sammy was gone, his smile and light erased from Cal's world. Cal set his jaw and wiped at the singular tear that rolled down his cheek, before he turned toward the other bodies and willed their spirits to rise. A moment later, nine restless souls met Cal's eye. He lifted his chin, a wicked smirk lifting his lips.

"Who wishes to seek vengeance for their death?"